BY HAROLD COYLE

HAROLD COYLE

THE TEN THOUSAND

A NOVEL

SIMON & SCHUSTER
New York   London   Toronto   Sydney   Tokyo   Singapore

SIMON & SCHUSTER
Simon & Schuster Building
Rockefeller Center
1230 Avenue of the Americas
New York, New York 10020

SIMON & SCHUSTER and colophon are registered trademarks
of Simon & Schuster Inc.

Designed by Irving Perkins Associates
Manufactured in the United States of America

10 9 8 7 6 5 4 3 2 1

Library of Congress Cataloging-in-Publication Data

Coyle, H. W. (Harold W.), date.
The ten thousand : a novel / by Harold Coyle.
                                         p.   cm.
1. Imaginary wars and battles—Fiction. 2. Soldiers—Europe—
                                    Fiction. I. Title.
                     PS3553.0948T46 1993
        813'.54—dc20   93–20151
                                         CIP

ISBN 0-671-77800-5

ACKNOWLEDGMENTS

I would like to thank the following for their assistance in making this book possible:

To Gerry Carroll, who is an author in his own right, for taking valuable time away from his own projects, family, and self-inflicted home improvement projects to look over my rough draft and comment on all that aviation stuff. Thanks, Gerry.

To Chet Burgess, one of Ted Turner's originals at CNN, for doing likewise and not only for commenting on the portions of the book concerning the media but for giving valuable advice on other areas as well. Most of all, however, I would like to publicly thank you for taking the time from what must have been a miserable schedule in January of 1991 to give me and Major Bill Little, both Desert Shield/Storm–bound, a great sendoff while we were cooling our heels and chewing our nails in Atlanta during the twilight period between peace and war.

Next, I would like to extend my appreciation to Michael Korda, of Simon & Schuster, who has served as a guide and shepherd in my writing career since my second book and Paul McCarthy of Pocket Books for his editorial comments and yeoman's work in making this book a readable commodity. Even though my name is on it and theirs aren't, no book is a one-person effort.

Finally, as always, I extend to my wife and children a special thanks for putting up with the long hours and all too frequent fits of passion that this book produced. Too often they absorbed the brunt of shots meant for others and still came back smiling. I can't think of anyone more deserving of my thanks and appreciation than those who kept me going by providing a gentle smile and encouraging word when I needed it. Thanks.

This book is dedicated to

GEORGE BANNON

and those of his generation who,

as riflemen, bore the brunt of World War II

CONTENTS

"Christianity has somewhat softened the brutal German lust of battle, but could not destroy it."
—HEINRICH HEINE (1833)

"If destruction be our lot we must ourselves be its author and founder. As a nation of free men we must live through all time or die by suicide."
—ABRAHAM LINCOLN (1858)

MAP 1: Germany and Central Europe

P R O L O G U E

**NORTH OF REGENSBURG, GERMANY
APRIL 1945**

The transition from night to day was subtle, almost unnoticed by the stunned survivors of the neighborhood. There were no birds chirping, no animals scurrying about to announce that a new day had started. The only difference that day was a slow, almost torturous, change from the cold oppressive darkness of night to a leaden gray sky that brought no warmth, no hope to those people who huddled in the corners of their shelters. Even the thought that the end of their nightmare was at hand brought no relief, no end to their strain. Six years of war and twelve years of National Socialism had crushed all emotions, all hope. All they had left that morning was eyes that had stopped seeing, ears that stopped hearing, and souls that stopped living a long time ago. It was truly the twilight of the gods.

In the corner of one of the basements, a mother and her five-year-old daughter huddled together. Only an occasional spasm or hacking cough shook the bundle of rags that covered them and differentiated the mother and daughter from the stack of corpses across the room from them. The mother was ever mindful that little separated them from the heap of dead. Whenever the little girl shook, the mother tightened her grasp on her in an effort to keep the girl from slipping away from the living. Though she no longer understood why she struggled to stay alive and keep her daughter warm and safe, it was all she knew, all that was left to her. Slowly over the past years everything that she had ever known and had ever loved had been stripped away and smashed as they had descended into a world of death and nightmares. Now only the five-year-old daughter and an eight-year-old boy who had once been her son were left. With the corruption of the boy's mind by the Hitler Youth, the mother had only had her daughter to keep her in touch with life and the living. With all the strength that she had left, the mother tightened her hold on her daughter. She would not let that life go.

Across the dark, dank basement the eight-year-old boy paced. Unlike his mother and sister, he was animated, alive, anxious to continue. The stench of rotting bodies and human waste that could not be disposed of mingled with the smell of burning wood and stagnant water. Such smells did not bother him. They, like many things, had to be endured. It was easy, he knew, to tolerate such inconveniences if you believed in yourself, the Fatherland, and the Führer. The smells, like the dead, were a part of war.

As he moved from one side of the basement to the other, his piercing gray eyes didn't see the torment of his own mother or the pile of bodies which, in accordance with regulations and emergency orders, he had dutifully segregated from the living and covered with a layer of lime. Instead they were fixed straight ahead and glazed over with images of soldiers and weapons, and tanks and planes, the implements of war that had made the Reich great and in the end would crush the Führer's enemies. Soon he and the other boys in his unit would have their chance to join his father, a tank commander who had fought the Russians and now faced the Americans. The thought of being able to fight and die for the Führer only served to increase the boy's excitement, an excitement that masked the rumble of heavy vehicles approaching.

Keeping as close to the rear of the Sherman tank as he dared, Private George Kozak kept his eyes open and his rifle at the ready. He hated going into towns and villages, hated it with a passion. There were so many places for the enemy to hide, so many places from which a sniper or a machine gun could suddenly appear. Out in the country, where it was more open, you didn't have to worry about basements and sewers or death from above. In a city the bastards could be, and usually were, everywhere.

Just the thought of a firefight caused Kozak to tense up. Sweat began to bead up and run in little rivulets from under his helmet liner band down his face. For a moment he considered unbuttoning his jacket but decided not to. Kozak knew that as soon as he paused, he would lose the protection of the tank. Another member of his squad would quickly move around him from the more exposed tail of the squad file and take Kozak's spot right up next to the tank, leaving Kozak in the open. Or if he turned his attention away from his search for the enemy to fool with his jacket, they might choose that moment to open up. No, Kozak thought, best to keep my eyes open and stay where I am. Something was about to happen, he could feel it. And when it did, he wanted to be ready. In a little over a month he would be twenty years old, an age not many of his friends had lived to see. Though he would still be too young to legally drink or vote back in Pennsylvania, his next birthday would nearly coincide with a rare event, completion of a full year in continuous combat. Of the ten men in his squad who had crossed the beach at Omaha three days after D-Day, Kozak was only one of three who could boast of seeing that much combat. The others had been taken away feet first. Kozak intended to see his birthday, as well as his first anniversary in combat, alive and in one piece.

That he didn't have any goals or even conscious thoughts of anything beyond his twentieth birthday never occurred to Kozak. While it was fashionable for politicians and dreamers to speak of a brave new world, such thoughts were foreign to the American rifleman in 1945. Like a million other infantrymen, Kozak's world was defined by the field of vision that the Sherman in front of him offered, and a future that was not his to control and was measured in minutes.

When the boy finally heard the grinding of the tanks and felt the rumbling of the earth, he ran to the window. "Papa, Papa! Mother, Papa has come home!"

From her corner the mother looked at the boy. Dear God, she thought, what a fool. What a poor godforsaken fool. Did he still believe that his father was alive? Did he still believe that the Nazis would be able to turn back the enemy? "Johann, that is not your papa. He is dead. He was killed last Christmas in Belgium with your uncle. It is the Amis. The Americans. They have come to put an end to this nightmare."

In a flash the boy turned to face her. "NO! You lie! You *lie!* Those are all defeatist lies! Papa is not dead. He is not dead. He will come back. You will see. The Führer has promised we will be delivered. You will see."

Turning away from his mother, the boy pushed a box under the basement window and stood on it, pulling himself up in an effort to see the tanks. The shock of seeing a tank he immediately recognized as an M-4A3 Sherman tank, followed by men in sloppy, dishevelled uniforms, was too much for the boy. The Americans! How could that be? How could his father let them come like that? First his father had left them. Then his mother, sister, and he had moved from their farm near Breslau to the dirt and filth of Regensburg. Then the bombers had come. And now the Americans themselves. Was this the end, like his mother had said? Was it really the end? And if it was, what was he to do? The Führer had called for all Germans to fight to the last. Was that what he was to do now? Fight the American tank? Without thinking, the boy reached down and grasped the knife he had been presented when he had joined the Hitler Youth. He was proud of that knife. It was a living symbol that connected him directly to his Führer. Now it was his only weapon. Questions of how best to use that weapon to do his duty for Führer and Fatherland now raced though the boy's eight-year-old mind.

The movement of a head bobbing up and down in a basement window not more than twenty feet away from him caught Kozak's eye. Shit! Without thinking, Kozak yelled, "Sniper on the right!" Running out from behind the tank, Kozak covered the distance from where he had been to the side of the basement window in a single rush. Even before reaching the relative safety of the side of the building next to the window, Kozak was pulling a hand grenade from his web belt. Behind him the rest of his squad dropped where they had been and trained their rifles on the window where Kozak was headed. The tank, oblivious to the infantrymen's actions, continued to rumble on down the street alone.

Once he had reached the window, Kozak held his rifle between his knees while he pulled the safety pin from the grenade and let the spoon fly off. With an audible snap, the grenade's striker hit the primer. After holding the grenade for three or four seconds, Kozak bent down and tossed it into the open window. As soon as he had released it, Kozak grabbed his rifle, stood upright, flattened himself against the side of the building, and waited for the explosion. Kozak had no intention of giving anyone who survived his grenade a chance to recover from its effects. As soon as he heard the muffled roar of the grenade, he stuck his rifle into the window and began to fire. Moving sideways across the open window, which was still billowing smoke, Kozak kept his rifle trained into the basement, squeezing off round after round as he continued to move. By the time he reached the other side of the window, the bolt of his M-1 Garand locked back and the follower assembly flipped out the expended clip.

For a moment he paused, flattening himself against the side of the building again on the opposite side of the window. When he had caught his breath, Kozak leaned over and looked into the window while the fingers of his right hand fumbled about his bandoleer searching for a new clip. The smoke from the grenade was still clearing. There were no sounds, no motions coming from the basement.

"Hey, Kozak! Anything?"

Kozak looked back at his squad leader, then down into the window again. Through the gloom and darkness of the room, all he could see was two stacks of bodies. There were still no motions, no sounds. Whoever had been moving about wasn't moving anymore. Relieved, Kozak relaxed, but only for a moment. The tank, his shield, was still rumbling down the street, leaving him and the squad behind and exposed. "No, Sarge. They're all dead."

Pushing himself up off the pavement, Kozak's squad leader looked about to ensure that all of his men were still with him, then shouted to them. "Okay, second squad, let's get moving. Now!"

Kozak didn't need to be told twice. Without another thought, he finished shoving a fresh clip into his rifle and turned his back on the basement window, running down the street to catch up with the tank. It was as if at that moment the Sherman tank was his only guarantee that he would live to see his twentieth birthday. And nothing and no one was going to stand between him and that.

OPERATION DESPERATE FUMBLE

C H A P T E R   1

6 JANUARY

Pausing just short of the crest next to a tree, Colonel Scott Dixon knelt on one knee, leaned against the tree, and began to pull the hood of his white camouflage parka up over his helmet. As he fiddled with the drawstrings of the white parka, Dixon scanned the crest of the hill to his front. Beyond it was the Ukrainian border. While one would assume that Dixon's head would be filled with concerns and thoughts about the upcoming operation, it was not. Rather the commander of the 4th Armored Division's 1st Brigade was at that moment feeling a twinge of guilt about insisting on being issued the white parka. After all, the odds of him, the commander of a maneuver brigade with two tank and two mechanized battalions, needing to use the white garment to hide from the enemy were remote. As he told the brigade XO when he was first given the parka, "If it gets to the point where this is the only thing that is protecting me, then someone has screwed up, big time." Despite the order from the division commander that only infantrymen serving in line companies and scouts receive the scarce article, the brigade S-4 had connived until he had obtained the coveted white parka. Now that he was actually using the camouflage properties of the parka during his personal reconnaissance of the Ukrainian border defenses his brigade would be crashing through in less than twelve hours, Dixon could justify having it. Of course, everyone who knew Dixon knew that he enjoyed having all the "neat" things, and no amount of justification could hide that. Still Dixon's staff felt no misgivings about indulging their commander. He was in their eyes worth it.

Scott Dixon, at age forty-six, was a complex man who had the ability to deceive those who met him with an easygoing manner. Physically he was equally unpretentious. A casual observer standing on the street corner of any large American city would never pick Scott Dixon out of a crowd as the commander of four thousand men and women. His five-foot, ten-inch body and medium build would be classified as average. The 170 pounds he carried about were well distributed, although there was a hint of a spreading waist when he wasn't wearing baggy fatigues or an oversized parka like today. Even if the observer were to look at Dixon's face from a distance, there wouldn't be anything of special note other than the fact that he wore his hair shorter than the average American male and his face still failed to betray the forty-plus years his body had clocked. Even the facial expression that would have betrayed his personality and emotions was carefully hidden from view. The only external feature that differentiated Scotty Dixon from any other middle-aged American male was his eyes. His eyes betrayed Scott Dixon.

Like many veterans who had seen war and knew that they had not yet seen their last, his eyes were often fixed in a sad faraway gaze. On those rare occasions when he allowed his mind to wander, the sadness in his eyes would deepen and glaze over with moisture as his mind's eye passed before him again and again a parade of faces and horrors of wars past. It was these memories and Dixon's determination to ensure that the parade didn't grow any longer that gave him the drive that made him a successful combat commander. And it was the sad realization that regardless of what he did, regardless of how successful he was, the parade would grow. For Scott Dixon knew that the one cruel hard fact that endured through the ages was that war meant killing and not all the killing was done by your side. It was this sad truth that gave Scott Dixon the one external characteristic that marked him as something different, something special. So Dixon, like so many other commanders in the past, stuffed his personal thoughts and emotions into a dark corner of his mind and revealed to friends, subordinates, and superiors only what they expected.

The crunching of snow behind him caused Dixon to turn as he absentmindedly finished tying his hood's drawstrings. It did not surprise him that it was the Russian colonel making his way up the hill to join him. Further down the slope Dixon could see his operations officer, also wearing a white parka, standing where they had parked their humvees. Cerro and the Slovak Army officer that served as their translator and liaison officer were talking to an angry farmer who had come up to chase them off his land. Cerro would, he knew, join them as soon as he had calmed the farmer down and sent him on his way.

As the operations officer for Dixon's brigade, Cerro spent, in his opinion, far too much time tied down at the brigade command post. Never missing a chance to get away from there and given a chance to play rifleman, crawling about in the snow, mud, and dirt, Cerro was, therefore, quite put out when Dixon had left him to deal with the farmer. Looking back down the hill at Cerro, Dixon smiled to himself and shook his head. Strange breed, the infantry, he thought. Of course, he totally discounted the fact that he, despite his twenty-two-year career as an armor officer, never passed up a chance to crawl around and play rifleman. Before turning back toward the border, Dixon noticed that Cerro had a white helmet cover, a commodity in even shorter supply than the white parka. Where in the hell had Cerro gotten that? More importantly, Dixon wondered, were there any more?

While the tall Russian colonel eased himself down into a kneeling position next to Dixon, Dixon turned his mind away from the trivial concerns of parkas and helmet covers to the matter that had brought these four men and their drivers to this spot. Between deep breaths and his efforts to pull the white hood over the brown pile cap he wore, Colonel Anatol Vorishnov spoke in a sigh, half to himself, half to Dixon. "This snow, it will be the death of me one day."

Twisting his head toward Vorishnov, Dixon raised an eyebrow. "I thought you guys loved winter and the snow. You know, General Winter, General Mud, and all that stuff."

Vorishnov laughed. "You, my friend, are a victim of propaganda and popular myths. When the wind blows, my nose and toes grow cold, like yours. And the snow pulling at my ankles is no lighter than that which you plow through. Unless, of course, one waits until someone else has beaten a path through it, like you just did."

Smiling, Dixon nodded. "Ah, now I understand why you took your time before following."

"We Russians, Colonel Dixon, at times seem to be dull and slow, but we are not stupid."

"Never thought you were, Colonel. Are you ready?"

Vorishnov grinned and motioned to Dixon. "After you, Colonel."

"Somehow, Colonel Vorishnov, I thought you'd say that."

"Do you think, Colonel Dixon, that your young major will be able to convince our curious Slovak farmer that we are simply sight-seeing?"

Dixon smiled. "Not to worry, Colonel. Major Cerro is a graduate of the Virginia Military Institute. That makes him more than qualified to fabricate tall stories."

Realizing that Dixon was still joking, Vorishnov smiled. There was a special affinity between Harold Cerro and Scott Dixon. Though both conducted themselves in a manner befitting the proper relationship between an operations officer and his commander, their regard for each other ran much deeper. Had they been peers, Vorishnov knew they would be best of friends. As it was, the conversations between Dixon and Cerro sometimes left one in doubt as to who the subordinate was and who the commander was. But then again, Vorishnov reminded himself, this is the American Army. They, he thought, had their own ways, not all bad, not all good. The one habit that both Dixon and Cerro seemed to share was a sense of humor that at times seemed inappropriate and irreverent. After having served in an army racked for a decade by social and political change, Vorishnov enjoyed the humor as much as Dixon did and participated whenever possible. "I thought in your country only the Irish could tell stories?"

"Yes, that is true. The Irish are gifted in that way. That is why Cerro had to go to a special school to learn." Looking over to the west, Dixon grunted. "We are losing the daylight. If we wait for Major Cerro, we will see nothing."

Vorishnov looked at the setting sun and agreed. "Yes, it would be a shame to come all this way for nothing."

Slowly Dixon began to make his way to the crest of the hill. It was a strange world that Dixon found himself moving through that evening. Even now, as his mind leafed through a mental file that stored the many concerns of command and the impending operation, Dixon could not escape the irony of the situation in which he found himself. Twenty years earlier, as a second lieutenant of armor, Dixon had been assigned to a unit tasked with defending West Germany against an attack from Soviet-led Warsaw Pact forces. It was east of Fulda, in central Germany, where he made his first trip to the border for recons. Then he commanded five M-60A1 tanks, tanks that could reach the breathtaking speed of twenty miles an hour on a downhill slope with favorable tail winds. His men wore the old-style World War II helmet, and the adversary he was looking for was Russian. Now, Dixon thought, the political situation and the world were moving as fast as the M-1A1 Abrams tanks that equipped the two armored battalions in his brigade. And his adversary today was as different as the uniform he had worn. Had someone told Dixon during his days at Fulda that he would be leading a combat command into the Ukraine, and using a serving Russian officer as an advisor, he and his fellow lieutenants would have considered him nuts. But it was about to happen.

When Dixon and Vorishnov reached the crest of the hill, Dixon was struck by the beauty of the scene before him. In many ways the mountains, forests, and high pasture lands, all blanketed in heavy snow, reminded Dixon of southern Bavaria. Even the small farmhouses and barns that dotted the countryside looked the same from a distance. But this wasn't southern Germany. This part of the world was, for the United States Army, new territory. The southern rim of the Carpathian Mountains dominated the horizon to their left and front as far as the eye could see. To their right, the forested and snow-covered foothills of the Carpathians slowly gave way to the Alföld plain, which eventually led into Hungary. Dixon, with a degree in history, understood the significance of what was about to happen and dwelt on that thought as he and Vorishnov settled down to study the border, which now lay less than one hundred meters from where they were. After a quick scan with their naked eyes, both men in silence hoisted their binoculars up and began to study the wire fence, the anti-vehicle ditch, guard towers, and the border crossing.

Except for the thin trail of smoke slowly curling up from the stovepipes in the guard towers and the guard shack at the border crossing, neither man could see any sign of unusual activity. There was no evidence of new excavations or weapons emplacements. Satisfied that there would be no surprises at the border trace itself, Dixon trained his binoculars on the road that ran from Slovakia into the Ukraine. There was nothing to indicate that it was mined or that any preparations had been made to crater it. After watching a Ukrainian customs official casually pass a truck overloaded with pigs without even bothering to check the papers the vehicle driver waved from a partially opened window, Dixon lowered his binoculars. He took one more look from horizon to horizon before he spoke. "Well, either they don't know we're coming or they are the coolest customers this side of the Rhine."

If Vorishnov didn't quite understand the term Dixon used, he understood his meaning. "Yes, I agree. It would appear, Colonel, that the buildup of Russian forces along their northern and eastern borders has fooled the Ukrainians. We will have tactical, and possibly operational, surprise in the morning."

Dixon glanced over at Vorishnov. He liked the big Russian. Forever correcting Dixon and his officers on the correct pronunciation of the names of Ukrainian towns, cities, and rivers, Colonel Vorishnov had an easygoing manner while maintaining a professional bearing and conduct. He was, Dixon thought, very Russian, never missing a chance to tell anyone who would listen about the greatness and beauty of his native land. Nor would Vorishnov's pride allow him to miss the opportunity to remind the Americans of the role that the Russian Army was playing in this operation. Although the only Russians who would actually enter the Ukraine during the upcoming operation were the advisors serving with all American units, it was fear of the Russian Army deployed along the northern Ukrainian border that would paralyze the bulk of the Ukrainian Army and allow the Americans to seize the two nuclear weapons depots near Svalyava. If nothing else, Vorishnov gave Dixon a peer, another officer of equal stature outside the normal chain of command, in whom he could confide and with whom he could compare ideas and thoughts. That Dixon would be glad to find a friend and confidant in a Russian officer was another sign that the world they were living in was, as Dixon's wife, Jan, often mused, "getting curiouser and curiouser."

Satisfied that he had seen all that there was to see from where they were, and noting the long shadows cast by the guard towers, Dixon nudged Vorishnov. "Well, I'm sold. Our friends down there aren't expecting us."

Without looking at Dixon, Vorishnov continued to study the border trace with his binoculars. "No, no. I don't believe they know what is about to happen. You should have a good morning tomorrow morning."

Dixon grunted. "It's not tomorrow morning and crossing the border I'm worried about. It's the road from Uzhgorod to Mukacevo that gives me the willies."

While still holding his binoculars up, Vorishnov twisted his head toward Dixon. "It is pronounced Moo-kay-see-vo, Colonel. And yes, I share your concern about that part of the operation. I still believe you are sending far too small a force south to block the Ukrainian armored brigade garrisoned at Uzlovaya. You are, in my humble opinion, placing too much reliability in your attack helicopters and the skill of the commander of that blocking force. I do not agree with your lovely young intelligence officer's assessment. After you strike across the border and move east, the Ukrainian brigade at Uzlovaya will move north to strike your exposed flank, not northeast to shield Mukacevo. And when that happens, you will need to shift portions of your main body south to deal with them. When that happens, you will find yourself involved in a meeting engagement in which they, operating on their own territory, will have the advantage."

Used to Vorishnov's corrections, Dixon let the comment about Mukacevo pass. But he defended his decision to use just one company as a blocking force. "Yes, I can understand your concern. Under most circumstances, I would agree. In this case, however, I feel justified in taking, what you consider, a risk. Captain Nancy Kozak, the commander of the blocking force, is a proven commodity. Even if the attack helicopters are grounded or diverted, we will have more than enough artillery in support to give Kozak the edge. Besides, with only two tank and two mech infantry battalions, I can't afford to disperse my force to protect against threats. If the Ukrainian armored brigade becomes a danger, then we'll deal with it."

Dixon paused, waiting for Vorishnov's response. Vorishnov, however, said nothing. He knew from Vorishnov's expression that the Russian remained unconvinced. The idea of placing that much confidence in an officer as junior as Kozak was to Vorishnov's mind foolish. But he said nothing, for this was not his brigade. He, Vorishnov told himself, had said his piece. Dixon, the commander, had made up his mind and was, he realized, prepared to pay the price if he was wrong.

When Vorishnov said nothing, Dixon sighed. I guess, he thought to himself as he looked at Vorishnov, old habits and ways of thinking are hard to break. With a shrug, Dixon looked away from Vorishnov and back at the border crossing before he spoke. "I think, Colonel, we are finished here. Let's head on back and see what the young'uns are doing."

Though Vorishnov didn't quite approve of the casual manner in which American officers conducted themselves, and didn't understand most of the names and references Dixon and his staff used, like the term young'uns applied to junior officers, Vorishnov understood it was all part of Dixon's style. And so long as Dixon and his subordinates were comfortable with it and it didn't interfere with the conduct of operations, Vorishnov felt there was no need to say anything. As much as it grated on him, the Americans, after all, had won more wars in the recent past than his own army. And as he had been taught from an early age, one does not argue with success.

"Yes, let us go back. My toes tell me it is time for some warm tea."

As the senators and congressmen filed into the White House conference room, the President did not leave her seat to greet them. Instead, Abigail Wilson was turned away from the door through which the congressional leaders entered the room, leaning over the arm of her chair, talking to her Secretary of Defense, Terry Rothenberg. That did not mean she was ignoring the congressional delegation. Wilson was far too astute a politician for that. Instead, from the corner of her eye she kept track of who was entering the room, making mental notes of the expressions on their faces and their deportment. Though she had already been well briefed on who would and would not be present, the seating arrangements, and which of the delegation were figureheads, and which were the real movers and shakers in Congress, her staff could not tell her what the attitude of the senators and congressmen would be at the time of the meeting. On this matter, Wilson was on her own. With the same well-practiced coolness that had catapulted her from the governor's mansion in Colorado into the White House, Wilson discreetly studied her opposition and prepared to meet them head-on, on her own terms, in her own time, in her own way. Of course, that was her intention. It did not, however, take into account Congressman Ed Lewis.

When the delegation was seated and Wilson's Secretary of State, Peter Soares, indicated that it was time to commence, Wilson looked over to him with a questioning glance. In her mind she had only counted off nine senators and congressmen. There were supposed to be ten. Soares, who had not been counting, wondered what Wilson was concerned about, and returned her glance with a blank stare. After seeing her nod to indicate that there was an empty chair catty-corner from her, Soares finally understood. He looked over to a presidential aide strategically located at the entrance to the room. With his face contorted, eyes pinched, and his teeth slightly exposed, an expression that reminded many of a rat, Soares tried to convey the message to the aide that someone was missing.

Unlike Wilson and Soares, the aide immediately became flustered when he saw Soares's expression and realized that there was something wrong. Straightening up, the aide turned and prepared to rush out of the room in search of the missing congressman. His progress, however, was stopped cold as he plowed into another man entering the room. The presidential aide literally bounced off the tall, lean frame of Ed Lewis, who, true to form, was taking his time about showing up for the "emergency" White House briefing.

Rather than being embarrassed, Lewis paused, flashing a slightly wicked smile as the presidential aide backed off and resumed his post. Once he was sure that he had everyone's undivided attention, Lewis bowed slightly. "My humble apologies for being so late." Looking over at the aide, Lewis's smile broadened. "It appears that the rush hour traffic is as bad in here as it is outside." This brought a few chuckles from his colleagues and a scornful look from Soares.

Wilson, though she was not happy that a congressman had managed to upstage her well-orchestrated opening, didn't bat an eye. Instead she lightly touched Rothenberg's arm as she broke off their private conversation and turned in her seat. So that she did not appear to be at a loss as to what to do while she waited for Lewis to take his seat, Wilson played with her notes, already carefully laid out in front of her. Pete Soares had been right, she thought. Lewis, when he wanted to be, could be a real asshole.

When he was sure that they were finally ready to start, Soares began the meeting. "As we all know, the Russian and Ukrainian governments have been unable to come to an agreement over the disposition of nuclear weapons stored in the Ukraine. The seizure of those weapons by the Ukrainian military in November and the Russians' demand that those weapons be returned to the control of the Commonwealth forces have resulted in an impasse. Economic sanctions, including the cutting off of all oil and petroleum products into the Ukraine, have resulted in hardships but no compromise. If anything, the actions by the Russians and the republics that still belong to the Commonwealth have only served to harden the determination of the Ukrainian government. Sovereignty and self-determination are, in their words, at stake."

Soares paused and looked at the assembled congressional delegation when he heard a sigh that sounded remarkably like "Shit." Lewis, who knew what was coming without having to be told, was already shaking his head. "Don't tell me, Pete. Let me guess. Our troops, deployed from their bases in Germany to the Czech and Slovakian republics in an effort to discourage the Hungarians from taking advantage of political upheavals between those two, just happen to be in a position to move into the Ukraine and secure the nuclear weapons in question. And, oh, by the way, the Russians, having publicly encouraged and praised our deployment into the Czech and Slovakian republics, have asked us to use those conveniently located forces to bail their sorry asses out of an embarrassing situation."

Angry at Lewis's rude interruption, Soares was unable to continue. Instead he stood at the end of the table and glared at Lewis. Seeing that the situation was about to get out of hand, Wilson intervened. "It's more than an effort to save the Commonwealth from public embarrassment. We have been able to confirm that the Ukrainian government has been approached by another, non-nuclear government about trading warheads for the economic support that the Commonwealth embargo has denied the Ukraine. With Ukrainian industry and transportation grinding to a halt due to the oil embargo, certain elements in the Ukrainian government have been reported to be taking the offer seriously."

Impatient, Lewis cut in. "So we are going to use military forces to do what the Russians haven't been able to do."

Noting that Wilson was now becoming irritated by Lewis's manner, Secretary of Defense Rothenberg took up the challenge this time. "Yes, Congressman Lewis, we are. At the request of the Commonwealth forces, surgical strikes, using our air and ground units currently deployed in eastern Slovakia, will be used to neutralize the threat. The two storage sites, both in the vicinity of Svalyava, will be seized by rangers who will secure the devices in question and prepare them for transport back to Germany."

Had Rothenberg hit Lewis between the eyes, he couldn't have gotten a more violent reaction. Lewis, having been a member of the National Guard for years and a veteran of the Gulf War, hated it when politicians used terms like "surgical strike" and "neutralize" as if they really meant something. Pushing himself away from the table,

Lewis became enraged. "Jesus, Rothenberg. Do you think you're about to present a case in court?" Lewis didn't wait for Rothenberg, who was now becoming upset, to answer. "We're not talking about your law firm back in New York filing a suit against someone. We're talking about war. Real people, our people, going through the Carpathian Mountains in the dead of winter to seize weapons that the Ukrainians are no doubt defending with their best units. And when that happens, when our good little American boys and girls come nose-to-nose with those good little Ukrainian boys in the mountains, there'll be nothing surgical about the outcome. For those of you who haven't been blessed with the experience, there's nothing surgical about being on the receiving end of a 750-pound general purpose bomb."

Like a tag team wrestling match, Wilson took over from Rothenberg. "Congressman Lewis, we appreciate your concerns and understand your feelings." Though angry at having her carefully prepared briefing upset by Lewis, Wilson maintained the calm, steady demeanor that had made her famous and politically unbeatable. "Believe me, we have looked at every option and weighed all the risks. If there were another way to resolve this, I would have been the first to try it. We cannot, however, allow continued nuclear proliferation. It is time to draw the line."

Lewis, about to comment on Wilson's melodramatic use of "It is time to draw the line," bit his tongue. This was no time, he thought, for personal attacks. Best, he reasoned, to stick to the critical issues at hand. Looking down at his hands, now folded in his lap, Lewis spoke in a low and controlled voice. "Do we know, Madam President, who this nation is? I mean, wouldn't it be easier just to tighten the blockade on the Ukraine?"

Taking his turn, Soares responded to Lewis without commenting any further on Lewis's question of the blockade. "No, Congressman, we do not know who has approached the Ukrainians. Our source within the Ukrainian government only knows that the offer was made and the details about the transfer of the weapons are currently being discussed."

"So, when in doubt, send in the Marines."

Wilson looked Lewis in the eye. "Yes, Congressman, something like that."

"What do the Czech and German governments have to say about this impending invasion?"

In a rather offhanded manner, one that surprised most of the assembled senators and congressmen, Rothenberg brushed off Lewis's concerns. "This is not a matter that concerns either of those governments directly. Besides, for reasons of operational security it was felt that the fewer governments involved the better. The request made by the Commonwealth directly to President Wilson is not a matter that directly concerns any of the other European countries at this time. After the operation is under way, they will be briefed. Given the purpose of the operation and its objective, they will see the wisdom of our decision and support us."

For a moment there was silence. Then Lewis in a rather subdued manner asked Rothenberg if he really thought that the Germans would calmly allow U.S. forces to use their country as a jump-off point for the invasion of another country.

Soares's response sounded like a lecture. "I need not remind you, Congressman Lewis, that it has been the policy of Germany since unification to disarm. This includes nuclear weapons." Soares paused to correct himself. "Especially nuclear weapons. Besides, since the foundation of the Federal Republic of Germany, the policies of our two nations have been as one. We, after all, were instrumental in bringing about the unification of the two Germanys. They will not, Congressman Lewis, forget that."

Lewis was about to remind Soares that it was our postwar policies, not to mention our occupation of Germany after World War II, that had created the division of Germany into two parts, but decided to let the matter drop. He was, he realized, howling at the moon. The decision to use military forces to cover for a lack of an effective foreign policy had been made. Dropping his head, Lewis folded his hands on the table and lapsed into silence.

Satisfied that the threat to her briefing had been beaten back, Wilson looked about the room. "There is much to cover, gentlemen. I do appreciate Congressman Lewis's concerns. They reflect very real and sincere feelings. I assure you, those concerns will be put to rest before you leave this morning. Now, Pete, if you would please continue."

Though he didn't appear to be paying attention to the colonel as he delivered his report, Chancellor Johann Ruff heard every word and understood what they meant to him and Germany. Outside the window he could see nothing of Berlin. Only a few stray flurries, illuminated by the lights of his office, heralding the coming of another winter storm, were visible. It was dark and bitter cold outside. Just like his mood, Ruff thought. Pivoting on his good leg, Ruff turned away from the foreboding scene and toward the two general staff officers who had brought Ruff news that he had not wanted to hear.

For a second he looked at the two officers. The contrast between them was remarkable. General Walther Schacht, chief of the General Staff's intelligence section, was comfortably seated in a chair with his long legs jutting out while his head, canted to the side, rested on the hand of his left arm, which in turn rested on the arm of the chair. It seemed to Ruff as if Schacht was bored as he listened to Colonel Gerhard Paul render his report. That, however, was only natural. Bavarians, Ruff thought, were easily bored when dealing with serious matters. Paul, a native of Leipzig and chief of Schacht's Eastern Europe Department, chose to stand while he briefed his Chancellor on the situation in the Ukraine. Everything about Paul was militarily correct. From his erect, almost ramrod stiff position of attention, to the clarity and conciseness of the report that he delivered, Paul was what Ruff expected soldiers to be. It had been, Ruff thought, a mistake to exclude the senior officers of the East German Volksarmee from the West German Bundeswehr at the time of unification. He was glad that he had finally been able to reverse that decision. It gave those officers raised in the lax atmosphere of the Bundeswehr worthy role models.

When Paul finished, the room fell silent as the two general staff officers waited for Ruff to speak. Shuffling over to his desk, Ruff stood next to it, leaning against the side of the desk in an effort to relieve the pressure on his bad leg. Though it would have been wise to sit, Ruff chose to stand during this meeting. It was, after all, a very serious matter. Besides, in his own way Ruff was testing General Schacht. It seemed to Ruff that if he, the Chancellor of Germany, was standing, then protocol would dictate that Schacht should also stand. But Schacht didn't, and therefore failed Ruff's little test.

"Are we sure, Colonel Paul, that the Ukrainians know nothing about this?"

Without hesitation, Paul responded to Ruff in a crisp, no-nonsense manner. "The Ukrainians have been mesmerized by the buildup of Russian forces. None of their intelligence summaries over the last four days even mention the possibility of action by the Americans. It is as if the Americans are not there, even though the Americans have made no effort to cover the deployment of forces into eastern Slovakia."

"Then it would seem," Ruff stated in exasperation, "that the Ukrainians, like us, have fallen for the American deception plan that their deployment into the Czech and Slovakian republics was an effort to discourage the Hungarians from grabbing land that probably is rightfully theirs."

Ruff's tone and manner reminded Schacht of a professor of history, not a chancellor. Lifting his head off his hand, Schacht shook his head as he spoke. "I am still convinced that the initial purpose of the American deployment into the Czech and Slovakian republics was nothing more than that, an effort to put pressure on the Hungarians. And by the way, they succeeded. Hungarian units have begun to move back from the Slovakian border." Schacht waved his hand over his head. "This new matter is entirely different. As much as I admire the Americans, I do not think that they are capable of such an effective deception operation. My American section, after careful re-examination, finds nothing to support such a claim."

"Whether or not it was planned, Herr General, the fact remains," Ruff shot back, "that the Americans have decided to take action unilaterally with forces supposedly committed to NATO and stationed in our country without bothering to consult us."

"Perhaps, Herr Chancellor, the Americans do not trust us." Both Ruff and Schacht turned toward Paul. When he saw that he had their attention, he continued. "This is in my opinion nothing more than a matter of operational security. And given the sensitivity of the operation and the involvement of nuclear weapons, I can appreciate the American concerns. A success will in their eyes justify their actions. It is the way Americans conduct business and in the past have waged war."

Paul's comments infuriated Ruff, as Paul had expected. Ruff exploded. "So long as those forces continue to trace their line of communications through Germany, using German rail systems and German facilities, the Americans have no right to act without first consulting us. No right! Justified or not, we will become implicated in this action if we allow the Americans to continue to use our nation as a springboard for their military adventures." Ruff, his face red, stopped. He needed to compose himself, to calm down. When he was ready, Ruff continued to question Paul. "Will the Americans be able to achieve their goal using only one reinforced brigade?"

Glancing from Ruff to Paul, Schacht watched and waited for Paul's response. "Their operation, from what we know, relies on speed and surprise. The ranger battalion, supported by special operations helicopter units, will have little trouble securing the two depots where the nuclear weapons are secured. This is a drill that they have practiced many times. The rangers will be reinforced later in the day by a dismounted infantry battalion airlifted into Svalyava. Together, rangers and infantry, supported by attack helicopters and close air support, will be able to hold the airhead while the weapons are evacuated. All of this will take less than forty-eight hours."

"Then, Colonel, why the ground attack?"

Now, Schacht thought, it was the colonel who was acting like a university professor.

"The ground attack is insurance, Herr Chancellor. If the weather prevents the removal of the nuclear weapons by air, the Americans will be able to open up a ground corridor that will be used to move the weapons as well as the rangers and the infantry out of the Ukraine. In addition, the Ukrainians will need to commit forces against the ground attack, forces that would otherwise be free to counterattack the American rangers. In the initial confusion of the American attacks, the Ukrainian commanders in the region may hesitate if they are unsure which is the main effort. It will take them time to gather intelligence, determine where the greatest threat is, and then develop plans and issue orders to deal with the situation. And while they do this, the Americans will be removing the weapons which they came for."

"And where," Ruff asked, "will the Americans take these weapons?"

Paul, not knowing, did not answer. For a moment this surprised Ruff. It should not have, since Paul's section was compartmentalized from other sections under Schacht's control. Schacht, wanting to put his energetic subordinate in his place without making a scene, allowed the pregnant pause to continue for a few more moments before he finally answered Ruff. "Sembach Air Base, Herr Chancellor. The Americans will use tactical airlift C-130s, I believe, to move the nuclear weapons either directly from the depot in the Ukraine or from a temporary site in Slovakia. From Sembach, the weapons will be transloaded to C-141s and flown to the United States for disposal."

"How sure, General Schacht, are you of your information?"

It was Schacht's turn to brag about his knowledge. "I was handed, this afternoon, a copy of the United States Air Force Europe's security and movement plan for what they are calling Operation Desperate Fumble."

Though Ruff was curious as to how such a document had been obtained, he decided not to pursue the matter, not now. There was much to be done, much damage that needed to be repaired. Although the American action had threatened to ruin one of his goals, their plans offered him, and Germany, the opportunity to achieve something even greater. Without any further discussion, Ruff dismissed Schacht and Paul. They had provided him with more than enough information for now.

When they had left, Ruff leaned over his desk and buzzed his personal aide on his intercom. "Is the Ukrainian ambassador here yet?"

A crisp, sharp "Yes, Herr Chancellor" came back over the intercom speaker.

"Has he been briefed yet?"

"Colonel Kasper is finishing that now, Herr Chancellor."

"Fine, fine. Please inform Colonel Kasper that I would like him to bring the Ukrainian ambassador into my office as soon as he has finished. And after you do that, inform General Lange that I will need to see him and his plans and operations staff immediately following my meeting with the Ukrainian." Without waiting for a response, Ruff flipped the intercom off and straightened up. That effort caused a spasm of pain in his right leg, a spasm that began from a knee long ago shattered by a grenade and never healed.

When the pain had subsided, Ruff opened a desk drawer and removed a highly polished wooden box. The box, measuring a little under a half a meter long, was trimmed with shiny brass hinges and a lock. Placing the box before him on his desk, Ruff reached into his vest pocket and pulled out a small key.

He paused for a moment after unlocking the box. For opening the box was to him a small ceremony to be cherished, something not to be rushed. When he was ready, Ruff slowly lifted the lid, revealing a black-handled knife in a black metal sheath nestled in blood-red velvet. Ruff ran his fingers along the knife, slowing when the tips of his fingers fell upon the Hitler Youth crest inlaid in the knife's handle. This knife to anyone else would be nothing more than a piece of metal, at best war memorabilia. But to Ruff it was his sole connection to his youth, a youth that came to a crashing end in April of 1945 when all of his dreams and all of his hopes, like his family, were brutally wiped away by an uncultured and brutish conqueror.

But even more than a link to his past, the black knife symbolized Ruff's quest born in the tortured mind and broken body of an eight-year-old boy who had nothing, not even his dreams. The idea of using this knife, his knife, to exact revenge had soon been replaced by practical concerns of survival in a devastated and defeated country. But the desire to exact that revenge was never far from Chancellor Johann Ruff's mind, just as his knife was never far from his side, ready to be used when the time was right.

C H A P T E R   2

---

7 JANUARY

While every wild gyration of the UH-60 Blackhawk helicopter caused Sergeant George Couvelha's heart to skip a beat, Specialist Kevin Pape, strapped into the nylon seat next to him, was leaning back and enjoying the ride. To Pape, being in a helicopter zipping along, through, and around every fold of the earth at high speed was the next best thing to sex. You could feel every maneuver, every twist, every turn. Pape especially enjoyed it when the helicopter went up and over hills. As the pilot came to a hill or ridge that could not be flown around, he would grudgingly pull his stick back, causing the helicopter to pitch up and forcing his passengers down into their seats. Once he was clear of the bothersome hill or ridge, the pilot would thrust his stick forward, causing the helicopter to dive, giving everyone on board a momentary lift. One could almost feel his internal organs, in particular the stomach, move up a few inches as if they were floating. While it was popular to compare the sensation of flying in a helicopter like this to a roller coaster, Pape thought such a comparison was all wrong. After all, as Pape liked to point out, roller coasters were safe. Almost no one ever died while riding on a roller coaster. A helicopter, however, being piloted by a twenty-two-year-old warrant officer, aided only by a navigational system built by the lowest bidder and night vision goggles that turned everything black and green, moving at one hundred plus miles an hour less than one hundred feet above the ground on a pitch black night, was an entirely different matter. That, Pape would gleefully point out to his drinking buddies, was a truly frightening experience.

Yet Pape felt no fear that night. Even when the pilot, misjudging a hill mass, almost stood the helicopter on its side, Pape didn't bat an eye. He was at nineteen a true adrenaline freak. No ride was too dangerous, no challenge too frightening. That was why he was a ranger. Rangers were always doing something neat, something that was just a little bit unconventional and a tad dangerous. Though, like everyone else in the United States Army, Pape had to tolerate the day-to-day routine BS, the rush of a mass parachute drop or a day on the rappelling towers more than compensated for the occasional tour of guard duty or post police detail. Besides, for him the rangers were just a beginning. When his current enlistment was over, he intended to re-enlist for Special Forces. In Pape's nineteen-year-old eyes, they were the ultimate danger junkies.

That he might not make it through his current enlistment was the furthest thing from Pape's young mind that night. He knew where they were going, and he knew what they were after. That there would be shooting was a given. After all, it was ludicrous to think that the troops guarding the nukes would just step aside and hand them over. As Pape's platoon leader pointed out, the first reaction of the Ukrainian guards when they saw a battalion of rangers armed to the teeth and spoiling for a fight come boiling out of the night wasn't going to be a challenge and request for a password.

It was therefore no surprise that the commander of the 1st Ranger Battalion, 77th Infantry, translated the line in his operations order directing him to use minimum force to mean swift, violent, and overwhelming firepower applied in the shortest amount of time. Such aggressive thinking was infectious and, to the rangers, welcome. Pape's company commander, carried away by what the first sergeant called the spirit of the bayonet, restated the phrase minimum force to mean using the fewest bullets in the shortest amount of time to kill the most Ukrainians. At their final briefing the young captain told his assembled troops that he expected them to "go in, blow away anyone that gets in our way, secure the nukes, and wait for the Air Force. No muss, no fuss."

So it was not surprising that young Kevin Pape, raised in the shadows of John Wayne, Clint Eastwood, and Rambo, drilled in the skills of war until he could perform without thinking, and fired up by bold, aggressive, and confident officers, should feel invulnerable to the point of being cocky. There was no room in his mind that night for the image of shattered bodies brutalized by grenades and automatic weapons. Pape's young nostrils had yet to inhale the stench of burned flesh or the contents of human bowels and intestines, mixed with warm blood, spilled at his feet. There was, in training, no way to simulate the screams of wounded and dying men that sounded more like wild animals than the cries of sons and fathers. Combat, only combat, brutal and bloody, can cure a young soldier's naiveté. Pape in less than fifteen minutes was about to receive his first treatment.

If Pape lacked the ability to visualize what was about to happen, Colonel Ed Martin, commander of the 404th Tactical Fighter Squadron, more than made up for him. Easing his F-117 fighter down to an altitude of 20,000 feet, Martin prepared to commence his final run-in. There wasn't actually much for him to do. Since takeoff, his fighter had for all practical purposes been on automatic pilot. All he needed to do to keep his aircraft on course was to keep the little green indicator on the display to his front that represented his aircraft's actual heading aligned with the command-heading indicator that the computer in the aircraft's navigational system told him he should be on. Even if Martin altered the airspeed or altitude, the navigational system's computer took this into account, made new computations, and transmitted a new command heading, if necessary, for Martin to follow.

As easy as that was, the actual bomb run would be, technically, easier. Once he had reached the point where he would initiate his attack, all the pilot of an F-117 had to do was activate the weapons controls, ensure the laser designator was on its mark, and then let his aircraft take over the bomb run. He would make what the designers called "a hands-off attack," meaning the firepower control computer, working with the navigational system computer, would do everything. Martin was just there to keep an eye on everything and make sure nothing went wrong. In theory a piece of cake.

For Martin, however, this mission was anything but a joy ride. Although he was the commander of the 404th, at that moment the only thing he commanded was the aircraft that he was in. And even that point, given all the computers and such, was questionable. In the past, the necessity of flying the aircraft, staying on top of the tactical situation, and keeping track of a wing man occupied the pilot's mind, leaving little time to dwell on fears, real and imagined. Glancing to his left and then his right, Martin looked at the night sky. He could not escape the thought that somewhere out there eleven other aircraft of his squadron, swallowed up by a bitter cold night sky, were boring down on their designated targets, alone, like his. It was times like this that made Martin regret not having a backseater that he could talk to. Now, Martin thought, if they could only come up with a computer that alleviated the apprehensions and concerns of a commander, he'd be out of a job, which at the moment didn't seem to be such a bad idea.

Below him, buried under tons of dirt, rock, and concrete in command and control bunkers and remote missile sites, soldiers of the Ukrainian air defense command sat monitoring their radar screens and sensors, searching for them. It was, Martin thought, a high-tech contest. After all, he and the rest of his pilots were betting that American technology would allow them to win the game of hide-and-seek against the best air defense system in the world. Given that, they had to win the intelligence war. They were betting that American intelligence was good enough to win the information battle, the results of which had been used to program his navigational and weapons-control panel for this attack. In that struggle, American intelligence agencies had to overcome Ukrainian counterintelligence and operational security measures designed to throw their efforts off far enough so that the real targets were missed. And even if Martin and his men made it to the correct target, there was always the question of whether or not the weapons they carried would do the job. What a waste, he thought, to come all this way just to put a hole in the ground.

Such thoughts cluttered Martin's mind as he approached the IP, or initial point, over Mukacevo. The price of failure was not an intangible that he had to leave to his imagination. During the Gulf War, Martin had had more than enough of an opportunity to see, up close and personal, what failure meant. His most vivid memory of the war was the loss of a close friend who misjudged his ability to bring his crippled aircraft home. In the midst of the air war, just when everything was settling down to almost a dull routine, Martin watched as one of the aircraft in the squadron he was assigned to came limping in after a raid over Iraq. Damaged by anti-aircraft fire, the pilot had lost some of his avionics as well as fuel. Still the pilot felt confident that he could make it. And he almost did. The pilot of the damaged aircraft actually made it to within two hundred meters of the runway before his lift and luck gave out. Martin, with two other pilots from the squadron, watched as the F-15E's landing gear bit into the desert sand just short of the runway and collapsed, sending the aircraft, still traveling at over one hundred miles an hour, tumbling forward, tearing itself apart. Despite his better judgment, Martin had run out to the aircraft, thinking that perhaps, somehow, his friend had miraculously survived. Miracles, however, were not in order that day. Like the F-15E, there was little left of Martin's friend.

A small chirp over Martin's headset wrenched his mind from the bright barren vistas of a past war captured forever by his mind's eye back to the bitter darkness of the present one. Looking at his console, Martin saw that a Ukrainian air defense search radar was sweeping the area. The electronic warfare system identified the radar as belonging to an SA-10 surface-to-air missile battery. It also told Martin that the radar had not yet detected him, that it was still in the search mode. Another tone, with a slightly different pitch, warned Martin that he had reached the IP.

For a moment Martin considered his situation. Although he was still undetected, as soon as he began his bomb run he would have to open the bomb bay door and allow the 750-pound laser-guided bomb he carried to swing down into the release position. Unfortunately, for the briefest of moments, the bomb, built without the benefits of stealth technology, would be visible to the SA-10 battery's search radar. That meant in turn that so long as the bomb was attached to his aircraft while Martin was getting his laser dot on target, the SA-10 battery could engage him.

The question of whether he should initiate his attack now or try a different approach, one that perhaps would not expose him to the surface-to-air battery, momentarily crossed Martin's mind. As quickly as that thought came, however, he pushed it aside. Martin, a full colonel in the United States Air Force and a squadron commander, had a critical job to do. To his front, just east of Mukacevo, at a range of ten miles and 20,000 feet below, lay the command and control bunker from which the district military commander would coordinate the defense of the Ukrainian province of Ruthenia. Destruction, or even the temporary crippling of that bunker, would hamstring the efforts of the Ukrainian commander to respond to the Army's ground attack. To break off his attack might be the best option. But there was no assurance that a different approach would be any safer. After all, if the Ukrainians took the time to set up a battery to cover one approach, it was logical that they would ensure all approaches were covered. Besides, only an attack from the southwest would ensure penetration of the main chamber. Another approach simply would not do the job.

With some effort, Martin began to compose himself as he turned his fighter into the attack. Scanning his instruments, Martin could feel his heart begin to beat faster while his breathing became more rapid. Slowly he began to block out all thoughts and feelings that did not concern his attack. Instead, Martin focused his full attention on the heads-up display to his front, checking the aircraft's heading, fire control reticle, airspeed, altitude, weapons status, and a myriad of other information. He was committed. He was in the attack mode. In another minute it would all be over, success or failure.

Without further thought, Martin opened the bomb bay door and allowed the bomb to swing out on a trapezelike frame that locked the bomb into the drop position. Almost at the same instant, the tone in his ear changed as the electronic warfare system told Martin that the SA-10 battery had radar lock. The target acquisition radar had been activated. Martin, however, ignored the tone. His mind and body were absorbed by the act of superimposing the laser designation reticle onto the ventilator shaft of the bunker below. That was at that moment all he needed to see, all he needed to worry about.

The blast of air let into the helicopter when First Lieutenant Frank Zack, the American ranger company executive officer, slid the door open hit Major Nikolai Ilvanich like a sledgehammer. Ilvanich, lulled into a deep sleep by the Blackhawk helicopter's vibrations, hadn't realized that they had reached their target. With the ease of a practiced veteran, Ilvanich, however, was fully awake and taking in everything. Nothing escaped him. He heard every word and saw every action around him. The executive officer across from him was in the door and ready to leap out as soon as the helicopter touched down. Behind him a nervous sergeant was fumbling with his gear while an excited soldier with fire in his eyes, named Pape, kept nudging him in an effort to get closer to the door. Ilvanich watched the young soldier as his fingers worked the action of his squad automatic weapon while he urged his sergeant to get moving. That young man's lust for battle,

Ilvanich knew, would be tempered as soon as he saw his first wounded man at his feet writhing and screaming.

When the helicopter came around the side of the mountain and began its descent, Ilvanich turned his attention away from Pape and leaned forward to study their target. Outside, framed by the helicopter's door, lay the landing zone. From where he sat, it looked small, mainly because it was small. To one side was the mountain that contained the nuclear weapons storage site. The landing zone was nothing more than a ledge measuring one hundred by two hundred meters that jutted out from the side of that mountain. In the glow of the security lights, Ilvanich could see the tunnel entrance, wide open at the moment. The entrance was protected by a small concrete bunker jutting out from the right side of the tunnel entrance overlooking a small maze of movable concrete road barriers set up in such a manner that anyone entering the tunnel had to zigzag through them single file. Across from it stood a cinder block building that provided protection for half a dozen or so guards responsible for patrolling the chainlink fence topped with barbed wire that ran along the entire outer perimeter of the ledge.

There was, as far as he could see, no movement on the ground, no guards visible. The security lights were still on, providing the helicopter pilots ample light with which to land. More importantly, there was no anti-aircraft fire. The surprise was complete. Barring a serious miscalculation, success was all but guaranteed.

Unsnapping his seat belt, Ilvanich readjusted his gear, pulled the zipper up on his camouflage parka, and pulled the folding stock assault rifle that he had slung over his shoulder around from his side onto his lap, resting his right hand on it. By the time the helicopter's wheels hit the ground with a thump, Ilvanich was ready.

In a second Blackhawk across from Ilvanich's, the scene was repeated. Before the Blackhawk's door gunners could open up with their M-60 machine guns, Captain Vernon Smithy's command of "LET'S GO, RANGERS" cleared the helicopter. In their haste to get out onto the ground and deploy, the rangers with Smithy masked the right door gunner's field of fire, preventing him from dropping the two Ukrainian guards standing behind the concrete barriers at the mouth of the tunnel that ran into the side of the mountain.

For a moment, the two guards hesitated, each one thinking the same thought: Stand and fight or flee? The shock of seeing four white-washed helicopters in a perfect formation drop out of nowhere and disgorge dozens of armed troops less than twenty meters away was overpowering. That they would never be able to stop them was obvious. That there was no escape from this flood of invaders was equally clear. All that remained for the guards to do, in the few seconds that it took their attackers to disembark and form an assault line, was to shut the huge steel blast door and warn the guards inside the mountain. After glancing at their attackers one more time, both fled for the bunker.

The faster of the two made it into the bunker and grabbed the phone to notify the guards inside the tunnel. The second Ukrainian guard followed after dropping down behind the concrete barrier and crawling to the bunker on his hands and knees. Once he reached the open doorway of the bunker, the second Ukrainian guard pulled himself up and faced the panel just inside the bunker door that controlled the lights and the blast door of the tunnel entrance. He only managed to hit the switch that started the thick steel door closing before a ranger tossed a grenade around the corner of the concrete barrier into the open door of the bunker.

The door gunner on the helicopter that carried Ilvanich and First Lieutenant Zack had no problems with the exiting rangers. Without any orders being needed, the twenty-one-year-old native of Tennessee opened fire, raking the cinder block building that served as a guard shack with a quick burst. The six Ukrainian guards stationed there, who were responsible for securing the outer perimeter fence, instinctively chose to fight, ignoring in their haste the door gunner's first burst. Pouring through the narrow door, parkas half on but weapons at the ready, they rushed out into the night to deploy and to repel the attackers. The lean country boy behind the helicopter's M-60 machine gun held his fire as he watched, waited, and shifted his gun to the right a little. When he fired again, he dropped the first three guards. The remaining three, seeing their comrades chewed up by machine-gun fire so quickly, were thrown into a panic. Caught in the open, between the onslaught of attackers and the chainlink fence they were supposed to guard, the remaining three guards turned to run back into their guard shack.

Kevin Pape stopped that. Holding the butt plate of his squad automatic weapon against his right hip, Pape trained his weapon on the first Ukrainian, who already had his foot in the door of the guard shack. Using his body to aim and direct the fire of his weapon, Pape opened up, holding the trigger down while he moved his entire body to the right, raking the file of Ukrainians. Like tin cans set on a wall for target practice, each of the Ukrainian guards was knocked back as Pape's hail of bullets swept down their file.

Following close behind Zack, Ilvanich watched the brief firefight with the six Ukrainians in the guard shack and the two guards at the tunnel entrance. All were dead or wounded in a matter of seconds. They were no longer a factor. But the two guards at the tunnel entrance, though they chose not to fight, had been far more effective than the six in the guard shack. In their haste, not one of them had even considered killing the floodlights that bathed the area around the mouth of the tunnel in a glaring green fluorescent light. That light, Ilvanich thought, was a gift to the Americans. It was a great aid to the demolition team, allowing them to prepare the charges that they needed to blow their way into the tunnel in record time. The light also made it easier for the rangers already on the ground to finish their deployment around the perimeter and assist in the landing of the next wave. Not killing the lights, Ilvanich thought, negated the sacrifice that the two guards at the tunnel had made.

Standing upright for the first time since landing, Ilvanich looked around and watched the American rangers. A little sloppy, he thought, but so far there were no problems that the Americans were not prepared to deal with. With nothing to do and no need to advise anyone, Ilvanich began to follow the ranger company XO. The ranger company commander, Captain Smithy, had more than made clear during the planning and preparation for the raid, that he had no use for Ilvanich. Ilvanich, though offended, had said nothing. He had no desire to add to Smithy's concerns. Smithy already was burdened with one Russian advisor, a slightly overweight major who had once been the deputy commander in charge of security of this storage site. Smithy didn't need a second advisor hovering over his shoulder.

Noting that Zack, the XO, had already moved into the guard shack in the company of two radiomen and a sergeant, Ilvanich followed to see what he was doing. Carefully stepping over a body that partially blocked the doorway, Ilvanich entered the guard shack. As he did so, he was overwhelmed by the warmth of the room and the bright lights that were still on. Dressed for combat in the cold, Ilvanich was made uncomfortable by the heat from the stove. He considered going back outside but decided to wait until he found out what Lieutenant Zack intended to do in there.

Zack, ignoring Ilvanich as his company commander did, went about the task of setting up the company command post. As soon as the radiomen set their radios on the table, Zack stripped off his heavy mittens, cocked his helmet back on his head, and grabbed the hand mike of the radio set on the battalion command net. "Swift Hawk Six. Swift Hawk Six, this is Alpha Five. Alpha is down and preparing to enter the briar patch. Over."

For a moment Ilvanich refused to believe that Zack intended to make this building the company command post. Not only was it the only landmark of importance with its lights still on, but it sat right in the middle of the primary approach leading onto the ledge that any Ukrainian reaction force would use to get to the tunnel fifty meters away. The comfortable and warm guard shack would in a matter of minutes become a death trap. Deciding that he wanted no part of that, Ilvanich called out to Zack, telling him that he was going to go outside.

Zack, with the radio's hand mike to his ear, waved to Ilvanich. "You go ahead and do that, Major," mumbling to himself after Ilvanich had turned to leave, "Shithead." Once outside, Ilvanich paused, shaking his head as he thought about Zack, repeating to himself, "Idiot, idiot."

Fifty yards away, by the tunnel entrance, Captain Smithy waited impatiently while the demolition team finished placing their charges. Though they had planned on such an eventuality, Smithy was upset that they hadn't been able to drop the guards before they closed the door. It would have been, he thought, so much quicker, so much easier.

To his rear, Smithy could hear the third and last wave of Black-hawks lifting off, telling him that the last of his company was in. Turning his head, he watched as the 2nd Platoon began to deploy to the left of the 1st Platoon, now in positions along the outer perimeter fence. The guard shack at the outer perimeter fence was where the two platoons came together and, because it was centrally located and easy to find, served as the company headquarters. Noticing the Russian airborne major standing next to the door of the guard shack, Smithy watched him for a moment. Smithy didn't like that Russian. While the fat major was a nuisance, he at least seemed friendly; and besides, his knowledge of the site had been and continued to be useful. Major Ilvanich, however, was different. He had a sinister air about him. Smithy had decided early that this man, laconic and stone-faced, was not to be trusted. As Smithy watched, Ilvanich moved away from the guard shack, unslinging his AK assault rifle and working its bolt while he looked around, observing the deployment of the 2nd Platoon. Wondering why he wasn't staying with Zack, as he had been told, Smithy was about to go over and find out when the sergeant in charge of the demolition team tapped Smithy on the shoulder. "We're ready to blow it, sir."

Anxious to get on with this, Smithy forgot about the Russian major and shifted his full attention to the matter at hand. Slapping the demo team leader on the side of the arm, Smithy yelled, "Okay, let's get this show on the road."

Turning, the demo sergeant cupped his hands over his mouth, yelling, "FIRE IN THE HOLE! FIRE IN THE HOLE! FIRE IN THE HOLE!" before giving one of his people the high sign to set off the charge.

Followed by the fat Russian major, Smithy moved around to the front of the protective barrier that had failed to save the two Ukrainian guards, yelling to the 3rd Platoon leader to be ready to rush the tunnel as soon as the charge went off. Ducking behind the concrete wall, Smithy prepared to wait until the blast door had been breached and the 3rd Platoon had completed their forced entry. While he waited, Smithy watched the members of 2nd Platoon who had not yet deployed seek cover. For the first time it dawned upon him that the floodlights were still on, bathing the entire area in light and making every move around the tunnel entrance visible for miles. Smithy was still debating whether this was good or bad when the demo charge went off.

At the other end of the tunnel, a group of Ukrainian soldiers peered over their hastily constructed barricade while they watched and waited nervously for their attackers to show themselves. Behind them, their commander, Captain G. Biryukov from the Ukrainian internal security forces, wondered what was going on outside. Except for a single panicked call from a guard at the entrance to the tunnel informing him that they were under attack, he knew nothing. In fact, Biryukov didn't even know that their assailants were Americans. Like everyone else in the tunnel, Biryukov assumed they were Russians. He had in fact even reported that to the reaction force. Efforts to report his situation to the commander of the Ruthenian military district using the direct line to the district command and control bunker east of Mukacevo had failed. That line, for some reason, was dead.

Nervously glancing around, Biryukov began to reconsider the wisdom of making a stand in the assembly chamber. At first he had considered surrendering this cavernous hall to the attackers and withdrawing his men to the two storage chambers below. That would have placed two massive barriers between his men and the Russians—the blast door at the entrance to the tunnel and the steel doors at both ends of the separate elevator shafts that serviced each of the two lower chambers. It had been a tempting thought, an option which he now regretted that he had not taken. To do so, of course, would not only have surrendered the assembly chamber, it would have meant splitting his meager force in half, with one group going down to protect the casings and triggering mechanisms in one chamber to the right of the assembly chamber while the others went down to protect the plutonium cores, the heart of the nuclear devices, which were kept in the other lower chamber to the left. In the end the fact that there were no communications facilities to the outside world in either of the lower chambers had tipped the scale in favor of holding on to the assembly chamber as long as possible. Besides, at the time Biryukov had made his decision, something that he had always found difficult, he had reasoned that if things went bad and the reaction force didn't make it to him before the Russians broke in, he could always retreat down to the other chambers. It was a safe compromise, one which he could justify to his superior.

When the thought that he would never have the need to justify it occurred to Biryukov as he watched and waited with his men, he called his deputy, a young lieutenant, and a sergeant over. Both men pulled themselves away from their positions at the barricade and trotted over to where Biryukov stood next to the elevator shaft leading to the chamber where the plutonium cores were stored. After the lieutenant and sergeant presented themselves, Biryukov looked at the main tunnel entrance, then at each of the two men before him. "Lieutenant Sorokovoy, give Sergeant Popel your key."

Startled by the order, both Sorokovoy and Popel turned and looked at each other wide-eyed before turning back to face their commander. The key in question was one of a pair that was needed to initiate the self-destruct sequence designed as a last-ditch effort to deny capture of weapons at the storage facility. According to regulations, only officers were permitted to carry the keys. Even under the most extreme circumstances, no one had ever thought of relinquishing control of a key except to another officer authorized to have it. So Biryukov's order was a shock to both his subordinates.

With both men staring at Biryukov, he took a deep breath. "Unless the main reaction force arrives in the next few minutes, we will lose this facility. My orders are to prevent the loss of any weapons. Since I am unable to contact the commander of the reaction force or the military district command post, I must assume the worst and prepare to execute my orders." Biryukov paused to let what he had just said sink in. "Lieutenant Sorokovoy, you will remain with the main force here on this level and hold for as long as you can. Sergeant Popel will accompany me with two men to the lower level and wait as long as we can before initiating the sequence."

Still stunned, neither Sorokovoy nor Popel responded at first. Instructions for activating the small atomic demolition device that would destroy the storage site in order to prevent compromise were classified top secret and were supposed to be known only by the officers of the guard. That every sergeant in the force knew how to do it was an open secret. Still, thoughts of the consequences of admitting it, even under these circumstances, caused the sergeant to hesitate.

An ear-splitting blast wrenched Biryukov's attention back to the far end of the tunnel. The Russians were attempting to breach the blast door. From somewhere to his right a sergeant yelled to his men, "Here they come!"

Biryukov looked toward the door, then back at his subordinates, yelling as he did so. "Lieutenant Sorokovoy, the key. Give the key to Sergeant Popel now!" Sorokovoy, also looking toward the tunnel entrance, pulled the key from around his neck and offered it to Popel without looking. Popel, knowing what all of this meant, took the key dangling from a chain and held it at arm's length as if it were a poisonous snake. Only Biryukov's shouted orders got him to react.

"All right, Lieutenant Sorokovoy, you have your instructions. Do the best you can and pray the reaction force reacts." When Sorokovoy was gone, Biryukov reached out and grasped Popel on his shoulder. "Come, Sergeant. Stay next to me. And whatever happens up here, we must make it down that elevator. Understood?"

After Popel nodded, Biryukov moved closer to the barricade. Like everyone else, he lowered his head and steadied his weapon. As he watched and waited for the assault force to come, a gray cloud caused by the explosion crept down toward them, filling the chamber with acrid smoke. Instead of a stampede of boots, however, the first noise that came from the gray cloud was a series of clicks and hisses. It took Biryukov a second to understand what was happening. When he did, his warning was cut short by a series of pops as the flash grenades went off and flooded the tunnel with blinding light.

Damn, he thought as he rubbed his eyes. Damn! You fool, you know better. You know the drill. Blind the defenders with smoke or flash grenades and then attack. It was a standard drill for the KGB strike teams. Still unable to see, Biryukov was alerted by a new series of pops and hissing sounds to the next step in the KGB drill. Reaching down, Biryukov grabbed for his chemical protective mask, yelling as he worked to pull it out of its carrier, "GAS! GAS! GAS!"

Though the second series of grenades were only HC grenades, white smoke, Biryukov and his men had no way of knowing and were not about to take a chance. Had they realized that the attackers were American rangers and not KGB, they might have forgone the hassle of putting on their protective masks. As it was, the smoke grenades worked better than Smithy could have hoped. The Ukrainians were struggling with their protective masks when Smithy's 3rd Platoon came out of the white cloud and fell upon Biryukov's men.

The run from the border into the center of Uzhgorod was fast, wild, and unopposed. Following the cavalry troop that led the 1st Brigade into the Ukraine, Company C, 3rd Battalion, 3rd Infantry, under the command of Captain Nancy Kozak, prepared to turn south on the road for Chop. While her driver kept the last vehicle of the cavalry troop in sight, Kozak stood upright in the open hatch of her M-2 Bradley infantry fighting vehicle, alternating between looking down at the map she held in one hand and up as she tried to read the street signs and look for landmarks she had been briefed on. Not wanting to miss her turn, Kozak paid scant attention to the scene around her. She noted that the streetlights were still on, indicating that the Ukrainians were taken by complete surprise, and wondered how long that would last. Kozak didn't pay any attention to the people of Uzhgorod, shaken out of a sound sleep by the rumbling of the cavalry troop's sixty-three-ton tanks, as they pulled the shades of their bedroom windows back to see who was invading their country this time. Kozak didn't even seem to be aware of a police car, lights flashing, as it came out of a side street, stopping just short of the main road leading from the border. The startled policeman driving saw the armored vehicles, slammed on the brakes, and immediately backed up without hesitation or looking behind him. Though the policeman had no idea who or why his city was being overrun by armored vehicles, he knew that at that moment there was little he could do.

When Kozak saw the turnoff, she keyed the intercom on her helmet and shouted to her driver to make a hard right. Gripping onto the lip of her hatch, Kozak hung on as the Bradley made the sharp turn that almost carried them into a line of parked cars that lined the street. Once they were on the road to Chop, Kozak leaned over and looked to her rear to make sure that the platoon following her also made the turn. In the bright light provided by the overhead streetlights, Kozak began counting vehicles as they made the turn until her own Bradley went around a slight curve that blocked her view. By that time, she had seen all four Bradleys of her 2nd Platoon, as well as the lead tank of the attached tank platoon, make the turn.

Satisfied that everyone in her company team would make the turn and that they were on the right road, Kozak turned to the front, looking at the shops and apartment buildings that lined the street on either side. There was little difference between the streets and shops here and those they had seen in Czech towns and villages. Those, in turn, had reminded her of the towns and villages in Germany, except that the German buildings were more modern, cleaner, and more colorful. Before turning her thoughts back toward her mission, it dawned upon Kozak that this whole region, with its buildings and dingy towns nestled in the hills and mountains connected by twisting roads, reminded her of Pittsburgh. Strange, she thought. In her two years in Germany she had been with armored columns running through towns and across the countryside without giving it a second thought. The idea of doing so in Pittsburgh, however, was totally beyond her. When the last of the streetlights whizzed by as her Bradley raced out of the narrow streets of the town and into the dark countryside, Kozak looked back at Uzhgorod one more time. I guess, she thought, these people are used to this sort of thing by now.

From the second-story window of his small bedroom, a middle-aged

Ukrainian shopkeeper watched the parade of armored vehicles roll by in the street below. Across the room, sitting up in their bed, his wife waited, struggling to overcome her fright and join her husband. Unable to do so, she called from the bed, "Josef, is it the Russians?"

At first he didn't answer. It had been a long time since he had served in the Red Army. But as a gunner on a tank stationed in East Germany, he had been trained well to recognize enemy vehicles. The sight of those vehicles right there under his own bedroom window was a shock. Finally, when he did answer, Josef meekly mumbled, "No, not Russians."

That statement made his wife's eyes grow large as she threw her hands up over her mouth. "Oh, my God, not the Germans, again?"

Turning, Josef looked at his wife. He was about to ridicule her for making such a silly statement, but then stopped. In this world of theirs, turned upside down, anything, including their worst nightmare, was possible. So instead of chiding his wife for making such a foolish comment, Josef walked across the darkened room, reassuring her as he did so. "No, it's only the Americans."

The high-pitched whine of a BTR armored personnel carrier racing up the road toward their position caused Ilvanich to turn his attention away from the echo of gunfire and grenade blasts coming from the tunnel and to the road outside the chainlink fence. It was the reaction force, finally. Looking at his watch, Ilvanich noted the time. Slow, he thought. They were too slow and now too late. A Russian reaction force, he reasoned, would have been there in half the time. How fortunate for the Americans, Ilvanich thought, that they are only pitted against Ukrainians and not Russians.

The American reaction to this new threat, however, was not slow. Along the perimeter fence, near the cinder block guard shack, one of the squad leaders shouted back to his platoon leader, "BTR on the road, coming up fast and dumb." At first Ilvanich considered the sergeant's report to be rather flippant and unmilitary. Then after thinking about it for a moment, Ilvanich chuckled. As he peered into the night beyond the glare of the bright security lights in an effort to spot the reaction force's BTR armored personnel carrier, Ilvanich decided that the American sergeant's report was in fact quite accurate. The Ukrainians were coming on too fast and in a manner that all but guaranteed their demise. Though dumb was not quite the word he would have chosen, Ilvanich reminded himself that the Americans had a unique unmilitary style that defied all logic and common sense.

Deciding that it would not be a good idea to stay next to the cinder block building once the shooting started, Ilvanich looked for a spot on the firing line along the chainlink fence that would offer both cover and a vantage point. When he saw what he was looking for next to a soldier with a squad automatic weapon, Ilvanich glanced down at his assault rifle to ensure that the safety was engaged before moving over to his new position. His pace was deliberate, not hurried, and he continued to look into the darkness for the approaching BTR.

Kevin Pape could feel himself getting excited. This was it! This was no bullshit, for a real enemy armored personnel carrier was coming after them. It wasn't a plywood panel like the ones they used on the squad assault range at Grafenwöhr. It wasn't a vismod, a mock vehicle with a fiberglass and sheet-metal shell made up to look like a BTR like the ones they went against at the maneuver training area at Hohenfels. This one was real, brim full of pissed-off Ukrainians who were coming after him and the rest of 2nd Squad. Pape didn't feel the cold. He didn't notice the Russian major settle down into a prone position next to him. All Pape's attention was focused where the road disappeared into the darkness as he listened to the noise of the BTR grow as it closed on their position. Flexing his right index finger, Pape lightly stroked the trigger of his weapon and waited.

To Pape's right, Sergeant Couvelha called out to his men armed with AT-4 anti-tank rocket launchers. "Billy, you fire first. And make sure you call out your range before you do." Couvelha twisted his head toward the second soldier. "Ned, listen up for Billy's range and watch where his rocket hits. Make your correction if you need to, then fire. Got it?"

Billy, intently staring through the sight of his rocket launcher, said nothing. He only nodded, a nod that Couvelha didn't see, not that he needed to. Billy was young but he was solid and dependable. Couvelha knew Billy had heard. Ned, a smile on his face, turned to Couvelha. "No sweat, Sarge."

Couvelha shook his head. Unlike Billy, Ned was a little too cool, too cocksure of himself for Couvelha, which is why Ned fired second. He was about to tell Ned that he had better pay attention to his front when Billy yelled, "RANGE, TWO HUNDRED METERS! FIRING!"

Billy's announcement gave everyone on the firing line a second to prepare themselves. Half of the men, looking elsewhere, hadn't seen the BTR as it emerged from the darkness. Even when he followed the road, Pape still could not see it. "WHERE? WHERE IS THE FUCKER? I DON'T SEE—"

The snap that announced the ignition of the AT-4's rocket motor, followed by a whoosh as the rocket left the tube, cut Pape short. Watching the rocket, Pape was blinded when the shaped-charge warhead made contact with the BTR head-on. The jet stream formed by the explosion of the rocket's inverted cone-shaped warhead cut through the armor of the BTR's front slope just below the roof. Missing the driver's head by inches, the jet stream hit the BTR's gunner square in the stomach after cutting through the ammunition feed chute that fed linked rounds to the BTR's 14.5mm machine gun. The driver was startled by the sudden explosion on the BTR's front slope, followed by the spray of molten metal thrown off by the jet stream as it raced past his head, and the screams of the gunner accompanied by the pop, pop, pop of 14.5mm rounds going off behind him. His first reaction was to slam on the BTR's brakes and duck his head, a motion that caused him to jerk the wheel to the left.

Watching where Billy's round struck, and noting that it appeared a little high, Ned laid the two-hundred-meter range line of his rocket launcher's sight on the center of the BTR, now slowing and offering an oblique shot as it turned. Lowering the muzzle of his AT-4 ever so slightly, Ned yelled out, "RANGE, ONE EIGHTY. FIRING," then let fly with his rocket. Though it was not a catastrophic hit, Ned's rocket ended any desire by the startled BTR's crew and passengers to stay with their vehicle. They didn't even wait for the driver to bring the BTR to a complete stop before hatches and doors flew open.

Checking himself, Pape flipped the safety off of his weapon with his thumb and continued to wait until the Ukrainian infantry squad began to spill out before he opened fire. Using the range announced by Ned to sight his weapon, Pape opened with a killing burst, hitting one Ukrainian before he could completely emerge from the BTR's side door. The Ukrainian's forward momentum, assisted by the shoving of the man behind him, cleared the line of sight for Pape to fire on the next man coming out the door. The second Ukrainian never realized that his companion had been hit, a fate that he soon suffered himself as Pape squeezed off a second short burst.

From inside the BTR, a flame shot out of the opened door, followed by a muffled explosion. A secondary detonation, probably an anti-tank rocket stored inside the BTR just like the one that had stopped it, went off, ending the short anti-armor ambush.

Seeing no more targets, Pape eased up, noticing for the first time that the Russian major was staring at him. While holding his weapon steady, Pape twisted his head and looked at the Russian lying less than a meter away from him.

Ilvanich smiled at the American soldier. "You did well. That was excellent shooting. Two five-round bursts, two men dead."

Pape smiled. "Piece of cake, Major. Piece of cake."

Ilvanich continued to smile. "Yes, I am sure it was." These Americans, he thought, take this too casually. What will happen, he thought, when things begin to go against them. "Now you need to prepare for a deliberate attack, dismounted this time, that will come up, oh, over there, to your right."

Pape looked over to where the Russian major was pointing. "How do you know that?"

Ilvanich smiled. "Because, my friend, two months ago I was doing the same thing at a site like this. Those men out there may be Ukrainians, but they read the same books I do. There is a gully, three hundred meters over there, that leads almost up to the fence. It is mined near the fence, but the BTR will use it to close on us and dismount its troops."

Not sure about the Russian next to him, Pape looked at the major for a few seconds, then grunted. "Okay, you're the expert." After which he shifted his weapon to the right.

Fifty meters below Ilvanich and Pape, another battle was being waged. In this one the Americans also held the upper hand, a fact that Biryukov could not ignore. The fight, for him and his small detachment in the assembly chamber, had been a disaster. Coming out of the smoke, the enemy had been among his positions before his men had gotten a shot off. At point-blank range the Americans had all but wiped out Biryukov's command. Only the quick thinking of one of his sergeants saved Biryukov from dying in that first rush with the rest of his men. Not that salvation was going to last long. Unable to move because of a wound that laid most of his side open, Biryukov sat with his back to the wall looking at the elevator doors that led back up to the assembly chamber. Only he, Sergeant Popel, who had dragged him into the elevator, and one other man made it to the lower storage chamber. Though the elevator was locked, Biryukov could hear the Americans working on the other side, preparing charges to force the elevator doors on their level. They had time, but not much. Once the American demolition team was finished, they would have to climb out of the elevator shaft before setting off their charges. After that everything would go fast. First, if they were smart, the Americans would drop grenades to clear the shaft and area by the door. Then the assault force would rappel down on ropes to finish Biryukov and his tiny command before they had recovered from the grenades. It was simply a matter of time before the Americans seized the weapons he was charged with guarding, unless he did something.

Looking down the long corridor to his right, Biryukov turned his mind away from the coming fight. Yes, he thought, it would be quick. Though some of the attackers would surely die this time, there was only so much that his two men could do. The Americans, Biryukov knew, had come too far to stop. They would gladly fill the elevator shaft with their dead in order to seize the warheads that sat in the chambers on either side of the long corridor. That the Russians had somehow gotten the naive Americans to do their dirty work didn't surprise Biryukov. His father had always told him that while the Americans acted like cowboys, they thought like boy scouts. Looking back at Popel, Biryukov coughed, spitting up small clots of blood. "If they do not hurry, I fear I shall miss their grand entrance."

The sergeant, his face betraying no emotion, nodded. "It shall not be long, Captain. I believe that they are climbing back up the elevator shaft. Once the demolition party is cleared, they will set off the charge. Then . . ."

In the silence, the soldier crouching next to the elevator shaft looked at the sergeant, then at Biryukov. His young face was contorted with fear and apprehension. He, like Biryukov and the sergeant, knew they had no chance. Still he refused to believe it. In his youth he refused to believe that there was no way out.

Coughing, Biryukov looked down the corridor again, then back at the sergeant. "Suppose, Sergeant, we decide not to cooperate with the enemy's plan?"

The young soldier piped up, "You mean we should surrender?"

Biryukov shook his head. "No. I doubt that they would be willing to take our surrender even if we were willing to offer it. After what happened up there, they have blood in their eyes." Biryukov paused, glancing once more down the long corridor before he continued without looking back at Popel. It was quiet, terribly quiet, like a tomb. "We must initiate the self-destruct sequence."

Popel didn't answer at first. Looking back at him, Biryukov forced a smile. "It is, Sergeant Popel, time to put your treasonable knowledge to use." Biryukov took his bloody hand away from his side and stretched it out. "As you can see, I cannot do it myself. I need your help, Sergeant." A spasm of pain went through Biryukov's body. Grabbing his side again, Biryukov forced himself to stifle a moan. When he could speak, Biryukov pleaded. "Please, Sergeant, hurry. We do not have much time. Do not fail me."

At the other end of the elevator shaft, Captain Smithy leaned over the open shaft, yelling to the last of the engineers struggling up the ropes to get a move on. This was taking too long for Smithy. The whole operation was not going the way he had wanted it to, and it was starting to piss him off. The gunfire from outside, barely audible to most of the men in his company that were in the assembly chamber, only served to increase Smithy's anger. Turning to the platoon leader standing next to him, Smithy blurted, "Why in the hell did those yahoos have to take the elevator down to where the warheads were stored? Geez, why couldn't they have used the other one? They really screwed this up." Smithy looked down the shaft and mumbled again, "They really screwed this up."

The platoon leader, not knowing if his company commander expected an answer, merely shrugged. How had the Ukrainians' action screwed up the operation? As far as the platoon leader could see, everything was in hand. They had cleared the upper chamber at the loss of one dead and three lightly wounded men. The initial portion of the Ukrainian reaction force was taken out by the rest of the company without any problem. And in a few minutes, after the elevator doors at the far end of the elevator shaft had been blown open, all they had to do was dump a few CS tear-gas and smoke grenades down the shaft, slide down the ropes, and clean up any Ukrainians who were still down there. The young platoon leader looked down the elevator shaft, then over at his commander, now pacing back and forth a few feet away, wondering what possibly could be wrong.

The attack by the second BTR had caught everyone, except Ilvanich, by surprise. No one had heard its approach. Even the riflemen

along the chainlink fence with night vision goggles failed to see the
second part of the reaction force as it advanced up a gully to the right
of the road. Only when a hail of 14.5mm rounds began to smack into
the cinder block guard shack did the men of 1st Platoon go to ground
and begin to search their assigned sectors in earnest.

"TO THE RIGHT. BTR WITH DISMOUNTED INFANTRY COM-
ING UP ON OUR RIGHT."

As if to underscore the warning, a hail of small-arms fire flew over
Pape's head from the direction of the gully that Ilvanich had pointed
out to him. Looking over to the Russian, Pape saw that Ilvanich had
his assault rifle up and was preparing to fire. "Son of a bitch! You were
right!"

Ilvanich did not respond to Pape's comment. He only issued instructions to the surprised American. "Remember, you are shooting
downhill. Aim lower than you normally would, otherwise your rounds
will go harmlessly over their heads."

Turning back to his front, Pape prepared to fire. "Yeah. Aim low.
Got it."

While Pape and Ilvanich were preparing to engage, First Lieutenant
Zack climbed out of a rear window of the guard shack, which was still
being chewed up by 14.5mm bullets from the BTR, and low-crawled
over to the entrance of the tunnel where the company's 60mm mortar
section was beginning to go into action. Excited and upset by the
sudden attack, Zack urged the sergeant in charge of the mortar section
to get a move on and start firing. The sergeant ignored Zack as he
continued to direct the men manning the two 60mm mortars. Only
when they were ready did the sergeant order his mortars to fire. With
his right ear covered by the radio's hand mike, and the index finger of
his left hand stuck in his left ear, the sergeant listened for corrections
from the 1st Platoon, shouting orders when he got them.

When he heard the sergeant yell to his mortar crews that they were
on target and to start pouring it on, Zack relaxed. Standing up, he
brushed away the dirt and fragments of cinder block that covered his
parka. There was nothing, he thought, that he needed to do at that
moment. Turning, he looked down the long tunnel and wondered how
his commander and the rest of the company were doing. He was about
to begin walking down the tunnel to find out when the earth beneath
his feet began to tremble. Believing that the Ukrainians were bringing
up tanks, Zack turned away from the tunnel to walk away.

He did not, however, get far, as the ground beneath him seemed to heave up. Not understanding what was happening, Zack turned back toward the tunnel opening and watched in horror as an immense, bright yellow fireball, propelled by a series of low-yield nuclear detonations, was forced up the elevator shaft, through the assembly chamber, and out the access tunnel straight at him.

CHAPTER 3

7 JANUARY

The casual early-evening business-as-usual attitude that had dominated the operations center of the Air Force's Space Command buried deep inside of Cheyenne Mountain, Colorado Springs, was gone. It had evaporated the instant that data from the DSP East satellite and the Nuclear Detection System sounded the alert that a nuclear detonation had taken place in the Ukraine. If anyone in the facility that night had been able to detach themselves from their duties and step back and watch, they would have noted two things. First, they would have taken great pride in the manner in which the event was handled. The equipment and systems responded without a problem. Information came into the operations center from satellites, remote sensors, and subordinate units where it was electronically routed to the appropriate Air Force men and women of Space Command in timely manner. Staff officers, given that information, analyzed it, made their assessments, and passed those assessments on to their superiors, both inside the Mountain and around the world. Everything, equipment and people, responded as programmed. It would, in fact, have been difficult for the unattached observer to tell the difference between this event and numerous drills conducted if it were not for the oppressive silence.

That silence, not obvious at first, spoke of the seriousness of the situation. For the first time since a bomb called "Fat Man" had been detonated above Nagasaki, a nuclear device had been set off in anger. Though initial information indicated that it had been only a small device, the size was immaterial. The nice clean surgical strike that the Pentagon briefers likened to the sure, precise prick of a rapier had turned into a radioactive bludgeon.

From his observation booth, the commander of Space Command sat looking down at the legion of staff officers and airmen as they went about their tasks in almost complete silence. Even the atmosphere in the observation booth, where senior officers normally congregated and held lofty discussions on world strategy during drills and training exercises, was heavy with gloom and apprehension. Only the buzz from the phone that provided a direct link with the White House War Room disturbed the ponderous quiet. Everyone in the observation booth watched as their commander, who had been sitting with elbows planted on the desk before him and his face resting between his open hands, sat up and reached out and grabbed the phone. His response was curt, almost plaintive. "Nolan here."

As the staff watched their commander, General Nolan visibly straightened up, telling them that he was in all probability talking to the President. It was several seconds, while Nolan listened to the caller, before his response confirmed that assumption. Finally he responded, shaking his head as he did so. "No, Madam President, there is nothing more that we can do from here at this moment. We have oriented every satellite that we can on the targeted area. It would not, in my opinion, be advisable to divert any additional assets away from their assigned missions. We must continue to monitor other areas of interest to determine what response, if any, the Ukraine, as well as other nations, are taking as a result of this event."

Nolan's aide found the use of the soft, rather nondescript word "event" to describe the detonation of a nuclear device rather foolish. Perhaps, he thought, using a softer word would make this disaster easier to deal with. Still he said nothing as he watched his boss nod his head. "I have been in direct contact with my British and French counterparts. While we all agree that we must be careful not to overreact, I must advise you that both the British and French feel the need to advise their governments that it would be in their own interests to increase their readiness posture." There was a pause before Nolan answered with a sigh. "Yes, I do believe the Brits and French spoke to each other before speaking to me. In my opinion, as the senior nuclear powers in Western Europe, they will coordinate their actions on behalf of the European Community." After another pause, Nolan simply hung up the phone and eased back in his chair, indicating that the President had terminated their conversation.

Nolan's aide watched his commander for a moment before speaking. "I'm sure, sir, it's times like this that make you wish you were somewhere else."

Nolan swiveled his chair around to face his aide. "No, Jack. You're wrong. For us, the worst is over. All we need to do is sit here, watch our scopes, and report what we see. It's the idiots who thought up this operation in Washington that have to explain away this mess and the poor bastards in the Ukraine that have to sort it out that I feel for. And believe me when I tell you, that the radiation from Svalyava won't even begin to compare to the political fallout that our noble administration is going to suck down as a result of this screw-up." Turning back to face the operations room, Nolan slumped down in his seat and mumbled, "No, today the Mountain suits me just fine."

Already at wit's end and nervous as hell, Second Lieutenant Tim Ellerbee all but jumped out of his skin when his platoon sergeant's tank, A34, sitting seventy-five meters to Ellerbee's left, fired. In an instant the stillness of the night was shattered by the ear-splitting crack of A34's 120mm main gun. Ellerbee's eyes flew open as he jerked his head up. Turning toward A34, he was blinded by the muzzle blast of A34's wing man, A33, who also fired. Recoiling from the effects of the sudden commotion, momentary blindness, and temporary disorientation, Ellerbee realized that he had fallen asleep. Despite the bitter cold that cut through his parka, despite the mission to secure the brigade's flank along the Latorica River, and despite his responsibility to cover the work of the engineer platoon as they prepared the highway bridge leading from Chop for demolition, Ellerbee had simply laid his head down on the machine gun mounted in front of his hatch and fallen asleep.

That he had fallen asleep should not have been a surprise. After all, the day before had been a busy one. Final precombat inspections and orders in their assembly area west of Michalovce consumed the entire afternoon. After a hot meal and nightfall, came a long, slow road march and occupation of an attack position just short of the Ukrainian border where final briefings were given and preparations made. With less than two hours of sleep, Ellerbee could have added to the normal apprehensions the emotions that all young soldiers going into battle for the first time experience. That strange feeling, a weird combination of fear of the unknown, apprehension, and impatience, crept into his tired mind every time there was a lull. That, coupled with the responsibilities of being a platoon leader and attached out with his platoon from his parent company to a mechanized infantry company, made for an almost overwhelming combination. At times, only his determination and pride kept him going. He was determined to show the mech infantrymen in the company his platoon was attached to that tankers were naturally superior beings. Just as important to Ellerbee was his male pride. He could not tolerate any sign of weakness, any indication that he was lacking as a man in any way when dealing with the commander of the infantry company to which his platoon was attached.

Such thoughts, however, were not on Ellerbee's mind at that moment as he tried to compose himself and figure out what was happening. Even before his night vision fully returned, he could make out that something on the south side of the river was burning. Twisting his head quickly this way, then that, Ellerbee was able to determine that his platoon sergeant, Sergeant First Class Ralph Rourk, had engaged some kind of vehicle on the far side of the river and had destroyed it. As he dropped down in his cupola, the first clear thought that came to mind was the hope that Rourk had not mistakenly engaged one of the engineer vehicles or a Bradley that was covering their work. His confidence that such a thing could not happen to him or his platoon evaporated as quickly as his confidence in his ability to understand what was happening. Hoping that his gunner had been alert, Ellerbee yelled, without bothering to key the intercom, "Tinker, did you see what Rourk fired at?"

Sergeant Tinker Shildon, Ellerbee's gunner, in his usual matter-of-fact New England accent and style, answered Ellerbee without moving his head away from the eyepiece of his primary sight or keying his intercom. "Yup. A tank. Looks like 34 got a tank. A T-80 from the looks of what's left of its turret."

Although every tank that wasn't American was a T-80 to Tinker, Ellerbee felt a rush of relief. At least his gunner was on the ball. Ellerbee's relief, however, was short-lived as the voice of the mech company commander came over the earphones of his crewman's helmet. "Alpha Three One, Alpha Three One, this is Charlie Six. Sitrep. Over." Even at that moment, when Ellerbee was still in the throes of confusion and near panic, the soft feminine voice coming over his tank's tactical radio bothered Ellerbee. It shouldn't have. He had told himself over the past three days that such trivial things should not bother him. After all, this was the twenty-first century, and women in combat arms had been a fact of life for many years. But it still did not seem right to him. The idea of going into battle with a woman, let alone listening to her orders, went against just about every convention his society had armed him with. The image of his company commander, standing at five foot eight, with big brown eyes that peered out from under the Kevlar helmet that hid long auburn hair and topped a well-proportioned body that wasn't an ounce over 135 pounds, did not even come close to what Ellerbee pictured as the typical infantryman.

Still she was his commander and at that moment demanding a report that Ellerbee was not prepared to render. Considering his options, Ellerbee tried to decide whether it was better to ignore her call while he contacted Rourk or to swallow his pride and admit over an open company radio net that he didn't know what was going on. Not that he needed to dwell on the subject for long. Taking a deep breath, Ellerbee keyed the radio net and blurted, "CHARLIE SIX, THIS IS ALPHA THREE ONE. WAIT, OUT." Without waiting for a response, Ellerbee released the lever on the side of his crewman's helmet that keyed the radio, reached over to the radio's remote control box, and changed the radio's frequency from the company command net to his platoon's radio net. She could wait, he thought. It was, after all, his platoon in contact.

A little less than a kilometer away, in a hidden position overlooking the bridge and river, Captain Nancy Kozak, commander of Charlie Company, 3rd Battalion, 3rd Infantry, sat perched on top of her Bradley. Looking out across the river at the burning hull of a T-80 tank, she thought a moment about Ellerbee's response. He didn't know what was going on. In her heart she knew without asking or needing to press the point. Easing herself down into her seat, Kozak looked over to her gunner, Sergeant Danny Wolf. There was a broad grin on Wolf's face. "The boy's fucked up, ain't he?"

Though Kozak didn't care for Wolf's referring to a second lieutenant as boy, she didn't say anything about it. Instead she nodded. "I think so. Let's find out." Bending over and twisting her body so that she was facing to the rear into the crew compartment of her Bradley, Kozak called out to Specialist Paul Paden, her radioman. "Pee, switch the aux receiver to the tank platoon's frequency."

Paden, whom everyone, including Kozak, referred to as Pee Pee, or Pee for short, was facing the radio. Acknowledging Kozak's order with a thumbs-up, Paden reached over to the auxiliary radio receiver and flipped the frequency control knobs until he hit the one assigned to Ellerbee's platoon. As soon as he did, the aux receiver's speaker came to life. "THREE FOUR, THREE FOUR, THIS IS THREE ONE. I SAY AGAIN, WHAT'S GOING ON OVER THERE? OVER." Ellerbee's voice was excited. Wolf chuckled. "Told you he was fucked up."

From a distance the report of a tank firing drifted over to Kozak's Bradley. Kozak ignored Wolf's comment and continued to lean over and listen to the aux receiver.

"THIS IS THREE FOUR. WE'RE ENGAGING SOME T-80 TANKS ON THE OTHER SIDE OF THE RIVER AT A RANGE OF 2700 METERS. OVER."

There was a pause. Then Ellerbee came on again. "THIS IS THREE ONE. DO YOU HAVE A GRID FOR THE LOCATION AND NUMBER OF THE T-80s? OVER."

Rourk's response to Ellerbee's request for a grid was quick, short, and final. "THREE ONE, I'M TRYING TO ENGAGE. I'LL REPORT WHEN I CAN. OUT."

Drawing in a deep breath, Kozak fought to control her anger. To have a subordinate cut her off as Ellerbee had, even in the heat of battle, was too much for her. After all, how could she, a company commander, coordinate and mass fires if her platoon leaders didn't submit accurate and timely reports? Stuffing her anger as best she could, Kozak told Paden to contact the engineer platoon and find out if they were under fire, then to contact 2nd Platoon, which was on the other side of the river covering the engineers, and find out if they were in contact.

Turning away, Kozak noticed that Wolf was grinning. "What's so funny, Sergeant?"

"Told ya the boy was fucked up."

Rather than become upset with Wolf, Kozak nodded. "You know, you're right, Sergeant Wolf. How about we go down there and straighten out poor Lieutenant Ellerbee?"

Wolf's smile disappeared in a flash. The thought of moving around in the middle of a firefight didn't seem like a good idea to him, especially since they would be going right where the enemy return fire was bound to be the thickest. He didn't, however, say anything. Kozak was serious. As dangerous as it would be, Wolf knew that it was the only thing, given Ellerbee's inability to control his platoon, that made sense. Besides, Wolf knew it was Kozak's style. In every training exercise, she simply could not stay out of the middle of things. Unable to get a clear view of what was happening from their position, Wolf had known in the back of his mind that Kozak's ordering them to move closer was only a matter of time.

"Sure thing, Captain." Turning away from Kozak, Wolf yelled over the intercom to Specialist Tish, the driver. "Hey, Terri, crank this bad boy up. The CO wants to go down and talk to them tankers."

The stunned silence that followed the explosion and the resulting fireball at the nuclear weapons storage site south of Svalyava seemed to last an eternity. The area outside the tunnel entrance was plunged into darkness as the security lights finally were snuffed out when the power to them was cut by the explosion. Like a gun's barrel, the access tunnel aimed the fireball and the main force of the explosion in a straight line across the open area out toward the road, wiping away the mortar section and leveling the cinder block guard shack before its force dissipated into the night. Members of the 1st and 2nd platoons who had been deployed along the chainlink fence or were off to either side of the access tunnel were unaffected physically by the explosion. Everyone else was either dead, dying, or simply gone.

Wide-eyed, Pape looked back at the tunnel. From the gaping mouth of the tunnel he could see the faint glow of fires burning inside. "What the hell happened? What's going on?" He was excited, almost screeching. Pulling away from the rocks and small berm of dirt that had provided cover to his front, Pape began to get up on his knees before Ilvanich's hand grabbed him by the shoulder and kept him from doing so.

"Back down. You must get back down. There may still be Ukrainians out there."

Though Pape continued to stare at the tunnel entrance, he lowered himself back behind the berm of dirt. Only after he was down did he turn to Ilvanich. "What the hell happened?"

That, Ilvanich thought, was obvious. But he didn't say that to the American, who was shaken and needed to be calmed, to be steadied. Doing so was an officer's job. Though he was a Russian officer and

Pape was an American, they were at that moment both on the same side due to the political requirements of their nations and practical considerations of the moment. Himself shaken by the turn of events, Ilvanich nevertheless took a deep breath and began to get up as he looked toward the tunnel entrance. "The Ukrainians in the tunnel have destroyed themselves and the nuclear warheads." Ilvanich placed his hand on Pape's shoulder again as he looked down into the young soldier's upturned face. Ilvanich could not see Pape's eyes, but he knew they were riveted on him. "You stay here and cover your assigned sector. Once the Ukrainians out there recover from their shock, they will be back. I will go over and find out what your commander is planning to do. Understood?" Even though Ilvanich didn't expect to find Smithy alive, he didn't want to upset Pape any more than he had to. Bad news sometimes needed to be taken in small doses.

Relieved that someone was doing something to find out what had happened, Pape gave a slight nod. "Okay, Major. I'll stay here."

The fact that this was the first time that Pape had acknowledged his rank was not lost on Ilvanich. As an afterthought, Ilvanich turned to his right. "You rangers along the fence, hold your positions. Keep alert, watch your sectors, and hold your positions. I will be back as soon as I find out what your commander intends to do." Twisting his head to the left, Ilvanich repeated his instructions, receiving a few grunts here and there from the darkness in acknowledgment.

Keeping low, Ilvanich backed away from the fence several paces before he stood upright and headed for the cinder block guard shack to find Lieutenant Zack. Moving through the darkness that his eyes were still struggling to adjust to, Ilvanich began to wonder if he would find Lieutenant Zack. That thought had no sooner occurred to him when Ilvanich's feet stumbled over something. Stopping, he peered down to see what it was. Unable to see, he squatted, reaching down with his left hand. It was, he found, a chunk of stone, smooth on one side but with jagged edges. Ilvanich realized that it was a piece of cinder block. To his front a pile of rubble slowly began to take shape as his eyes finally began to adjust to the darkness. Glancing to the left at the tunnel entrance, then following the direction that the force of the explosion would have followed until it reached the pile of rubble, Ilvanich realized that the guard shack, and everyone who had been in it, was finished.

The fact that he had been right and the ranger company executive officer wrong about the guard shack was no comfort to Ilvanich, for he quickly realized that along with Zack the radios for the company command net and the battalion command net were also probably smashed. Russian tactical radios, Ilvanich thought, especially those used by airborne units, were generally more robust than their users. Hoping that the American radios had the same qualities, he slung his assault rifle over his back and moved forward into the rubble to search for those radios.

He had just started pulling away sheets of roofing when a voice with a slight quiver behind him called out, "Zack! Lieutenant Zack! Is that you?"

Ilvanich did not stop. He was near where he thought the radios should have been. Instead he responded to the voice as he continued to work his way down through the pile of broken blocks and metal sheets. "No. I think Lieutenant Zack is dead. Who are you?"

"Fitzhugh, Lieutenant Fitzhugh, 1st Platoon. Are you the Russian major?"

Ilvanich continued to dig away, feeling his way about in the darkness, heaving broken cinder blocks out of the way and working around anything soft that his gloved hands came across, since anything like that was a body or body part, something that he was not interested in at that moment. "Yes. Are you the next senior officer after Lieutenant Zack?" There was silence. "Well, are you or aren't you?"

Fitzhugh's response was slow and halting. "Well, no, not really. You see, Lieutenant Jacobsen, the platoon leader for 2nd Platoon, he was next. Then Burglass of 3rd Platoon. Then me."

"Well, then, go find me one of those two and have him come over here. And while you're at it, send over some men to help me find the radios."

Fitzhugh didn't move. Instead, he turned and looked at the tunnel entrance. In the darkness he saw or heard nothing coming from it. He thought for a moment, then turned back to Ilvanich, who was still digging away. "They were both in the tunnel, I think, with the old man."

For the first time, Ilvanich stopped what he was doing and twisted his body to face where he thought Fitzhugh was. "Well, if that is the case, then that makes you the senior surviving officer, doesn't it?"

The dark, faceless form that stood a few feet from Ilvanich didn't reply. Ilvanich was becoming annoyed. "You are the next in command. Do you understand that, Lieutenant?"

Fitzhugh's response was low, barely audible, and almost plaintive. "Well, yeah, I guess I am. I mean, if everyone is really dead. I mean, they might not all be dead. Maybe—"

Ilvanich tossed a cinder block he was holding to one side and moved over to Fitzhugh's form. Grabbing both arms with his hands, Ilvanich shook Fitzhugh. "All right, Lieutenant, calm down. Just calm down and think for a moment. Maybe they are not dead. Maybe they are still somewhere around here. I do not think so, but anything is possible. That, however, is not important. What is important is that they are not here able to command what is left of the company. You and I are here and able to command. That, right now, right this moment, is all that matters." Ilvanich paused, letting that thought sink in before continuing. "Until one of the other officers shows up, the rest of the company is depending on us. Do you understand me, Lieutenant?"

Ilvanich felt Fitzhugh straighten up. Still unable to see the expression on the lieutenant's face, he had no idea what Fitzhugh's response was going to be. When it came, it surprised him. "Yes, sir. I understand. What do you want me to do?"

Ilvanich suddenly realized that Fitzhugh, confused and unsure of himself, was relinquishing command of the company to him. He had not expected that. He wasn't sure that he wanted that. How would the American sergeants and soldiers respond to taking orders from a Russian? That thought, however, was quickly replaced by Ilvanich's own logic. The American lieutenant was shaken. It would be some time before he would recover enough from the shock of becoming the company commander of a shattered company before he could be effective. He himself had just said they were the only ones who could command. So Ilvanich quickly decided to push aside his concerns and assume command, something that he had already done instinctively. "All right. First pass word down the line that everyone is to hold their positions and put on their protective masks. There is, no doubt, fallout from the explosion. Have your platoon sergeants get a head count, and then you and the platoon sergeants report here to me with that status. And bring three men to help me find the damned radios. Clear?"

Fitzhugh pulled his right arm away from Ilvanich's grasp and saluted. "Yes, sir. I got it." He turned and began to go back to his platoon, then stopped. Ilvanich paused to see what he wanted. "Major, I'll be okay. I'm just a little, well, I—"

Ilvanich felt a slight pang of sympathy for the young American officer. He had felt the same way once, had been through the same experience. Command in battle is not easy. It was, Ilvanich knew, even harder the first time. "Yes, I know. Now go. We must hurry."

Standing along the side of the road leading out of Uzhgorod, Dixon, with Cerro at his side, watched an artillery battery rumble by them. "Hal, this is taking too long. It's taking too damned long."

Cerro watched another M-109 self-propelled howitzer roll by without responding as Dixon continued his one-sided conversation. "We have too much shit going forward. This is a raid, like you said, not an invasion. Most of these units look like they're making a permanent change of station move."

Dixon paused to watch an ammo carrier for the self-propelled gun trundle on by. "Well, Hal, it's too late to do anything about that now. Make a note, will you, to get ahold of the task force and battalion ops officers and have them give you a list of exactly what they took along. It's obvious that the commanders in this brigade still don't understand the meaning of essential vehicles only."

Like in a tennis match, as soon as the ammo carrier passed and the next self-propelled gun came closer, both Dixon and Cerro snapped their heads to watch its passing. With nothing better to do at that moment, and needing to escape the cramped confines of their command post carrier, Dixon and Cerro had left those tracks, leaving captains and sergeants to monitor the incoming status reports. Wandering to the side of the road, the two officers watched the follow-on elements of the brigade pass. Watching columns of military vehicles roll by, Cerro had once thought, was sort of like watching television. It was repetitive and required no thinking, a mindless diversion that was therapeutic, the perfect way, he had found a long time ago, for a commander to give his mind a rest while appearing to be doing something and showing his face. Everyone, even the notorious Scott Dixon, needed a break. Like Dixon, Cerro had stood on the side of the road watching vehicles of every description and size go by while allowing his brain to simply drift about and rest. Dixon's comments, his first in almost five minutes, were followed by a couple more minutes of silence as his brain drifted free again.

Dixon was busy watching the first of a long line of five-ton cargo trucks begin to roll by when Cerro heard the rapid approach of footsteps and crunching of snow behind him. Turning, he saw one of his young captains, a slip of paper in his hand that Cerro assumed to be a message form, headed for him. "Looks like a dispatch from the field, sir."

It took Dixon a moment to catch on, first looking over at Cerro, then at the approaching staff captain. "Hmm. Must be an update from 3rd of the 3rd on the fight at the Latorica River. Seems like the Youkes aren't wasting any time moving their forces from Chop."

"Won't do 'em any good, Colonel. Not with Kozak on the prowl."

The arrival of the staff captain cut off Cerro's retort. Momentarily out of breath and excited, the young captain looked at Dixon, then glanced at Cerro. Cerro nodded for him to go ahead and report directly to the colonel. Dixon, feeling good, returned the captain's salute and quipped, "Well, what news from the Old Guard down at the Latorica River?"

The captain shook his head as he reached out to offer Dixon the small slip of paper he had been carrying. "No updates from the Task Force 3rd of the 3rd after their report that they had defeated the advanced guard detachment. This report is from Tenth Corps headquarters in Prague, sir. They picked up a report over Sky Net from SAC. Satellites have detected what they believe was a nuclear detonation south of Svalyava. Corps has advised all units involved in Operation Desperate Fumble and east of Prague to commence nuclear survey and monitoring."

Dixon had said nothing. He had suspected that something would go wrong. He constantly reminded his commanders and staff that things never go exactly the way they were planned, which, according to his admonishments, was why commanders were always needed to be forward and staff officers thinking. In the back of his mind, Dixon had been waiting for the hidden flaw of this operation to pop up and rear its ugly head. That it came in the form it did was a shock that neither he nor Cerro had imagined.

Cerro, taken aback by the captain's announcement as much as Dixon, responded first. Folding his arms across his chest and looking down at the ground, Cerro grimaced. "Well, so much for stealth and cunning." Looking up at the captain, he asked if there was anything else.

"No, sir. We asked for additional information, but the people at corps gave us a wait-out. I don't think they had a good handle on everything yet." Then as an afterthought he added, "The sergeant major is having Sergeant Godwin prepare an effective downwind message and frag order for all units to initiate immediate survey and monitoring. By the time you get back, it should be ready."

Dixon reached out and put his hand on the captain's shoulder. "Well, don't wait for us. Get back there and get it out over the air. Use flash-override if necessary. Now go."

After a hasty salute, the captain turned and trotted off back to the command post carriers.

For several seconds, Cerro watched Dixon in silence. Dixon was thinking, mentally absorbing the latest development and considering what actions, if any, he needed to take. Finally Cerro spoke. "Colonel, should we consider delaying the deployment of the brigade trains forward in case someone decides we need to unass the Ukraine in a hurry?"

Dixon thought about Cerro's question as he turned and looked at the unending line of trucks moving east. "Too many goddamned vehicles," he mumbled. "We've got too much shit for our own good." Then he looked at Cerro. "Let's wait and see what's happening before we get all excited and start altering the equation. Come on, let's go. Break's over, Hal. Back on your head."

The last of the three tanks of the advanced guard detachment had been destroyed by the time Kozak reached Ellerbee's position. Pulling up next to his tank, Kozak had dismounted and climbed up on Ellerbee's tank, where she listened to his report. When Ellerbee was finished, Kozak went over with him what she expected from her subordinates in the way of reports. Though she was composed by the time she got back into her Bradley, Sergeant Wolf knew that the red in her cheeks wasn't all due to the cold and wind. Watching her as she put her combat crewman's helmet on and stared blankly to her front, Wolf decided she needed a little humor. "Well, ma'am, I guess it's true."

Caught up in her own thoughts, Kozak gave Wolf a quizzical look. "What are you talking about, Sergeant Wolf?"

Wolf smiled. "You know, ma'am. Hell hath no fury like a woman scorned."

Kozak suppressed the urge to laugh. "Where in the devil, Wolf, did you hear that one?"

"The first sergeant. That's what Top always says when you go off and chew someone out after they've pissed all over your leg."

Though military etiquette frowned on sergeants talking to their commanders in such a manner, Kozak seldom corrected or restrained Wolf or any of the members of the crew of Charlie 60, her Bradley. She in fact encouraged open and free discussion as a means of both relieving the tensions that sometimes became unbearable in C60 during operations and as a way of finding out what the latest rumors and gossip in the company were. Still they had their limits. And vulgarity was, for her, pushing the limits of acceptability.

"Sergeant Wolf, you are not the first sergeant. And I didn't chew Lieutenant Ellerbee out. I merely ensured that he understood what I consider to be proper reporting procedures."

Wolf gave Kozak a knowing smile. "Okay, ma'am, I understand. Where to now? Back up the hill?"

"No. Let's head for the bridge and find Lieutenant Matto. We need to see how her engineers are doing. Those three T-80 tanks no doubt weren't alone. I expect we'll have some more company soon."

Serious now, Wolf keyed the intercom switch on his crewman's helmet. "Yo, Terri. Crank it up and move on down to the bridge to where we were before."

Terri Tish, known by most of the company as Terri Toosh, responded by cranking up the Bradley. Despite the fact that she was small in stature, Wolf had known few drivers, including himself, who could make a Bradley perform like Terri. Though he still kidded her about women drivers, his comments, like those he made with Kozak, were lighthearted.

At the northern approach of the bridge, Second Lieutenant Elizabeth Matto stood next to the ancient M-113 armored personnel carrier that served as her command post track and ammo carrier. While the ton-and-a-half trailer attached to the personnel carrier restricted its maneuverability, the extra demolitions and barrier material she could carry in the trailer made it too important to be left behind.

In the distance she could see the sappers of her platoon going about their tasks. On the south end of the bridge, an M-9 armored combat engineer vehicle, called an ACE, was cutting a hasty anti-vehicle ditch on either side of the roadway leading up to the bridge, while a squad of her people finished emplacing a cratering charge on the roadway itself. On the bridge, another squad worked on placing demolition charges. She intended to drop two sets of the bridge's supports as well as three sections of roadway in order to create a gap too large for the Ukrainians to bridge with an armored assault bridge.

Though the work was taking longer than she had anticipated, it was progressing well and nearly completed when Matto heard the whine of Kozak's Bradley approaching. Turning to her platoon sergeant, Matto told him to make a quick check along the line and hurry the demo teams up while she stayed where she was and "entertained" the CO.

Kozak, however, wasn't interested in being entertained. After pulling up next to Matto's personnel carrier and dismounting, Kozak came up to Matto for a report on their progress.

Matto rendered her report while they both watched the engineers on the bridge. In the light of a pale moon that just barely cleared the high ground behind them, they could even see the M-9 ACE as it continued to laboriously hack away at the frozen ground. "Well, ma'am, it'll be another ten, maybe fifteen minutes until the highway bridge will be ready to be dropped. The cratering charge on the southern approach to the bridge is in place and ready, but the anti-tank ditch extended to the riverbank won't be finished for at least another half hour. I believe the railroad bridge upstream is ready to drop now."

Kozak listened to Matto's report in silence. When Matto was finished, she began issuing orders. It was, to Matto, almost as if she had already decided what she intended to do before hearing the status of the work. "Go ahead and stop the anti-tank ditch. We don't have a half hour. Use a very hasty minefield to close the gap if you can do it in ten minutes, which is all the time you have to finish the job on the bridge. I'm going to order the infantry platoon back now. The brigade's shifting a company of attack helicopters covering the advance on Mukacevo to a battle position just northwest of here to give us some support. Between them and the mines, we can do without the anti-tank ditch."

Not waiting for a response, Kozak began to turn to hurry back to her track when Matto stopped her. "Captain, we can't surface-lay the mines and then set off the cratering charge. The detonation and debris from that charge will set off most of the surface-laid mines. We'll have to set off the cratering charge, then go back and lay the mines."

Kozak looked at Matto, then at the bridge, and then back at Matto. "Okay. Forget the mines. We don't have that kind of time. Do whatever you need to do in order to blow everything in ten minutes."

Saluting, Matto turned and trotted off toward the bridge, calling out for her platoon sergeant as she went. Kozak watched and listened for a moment. Her voice, like Kozak's, came out as a screech whenever she tried to yell, which was why Kozak seldom yelled. It was, she had been told by one of her sergeants years ago, both irritating and at the same time a source of amusement to the men under her command. So Kozak had learned to give orders and direct her subordinates in a way that all but eliminated the need to yell and shout. When shouting was necessary, she had one of her male NCOs do it for her when possible. Although few people in her company knew why their young female captain with a slightly crooked nose seldom yelled at anyone, most of the men and women in her command preferred it that way. It showed, one senior sergeant once said, that she had respect for her people as well as for their eardrums.

When she reached her Bradley, Kozak stopped next to it and called for her gunner. Because of her accent, Kozak didn't emphasize the "l" in Sergeant Wolf's name, which resulted in her calling him Woof most of the time. As she stood there calling for Wolf to pop his head up while trying to keep from screaming, a young engineer fifty meters away stopped what he was doing and looked over to see who was going "Woof, woof." From where he stood, it looked as if Kozak was baying at the moon. That sight, in the middle of what had been a tense and exhausting night, caused the young engineer to burst out laughing. His squad leader, wondering what was so funny, stopped what he was doing. "Are you losing it, Havarty, or is it a private joke?"

Havarty continued to laugh as he pointed at Kozak, who was still calling to Sergeant Wolf. The squad leader snickered, then wiped the smile from his face. "So? What's so strange about that? What do ya expect? She's an officer and an infantryman. Insanity and strange habits go hand in hand when you mix those two. Now get back to work before I sic her on ya."

*　　*　　*

While they waited for the platoon sergeant of 2nd Platoon to arrive, Ilvanich checked out the radio that two men had pulled out from under a pile of wreckage. Even though he had made a point of watching how the radiotelephone operators performed their checks and used their equipment, Ilvanich soon found that it was impossible to put the radio into operation. The electromagnetic pulse that had preceded the nuclear detonation had fried every transistor in the radio.

Tapping him on his shoulder, Fitzhugh got Ilvanich's attention. Pushing the worthless radio away, Ilvanich turned to see why Fitzhugh interrupted him. "Major, we found Lieutenant Zack over by the tunnel. He's dead too."

Nodding, Ilvanich turned back to look at the radio. Unable to contact anyone, and realizing that they could not stay where they were, Ilvanich decided that he had to do something soon, before the Ukrainians recovered and came forward to investigate, or radiation levels exceeded permissible levels.

Standing up, Ilvanich looked at the remaining leadership of the ranger company gathering about him before he responded. Unlike Fitzhugh, Ilvanich doubted if the sergeants were sure about his taking over. In the pale moonlight, Ilvanich could see it in their eyes. Except for the scurry of men and medics tending to wounded about them, there was an eerie silence as he did so. While there was what he thought was a glimmer of doubt, Ilvanich also saw that they were there in response to the orders he had issued, through Fitzhugh. If there was one thing that he was sure of, it was that they were professionals and understood their situation. They understood what had happened, they understood that Fitzhugh wasn't ready to assume command under such circumstances, and they understood that if something wasn't done soon, none of them would make it out alive. Deciding that this moment was as good as any to find out how receptive the leadership of Company A was to him as their commander, Ilvanich began to issue his new orders. As he did so, he watched how the gathered sergeants reacted to him.

"The electromagnetic pulse has destroyed these radios. Unless there is another radio somewhere here that can reach battalion, we have no means of contacting them." Ilvanich paused to let that fact soak in. "The blast, I am sure, has also released radiation, some of which will be residual. That means we cannot stay here for very long. And no doubt once they get over their own shock, the Ukrainians will be back in force." Again Ilvanich paused. Now as he prepared for the moment of truth, he drew in a deep breath. "With the weapons which we came for destroyed or buried, there is no reason for us to remain in place and accumulate radiation. Follow-on forces will no doubt be diverted to the other weapons storage site by either the battalion commander or corps. While your battalion commander will no doubt organize a survey and monitoring team to come over here and check out the situation here, that will take time, time in which we will continue to be exposed to radiation and the danger of a counterattack. I do not believe it is a good idea to wait and depend on what others may or may not do. So we are going to move out from here."

The reaction by the sergeants, though muted, was positive. The decision to move, regardless of who made it or who led them, was welcomed. Not only would they escape the stench of burned bodies that was beginning to permeate the area, but they would move away from the invisible enemy, radiation, that each suspected would soon saturate the area. Ilvanich allowed himself a few seconds to enjoy his success. Then, as was his habit, he got back to the matter at hand. "All right, if you have no objections, we must get on with this. Now give me a complete account of your units, their conditions, and positions. Then we will go over how I expect the next thirty minutes to go and what we will do."

Without hesitation, the leadership of Company A gathered around to render their reports and hear their commander's orders.

After a brief discussion over a map with Fitzhugh and his senior sergeants, Ilvanich decided on where they would go and the formation they would use. As they prepared to break up and head back to their platoons to pass the word, one of the sergeants stood up and stared at the tunnel behind him. "Major, I think we need to go in there and see if there are any survivors."

This comment caused everyone to stop what they were doing, for each of them, except Ilvanich, had been thinking the same thing. Looking first at the tunnel, then at Ilvanich, they waited for his response.

Ilvanich looked at the tunnel, and then at the faces of his leaders. It was, he knew, foolish to go in there. No one, he knew, could have survived the blast. Even if they had somehow miraculously survived the fireball, that same fireball would have eaten every cubic centimeter of air in the tunnel and replaced it with superheated gases. Exposure to that, even for a second, would be enough to destroy a man's lungs. After considering his response, he was about to point this out in graphic detail, but decided not to. The men in that tunnel were their comrades and friends, people they felt a responsibility to. "You realize that the chances of anyone being alive in there are nil."

The sergeant who had brought up the matter nodded. "We know that, Major. But we have to try. Otherwise I'd never again be able to face the wives and kids of people I know in there." There was a pause before he added, "We have to try. You understand, don't you?"

No, Ilvanich thought, he didn't understand why a man was willing to go and confirm something that he already knew. "What is your name please?"

"Rasper, Sergeant First Class Allen Rasper. Platoon sergeant for 1st Platoon."

"You realize, Sergeant Rasper, that whoever goes in there will absorb more radiation, perhaps a lethal dose."

The only response by Rasper to Ilvanich's observation was to repeat his comment. "Sir, we have to try."

Realizing that Rasper's comment was more of a statement than a plea, Ilvanich decided to give in. Although he knew it was not meant to be a test, to refuse this request, as insane as it was, would jeopardize his tenuous position as their temporary commander and could lead to further disaster. "All right, we will go. But we go with a radiacmeter. Once the radiation level becomes too high, we turn back. Agreed?"

Rasper and the others nodded.

Ilvanich looked about the group. "Who is going with me?"

Caught off guard by the idea that Ilvanich was going, the Americans looked at each other for a second. Then Rasper stepped forward. "I'll handle the radiacmeter, Major."

Ilvanich reached out and put his hand on his shoulder. "Good, good." Then he turned to Fitzhugh. "While we're in there, you are in command. You are to prepare the company to move from here as soon as we return. Bring your map and come over here."

Moving up next to Ilvanich, Fitzhugh turned his small flashlight onto a map he held between himself and Ilvanich. Ilvanich, a professional soldier to the core, had already considered their situation and had come to a decision. Using his finger to trace a line on the map, Ilvanich issued his orders. "We will move to the south, along the side of the mountain to a point here. That line of march should take us away from the downwind area of this mess, away from where I expect the Ukrainians to launch their next attack, and take us to a landing zone, here, that we can defend. Have the company ready to move when I return. Understood?"

Fitzhugh nodded. "Yes, sir. Understood."

"Good, now get moving." When the rest of the leaders had gone, and while Rasper checked out his radiacmeter, Ilvanich dug about the ruins of the guard shack looking for some rubberized ponchos he had come across before. Finding them, he pulled two out, tossing one to Rasper. "They will not give us much protection, but it will help. We can discard them after we are finished."

Rasper put on the poncho Ilvanich had handed him and his protective mask. When he and Ilvanich were ready, the two men tromped off into the gaping black void that reeked of burned flesh. For a moment every eye in the company was on them as each man shared two common feelings: that someone was going to at least search for survivors and, at the same time, relief that they were not the ones going in.

"Colonel Dixon, the corps G-3 is on the line for you."

Dixon, seated in front of the operations and intel maps between Cerro and his intelligence officer, leaned way back in the folding chair he was seated in until the front legs of the chair left the ground and his back began to arch forward. Reaching behind him blindly with his right hand, he opened it and waited for the phone. Behind him, the operations duty officer got up, leaned over the table he was at, and placed the phone receiver in Dixon's outstretched hand. As soon as Dixon had a firm grasp on it, the duty officer grabbed the phone line and began to feed more toward Dixon in anticipation of Dixon's returning back forward. Even this effort, however, did not help as Dixon, already talking on the phone, dragged the receiver across the duty officer's table, creating an avalanche of pens, pencils, notebooks, clipboards, coffee cups, and scraps of paper onto the ground. While Dixon was oblivious to this, Cerro shot the duty officer a dirty look while Command Sergeant Major Duncan grabbed the operations sergeant by the arm and quietly reprimanded him for failing to keep the duty desk neat and clear of unnecessary trash and clutter.

"Dixon."

The corps G-3's voice betrayed how tired and harried he was. "Scott, we have to pull the Apaches from you. Things aren't going well for the rangers, and they may need the attack helicopter support."

Dixon grunted. "Yes, sir. I understand that, sir. But that, sir, puts my flank guards in a tight spot. I expect that reserve brigade from Uzlovaya to plow into our southern flank any minute. I've only got one company down there. Taking away the Apaches leaves me little choice but to pull more forces from the drive on Mukacevo to cover my flanks."

The corps G-3 wasn't moved by Dixon's argument. Not that Dixon expected him to be. "I know, but you need to remember, you're only a supporting attack. The corps commander never expected you to make it to Mukacevo."

"Yeah, I know. We're the red cape and it's our job to keep the bull busy while the rangers cut off his nuts. Well, tell Big Al that he had better hurry before we lose ours."

The corps G-3 laughed. "You know what Big Al will say to that."

Dixon laughed too. "Yeah, I know. He'll look at you and say, 'What's Dixon worried about? He doesn't know what to do with 'em anyway.' "

Turning serious, the G-3 asked Dixon how his brigade was doing. "We're in good shape. No surprises, no problems yet that we didn't anticipate. Other than the fact that the Youkes are reacting faster than we had thought they would and my battalion commanders are moving into the Ukraine with everything that their units own plus, we're doing quite well. Loss of the Apaches may slow us down later, but for now, no problems."

The corps G-3, satisfied with Dixon's assessment, promised him that he would return control of the Apaches as soon as they were finished supporting the extraction of the ranger company. Failing that, the G-3 promised Dixon that the Air Force would have some A-10s on station at dawn to sweep the road and high ground ahead of his brigade.

Finished, Dixon held the phone over his head, waiting for the operations duty officer to take it, while he turned to Cerro. "Well, you heard?"

Cerro nodded. "We lose the Apaches. Okay, no problem. Do we shift another company down to the Latorica?"

Dixon, relieved of the phone, folded his arms and looked at the map for a moment as he thought. "No, not yet. Hal, contact the 2nd of the

35th Armor. Tell them I want a string on one of their companies, tank heavy. Their mission, if I need it, will be to move south to reinforce or relieve Kozak at the Latorica."

"Do we want to shift priority of fires to Kozak's company?"

Dixon thought about that, then shook his head. "No, not yet. But I do want you to have one of the OH-58 Delta scouts move south and keep an eye on things down there." Dixon turned to Cerro and pointed his finger at him. "Be prepared to shift priority of fires if things get really tight down there, but don't do so without my permission. With the Apaches gone and the A-10s unavailable until dawn, we may need the artillery to blow through any roadblocks further down the line. Our main effort still remains keeping the pressure up on Mukacevo and drawing the Ukrainians' heavy forces away from the rangers. The best way we can do that is to keep moving. Kozak will have to do the best she can with what she has."

Turning toward the map, Cerro looked at the blue map symbol that represented Kozak's company. Sitting at a point just north of the Latorica River, where the road to Chop crossed it, the small blue company marker was threatened by an ominously large red marker that represented a Ukrainian tank brigade. The intelligence duty officer, having posted the Ukrainian brigade symbol, had drawn a large red arrow pointing from it right at the center of the symbol that represented Kozak's company. Cerro mused as he continued to look at the map, "Well, young Captain Kozak has her work cut out for her."

Dixon said nothing at first. Instead he stood up and stretched, his hands reaching the canvas roof of the forward command post's tent extension. "Hal, I got the feeling that before this thing is over, we'll all have our hands full." Dropping his arms, he put his hands on his hips and looked about his command post, then back to Cerro. "Get on the horn and let 3rd of the 3rd Infantry know the Apaches are going away."

Turning to Command Sergeant Major Duncan, Dixon informed him that he and Colonel Vorishnov were going forward in his tank .

Without another word, he walked out and let his staff go about issuing the orders and instructions necessary to deal with the brigade's new situation.

CHAPTER 4

7 JANUARY

The attack on Kozak's position north of the Latorica River was slow to develop, reflecting the Ukrainian brigade commander's surprise that American forces were already deployed so close to Chop, his uncertainty of the precise location and composition of those forces, and his standing orders. While the loss of his entire advanced guard detachment of three tanks before they could provide him with any detailed information was regrettable, at least the initial garbled report of their platoon leader gave him something to work with. The report that they were being hit by long-range tank fire, and subsequent reports from a recon unit that arrived moments later, confirmed that the engagement had taken place two thousand meters south of the bridge. Based on the information he had at hand, he assumed he was facing a flank screen by an armored cavalry unit. That would account for the speed with which the Americans had arrived at their positions and the presence of tanks. A deliberate attack, he decided, rather than a hasty one, would therefore be more effective, since a series of progressively larger hasty attacks would only allow the Americans to grind up his combat power a little at a time. One full-blooded and coordinated attack, with all the combat power he could bring to bear, would not only scatter the screening force, it would leave his forces in the proper formations for further attacks north toward Uzhgorod.

There was, of course, the problem of crossing the river. Destruction of the highway bridges complicated his mission. As the Ukrainian brigade assembled west of Chop, its commander and his staff pondered their options at the junction where Highway 17 turned north toward the Latorica. As throngs of frightened refugees struggled to get around, past, or through the tanks and personnel carriers of the brigade, the brigade commander realized that only two real choices existed. He could either move his forces to the east and cross at another site or conduct an assault crossing north of Chop.

His choice of options, however, was limited due to his literal translation of his standing orders. If, those orders stated, an attack originated from Slovakia, he was to deploy his brigade from their garrison at Uzlovaya to Chop. From there, he was to cross the Latorica via the highway and railroad bridge, which the orders assumed would be intact. Once assembled on the north side of the Latorica, the Ukrainian brigade was to attack north along Highway 17, into the flank of the invading force, using Uzhgorod as their objective. Unable to contact the commander of the Ruthenia Military District, the Ukrainian brigade commander felt he had little choice but to carry out his standing orders to the letter. Other units throughout Ruthenia depended upon the success of his operations. Besides, as one of his staff officers commented during their discussions, the number of refugees was multiplying by the hour. Using vehicles of every description, they were clogging the roads throughout the area, as well as the streets of Chop. It was, the staff officer pointed out, at best questionable if they could turn the brigade around and countermarch it back through Chop to a crossing site east. Seeing that his brigade was already 70 percent assembled south of the Latorica and ready to strike north, the brigade commander decided to follow through, trusting his luck and the skill of his soldiers.

Although Kozak had lost the support of the Apache attack helicopters, that did not mean she and her company had been abandoned to their fate. Instead, Hal Cerro began to concentrate those assets available to the brigade that were not directly involved with the operations at the nuclear weapons storage sites. The first asset turned south in support of Kozak's unit was an EH-60A Quickfix, a tactical communications intercept, direction-finding, and jamming system mounted in a modified UH-60 Blackhawk helicopter with the Quickfix. It was used to search for and locate signals from tactical radios, and Cerro, working through the brigade's intelligence officer, prioritized the tasks of the Quickfix to finding and locating the command element of the Ukrai-

nian brigade moving from Uzlovaya and then the fire direction center
of its supporting artillery battalion. Since the Ukrainian brigade was
on the move and would have to use the radio to coordinate its subordinate units, Major Lea Thompson, the brigade S-2 that Dixon had
nicknamed Princess Lea, felt that they would have no problem locating either of their designated targets once contact was made with
Kozak's unit.

In addition to the Quickfix, Cerro checked with the brigade's fire
support coordination officer, or FSCO, to ensure that they were ready
to provide counterbattery fires as well as defensive fires. An artillery-
man, Major Salvador Salatinni, known as Big S, never missed an opportunity to promote his fellow red legs. Taking Cerro over to his map
board in the brigade forward CP, Salatinni briefed him on the deployment and preparations of the two artillery battalions supporting the
1st Brigade. One battalion, he pointed out, which was deployed south
of Uzhgorod, was in place and prepared to fire in support of Kozak. To
counter enemy artillery, AN/TPQ-36 and AN/TPQ-37 Firefinder radars were deployed and oriented to the south.

Although Cerro understood the mission and capabilities of the Firefinder radars, Salatinni explained again, as he often did, that as soon as
a single enemy artillery round was fired, the Firefinders would be able
to detect the incoming enemy projectile and then, assisted by computers, determine the location of the gun firing that projectile before
the projectile impacted. Cerro, seeing Salatinni caught up in his own
briefing, let him continue as he explained that the information from
the Firefinder radars would be fed directly into their artillery battalion's TACFIRE fire control computer system. The TACFIRE computer would then, according to the way division artillery had it
programmed for this operation, automatically pass the information
concerning the enemy artillery locations to a platoon of multiple
launch rocket systems, or MLRSs, that were supporting the brigade.
The MLRS platoon, with three launchers, would dump one pod's
worth of rockets on each enemy artillery battery located. This, Salatinni emphasized, meant that a six-gun Ukrainian artillery battery
would be attacked by twelve rockets. Since each rocket contained 644
submunitions, or bomblets, every enemy artillery battery would be
attacked by 7,728 submunitions. Or, Salatinni said with a broad smile
and dancing eyes, put another way, each enemy gun would be attacked by 1,288 submunitions.

Cerro, his mind dulled by lack of sleep and dealing with the usual unending parade of problems and concerns that operations officers deal with, merely nodded or grunted as Salatinni bombarded him with facts, figures, and explanations. It was amazing, Cerro thought as he listened, how artillerymen not only got so caught up in memorizing all those numbers and technical details, but took it upon themselves to educate those unable to repeat that data. When Salatinni was finally finished, Cerro looked Salatinni in the eye. "S, I appreciate the briefing. I would like to clarify one point, however."

A smile lit across Salatinni's face. "Sure, Hal. What is it?"

"Is the artillery ready?"

The efforts of Cerro and the 1st Brigade staff were, at that moment, completely unknown to Captain Nancy Kozak and Company C, 3rd of the 3rd Infantry. After having parked their Bradley in the lee of a stone barn, the crew of C60 settled in to watch and wait. Perched high in the open hatch of C60, her M-2 Bradley, there was little for Kozak to do but to watch and wait. Across the river she could see very little. The cold, pale moon, hanging low in the sky behind their positions, was reflected off the white snow, turning everything gray and creating deep, dark shadows. She could hear, however, what she couldn't see. From deep in those shadows, the sounds of tracked vehicles winding their way slowly and laboriously along forest trails drifted across the river. The crisp, cold night air seemed to magnify those sounds, making it difficult to accurately judge the precise location or size of the approaching enemy. With nothing to do but wait for the Ukrainians to show themselves, Kozak waited and watched. At that moment, she had the feeling that her company had been deployed on its own to defend the far side of the moon.

The rest of her crew shared her foreboding. After a night of furious activity and no sleep the lull and silence left each member of the crew to deal with his or her own fears, apprehensions, and natural desires to drift off to sleep as best they could. Wolf, peering through his thermal sight, slowly traversed the turret as he searched the tree lines across the river for the enemy. Here and there he could see indications of vehicle concentrations as the exhaust from those vehicles heated the trees they sat next to. The sap in those trees, heated by the vehicles' exhaust, spread that heat throughout the tree. As a result, some trees were warmer than those trees which were not near any vehicles. Wolf's thermal sight picked up this temperature difference and provided him with a good idea of where the enemy were. With a map in his lap, he kept himself occupied by trying to correlate his sightings through the thermal sight with their location on the map. Every few minutes, when he had some substantial change, he would pull on Kozak's pant leg. After Kozak bent down, Wolf would show her what he had. Making a mental note, Kozak would acknowledge his efforts, then return to her position in the open hatch from which she would study the areas Wolf had pointed out.

Both Tish, the driver, and Paden, the radioman, were less vigilant. Not that there was much for them to do. Though Kozak should have had one of them out on the ground to provide security, she didn't want to scatter her crew or expose them to the artillery barrage she expected to precede the Ukrainian attack. When it came, Kozak wanted to be able to move and move fast. People wandering about in the dark in the middle of an artillery barrage would handicap her just when she would need them the most. Besides, Kozak reasoned, she was in the middle of the tank platoon. Ellerbee's security measures, which weren't the best, at least provided her Bradley with some degree of local security. So Tish and Paden stayed put in their assigned positions, drifting in and out of fitful periods of sleep.

Thirty meters away, Second Lieutenant Ellerbee had no trouble staying awake. There was, of course, the incident earlier that morning that had given him the scare of his life. Every time he thought about it, he felt anger and embarrassment over the fact that he had not only been asleep during his first fight, he had fumbled the most basic of all leadership requirements, timely and accurate reporting. The consequences of that incident were immediate and embarrassing. The visit by the mech infantry company commander, during which he received a not so subtle lecture on what a platoon leader was expected to do in combat, was bad enough. That Ellerbee had expected. Even the relocating of the company commander's Bradley over to his position was not totally unexpected. Though it showed that she lacked confidence in his abilities to report to her in a timely and accurate manner, Ellerbee could have dealt with that slight too.

What really bothered Ellerbee, though, was the fact that he had failed in front of a woman. As a professional officer, such thoughts weren't supposed to even enter into the equation. He was, after all, an American soldier, an officer at that, serving in an organization that had been totally integrated for years, in which individuals were to be judged, as he had been taught, on their abilities, not their sex, color, or background.

That, Ellerbee had found, was far easier to discuss than it was to practice. He was, he knew, not a sexist. His mother and father had both provided him and his brother with what was considered to be the politically correct role models for an upper-middle-class American family. He enjoyed the company of women and had during his high school and college years never lacked for a date. Ellerbee was even able to accept the presence of females in his college ROTC detachment, although he, like the other members of that unit, found it hard to keep from snickering when new female cadets were learning to issue orders during drill and ceremony practices. The usual retort by the cadet detachment commander at such times, for the unfortunate female cadet to "bang 'em together like you had a pair," was always greeted with hoots and catcalls from the male cadets in the ranks.

It wasn't until Ellerbee arrived at his first assignment that he found himself confronted by what many old-timers simply referred to as "The Issue." Five years after the first females entered combat arms, there was still an unofficial debate raging over the issue, a debate Ellerbee found himself in the middle of. Quite by accident, he was assigned to what his platoon sergeant, Sergeant First Class Rourk, called a pure platoon, meaning that there were no females assigned to it. When Ellerbee asked how that could be, especially since 10 percent of the company was female, Rourk smiled and winked. "Well, sir," he said, "the first sergeant and I have an understanding. When replacements come in, I get first dibs on them." Even Ellerbee understood what that meant. Though he knew that such a practice was not in the spirit of the Army's policy concerning integration, he said nothing. Dealing with replacements, after all, was sergeants' business. So Ellerbee allowed Rourk to continue to manipulate the system.

As innocent as that was, Ellerbee soon found himself adopting Rourk's viewpoint, an effort that was reinforced by other officers in the battalion and unconsciously by his own company commander. Whenever the officers of the battalion gathered socially, Ellerbee noticed that for the most part the male officers gravitated together while the female officers did likewise. In these small social groups, the business of the day was discussed, with one or more male officers inevitably complaining about the latest "female" problem in his unit or section. Ellerbee, as anxious to be accepted by his fellow officers as he was to be accepted by his platoon sergeant, said nothing. He was, after all, new and was learning. Since his platoon was "pure," many of his fellow officers would end their complaint sessions by looking at him, shaking their heads, and saying, "Ellerbee, you're lucky. I don't know how you keep your platoon pure. But whatever your method, keep it up. It'll save you a lot of heartburn."

On duty, Ellerbee found himself being compared to the platoon leader of the 1st Platoon, a Second Lieutenant Christine Johnson. Assigned to the company eight months before Ellerbee, Johnson had earned the grudging respect of Ellerbee's company commander. During their annual gunnery cycle, three of her four tanks qualified distinguished. This was followed up by a rotation at the Combined Arms Training Center during which Johnson's 1st Platoon performed brilliantly. Unable to argue with success, everyone assumed Johnson was a shoo-in to be the next company executive officer. So it was quite natural that Ellerbee's company commander, as well as the battalion commander, held Johnson up as the role model for newly assigned platoon leaders.

Ellerbee found he was unable to deal with this comparison. How, he asked himself, could anyone possibly expect him, an independent and successful man, who was no slouch when it came to looks and athletic ability, to pattern himself after a girl? At five foot five and 145 pounds, Second Lieutenant Christine Johnson was, to Ellerbee, nowhere near the ideal image of the great warrior that his commander seemed to think she was. As hard as he tried, he could not get beyond Johnson's big brown eyes and round face that was forever framed by long wisps of hair that always managed to free themselves from under her helmet or hat. Johnson had an easygoing, unassuming, and cooperative manner. Coupled with an adeptness when dealing with the people in her platoon as well as her superiors, she became quite popular with her commander and, to no one's surprise, to the men and women in her platoon. Still Ellerbee could not bring himself to see beyond the physical. His reaction was an emotional one, one that was reinforced by the attitudes of his platoon sergeant and other male officers in the battalion who refused to put "The Issue" to rest.

So it was no surprise that as Captain Nancy Kozak was busy pointing out to Ellerbee that he needed to do a better job of reporting the next time, her words were blocked out by Ellerbee's own thoughts.

Over and over in his mind, as he stood there listening to her, Ellerbee kept telling himself that he didn't need to take this from a damned woman who shouldn't have been there in the first place. Even after she left, Ellerbee found himself unable to concentrate on the matter at hand. Instead of maintaining the presence of mind that would be needed to deal with the coming fight, Ellerbee went over and over in his mind the earlier engagement, ending each review by mumbling to himself the same question. "Who," he quietly asked himself, "does that bitch think she is?"

With his mind occupied with thoughts that ranged from self-pity to anger, Ellerbee was too busy to notice that the yellow low battery indicator light on his control panel had lit up.

Major Nikolai Ilvanich and the survivors of Company A, 1st Ranger Battalion, whom he now commanded, had no such difficulties when it came to keeping their minds on their current situation. Ilvanich's decision to move down the hill and away from the storage site had been accepted by everyone in the company without a murmur of protest. Besides, as Ilvanich pointed out to Lieutenant Fitzhugh before going into the tunnel with Rasper, there was always the possibility that the commander of the relief force would still attack. Not knowing how badly the facility had been damaged, the Ukrainians might still press home an attack, if for no other reason than to eliminate the raiders and find out exactly how much damage had been done to their precious nuclear weapons. Ilvanich therefore cautioned Fitzhugh that while he prepared the company to move, Fitzhugh was to pay attention to security of his force and be ready to go back into defensive positions if necessary. Fitzhugh had just finished making his rounds of those positions when Ilvanich and Rasper emerged from the tunnel.

Both Ilvanich and Rasper covered the final steps toward the entrance of the tunnel in quick, long strides. Neither man stopped to talk to Fitzhugh, who was waiting for them as they emerged from the tunnel. Instead, Rasper peeled off to the left while Ilvanich, barely slowing, went to the right, throwing himself against the side of the mountain. Once clear of the entrance, Rasper tore off his protective mask and threw it away from him in one quick motion as he bent over and began to throw up. Looking over at Rasper, Fitzhugh became

alarmed. The first thing that came to his mind was radiation poison-
ing. Rasper, still bent over double, continued grasping his knees as his
stomach muscles spasmed in an effort to expel their contents.

The Russian major, Fitzhugh thought, had been right. Rasper had
absorbed lethal doses of radiation and was dying. Turning to Ilvanich,
he saw that the Russian major had also ripped his protective mask off
and was standing with his back against the side of the mountain,
wide-eyed and staring off into the distance. Even in the pale moonlight, Fitzhugh could see the major's face had no color and that he was
struggling to keep from throwing up. Overcoming his initial shock,
Fitzhugh slowly walked over to Ilvanich. "Sir, is there anything I can
do?"

Ilvanich didn't hear Fitzhugh. He didn't hear Rasper either as he
struggled to control his dry heaves and shaking. He merely stood there
unable to erase the image of twisted and disfigured bodies, burned
beyond recognition, that hung before his eyes. Dear God, he thought
over and over. How could we do such a thing to ourselves? How could
sane men who claimed to be responsible leaders order their sons to
such a death? It was not possible, not possible. Such murder, cloaked
in the guise of political necessity and patriotism, transcended insanity. Such madness defied logic. There was no logic that could justify
what had happened there that night. And again Ilvanich thought, Dear
God, how could we do such a thing to ourselves?

Despite his years as an officer and experiences in combat, the overwhelming horrors that had greeted both him and Sergeant Rasper
overcame any self-control that the two men had. With Ilvanich in the
lead and Rasper following, the two men had almost made it to the
elevator shafts. Their pace was slow and careful as Ilvanich with a
flashlight worked his way around obstacles, barriers, and bodies, bodies that were burned to varying degrees. Some were missing limbs or
heads. Most, burned black, were still smoldering, filling the air with
the sickly-sweet smell of burned flesh.

Just before they reached the elevator shafts, Ilvanich stopped short.
To his front, rock, shattered concrete, and debris formed a wall that
blocked access and brought their search to an abrupt halt. As he studied the rubble before him, Ilvanich hoped that it would seal the further escape of radiation from the storage chambers below. If nothing
else, he thought, this brought their search to an end.

Ilvanich was just about to announce his intention to turn around when the beam of his flashlight fell upon one body partially buried in the rubble. With the uniform ripped away and burned, there was no way of telling which side he had belonged to. Not that it mattered. What struck Ilvanich was the expression on the face, a face that seemed to be looking right at him. Most of the skin and muscle on the face was peeled away by the force of the explosion and the fireball. What struck Ilvanich, as he stood there unable to turn away from the mangled body, was the skeletal grin that stared back at him. It was to Ilvanich as if the corpse was laughing at him, a laughter he could almost hear ringing in his ears. Slowly, uncontrollably, Ilvanich's hand began to tremble as he suddenly imagined that the corpse was laughing at him and everyone who had survived. The corpse was laughing at them because they were alive and had not yet seen the end of their suffering.

Only with the greatest of efforts did Ilvanich manage to tear himself away from his dead tormentor. Pivoting, he began to move back toward the entrance of the tunnel, brushing Rasper with his shoulder and blurting as he did so, "We have gone far enough."

Rasper, his eyes glued to the radiacmeter in an effort to avoid seeing the bodies that littered the floor of the tunnel and assembly area, said nothing as he turned and followed Ilvanich. He was sorry that he had not listened to the Russian. He was sorry that he had insisted on coming in the tunnel. Not in his most tortured nightmares had he imagined anything could be like this. Such thoughts soon gave way as he struggled to hold down the contents of his stomach that the bile in his throat told him was coming.

After shaking Ilvanich, Fitzhugh finally got a response. Slowly Ilvanich turned his head and faced the young lieutenant.

"Sir, the company is ready to move."

Ilvanich blinked, then nodded. "Fine, fine." He looked over Fitzhugh's shoulder to where two men were helping Rasper. "Is the sergeant all right?"

Fitzhugh looked over his shoulder, then back to Ilvanich. "I don't know. Did you suck down that many rads that fast?"

"No, that is not radiation sickness. It is sickness of the heart."

There was a pause while Ilvanich looked toward the tunnel entrance. "If, my young friend, we could take the leaders of your country and mine, hand in hand with the leaders of the Ukraine, for a walk down that tunnel, we would have no more talk of wars."

Fitzhugh looked into the dark, gaping entrance of the tunnel, wondering what could possibly turn two veteran soldiers like Ilvanich and Rasper into emotional basket cases. Whatever it was, it was better that he didn't know.

Pushing thoughts of the tunnel aside, Ilvanich forced himself to turn his attention to the current situation they faced. "You said the company is ready to move?"

"Yes, sir. We were just waiting for your return."

Ilvanich pushed himself away from the wall. When he had his balance, he looked at Fitzhugh. "Good, good. Now get the company moving. I will be along in a minute."

Fitzhugh saluted, turned, and walked away, passing the word for the 1st Platoon to mount up and move out. When he was gone, Ilvanich looked back into the tunnel one more time before he shook his head, then walked over to Rasper to see if he was ready to go.

The first volley of 152mm rounds impacted to the rear of Ellerbee's platoon, just short of the roadblock next to a farmhouse being manned by Second Lieutenant Matto's engineers. Like a great trigger, those eighteen artillery rounds catapulted hundreds of soldiers, both American and Ukrainian, who were spread out over an area that encompassed a couple hundred square kilometers, into action.

On C60, Kozak automatically turned to her rear, looking to see where the rounds impacted, before dropping into the turret. Wolf, without needing to be told, yelled to Tish to crank up the engine. Tish, like Wolf, didn't need to be told either. Her finger was already on the starter when Wolf yelled. Paden's eyes popped open as if he had been hit by an electrical shock. In a single glance he checked the frequency settings on both the receiver-transmitter and the auxiliary receiver to ensure that they were set on the correct radio nets. Then, knowing that Tish would be starting the Bradley, he reached up and turned the radios off until after the engine turned over.

When she heard the sound of the radio click back on over her earphones, Kozak waited a second before she pushed the push-to-talk lever on the side of her helmet with her thumb. Listening for the beep that told her the radio was in the secure mode, Kozak notified battalion that they were receiving artillery fire on the tank platoon's position.

Even before Kozak began to transmit her initial report, Sal Salatinni knew the Ukrainian barrage had commenced as the Firefinder radars lit up the 1st Brigade's TACFIRE net with the information that the rocket launchers designated for counterbattery fire would need. Since the mission was already planned for, there was no need for anyone in the division artillery chain of command or at the 1st Brigade to intervene. Salatinni sat in his command post carrier where he monitored the process, yelling out to Cerro that the show was about to begin as he waited for the rocket launchers to acknowledge receipt of mission and confirmation that they had fired.

Ten kilometers from the brigade command post and twenty kilometers behind Kozak's position, the three-man crew of each of the rocket launchers was alerted that they had an incoming mission. Huddled in the armored cab of their launchers, the MLRS crews watched and responded as their computer display took them through the launch sequence. The TACFIRE computer at the field artillery battalion to which the MLRSs were attached assigned each of the three rocket launchers a separate target based on the known location of the rocket launchers and the target locations identified by the Firefinder's radar and computer. When the rocket launcher's computer finished receiving the data and was ready, it cued the crew to initiate the firing sequence.

Outside the rocket launcher there was no sign of human life, no indication that men were involved in the killing drill that was taking place. Like a great robot, the boxlike rocket pod swung about, aiming its twelve missiles toward the Ukrainian artillery batteries currently engaged in their own killing drill thirty kilometers away. When the computer sensed that the rocket pod was locked onto the proper elevation and azimuth, it gave the crew of the rocket launcher a green ready-to-fire light. A simple flick of a switch lit up the night sky as a ripple of twelve rockets issued forth out of each pod and streaked south toward their designated targets. No sooner had the last rocket left the launch pod, than the pod was returned to the travel position and the MLRS moved out, headed for a new spot where it would reload and await its next mission.

To the south, no one in Kozak's company saw or heard the rockets pass overhead. Kozak's people were too involved in preparing to receive the attack that the Ukrainian artillery had announced. Nor did the Ukrainian assault elements and their supporting tanks see or hear the incoming American rockets. The attention of the men making the assault or supporting it was riveted to their immediate front, looking for targets across the river or at the hundred or so meters of open ground between their jump-off points at the river's edge. The rockets, while they would influence their fight, belonged to a separate battle, an artillery duel that the Ukrainians lost before they even realized that it had been initiated.

After reaching the apogee of their flight, the rockets began their descent, each one spreading out and away from the others that it had been fired with. When the clamshell-like warhead of each of the rockets burst open, spewing its 644 bomblets, the Ukrainian gunners were in the process of preparing to load the fourth round of their barrage. None of the guns, however, managed to fire that round as the bomblets saturated an oblong beaten zone encompassing an area a little over one kilometer in size. The resulting devastation was not as complete as Salatinni would have liked, leaving several guns, vehicles, and artillerymen untouched. Left alone and given time, the Ukrainian artillery battalion would be able to recover some of its ability to function. It was, however, in military terminology, effectively neutralized and would no longer play a part in the battle that was developing along the Latorica.

The artillerymen supporting 1st Brigade were not finished. Their work, in fact, was just beginning. Even before the first MLRS rocket left its pod, the 155mm artillery battalion was receiving its firing orders over the TACFIRE net.

Bursts of radio traffic were heard on the frequencies that the brigade S-2, Lea Thompson, believed to be the Ukrainian brigade command net and artillery net, caught by the EH-60A Quickfix helicopter just after their artillery began to fire. Though each message was only a few seconds in length, together they were enough to fix the Ukrainians' locations. The electronic surveillance package on board the helicopter received and processed the signals using the targeted frequencies and recorded that information in its computer as back azimuths, or lines leading from the helicopter back in the direction from which the signals originated. After several seconds, this computer had accumulated several back azimuths, since the helicopter was moving and the source of the signal was not. Using its own internal mapping system, the computer plotted all the back azimuths and compared them. The point where all the back azimuths came together gave it, and everyone who had access to the computer's data down-link, the precise location of where the signals originated.

Lea Thompson compared the new location provided by the EH-60A helicopter with the one they had previously suspected to be the Ukrainian brigade command post based on earlier signal intelligence. When she saw that they matched, she became excited. "We've got 'em. We've got their CP." Bounding out of her command post carrier, she went over to Cerro. "Hal, we should fire on the Ukrainian brigade CP now, while we have it."

Salatinni, hearing Thompson's request, stuck his head out of his command post carrier. "1st of the 66th Field Artillery is ready to fire that mission. Do we have a go?"

Cerro looked at Salatinni, then at Thompson. For a second he wondered if they appreciated what they were about to do. Did they really understand that through their actions they were about to dump several hundred pounds of steel and high explosives on a group of real human beings? And did they know what would happen to those human beings when that happened? How could these staff officers, so far removed from the actual killing, appreciate what they were doing? But as quickly as those thoughts passed through his head, they left, allowing the brain of the operations officer to re-engage. Without further hesitation, he turned back to Salatinni. "Go ahead, Sal, fire it."

Pulling his head back into his track, Salatinni nodded to his sergeant seated at the TACFIRE console. A simple "Send it" was all he needed to say to initiate the fire mission.

At the fire direction center of the 1st of the 66th Field Artillery battalion, the TACFIRE printed up the mission, giving the target location, a description of the target, recommendation as to the type of ammunition to be used and number of rounds to be fired, and which of the battalion's three batteries was to fire the mission. The officer on duty reviewed the information and recommendations. Deciding to accept the TACFIRE's recommendations, he hit a button that sent the necessary data to the battery it had selected to fire the mission.

Seven kilometers away from the battalion fire direction center, Battery B, 1st of the 66th Field Artillery, received the fire mission. The same data that had been displayed at battalion was displayed at Battery B. The executive officer of Battery B saw no need to change the orders to engage an enemy command post as a point target with two volleys of dual purpose improved conventional ammunition. Like the officers on duty at the other command posts, he accepted the mission and computer recommendations by simply hitting a button. Electronically, the battery's computer sent out the elevation and azimuth needed by each gun, information that it had already calculated and had ready.

Even at the guns, computers were standing by ready to work. Upon receiving the elevation and azimuth from the battery's TACFIRE computer, the guns' own computers processed that information and translated it into action. Each gun commander ordered up the appropriate round of ammunition to be fired by reading it off of the computer's display. As the ammo bearers prepared and then passed the rounds to an assistant gunner who loaded the round, the gunner checked about the gun to ensure there was nothing in the turret of the M-109A5 howitzer that would get in the way when he fired. When the round and propellant were loaded and everyone was clear of the gun, the gunner hit the button that fed the elevation and azimuth into the howitzer's gun-turret drive. With quick, smooth movements, each of the eight guns of Battery B was laid on target. When all guns reported in that they were ready, the battery executive officer gave the order to commence firing.

The impact of those rounds across the river from Company C's position caught Kozak's attention, but she didn't bother herself with wondering who had fired them and what they had hit. As far as she was concerned, at that moment that artillery barrage wasn't important to her fight. Kozak had no idea how much the field artillery in her support had already begun shifting the odds of success back into her favor. In a span of minutes, before the first Ukrainian BMP had left its concealed position to commence the assault, the Ukrainians had lost their ability to bring indirect fire against her company. Equally important, the commander and much of his battle staff were also out of action. Although the initial American artillery fire missions had not touched any of the Ukrainian assault elements, when those elements came they would be without artillery support and would have no command and control element capable of directing the battle.

What was important to Kozak at that moment was the report that there were enemy tanks on her left flank taking her 1st Platoon under fire. There was also activity reported by her 2nd Platoon on the right. Kozak knew that there were enemy vehicles on both her flanks. Reports before the enemy attack of noise and numerous thermal hot spots in the woods across the river had alerted her to that. What she didn't know yet was whether the Ukrainians were trying to make a demonstration on one flank in order to keep her from shifting forces before the battle to the flank where the main attack was coming, or if they intended to hit both flanks with an attack.

From her position, Kozak could see the flashes of fire as enemy tanks on her left fired into the wood line where her 1st Platoon was located. Initial reports from Second Lieutenant Sylvester Ahern, platoon leader of that platoon, indicated that the Ukrainian tank fire was inaccurate and ineffective. They were, Kozak thought, firing blind. To her right, where the other enemy concentration had been reported, there was nothing. The platoon leader of her 2nd Platoon, Second Lieutenant Marc Gross, reported that while his dismounted infantry near the river line could hear numerous vehicles cranking up, they had no visual sightings yet and were not under fire. Although she didn't want to commit yet, Kozak was convinced in her heart that the action on the left was the demonstration and that the main attack would fall on her 2nd Platoon. Keying the radio, she ordered Ellerbee to stand by and be prepared to shift his entire platoon to the right in support of 2nd Platoon or as a counterattack.

When Ellerbee acknowledged, Kozak didn't bother to wonder why his radio transmission was so weak even though his tank was only thirty meters away. Instead, Kozak yelled to her crew, "Okay, gang. Show time. We're going over to 2nd Platoon."

Wolf, expecting that order, was going to make a comment, but didn't. Somehow, the gravity of the moment and the sudden welling of tension that one feels before entering battle made humor and glib remarks seem inappropriate. So Wolf, like the rest of C60's crew, remained silent as they responded to Kozak's orders and prepared to engage the enemy. Pulling back away from their position under Kozak's direction, Tish maneuvered C60 through the woods and down to where 2nd Platoon's dismounted infantry waited.

CHAPTER 5

7 JANUARY

When the first wave of Ukrainian BMP infantry fighting vehicles broke from their cover and began to rush down to the riverbank, Lieutenant Marc Gross and his 2nd Platoon were ready. From his position with the dismounted element of his platoon just inside the wood line along the river, the moonlight and shadows made the Ukrainian infantry fighting vehicles look more like crocodiles slipping into the water than fighting machines. He would wait, he decided, until they were in the water before he gave the order to fire.

Word that the attack had commenced caught C60 still halfway between Ellerbee's and Gross's position. Doing the best she could to steady herself in the open hatch of her Bradley as it bucked and bumped down the forest trail to the river's edge, Kozak began to issue orders to her company. After acknowledging Gross's initial report, she ordered her executive officer, First Lieutenant Patrick Goldak, to pass that report on to battalion. When Goldak acknowledged, Kozak called her fire support officer, Second Lieutenant Eugene Fong. She instructed him to request that the final protective fires plotted in front of 2nd Platoon, together with another mission into an area where they suspected the enemy tanks would be supporting the crossing, be fired immediately. When he gave her a "Roger. Out," Kozak called Ellerbee. Knowing that the bulk of his platoon could not engage the enemy vehicles from where he was, she ordered him to flex his platoon to the right, into 2nd Platoon's area as planned. Ellerbee, unlike the others, did not immediately respond. Repeating her orders to Ellerbee, Kozak finally got a response from Ellerbee's platoon sergeant, Sergeant First

Class Rourk. Although she had no idea why Ellerbee had not responded himself, Kozak let the matter drop. As a final check, Kozak radioed Lieutenant Ahern to make sure that there was not an attack developing to the front of 1st Platoon. Ahern confirmed Kozak's assumption, reporting that enemy tank fire was continuing but that he saw no sign of an assault developing where he was.

Finished with her orders, Kozak looked about her to ensure that Tish was still headed in the right direction, then called back to Gross requesting an update on his engagement. His response was quick and short.

"CHARLIE SIX, THIS IS TWO SIX. WE HAVE TWO ZERO PLUS BMPS IN THE WATER. WE ARE ENGAGING NOW. OVER." As if on cue, Kozak heard a series of muffled bangs over the roar of C60's engine as Gross's platoon fired their first volley of anti-tank rockets and TOW wire-guided anti-tank missiles.

Though they had anticipated some return fire during their assault, the rocket and missile fire startled most of the commanders of the assaulting BMP infantry fighting vehicles. Here and there, a BMP swerved a little to the right or left or slowed down slightly as the drivers also reacted to being taken under fire. Recovering their own composure, the commanders of the erring vehicles issued sharp reprimands to their drivers before turning to search for the source of the enemy fires.

As his BMP infantry fighting vehicle approached the river, the Ukrainian commander of the assaulting battalion was momentarily taken aback by the volume of enemy fire that had lit up the northern riverbank. He had been told by his brigade commander that they were being opposed by a single armored cavalry platoon equipped with tanks. The telltale signatures of rockets and anti-tank missiles coming from the wood line and high ground beyond told him different. Grabbing his radio hand mike, he called to inform his brigade commander of the true situation and request immediate artillery support. There was, however, no response to his calls. Neither his brigade commander nor his operations officer answered. Giving up, he tried to call the artillery support officer at brigade. That effort too met with failure. In frustration, he turned to his own artillery support officer and ordered him to contact the supporting artillery battalion and tell them to shift their fires to his front. Having anticipated that order, the artillery officer looked up at his commander and reported that he was having no luck at contacting the artillery battalion or its firing batteries.

In frustration, the battalion commander cursed, turning back to see how the two companies of his first assault echelon were doing. His eyes were greeted by the vision of burning vehicles, some still in the river, sinking or lazily turning around and around as they drifted downstream, out of control. Most of the first assault wave, however, had already reached the far shore and were beginning to pull themselves out of the water. With nothing further to be gained from staying where he was, the battalion commander ordered his driver to move out and join the second assault echelon, consisting of one company of infantry fighting vehicles, which were just beginning to emerge from their hide positions and head down to the river. With a little luck and some pushing, they could still succeed.

When the enemy infantry fighting vehicles reached the north bank of the river, they broke into two groups. One group moved straight for the woods where Gross and his dismounts were. A second group of eight vehicles to the left charged into a gap in the woods that led to the high ground where Gross's platoon sergeant was located with the platoon's Bradleys. Unable to control both fights, Gross concentrated on the group entering the woods while leaving his platoon sergeant to deal with the others running through the gap.

Though the dismounted infantry with Gross had managed to stop two of the assaulting BMP infantry fighting vehicles while they were in the river with their first volley of anti-tank fire and three more BMPs at the riverbank as they were pulling themselves out of the river, that still left seven Ukrainian BMP infantry fighting vehicles bearing down on the dismounted infantry of 2nd Platoon. Within seconds of reaching the riverbank, those seven BMPs were up, out, and right into the middle of the platoon's position. From firing ports along the sides and in the rear of the BMP infantry fighting vehicles, the Ukrainian infantry squads inside the BMPs opened fire as the BMPs entered the woods where the American positions were. Together with the fire from the mounted infantry, a 30mm cannon, and a 7.62mm machine gun mounted in its turret, each BMP laid down fire that began to having a telling effect on 2nd Platoon.

While the Ukrainian fire was wild and blind, its sheer volume, along with the chaos created when the BMPs themselves came tearing through their positions, was more than enough to break up 2nd Platoon's ability to offer organized resistance. For several terrifying seconds each of the dismounted infantrymen with Gross, as well as Gross himself, was on his own. The noise and confusion created by the appearance of the large steel fighting vehicles crashing through the woods only inches away, while spewing fire from every direction, was terrifying. For several critical seconds, each man and woman had to decide for himself whether to stay put, doing nothing while the Ukrainian BMPs passed, fight the BMPs as best they could, or flee.

To his left, Gross heard a piercing scream. To his right, someone was yelling for a medic. The shouts of squad leaders were punctured or cut short by the noise of gunfire and the grinding engines of enemy vehicles as they crashed their way through the woods. His platoon was taking casualties, and at that moment there was nothing that he could do to stop the enemy or help his people who were in trouble. Suddenly the real problems of being a combat leader hit home. For several critical seconds Gross would have to trust that his squad leaders and every individual rifleman in those woods would continue to perform their assigned duties while ignoring the pain and suffering of their friends and comrades. In those seconds, with enemy vehicles everywhere, there was nothing that Gross or the infantry squad leaders in the woods with him could do to control the people under their command. If he failed to keep his head and suppress his own fear and panic, or the discipline and cohesion of the unit failed, the platoon would fall apart and cease to be a fighting unit. If his nerve and the cohesion of his platoon held, then Gross and his sergeants had a chance to reorganize the platoon after the BMPs had passed and continue to resist. Jumping out of the path of a BMP that rolled on past him like a rogue elephant, Gross prayed that, one, he survived the next ten seconds, and two, he found something left to command at the end of those ten seconds.

The problem facing Ellerbee at that moment was, for him, equally distressing, though not nearly as hazardous. When he heard Kozak's order to flex his platoon to the right, Ellerbee yelled down to his driver to crank it up and prepare to move out. Turning off his radio during the starting sequence, Ellerbee held his hand on the radio's on-off switch while he waited for the sound of the engine turning over. When Wilk, his driver, hit the starter button, however, the only sound they heard was a clunk as the lights in the turret all but died out. "JESUS, LIEUTENANT! THE BATTERIES ARE DEAD!"

Startled by that announcement, Ellerbee let go of the radio's on-off switch, leaned down, and yelled, "WHAT DO YOU MEAN, THE BATTERIES ARE DEAD?"

"THEY'RE DEAD! DRAINED! NO POWER TO START THE TANK. WE NEED A SLAVE."

While Ellerbee sat there dumbfounded, Tinker Shildon turned around in the gunner's seat, faced Ellerbee, and began to pull his crewman's helmet off. "There's a slave cable on Rourk's tank. I'll go get it." Though his voice wasn't excited, Shildon was up and out of his seat in a flash. Squeezing past Ellerbee, the breech block of the 120mm main gun, and the loader, Shildon didn't stop until he was halfway out of the loader's hatch. Then his voice betrayed his shock and surprise. "WHERE IN THE HELL ARE THEY GOING?"

Shildon's comment threw Ellerbee. As he scrambled in an effort to get his head up and out of his hatch to see what Shildon was yelling about, Ellerbee yelled, "WHO? WHERE'S WHO GOING?"

"Sergeant Rourk and the rest of the platoon. They're moving out!"

Like a floating toy held under water in a bathtub and suddenly released, Ellerbee popped up and looked about just in time to see the taillights of Rourk's tank and his wing man disappear in the woods to their right. Instinctively Ellerbee reached up and keyed the push-to-talk lever on the side of his crewman's helmet to activate the radio. When nothing happened, he suddenly remembered that he had switched the radio off and had failed to turn it back on in the confusion following Wilk's announcement that they had no power. Just as he was prepared to drop down and turn the radio on, Ellerbee saw his own wing man's tank, A32, go screaming right behind him. Jumping back up, Ellerbee pointed at A32 and yelled to Shildon, "STOP HIM, TINKER. STOP HIM."

Pushing himself up and out of the loader's hatch, Shildon scrambled to the edge of the turret roof, climbed over the crew's personal gear stored in the bustle rack at the rear of the turret, hit the back deck with both feet, and took a flying leap onto the frozen ground, yelling at the top of his lungs as he did so. His efforts, however, were for nought. By the time he got up and began chasing A32, that tank, like Rourk's and his wing man's, was gone, swallowed up by the dark woods. Stopping, Shildon looked at the woods where A32 had disappeared, then back at the dark form of Ellerbee, who was hanging halfway out of his hatch. In the distance, both Shildon and Ellerbee could hear the battle at the riverbank.

Remembering that the engineer platoon was down the road a few hundred meters, Ellerbee yelled over to Shildon, "TINKER. Go down the road. Find the engineers at that farmhouse and see if they have someone who can come up and give us a jump start."

Looking through the woods toward the road, Shildon paused for a moment as he considered going back to the tank for his field jacket and helmet. A series of explosions from 2nd Platoon's positions and the thunk-thunk-thunk of 25mm cannons firing told him he didn't have time for that. Turning, he began to run. As he had before, Ellerbee sat there and watched Shildon disappear into the darkness, like the other tanks in his platoon had. Bad luck, he thought, piled on top of more bad luck, had left him and his disabled tank on the hill while Gross and the infantrymen in his platoon fought for their lives. Pounding his fist on the edge of his open hatch, Ellerbee began cursing out loud at Kozak and the incredible bad luck that had brought him to this spot.

No one in 2nd Platoon, or Kozak, realized that Ellerbee was out of the fight. Even Rourk, who had acknowledged Kozak's order and had passed it on to the platoon, had no idea what had happened to his platoon leader. What he did know was that the infantry was in trouble and that his platoon leader had failed to respond. Assuming that his lieutenant was too busy trying to get himself and his tank ready to move, and that he would follow when he could, Rourk took over the platoon and moved out in response to Kozak's order. There would be time later, if they won, to listen to Ellerbee's excuses. Right now, all Rourk knew was that the grunts were in deep shit and needed help.

Clear of the river and in the woods, the commander of the Ukrainian company that was overrunning Gross's dismounted infantry had three simple choices and not much time in which to make his decision. He could stop in the middle of the American position in the woods, dismount his own infantry, and try to wipe out the enemy. Since he really didn't know how many of his BMPs had made it, and his own company was as disoriented and confused at that moment as the enemy they were overrunning, he quickly decided against that. His next option was to move out of the woods and stop there. By doing so, his company would be clear of the enemy positions and in the open. The Ukrainian commander would then have time to dismount and organize his own command before going back into the woods to clear out the enemy. That, however, didn't seem like a good idea, since there had been reports of enemy tanks in the area. They, he thought, might be on the high ground, ready to engage his company as

soon as it emerged from the woods. To stop there would only make
the job of the enemy tanks easier. The final option available to him,
as the Ukrainian commander saw it, was to forget about the Americans in the woods by the river line and just keep advancing toward the
high ground. There, in the woods overlooking the bridge and open
areas near the riverbank, he could deploy his company and cover the
engineers as they put their bridge across the damaged highway bridge.
Once that bridge was in place, the two tank battalions of the brigade
would be able to cross over and join him. Then they could deal with
the enemy tanks. That, he decided, would be the most advantageous
decision for his company and the entire brigade.

The impact of the conditions under which the Ukrainian commander had to make this decision played no small part in his choice.
In the small, cramped confines of his own BMP's turret, he could see
precious little of the outside world, a forested world that was as black
as the ace of spades and illuminated at random only by an occasional
flash of gunfire or an explosion. The grinding of his BMP's engine,
mixed with the chatter of the machine gun and the thunk-thunk-
thunk of the 30mm cannon in the same turret he sat in, mingled with
the firing of other BMPs outside. Added to this was an occasional
bing-bing-bing as bullets, both enemy and friendly, ricocheted off the
outside of his BMP. Under such conditions, coupled with his temporary loss of control over his company and the tension and stress of
combat, it was a wonder that the Ukrainian company commander was
able to think at all. But he could and did. Without any hesitation, he
ordered his remaining vehicles to continue to advance through the
woods and up to the high ground beyond. The follow-on company, he
decided, could deal with the mess in the woods. He wanted to get out
into the open where he could fight his company.

After skirting the edge of the tree line where Gross and his dismounts were located, Kozak was about to order Tish to make a left
and head into the woods when Wolf yelled that he had acquired two
BMPs to their front. Dropping down, Kozak put her eye to her sight.
In the center of her sight, at a range of less than four hundred
meters, Kozak saw the distinctive image of two BMPs moving across
their front through the gap toward the high ground. "GREAT! WE
MADE IT." Excited, Kozak began to issue her fire command.
"DRIVER, STOP. GUNNER—ARMOR PIERCING—BMPS—RIGHT
BMP FIRST—"

But before she could give the order to fire, something moved in front of their sights and blocked their view of their intended targets, causing Wolf to yell, "WHAT THE—?"

Popping her head out of her hatch, Kozak was greeted by the image of three BMPs in a line emerging from the woods she had intended to go into. The nearest BMP, perpendicular to their line of fire, at less than ten meters, was blocking their line of sight. Kozak screeched, not bothering to key the intercom, "BMPS! BMPS! FIRE! NOW!"

Realizing what was happening, Wolf jerked the trigger, sending a volley of 25mm armor-piercing and high-explosive rounds into the flank of the Ukrainian company commander's BMP. At that range, none missed.

With her head still up, Kozak was blinded by the impact of her own Bradley's rounds on the side of the BMP. The sound of the firing of the 25mm cannon and the impact of those rounds was mixed with the wild screams of the men and the explosion of stored ammunition inside the BMP Wolf was riddling. In a second, Kozak regained her senses. "CEASE FIRE, CEASE FIRE." Wanting to put some distance between her and the BMP they had just destroyed, so that they could maneuver around and engage the other two BMPs beyond it that continued to move forward, Kozak yelled to Tish, "DRIVER! BACK UP, BACK UP, BACK UP!"

Responding to her commands, Tish jerked the Bradley into gear and started moving the vehicle backwards. They had not moved more than five meters when a stream of tracers emerged from the woods to their left and streaked across the front of Kozak's Bradley. Startled, Kozak looked over, just in time to see the nose and barrel of a BMP come out of the woods, almost ramming into the front left fender of Kozak's own Bradley.

"WOOF! BMP! LEFT, FIRE! FIRE! NOOOOW!"

While Tish was still backing up, Wolf traversed the turret, firing blindly as he did so, hoping to hit the enemy vehicle that Kozak was screaming about. When the image of the BMP's turret came into his sight, Wolf adjusted his fire and began to pump round after round into the turret of the enemy vehicle. As before, there was little chance to miss, and the effects on the enemy BMP were immediate and telling. When he was satisfied that the turret was wrecked, Wolf let up on the trigger, lowered his gun, and then raked the length of the BMP where the infantry squad sat with another volley.

As she watched to both her flank and front, Kozak ordered Tish to turn on the smoke generator, hoping that the veil of smoke would buy her some time to sort out what was going on.

As they broke out of the tree line, Rourk's gunner saw Kozak's Bradley, still backing up, and the BMPs to its front. Even as he yelled to Rourk, the gunner laid his sight on the first undamaged BMP he saw. Rourk didn't need the aid of a night vision sight to make out the forms of enemy BMPs and Kozak's Bradley. Without hesitation, Rourk yelled down to his gunner, "Get the first BMP, to the right of the burning BMP, now."

Used to Rourk's informal fire commands, the gunner gave the crew warning that he was about to fire by yelling, "ON THE WAY." With the aiming dot of his sight reticle laid on the center of mass of the enemy BMP, now moving around the burning hulk of the first BMP that Kozak had engaged, the gunner hit the laser range finder button, watched for a return, and then fired. At a range of less than two hundred meters, the hypervelocity, armor-piercing, fin-stabilized round ripped through the BMP and went screaming out the other side almost without pause. Seeing the effect of his first round, Rourk ordered the loader to switch to HEAT, high-explosive anti-tank rounds, before ordering his gunner to traverse right and engage the next BMP.

His wing man, however, pulling up next to Rourk's tank, got that one first. Like Rourk's, A33's gunner fired the armor-piercing round that was in the chamber. Though it was a waste of a good armor-piercing round, it was much quicker to empty the chamber by launching the round through the tube than having the loader try to unload it. And besides, in combat no one argued with a kill, even if the wrong ammunition was used.

Glancing back to see who had delivered her from the jaws of death, Kozak saw the two M-1A1 tanks to her rear. Directing Tish, she ordered her to stop making smoke and to continue to back the Bradley up until they moved in between Rourk's tank and a third M-1A1 that had come out of the woods. All the while, Wolf continued to search for more targets, and Rourk's three tanks continued to engage the last of the BMPs that had overrun Gross's position.

The engineers manning the roadblock peered out of the window of the farmhouse into the darkness as they listened to the sounds of the battle down by the river drift through the woods toward them. After the sudden and terrifying exposure to enemy artillery fire just short of their position, followed by the noise of battle that seemed to be coming closer and closer toward them, every noise, every motion, real and imagined, caused the engineers to jump. Left out there on their own, with no idea of what was happening, the engineer squad leader and his seven soldiers struggled to control their fears as they maintained their vigilance. Outside in a nearby field, the bellowing of a cow injured by the artillery barrage served to remind the engineers that this was for real, that there was a real enemy out there intent on killing them. Across the room, huddled in the corner of the farmhouse, the owner of the house, his wife, and two young children watched the engineers. At that moment in the darkness of the room, listening to the sounds of an approaching battle, it would have been difficult to tell who was more frightened.

"Sarge, Sarge. To the front. Something's coming up the road." The warning, shouted by the gunner manning an M-60 machine gun, didn't need to be repeated. While his people aimed every weapon they had down the road, the squad leader wondered how long he should wait before challenging the approaching intruder.

Having no idea where the engineer roadblock was, but knowing that this was no time to screw around, Shildon kept running for all he was worth. Huffing and puffing, he made it up the last incline, picking up speed as he continued to pump his legs. Absorbed by his own exertions and unable to hear very much due to the pounding of his feet on the pavement and his labored breathing, Shildon didn't hear the half-hearted challenge given while he was still fifty meters from the farmhouse.

The realization that the intruder running at them had increased his speed, rather than stopping when he was challenged, left the engineer squad leader little choice. Without a second thought, he lifted his rifle to his shoulder and passed the word to open fire.

For a moment there was a pause in the action, a pause that allowed Kozak to catch her breath. It took her several seconds to calm down enough to look around and assess her situation. To her right sat Rourk's tank. Beyond that she could see another M-1A1 tank. To her left, just a few meters away, was a third tank. That she didn't see a fourth tank didn't occur to her. What did occur to her was that the tanks had arrived just in time, destroying four more BMPs that had continued moving out of the woods while C60 had been fighting its own little battle. What chance, she thought, would she have had of surviving if the tanks had not arrived when they did. After pushing that thought aside, and finally composed enough to speak, Kozak made a crew check. Like her, most of her crew had been stunned into silence by their close brush with death. Only Paden, who had been in the rear compartment and unable to see out, had no clear idea of exactly what had happened. The reactions of the others, however, had been enough to convince him that things had been very, very tight.

Satisfied that all was in order where she was, Kozak attempted to contact Gross in an effort to find out what was happening within 2nd Platoon. Sitting in the low ground, one hundred meters behind the woods, Kozak was unable to see the river or the gap beyond. But she could hear the sounds of small arms coming from the woods she had just fled from and Bradley cannon fire from the high ground far off to her right. Artillery seemed to be impacting somewhere off in the distance, beyond the woods and near the river. She couldn't tell whose artillery it was, let alone what it was hitting. Finally ready, Kozak began to find out.

The first person to answer Kozak's call for sitreps was Gross's platoon sergeant, sitting up on the high ground with the platoon's Bradleys. His report was quick and harried. "CHARLIE SIX, WE ARE ENGAGING A WHOLE BUNCH OF BMPS TO OUR FRONT. WE HAVE DESTROYED AT LEAST TEN, BUT THERE ARE MORE MOVING UP NOW, OUT OF THE RIVER. ENEMY RETURN FIRE IS BECOMING HEAVY AND ACCURATE. CHARLIE TWO TWO HAS BEEN HIT AND IS OUT OF ACTION. I MAY HAVE TO PULL BACK FROM HERE. OVER."

Realizing that he was facing the second-echelon company, Kozak looked over to Rourk's tank, then keyed the radio. "CHARLIE TWO FOUR, THIS IS SIX. HOLD YOUR POSITION. I AM COMING UP ON YOUR LEFT WITH THE TANKS. WE WILL HIT THE ENEMY SECOND COMPANY IN THE FLANK. DO YOU COPY? OVER."

Gross's platoon sergeant, in the midst of an engagement, only managed a quick "WILCO."

That, however, was enough. While facing Rourk's tank, Kozak radioed him. "ALPHA THREE FOUR, THIS IS SIX. DID YOU MONITOR MY LAST ORDER TO CHARLIE TWO FOUR?"

Rourk waved while he answered over the radio. "ROGER THAT, SIX. WE'RE MOVING OUT NOW." Taking his cue from Rourk, the driver of his tank began to move forward.

When the tank to the left began to move, Kozak called to Tish over the intercom. "Okay, let's try this again. Tish, move out and try to keep abreast of the tank to your left."

As Kozak and the tanks began to pass to the rear of his position, Marc Gross was still in the process of pulling his dismounted squads back together. Reoriented by Gross to the front and right, squad leaders called out to their men, who were scrambling and stumbling about in the woods torn up by the first wave of BMPs. While the platoon medic and a lightly wounded infantryman paused to help some of the more severely wounded, the rest of 2nd Platoon's dismounts homed in on the sound of their squad leader's voice. This effort was complicated by the presence of one BMP that had earlier run through his position and, unlike the others that had left the woods, had turned back. Realizing that he would be unable to ignore the presence of that BMP, Gross ordered the squad leader of his 2nd Squad to take his men and go back to find and destroy it. With that problem taken care of, Gross turned his attention to the efforts of his other two squads. Both had taken casualties, but for the moment both were preparing to re-engage enemy BMPs going past them into the gap.

The BMPs moving through the gap offered the anti-tank gunners flank shots at less than fifty meters and provided Gross's men with perfect targets against which they could vent the rage they felt after being overrun. Seeing there was nothing more that he needed to do, Gross ordered the squad leaders to fire at will. After the first anti-tank rocket was launched, Gross called for his radioman, took the hand mike from him, and called to his platoon sergeant for an update.

Back on the hill where Kozak had left him, Lieutenant Fong listened to the reports to Kozak and plotted them on his map. Even though she hadn't asked for it, Fong decided that Kozak would need some artillery to support her counterattack. Satisfied that he had a handle on the situation, he told his sergeant to contact the supporting artillery battalion and request fires on two preplanned targets that would cover the gap. The sergeant, leaning over to confirm the target numbers Fong had given him, asked if they wanted to cease their bombardment of the enemy tanks that had been supporting the river crossing. Fong looked at the sergeant, then at his map. "Tell the FSO at battalion that if the guns can fire both missions, then yes, keep up suppressive fires on the enemy tanks. If not, shift all fires into the gap."

Giving Fong a thumbs-up, the sergeant began to process the call for fires using his digital message device, a keyboardlike device that tied directly into the TACFIRE system used by the artillery. While the sergeant did that, Fong called Kozak on the Charlie Company command net, notified her of his actions, and reminded her that the artillery was on the ball and doing its job.

Stuck in the middle of a cluster of BMPs, the Ukrainian battalion commander realized that they were in trouble. Opening his hatch, he watched as the anti-tank fire he had assumed had been silenced resumed. He was about to order the follow-on company commander to shift one platoon over to engage the enemy anti-tank gunners in the woods on their flank when that company commander called over the radio net that enemy tanks were coming up from behind the woods. Jerking his head to the front right, the battalion commander watched as two BMPs on the right were blown up by enemy tank fire. Hit from the front by enemy Bradleys on the high ground, and now by tanks and dismounted infantry on the right, he saw no choice but to order all surviving vehicles to move left and take refuge in the woods on the other side of the gap.

By now it was too late to salvage much. Command and control of the battalion disappeared in a matter of seconds as the second-echelon company collided with the remains of the lead assault company and mingled, just as Kozak with the tanks came up on the flank and opened fire. That this happened just as the dismounted infantry with Gross opened fire and the first volley of artillery began to rain down on the gaggle of BMPs was pure luck, nothing but pure luck. But luck, as Ellerbee had found out, was at times just as important in war as good planning and training.

Using the woods to mask her command from the supporting Ukrainian tanks still sitting on the other side of the river searching for worthwhile targets to engage, Kozak began the methodical process of destroying the remains of the Ukrainian motorized infantry battalion.

The final act in Ranger Company A's drama that night was, by comparison to Kozak's fight, anticlimactic. The movement of the ranger company down away from the tunnel was unopposed. Ilvanich's prediction that the Ukrainians would shift their efforts to the right of where the reaction force had been defeated appeared to be correct. Ilvanich, finally able to shake himself out of his despondency, joined the end of the column. Within minutes of moving off of the ledge where the tunnel entrance was located, he was able to concentrate again. The cold morning air, the physical act of moving in the company of soldiers, and the simple fact that they were finally leaving the tunnel that reeked of death were invigorating. By the time he had moved a kilometer, Ilvanich began to feel that he was back in control of himself and the situation. That did not mean he had forgotten. No, Ilvanich knew better than that. It only meant that for the moment the images, the sights, and smells that he had witnessed that night were relegated to the recesses of his mind where they would lie dormant. Someday, Ilvanich knew, they would be back. Like thieves in the night, they could creep back into his conscious mind. There they would try to rob him of his sanity and stability, just like the other images of past battles that he struggled to restrain and suppress and on occasion did. Regardless of what happened, regardless of who won, Ilvanich knew that this war would never end. Only death, he knew, would bring an end to his suffering.

As the single file of men, burdened by wounded comrades and heavy weapons, snaked its way along the side of the mountain, Ilvanich began to make his way to its head. The rangers, each left to deal with his own thoughts, pushed on in silence, reminding Ilvanich of members of a funeral procession. They needed to be touched, he thought, touched by a word of encouragement, a smile, a hand from another living human being. So as he moved forward, followed by Sergeant Rasper, Ilvanich took the time to pat each man on the back or grab his arm and say something, anything, in an effort to shake the men in his command out of their stupor. The presence of Rasper following on Ilvanich's heels and doing the same as he was overcame any reservations that the rangers in Company A had about the Russian major.

By the time he reached the head of the column, Ilvanich was feeling better about his decision to move overland in an effort to link up with the rest of the ranger battalion at the other storage site. Fitzhugh, who had been at the head of the column, was slowly picking up the pace as the shock of the morning's operation wore off and the soldiers of Company A began to regain their balance. When he came up next to Fitzhugh, Ilvanich placed his hand on Fitzhugh's shoulder. "We must not speed up too much, or the men carrying the wounded will soon be lagging behind."

Fitzhugh looked over at Ilvanich and nodded. "Oh, yeah. Sorry, Major. I guess I was getting carried away. You know, put as much distance between us and that place."

He was doing better, Ilvanich thought. The young lieutenant was overcoming the paralysis of fear, shock, and panic. Looking back at the column struggling through the dark, snow-covered landscape, Ilvanich knew that it had been a good move to get out and away from the tunnel. Smiling, Ilvanich returned Fitzhugh's nod. "Yes, I share your desire. But not at the expense of losing our wounded. We must make it all together or not at all. Now just keep heading along the base of this hill until we hit the Svalyava road. From there it will be a short march through the woods and up a hill."

Though he still had no contact with the American battalion commander, or anyone else, Ilvanich trusted that the American battalion commander would react in the same manner as a Russian commander would in the same situation. Eventually he would use the scout helicopters, or perhaps even the attack helicopters themselves, to conduct a search for survivors and attempt to assess the situation. While it was always possible that those helicopters would find them, Ilvanich could not count on that. It was important, Ilvanich knew, to do something, something positive. To have waited for someone to find them and come to their rescue was against everything that Ilvanich had been taught. All he had to do was to keep his company together and out of harm's way until they were found or they reached the other rangers.

A feeling of nausea overcame Ilvanich, causing him to slow his pace, then stop. Fitzhugh didn't notice the sweat that was beading up on Ilvanich's forehead. Nor did he stop when Ilvanich halted. Fitzhugh simply kept trudging along through the snow and into the darkness, leaving Ilvanich alone. Ilvanich managed to compose himself, fighting back the nausea that he had feared would come since it was usually the first symptom of radiation sickness that manifested itself.

A series of explosions coming from the direction of the tunnel caused Ilvanich to turn around. In the darkness he could see that the Ukrainians were laying down a barrage on the ledge in front of the tunnel they had just left. Looking about, he noticed that the entire column had stopped and turned to watch. They, as he did, realized how close this entire affair had been. Overcoming his own concerns, Ilvanich called out to his command, "Those are 120mm mortars. The Ukrainians still believe we are at the tunnel and they are preparing to attack. So long as we do not do anything foolish, we will be safe until the helicopters find us or we reach our own lines." Looking at Fitzhugh, he ordered him to keep moving. "That fight," he reminded his men as they began to pass him, "belongs to the attack helicopters now. Our mission is almost over."

By the time Dixon rolled up in his tank, the forward command post was almost ready to move. Cerro, who had been standing out of the way, watched Dixon as he stood on top of the turret shaking the ice and snow off of his parka. After handing the parka to his gunner, who had moved up into the commander's hatch while Dixon prepared to dismount, Dixon stretched. Bringing his hands down to his hips, he looked about before he started to dismount. Behind Dixon on the horizon the sun was just beginning to make its appearance. To Cerro, Dixon, standing erect on top of his tank, hands on his hips and legs spread shoulder width, looked like a feudal lord surveying his conquests. That analogy, Cerro thought, wasn't far from the truth.

Three hours after crossing the border, the lead elements of 1st Brigade, 4th Armored Division, were about to enter the city of Mukacevo, ahead of schedule and despite predictions that they would never make it that far. The Ukrainian tank brigade from Uzlovaya, a threat that had been a major concern before the operation, had been met and turned back. Even at the moment, air strikes were going in to ensure that it would be unable to recover from the pounding that it had received at the hands of 3rd of the 3rd Infantry. And the militia units throughout the region were for the most part ineffective. Unable to coordinate their activities, resistance was minimal. Only one roadblock on the road to Mukacevo had been encountered after crossing the border. A hasty attack by 1st Battalion, 37th Armor, the brigade's lead element, had easily pushed it aside. Yeah, Cerro thought, Dixon was at the moment lord and master of all he saw.

Walking over to Dixon's tank, Cerro was greeted with a smile. "Hell of a fine day to be a tanker, Hal. How's the staff business going?"

Dixon was animated. Strange, Cerro thought, how a ride in a tank, a chance to join in on the rush against an enemy position, and the dawn of a new day can wipe away all the fears and exhaustion that seemed to grow in the darkness of night. There was nothing that could make a man feel more alive than to put one's ass on the line and survive. Strange breed we are, he thought. "You need a quick update, sir?"

Looking down from his commanding height, Dixon smiled. "Of course. You have one?"

"Well, sir, we seem to be in the middle of a lull right now. Our lead elements are on the outskirts of Mukacevo with no signs of resistance other than a few hasty roadblocks that no one seems to be interested in defending. Kozak and her crew down on the Latorica are in good shape. They haven't had any contact in a couple of hours and have managed to re-establish their blocking positions. Further to the east, the ranger company from the storage site that got trashed linked up with the rest of their battalion at the second site. According to corps, they've already started lifting out the nukes from that site. Since nothing seems to be in the wind, I thought this would be a good time to jump the CP forward to Mukacevo. I was just getting ready to jump forward to the next location when you came up. We'll be on the road in another fifteen minutes."

Slapping his hands on his chest, Dixon took a deep breath. "Well, don't let me stop you. I'll get one of your loyal minions to give me an update."

Cerro saluted. "Okay, I'll leave you here to gloat, sir."

Dixon laughed. "Do I detect, Major, some sour grapes?"

"No, sir, not at all. You're the boss and you have every right to roam about the countryside wherever you please while I keep the galley slaves in line."

Dixon, a smile lighting up his dirty face, looked at Cerro. "Don't worry, Hal. Your day will come. I assure you, after this you'll be a shoo-in for battalion command. And when you get your battalion, I hope that you get an operations officer that's just as obnoxious as the one I've been saddled with."

"Okay, sir. I get the message. I'll meet you up the road." Exchanging salutes, Cerro turned and began to walk away, then paused. "Oh, one more thing, Colonel. There's a storm brewing in the west."

Dixon's face now showed a moment of concern. "Any chance of its affecting us?"

Cerro shook his head. "Too early to tell, sir."

Looking at the dark sky to the west, Dixon thought about it for a moment, then smiled again. "Well, there's nothing you or I can do to stop it if it decides to come our way. No need to worry about something that's beyond our control. We have more than enough to deal with here. Now, break's over. Back on your head."

PART TWO

THE GERMAN CRISIS

C H A P T E R   6

7 JANUARY

After a second review of the script her producer, Charley Mordal, had provided her for the twelve noon broadcast, Jan Fields-Dixon decided that more changes needed to be made. Although it never ceased to amaze her how little information their news program actually put out over the air, today's script, concerning what the script referred to as the American incursion into the Ukraine and the first use of a nuclear weapon since 1945, was particularly bad. With script in hand, Jan headed for the producer's desk, which was no easy task, especially on a day when a news story like this broke. The normal well-paced and measured chaos and pandemonium of the central newsroom was intensified tenfold. Jan had once theorized to a fellow correspondent that the importance of a news story could be measured by the amount of shouting and yelling that took place behind the camera. Few in the business disagreed with her.

Winding her way through and around a maze of computer desks and long consoles manned by stern-faced technicians and harried assistant editors, Jan bobbed and weaved as she attempted to keep from being knocked down or overrun by people running about with as much direction and purpose as headless chickens. It was for this reason, despite criticism from her boss, that Jan wore her sneakers most of the day. "Only a fool," she was fond of replying to his comments, "would willingly wear three-inch heels while playing stickball in heavy traffic." Besides the practical benefit, Jan enjoyed tweaking the nose of authority when in her opinion those wielding that authority were being a tad bit dumb. So Jan's sneakers served as a visible symbol of willingness to challenge stupidity that others freely accepted as "the way things are."

When he saw Jan headed his way, the first thought that entered Charley Mordal's mind was to flee. After a struggle of ten hours trying to pull together a coherent package that somehow brought all the elements of the latest crisis into focus, the last thing Mordal wanted to do was get into a pissing contest with Jan. Flight, however, would not save him. Once Jan achieved what everyone called target lock, there was no escape. That didn't keep the others who had been gathered around Mordal's desk from taking flight. Like cockroaches scattering when the light went on, the people who had been with Mordal were gone before Jan reached his desk.

Without hesitation, Jan carefully moved a stack of papers and computer printouts out of the way before sitting on the corner of Mordal's desk. Crossing her legs, Jan leaned forward, resting her left arm on her leg, leaving her left hand to dangle over her knee. Settled, she held the script in front of her with her right hand. "Charley, we *really* need to take a serious look at this script. It is, to use a cliché, a mile wide and an inch deep."

Exhausted from his efforts, Mordal slumped back in his chair and stared at Jan before answering. It was times like this that made him wonder if it was worth the pain that he and the rest of the editorial staff had to endure in order to work with this woman. She was by any measure attractive. Jan's long brunette hair sported soft bangs that brushed across her forehead so they fell just above her right eye, while framing her oval face with gentle waves that cascaded softly about her shoulders. Jan used little makeup, just enough to highlight her high cheekbones and big brown eyes, which were her favorite feature. Coupled with a firm, persuasive manner, Jan used her eyes like a weapon.

Looks, however, were not Jan's strongest point. Her skills as a correspondent were what made her. With more credentials to her credit than fellow correspondents with twice the time in the business, Jan had an ability to communicate the news that few came close to matching and none surpassed. It was as if, someone had said, she had been born for this. Still this didn't make dealing with her any easier, especially when she thought that she was right.

Mordal's exasperated response was not exaggerated. Lifting his right hand as if he were trying to fend her off, Mordal avoided looking into her eyes as he answered. "Jan, I've been up since one o'clock this morning. I have personally looked at every piece of information concerning our President's little tantrum—"

In a voice that sounded like a schoolteacher's, Jan interrupted Mordal. "Charley, I would *hardly* call the invasion of another country, an invasion that, oh by the way, resulted in the detonation of God knows *how* many nuclear warheads and an outcry from our European allies, a 'little tantrum.' "

Mordal was tired, harried, and in no mood to be lectured to. "Look, Jan. You have the best of what would otherwise be called a handful of shit. No one is talking. Not the White House, not the State Department, and especially not the Pentagon. All we have right now is a whole lot of bits and pieces that, unedited and strung end to end, don't come out to more than five minutes' worth of airtime."

"So," Jan retorted, "your solution is to have me chat with a bunch of pseudo-experts who know less than we do and prove it every time they open their mouths."

Looking her in the eye for the first time, Mordal nodded. "Yes. Something like that. Why, do you have a better idea?"

Mordal had no sooner said that than he regretted doing so. "As a matter of fact, Charley, I do. It seems that the Germans are being quite silent about the whole affair. In fact, except for this one short piece here from Reuters stating that German forces were placed on alert this morning within minutes after the American invasion began, we have nothing concerning Germany."

"So? What's the big deal? I mean, it's obvious that they and the rest of Europe are as embarrassed about the whole thing as we are. You know, big American operation goes haywire, radiation contaminating Swiss moo cows, fear of three-headed children being born paralyzing Central Europe, Chernobyl revisited. You know, the usual."

Jan made a face. She ignored his attempt to mock her and continued to press her point. "Charley, you don't think about your own stuff or try to put any of it together, do you? Over the last year and a half, the Germans and the Ukrainians have been building what the German Chancellor called last July 'a new basis for both political and economic cooperation in Central Europe between our two great nations, nations that together can bring East and West together and strength and unity out of chaos.' When you consider the amount of money the Germans have invested in the Ukraine, you can't deny that politics and national interest follow. For instance, the joint proposal that the

Chancellor of Germany and the President of the Ukraine put forth last spring, when the Czech and Slovakian republics threatened to resort to armed conflict to resolve their differences, that Germany and the Ukraine intervene to prevent war. With that level of cooperation, one would expect some kind of reaction from our friends the Germans."

Mordal shrugged. "Okay, granted, the Germans like the Ukrainians. But the Germans are our allies. They have been for more than fifty years. Given a choice, who do you think they're going to side with?"

Jan straightened up as she continued to look at Mordal. He really didn't understand. She was about to remind him that the Germans had been reluctant allies from the start, and had been pushing to get U.S. forces out of Central Europe since the unification of East and West, when an assistant editor came running up to Mordal's desk. "Gee, Charley, I hate to bother you and Jan, but we just got word that the President will be making an announcement at noon."

Looking over to the bank of clocks on the wall, then at his own wristwatch, Mordal mumbled, "Well, that's just great! Just outstanding! Thirty-five minutes to airtime and everything goes into the shitter." Standing up, he looked at Jan. At least, he thought, this gave him a great way to end a conversation that he really wasn't interested in. "Look, Jan dear. You may have a wonderful story line there. But right now we have thirty or so minutes to rearrange everything. We'll talk about this later." Motioning to several technicians and assistant editors, Mordal turned his attention to his new problem. "Once we got a handle on this, Jan, I'll get back to you. For now, plan on introducing your program at noon like normal. Then announce that we'll cut to the White House briefing room. Jimmy will take it from there. And hang on to that script just in case this falls through or the President's announcement is mercifully short. I'll have Debbie display any changes on the TelePrompTer."

Though she wasn't pleased that she had failed to make her point, Jan nodded and got up off of Mordal's desk. News, after all, was news. And while she truly believed that she had a good story line that needed to be pursued, this was not the time to do it. "Okay, Charley, I'll go get myself ready and leave you to deal with the alligators."

As President Wilson's entourage entered the small room off to the side of the press briefing room, a technician signaled one of the aides attending the President. Walking over, the technician whispered, "The President's secretary is on the line. She says that the German Chancellor is on the line requesting to speak directly to President Wilson."

Wilson's aide frowned. "How much time do we have before we go on?"

The technician looked at his watch, then at a wall clock. "Three minutes."

Tilting his head down, the aide thought a moment. Then, making a decision that he thought was best but one which was well beyond his pay grade, the aide spoke with an assumed air of authority. "Tell the President's secretary to contact Secretary Soares's office at the State Department and have the Chancellor's call transferred over to him." Without any further thought, and not wanting to clutter the President's mind with any thoughts other than what she was about to tell the American public, the aide let the technician and in turn a secretary handle the German Chancellor's call.

The aide, unfortunately, had forgotten that Secretary Soares was in the middle of a meeting with the members of the UN Security Council in New York at the moment. Soares's secretary, knowing that the meeting at the UN was important, didn't want to forward the call to New York for fear of interfering with it. She therefore recommended that the call be transferred to the next man in Wilson's inner circle, the Secretary of Defense.

While Chancellor Ruff of Germany was being kept on hold and aides and secretaries across Washington, D.C., were passing his call about like a football, Wilson's press secretary came up to her side. "Here's the revised script as it will appear on the TelePrompTer, Madam President."

Wilson, oblivious to the fumbling of her staff and the staffs of her cabinet, prepared herself for the press. Taking the script in her right hand, Wilson reached across with her left hand and put it on her press secretary's arm. "Please do me a favor, Maggie, and don't make a face this time if I stray from your prepared text. You know how I love to play the room."

"Oh, no problem, Madam President, you go right ahead and improvise all you want. You know you're at your best when you do that."

Yes, Wilson thought. She always did her best when she trusted her instincts. As she watched the big hand of the clock inch toward twelve, she regretted that she hadn't trusted her instincts on this current issue. While Pete Soares was a great political advisor and Terry Rothenberg was a shrewd lawyer, they needed to think more on their own and not take as gospel everything their advisors in the State Department and the Pentagon fed them. They had made too many mistakes on this one and needed to make sure that didn't happen again, provided, of course, she could pull their collective chestnuts out of this fire.

"One minute, Madam President."

Drawing two deep breaths, Wilson flashed her best campaign smile and prepared to step into the lions' den.

"Damn them. DAMN THEM TO HELL!" Lunging forward over his desk, Chancellor Ruff thrust his finger at his military aide. "You go and find the lowest bathroom attendant in this building. Have him get on the phone and tell that little fat Jew Secretary of Defense that if I wanted to talk to him, I would have called him." Pushing himself away from his desk, Ruff looked at Colonel Hans Kasper for a moment. "Who does that whore think she is dealing with? Does she believe that Germany is still a vassal state, to be dealt with at *her* convenience?"

Kasper did not flinch. He had no intention of finding a bathroom attendant, since there were none in the building, and, more importantly, Ruff's comment was simply part of an elaborate play being enacted for the benefit of members of the cabinet who were not privy to the script. Ignoring Ruff's last comment, Kasper excused himself, playing his role to the hilt. "I will personally tend to the call immediately, Herr Chancellor." Pivoting smartly on his heel, he left the room to Ruff and the cabinet members that had assembled in his office.

When the door was closed and he had regained his composure after his well-controlled outburst, Ruff turned to the members of his cabinet. Though he had no idea of the folly in Washington that had resulted in what Ruff considered an insult, the timing of it couldn't have been any better for Ruff. "That, my friends, is what the Americans think of us. That is why it is time, in my opinion, to bring this unnatural state of affairs to an end. We no longer need an army of occupation to remind us that they defeated us. We no longer need to have foreigners rub our noses in the sins of our fathers. The past is over." Ruff pounded his fist on the desk to emphasize his point. "OVER! OVER! It is time that *WE* made the Americans understand that."

Across from him, the members of his cabinet listened to him in silence. Some showed their agreement with a simple nod or a gesture. Others, uncomfortable with Ruff's manner and what they believed his line of thinking, grimaced or shifted restlessly in their chairs. This did not surprise Ruff. He already knew who could be trusted and who needed to be kept in the dark. In time, everyone, even the dullest idiot, would come to understand what he was after. But he expected by then to have presented the German people a fait accompli, one which, when they came to understand what was at stake, they would support. Until then Ruff had to ensure that they continued to pretend that they were what his Foreign Minister, Bruno Rooks, called the innocent rape victim.

Standing up, Ruff looked about the room, then turned his back to the members of his cabinet as he limped across the room to a window. The storm that had started that morning continued unabated.

From behind him, Thomas Fellner, the Interior Minister, was the first to speak. "I believe we need to send a high-ranking representative to the United States, preferably Herr Rooks. He could be there by tomorrow morning to meet with President Wilson. Once we understood what they had in mind and what they intended—"

Pivoting, Ruff thrust his right arm down, jabbing his index finger toward the floor to emphasize his anger as he shouted, "NO! NO! I will not send a member of my government hat in hand crawling to that bitch, for any reason. Not tonight, not tomorrow, NOT EVER!" Folding his arms across his chest, Ruff took a deep breath and threw his head back before he continued. "Think, Thomas, think. Think of what that would tell the world. The leaders of the other nations in Europe would see that and say, 'Ah, see how Germany, the good little client state, runs to the United States for instructions.' Is that what you want, my friend? No. Germany is the offended party. Germany is once again captive to a unilateral American action that has gone astray." Taking a few steps forward, Ruff thrust his right arm up, finger pointed to the ceiling. "No, my comrades. Germany will not roll over like an obedient puppy dog, allowing the Americans to come and go as they please. Not this time. Not while I am Chancellor."

As if on cue, Rudolf Lammers, the Minister of Defense, spoke out. "What other options, Herr Chancellor, do we have? As we sit here beating our chests in righteous indignation, the Americans are already flying nuclear weapons into our country from the Ukraine. This is an act, if I may remind all of you, which is in clear violation of every disarmament agreement we and the United States have been party to since the collapse of the Eastern bloc. By tomorrow morning, if we do nothing, the weapons will be transferred to larger aircraft and flown back to the United States. The Americans will have, as a result of their deception and our ineptitude, achieved their objective, at our expense."

"That," Ruff added, "is exactly my point. While we sit here wringing our hands, wondering what to do, the Americans forge on with their plan. We must act. We must take action to ensure that the United States, as well as the rest of Europe, understands that we are not a puppet on a string to be jerked about whenever it pleases them. German sovereignty and self-determination, not to mention our pride and integrity, must be respected."

As in the past, Fellner raised the voice of concern and caution. Not that Ruff didn't expect it. In fact, he had counted on Fellner to do so. "What, Herr Chancellor, do you propose to do at this point? Outside of official protests, the only other option that I see is direct action against American operations within our borders. Are you proposing that we take such measures?"

Fellner's comments could not have been any more timely or better put than if Ruff had written that part of the script himself. For Ruff, the fact that Fellner, the voice of reason within the German cabinet, a man viewed by everyone in Germany and Europe as being the epitome of what a good peace-loving German should be, was the first to mention direct action was critical. For several moments, Ruff let Fellner's comments hang in the air, acting as if he were thinking about them. When he was ready, Ruff moved back to his desk, limping slightly. When he spoke, Ruff looked down at the floor, voice soft, reflective, almost as if he were speaking his thoughts rather than addressing his ministers. "That, my friends, is what we must now discuss." Then, as if a moment of indecision had passed and he had regained his resolve, Ruff looked up. "If you would, there is much to do and not much time. I would like to speak with Herr Rooks and Herr Lammers for a few minutes in private." As the cabinet members began to rise from their chairs, Ruff called out, "Excuse me, gentlemen. I am sorry. I have forgotten that I am scheduled for a press conference that should have started five minutes ago. We must as soon as possible inform the German people about what is happening in order to calm their fears and let them know that we are doing something." Looking around the room as if he were trying to decide who should serve as his substitute, Ruff stopped when his eyes came to rest on Fellner. "Would it be possible, Herr Fellner, for you to take it for me?"

Though he would have preferred not to, Fellner nodded. "Yes, Herr Chancellor, I will. How much do you want me to tell the press? Is it appropriate at this time, Herr Chancellor, to mention that we are considering declaring a state of emergency?"

Ruff struggled to conceal the joy he felt when Fellner mentioned a state of emergency. Such a declaration would allow Ruff as the Chancellor to take action without having to consult the Bundestag. "Do as you see fit, my friend. It just might be wise to bring out some of the concerns we have expressed in this meeting."

Rooks and Lammers looked at each other with a knowing glance when Ruff made that comment.

After a moment, Fellner agreed. "Yes, perhaps it is best if we begin to tell the German people the truth and prepare them."

"Yes," Ruff repeated solemnly, "I suppose you are right."

When the rest of the cabinet was gone, Colonel Kasper entered the room. "Herr Chancellor, General Lange and General Schacht are waiting."

Waving his hand, Ruff ordered Kasper to show them in. Walking over to Rooks and Lammers, Ruff shook their hands. "It has begun, my friends, it has finally begun. Now all we need to do is to see if the commander of the 1st Parachute Division can deliver as he has promised."

Both Ruff and Lammers knew there was no need to discuss options. The direct action that Fellner had mentioned had already been decided upon several days before. Orders to the units involved had already been issued. Units of the Bundeswehr that were to execute those orders were on the move at that very moment. The meeting between Ruff, Rooks, Lammers, and his military chiefs was nothing more than a final review of the situation and any last-minute coordination that needed to be made.

If all went well, within twelve hours Germany would be a nuclear power.

The evacuation of the remnants of Company A back to the heart of Slovakia brought little comfort or joy to the survivors. While it was reasonable that they would be treated separately and kept for a while due to their exposure to radiation, the treatment that the rangers of Company A received by everyone they came across was, in Ilvanich's mind, inexcusable. The danger from any radiation that the rangers had come into contact with in the Ukraine had long since been dealt with. That did not stop treatment, however, which Ilvanich considered to be cruel and unjustifiable to the men who now looked to him for answers.

Unable to restrain himself any longer, Ilvanich finally overcame his reluctance to complain and began to exert himself in the manner that was more natural to him and befitted the situation. Almost springing up from the cot where he had been sitting simmering, Ilvanich turned to Fitzhugh and the platoon sergeants who sat gathered around the cot next to Ilvanich's, picking through their cold MRE meals in silence. The Russian major's sudden move, coupled with the determined look on his face, brought a hush throughout the cot-filled tent that served as a ward for the survivors of Company A.

Looking down at the upturned faces, Ilvanich began to speak, loud enough so that everyone in the tent and the adjoining tent where the nurses were on duty could hear. "This treatment is abominable. We are not lepers, and I cannot sit here and watch you people be treated as such." Finished, Ilvanich marched to the entrance of the tent that led to where the nurses were.

The sudden shouting startled Captain Hilary Cole, senior nurse on duty. Like most of the staff of the 553rd Field Hospital, she had mistaken the sullen discontentment of the rangers for shock and grief. Cole had just managed to stand up and turn to the tent flap that separated the tent where her station was from the tent where the rangers were when the flap was pulled open from the other side. Pausing, Cole watched as the one who had been identified as the Russian major entered her tent with a determined look that bordered on anger. Close behind him, in his shadow, came the young second lieutenant. When the Russian was in front of Cole's desk, he stopped, causing the lieutenant to take one short step to the Russian's left.

Still unsure of the relationship between the Russian major, whom all the rangers took their orders from, and the American lieutenant, Cole looked from one to the other. Though he was dressed in the same maroon bathrobe that the rest of the rangers were wearing, there was no mistaking that the major was the officer in charge. "What seems to be the problem, Major?"

Cole's soft voice, her blue eyes set in a thin heart-shaped face that was framed in blond hair that Ilvanich thought was too short, momentarily took the edge off of his anger. Looking down at her, Ilvanich thought for a moment, reframing his angry demand into as diplomatic a request as he could manage. "Please inform your commanding officer that I must speak to him."

For a moment Cole looked at the Russian, wondering whether she should find out what he wanted or just go ahead and do as he demanded. Looking into his eyes, dark eyes that were fixed in an unblinking stare, she decided to simply pass the message. Picking up the phone on her desk, Cole dialed the commander's office.

Saying nothing and betraying no reaction, Ilvanich listened as the nurse passed on his demand. "Hi, Anna? Is the colonel in? Good. No, I don't need to talk to him, but the Rus— I mean the major in charge of the rangers would like to talk to him now. No, I don't know, but I think he better come over right away. The Rus— I mean the major is waiting here in my office." There was a pause while Cole waited for an answer. During the pause, she looked down at the phone, avoiding Ilvanich's stare. "Great, I'll tell him." Hanging up the phone, Cole looked at Ilvanich, forcing a smile. "The colonel will be over in a minute. If you would return to your area, I'll call you when he is here."

Cole's request brought back Ilvanich's anger. Clenching his fists and narrowing his eyes, he almost hissed when he spoke. "We are not some kind of dangerous things that you can stuff into isolation and forget. Those things in there are your fellow countrymen, elite combat soldiers. Those soldiers have been through a lot in the last seventeen hours and deserve to be treated like the men they are."

For a moment Cole felt the urge to back away from the angry Russian but didn't. "Major, I have my orders. You and your men are to remain in isolation until we can evacuate you back to Landstuhl in Germany." From the other end of the tent where Ilvanich stood, two military policemen who had been posted outside came through the tent flaps when they heard Cole's and Ilvanich's exchange. When she heard them, Cole turned around, motioning that they were to stop where they were and keep out of this for the moment. For several awkward seconds they all looked at each other, wondering what to do next. Only the appearance of Colonel Sandy Holleran, commanding officer of the 553rd, broke the stalemate.

The white doctor's coat that hung over his standard-issue battle dress fatigues was open in the front, accentuating a waistline that was several inches larger than was militarily acceptable. But Holleran was a doctor, a good one who even had a knack for command. So his weight, though deemed somewhat excessive, as well as hair that was slightly too long, was overlooked. When he was in the tent, Holleran looked about. Seeing that everyone was on edge and ready to jump, he decided to take it slow and easy. With a quizzical look he turned to Cole. "What seems to be the problem, Captain?"

Though there was no emblem of rank showing, Ilvanich assumed, by the doctor's demeanor and the deference the MPs showed when he entered, that this was their commanding officer. Coming to a position of attention, Ilvanich spoke before Cole could answer. "Sir, I requested a meeting with you to discuss the manner in which my men have been treated."

Without pausing, Holleran walked up to Cole's desk, grabbing a chair for himself and motioning for Ilvanich to take a seat across from him. Holleran watched as the Russian major moved over, followed by the young American lieutenant who stood behind him. Though he had no idea how it came to be that this Russian had become the commander of an American ranger company, there was no doubt, from what he had heard and what he saw, that the rangers accepted him as such, and Holleran spoke as if this were a natural everyday occurrence. Turning his mind to the matter at hand, Holleran opened the conversation. "Before we get started, I must tell you, Major, in all candor, that the situation we are facing here is entirely new to me and my staff. None of us have ever had to deal with radiation casualties."

Ilvanich leaned forward and cut Holleran off. "We are not casualties. Yes, we have been exposed to radiation, but none of us are suffering from any adverse effects." Ilvanich, of course, was lying. Several hours after reaching the rest of the ranger battalion, both he and Rasper had thrown up. Speaking in private to Rasper, Ilvanich told him that they were both suffering from the effects of radiation. Rasper, his face showing no signs of emotion, merely looked down at his boots and nodded as he spoke, "Yes, sir, I know." Then looking up at Ilvanich, with the hint of a plea in his eyes, Rasper asked if Ilvanich would keep it quiet. Other than the nausea he felt, Rasper said that he was all right. So the two men kept their problem to themselves. There was, they felt, no need to panic the rest of the company or anyone else.

That, however, didn't keep everyone they came into contact with from keeping them at arm's distance. This Ilvanich understood. It was expected, since the rangers under his care carried with them radioactive fallout on their clothes, equipment, and even their skin. Before entering the ranger battalion perimeter, Ilvanich had the rangers of Company A halt in a wood lot. There they discarded their outer clothing, overshoes, web belts and suspenders, and anything that was not absolutely critical. Ilvanich then had them do a hasty decontamination of all the equipment they retained, including their protective masks and weapons, by rubbing them down with snow. Still their actions did little to still the fears of whoever came into contact with them. From the beginning everyone, from the battalion commander on down, treated the survivors of Company A as if they were infected with a deadly plague.

Ilvanich leaned back in his seat as he recounted to Holleran their travails. "First, the ranger battalion commander places us outside their regular perimeter. Though we were covered by interlocking fires from the rest of the battalion, my men sat there looking at me and then back where the rest of the battalion was wondering what was going on. When the helicopters came, stripped of everything, including seats, so they could be decontaminated easier after we were delivered, the crews treated us like we all had the AIDS virus. If it wasn't for the intervention of one of the crew chiefs from a medical evacuation helicopter who gave us the rations from his own crew, none of us would have had anything to eat."

Slowly, as he spoke, the anger that Ilvanich had contained all day began to boil out. "Then, when we arrived here, they were ordered to land over three kilometers away in order not to contaminate the camp. The pilot of the lead helicopter informed me of this, but then at the last minute he ignored the order. For his troubles and kindness he was reprimanded in front of his crew when we landed."

Aware of this, Holleran winced. He was aware of this incident and had been angered over it. That he hadn't been there himself was an error in judgment on his part that he had regretted then and even more so now. It was becoming clear as Ilvanich rattled on and on that Holleran's absence had been interpreted either as a lack of interest or fear.

Not finished with his litany of errors, Ilvanich continued. "Once on the ground, we were greeted by a squad of military police, all in protective clothing and masks, who escorted us to the showers under armed guard." Looking up at Holleran, Ilvanich pointed a finger at him. "Now the first shower was necessary and welcome. The second shower, even though the hot water was gone, was tolerated. But the third shower, in freezing water, was too much." Dropping his hand, Ilvanich pulled at the bathrobe he wore. "And when we were finished, instead of being issued proper uniforms, we are given these things. Half of my men are freezing because of the stupidity of your staff."

Up to now, Holleran had said nothing. But when Ilvanich started calling his staff stupid, Holleran had to speak. "As I told you, Major, this is all new to me and my staff. If we—"

Ilvanich didn't let him finish. "You don't understand, do you? None of you do. Do you realize that those soldiers in there, the elite troops of your army, are the first soldiers to face the use of a nuclear weapon by a hostile force? Do you realize that we had to turn our backs on over a third of their comrades and leave them buried under radioactive rubble, never to be retrieved? Can you imagine what is going through their minds?" Ilvanich jumped to his feet, his arms waving as he spoke. "No, of course you can't. You weren't there. You didn't have to look in their eyes and see their terror as they smelled the burnt flesh of their dead friends and comrades. To you, we are nothing but mutants, strange new specimens that need to be studied in isolation. Well, Colonel, I am telling you, in terms that I hope even the dullest recruit can understand, that unless you start treating your own countrymen like the soldiers they are, with a little compassion and understanding, you are going to find yourself with a ward full of mentally unstable people that neither I nor your MPs will be able to control."

There was a pause when Ilvanich noticed that everyone was standing staring at him. He had said everything he had wanted to. Perhaps it did not come out as well as he would have liked, but, given the emotions of the moment and the need to speak in English, he had done the best he could. Satisfied, Ilvanich folded his arms across his chest and took several deep breaths in order to compose himself.

At a loss, Holleran first looked at Captain Cole, then back at Ilvanich. Slowly he began to shake his head. Jesus, he thought, did we ever screw this one up. Holleran took a step toward Ilvanich and put his hand on the Russian's shoulder. "Major, I really don't know what to say except that I am sincerely sorry for this, all of this. What can we do to correct this problem?"

Looking into the doctor's eyes, Ilvanich saw that he was fighting back tears. He meant it, Ilvanich thought. He meant what he said. For a moment he considered apologizing, but found he was unable to think or speak clearly. This day, even for him, had been too much. Pointing to Fitzhugh, Ilvanich mumbled that the lieutenant had a list of their immediate needs and then left the tent. Unable to continue after having worked himself into such a state of anger, he turned and headed back to the ward tent to sort himself out while Fitzhugh pulled out a sheet of paper from his bathrobe pocket and Holleran prepared to take notes.

Caught by Ilvanich's sudden return, the men of Company A fell over each other as they tried to clear the entrance when Ilvanich parted the tent flap and re-entered the ward tent. Once he was inside and saw that the men had been crowding around listening to his speech to the colonel, Ilvanich stopped. The American rangers stopped too, looking back at him for several seconds. Finally Rasper stepped forward and offered his hand to Ilvanich. "Major, I know I speak for the rest of the men when I tell you that we will follow you anywhere, anytime."

To a civilian, such a comment would have seemed strange. But to Ilvanich, who had served in the Soviet and Russian armies' elite units his entire military career, Rasper's comment was the highest praise that one soldier could give to another. Overwhelmed, Ilvanich could only nod as he took Rasper's hand and muttered his thanks. Though he knew that there would be other problems, for the first time he felt that the worst was over.

With men like this, he thought, anything was possible.

Like the toy dog that some people put in the back of their cars whose head bobbed up and down as the car moved, Jan simply nodded as she listened to a retired Army colonel go on, and on, and on about what he thought was happening in the Ukraine. What an idiot, she thought. Scott told me he was a blowhard. Now, Jan thought, the whole country knew. When the tiny light in front of Jan flashed on telling her it was time for a commercial break, Jan gladly interrupted. "Excuse me, Colonel, but we have to take a break at this time." Jan turned away from the monitor she had been watching to the camera to her front. "We've been talking to Colonel Edward J. Littleton, Jr., an expert on U.S. forces in Europe. We will return to him to continue our discussion of American operations in the Ukraine in a minute. First, a word from your local cable network."

When she was sure all the cameras in the studio were off and the mikes were dead, Jan's shoulders slumped forward. "God, Charley, where do you find these people? In the classified ads of a grocery store tabloid?"

From the booth to her side, Mordal laughed. "No, Jan dear. We send someone down to the unemployment office to screen the applicants. I thought you liked Army colonels?"

Her marriage to a colonel in the Army had amazed many in the business, since soldiers and the media were traditionally antagonists. Always a good source of amazement, Jan loved to shock people when she got the chance. "Charley, I like to sleep with colonels, not talk to them. You should try sleeping with one. You might like it."

The cameraman in the studio covered the mike in front of his face. "How do you know he hasn't, Jan?"

Jan glanced over at the cameraman, trying hard not to laugh. Not understanding what the joke was, Mordal keyed his mike. "Jan, dear, unless you have a better idea, you're stuck with our retired paper warrior."

"Well, now that you mentioned it, Charley, I do have someone in mind."

"You set me up, didn't you?"

Jan, feigning innocence, sat upright. "*Moi,* dear Charley, set you up?"

A technician leaned over and gave Mordal a fifteen-second warning. "Jan, you have ten seconds to tell me who this wonderful guest is."

"Ed Lewis. After I'm through here, why don't I trot over to his office with a crew and interview him. I'm sure he'll have some wonderful comments to make about this."

"Five seconds, Charley."

Mordal considered her suggestion, then nodded. "Okay, Jan, you're on. I'll get someone on it right away." When the light came on indicating they were back on the air, Mordal settled back in his chair to watch Jan go to work. She might be a pain in the ass, he thought, but he couldn't help marveling at the way she worked. She was not only damned good at what she did, she had a great mind. Turning to his assistant, he asked her to contact Congressman Lewis's office and see if they could arrange for Jan to interview him later in the afternoon. While his assistant started making the necessary calls, Mordal returned to watching the retired Army colonel, who was using a map displayed on a screen to draw circles and lines as he attempted to describe the military operations in the Ukraine. His actions and diagrams, reminding Mordal of a sportscaster doing a Monday Night Football game, caused him to chuckle. Jan was right, he thought. This guy is rather comical.

While it was customary for the first soldier who saw Dixon enter the command post to shout, "At ease," no one bothered to stop what they were doing and come to attention. Dixon didn't expect them to and they knew it. The announcement, akin to the old naval tradition of calling all personnel on the bridge to attention whenever the captain came on or exited the bridge, made to honor the appearance of a senior officer, required everyone in the room to come to attention until released by the senior officer so honored. "Best you stay in practice," Dixon would occasionally kid his staff, reminding them that "you never know when you may get someone in command of this gang of thieves who takes that shit seriously."

Once he had pulled his gloves off and his hood back, Dixon began to make his way through the crowded command post to the hot stove in the corner. As he negotiated his way around tables, chairs, and members of the staff, someone shoved a steaming cup of coffee in front of him. Dixon turned to see who it was to thank him and quietly remind him that they needed a second cup of coffee. The soldier looked behind Dixon and winced when he saw Colonel Vorishnov. They still weren't used to taking care of two colonels. After mumbling a short apology, the soldier ducked back into the command post carrier to fetch the second cup.

Vorishnov, who was following Dixon and had heard Dixon's comments, acted as if he hadn't. It would have been, he knew, impolite to do so, especially since Dixon had gone to great extremes to make

Vorishnov not only feel comfortable in the American command post, but an equal. Even in Dixon's absence Vorishnov was treated by the 1st Brigade staff in the same manner in which they treated Dixon himself. Vorishnov marveled at this. In his heart, he knew that he could never have dealt with a liaison officer from another army, regardless of rank or mission, in the same way in a Soviet or a Russian command post. Vorishnov had seen all too often how the unnatural xenophobia, the fear and hatred of foreigners, coupled with arrogance, often unfounded, handicapped the ability of Russian officers in their dealings with their counterparts in other armies. Even when he had been a commander, Vorishnov had known better than to insist on such equal treatment for foreign officers, lest he cause his subordinates to suspect his loyalty and judgment. Though Vorishnov wasn't naive, and knew that not everyone in the command post of Dixon's 1st Brigade accepted him with open arms, Dixon was sincere and Vorishnov was actually enjoying the assignment.

Moving to two free seats set around a stove in the corner of the command post, Dixon and Vorishnov joined Lieutenant Colonel David Yost, the brigade executive officer, and Command Sergeant Major Duncan. Neither man stood as Dixon and Vorishnov took off their heavy overgarments and draped them over the backs of the unoccupied chairs. Finished, Dixon surveyed the comings and goings of the staff before he sat down. "Well, I guess everyone's gotten over the nuke scare."

Yost grunted. "Everyone that's not a ranger. According to corps, those boys are still pretty badly shaken. The company at the site that was trashed took over 40 percent casualties, including all but one officer." Looking over to Vorishnov, Yost smiled. "And, in the spirit of cooperation, the senior Russian liaison officer with that company assumed command of the company, reorganized it, and led them out. The corps commander was most impressed with that."

Dixon shot both Yost and Duncan a knowing smile, appreciating that such a report would more than vindicate his insistence on including Colonel Vorishnov in all aspects of the operation as an equal. Before Vorishnov's arrival, Dixon had told his staff that they could learn a lot from the Russians and, man for man, they were just as good. Now, Dixon thought, the last of the nay-sayers in his own command post would be convinced by the ranger incident. "The last report," Dixon noted, "was that we had no fallout in our area of operation. That was at the eighteen-hundred-hour update. Any change?"

"No," Yost responded, shaking his head. "The storm that's moving in from the west is sweeping everything east. Besides, follow-up reports indicate that the leakage of radiation from the site is minimal and well within acceptable levels."

"Ha, I love it. Minimal. Who made that statement, some pencil-necked analyst tucked away safely in the basement in Langley?"

Unable to follow, Vorishnov looked at Dixon, then Yost. Seeing that the Russian colonel was puzzled, Yost explained Dixon's comment. "Langley, in the state of Virginia, Colonel Vorishnov, is where the CIA headquarters is."

In an instant Vorishnov understood and joined the laughter. "Oh, yes. I understand. I see that we share a common appreciation for the abilities of our national intelligence communities." The appearance of a cup of coffee in front of his face caused Vorishnov to pause while he took the cup and thanked the soldier who had brought it over. Taking a sip, Vorishnov continued while Dixon and the others politely listened. "In Moscow, as late as six months ago, our people released an intelligence summary that stated categorically that all nuclear weapons that had been in the Ukraine before the Commonwealth treaty were accounted for and destroyed. It even included a detailed description of how and where each weapon, by serial number, had been disposed of. Only the defection of a Ukrainian intelligence official, upset by the efforts of his government to sell several of their hidden devices, alerted us to the fact that some of the weapons still existed."

When Dixon spoke, his tone was serious. "Did anyone ever find out what country was involved in that deal?"

Holding his cup of coffee in both hands in his lap, Vorishnov looked down at it for a moment before answering. That subject had been a matter of great debate once the report had been confirmed. Everyone had their suspicions but little solid information to confirm them. Vorishnov, like many of his fellow officers, tended to believe the worst-case scenario presented by the Russian Army's chief of intelligence. Looking up at Dixon, Vorishnov, however, decided not to share those beliefs, especially since Dixon's command traced its line of communications through that country, and the United States Army in Europe depended heavily on Germany for support. How ironic,

Vorishnov thought. If the suspicions were true, that support was denying the Germans the very weapons they were after. There is, he thought to himself, a God after all, smiling down on Mother Russia.

Like a shadow cast by a cloud momentarily blocking out the warm sun, Vorishnov's pause and his change of mood told Dixon that Vorishnov knew something that he could not or did not wish to share with him and the other Americans. Knowing it was time to change the subject, Dixon took a sip of coffee, then turned to Yost. "Any change since the last update?"

"Negative. All units have assumed a hasty defense, per the corps order, and are ready to resume offensive operations or, on order, commence our withdrawal from the Ukraine. No new contacts since those reported at the eighteen-hundred-hour briefing and Major Thompson says that it looks like nothing is brewing on the horizon. Our biggest concern at this moment is the storm."

"More snow?"

Yost grunted. "At least six inches, probably more."

"Well." Dixon sighed as he put his cup of coffee on the ground next to his chair and stretched out. "You tell Princess Lea that I don't want her to talk to me until she has a better weather forecast."

Duncan laughed. "In this part of the world, sir, that will be a long, long time."

Standing, Dixon looked down at Duncan. "You better hope not, Sergeant Major. Otherwise you'll find yourself shoveling a hell of a lot of white stuff."

"Well, sir," Duncan retorted, "that will sure beat all the brown stuff your staff has been shoveling around here lately."

Yost turned to Duncan. "Sergeant Major, you leave my staff alone. They try hard."

"Oh, yes, sir, they do try hard. Exactly what it is they're trying to do, however, is beyond me."

Watching his XO and sergeant major rib each other caused Dixon to shake his head. "Now, now, children, don't fight. I'm going to get some sleep. Be nice to each other while I'm away."

While Yost smiled, Duncan protested, "Gee, Colonel Dixon, do we have to?"

Although Vorishnov understood that the Americans often engaged in casual and meaningless humor, it was hard for him at times to know when the subject and the mood had changed. They did quickly and with almost no clue. Even the detonation of a nuclear device by the Ukrainians and the political firestorm that would surely follow didn't seem to diminish this desire to act in a manner that his fellow Russian officers would consider unprofessional. It was no wonder, Vorishnov thought, that so many of his contemporaries refused to take seriously America's ability to wage war.

Standing up, Yost stepped closer to Dixon. Lowering his voice, he informed Dixon that the commander of the 3rd Battalion of the 3rd Infantry, Lieutenant Colonel Richard Zacharzuk, wanted to talk to him as soon as possible on a personnel matter.

"Let me guess. He wants to talk to me about Second Lieutenant Ellerbee, doesn't he?"

Surprised, Yost looked at his commander and nodded. "Yes, sir, exactly. How did you know about that?"

Moving his hands and arms as if he were working levers and dials, Dixon boomed in a sonic voice, "The Great Oz knows all and sees all." This sudden disturbance of the command post's dull late-night routine caused everyone in the command post to momentarily cease what they were doing as they looked over to see what their commander was up to now. Stopping his wild motions, Dixon looked about, smiled, then turned back to Yost as he continued the conversation in a low voice. "Besides, Jim Tuttle collared me on the road and gave me the 2nd of the 35th Armor's side of the story already. What do Rick Zacharzuk and the company commander involved say about Ellerbee?"

"Both Rick and Nancy Kozak, Ellerbee's company commander, want Ellerbee and his platoon sent back to 2nd of the 35th Armor immediately. Rick says the kid's a sorry excuse for an officer. Kozak doesn't want him endangering her command."

Dixon moaned. "I was hoping to avoid getting into that tonight."

Yost shrugged. "You'll have to admit, sir, getting one of your own men killed and losing control of your unit in the middle of a battle does make Ellerbee look like a problem."

"David, I agree. But we don't know what happened. We have only the stories of two battalion commanders, both of whom are tired, in the middle of a combat zone, and neither of whom was there, making judgments. I refuse to make any changes or to relieve an officer without at least a cursory investigation." Dixon paused as he thought. "The situation down there has stabilized, so there is little likelihood that 3rd of the 3rd will be engaged in a serious fight for a while. Contact both commanders involved and inform them that I have no intention of changing the task organization or relieving anyone at this time. Ellerbee will stay exactly where he is, doing his job, until I can personally look into this matter with a clear head and with all the facts in hand. Clear?"

"Loud and clear, sir."

Taking a deep breath, Dixon looked around the command post one more time. "David, Colonel Vorishnov and I have been on the road most of the day. We're going to get some sleep. Unless something exciting happens, no one's to disturb me until at least oh five hundred."

Duncan stood and turned to Yost. "I'll inform the duty NCO, sir, and then take the colonels to their quarters."

Satisfied that all was in order and that his presence was not required, Dixon began to gather up his gear and put his parka on. "I hope, for the sergeant major's sake, we don't have to make a major trek to find my bed. I'm beat." Turning to Vorishnov, Dixon winked. "It's hell getting old, isn't it."

Vorishnov smiled. "I wouldn't know, Colonel Dixon."

Caught off guard by Vorishnov's subtle humor, Dixon shook his head. "God, it's time for me to leave." Turning and walking toward the exit, Dixon, followed by a smiling Vorishnov, mumbled, for the amusement of the staff still on duty, "I get no respect, no respect at all."

Shown into Congressman Lewis's office, Jan Fields-Dixon was greeted with a warm smile and a handshake. "It's been too long, Jan. That's why I asked the President to invade another country. Seems that's the only way to get you to come and see me."

Taken aback by Lewis's warm smile and relaxed manner, Jan returned his smile and took a seat. For a moment she just stared at him, almost as if she expected something to suddenly change. When he became conscious of her staring, Lewis blinked his eyes. "What? What did I do wrong?"

Caught off guard again and suddenly aware of her staring, Jan shook her head and laughed. "Oh, gee, Ed, I'm sorry. It's just that I expected something entirely different. Your mood, that is."

Lewis chuckled as he grabbed the arms of his chair and leaned back. "You and my wife, Amanda, must have been talking again. Every time she hears something on the news, she calls me to tell me to calm down."

"Well, Ed, I must admit that you do have a reputation for shouting first, loudest, and longest whenever the administration, as you are so fond of saying, oversteps the bounds of logic and sanity."

Again Lewis chuckled. "Well, of course. It is a reputation well earned and, if I may say so, to my benefit."

Jan cocked her head and looked at Lewis questioningly.

With a devilish grin that he used to disarm opponents and put friends at ease, Lewis let Jan ponder his statement for a moment before he spoke. "You see, Jan, it's all a trick. In the beginning it wasn't. When I first came to Hell on the Potomac, I truly did get myself worked up and upset every time the administration or my fellow congressmen did something I thought was dumb. Hell, for the first year I was in a constant state of righteous rage. Then, shortly after the Mexico affair, I saw the light."

"Ed, don't tell me you were born again."

Lewis laughed. "No, nothing as dramatic as that, although I imagine that would be good for a few votes back home in Tennessee. No, after thinking about how close we came in Mexico to the end, I remembered an Arab saying we used all the time in the Persian Gulf."

Jan pointed, holding back her excitement. "Don't tell me. Don't tell me. Let me think about it for a moment. Something about Allah and hands off, or something like that. Scott says it every time he wants to get out of doing something."

"Inshallah, it is God's will."

"That's it. What is it with you guys? Did they brainwash you over there and stencil that saying on the inside of your head?"

"No, nothing like that, I think. Anyway, as I was saying, after Mexico I thought a lot about what I was doing here in Washington, both as a representative for the people of Tennessee and for myself. To tell you the truth, Jan, I really didn't like what I was doing either."

The sudden reference to Scotty caused Jan to pause. He was there in the thick of it. Though the Army had not announced yet what units had been involved in the operation, in her heart Jan knew Scotty was there. Like the good worker who was rewarded by being given more work, Scott Dixon's superiors had a habit of throwing him into the breach whenever there was a nasty and difficult job to do. That his brigade was the one selected to provide the ground force was merely an accident of geography and the sector Scott's brigade had as part of the peacekeeping effort in Slovakia would never wash with Jan. While Scotty referred to his constant overuse as "No rest for the wicked," Jan always responded by claiming that the Army was good at beating dead horses. That she had used the analogy of the dead horse caused her a sudden pang of regret, one that Ed Lewis noticed. Seeing that the congressman was staring at her while she reflected on her accidental indiscretion, Jan forced herself to return to the matter at hand. With a forced smile, Jan picked up where she had left off. "So you were born again."

Looking up at the ceiling, Lewis thought about Jan's sudden change in mood and her statement before answering. He knew what was going on in her mind and for a moment thought about offering her some comfort or reassurance. But since she had chosen to press on with the interview, Lewis decided to follow along and not press the personal issues. There might be a time, after he knew more about the situation, when he might need to do so, but this was not it. "I guess in a way you could say that." When Lewis looked back at her, he did so with a serious, reflective look. "It was more of an awakening. I suddenly realized that I was in my mid-forties. That I had two children in college with one about to be commissioned in the Army. That I had a wife who loved me and cared for me that I had lived with but had not talked to, I mean really talked to, in years. I suddenly realized that I was becoming like everyone else in this town, a self-centered, government-inspected, grade-A cynic."

Jan was touched by the confidence that Lewis was showing by telling her this. Ordinarily, politicians didn't discuss their feelings in such an open and casual manner with a member of the media. But Ed Lewis and Jan Fields-Dixon had a relationship, a bond of friendship, that was important to both of them. After barely escaping with their lives from a brush with terrorists during the second Mexican Revolution, the two had developed a close friendship that neither let the business of news and politics interfere with. So as they spoke in the quiet privacy of Lewis's office before starting the interview, it was as friends. "Sounds like midlife crisis to me, Ed."

"Perhaps, Jan, that is what it was. All I know is that I realized that I was impaling myself on every crisis and every stupid issue, often to no effect, without thinking about what it was costing me or my family. So I told myself, 'Self, this is dumb!' That is when I remembered the old Arab saying and finally understood what it meant." Sitting up, leaning across the desk, Lewis looked at Jan, wide-eyed and smiling. "Now, before I jump into the fray, I ask myself, 'Can I make a difference now, or should I wait? And when I do, what can I do to help?' "

"With age, Ed, comes wisdom?"

He nodded. "Something like that. Now I don't think you came down here with a camera crew just to listen to an almost old man wax philosophical about the meaning of life. What do you want to discuss in the interview?"

Opening a notebook that she had on her lap, Jan went over some of the questions she had intended to ask, in no particular order, explaining that she had no clear idea yet what she would emphasize. Therefore she intended to skip around with questions until they hit upon something that they could develop into a coherent and intelligent on-camera discussion. Lewis, in full agreement, listened to Jan's questions, making short comments as the mood struck him, or giving her a thumbs-down when she hit him with one that he really didn't want to answer. This continued for several minutes until Jan asked him about Germany. Like a bull tweaked by a cattle prod, Lewis jerked and sat upright. Pointing his finger, his eyes narrowed. "There's going to be trouble with them. Mark my words, Jan. Big trouble."

Lewis's strong reaction to a subject that Jan was interested in exploring excited her. Lowering her notebook to her lap, Jan asked Lewis to explain.

"Well, in the first place, the administration has really screwed up how they've handled the Germans from the beginning. I get the impression that Soares and the rest of his crew at the State Department haven't woken up to the fact that the Germany we are dealing with today is not the same Germany we tried to play big brother to in the fifties. After fifty years of atoning for the sins of their fathers and living in the shadow of the Iron Curtain, the new Germans feel that it is time that they assumed their rightful place in the world as the leaders of Central Europe."

Lewis eased back a bit in his chair and toned down his comments, but kept on the subject of Germany. "Now I don't think we need to worry about anything as dramatic as the Fourth Reich or something like that. Still—"

"Then, Ed, you feel that the Germans will do more than they already have?"

"I don't see how they can't. They are a proud, sometimes downright arrogant people who pride themselves on their independence and culture. They defeated the Romans and survived the Thirty Years' War that left their entire country devastated and one third of their population dead. In modern history, Napoleon couldn't crush them, and they've come back from the brink of oblivion after suffering the worst military defeat in history in 1945. While we've been busy elsewhere dealing with other problems, the Germans have been pulling themselves together, working to overcome years of internal strife and the stigma of the Holocaust. They are ready, Jan, to leap back to the forefront of world politics, with a vengeance."

"What do you think they will do?"

Lewis shook his head. "God, I wish I knew. I doubt that they will allow us to violate the nuclear-free-Germany treaty with nothing more than a harsh public reprimand, which by the way is what Soares is trying to convince the President is exactly what the Germans will do. No, Jan, our friend the Rat has no idea what he is dealing with." Lewis paused, looking down at his desktop for a moment. In his mind's eye, he could see the image of Soares with his pinched ratlike face that had earned him his nickname. The man, Lewis thought, was worse than an idiot. He was an idiot in an important position, which made him, in Lewis's eyes, a dangerous idiot.

Looking up at Jan, Lewis continued. "To answer your question, I don't know for sure what the Germans will do. Unfortunately, no one here in Washington does either. The Germans are, as Elmer Fudd likes to say, 'being very, very quiet.' " Lewis paused, thought for a moment, then continued. "Whatever it is, it will be both forceful and something that we cannot easily ignore."

For the first time, Jan became concerned, and her voice showed it. "Military action? Do you think the Germans will take some kind of military action?"

Again Lewis shrugged. "Maybe. But who knows. What I do know is that it is never a good sign when two nations who have their horns locked together over an issue stop talking to each other. Why Ruff has chosen now, of all times, to refuse to be reasonable, as he always has been in the past, is beyond me. This, coupled with Ruff's statements to his own press and his failure to respond to our State Department's communiqués, baffles me the most."

For a moment, both Lewis and Jan sat there in silence. Finally Lewis leaned forward and placed both hands, folded, on his desk as he flashed the best smile he could manage. "Now, I don't mean to rush you, but I do have one more appointment this evening, and Amanda is expecting me home by seven for dinner."

Jan looked at her watch. "Yeah, time is sort of slipping away. I'd like to get this on the air by tonight. Okay, Ed, get yourself ready, and I'll get the crew in here to shoot."

Like all members of the German Army's 1st Parachute Division, the young soldiers of Number 2 Company, 26th Parachute Brigade considered themselves the best of the best. This, of course, was due to the efforts of their officers and sergeants, all professionals who were forever vigilant, watching, checking, and ready to correct even the slightest infraction of the regulations or slackness. They took their duties seriously. Which was probably why on the night of this operation the soldiers of Number 2 Company were so involved in their company commander's final inspection that no one noticed their brigade commander, Colonel Johann Haas, for several minutes.

As was his way, Haas had come forward alone to watch the final preparations and see his men across the line of departure when it was time. Known as the phantom, Haas made it a practice to move about in the night during exercises in the field checking on his men and ensuring that all was in order. On this night, the first time that his unit would be called on to execute the tasks it had trained long and hard for, Haas was everywhere.

When one of the sergeants noticed Haas, he passed the word to his company commander. When the word reached the young commander, he paused, then continued to complete the inspection of the weapon he held. Finished, he returned the weapon to its owner and left to present himself to Haas.

In the moonlight that filtered through the pine trees and fell on Haas and the company commander, it was difficult to tell the difference between the two men. Except for the fact that the company commander wore his helmet while Haas, despite the cold, wore his maroon beret, the two men were dressed and armed identically. Even the close-cropped hair and stern no-nonsense expression that masked both men's faces as they spoke looked alike. This was due in a large part to the habit young commanders had of emulating their senior commanders. Commanders throughout history have always provided the role model for their subordinates. Those subordinates were expected to watch and learn so that one day they could assume positions of greater authority when their commander either moved on to other assignments during peacetime or, in time of war, became a casualty. The commander, as part of his duty, was held responsible for providing the best possible example in everything he did, in thought, word, and deed. This, however, was more difficult than one would imagine, as Haas was finding out that night. He especially had difficulty controlling his thoughts.

The shock of seeing the Chancellor's own military aide, Colonel Hans Kasper, at the headquarters of the 26th Parachute Brigade bearing sealed orders for Haas could not match his shock when he saw what those orders were. For the longest time, as Kasper spoke, Haas could not help but wonder if this was not some kind of test, a hypothetical drill to test his loyalty or the readiness of his unit to respond to unplanned emergencies. Even after he convinced himself that Kasper was serious, that this was real, Haas still had difficulty accepting it. Still, he did not allow those doubts to interfere with the performance of his duties. The orders all appeared to be authentic. The verification, which Kasper offered, checked out. All *was* in order. So Haas hid his personal fears and doubts behind his commander's mask and prepared his unit to execute their assigned duties as ordered.

In those few moments before midnight, with less than two minutes to go before those orders became a reality, Haas still was unable to quiet the apprehensions he felt. Though attired alike, the thoughts that ran through the minds of the two commanders facing each other were worlds apart. The company commander's mind was cluttered with all the very real and necessary practical matters that need to be considered when hurling over one hundred men into combat. Enemy dispositions and weapons, tactics and maneuvers necessary to overcome or neutralize them, the effectiveness and readiness of his own weapons, coordination for support of his unit by other elements involved in the assault, as well as numerous other considerations were of paramount concern to the company commander.

Haas, however, saw beyond the immediate operation. As a graduate of the famous Kriegsakademie and an officer impatiently awaiting his reassignment to General Staff duty, Haas could not easily push aside the possible worldwide political effects of what his unit was about to do. The other European powers, especially the French and Poles, would react. And the Americans, with forces actually deployed throughout Germany, would not simply roll over and accept the German action, no matter how just or reasonable their demands. The Americans, he knew, viewed international law as an instrument to be applied when it served them, and ignored when it didn't.

Then there was his friendship with the Americans themselves. Even as he stood there listening to his company commander review his preparations to assault an American installation, Haas wore the American airborne wings he had been awarded after three grueling weeks of training in the hot Georgia sun. Many of his fondest memories as a soldier were of when he served side by side with the people he had now been ordered to attack, an attack he still felt was wrong.

But what was he to do? That, in the end, was the great dilemma that tore at his mind. According to the Bundeswehr's own interpretation of an officer's duty, Haas was obligated to conduct himself in accordance with his conscience. If given an order that he felt was morally wrong, it was not only his right but his duty to refuse to obey it. When the Bundeswehr was formed in 1955, the old Prussian tradition of moral choice when deciding right from wrong became a critical piece of an officer's selection and training. Throughout his military education, the July 20th plotters who had attempted to assassinate Hitler were used as examples of officers who refused to go against their conscience. As he stood there half listening to his subordinate, the words of one instructor kept ringing in Haas's ears, almost as if they had just been spoken. "While loyalty to your nation is, and should always be, uppermost in your mind, you must never forget that morality and conscience must be your final guide, the decisive element when deciding right from wrong."

Yet such theories, Haas thought, seemed out of place here on this cold and bitter night. He had no one to turn to for guidance, no one to discuss the issue of right and wrong with. To base a military decision on a feeling, regardless of how strong, was, to say the least, rather difficult. Yet at that moment in the cold darkness just before midnight, that and his own conscience were all he had with which to weigh the matter at hand and make a decision. Before the Battle of Leipzig in 1813 with the French, the Prussian King told those soldiers who could not in good conscience fight in the upcoming battle that they were free to leave. He did not want to create a conflict in the conscience of those officers who had served with the French when Prussia, as an occupied and reluctant ally, had been aligned with France in her war against Russia. Haas didn't have someone offering him such a choice. His superiors in distant Berlin had only given him his orders.

He was still pondering those lofty matters when the young company commander finished his briefing. Glancing down at his watch, and impatient to return to his unit, the company commander asked if there would be anything else. Without responding at first, Haas looked at the company commander for several seconds in order to refocus his mind on the situation at hand. Unable to come to any firm decision, Haas simply shook his head. With an expressionless face, Haas replied, "No, there is nothing else. You have your orders."

The company commander, glad that there were no last-minute changes, saluted and left Haas standing alone, troubled how easily he had uttered the words "You have your orders." For the first time he understood how his father had felt in the last war. Now, as if a great veil had suddenly been lifted from his eyes, he knew what had happened in 1939. And as he walked away, Colonel Johann Haas, commander of the elite 26th Parachute Brigade, felt shame.

CHAPTER 7

8 JANUARY

Although there was absolutely nothing that he could do, Major General Earl Lowery couldn't tear himself away from the operations center. All across Sembach Air Base, men and aircraft sat silent under a newly fallen blanket of snow. Only in the operations center was there any appearance of any sort of activity. And even here that activity was, to put it mildly, minimal. At 2:30 A.M., with operations temporarily suspended due to weather and failure of the German government to provide clearance for American military aircraft, there wasn't much to do. Still Lowery remained. Like a captain lashed to the bridge of his ship in a storm, he watched, listened, and waited.

With his lanky six-foot, five-inch frame sprawled in a swivel chair and his feet propped up on the edge of the picture window that separated the command group booth from the operations room below, Lowery vacantly stared at the activities of his staff. Seated at rows and rows of desks arranged like a dark, sinister amphitheater, those junior officers, mostly majors, captains, and lieutenants, sat staring at either their own computer monitor or at the large tote board at the far end of the operations center that showed the status of the airfields, squadrons, and a host of other facilities that made up the United States Air Force's European Command. Though Lowery, commander of all Military Airlift Command units and personnel in Europe, normally confined his interest to the missions and needs of his command, tonight he was interested in everything that was happening in the European Theater of Operations, or ETO.

Not much was happening, nor was anything, at that time, supposed to be happening. In accordance with the Air Force directive covering the current operation, Desperate Fumble, airlift operations from Sembach would not resume until after daylight. Only then would Lowery and his command be able to get rid of the nuclear devices flown in from the Ukraine during the previous day. Until then, "The Devices" sat in three hangars under heavy guard.

It was while he was inspecting the devices in the hangars earlier in the evening that Lowery was struck, as soon as he walked in the door of the first hangar, by how similar the heavy metal protective shipping containers were to aluminum military coffins. Stopping short, he looked about the room at the rows and rows of containers, each separated from the other by several feet. The air security personnel, rifles slung but ready, walking solemnly up and down the rows could just as easily have been an honor guard. Startled by this comparison, Lowery stood there for several seconds unable to think about anything other than his first real mission as a newly assigned C-130 co-pilot. Lowery, out of the Air Force Academy for less than a year and just finished with flight school, was sporting shiny new first lieutenant bars on his shoulders when he went to Viet-Nam in the late spring of 1968. Dispatched to Da Nang from Bien Hoa, the glamour and excitement of being a serving officer in an active theater of operations was turning out to be all he had imagined. Even his normal dour Oklahoma demeanor couldn't hide the enthusiasm he felt at finally being part of the action.

That enthusiasm soon evaporated when he received his first cold slap of reality. Instructed by the pilot to go over to the hangar where the cargo for their return trip was being processed, Lowery had walked into a large hangar very similar to those at Sembach to find the loadmaster. He found the master sergeant standing in the center of rows of aluminum shipping containers inventorying them with an Army sergeant. Lowery all but skipped over to the two sergeants, occasionally tapping some of the containers with his hand as he went by. When he reached the sergeants, smile on his face, Lowery asked how things were going.

The loadmaster looked up from his clipboard and gave Lowery a condescending smile. "Oh, pretty good, pretty good. Sergeant Johnson and I were just making sure that everything was in order. After all, the last thing we want is to give some gray-haired old lady the wrong box."

Lowery, not understanding what the loadmaster was talking about, asked him what he meant. Realizing that the young lieutenant didn't know that the metal containers he was about to load on their aircraft were coffins, the loadmaster decided to introduce the new lieutenant to the reality of war. With a grin on his face, the loadmaster announced, "Well, sir, for your very first mission, you are being given the rare privilege of granting the fondest wish that every GI and airman in Nam harbors. You are going to fly home, at no expense to the families, ninety-six fathers and sons." Then the loadmaster allowed his grin to change into a feigned look of concern as he looked about the hangar. "Of course, I really don't think this was what they had in mind."

Only then, as he too looked about, did Lowery understand what the sergeant was saying. In a flash, the jaunty, almost childish grin on Lowery's face was replaced by a look of horror. When the loadmaster saw this, he grinned. After having listened to Lowery harp on the virtues and benefits of his strong Baptist upbringing all the way from Travis Air Force Base in California to Bien Hoa, the loadmaster saw his chance to get even. Patting Lowery's shoulder, the loadmaster looked about the hangar. "Oh, don't worry, sir. Sergeant Johnson here assures me that there will be no second comings from this group."

Equally appalled by the idea that he was surrounded by the bodies of so many of his countrymen and the ease with which the two sergeants made fun of the dead, Lowery turned and fled from the hangar. It would be a long time before he could forget the ring of the sergeants' laughter echoing in the hangar filled with coffins as Lowery tried to run away from the reality of his profession.

Lowery watched in silence as his young staff officers in the operations room below went about their duties. Pulling his long arms into his sides, he linked his bony fingers together over his stomach, keeping his own counsel as the images of that day in Bien Hoa ran through his mind. Behind him, his senior staff officers sat, like Lowery, watching the comings and goings of the officers in the ops center. A few gave in and nodded off to sleep at their desks. None of them really knew their commander on a personal level, since he kept to himself, and his laconic manner and fundamentalist religious beliefs let few people past his professional side, but they did know of his reputation, which started in Viet-Nam during the height of the siege of Khe Sanh. It was rumored that Lowery, unable to stay out of the action, requested and was granted a transfer out of the C-130 squadron at Bien Hoa to one that was resupplying the Marines at Khe Sanh. It was during this assignment that Lowery made his mark. For in the spring of 1968, Lowery flew every mission he could, day and night, into Khe Sanh during the height of the siege, bringing in desperately needed supplies and hauling out the wounded. He stood out from the many pilots who made that run, because he was one of the few pilots who always brought his aircraft to a full stop, even when in the middle of NVA artillery barrages, to allow the corpsmen and litter bearers of the besieged garrison to run out to load the wounded. This single-minded, almost obsessive drive to deliver the goods to the troops in forward areas, whether in war or in peace, made him very popular with Army and Marine commanders and a demanding taskmaster. From their first introduction to him, new officers in his command were told over and over again, "We make a difference, through hard work and dedication to duty. And if we don't get it right the first time, those poor bastards on the ground will pay for it." Though his senior staff officers, like Lowery, could do nothing at the moment, the apprehensions and uneasiness of a commander can be as contagious as confidence. So they sat there watching Lowery sit where he was, wondering what heinous new missions he was pondering that would task them to the limit.

The buzz of a phone, though muted, startled several of the senior staff officers who were close to dozing off. When they saw that it was not their phone ringing, everyone in the command booth turned this way and that to see whose phone was ringing. Only after they saw Colonel Horst Maier, the Luftwaffe liaison officer to the Military Airlift Command, pick up his phone did everyone, including Lowery, go back to their own thoughts.

Seeing that it was the encrypted direct line to the Luftwaffe's own military airlift command, Maier answered in German, "Maier here."

On the other end of the line he heard the familiar voice of an old classmate and fellow officer. "Hello, Horst. This is Rudi, Rudi Poersel. Do you recognize my voice?"

Taken aback by this strange introduction, Maier frowned. "Why of course, Rudi, I recognize your voice. What are you doing in Frankfurt? I thought—"

Poersel cut Maier's question short. "Horst, I am not in Frankfurt. I am in Berlin. We have been patched into this line." There was a pause as Maier heard his old friend take a deep breath before he continued.

"Listen, Horst. I am about to put General M. G. Gorb on the line. And believe me, this is General Gorb and I am in Berlin."

While Maier waited for the chief of staff of the Luftwaffe to come onto the line, his surprise turned to concern. "Colonel Maier, this is General Gorb. Do you believe me?"

Pulling the phone away from his ear, Maier stared at the receiver for a second before putting it back to his ear and acknowledging, "Yes, General Gorb, I believe you are who you say you are. What, sir, may I do for you."

In a hushed monotone voice, Gorb began to speak. "This is critical. You do not have much time, and you are to tell no one where you are what you are doing. If you fail, the consequences for both the Americans at Sembach and the German people will be immeasurable. Do you understand?"

For the first time, Maier said what he was thinking. "No, Herr General, I do not understand, but I am listening."

"Believe me, Colonel Maier, I understand your concern at being approached like this. Unfortunately, there was no time to do things any differently. But I have been assured that you are reliable and will do what is right."

This last comment only served to heighten Maier's fears. Unable to think of anything else to say, he responded automatically. "Of course, Herr General. You can count on me to follow your orders to the best of my abilities."

Still in a hushed voice, Gorb continued. "Good. That is all I ask of you. Now as soon as you hang up, you are to go to the entrance of your command and control bunker. There you are to wait for Colonel Johann Haas, commander of the 26th Parachute Brigade. Once he presents himself to you, you are to take him to General Lowery and serve as a translator. Is that clear?"

As surprising as it was to be talking to the chief of staff of the Luftwaffe at this hour, the idea of Maier finding the commander of an elite parachute unit wandering around outside his bunker in the middle of the night while such a sensitive operation was under way was incredible. "How, Herr General, is this Colonel Haas going to make it to the bunker entrance? I myself reviewed the list of German personnel authorized to be on Sembach during this, ah, operation, and I do not recall seeing any Haas on it."

"How Colonel Haas gains access to the American air base, Colonel,

is neither your concern nor mine. You are only to meet him at the
bunker entrance, get him to the American general as soon as possible,
and follow Colonel Haas's orders without question, without hesitation. Those are your orders. Do you understand?"

Maier was dumbfounded. Unable to speak, he held the phone to his
ear until Gorb repeated his last question with greater force than before. "Colonel Maier, do you understand your orders?"

Without thinking, Maier responded, "Yes, Herr General. I understand. Is that all?"

"Yes, that is all. Good luck." With that, Gorb hung up, leaving
Maier sitting there staring at the phone with a look of disbelief and
thinking how stupid his last comment, "Is that all?" had been. Damn,
he thought as he looked about the room, wasn't that enough?

Maier was about to jump up and leave, then paused. If, he thought,
his friend and the man who claimed to be General Gorb were calling
from Berlin, he could easily find out. Picking up the phone again, he
listened for it to automatically dial through. When the duty officer at
the other end picked it up and identified himself, Maier asked the
duty officer in Frankfurt if he could check to see if a priority call had
been relayed from Berlin through their circuits to him in the last five
minutes. "I do not need to check," the duty officer responded. "Yes,
Colonel, there was a call from the chief of staff's office. Why do you
ask? Do you need to call him back? I can have the operator patch you
through directly into General Gorb's office in a couple of minutes. No
problem now that we know how to do that."

For a moment Maier considered doing just that, then decided against
it. "No, that will not be necessary, thank you."

Slowly replacing the phone receiver, Maier stared at it absentmindedly for several seconds. Finally, after convincing himself that the call
had been real and the order was valid, he stood up. Tugging at the hem
of his uniform blouse, he looked about the room to see if anyone was
looking at him with suspicion. Satisfied that no one was paying any
attention to him, Maier turned and left the command booth.

As the door closed behind Maier, the air division operations officer
turned to the division intelligence officer. "Where's he going?"

Not having noticed that anyone had left, it took the intelligence
officer a couple of seconds to figure out who the operations officer was
talking about. When he finally did, the intelligence officer merely
shrugged. "If he's smart, he's going to bed, like we should have an
hour ago."

Emerging from the well-lit entrance, Maier was struck by the piercing cold. Beyond the powerful beams of the security lights, he could
see that the snow had stopped and that it was still dark. Actually, he
corrected himself, it was dark again. A whole day had come and gone
without his seeing any of it. He detested days like this when he would
go into the bunker before the sun came up and wouldn't leave until it
was gone. Not only did he get the feeling that he had lost a day, it
compounded the depression he always experienced when working in
an underground facility all day. As an officer and transport pilot in the
Luftwaffe, he felt that flying was his natural element and that living
in a hole in the ground was a practice best left to the Army.

He was just beginning to debate if he should go back to the doorway
to wait when the figure of a man moving toward him suddenly appeared just beyond the light. Pausing, Maier watched as the figure,
marching as if on parade, headed straight for him. When the sentinel
on duty at the entrance also saw the figure, he came out of the warmth
of his shelter, unslinging his rifle as he did so. Maier, however, raised
his hand and signaled to the sentinel. "All is in order. I have been
expecting this man."

The sentinel, caught off guard, looked at Maier, then at the figure as
it continued to close on them. "No one at the first guard post called
me to tell me about anyone coming through, Colonel. I'm going to
have to hold him here until I can check this out."

Angrily Maier turned and shouted, "We do not have time for that,
airman. I will vouch for this man. He is a colonel in the German Army
that your commanding general has been expecting. If there is a problem with your access roster, we will adjust it later."

The sentinel paused, peering into Maier's eyes while he debated
whether to hold the two Germans and call the commander of his relief
or to accept the German colonel's story. Not that he doubted the
colonel's story. From the beginning, this whole operation had been a
real zoo, with scores of strange colonels and generals from the Military Airlift Command coming and going without anyone checking
their credentials. All that had been necessary, for the sake of expedi-
ency, was for a regular member of the staff assigned at Sembach to
verbally verify that they were okay and they were passed through.
That the Germans would do the same didn't trouble the sentinel. The
only thing that caused him to pause was the fact that the German
Army colonel, now only a few feet from them, had come from the
direction of the hangars, not along the walkway that led to the only

entrance through the fence that formed an outer perimeter for the command and control bunker.

Seeing the airman's hesitation, Maier decided to push his bluff a little further. "Is there a problem with that, airman? Or must I call General Lowery and have him personally confirm the fact that he is now waiting for Colonel Haas?"

After taking one last look at the German Army officer now standing in front of them, and then back at Maier, the airman took a step back. At 2:45 in the morning, the last thing that the airman on guard wanted to do was to rouse Lowery's anger. Rather than press the matter, the sentinel brought his weapon up into the proper position for saluting when under arms and told both German colonels that they could pass. Haas, sensing that there had been a bit of trouble, gave the American airman a casual salute and followed Maier, saying nothing as he went.

Once in the corridor leading to the command booth, Maier told Haas in German of the call from Berlin and repeated General Gorb's skimpy instructions. Then he stopped, when he saw no one was in the corridor. When Haas also stopped and faced him, Maier blurted, "What in heaven's name is all of this about? How in the devil did you get onto this base and are you—"

Haas, his face frozen like a mask, cut Maier short. Not only was there an urgent need to get on with this, but Haas held all aviators, regardless of rank or branch of service, in contempt. They were, to him, a combat commander who was expected to perform anywhere, anytime, under any conditions, overpaid and underworked prima donnas. "You are to take me to General Lowery immediately and introduce me as the commander of the 26th Parachute Brigade. When I speak, you will translate everything I say, word for word and without the slightest hesitation. Is that clear, Colonel?"

Maier felt himself flush with anger at Haas's demeanor and tone. Haas saw this but did not relent. "Colonel, I am sure that your superiors informed you that you were to do *exactly* what I tell you and that we had little time. Now, either you take me to Lowery without any further delays, or I will find him myself."

There was no trace of apology, no sign that Haas had any intention of telling him anything. Instead, all Maier saw was a harsh face, a face as harsh as the man's words and manner. Without another word, Maier started toward the command booth, then Haas spoke. "And remember, you will translate everything without any modification. If you don't, I will know. I am fluent in English."

Maier let that matter drop. There were, after all, many German officers who resented the old regulation that had required all senior officers to learn English in order to work with their American allies even though it was the Americans who had come to Germany. Haas's refusal to speak English, Maier thought, was either a matter of pride or, more than likely, was to show that this action was being done in the name of the German nation and, as such, should be presented in German, even if it was just a formality. Resigned to the fact that he would not learn what this was all about until Haas was in the presence of the American general, Maier continued down the corridor with Haas following.

Lowery was shaken out of his gloomy thoughts by the sound of boots coming up behind him and his operations officer shouting Maier's name. Pushing himself off of the wall to his front with one foot, he swung his seat around, stopping just as Maier and Haas reached him. Behind them, he could see that his operations officer had left his desk and was headed over to join them.

For a moment no one said anything as Lowery looked the German parachute officer over. His ruddy face and the muddy snow on his boots melting into a puddle at his feet told Lowery that this man had just come in from the outside. Except for the maroon beret the German Army colonel wore pulled down low on his forehead, everything from the stern expression to the submachine gun slung over his right shoulder and partially hidden under his right arm told Lowery that he was ready for battle. He was about to ask what this was all about when Maier, without looking into Lowery's eyes, barked an introduction. "General Lowery, this is Colonel Johann Haas, commanding officer of the 26th Parachute Brigade. I have been ordered to present him to you and translate."

From behind Maier and Haas, the operations officer yelled, "Now just hold it here a minute. Just hold everything a cotton-pickin' minute. Colonel Maier, what in the hell do you mean bringing this—"

Looking down at Lowery, Haas fixed his gaze on Lowery's upturned eyes. In a voice that was firm and told Lowery that he was not to be trifled with, Haas began to speak German in a rather slow and deliberate manner. Lowery, whose German barely enabled him to order a beer and Wiener schnitzel on his own, glanced over to Maier as he waited for the translation. From the expression on Maier's face, now growing visibly pale and taut, what Haas had to say really bothered Maier. When Haas was finished, rather than translate, Maier turned his head to face Haas. Haas, who had been looking at Lowery, returned Maier's stare when he did not hear him translating. The look that he gave Maier was cold, uncompromising, and angry. Finally, Maier drew a deep breath, looked down at Lowery, and with a great effort began to speak.

"General Lowery, in order to prevent unnecessary bloodshed, Colonel Haas requests that you immediately order your security personnel guarding the nuclear weapons under your control to stand down and return to their barracks."

Only the muted conversations of junior staff officers in the operations room below could be heard in the stunned silence that followed Maier's translation. No one moved, no one spoke as all the colonels on Lowery's staff looked first at Haas, then at Lowery. Finally overcoming his own shock, Lowery slowly stood up in front of Haas. When his entire six-foot-five frame was erect, he looked down at Haas. "On whose authority are you making this demand?"

Haas, looking up at the American general, didn't wait for Maier to translate from English to German before he responded. Finished, Haas glared at Lowery while Maier, having ceased all conscious thought, mechanically translated. "I have been ordered by Chancellor Johann Ruff to seize the nuclear weapons that *your* government has brought into *my* country in violation of the Berlin Accord signed by both your government and mine."

That Maier didn't translate Lowery's question before Haas responded did not escape the general's notice. This colonel, Lowery thought to himself, was being very formal and very hard-nosed about this. It was, Lowery thought, as if Haas felt it was beneath his dignity as a representative of the German government to lower himself to speaking English. Well, Lowery thought, two can play hard-ass. "I hope, Colonel, you realize that I don't have the authority to turn the weapons over to you or anyone else. Nor am I in a position to open negotiations concerning their control. This is a matter that must be taken up between our governments through the proper channels."

Without a pause, Haas responded and Maier translated. "You do not seem to understand, General. I am not here to negotiate. Nor am I here to ask you to turn those weapons over. I am merely asking you to have your people step aside and relinquish control over something that I am prepared to take by force of arms."

Lowery was about to shout that Haas wouldn't dare, but then thought better. This was simply not the kind of thing that the Germans would try to bluff their way through. If Haas was standing there defiantly, then he had to be in a position to fulfill his threat.

Lowery was still pondering how best to respond when the operations officer pushed his way between Maier and Haas. "Just who in the hell do *you* think you are, mister, coming in here and making that kind of demand? Who do you think you're dealing with? Your people, if they're out there, will be cut to ribbons if they even think about stepping foot on this base."

Haas stomped his boots, shaking off more mud and snow onto the floor, then gave the operations officer a knowing smile before he answered. Maier, now behind the operations officer, translated over the officer's shoulder. "Colonel Haas asks me to point out that he, like his men, had absolutely no problem making their way onto this base." Then, turning back to Lowery, the smile gone from his face, Haas looked at his watch before he spoke.

Lowery listened as Maier, now calmer, carefully provided his translation. "You have, General, less than ten minutes in which to make your decision. After that, my men, already in their assault positions *in* and around the hangars, without the need for any further orders from me, will wipe out your entire guard and the reaction force. Even if you were to alert your people now to the danger, there is nothing that they could do to change their fates. We are, as you would say, locked, loaded, and on automatic pilot."

Looking down at the puddle of mud and water on the floor and then into Haas's eyes, Lowery's heart began to sink. Suddenly, the image of the hangars and their contents flashed before his eyes. This was immediately followed by the vision of the rows and rows of coffins in Da Nang. Without realizing it, Lowery let out a soft moan as he let his six-foot-five frame sink back down into the chair behind him. No, he thought, he couldn't let that happen. There was simply no way that he could allow young airmen, his young airmen, to die for nothing. Looking up at the German parachute colonel, he knew he was beaten, for General Earl Lowery didn't have it in him to make the kind of command decision that would in effect be the death warrant for an untold number of soldiers and airmen.

Spinning about to face his desk, Lowery grabbed the phone, then paused. "What's Harrison's number?" General Bret Harrison, U.S.

Army and commander-in-chief, United States Europe Command, was Lowery's immediate commander for this operation.

Without needing to look, Lowery's aide rattled off the phone number.

Punching in the numbers, Lowery looked down at the phone while he was waiting for it to be answered on the other end, knowing that every eye in the room was riveted on his back. When the phone was picked up, an operations duty officer at Harrison's headquarters identified himself. Wanting to get the duty officer's attention and cut straight through to Harrison without long-winded explanations, Lowery used the code word reserved for the loss of aircraft bearing nuclear weapons. "This is General Lowery at Sembach. Inform General Harrison we have a Broken Arrow and I must speak to him immediately."

Without hesitation the duty officer said, "Yes, sir," and transferred the call to Harrison's quarters. Roused from a fitful sleep, Harrison's response was groggy and gruff. "Harrison."

Despite the fact that time was pressing and he felt the urge to blurt everything out, Lowery knew Harrison's mind would be clouded by sleep and would need a few seconds to comprehend what he had to tell him. Therefore, when Lowery spoke, he did so slowly and deliberately. "This is Lowery at Sembach. I have just been informed by the commander of a German parachute brigade that his brigade is deployed in and around Sembach with orders to seize the nuclear weapons here at Sembach, by force if necessary."

Harrison, wide awake now, shot back, "Did he say who gave him those orders?"

Lowery, hunched down over the phone, shook his head. "He claims to be acting on behalf of the German Chancellor."

"Have you been able to check this out?"

Shaking his head, even though Harrison couldn't possibly see this, Lowery responded as he looked at his watch. "There isn't time, General. The German colonel here claims that his assault units are in position and ready to strike within the next five minutes."

From behind, Haas corrected Lowery using perfect English. "Three minutes, Herr General."

Spinning in his seat, Lowery shot Haas a look that could have killed. "Three minutes, sir. We have three minutes."

"Jesus Christ, man, is he serious?"

Lowery, still facing Haas, glanced down at the manner in which

Haas cradled his automatic weapon. "I do not believe, General Harrison, that this officer is bluffing." Then, Lowery asked the question that Harrison was expecting. "What, General, are your orders?"

With less than three minutes to go Harrison knew there was no time for consultation with anyone, not even his own staff. In a heartbeat he knew he had three choices. He could tell Lowery to stand fast and call the German's bluff. If it was a bluff, nothing would happen. If it wasn't a bluff, then Harrison would be responsible for unleashing a chain of events that neither he nor Lowery would be able to control. Not knowing exactly what and who was involved, this would be a blind crapshoot of the worst kind. Though he could have justified making such a call, Harrison had no way of knowing what forces such a bloodletting would unleash.

The second choice would be to tell Lowery to stand his guard force down, let the Germans have the weapons, and allow the diplomats in Washington and Berlin to sort this out through negotiation. Though the thought of turning nuclear weapons over to a foreign power without firing a shot was against everything American commanders had been taught, Harrison tempered this position by reminding himself that these were Germans. Given the fact that the Germans were an ally, and there had been arrangements in the past to issue German nuclear-capable forces nuclear devices under certain conditions, Harrison could see little danger here. The Germans, after all, were a civilized and friendly power.

The final choice was to leave the choice up to Lowery. This, Harrison knew, was both an acceptable one but one that was a cop-out. Lowery was Military Airlift Command, a transporter. Operational decisions of this magnitude were not normally his to make. Harrison, on the other hand, had always prided himself on his ability to make swift and decisive decisions. As a combat commander, trained to think fast and react, decision making was second nature to him. In the past, his decisions had been good ones. Now, faced with perhaps the greatest single one, Harrison reacted in the only manner in which he could.

There was, he suddenly realized, no choice at all. "Lowery, you are the senior commander on the spot. You must use your judgment and do what is best. I recommend that you pull your guard force back and do not resist the Germans. Try to keep them from removing the weapons from Sembach, but not by force of arms."

Troubled by Harrison's comment "I recommend," Lowery's response was cautious. "Sir, am I to interpret this as an order?"

Angered as much by his own attempt to pawn off the final decision to Lowery as by Lowery's question, Harrison shot back, "Yes, General Lowery, that is an order. Turn the weapons over to the Germans now."

Taking three deep breaths in an effort to compose himself, Lowery replaced the receiver and turned to his aide seated at a desk behind him. "Jim, get me Major Harkins on the phone immediately." Then, turning to Haas, Lowery informed the German of the decision. "I am ordering my guard force and ready reaction force to stand down. Please order your men to hold their fire."

Though pleased, Haas hid his relief that force had not been necessary. Looking over to Maier, Haas called out in English, "Dial 026 on your telephone, Colonel Maier. A Major Kessel will answer. Tell him Case White is in effect." Turning back to Lowery, Haas saw the look of bewilderment in his eyes. While Maier complied, Haas explained. "We have, General, tapped into your base phone system. I thought it would make it much easier to run this operation." What Haas didn't tell Lowery was that the five-minute limit had been a bluff. Major Kessel and the assault force were under strict orders to hold their positions until either Haas ordered them to move or they heard shooting or a commotion coming from the base command and control bunker.

Captain James Wilks, the aide-de-camp to Lowery, automatically picked up the receiver of the phone in front of him and began to punch up the number for Major Harkins, the commander of the security forces on Sembach, then stopped. Looking up at Lowery, then at Haas, Wilks thought about what he was about to do. It suddenly dawned upon him that his boss, a man that he greatly admired and whom he had looked to as a means of furthering his own career, was about to surrender over one hundred nuclear weapons to a foreign power. Without so much as a show of resistance, Wilks thought, Harrison and Lowery were prepared to violate one of the most basic principles that the United States Air Force had operated under since becoming a nuclear power, which was to safeguard those weapons at all costs. That, coupled with the thought that such a move would make Germany, the nation that had started two world wars in pursuit of world domination and had murdered over twelve million men, women, and children in concentration camps, a nuclear power, seemed too much to accept.

Though he suspected, like everyone else in the command booth, that resistance would probably be pointless, the idea of simply throwing his hands up and doing nothing to stop the Germans was unthinkable. Such a decision, he believed, should not be made by Harrison or Lowery, regardless of how many stars they had. Slowly Wilks replaced the receiver on its cradle and stood up.

Dumbfounded, Lowery looked at Wilks for a second before he realized what Wilks was doing. Recovering from the shock of his aide's insubordination, Lowery repeated his order. "Captain Wilks, I am *ordering* you to call Major Harkins now."

Wilks said nothing. Instead, he simply stepped back away from his desk and assumed a rigid position of attention. Even when Haas reached for his automatic weapon and trained it on him, the young aide stood his ground.

Incensed at his aide's insubordination, pushed to the breaking point by the tension of the moment, and galvanized by Haas's hostile reaction, Lowery jumped to his feet and began to yell. "*Damn* you, Captain. Damn you to hell. I gave you an order." Still Wilks did nothing.

Below the command booth, several of the officers in the rear rows of the operations center, hearing Lowery's muffled shouts reverberate through the thick glass window of the command booth, turned to see what had gotten their commander so upset. Unaware of what was going on, they watched wide-eyed as Lowery lunged across the command booth and bodily pushed Wilks out of his way with one hand while grabbing a phone with his other. After punching up a number and while he waited for the person on the other end of the line, the staff officers in the operations center could see Lowery glaring at Wilks, still standing at attention, and clearly hear Lowery yelling at him, over and over, "Damn you, Captain. Damn you to hell."

Charley Mordal didn't even give Jan a chance to say hello before he blurted out, "Jan, you were right! You were the only one who saw it coming."

Though she was used to being called like this in the middle of the night at her Gaithersburg, Maryland, home, Jan's reactions were far from automatic. Where her husband, Scott, could jump out of bed and be fully alert before his feet hit the floor, Jan's mind needed time to come to life. Still not fully awake and having no idea what Mordal was talking about, Jan blinked her eyes a few times, looked at her alarm clock, and yawned before responding. "Of course I was right, Charley." Then after thinking for a second, she added, "Exactly what was I right about this time?"

"The Germans. Jan, can you believe it? The Germans apparently overran the Air Force base in Germany where the nukes were waiting for transport back to the States and seized them. You and Lewis seem to be the only people in this town that saw that coming. You're incredible."

Jan didn't really hear anything after Mordal mentioned that the Germans had overrun an American base. For several seconds all she could think about was Scott and his safety. Where was he? Was the American Army already involved? Those and other questions rushed through her mind as Mordal, more animated than Jan had ever heard him before, rattled on and on. Knowing that sitting there in her bedroom wondering and worrying would accomplish nothing, Jan cut Mordal off. "Okay, Charley, thanks for calling. I'll be down at the studio in less than an hour."

Without so much as a good-bye, Jan hung up, leaving Mordal wondering why she was coming to the studio at that hour. After thinking about it for a moment, though, he decided that perhaps it wasn't a bad idea. His only regret was that he hadn't thought of it first. Of course, Charley Mordal didn't realize that Jan wasn't going into the studio out of dedication to the network or her profession. Her motives that night were purely selfish. At the World News Network headquarters in downtown Washington, D.C., she would have firsthand access to every major news agency in the world and sources of information that rivaled the CIA's and FBI's. In the avalanche of information and news that would flow into WNN headquarters, Jan hoped to find a scrap of news about the only person in the entire world that she really cared for, a man who by his nature and profession was bound to be in the middle of things in Germany. Though she could do nothing to change things or help him, at least she would know what was happening to him.

Bounding out of bed, Jan dashed to the bathroom. As she stood before the full wall mirror quickly combing her hair into a presentable style, she glanced down at the black nondescript comb, green toothbrush, and unused razor that sat next to the second sink that was Scotty's. Though he hadn't been able to tear himself away from his command in Europe for months, Jan, out of habit, kept his personal things in order and handy, just in case. For despite her reputation as a hard-nosed news correspondent, Jan Fields-Dixon was an eternal optimist. Scott, she knew, would somehow find his way out of this mess, just as surely as the politicians in the White House would find a way to suck him into it.

Suddenly the focus of everyone in Washington shifted from an obscure spot on the eastern fringes of Europe to the heart of the continent. Overwhelmed by the new German crisis, matters concerning the Ukrainian crisis were relegated to other senior members of the State and Defense departments while President Wilson and key members of the National Security Council met to discuss and deal with the German crisis.

As was her style, Abigail Wilson had listened to what everyone had to say concerning the matter at hand, in this case the German crisis, without comment. When she was satisfied that everything that needed to be known had been presented, she gave her initial guidance and then sat back and let her staff, in this case the Security Council, work out a solution. From her seat, Wilson watched the process in action. A steady stream of people, some in uniform, some in shirtsleeves, flowed around and past her, coming and going, sometimes giving the impression that they had no apparent direction or purpose. Every now and then one or more of these people would stop another in midstride and hold a quick hushed impromptu discussion where they stood. Finished, they would part and continue to pursue whatever mysterious errand they had been on. Elsewhere in the room small clusters of people were huddled discussing some matter or the other. The whole scene unfolding before her gave Wilson the feeling that she was sitting in the eye of a hurricane. After thinking about that analogy for a moment, she decided that it didn't do justice to the current situation. What she had started, Wilson decided, was shaping up to resemble more and more a firestorm. How to stop that firestorm, which at that moment was completely out of their control, was the question she pondered and the throngs of people around her debated.

For several minutes Wilson studied each of her key staffers, people who had led her into the Ukrainian crisis and now were expected to find a solution to a new crisis in which all its attendant problems had yet to come to the surface. Off to her right, Peter Soares was holding court with her foreign affairs advisor and a number of serious-looking State Department bureaucrats. The expression he wore and the manner in which he held himself or threw his arms about to make his point reminded Wilson of when he had been running Wilson's gubernatorial and presidential campaigns. Watching, she had no doubt that his line of thinking and the approach he was using to deal with this crisis were similar to those he had used then. Unfortunately, this was not a political campaign. For a moment Wilson wondered if his ability to negotiate the American political landscape for diplomatic skills and his knack for organizing campaigns for leadership gave him the insight necessary for dealing with this issue. In her heart she knew that his tried-and-true methods, those that had gotten her into the White House, would be of little use in resolving the expanding German crisis, one which his decisions had precipitated. The fact that the Ukrainian operation had turned sour, despite his assurances, introduced an element of uncertainty into Wilson's mind that was now tainting her trust of anything that Soares said.

To her front, among a cluster of generals and admirals, Terry Rothenberg sat. His long face, with drooping eyes peering through a pair of bifocals tottering on the edge of his nose, had never looked so long. As Wilson sat there watching him turn his head this way, then that, as one senior officer after another talked, she knew that Rothenberg was as much out of his element as Soares was. The brilliance that had made him New York City's successful contract lawyer failed to provide him with the tools he needed to deal with the harsh military decisions that were demanded when war threatens. Rothenberg, like Wilson herself, was often reduced to listening to his experts, both military and civilian, toss about one option after another, never knowing for sure who was right or even if there was a right answer.

As she sat there, Wilson began to suspect that the people in the room, the same ones who had assured her that the plan to secure the nuclear weapons was sound and gave her a 95 percent probability of success, were not up to dealing with the German crisis. Like Rothenberg, Wilson had come into her office with only a very basic understanding of military affairs and trusted the experts and professionals to deal with the details. Now, like Rothenberg, she felt betrayed by those experts and was at a loss as to where to turn for the help and advice that she, and the nation, so desperately needed.

Knowing that it would be several hours before anyone had a good handle on the situation, let alone viable options, Wilson decided to seek advice from a source that many would consider inappropriate. With a slight motion of her right hand, Wilson signaled the aide seated behind her. Leaning forward, the aide listened. "Tom, have the car pulled around front immediately."

Knowing that as soon as he gave the order for her limousine to move, William J. Balick, the head of the White House Secret Service, would want to know, the aide asked Wilson what her destination would be. Balick, more commonly known as Billy B, had to know where the President was going so that he could plan a route and then scramble teams along it in advance to scout it and to provide security at her destination.

Wilson knew the reason for the aide's question but ignored it. The one thing that bothered Wilson the most about being in the White House was the manner in which everyone tried to control her comings and goings. It was as if everyone, especially the Secret Service, was trying to force her into an airtight, bulletproof, controlled-access bubble. To a person who had known unlimited freedom all her life, such attempts were stifling, almost suffocating. From her earliest days as a child, Wilson had enjoyed coming and going as she pleased, often roaming her parents' large ranch in Colorado alone on foot or horseback. Half jokingly, Wilson had told a friend before leaving Colorado for the White House, "My mother and I have spent most of our lives in an effort to escape from having men dictate what we could and could not do. I'll be damned if I'm going to let them do it to me in Washington."

While understanding the need for security, Wilson felt that the Secret Service men were far too compulsive and restrictive. Though she seldom felt the need to remind people of her office or title, when it came to the Secret Service, Wilson took every opportunity to remind them of who the President was. Wilson's response to her aide, therefore, was short and sweet. "It will just be you and me. Now we haven't got much time. It's late and getting later."

In an effort to make sure that she was making a conscious decision about her security, the aide rephrased his question. "And where should I tell Mr. Balick that we are going?"

Wilson stood up, causing most of the people in the room to stop what they were doing and turn to look at her. "Please tell Billy B that I am going out into the night with a lantern in one hand in search of an honest man and my hat in the other."

Unhappy with her response, for the aide knew that Balick would ride him for not getting a straight answer, the aide glumly shook his head and called the White House garage to relay the President's order. Looking over to Vice President Kevin Wojick, in the middle of a conversation with several members of the Security Council, Wilson called, so that everyone in the room could hear, that she was leaving. Then, before she walked out, Wilson added, "Mr. Vice President, I leave you here to deal with this, this debating society. I will be back in two hours. If in that time you are able to get Chancellor Ruff on the phone and he is willing to speak with me—I mean really speak to me and not simply rehash his 'wounded national pride' speech again— contact me immediately." Wilson turned to leave, but then paused. Over her shoulder she added with a bitter note in her voice, "And if you can't have something that makes sense ready for me to listen to by then, please turn out the lights and lock the door before you *all* leave."

From across the room, Soares watched Wilson leave. That she, like everyone else on the crisis action team, was tired and very much on edge didn't matter to Soares. It had been a mistake, he now knew, to put a woman like that in the White House. She neither understood the fine rules of the game nor how to conduct herself with the dignity that the office of the President of the United States demanded. While even he had to admit that she often displayed an intuitive knack for resolving difficult problems, her methods of dealing with men of high position, such as himself, were often irritating to the point of disrespect. The party, Soares had decided long ago, had been wrong. The nation wasn't ready for a woman President, especially this one.

It wasn't until she reached Bethesda that the idea of stopping by to see Ed Lewis dawned upon Jan. Though she suspected that he already knew about the German seizure of the nukes, there was always the off chance that he might have gone to bed early. After all, she thought, with his newfound view on life, he just may have gone overboard and started getting all the sleep he needed.

When she turned down the street where Lewis lived, Jan was surprised to see a number of cars sitting in front of Lewis's house and
what looked like every light in the place turned on. At first, thinking
that he was having a party of some kind, Jan wondered if her attire
would be appropriate. Then she dismissed that idea as being foolish.
Amanda and Ed Lewis weren't the late-night party type. When she got
closer, Jan saw two men standing on the porch and caught a glimpse
of another as he disappeared around the house. Her dismay suddenly
turned to alarm when she realized that there may have been some
kind of emergency or threat. If that was true, Jan thought, then maybe
this was the wrong time to pay a visit. But again she dropped that idea.
She was, after all, a friend of the family and, almost as important, a
news correspondent. As was her habit, once she had made up her
mind, Jan pushed forward with the single-minded determination of a
charging rhino.

Already upset with the President's sudden and mysterious foray
into the night, the members of the Secret Service team that accompanied her were on edge and very nervous. Denied the opportunity to
perform a detailed recon of Lewis's house, they attempted to clamp
down on everything that went on in the house while President Wilson
was there. They, of course, had not counted on Amanda Lewis. Roused
out of bed by the sound of voices and the pounding of feet downstairs,
Amanda threw on a robe and came down to find her house overrun by
stern-faced men and women. One group was in the middle of searching rooms and scanning them with electronic devices while another,
who had taken over the dining room as a command center, was busy
moving furniture around. One overzealous agent, seeing Amanda de-
scending the stairs, moved toward her in an effort to head her off. He
pulled out his badge, flashing it in her face. "I'm sorry, ma'am. Agent
Bradshaw, Secret Service. I'll have to ask you to go back upstairs and
remain there while the President is here."

Unimpressed by Bradshaw's badge, and angered at being ordered
about in her own house, Amanda looked Bradshaw in the eye. "Young
man, I am sure you have your duty and your orders. But this is my
house. And if you want to walk out of here under your own power, I
suggest you let me by."

Taken aback by the defiance shown by this five-foot-four, 120-
pound woman in a bathrobe, Bradshaw was about to call for his su-
pervisor when Amanda pushed by him and headed into the kitchen to

make coffee. Not easily put off, he followed her, asking her to go back upstairs. Bradshaw's persistence only served to irritate Amanda. Stopping just short of the kitchen, she turned on Bradshaw. With an angry look on her face and her finger pointed at his nose, Amanda Lewis shouted so that everyone in the house could hear. "Look, Mr. Special Agent whoever, if you or your friends here dare threaten me one more time, I'll run the whole lot of you out into the snow. Now back off." Without another word and before Bradshaw could respond, Amanda pivoted on her heels and marched into the kitchen, where two other Secret Service men gave her a wide berth when they saw her coming.

Frustrated, his face red from embarrassment, Bradshaw turned around just in time to see Jan come through the front door at the other end of the hall. Without so much as a pause, Jan headed straight for the door of the study where she knew she would find Lewis. Recovering from his brush with the congressman's wife, Bradshaw hurried down the hall to head Jan off. Shoving his arm in front of Jan's face just as she was about to open the door, Bradshaw yelled in Jan's ear, "Hey, you can't go in there."

Already charged up from having to deal with the Secret Service men at the front door, Jan backed off half a step, turned to face Bradshaw, and thrust her finger up at his face. "Look, mister, I'm in no mood to play cowboys and Indians with a troop of overgrown boy scouts. Either move it or lose it."

Tiring of being abused by pushy women, Bradshaw was about to grab Jan's arms to push her away from the door when Jan lifted her right foot and brought the heel of her boot crashing down on the toe of Bradshaw's shoe. Shocked by her sudden attack, caught in midstride, and overcome by immense pain, Bradshaw lost his balance. While he was trying to grab his injured foot with one hand while flailing the other one about in an effort to find something to grab to keep from falling, Jan pulled the sliding door of the study open and popped in.

Though she knew that the President was there, it still came as a surprise when Jan saw Wilson seated among the haphazard stack of books, files, and stray papers that Lewis found comforting. Lewis, seated at his desk with his feet propped up, looked over to Jan. "Welcome, Jan. We were just talking about you when we heard your rather vocal introduction to the President's bodyguard."

Jan blushed slightly, looking over at Wilson and then at Lewis. "I apologize for intruding like this, Ed, Madam President, but I was on my way into the office and thought you might not have heard the latest news from Germany yet. And then when I saw all the people running about your house, I was worried that something had happened to Amanda or you."

With a smile, Lewis invited her to take a seat, if she could find one. Wilson, surprised by Jan's appearance, glanced over at Lewis after he made the offer to Jan to join them. Noticing Wilson's look of concern, Lewis took his feet off the desk and leaned toward Wilson while Jan searched for a clear place on the floor to dump a stack of books she had removed from the least cluttered chair. Without waiting for Jan to finish, Lewis started in on the President. "See, that's just the kind of thing you are going to have to stop doing. Geez, Madam President, the whole world knows we've screwed the pooch on this one. So why hide it? It's time you came out, just like you did with me, with hat in hand and told the truth, the whole truth, and nothing but the truth."

Though her predecessor had warned her that Lewis could be a dangerous political adversary, not to mention brash and downright disrespectful on occasion, Wilson appreciated that Lewis had much going for him. Everyone in Washington agreed that he was one of the few people in Washington she could trust in a pinch. The former President himself, despite his warnings to Wilson, had used Lewis during a particularly sensitive crisis with Mexico. Through this and other such coups, Lewis had earned a reputation for being one of the most politically astute and respected authorities on international affairs in Washington. There had even been serious discussion about asking Lewis to serve as Wilson's Secretary of State instead of Soares.

Suspecting that Chancellor Ruff wasn't in a mood to listen to either her or Soares, a man many Europeans had difficulty dealing with, Wilson decided that she would take the former President's advice. Of course, she also remembered his warning: "Lewis has a tendency to come on like a down-home good old boy, so don't be offended by his manner." Taking Lewis's comments in stride, Wilson was about to respond, when her comments were pre-empted by another interruption at the study door. This time it was the appearance of Agent Bradshaw.

Barreling in, Bradshaw looked at Jan, now seated across from Wilson, then at Wilson, before he began to apologize for letting Jan in. Wilson, however, was tired of being interrupted, first by Jan, now by

Bradshaw. Already uneasy about coming to Lewis like this and the manner in which he was treating her, Wilson, in a momentary flaring of her temper, cut Bradshaw short. "Look, Bradley, or Banden, or whoever you are, get out of here and close the door."

Totally frustrated and in pain, Bradshaw closed the door, catching a glimpse of Jan just as she canted her head, smiled, and waved 'bye to him.

Pausing a moment to pick up her train of thought, Wilson continued where she had left off. "In principle, I agree with you, Ed. But . . ." Wilson hesitated as she glanced at Jan. "Even you understand that there are things, military matters and ongoing delicate diplomatic discussions, that we cannot go public with."

Lewis rolled his eyes as he settled back into his chair. "Oh, please, Abby. You don't need to remind me of that. Even Jan here, one of the foremost correspondents in the world, understands the necessity of keeping secrets, *real* secrets, a secret. But don't, if you hope to salvage any shred of credibility and trust, hide everything, big mistakes and small, behind the cloak of operations security. The American people are a lot more sophisticated than your advisors give them credit for. Yes, the operation, aptly named Desperate Fumble, succeeded in disarming the Ukrainian nuclear arsenal, as you intended. No one is arguing that point. But it was not the most successful military operation in American military history as Rothenberg keeps telling the media. We succeeded, not in the manner in which we had hoped, and at a much higher cost than expected, but we succeeded. That, Madam President, is what your Secretary of Defense *should* have said."

"All right, you have made your point. That was, I agree, poorly handled. Expressing regrets concerning that matter, however, does nothing to solve our, excuse me, my current problem. I was hoping, Ed, to use you in much the same way that my predecessor used you to resolve the Mexican problem."

Anxious to say something but knowing that she was there only by the grace of luck, her own tenacity, and Ed Lewis's blessing, Jan held back. There would be ample opportunities, she knew, to develop this incredible stroke of luck into a useful story later. For now, Jan was more than content to stand on the sidelines and watch history in the raw unfold before her very eyes.

Lewis was looking down, contemplating Wilson's offer, when he heard his wife outside the study bark, "Young man, make yourself useful and open the door like a good boy."

Everyone in the study looked up as Bradshaw, a sheepish, downcast look on his face, opened the door and allowed Amanda in carrying a tray with a coffeepot, cups, saucers, and such. Hesitating, Amanda looked about in vain for someplace to set the tray. Jan, seeing her predicament, jumped up. "Here, Amanda, let me make myself useful. I'll hold this while you serve." Though Lewis could see that Wilson was not exactly pleased at being interrupted like this, she said nothing as Amanda, followed by Jan with the tray, served her, then Ed, and finally poured Jan a cup and emptied a sack of artificial sweetener in it. Finished, Amanda took the tray from Jan, who retrieved her cup while she thanked Amanda, who excused herself and went back to the kitchen.

Watching Ed while she sipped her coffee, Jan knew that he would accept the President's challenge. While Ed might wear the livery and speak the language of a Washington politician, he was, Jan knew, a warrior at heart. Like her own husband, Scotty, Lewis had a streak of dedication to God and country that ran through and through. And like Scotty, Lewis could no more ignore a call to duty than she could stop the new day from dawning. The only reason Lewis was taking so long to respond to Wilson's offer was because the wheels in his mind, figuring out what he would ask for and what he would insist on, were already turning. Either that, Jan thought, or he was screwing with the President, making her stew a little longer in her own mess before granting her request that he help salvage her political future.

Setting his cup down on the saucer, Lewis silently wished that Amanda had used the regular everyday coffee mugs, the ones with all the chips and stains, rather than the good china. It would have, he thought, made for a more humbling experience for the President. Looking over to Wilson out of the corner of his eye, Lewis asked what exactly she had in mind.

"To tell you the truth, I was hoping to discuss that with you. Like I told you in the beginning, the entire National Security Council, to a man, is thrashing about the streets of Washington like a herd of beached whales. I need someone with a clear head and experience in matters like this to get us back on track and headed in the right direction. Besides . . ." Wilson paused and looked down at her lap for a moment before looking into Lewis's eyes with what he took to be a sincere, heartfelt plea. "I need someone whom I can trust, someone that the American people and the media can trust, and someone unconnected with the Ukrainian fiasco."

Lewis was about to add, "And someone who is politically expend-able," but didn't. Instead, Lewis nodded. His response was short, pos-itive, and sincere. "Madam President, I will do everything I can for this nation." Shrugging his shoulders, he added, "At a time like this, how can anyone do otherwise?" Then, before Wilson had an oppor-tunity to thank him, Lewis turned to Jan. With a jaunty ring to his voice, he asked, "Jan, you think you can be ready for an all-expenses-paid trip to Berlin in, oh, say six hours?"

Jan smiled. "Ed, I'm surprised you would even ask such a foolish question. Name the time and place, and I'll be there, with rings on my fingers and bells on my toes."

Lewis, his face now serious, added a cautionary note as Jan stood up to leave. "I have a feeling, Jan, we, the nation, aren't going to get off as easily as we did in Mexico. The Germans, I suspect, have a long agenda of their own that they have been sitting on for quite some time. Despite what some people think, we and our German friends have little in common, and the detonation in the Ukraine and the nukes we brought into their country aren't going to do anything to endear us to them." Standing, he looked down and shook his head. "No, the Germans wouldn't pull something like this on the spur of the moment unless they were sure they could get away with it. There's more to this than meets the eye." Looking up at Jan, then over to Wilson, Lewis sighed. "We aren't going to walk away from this one without paying a price, a heavy, heavy price. I just hope we can afford it."

C H A P T E R   8

10 JANUARY

Neither the pale sun struggling to rise in the cold southeastern sky nor the tasteless breakfast being served from the back of a mud-covered truck that morning brought relief to or dispelled the gloom of the near frozen soldiers of Number 4 Company, 26th Panzer Battalion. Sitting on the turret of his Leopard II tank with his feet dangling over the side, their commander watched his men huddle together to share both their body warmth and rumors as they waited to file by the mess truck and be served. Unable to do anything to improve the lot of his soldiers or explain the reasoning behind their sudden deployment to the border, Captain Friedrich Wilhelm von Seydlitz was content to simply sit where he was and wonder, just like his sullen, unhappy soldiers did, what was to become of them. As he did so, he couldn't help but wonder if his ancestor and namesake, Frederick the Great's youngest and most successful cavalry general, had ever experienced the same uneasiness and self-doubt that he did that morning. Probably not, he thought ruefully.

Such comparisons were easy to make. Everyone, as far back as he could remember, used the famous Prussian general or the captain's great-grandfather, Generalmajor Walter von Seydlitz-Kurzbach, as standards against which to measure young Seydlitz. As he grew, that tendency continued, exacerbated by the fact that Captain Seydlitz was the spitting image of the hero of Rossbach. Inheriting the same tall and lean physique, right down to the light, almost sleepy eyes, Captain Seydlitz could easily have put on the straw-yellow uniform of the

Rochow Cuirassiers that von Seydlitz had worn in 1758 and been mistaken for the great cavalryman.

But the similarity was only skin deep, or so young Seydlitz thought. He lacked the decisive nature that had allowed his ancestors to make their mark on German military history. His great-grandfather, commander of the 51st Corps at the Battle of Stalingrad, hadn't hesitated to stand up to Hitler, despite the possible consequences, when he knew he was right. No, young Seydlitz thought as he pulled the hood of his parka up to shield himself from the frigid wind that cut through him, the name Seydlitz and a smattering of genes handed down from generation to generation did little to prepare him for this.

Not that there was much that his company could do at that moment, other than eat breakfast. The decisions that would determine whether he would lead his thirteen Leopard tanks back to their kaserne in Wieden or into battle here, along the Czech-German border, with their former ally would be made by politicians in Berlin and Washington. The fact that he, unlike his ancestors, had no control over his own destiny was just as difficult to accept as his orders to prevent all American military traffic from crossing out of or into Germany had been. In agonizing over this last matter, Seydlitz knew he was not alone. He couldn't think of a single German who would say the Americans had been right in using Germany as a base for their adventure into the Ukraine. Nor could he imagine any of his countrymen coming to the defense of the Americans' decision, which most took as an insult, to bring nuclear weapons into their country without the knowledge or permission of the German government. It was, in the words of Seydlitz's brigade commander, as if the Americans were deliberately trying to provoke them.

Still, the deployment of the entire brigade to the border three days ago, coupled with the announcement from the Chancellor's office in Berlin that the reserve battalions of Seydlitz's brigade, as well as other brigades, were liable for immediate recall, seemed unnecessarily provocative on Germany's part. Diplomatic, not military, action was what his government should have been using to resolve the issue. Yet nothing, at least nothing that he knew of or had heard on the radio, even suggested that Chancellor Ruff or the Americans were interested in pursuing active talks. Instead, as the brigade watched and waited for the Americans to test the resolve of the German government, a test every officer and soldier in the brigade knew would come, Berlin continued to issue new pronouncements, new directives, and new deployment orders that could only serve to increase rather than decrease the tension. So, as for many of his fellow officers, the news that a parachute brigade had seized the American air base where the nuclear weapons in question had been only brought dread and foreboding. For the Army better than anyone else knew that the Americans could not ignore the German challenge. Unless cool heads and common sense were allowed to prevail, it would, Seydlitz knew, have to come to a fight.

With his mind cluttered by such weighty concerns, Seydlitz did not notice the driver of his tank as he carefully climbed on board, taking great pains not to spill the contents of his commander's breakfast. Only after he offered the steaming plate of food did Seydlitz acknowledge him. Forcing a smile across a face still clouded by deep worries and personal doubts, Seydlitz thanked his crewman and took the plate. Looking down at the plate, Seydlitz made a face, then asked his driver what, exactly, he'd been handed.

The loader smiled. "Well, Herr Captain, when I was training at Münster, my cadre sergeant told us never bother asking where we were going, since we had no choice in the matter anyway, never ask what we were going to do when we got there, because chances are the officers taking us there probably didn't know either, and never, never, never ask an army cook what he is serving, because even they didn't know what it used to be."

Seydlitz looked at his loader and laughed. The German Army didn't need to spend millions and millions of marks on training its officer corps, Seydlitz thought, in military theory and tactics. His loader, with just a few weeks of training, understood things far better than he did. All that was necessary, it seemed, was for officers to act more like their crewmen; shut up, go where you were told, don't worry about what's going to happen, and eat what you are given. For a lowly panzer captain such as himself to worry about anything else was, Seydlitz realized, a waste of time.

After two days of nonstop lectures and one-way speeches, Ed Lewis was ready to give up. Actually, he thought, as he listened to Chancellor Ruff, there was nothing really to give up, since that phrase implied that there had been a two-way struggle. If anything, there had been no room, as far as the Germans were concerned, for any kind of open dialogue. From the beginning of his round of official and unofficial meetings, Ed Lewis had been stonewalled by a solid party line that none of the German players were deviating from. From Thomas Fellner, Minister of the Interior, and to the left of the political spectrum, to Rudolf Lammers, the Minister of Defense and a staunch conservative, the only difference in their presentations had been the intensity of the speaker's emotions.

Not that even that point made a difference. Even now, as he listened to Chancellor Ruff go over the same ground covered by the members of his cabinet, Lewis was reminded how much he disliked listening to German. It was to him a very harsh language. The sharp, crisp manner in which the northern Germans spat out their words almost seemed to assault his ears. Though he imagined that he was just being a little hypersensitive because of the content, Lewis found his mind wandering as he tuned out Chancellor Ruff, just as President Wilson had when it had become obvious to her that direct talks between her and Ruff were fruitless. So, instead of paying attention to what was being said, he found himself wishing that it had been the French and not the Germans who had precipitated this crisis. The French language at least was more pleasing to the ear.

The American congressman's lack of interest in what he was saying was not lost on Ruff, and it angered him. It angered him more than the fact that a mere congressman, and not a member of the President's own council, was picked to come to Germany to hear them out. Well, Ruff thought, if the Amis are going to hold us in such low regard, then perhaps I can do something to make them see this whole affair in a new light. Standing up, Ruff caught both Lewis and the German translator by surprise. "I see, Herr Congressman, that you are tiring of hearing the same thing over and over again. Perhaps you do not believe our resolve."

Caught off guard and regretting that his disinterest had been so obvious, Lewis sat up and began to apologize. He was, however, cut short as Ruff began to speak without pause, making it difficult for the translator to keep up. "The realities of world politics and diplomacy in the modern world are both harsh and obvious. For years the great struggle was, as many have pointed out, between the haves and the have nots. But what few people have understood, or cared to understand, was that when the terms 'have' and 'have not' were used by the

United States and the former Soviet Union, the speaker was not talking about monetary or mineral resources. No, Herr Congressman,
have and have not, when it came to determining who would be listened to and who could be ignored, meant having the bomb or not
having the bomb." Ruff paused, allowing this statement to take root
as he limped from behind his desk over to a wall where a map of
Germany, with its 1938 borders lightly highlighted and extending
from its current borders, was displayed. Stopping next to a German
flag, Ruff turned back and looked at Lewis, ready to continue where he
had left off.

"During the eighties, a great famine swept through much of Africa.
Though the United States was concerned, officially it did little. The
result, Herr Congressman, was millions of deaths, deaths of innocent
women and children that were recorded on film and shown almost
nightly in every home in America. In the early nineties, after the
collapse of the Soviet Union, when the new republics of the Commonwealth faced the same fate, the nations of the world, led by the
United States, tripped over themselves in an effort to rush aid to
the poor Russians. And why, Herr Congressman, such a difference?
The reason is obvious. Ethiopia had no nuclear-tipped missiles that
could reach the United States."

Lewis, shifting in his chair, finally found a chance to speak as Ruff
paused. "That, Herr Chancellor, is a rather cynical view. Surely you
must realize that—"

With a clearly discernible edge in his voice, Ruff cut Lewis off.
"This, Herr Congressman, is a very cynical world. Only those who are
willing to accept that and deal with the reality of things as they are
and not as they would like them to be will survive. Fifty years ago,
Germany was a broken country. Mentally and physically we had
reached the zero point. There was nothing. *Nothing.* Even worse, Herr
Congressman, if such a thing can be imagined, was the contempt with
which your countrymen, cloaked in self-righteousness, came into our
country and judged our people according to a morality that even your
own government could not live up to. We sat helpless, broken, and
exhausted, while you systematically created the theory of collective
guilt and then proceeded to drag the German people, their culture, and
their history, through the filth as if we were nothing but animals. And
then, to add hypocrisy to hypocrisy, when it suited your needs, when
the communists suddenly turned from friend to enemy and your busi-

nessmen needed new markets to exploit, we became acceptable again. But in your eyes, and in the eyes of the American politicians bought and paid for by the Jews, we never were, and never could be, your equal, worthy to sit down with you and share as equals. Well, Herr Congressman, we have paid for the sins of our fathers. For fifty years we have sat quietly while your countrymen pointed to us and told us that we should be ashamed of ourselves on one hand while using our people and our nation to achieve your political ends. It is time now that we turn our backs on the past and look to the future, to the new order in Central Europe, an order that has no room for the hypocrisy of American politics and meddling."

Lewis, for the first time since arriving in Germany, found himself becoming uneasy. The words "new order" and the mention of the Jews in a negative connotation caused Lewis to visibly twitch. Satisfied that he was having the desired effect, Ruff continued, speaking now in a rather matter-of-fact tone. "I have been informed that your President demands that we turn the nuclear weapons we seized from Sembach back over to your control. That, in our view, would be akin to a policeman returning stolen goods to a thief and helping the thief load them into his car. Your nation has no legal right to those nuclear weapons. None. That you think you do is simply another example of the contemptuous self-righteousness that you use to cloak your misguided and haphazard foreign policy. Rather than return those weapons, it is the decision of this government to keep them and incorporate them into a Central European arsenal that will allow all the nuclear 'have nots' in this part of the world to deal with the United States on an equal footing. Even you, Herr Congressman, can understand that."

After considering his response for several seconds, Lewis began to speak slowly, carefully choosing his words. "This is, I am sure, a matter that concerns more than the United States. You realize that the other nuclear powers in Western Europe, the French and British, not to mention the Russians to the east, are very concerned about a new nuclear power in Europe." Lewis was about to add "especially a nuclear arsenal controlled by Germany," but decided not to.

Ruff chuckled, having anticipated Lewis's comments and understanding that the concern was for a nuclear Germany. "The French, with over one fifth of their population clustered around Paris, not to mention all their vital government and business centers, would not risk any rash and precipitous action against us. Even the detonation of two or three devices in the Paris metropolitan area would make the devastation and deaths of both world wars seem trivial in comparison. And the British, with their traditions of de facto recognition of reality and their own problems in controlling the Irish and Scottish minorities within their own island empire, will accept our new position with hardly more than an official protest."

Determined to show that he was not intimidated and that he, as well as the United States, could not be easily bluffed, Lewis leaned over and tried to take up the attack. "Look, Herr Chancellor, you know as well as I do that those weapons as they sit right now are of no value to you. You didn't even secure the codes necessary to activate the devices. According to our experts, it would take a great deal of effort, not to mention a small amount of luck, to make use of the weapons you have. I do not see what advantage your government hopes to achieve with such a hollow threat."

If it had been Lewis's intent to upset Ruff's well-orchestrated lecture, then the smile that lit Ruff's face showed that it had not had the desired effect. Shaking his head, Ruff continued to smile. "You think, Herr Congressman, that we are fools. You have been treating us like naughty children for so long that you assume that we cannot think or act on our own behalf. Well, let me assure you that we are not children. And the game that we are now playing out here and out there is no child's game. So that you understand, in terms that even your President can comprehend, we are not only capable of retaining those weapons and using them, but we are more than willing to do so."

The look on Lewis's face betrayed his shocked disbelief. Ruff, seeing that his words had struck at Lewis's heart like a dagger, gave that dagger a twist. "You see, Herr Congressman, the Ukrainian government has provided us with the necessary codes and information for activating the weapons. As we speak, technical advisors from the Ukrainian Army, an army which you attacked and embarrassed, are working with the Bundeswehr and Luftwaffe to retrofit those devices to suitable delivery platforms. We are, you see, quite prepared and ready to deal with the United States or any nation from a position of strength. The German Revolution of 1989 has reached its logical conclusion. We are, and by every right, a world power. And neither you, your President, nor your tiny Army freezing in the Czech Republic and Slovakia, can change that, without paying a price that is, by any measure, too much."

When Chancellor Ruff was finished, Congressman Ed Lewis walked out of the Chancellor's office as if in a daze. He didn't even acknowledge Jan Fields-Dixon's presence as she hurried to join him. Only after he had thrown himself into the back seat of their Mercedes limousine and had allowed himself to sink, physically and figuratively, into the seat did his blank, pale expression change. Even then, his new expression was one that betrayed Lewis's sense of despair and hopelessness to Jan. Knowing that in due time Lewis would tell her everything that he was authorized to tell her, and probably more, she left him alone. Whatever had been said in the private meeting between Lewis and Chancellor Ruff had crushed Lewis's hope of a quick and amiable settlement. Reining in her correspondent's curiosity, Jan simply sat, like Lewis, watching the sights of Berlin rush by them as the limousine took them to the American embassy before their return home. She had, after all, been invited along on this trip by Lewis to serve as another set of eyes and ears to help him observe the mood of the German people as well as their elected officials. Though it was not normal for a politician of Lewis's status to entrust such a task to a member of the media, the special bond of friendship and trust that existed between Lewis and Jan, as well as her ability to see things that others missed, made Jan Fields-Dixon an invaluable asset.

Finally, after traveling awhile in silence, Lewis turned to Jan and exclaimed in a low, almost plaintive voice, "We're going to have to fight these people. I can't see any other way out." Looking out the window at the streets filled with scores of Berliners going about their daily tasks, Lewis repeated his statement, almost to himself. "We're going to have to fight these people." Then, as an afterthought, he added, "Again."

Both Lewis's demeanor and his pained comments shocked Jan like nothing had in a long time. Mistakenly referred to as a pacifist, Lewis had spent his entire political career, ever since resigning his commission in the Tennessee National Guard, fighting anyone who dared advocate the use of military force as a substitute to bankrupt foreign policy or as a solution to an international crisis. The American military was created and maintained, he was fond of saying, to safeguard American security, not to export and impose American principles or to make the world safe for corporate America. The United States, he told his opponents, had no right to impose its views or order on anyone, for whatever reason. Lewis's comment, therefore, was one that Jan was ill prepared for.

The quiet business-as-usual attitude of the Berliners along their route was absent as the limousine carrying Lewis and Jan pulled up to the entrance of the embassy. Double lines of police, stern-faced and in riot gear, stood posted at both ends of the street and in a semicircle around the embassy's main entrance. Though the throngs of people that faced the police were quiet, content at that moment to merely hold their signs and shuffle about in the slush in an effort to stay warm, Jan could see that both sides stood braced, ready for action. Even inside the embassy compound, the Marine detachment, in battle gear and armed alternately with rifles and shotguns, stood ready to deal with all comers.

If Lewis noticed any of this, he showed no concern. When the limousine stopped in front of the foyer, Lewis headed into the building, hands buried deep in the pockets of his overcoat and head bowed. Even when he was inside, he ignored the embassy staff as he headed down the corridors and up the stairs, followed by Jan, to the office he had been using over the past two days. Once there, he went to a chair overlooking the main embassy courtyard, where he sat staring vacantly out the window, without bothering to remove his coat. Seeing that he was, to say the least, uncommunicative, Jan left him to go in search of coffee and something to eat. Food and drink, she thought, might help him overcome his gloom. And if it did nothing for him, at least Jan's search for it gave her something to do with her nervous energy.

When she returned with a serving tray filled with breakfast pastries, coffeepot, and cups and saucers, Lewis finally began to stir. Whether it was the clanking noise of the cups and plates on the tray that Jan intentionally made or the smell of the fresh-perked coffee that brought Lewis about didn't matter. As she poured a cup for both of them, Lewis stood up, slipped his overcoat off, jammed his hands into his pants pockets, and walked over to Jan. Accepting a cup fixed just the way he liked it from Jan, Lewis watched her as he waited until she had prepared her own cup and stood facing him. Finally ready to speak, he looked Jan in the eye, took a sip of coffee, and smiled. It was, to Jan, a tired, unhappy little smile.

"You know, Jan, I'm constantly amazed by the way you and Amanda go about through this world each in your own way, but very much the same."

Struck by this strange comment, Jan wondered if she had missed something. But she knew she hadn't, so she said nothing, allowing Lewis to ramble on between sips of coffee.

Lewis chuckled. "I can see by your expression you're wondering what in the hell I'm talking about. Well, to tell you the truth, Jan, I'm not sure, at least not right now. You see, both you and Amanda are willing to accept people and things for what they are. Both of you, each in your own way, work with what you have, trying to keep things together and in harmony. Me, I guess I'm no better than every other guy who set out with what he thought were the ideals and principles that were the only true way to everlasting peace and happiness for the whole world, ready to cram them down the throat of everyone that disagreed with him." Lewis paused as he set his cup down and poured himself more coffee. "Well, Jan, it's hard for a man like me to suddenly realize that he doesn't have all the solutions, all the answers. I feel . . . I feel like Superman must have felt like the first time he was exposed to kryptonite."

For the first time since leaving the Chancellor's office, Jan spoke. "I take it, Ed, that the Germans are not ready to negotiate?"

His tone and demeanor betrayed the incredulousness he felt. "Negotiate? That, Jan, is the wrong word. I think the Germans call it *Diktat*. No, Jan, there doesn't seem to be a man in this city, from Ruff all the way down the line to Interior Minister Fellner, the one who was supposed to be reasonable, interested in negotiating. Instead, all of them, to a man, have a list of grievances and conditions that they insist must be worked out before serious discussions between our two governments can start."

Caught up now in Lewis's discourse, Jan asked what exactly those conditions were.

Raising an eyebrow as he took a sip of coffee, Lewis slowly replaced the cup onto the saucer and stared at it for a moment before answering. "Oh, though there are a whole bunch of little bones of contention that vary in importance depending on who you talk to, everything comes down to two really big items that all the Germans seem to agree on."

"And they are?"

Lewis, his eyes betraying no emotion, looked at Jan as he spoke. "First, all U.S. military forces must, and I emphasize the word they used, must withdraw from German territory by this July."

"But we can't simply up and leave in less than six months. They can't be serious. Are they?"

"Quite, Jan. They have been watching the American political landscape and they realize that few Americans would object to our pulling our troops home as part of an effort to reduce our annual military budget. After all, we have been after the Europeans for years to assume a more active role in their own defense. Here on a silver platter they give us the very thing that many of our fellow countrymen have been demanding."

He was, Jan realized, right. Chancellor Ruff knew that the Wilson administration would have a hard time justifying the continued retention of American forces in a Europe free from the specter of worldwide Soviet domination. "And the other demand, Ed?"

With a sigh, Lewis looked down at the floor, then back into Jan's eyes. "There, I'm afraid, they have us again. You see, Chancellor Ruff believes that Germany, in order to maintain its position in the European community as one of the leading states, must be able to stand side by side with the other states as an equal in fact as well as in word."

"How can we, the United States, help them achieve that? Most of the European community already acknowledge Germany's role in the new Europe."

"Jan, Ruff wants more than a verbal acknowledgment. He wants the horsepower to back it up. He believes that Germany, in order to be taken seriously, must be allowed to join the most exclusive club that all nations who want a say in shaping this world must belong to. In short, Jan, Germany, or I should say Chancellor Ruff, wants nothing less than for the United States of America to accept her as a nuclear power, free to retain the weapons she already has and develop her own as she sees fit."

Though she knew that she should have seen it coming, Lewis's articulation of that demand startled Jan. Dark, sinister images flashed through her mind as she stood there in silence trying to grasp the significance of what Lewis had said. Finally able to speak, she looked up at him. "But we can't do that. I mean, we can't agree to any of that."

Lewis slowly set the cup and saucer he was holding down on the tray, then thrust his hands into his pants pockets. "I know, Jan, I know."

Both Jan and Lewis were standing there looking down at the floor in silence when a member of the embassy staff knocked and entered the room. She paused, however, when she saw both Jan and Lewis standing motionless around the small table in the center of the room. "Oh, excuse me. I am sorry for interrupting."

Shaken out of his grim thoughts, Lewis looked up at the staffer. "Oh, no, you weren't interrupting. What can I do for you?"

"The ambassador was wondering when you would be returning to Washington. You had mentioned last night that you wanted to depart this afternoon after one more round of discussions with Chancellor Ruff. Is that still correct?"

Lewis thought about that for a moment before answering. "No, there has been a change. Please ask the ambassador if he would be so kind as to make the necessary arrangements for me to go to Prague to meet with the commander of the Tenth Corps."

While the embassy staffer acknowledged Lewis's request, Jan looked up at Lewis with a quizzical look on her face, but said nothing until the staffer was gone. "What are we going to Prague for?"

Lewis shrugged his shoulders. "Don't know right now. But we have a few hours to figure that out. Now if you would excuse me, Jan, I need to call the President, pay the ambassador my respects, and pack."

After crossing over to the north bank of the Uh River, Nancy Kozak ordered her driver to move off the road. Taking up a position from which she could see the northern approach of the bridge she had just crossed, Kozak settled down to wait for the last of her company to cross the river before they continued their withdrawal into Slovakia. She, like the rest of her company, would be glad to see Slovakia again, where they would be able to rest and relax. Their mission as the flank guard for the 1st Brigade's southern flank had been, except for the initial six hours, tedious on one hand while at the same time, due to their exposed position on the brigade's flank, nerve-racking. Once the Ukrainian armored brigade's effort to force a crossing against Kozak's company had been rebuffed and the Air Force had worked it over during the day, the remnants had been content to slip away to the southeast and establish blocking positions north of Uzlovaya. They still, however, were a threat that could not be ignored.

Nor could Kozak and her tiny command ignore their unusual position as accidental liberators. Without realizing it, Kozak's company, as well as the rest of the brigade, had found itself smack in the middle of the Ruthenian struggle for independence from the Ukraine. Never having heard of Ruthenia, Nancy Kozak, through broken translations provided by the farmer whose home the engineer platoon had occupied, learned that Ruthenians, who held that they were ethnically different from the Ukrainians, made up the bulk of the population around Uzhgorod, the historical capital of Ruthenia. Unhappy with the Ukrainian government's decision to prevent closer ties with their ethnic brethren in Slovakian Ruthenia, the Ukrainian Ruthenians had been agitating for independence. The sudden appearance of American forces fighting the Ukrainians naturally was viewed as an answer to their prayers. That neither Kozak nor any of her soldiers knew of the problem didn't seem to matter to the happy Ruthenians. As the farmer explained, front-line soldiers, regardless of which flag they serve under, are seldom told the real reasons behind their orders. Unprepared for this sudden attention and civil-military problem, Kozak had no idea what to do. After trying to explain that they were not there on behalf of the Ruthenians, she gave up, letting the farmer and all his relatives, and other farmers and villagers from the area who came to visit their "liberators," believe what they wanted. Besides, the Ruthenians, despite their obvious difficulties in making ends meet, were always ready to give Kozak's soldiers fresh bread, sweets, and warm home-cooked meals. Though she felt bad knowing that they were accepting the gifts from the Ruthenians under false pretenses, Kozak saw no way of stopping it. So she let it go and tended to the military matters for which she was trained.

Not that there was after the seventh of January a great deal to do professionally. After being repulsed in their predawn assault, the Ukrainian armored brigade, stalled on the south bank of the river, was worked over by the aging but venerable A-10 Warthogs. Coming in low and slow, the A-10s nailed anything that even looked like it was of military value. When the Ruthenian farmer later told Kozak that a number of refugee columns flowing out of Chop had been shot up by accident, Kozak questioned the air liaison officer who had joined her company about it. He shrugged off the concern by flatly stating that there was always the possibility of collateral damage when operating in densely populated areas. When asked by Kozak exactly what he meant by collateral damage, the Air Force captain looked at her as if he didn't believe she had to ask, and then answered in his casual, matter-of-fact manner, "Oh, it's damage to civilian structures or personnel, usually civilians that are in the vicinity of the target but aren't part of the strike's objective." Seeing an expression of disapproval creep across her face, the Air Force captain continued. "You know, when an A-10 comes rolling in at treetop level at over four hundred miles an hour, the pilot doesn't have a whole lot of time to separate the wheat from the chaff. When enemy tanks and refugees are sharing the road, collateral damage is unavoidable." Though she didn't know exactly how to feel about this, Kozak was glad to find out that the Ukrainians had given up their efforts to stay in close proximity and had pulled back from the river in an effort to escape the pounding from the air. There was a price that needed to be paid by someone, she realized, for everything.

With the immediate threat removed and casualties from the first day's fight tended to, Kozak turned to reorganizing and resting her company, while at the same time maintaining her command at a high state of vigilance. For the infantry and engineer platoons, this was no problem. Though the infantry platoons, as is traditional, suffered the majority of the casualties, their morale was high and they remained motivated and ready. This, however, was not the case with the tank platoon. Though it did play a pivotal role in the final defeat of the Ukrainian assault river crossing, the poor performance of their platoon leader, and the loss of one of their own to friendly fire, left a pall hanging over the entire unit.

Kozak did little to dispel this. Had it been a training exercise, she would have been able to shrug off Lieutenant Ellerbee's errors, just as she had done with other new lieutenants. But Kozak had lost her objectivity. Her own brush with death during the fight along the Latorica River, coupled with the accidental death of Ellerbee's gunner to friendly fire, a death that she viewed as both tragic and avoidable, had destroyed her ability to view Ellerbee in the detached and professional manner that she knew she should. As hard as she tried to reason with herself, Kozak continued to discover that she was, after all, very human. Though her mind told her that such errors and transgressions were unavoidable in the heat of battle, she found that she could not forgive Ellerbee for the very real professional shortfalls that had almost cost her and her crew their lives, and what she perceived as a poor attitude.

Having determined that she would never be able to fully accept Ellerbee as a responsible combat leader, Kozak did little to hide the contempt in which she held him. It showed in the manner in which she ignored him and the disdain in her voice when she spoke of him. When Kozak called for a meeting of all platoon leaders the night after the battle, she made it a point that she wanted Ellerbee's platoon sergeant, Sergeant First Class Rourk, to accompany him to the meeting. When, after the meeting, Rourk asked to see Kozak alone, pointing out that it was foolish for both him and Ellerbee to come to her meetings, Kozak didn't bat an eye. She simply looked straight at Rourk and told him, "Yes, you have a point. In the future leave him behind."

Kozak's efforts to remove Ellerbee or his platoon were frustrated by the brigade commander. His order that Ellerbee and his platoon stay where they were until he had an opportunity to personally review the situation pleased neither Kozak nor Ellerbee. When she went to Lieutenant Colonel Rick Zacharzuk, her battalion commander, to request that he request that the brigade commander reconsider his decision, Zacharzuk, nicknamed Ricky Z, refused to bring the matter up to Dixon. "Things are getting a little hairy right now, especially with this German thing," he told Kozak. "Though I agree with you, I'm afraid the brigade commander has one hell of a lot on his mind. Until we're out of Ukrainian territory and the situation in Germany is clarified, I have no intention of bothering him with this." Then, noticing that Kozak's shoulders physically slumped when he told her that, Ricky Z tried to soften the blow. "Look, Nancy. In another day we'll be back in an assembly area in Slovakia. Once we're there, I don't care if you surround Ellerbee and his tanks with barbed wire and post guards on them. I imagine we'll sit there while the powers that be sort out all the hard feelings between Berlin and Washington and all the little nukes are back in hand. Until then, you'll have to make the best of a bad situation."

As if her dark thoughts had conjured them up out of the river, Kozak heard Ellerbee's tanks rumble across the bridge and begin to close on the spot where her Bradley sat. Though she knew she was being petty and unprofessional, Kozak couldn't hide the feeling of disdain she felt every time she thought about Ellerbee. The mere image of the tanks passing her position, great black hulks against the dark overcast sky, caused Kozak's blood pressure to rise. Counting them in order to make sure that they were all clear of the bridge before she gave Lieutenant Matto permission to blow the bridge, only Ricky Z's promise to get Colonel Dixon to resolve the Ellerbee issue as soon as things settled down allowed Kozak to carry on in what she considered to be an intolerable situation.

Any regrets that still lingered in Scott Dixon's mind over his being pulled away from his brigade during the final stages of its withdrawal from the Ukraine were forgotten as his helicopter landed in the military compound at Milovice that had once served as the Soviet Army headquarters in Czechoslovakia. For there, just outside the circle marked in the well-packed snow that served as a helipad, stood his wife, Jan. Struggling against his natural desire to run up and grab her about the waist, Dixon deliberately lumbered on over to where she stood. With a smile on his face, Dixon walked up to her. "Hi, honey. I'm home. What's for dinner?"

In no mood for Scotty's playful humor or small talk, Jan simply stepped up to him, pushed the hood of his parka back, took his face in her hands, and kissed him. For several seconds, during which Dixon reached around Jan and pulled her body against his, they stood there ignoring the stares of military personnel coming and going and the bitter cold wind that whipped past them. When their lips finally parted, Dixon looked at Jan's beaming face. "We'd better stop this and go in before we freeze in this position."

Jan, her face aglow, sighed. "Would that, Colonel Scott Dixon, be so terrible?"

Giving Jan a gentle squeeze that she hardly felt through the layers of winter clothing, Scott chuckled. "Well, I could think of worse fates. But," he continued with a disappointed sigh, "I doubt this is what Big Al had in mind when he ordered me to come here."

Big Al was the nickname given to the Tenth Corps' five-foot, three-inch commanding general, who had been the division commander of the 16th Armored Division when Scott Dixon was the division's operations officer and Jan Fields was just living with him. An aviator by trade, Big Al Malin enjoyed Jan's charm, wit, and the attention she showered on him. When she finally married Dixon at Fort Hood, Big Al gave her away at the ceremony. This was a task he doubly enjoyed, since he cherished Scott Dixon's ability as an operations officer and as a thinker. Dixon, Big Al was fond of saying, was a true military artist who shared his love of military history.

Holding each other close, Jan and Dixon slowly walked over to the building that was serving as the Tenth Corps' headquarters in the Czech Republic. "I was told less than five minutes ago that you were coming in straight from the Ukraine, Scotty. All Ed Lewis told me was that if I wanted to see you, I had better get out here ASAP."

Surprised more by the mention of Lewis's name than her presence, Dixon slowed a little. "What, may I ask, is our friend from Congress doing here at this time of night? Don't tell me. Congress found some facts missing again and he was sent to find them."

Jan slapped Dixon's behind. "Scott, get serious. The President asked him to go to Germany to lay the groundwork for negotiations between us and the Germans over the question of the nukes and the German demands that we pull out of Germany."

Dixon chuckled. "Yeah, Herr Ruff really pulled a slicky one over on us." Then, holding Jan at arm's distance, he looked at her. "And I suppose you, of course, just happened to be in the neighborhood when the President asked Ed Lewis to come over here and you asked if you could tag along."

Looking over at him, Jan smiled. "As a matter of fact, that's exactly what happened."

A look of disbelief flashed across his face. "A likely story. I suppose you expect me to believe that."

"You can believe what you like, Scott Dixon. But it happens to be the truth. Cross my heart and hope to die. Now, tell me, what are you doing here?"

The appearance of two officers at the door they were headed for, both of whom Dixon recognized as being from the corps operations section, caused Dixon to stop. "I really don't know, Jan dear. But I've got a feeling we're about to find out."

Giving her husband a final squeeze, Jan said nothing as the two officers came up to Dixon and asked him to follow them.

While Jan took a seat in Big Al's outer office across from his aide-de-camp, Dixon was told to go on into the commanding general's office. There he found Ed Lewis and the general, sitting in armchairs, deep in conversation. Pointing to a pot of coffee sitting on a side table, Big Al, without any show of ceremony or formality, told Dixon to grab a cup, pull a chair on over, and join them. As Dixon pulled his seat up next to Ed Lewis, he greeted Lewis with a slight nod. Lewis, on his part, forced a smile and returned his nod. He was tired, Dixon thought. But it was more than a simple lack of sleep. His whole face, his eyes and cheeks, seemed to be drooping, almost as if the hidden thoughts weighing heavy on his mind were dragging his face down. Noticing that Dixon was staring at Lewis, Big Al started. "The congressman, Scotty, has just come from two days of nonstop discussions with the German government in Berlin."

Taking a sip of coffee, Dixon shook his head. "I'm sorry, sir. I've heard all kinds of rumors, but with operations still under way in the Ukraine, I've haven't really been paying much attention to what's going on outside my brigade."

"In a nutshell," Big Al started, "the Germans not only seized the weapons that the rangers took at the one storage site that didn't get trashed, they've been able, with the help of the Ukrainians, to remilitarize them. The Chancellor and his minions have informed the congressman here that they not only intend to keep them but are ready to use them if we, or anyone else, try to take them away."

Somehow, Big Al's comment didn't surprise Dixon. The use of nuclear weapons held no special horror for Dixon. It was to him simply another weapon. Having spent most of his adult life in the study of how best to destroy his fellow man, the proper employment of nuclear weapons had always been part of the equation. So the mention of them didn't cause him any great alarm or apprehension. In fact, nothing that Big Al said really surprised Dixon. To his analytical mind, it all made sense. Germany had been for years posturing itself for a more central role in the leadership of the European community. The revolutions of 1989 and the fall of communism that had opened up Eastern Europe had, by a simple fact of geography, placed Germany in the pivotal role as the gateway to the East. All that Germany needed to achieve big-power status was the hardware, which, thanks to the United States, it now had.

Looking over at Lewis's face, then back to Big Al, Dixon commented, only half in jest, "I take it this is the good news."

Easing back into his seat and taking a sip of coffee, Big Al grunted. Like all senior officers, Big Al found that officers who could think clearly and speak their minds without being mesmerized by a general's stars or a radically new situation were a rarity. Scott Dixon was one of those officers, and Big Al used his talents and mind whenever he got the chance. "As always, Scotty, you're ahead of the game. It seems that our former friends and allies in Berlin, Chancellor Herr Ruff in particular, already have an agenda in mind that their newfound power will enable them to implement immediately."

"And that, sir, is?"

Big Al looked up at the ceiling. "Oh, nothing less than the complete withdrawal of all U.S. forces from the Federal Republic of Germany, beginning with the Tenth Corps."

In an effort to make light of the situation, Dixon quipped, "Well, we'll be a little late for Christmas, but if he can pull that off, most of my people will vote for Ruff. Besides, some of Congressman Lewis's friends back in D.C. will be all for it. Less money for defense, more for social programs and all that great political rhetoric." Taking a sip of coffee, Dixon gave the appearance of absentmindedly mumbling a final snide comment. "Gee, now that I think of it, I wish I had voted for that guy."

Tired and still upset over his final meeting with Ruff, Lewis did not appreciate Dixon's attempt at humor, and his tone made that obvious to both Dixon and Big Al. "Colonel, the Germans, at gunpoint, forced their way onto an American military installation and seized nuclear weapons, weapons which, by the way, our nation has worked to control and limit."

Undaunted, Dixon countered. "Of course, one could always look at the flip side of this issue. We did, without prior consent, move nuclear weapons back into Germany in clear violation of the Berlin Accord of two years ago that specifically prohibits the storage of nuclear weapons in or their movement through Germany. We, the main backer of a nuclear-free Central Europe, were the first to break the rules. Seems to me that if this went to a court of law, the Germans would have a strong case."

Lewis replied sharply. "Unfortunately, Colonel, this matter isn't going to be resolved in a court of law. The Germans fully intend to force the United States into a showdown, one in which we either have to back away from or respond with force."

Seeing that the discussion between Lewis and Dixon was beginning to get out of hand, Big Al decided it was time to get back to the reason for the meeting. "Gentlemen, all of this, I'm sure, will make a great story and debate back in Washington. But that is not our concern. Whether we're right or they're right is, for me, unimportant. What is important, Colonel Dixon, is that one of the conditions the Germans are insisting on is that this corps be disarmed prior to its withdrawal from Europe."

Dixon looked at Big Al, then Lewis, and finally back to Big Al. "They, of course, are kidding, aren't they? I mean, even they understand that to do so would be tantamount to unconditional surrender, an insult to the Army and the entire nation."

"I think," Lewis interjected, "that's the idea. Sort of a public emasculation. And if Ruff does it, he'll become a national hero, Germany's twenty-first-century Arminius."

For a moment Dixon tried to place the name Arminius but couldn't. Big Al helped him out. "The Teutoburger Wald."

In an instant Dixon understood. By the year A.D. 9 the Roman Empire had been trying for twenty years unsuccessfully to civilize the Germans east of the Rhine River. During their annual movement from their summer quarters on the Weser River near where modern Münden stands, to winter quarters, the three legions and six cohorts of Quinctilius Varus, the Roman governor of Germany, as well as Roman merchants, bureaucrats, family members and such were attacked by the German tribes. Arminius, a leader of the local German tribes and supposedly a friend of the Romans, led the Germans against the Romans. In a three-day running battle that took place in the then heavily forested Lippe Valley, the German tribes under Arminius wiped out 18,000 Roman soldiers and 12,000 Roman merchants and bureaucrats, leaving a mere hundred Romans to return to Rome to spread the story of German power. That battle not only halted the eastward expansion of the Roman Empire and began its downward spiral, it left Germany free to develop its own culture without the latinizing influence that so dominated other Western European cultures. Known simply as the Battle of Teutoburger Wald, it is held by many as the beginning of German history and nationalism, with the Germans regarding Arminius in the same manner as Americans do George Washington's role in the American Revolution.

After thinking about the analogy for a moment, a now sober Dixon looked at Big Al. "He can't be serious, can he? I mean, even the Germans must realize that this is the twenty-first century."

"They do, Colonel," Lewis took up. "Believe me, they do. Which is why instead of using the wicker shields and javelins Arminius's warriors used against the well-armed and disciplined Roman legionnaires, Chancellor Ruff intends to rely on nukes."

"And the German public is going to buy this line and back him?"

"Ruff seems to think they already have, Colonel. His election to office on a conservative Germany-for-Germans platform has been interpreted by many, including Ruff himself, as a mandate which he has taken seriously. That, coupled with our own diplomatic blunders in the past few days and his decisive actions have made him quite popular with conservatives in Germany, for the moment. You see," Lewis added, "unlike the Americans, who classify the last presidential election as ancient history, the Germans, like most Europeans, have a strong sense of history. We were reminded of this in the early nineties when tiny tribes with flags long forgotten by most people suddenly took advantage of the political upheavals in Central Europe and popped up all over the map of Central and Eastern Europe. This resurgence of tribal nationalism makes the analogy of Arminius more appealing to the Germans, a proud and homogeneous culture with a long history."

"In short," Big Al added, "we're out here on a limb, and Herr Chancellor is hacking away at it like crazy."

Dixon threw his hands out. Knowing that Big Al was using this as a skull session in which he wanted any and all ideas to be thrown out, discussed, and examined as they searched for a solution, Dixon took the lead. "Okay, fine. So we hunker on down here, enjoy a nice pleasant winter vacation in the Czech mountains while things cool down and the politicians settle down to some serious talks."

Shaking his head, Lewis sighed. As the political consciousness of the group, Lewis responded. "I wish, Colonel, it was that easy. When I spoke to the President earlier this afternoon, she informed me that the Czech ambassador had already approached her and has, on behalf of his government, requested that the Tenth Corps leave his country immediately. The Germans, and apparently the Ukrainians, according to the CIA branch chief in Berlin, have already been at work. Seems they have been reminding the Czech and Slovak governments that Germany and Ukraine have borders with them that are considerably longer than their borders with the United States."

Dixon thought about that for a moment before responding. "Well, nothing like strategic blackmail. What about the Poles? Will the Poles let us pass to the Baltic coast and home?"

"That avenue," Lewis said, "is being explored, but it doesn't look promising. The Polish government is still miffed over the amount of aid that we have poured into Russia at their expense. Besides, not only have the Germans been working on them, but a withdrawal through Poland would be for the Germans a moral victory. I can see him now," Lewis continued, waving his hands about as if he were delivering a speech, "standing on a podium, the new little Hitler, proclaiming to the whole world how the vaunted American war machine had slithered away behind the benevolent protection of the Polish Army rather than face certain defeat at the hands of a unified German Army."

Dixon rolled his eyes. "Oh, what a wicked web we weave. You know, this is sounding more and more like Peyton Place goes to the UN instead of an international crisis." Then looking at Big Al and Lewis in turn, Dixon said, "I take it someone here has a brilliant idea that will magically resolve this whole goat screw."

"Well, Scotty," Big Al declared, "I'm glad you asked. Do you recall the story of Xenophon?"

Both Dixon and Lewis looked over to Big Al. He had the hint of a smile on a face that betrayed no real concern. He's got something in mind, Dixon thought, and he's been setting us up for it. Realizing that Big Al wanted him to act as a lead-in to his plan, Dixon responded. "Yes, of course. The March of the Ten Thousand. Around 400 B.C. a force of ten thousand Greek mercenaries in the service of the King of Persia was betrayed and left high and dry in the center of what is today Iraq. Rather than surrender their arms, as the Persian King demanded in return for their lives, the Greeks closed ranks and marched back to Greece, through Kurdistan, I believe, taking on all comers."

Big Al's smile broadened. "Your memory is good, Scotty, almost as good as Congressman Lewis's."

Allowing the compliment to pass over him, Dixon continued to play his role by articulating what he thought Big Al was hinting at. "Let me see if I'm following. What you're proposing, General, is that we tell the Germans to piss off, then we form up and march to Bremerhaven."

"Actually, Scotty, it was the congressman's idea. You see, he wanted to go back to Washington with a military option in his hip pocket."

Looking at Lewis in surprise, Dixon was about to speak when Lewis cut in. "I know what you're thinking, Colonel. Can it be true the great pacifist, champion of diplomatic solutions over military adventures, is in reality a hawk in dove's clothing? Well, I'm afraid that I'm a victim of the thirty-second campaign commercial. I have been and always will be a believer in responsible government and reasonable, intelligent, and responsible policies. That I've opposed the American policy of shoot first and talk later is a matter of record. But there comes a time, such as this, when there is no room for talking, when the long-term dangers justify the risk, that military force is justified."

"That," Dixon countered, "is all well and good. But let's face it. This is the twenty-first century, not 400 B.C. And the country we are talking about tromping through is a highly civilized, densely populated nation that, oh, by the way, is armed with the latest technology, not to mention the odd nuke here and there. We're not talking about the Teutoburger Wald or the March of the Ten Thousand through the mountains of Kurdistan here. What you are proposing, Mr. Congressman, is a head-to-head confrontation between two mechanized armies smack dab in the middle of the most populated corner of Europe." Dixon sat back and shook his head. "I'm sorry, sir. I'm afraid I don't really see a viable option here. I'd just as soon ask the people in my brigade to click their heels together and mumble, 'There's no place like home' three times as ask them to participate in such a hare-brained operation."

Big Al grinned. "I love the way you get right to the heart of the matter, Scotty. Which is exactly why I asked you to come here and help me draft a concept for the operational plan that Congressman Lewis will carry back to Washington. Since both the congressman and I agree that the Pentagon's Polish option and their idea of flying our personnel out of here and leaving all our heavy equipment behind will be non-contenders, we need to provide the President with something that makes sense."

Looking back and forth between Big Al and Lewis, it began to dawn on Dixon that they were serious. "And you both think that marching the entire corps from one end of Germany to the other in the dead of winter makes sense?"

When Big Al spoke, his voice was quiet, yet firm. "I hope that this proposed bout between the modern German Arminius and me, the American version of Xenophon, can be avoided. That, however, is out of our hands." As Big Al shifted in his seat, Dixon knew that his last comment was mostly for Lewis's benefit. Such a wish was a mere dream that no one, especially the commanding general, should base his plan on. If and when American forces crossed into Germany, there would be a fight. Dixon knew it and he had no doubt that Big Al knew it too. After a moment of silence, Big Al continued. "What is within our power is our ability to give our national leaders our best opinions and a viable option that they can use if all else fails."

Staring down at his coffee cup for several seconds, Dixon thought about everything that had been said. As he did so, the sheer audacity of what Big Al was proposing began to take hold. For a second, the image of Chancellor Ruff attired as an ancient German chieftain in his Leopard II tank, and Big Al wearing the helmet and breastplate of an ancient Greek general mounted atop an M-1A1 Abrams, bearing down on each other on a wide-open stretch of autobahn, flashed through Dixon's mind. The whole idea was so insane, Dixon suddenly realized, that it just might work. Besides, the other alternative, the idea of ordering his soldiers to meekly lay down their weapons and go home like a herd of sheep, was a thought that was so repugnant that he couldn't even dwell on it. Looking up at Big Al, Dixon smiled. "Hey, General! What a wonderful idea. Glad I thought of it. When do we start?"

CHAPTER 9

11 JANUARY

"That's it? That's all the short little bastard had to say? Who in the hell does he think he is?"

From where she sat, Abigail Wilson snapped at Soares. "Pete, I would appreciate it if you let Congressman Lewis finish."

Pete Soares had never gotten used to what he in private referred to as Wilson's "naughty boy" manner of dealing with her own cabinet when they got out of hand. After all, he was, as he told his close friends, a forty-eight-year-old man, one that was very successful and powerful. He didn't need a mother to tell him how to act or talk. Still, in public, he paid heed to Wilson's reprimand. She was, after all, the President, although he never would admit to himself or anyone else that he was her subordinate. Screwing his face in the peculiar fashion that had earned him his nickname, "The Rat" eased back into his chair as Lewis prepared to pick up where he had been when Soares had interrupted.

"What exactly," Lewis shot back at Soares, "would you have him say? As far as he's concerned, he and every soldier in his corps is a political hostage. Lieutenant General Malin is not only a soldier, he is the senior officer in command of a combat command whose very existence is endangered. His insistence that this administration, the very same one that precipitated the crisis, take immediate and decisive action to resolve that crisis in a manner that does not compromise the prestige of the United States or the United States Army is, as far as he's concerned, reasonable."

From across the table, Terry Rothenberg, the Secretary of Defense, shook his head. "He knows better than anyone else that the United States will use nuclear weapons only as a last resort and only if there is a direct threat to this country. While I sympathize with his position, I cannot advise you, Madam President, to take any military action against the German government. None of the other NATO allies, either collectively or individually, would support us. They, like the Germans, view the current crisis as regrettable, but one which is of our own making. And, like the Germans, they believe that the final solution must be arrived at by the Europeans themselves. Though in private the ministers of defense in both France and Britain are quite upset that the Germans are now nuclear capable, they do not feel that seizing them by force is the answer. Even if it means abandoning all of General Malin's heavy equipment and losing face. In the words of Harold Lloyd, the British Minister of Defense, 'You Americans have done quite enough already. We would thank you very much if you would just quietly leave and let us sort this out between ourselves.' "

"Surely," Soares hissed, "*that* arrogant little shit doesn't think we're simply going to stack arms, stick our tails between our legs, and go home? I mean, the British, of all people, should know that appeasement does not buy peace."

With a glare that could have cut a stone, Wilson got Soares to stop talking. When she was ready, Wilson spoke with a calm, measured voice. "I am inclined, as distasteful as it is, to agree with Terry and the Joint Chiefs of Staff. Without the political and military support of our European allies, resolution of this crisis through military action is out of the question. As far as I am concerned, it's time we stopped playing John Wayne and started dealing with the rest of the world as intelligent human beings who are no better and no worse than we." Then, looking about the table, she added, with a hint of sarcasm in her voice, "Who knows? Maybe that will work."

Fighting the urge to roll his eyes in disgust, Soares could only think how big a mistake it had been to allow a woman in the White House. Regardless of what the surveys and political polls said, he knew in his heart that June Cleaver, the nickname Wilson's opponents in her own party had given her, didn't belong in the Oval Office, unless, as Soares had once jokingly said, it was to vacuum. Standing up, Soares collected his notes. "Well, I guess that's it! We knuckle under."

Wilson countered, her voice firm and clear. "Unless things change dramatically in the next day or two, there is no other way out. We tried to ride a hungry tiger and were thrown. Now it's going to eat us all for sure." For a moment she looked about the room. Then, as was her style, she summed up her view of where they stood. "We are, gentlemen, three days into this crisis and, as of yet, we have no viable options. Repeated attempts to establish direct talks between Chancellor Ruff and myself have failed. Instead, he has been repeating dogmatic speeches better suited for the evening news than dealing with us. That, coupled with Chancellor Ruff's unconditional rejection of both the British and the French offers to mediate, is, to me, a clear sign that he personally has no intention for the moment of considering alternatives. Efforts by our respective State departments to establish a basis of talks have been politely ignored. And now, my back-door approach using Senator Lewis has been slammed in my face."

Wilson paused while she allowed her summary of the situation to soak in. "So, gentlemen, we are back at square one. Your job, Terry and Pete, is to go back and, with everything that has transpired over the last three days, reassess where we stand. By eight in the morning, present those new assessments to us and any new options for resolving this crisis that those assessments may point to. And as you do so, please bear in mind that we must, gentlemen, make sure that the tiger we've latched onto doesn't eat too many innocent people. Now, if you both would excuse me, I would like to speak with Ed Lewis in private." Again Wilson paused.

Uneasy about Lewis's role as an official envoy of Wilson to the German Chancellor, Soares was about to protest this private meeting but decided not to bother. If, he thought, she was prepared to throw her political career in the shitter by giving in to the Germans, it was her affair. He didn't need to join her. If anything, the more distance he put between himself and her the better. He had worked to get her there at the urging of the party bosses against his better judgment. It was time, Soares decided, to start looking for a suitable replacement, one whom he could back and who, in turn, would help him further his own career.

When the room had cleared, Lewis sat back and waited for Wilson to speak. "Well, Ed, did we do all right?"

Looking about the room, Lewis paused before he answered. "I

trust, Madam President, that we are not being monitored or re-corded?"

Wilson shook her head, a little annoyed that he would even ask. "What makes you think that I would allow such a thing?"

A sheepish smile lit across Lewis's face. "Oh, I suppose every time I get involved in anything that's a little covert, I get slightly nervous. It's a throwback to the sixties. You know, Big Brother, J. Edgar Hoover, and the Nixon tapes."

"If we are, then a lot of heads will roll. Now, to the point. Do you in your heart really believe that General Malin can pull this off?"

"As I told you before, Big Al, excuse me, I mean General Malin, and everyone involved in the plan fully understands that this entire en-terprise is a series of risks. In fact, from beginning to end, and every step along the way, it is all a series of gambles. We're gambling that the Tenth Corps can break back into Germany without a fight. We're gambling that the Germans, both in Berlin and in the field, will be so confused and thrown off by your apparent acceptance of their de-mands, followed by General Malin's actions and the ground opera-tions, that they may, at least in the beginning, hesitate and step aside rather than fight. We're gambling that the other European countries buy Malin's role as a renegade commander acting on his own accord, and continue to work with you. We're gambling that General Malin's propaganda machine will erode the support of the Bundeswehr and the German people for Ruff and his government, giving Malin and his soldiers an open road north. And we're gambling that General Malin can get the Tenth Corps to the coast, where it can be resupplied and, if necessary, reinforced for future operations. Yes, we can pull it off, provided everyone involved keeps coming up with a good roll of the dice."

Wilson looked at Lewis intently. "What is the worst-case scenario?"

In a cold, unemotional voice, Lewis answered. "The worst thing that could happen is that the German Army and people rally around Ruff's Deutschland Über Alles cries, stopping the Tenth Corps and wiping it out in the heart of Germany."

"And if we can pull this off, what's the best we can hope for?"

"Big Al and his corps make it to the coast as a fighting force, ready to be withdrawn from the continent or, if the situation dictates, re-inforced. This would give back to you a viable military option as well as discrediting Ruff's government. There is the outside possibility, depending on how the Germans themselves view this whole affair as it unfolds, that Ruff's government could be replaced by one willing to hold reasonable negotiations with you."

"I would think that the Germans, and even our allies, would see this 'mad general' ploy in a heartbeat. I mean, after all, the Europeans are past masters at diplomatic duplicity, aren't they?"

Lewis nodded. "That's right. And they still like to think of us as fumbling babes in the woods when it comes to playing diplomatic hardball. Which is why this screwball idea is so good. We're the crazy Americans, cowboys of the free world. Most Europeans agree that anything and everything is possible when dealing with us. But a subtle, intricate plot on a scale such as this, in the eyes of most Europeans, is beyond us."

For several minutes Wilson sat at her desk and looked down at the blank blotter, deep in thought. Finally, without looking up, she spoke, as if she were thinking out loud. "Without going to the Joint Chiefs, I am not militarily astute enough to determine on my own if General Malin and his people can do, from a technical standpoint, what they say they can. I have only your word and his. Nor can I or anyone else accurately predict at this time what Ruff and the German people will do. I can't imagine them simply stepping aside and letting General Malin's corps roll merrily through their country."

Lewis cut in. "As I told you before, Abby, there will be a fight. The best Big Al said that he hopes for is that it doesn't occur until he's within striking distance of the coast and that only a portion of the German Army, for whatever reason, can be brought to bear."

Looking up at Lewis, Wilson thought for a moment before she asked her next question. "And what do I tell the other European leaders? The Germans will no doubt work hard to get them involved on their behalf."

"That's where the renegade general role comes in. After you order Malin to stand down and prepare to fly his people out of the Czech Republic and Slovakia and he refuses, you simply tell Ruff that Big Al's actions are the acts of a madman and request that he allow you, working in cooperation with the German government, an opportunity to resolve the crisis. This stance should throw the German government off balance for a while, forcing them to act with some restraint and remove the specter of escalation without actually removing the threat."

Wilson shook her head. "I don't understand."

"It's all mirrors and smoke at this point. You see, Big Al will be more of a marauding band than a national army that represents our nation or its policy. By condemning his actions and doing all you can from a distance to help the Germans police up this rampaging corps, without actually doing anything, you can help temper the German response. Big Al, your position will go, and not his soldiers, is the criminal. Therefore, you can promise the Germans that if they allow the Tenth Corps through without resisting them, you will pay for any damages and bring the responsible culprit, i.e., General Malin, to justice just as soon as you have him in custody. Big Al, of course, will at some point promise to turn himself over to a representative of the American Department of Justice just as soon as he has gotten his soldiers, whom he is responsible for, and their equipment to the coast."

"And what if," Wilson countered, "Ruff and the Germans don't buy this line of manure?"

"Simple. You point out to Herr Ruff that you cannot sit back and allow the German government to endanger the lives of Big Al's soldiers, who are confused and misguided, simply because their commander is wacky and disobedient. If, you will tell Ruff, the Germans threaten to apply undue force and cause needless American deaths, you, as their commander-in-chief and President, will have no choice but to do everything in your power to help those poor misguided and innocent soldiers."

Again there was silence as Wilson considered what she thought was a crazy idea. When she looked up at Lewis, her face showed her skepticism. "Do you *really* expect the Germans to believe these lies? Do you really think we can fool anyone?"

Pointing to the door, Lewis smiled. "You already have started sowing the seeds of your own deception, Abby. Right now, Soares and Rothenberg are going about preparing the necessary orders and instructions that will, if you don't accept General Malin's plan, fulfill the German demands. There's no doubt that the media, leaky 'official' sources, and German intelligence will pick all of this up. As long as you keep them in the dark, they will be your best cover."

"What about the nuclear devices, Ed? How do we resolve that one?"

Shaking his head, Lewis threw his hands out. "Haven't got a real good answer on that one yet. I've been thinking about it, but I'm afraid that there's no one solution that will solve all our problems at once. So I recommend that we deal with the most immediate problem first, the Tenth Corps."

"You don't think the nukes are a problem?"

"A problem, yes. The most important one, no. After all, who, Madam President, are the Germans going to use them against and where? If they go for the Tenth Corps before they enter Germany, they, the Germans, start the war and drag the Czechs and Slovaks and God knows who else into the fray. Even their friends the Ukrainians would be pissed, especially when you consider that radioactive fallout from Ukrainian bombs detonated on Czech soil will drift east into Ukrainian territory. And if the Germans wait until the Tenth Corps enters Germany, that would mean punching gigantic radioactive holes in German soil." Lewis shook his head. "No, I'm afraid not even Hitler would have been that dumb. After all, despite the fact that they had nerve gas during World War II and we didn't, the Germans still didn't use it for fear of retaliation. We know where the nukes are. We even know who's guarding them and, for the most part, how. The CIA's been pretty good about keeping up with that. So if you accept my premise that the Germans won't use them on their own soil, the nukes are for the moment a minor concern."

Lewis's statement that the nukes were a minor concern caused Wilson to roll her eyes. Only after considering everything that he had said was she able to accept Lewis's analysis as valid. Calm again, Wilson looked down, pondering Lewis's assessment in silence. Finally she looked over at him. "You realize, Ed, that after all this is over, even if we do pull it off, our political careers will be over."

After a short pause during which Lewis's face lost all expression, he spoke. "Madam President, yesterday I sat as close to Chancellor Ruff as I am now to you. I looked into his eyes and listened to his words. I cannot express to you my feelings of horror and dread. What the words did not convey, his eyes and the tone of his voice did. I felt as if I were staring into a dark bottomless pit. As I thought about that pit, suddenly I realized that I was listening to the same words our fathers and grandfathers had listened to in 1933. I do not mean to lecture you, Abby, but I must tell you, our fathers had to see the same dark pit. *They had to.* But they didn't know what was at the bottom of it. We do. You know and I know. That pit is filled with over thirty million corpses. And those corpses are there because our fathers took the safe, sure road. They tended to their political concerns and ignored their responsibility to the human race. They saw the face of evil and turned their backs on it. Can you do the same?"

13 JANUARY

Roused from a fitful sleep, Chancellor Ruff didn't bother dressing before going down to the den where he was told Colonel Kasper was waiting. When he entered, Ruff immediately regretted not having taken the time to dress. Kasper, in full uniform, jumped to his feet as soon as the doors of the den were slid open for Ruff. Another colonel, whom Ruff had seen once at the headquarters of the Bundeswehr, also came to a rigid position of attention. Concealing his embarrassment at being presented in nothing but pajamas, bathrobe, and slippers, Ruff headed right to his desk, where he took a seat before addressing the two officers.

Pivoting in place, both colonels waited while Ruff took his place behind his desk and lit a cigarette. Finally Ruff, after taking a long puff, looked up at Kasper. "Well?"

Kasper's usual clear, sharp manner was not dulled by the early hour. "Herr Chancellor, may I present Colonel Gotthardt Mahler of General Lange's personal staff."

Without pause, as if rehearsed, Mahler presented himself. "Herr Chancellor, General Lange regrets not being able to report to you at this time. He is currently reviewing the situation and will, after the morning briefing, report directly to you in person."

Waving his hand with the cigarette in it, Ruff indicated that Mahler was to continue. "Sir, we have been able to confirm that the American Tenth Corps is in motion, with logistical elements moving north from Prague." Stepping forward, Mahler laid on Ruff's desk a small map showing the northern Czech-German border. As he continued to speak, he pointed to red military symbols marked on the map. "They have commenced establishing forward logistical bases in the vicinities of Chomutov, Teplice, Decin, and Liberec." Leaving the map in front of Ruff, Mahler stepped back, allowing the Chancellor to study the map and the strange military symbols that had no meaning to him as he thoughtfully puffed on his cigarette. Finally he looked up at Mahler. "And what, Colonel, is General Lange's conclusion?"

Kasper had warned Mahler that the Chancellor had only a cursory layman's understanding of operational matters, telling him that he needed to be very specific, without being insulting, when explaining the military situation to Ruff. So Mahler was careful to respond in such a manner that his answer didn't sound like a lecture. "General Lange believes that we are seeing the beginning of a redeployment in preparation for ground operations against Germany."

Looking up at Mahler with narrow, inquiring eyes, Ruff took a puff from his cigarette. "You are aware, I am sure, that President Wilson of the United States has stated that she is committed to defusing this situation and begin the withdrawal of American forces from Europe as soon as the disposition of American equipment and weapons can be arranged with the Czech government. Could this move not be part of that effort?"

With no need to consider Ruff's question, Mahler responded. "That, Herr Chancellor, is possible but unlikely. General Schacht reports that none of his sources in the Czech Republic have found any evidence that American combat units are preparing their weapons or equipment for demilitarization. If anything, his latest intelligence indicates that the Tenth Corps' combat units are preparing for sustained combat operations. Our agents who have been able to observe American units around Prague and Pizen all speak of units stripping away all unnecessary vehicles and equipment while distributing large quantities of combat rations, lubricants, and spare track parts to combat vehicles. Yesterday the corps logistics officer submitted a request to the Czech Army office of logistical operations for all the fuel cans it could spare, to be delivered to the main corps support area within forty-eight hours."

Ruff was careful in wording his question so as not to appear totally ignorant of military matters. "Yes, this all seems to belie what the American President is saying. But I cannot simply come out and declare her a liar based on the movement of a few supply units. Can I, gentlemen?"

Kasper, understanding the real question behind his Chancellor's question, responded. "This is normal procedure for American forces. Some of their officers call it a slingshot. When the situation allows, logistical units and the bulk of the supplies to be used during the initial phases of an offensive operation are moved as far forward as possible in advance of the combat units. The combat units themselves are kept as far back as practical and dispersed. Only at the last moment are those units launched forward. When the combat elements do come forward, they all pass through the pre-established logistical points where they refuel and then move immediately into the attack. In this way the logistical system, normally the bulkiest and most cumbersome part of an army, is already set in place, leaving the roads free for movement of the combat units and able to support combat operations from the very beginning. It is a system the Americans have practiced here in Germany during Reforger exercises and used quite successfully during the first Gulf War."

Finishing his cigarette, Ruff crushed it in an ashtray and looked at the map again. "How soon before we know for sure when and where the Americans will strike, if indeed they intend to strike?"

Picking up where Kasper left off, Mahler responded. "The next elements that move forward, if the Americans stay true to their doctrine, will be corps and division artillery units. Like the logistic units, by moving them forward first, the artillery units will be off the roads and ready to support the maneuver units when they come through. As for the likely axis of advance, when I left we were looking at three major avenues of advance into eastern Germany." Leaning over Ruff's desk, Mahler used his index finger to show Ruff where he was talking about. "One, here, north from Chomutov toward Chemnitz. Another, here, from Teplice into Dresden with a possible supporting attack from Decin also north toward Dresden. There is also the remote possibility that an end run may develop here, from Liberec, through Poland, toward Görlitz."

Mention of the move through Poland surprised Ruff. "They wouldn't dare."

Resuming his position of attention, Mahler responded in a matter-of-fact manner. "It has been confirmed, Herr Chancellor, that General Malin, the commanding general of the Tenth Corps, paid a personal visit to the Polish embassy in Prague yesterday afternoon. This was followed last night by the appearance of the Polish military liaison officer at Tenth Corps headquarters. While such an operation is questionable, General Lange cannot ignore that possibility. He has instructed his planning staff to take such a contingency into account when planning for the redeployment of our forces to counter the American threat."

"When, Colonel Mahler, does General Lange intend to present a full report and his recommendations to me?"

Lifting his right arm to eye level, Mahler studied his watch for a moment before answering. "In four hours, Herr Chancellor. There is an intelligence update by General Schacht's section for the senior members of the General Staff scheduled at 0630, followed by a final review of the draft operational plan to the full staff at 0700 hours. That will take no more than thirty minutes. After that, Generals Lange and Schacht, along with the chiefs of their planning staffs, will be prepared to report to your office at 0800 to brief you and your cabinet." Then, as an afterthought, Mahler added, "Will that, Herr Chancellor, be satisfactory?"

With a wave of his hand, Ruff told Mahler that eight o'clock was satisfactory. Thanking the two colonels, he dismissed them. When he was alone, Ruff looked down at the map on the desk before him. So, he thought to himself in the silence of his den, the Americans come again. That thought brought his black-sheathed Hitler Youth dagger to mind. After lighting another cigarette, Ruff leaned back in his seat, taking a long drag as he looked up at the ceiling. Though his eyes were open, he only saw the images of a dark, gray corpse-filled cellar in Regensburg in April of 1945. Every detail, even the smell of that cellar, was as keen to him at that moment as if it had just been yesterday. He could even feel the pain in his leg almost as intensely as he had when the wound was fresh on that distant day. "This time," he said to himself with a hint of self-satisfaction, "*I* shall be ready."

Arriving at the rail yard in Milovice just as Nancy Kozak's company was finishing breakfast and getting back to loading their vehicles onto rail cars, Scott Dixon and Colonel Vorishnov joined Kozak for breakfast and watched the operation. Using the hood of Kozak's humvee as a table, the three officers ate their breakfast of runny eggs, soggy toast, and limp bacon while Kozak briefed Dixon on the status of her company between mouthfuls. Not that he didn't already know its status, as well as that of all the companies under his command. Dixon's own staff had already given him an update on that less than an hour before. It wasn't the information he was interested in at that moment. What he was really looking at was Kozak's attitude and the attitude of the soldiers in her command. That was something that didn't show up on the charts and graphs at brigade headquarters. For this piece of critical information, Dixon relied heavily upon his own eyes and ears. With what they had to do, Dixon had to be sure that everyone in his command was mentally as well as physically ready. So, informing Dave Yost, his executive officer, that he had had enough staff briefings and planning sessions at both corps and his own command post to last a lifetime, he and Colonel Vorishnov hopped into Dixon's humvee and fled the organized chaos of a brigade headquarters in the throes of planning and preparing for the invasion of Germany.

Referring to notes in a spiral notebook covered with a personalized camouflaged carrying case, Kozak alternated between eating and re- counting item by item the status of her command and her concerns. As she did so, Vorishnov watched her in fascination. He watched how she held her fork, how her full, shapely lips moved when she spoke, how she held her head slightly to the side with a few stray wisps of her long hair falling out from under her helmet. Such a lovely girl, he thought, involved in such a cold, brutal business. A veteran himself, Vorishnov wondered how such a beautiful creature as this woman could maintain her femininity and still continue to do what was nec- essary. Vorishnov was just beginning to imagine what Kozak would look like in an elegant black gown with a jeweled necklace draped about her slender neck instead of the dirty collar of an olive drab wool sweater, when her company first sergeant came up behind her and interrupted her briefing by loudly clearing his throat.

Without showing any indication that she was upset over the first sergeant's interruption, Kozak paused and turned toward him. "Is ev- eryone back at it, First Sergeant?"

Making a slight grunt, First Sergeant Gary Stokes's reply showed his disgust. "Well, ma'am, like my old man use to say, 'Ya can teach 'em, but ya can't learn 'em.' "

She looked at him for a moment with a patient, calm expression on her face while she waited for Stokes to continue. "It's the same old story, Captain Kozak. As soon as someone starts shooting, half of what we tried to teach these people goes out the window." Looking at Dixon, Stokes threw his hands up in disgust. "I mean, the second we go into combat, everyone thinks, Hey! Fuck it, man, this is war, and all the discipline and accountability we try to instill in these guys is forgotten."

"What exactly," Kozak asked, "is the problem?"

"Tie-downs and chock blocks, ma'am. There isn't a complete set of either in the entire company."

A worried look crept upon Kozak's face. "You mean there isn't a single vehicle in the *entire* company with everything it needs for rail loading?"

Knowing that she was asking about her own Bradley, Charlie 60, Stokes shook his head. "None, *nichts.* I personally checked."

Vorishnov noticed the embarrassed look that caused her cheeks to blush slightly. Turning to Dixon, she asked if she could be excused, stating that she needed to look into the matter of tie-downs immediately. With a knowing smile, Dixon nodded and told her no problem. After they exchanged salutes and both Kozak and Stokes were out of earshot, Vorishnov commented, still watching Kozak's hips sway despite the bulky parka and field gear, "You know, that could never happen in the Russian Army."

At first Dixon thought that Vorishnov was talking about the crews losing their tie-downs. After noticing, however, the manner in which Vorishnov was looking at Kozak as she walked away, Dixon understood that he meant women leading combat units. Dixon chuckled. "That, Colonel, is your loss."

Taking a sip of his now lukewarm coffee, Vorishnov stared at Dixon with a quizzical look. "Do you honestly think so?"

"Colonel, I know so. Some of my best troopers are female. They're for the most part sharp, dedicated, and with few exceptions, far more astute when it comes to dealing with people. Besides, overall, they have a very real civilizing effect on the units to which they belong."

Vorishnov watched Kozak go about her business as he continued to speak to Dixon. "Our intelligence officers like to tell us that the presence of so many women in your units is making them soft, that they are feminizing your army."

Dixon smiled knowingly. "Well, your intelligence people can believe what they want. I personally know of several Iraqi officers who would beg to differ with that conclusion. I'll be the first to admit there are problems. After all, as the saying goes, boys will be boys, and girls will be girls, especially when you put them together. But it's all part of being a democracy. Everyone has a right to make it in the world as far as they can go."

Turning toward Dixon, Vorishnov took another sip of coffee. "I think, Colonel Dixon, in this case I must agree with some of my fellow officers. Allowing women in combat units is a little too much democracy."

Dixon was about to counter when a soldier who had been serving breakfast came up. "Colonel, we're closing up the chow line. I thought you'd like some hot coffee before we pack it away." Taking advantage of the offer, both Dixon and Vorishnov presented their cups to the soldier, who filled them well past the brims. Only the heavy gloves they wore to protect their hands from the bitter cold morning saved both officers from getting their hands burned by the steaming coffee.

As they waited for their fresh cups of black coffee to cool down, which didn't take long, Vorishnov mused, "You know, Colonel Dixon, I served as a staff officer at the Group of Forces, Central Group, here in Czechoslovakia, when it was Czechoslovakia."

"Yes, Colonel, I knew that. That is why I asked that you remain with my brigade. Who better to advise me and my staff on this operation than a man who planned to come crashing through the Cheb Gap just like we plan to."

Vorishnov looked over to Dixon. "I would like to point out, Colonel Dixon, that when I was at Central Group, I never remember coming across any plans that called for throwing an entire brigade across the Czech-German border strapped down on a train."

"Four trains, to be exact. That, Colonel, is my little innovation. Got the idea from studying the Korean War. On the first day of that war, one of the North Korean Army units took advantage of their complete surprise over the South Koreans. Just before dawn they replaced the section of tracks that had been torn up when the north and south separated and rolled right into their initial objective in rail cars."

Vorishnov held his left index finger up as he prepared to make his point. "Ah! Yes, that is important to remember."

Puzzled, Dixon looked at Vorishnov. "What is important?"

"The North Koreans. They didn't just board a train and roll into enemy territory. They prepared their way by laying tracks across the point where the rail line was broken." Vorishnov dropped his arm, taking a sip of coffee while he allowed Dixon to think for a minute.

"Well, Colonel, you have me. You, of course, know that the rail lines are intact. The Germans have not stopped civilian traffic. I doubt if they will, since this is still just an affair between the United States and Germany. So I don't get your point."

"You are quite right. There is no need to lay rail. But that does not mean that you cannot, as you say, grease the skids a little so that your command can slide into Germany just a little easier."

Dixon looked at Vorishnov as he tried to figure out what the Russian was up to. Finally he shrugged. "Obviously you have something in mind. I am, as the saying goes, all ears."

"There is, serving with one of your ranger companies, a Russian major who, while I was serving here in Czechoslovakia, commanded a Desant, or special purpose air-assault detachment in the Central Group. He speaks German fluently and is passable with his Czech. One of his tasks as a Desant detachment commander was to travel throughout southeastern Germany posing as a truck driver in order to learn all he could of the area in preparation for the day when he would lead his detachment there in advance of an invasion of Germany." Then, realizing what he had said, a sly smile lit Vorishnov's face as he quickly added, "If, of course, aggression by NATO had forced the peace-loving Soviet Union to launch such a counteroffensive."

Dixon grinned at Vorishnov's sudden backpedaling on the invasion issue. "Of course."

Continuing with his discussion, Vorishnov quickly got to the point. "This major, Major Nikolai Ilvanich, also happens to be in temporary command of the ranger company he is with. Given his experience as a commander of a Desant detachment, his knowledge of our proposed area of operation, and the group of elite soldiers in hand, I have little doubt that he could give your brigade the extra margin of safety that it will need to make this operation a reality. Besides, he and his company are being held at a hospital just north of here as if they were prisoners. I see no reason why we should not put them to good use."

Dixon, always one to take advantage of every opportunity to stack the odds in his favor, liked the idea. Before saying so, however, he asked Vorishnov if Ilvanich, a Russian, would risk his life in an American operation, leading American troops.

A smile came to Vorishnov's face. "When I was a student at the General Staff Academy, we had a tactics instructor who enjoyed a little joke now and then. One day he presented a tactical problem to our class. We were told to place ourselves in the role of a tank division commander who had broken through the main NATO defensive belts and was headed west to the Rhine River. Our problem was that two NATO divisions were being thrown against us, with a German armored division coming at our flank from the south and an American armored division advancing from the north. The instructor asked us to determine which threat we should deal with first, the German division or the American, and then explain our reasoning. A classmate of mine, a very clever if arrogant fellow, quickly finished weighing the pros and cons of both options. He stood up and announced that we must turn against the German division first. The tactics instructor, making a great show of it, pounded on his desk and yelled, 'No, no, no. You're wrong!' Shocked, and a little embarrassed, but determined to prove his point, my classmate started to enumerate the reasons for his decision. Again the instructor cut him off, yelling this time, 'The Americans, you must deal with the Americans, first and always.' Frustrated, my classmate finally blurted, 'But why? Why always the Americans? Why leave the Germans till later?' With a sly grin the instructor stated, 'That is obvious. As soldiers, we must always deal with business before pleasure.' "

Dixon chuckled. He had heard the same story, but with different nationalities, before.

Then suddenly Vorishnov's entire demeanor changed. When he spoke, his tone was cold and serious. "A resurgent Germany armed with nuclear weapons is something that Russia cannot live with. This fight which we are about to enter is not simply between the United States and Germany. It is a struggle to crush an evil thing in the womb, before it can endanger decency and humanity again."

Vorishnov's sober statement didn't need any further comment. After taking one last look around, Dixon turned to Vorishnov. "Well, the corps commander promised me anything that I wanted. Let's take a ride over to that hospital where they're holding your major hostage and see if he's interested in having some fun."

From his tank, Second Lieutenant Ellerbee watched his brigade commander and the Russian colonel climb into a humvee and drive away. As they did so, his heart sank. Ellerbee had been sitting there for the better part of an hour watching Colonel Dixon, trying to screw up enough courage to go over and protest the manner in which he and his platoon were being treated by Captain Kozak. But just as he was about to, just when he had built up enough gumption, Ellerbee talked himself out of it. No, he reasoned, odds were, if he did, the colonel would ignore him. Or, Ellerbee told himself, Colonel Dixon would tell him that, based on his personal performance in the Ukraine, he deserved it, or that Kozak, as the commander, could run her company as she saw fit. No, he convinced himself, it would be futile to complain.

Then, when he had given up, Ellerbee saw Dixon looking right at him. Maybe, just maybe, Ellerbee thought, the colonel would recognize him, come over, and ask him how things were going with his platoon. Now, Ellerbee reasoned, if the colonel asked, then it would be all right to complain. Then it wouldn't sound like sour grapes or simple bitching. He had been told once that so long as the senior officer asked, it was okay to give an honest answer. Ellerbee had no sooner psyched himself up when a soldier who had been serving breakfast to the company came up and offered the two colonels some more coffee. Dixon turned his head away from Ellerbee, accepted the coffee, and continued his conversation with the Russian colonel.

Ellerbee was still sitting on top of his tank bemoaning his fate and freezing when Dixon and Vorishnov drove off. Sighing, Ellerbee quietly resigned himself to his fate. He would be stuck there, serving under an airhead female captain who treated the male soldiers in her command like trash during an operation that had about as much chance of succeeding as a snowball's chance in hell. This was not, Ellerbee thought, what he had joined the Army for. This was nothing but horseshit, pure and unadulterated horseshit.

Having completed his morning inspection of his now widely dispersed company, Captain Seydlitz was about to settle down to enjoy the wurst and roll he had picked up in a town along his route when his battalion commander's vehicle came into sight. Quickly stuffing the food back into its bag and dumping it behind the seat of his small open-air Volkswagen jeep, Seydlitz prepared to greet his commander. How fortunate, he thought, his timing had been. It was good that he had inspected the company before the battalion commander arrived to conduct one of his notorious unannounced inspections. Of course, there was always the possibility that his platoon leaders and tank commanders had failed to correct the deficiencies that Seydlitz had discovered in his own inspection. Not that it mattered to him, for as long as he had done his duty as an officer and troop commander, he could not be faulted.

When the battalion commander's vehicle stopped, the commander didn't bother to get out before he started talking to Seydlitz. "You have one hour to prepare to move your company, Captain." Elated over his battalion commander's announcement, Seydlitz reached down and grabbed his map case on the seat of his jeep before hurrying over to his commander's vehicle. Giving Seydlitz time to open his map before he began to rattle off his orders, the battalion commander looked about. "Can you be ready in an hour?"

Seydlitz, glad to be able to do something to break up the dull routine of dry fire drills and inspections, all but shouted out in great enthusiasm, "If necessary, Herr Oberst, we will be ready in five minutes."

The battalion commander's response sounded more like a warning than encouragement. "You wouldn't be so excited if you understood the magnitude of the mess our fearless Chancellor in Berlin has created."

Standing before his commander, Seydlitz stared at him, wondering what exactly his commander was talking about. Seeing the puzzled look on his subordinate's face, the battalion commander, as a way of venting his own frustration and at the same time informing him what was in store for their commands, began telling Seydlitz everything that he knew at that moment. "We will assemble the battalion here," he said, pointing at a spot northeast of Marktredwitz on the map Seydlitz held. "From there we will move to an assembly area southeast of Chemnitz via the E51 and E441 autobahns. By the time we arrive there, the brigade commander expects to be in receipt of further orders that will tell us where we go from there and what will be expected of us."

The battalion commander paused before he explained these new orders to his attentive but bewildered company commander. "It seems that despite what the American President is saying, and the moves by American units left here in Germany appear to support her position, the Americans in the Czech Republic are massing on the Czech border south of Chemnitz and Dresden. There exists, according to Army intelligence, the very real danger of a move by the American corps into Germany aimed at recovering the nuclear devices we seized from them."

Seydlitz thought about that for a moment before he asked the question that had been bothering every German officer, from General Lange right down to Seydlitz's battalion commander. "And what, Herr Oberst, are we expected to do if the Americans do make such an effort?"

He did not get an immediate answer. Instead, the battalion commander pondered the question himself. When he and the commander of the other active duty battalion had met with their brigade commander earlier that morning to receive their orders for the pending move, that very question had been debated for over half an hour. After years of working hand in hand with the American Army, the very idea of suddenly turning on them was a shock. While the division order pointed out several times that it was their duty to defend Germany against any and all invaders, there was a very real question as to whether the Americans, a member of NATO with basing rights in Germany, would really be invading Germany or simply be violating their status of forces agreements, agreements signed by both nations that governed the stationing of forces in Germany that were still technically in effect. The brigade commander, only half jokingly, commented that if the Americans came forward in road march columns and not in battle formation, then this would be a simple matter for the police. "In that case," he blandly stated, "all the police will need to do is arrest the senior commander for conducting a road march without permission or proper documentation." Such attempts to make light of their moral dilemma, however, did not answer their question. Finally the brigade commander ended the session by stating that it could come down to each commander doing what he believed was morally correct given the situation he found himself in. To this he added a warning. "Until that time comes, if it ever does, we will carry out our orders."

Seeing that his commander was lost in his own thoughts and that no answer was forthcoming, Seydlitz came to attention. "Will that be all for now, Herr Oberst?"

Looking up with sad eyes, the battalion commander shook his head. Then, as an afterthought, he added, "Be prepared for long delays and no resupply once we get started. For the first time since the last war, the German Army will have two corps and six divisions, with all attached and supporting active duty units, in motion at once, and all headed in the same direction. Added to that we may see reserve units, provided the Chancellor is given his wish and the permission to activate them, scrambling to join up with their parent brigade. And," the battalion commander added with a flourish, "just to make this whole affair more challenging, American logistical and support units that were left in Germany are already on the road. They will be converging on the Grafenwöhr and Hohenfels training areas from all over southern Germany in preparation for storing their equipment and leaving Germany per the Chancellor's demands."

Unable to think much beyond the scope of his own thirteen Leopard II tanks, Seydlitz could not imagine why, given Germany's excellent road system, such movements should be a problem. No doubt, he thought, his commander was simply exaggerating. Then another thought came to mind. "Who, Herr Oberst, will replace us here at this border? If we leave here, the Americans will be free to slip into Bavaria."

Looking at Seydlitz for a moment, the battalion commander shook his head. "That, Captain, is highly unlikely. If the Americans intend to march to the sea for ports of embarkation, or try for the nuclear devices as the General Staff suspects, they would be taking the long way around by going through here. Everything points to an effort to break out of the Czech mountains onto the North German Plain where there is room to maneuver, and then to the sea. Besides, by marching through Bavaria, the Americans would never come close to the storage sites west of Berlin where the nuclear devices are. But," he added, "just in case, the 1st Mountain Division will be deploying north from the Austrian border to replace us, although their primary mission will be to keep the American units assembling at Grafenwöhr and Hohenfels from slipping across the border to join the Americans already in the Czech Republic."

Visualizing a map of Germany in his mind and considering the logic of what his commander had told him, everything made sense to Seydlitz. Though the 1st Mountain Division lacked the ability to stand up to a mechanized force, it would have more than enough to contain the American support units assembling in Grafenwöhr and Hohenfels. Satisfied, he pointed out that one of his platoons manning a roadblock ten kilometers from where they stood was out of radio contact due to a mountain that blocked radio transmissions. Since he would have to drive over to that platoon's location to contact it, and he had less than an hour to get moving, Seydlitz asked his battalion commander if he was finished with him.

Unable to provide his subordinate any further information or guidance, the battalion commander told him no, there was nothing else, and left. Seydlitz, like thousands of junior officers like him, began to set into motion the German Army's great leap into a nebulous situation, unsure of itself, its role, and, most importantly, where its duty and loyalty truly lay.

13 JANUARY

With the babble of the World News Network early-morning report providing background noise, Ed Lewis and his chief assistant sat down to go over Lewis's schedule for the day. Neither man paid much attention to the news commentator until he announced that they were cutting over to the White House, where the President's press secretary was about to hold a short press conference. For the first time, Lewis acknowledged that the television was on, asking his assistant to turn the volume up. As he did so, Lewis settled back in his seat, propped his feet up on his desk, and prepared to listen to the latest official statement from the White House.

The prepared text was, as usual during such situations, rather bland and contained few specifics. In a nutshell, all it announced was that President Wilson had ordered the immediate withdrawal of non-essential American military personnel and their dependents from Germany. Dependents, alerted the day before, were already flooding into points of embarkation. The Army and Air Force support units still in Germany that had not participated in the Czech operation had begun to concentrate at the Grafenwöhr and Hohenfels training areas, where they were, according to the presidential spokesman, to prepare their equipment for temporary storage. Lewis, of course, already knew all about these actions. What he was waiting for was the question-and-answer session. Only then would he be able to gauge how well Big Al's movements and his grand deception plan were succeeding.

The news correspondents in the White House briefing room didn't waste any time. The CBS White House correspondent was on his feet firing away before the President's press secretary could acknowledge him. "There are reports from Reuters this morning that the American forces in the Czech and Slovak republics, rather than preparing to stand down to a lower state of readiness, are in fact massing on the Czech border south of Berlin. The Reuters report claims Chancellor Ruff and his government view these moves as both threatening and provocative. The German Army, according to the report, is redeploying forces to counter this threat. How do you explain this in light of what you just stated?"

The press secretary shuffled his notes before looking down at the CBS correspondent. "I am sure you are well aware that tensions are quite high over there. I have no doubt that the Germans are overreacting to harmless moves. No doubt the forces that this news story, which I have not seen, is talking about are those that were involved in the Ukrainian operation and are simply completing their withdrawal from that country."

The CBS correspondent, as well as most of the other reporters and correspondents in the room, wasn't satisfied with this explanation. Pressing his point, the CBS correspondent countered. "While what you say may be true, why would those forces be shifted all the way to the German border and not around Prague or Pizen where the rest of the Tenth Corps was deployed? And what of the reports from Prague yesterday of massive movement of American forces out of that city headed north?"

The presidential press secretary was now beginning to become visibly uncomfortable. "I am sorry, but those are questions best asked of the Pentagon. We do not keep track of every unit here. Now if we could continue."

The press secretary pointed to a reporter from the *Washington Post*, who jumped up and hammered him. "If, as you say, the President is in fact meeting all the demands of the German Chancellor, how do you explain the news story being aired by WNN this morning of Chancellor Ruff's public statement that the movement of American forces is designed to threaten Germany and is not, as President Wilson's statement claims, meant to defuse the situation?"

The frustrations of the presidential press secretary were obvious as he grasped the podium with both hands and glared at the *Washington Post* reporter for several seconds before even attempting to answer his question. Satisfied that all was beginning to unravel as they—Wilson, Big Al, and he—had hoped, Lewis told his assistant to turn the television off before they continued.

This request struck Lewis's assistant as strange. Lewis, a confirmed news junkie, always had someone, if he couldn't, listening to the WNN channel. It was therefore strange that he should give up watching such an important White House briefing. Perhaps, he thought, Lewis had simply given up on this situation. Maybe he was disgusted and didn't want to hear any more for fear it would only upset him. That theory, however, was shot when the assistant, after getting up and turning the television off, turned around and saw Lewis roll a pair of dice across the blotter on his desk. When the two cubes stopped rolling, he looked at the results and mumbled, "Not good. Hope Big Al has better luck." Then, with a smile, he looked up at his assistant as he scooped the two dice up and dropped them in the top drawer of his desk. "Well, let's get back to the schedule."

They had just begun to do so again when the buzzer on his phone interrupted. Without waiting, Lewis mashed down the button that was blinking and picked up the receiver, almost as if he had been expecting the call. From where he sat, Lewis's assistant listened to the one-sided conversation in an effort to determine whom it was with and what it was about.

"Yes, Abby, I saw him . . . Yes, he did good. . . . No, I don't think there's anything more that needs to be said at this time. The ball's in Big Al's court and it's almost time for him to serve. . . . Yes, I'm packed and ready. I can be over there in half an hour and go straight to Andrews as soon as we're finished. . . . No, I haven't had any second thoughts about this. I was already well past that yesterday and working on third and fourth thoughts. . . . Okay, if there's nothing else, I'll unplug from here and beat feet to the White House. . . . Yeah. Okay, good-bye, Madam President."

Replacing the receiver, Lewis looked at his assistant. He had the faint trace of a self-satisfied smile on his face. "Frank, cancel all appointments for the rest of the day, tomorrow, and the next day. I'm headed back to Berlin. Please tell Mary on your way out to call my wife and put her through as soon as she's on line."

Without any further discussion, Lewis leaned back in his seat while his assistant got up to leave. The last thing he heard before he closed the door to Lewis's office was the faint noise of two dice rolling across the blotter on Lewis's desk.

14 JANUARY

After spending eighteen hours bundled up in the back of an unheated truck with six other nurses and half a ton of assorted equipment, traveling the length and breadth of the Czech Republic, Hilary Cole expected to find more than an open snow-covered field at the end of their ordeal. She had been hoping they would find some kind of reception station or facilities. But there were none. The advance party that had been sent out six hours ahead of the main body, she found out as she danced around in the snow trying to hold the contents of her bladder just a little longer, had been there and left. Not only was nothing set up and ready for them, that news meant that they were going to need to load back up into the rear of a truck that offered all the creature comforts of a shipping crate and continue their long odyssey through the cold, dark winter night with no idea of where they were going or when they would get there.

Though she didn't really understand what was going on in Washington and Berlin, Hilary Cole knew that things were badly screwed up and no one seemed to know what was going to happen next. Though she understood all too well that the political games being played out between her government and the Germans controlled her future, as well as the future of every man and woman in the 553rd Field Hospital, they were of little concern to her at that moment. What was foremost on her mind was finding someplace where she could find some privacy, for she knew if she did not relieve herself soon it would come gushing out of its own accord. And that, she knew, would only make the miserable conditions she had no choice but to tolerate even worse.

Looking about in the dark, Cole saw nothing that even remotely resembled a building or structure. As she held her arms close to her chest, half trying to protect herself from the bitter cold wind that cut through her like a knife, a voice from somewhere in the dark shouted for everyone to mount up and prepare to move. "No!" she shouted. "They can't be serious. They can't."

Another nurse next to Cole gave out a soft, low whine. "Oh, Hilly, they've got to be kidding. I can't take another hour in the back of this damned truck. Can't we just . . ."—she looked about—"well, can't we just stay here and rest? They *have* to let us stop somewhere and rest, don't they?"

As the sound of truck engines coming to life began to spread down the column, Cole realized that there would be no rest, at least not here and not now. Though she was hard pressed to conceal her own disappointment, Cole did her best to comfort her friend. "Look, Pat, if this next little jaunt down the road gets us closer to Germany and out of this miserable country, I'm all for it. Besides," Cole continued, spreading out her arms and turning to her left and right, "there isn't a decent place within miles. That truck may be miserable, but at least it's headed in the right direction."

Slumping over and holding her arms tightly across her chest, Pat began to move to the truck. "Personally, I think it's a great idea to go home. The only thing I can't understand is why do they need to make it so damned uncomfortable for us while we're doing so."

Cole sighed. "Because, dear, this is the Army. You know, where every day is an adventure?"

"Well, Hilary, would you make sure that our next adventure is someplace where the sun shines and it never snows?"

Cole, though still dejected and cold, couldn't help but laugh. "Sure, Pat, sure. I'll be sure to tell the colonel that as soon as I see him. Now get those hips in motion, girl, and climb back on up. I got a feeling this is going to be a long night."

If Big Al was nervous and uneasy about what he was about to do, Ed Lewis saw no sign of it when they greeted each other in Big Al's office. If anything, Big Al was as jovial as ever. "So, how're the boys in Berlin taking the news?"

Lewis, caught up in Big Al's cheerful, easygoing mood, smiled and shook Big Al's hand. "They're hoppin' mad. Fortunately for us right now, they really don't know which way to hop."

Still holding Lewis's hand, Big Al looked into Lewis's eyes. "Then, I take it, they're buying the renegade general story."

With a satisfied smile, Lewis nodded. "Hook, line, and sinker. Right now I imagine Ruff and the German General Staff are in the throes of playing a thousand and one 'what if' drills. Ruff's last words to me as I left were 'If your President can't control her generals, the German Army can.' "

Letting go of Lewis's hand, Big Al motioned Lewis to take a seat. "Then all I need is some bad weather, and away we go."

Taking his seat, Lewis responded with a note of satisfaction, "And if the forecast holds, you'll have that tomorrow night. Light snow, overcast, and near zero illumination." Then as an afterthought, Lewis asked, a bit worried, "Will Dixon and his Trojan horse be ready?"

Nodding, Big Al smiled. "Congressman, we're loaded, locked, and cocked. All I need to do is say 'bang,' and we're gone." Then it was Big Al's turn to get serious. "Tell me, how are things on the streets of Berlin? What's the German public reaction to all of this?"

Leaning forward in his seat, Lewis placed his elbows on his knees and clasped his hands together. "As you know, the German Parliament is in an uproar. Between their debates on the wisdom of keeping the nukes and demands by the left that they, the Parliament, assert their authority in an effort to curb Chancellor Ruff, the members of Parliament have been unable to agree on any solutions to any of the problems Ruff has presented them. Though I believe most Germans will support some kind of action against our violation of German national integrity, many feel that Ruff's actions and demands are a little too extreme and provocative. That's why the Parliament is try-ing to block Ruff's call-up of the reserve units. They feel that if they can reduce his military options, he will be forced to enter into serious negotiations."

"And what," Big Al asked, "are the chances of that?"

Lewis simply shook his head. "This whole thing has now become a great power struggle for Ruff, both an international contest as well an internal one. All of Germany, including the Bundeswehr according to our military liaison officer in Berlin, is torn right down the middle. As the specter of armed conflict becomes more and more a possibility, the debates, public and private, are becoming more and more heated. Only in the eastern part of the country is there a clear consensus in favor of Ruff."

This statement caused Big Al to slap his knee. "Dixon was right. Damned if he didn't call that one right on the money. I just hope the German intelligence chief isn't as devious as Dixon."

Lewis looked at the general for a moment, wondering what he was talking about. Seeing Lewis's look, Big Al explained. "Eastern Ger-many was of course for years communist. Since the late 1940s the people have been raised to hate the United States and Americans. Old Scotty pointed out that while a run through eastern Germany would be the shortest route to the sea, militarily and logistically sound, it would be right through the middle of a population whose sympathy would be, at best, questionable. In Bavaria and central Germany, where American forces were stationed for years, we would find greater support from the people. They, after all, are used to us. Our pledge to pay for all damage to personal property and our calls for noninterfer-ence will be more credible there than they would be in what used to be East Germany."

"That," Lewis said, "makes sense and follows what the CIA chief in Berlin told me. It appears that the government officials and parlia-mentarian representatives of the southern states, especially Bavaria, are openly criticizing what they call Berlin's dangerous provocations.

This division seems to be reflected, though somewhat muted, within the Bundeswehr itself."

"I'm counting on that, Congressman. The muddier we can keep the international and internal waters, the better our chances."

Interrupting, Lewis held his hand up. "There's one thing that puzzled both the CIA chief in Berlin and me. How, exactly, General, did you manage to get the Poles involved in your deception plan?"

This brought a big smile to Big Al's face. "Long story. You see, my grandfather was a Polish immigrant by the name of Malinoski, Stanislaw Malinoski. When he came to America at the turn of the century, he quickly discovered that in order to get ahead in America you needed to be a citizen and have an Anglicized name. He figured that if he joined the Army, which was then looking for a few good men to fight in the Philippines, using the name Stanley Malin, he could get both. Well, he did, as well as a career. When he came back, he was a sergeant, earning a comfortable living and having prestige that his fellow Polish immigrants didn't have. So he stayed in the Army, married, raised two sons, and started a military tradition. One son, my father, went to West Point and graduated in time for World War II. Between World War II and Korea, he had me, who followed his footsteps."

Lost, Lewis just nodded.

"When the American embassy held its New Year's Day reception, I met the Polish ambassador. After telling him this story, he embraced me like a long lost brother and invited me to the Polish embassy to join him for lunch whenever it was convenient. Knowing that German intelligence would be watching me like a hawk, I decided to take the ambassador up on his offer the other day. It appears that the Germans followed. But"—holding up a finger and with a smile on his face, Big Al added—"just in case they missed that, I invited the Polish military liaison officer out here to join me for dinner that night and to tour my headquarters."

Settling back into his chair, Lewis shook his head in disbelief. "And you moved some units to Liberec, near the Polish border, just to make sure the Germans drew the right conclusions."

Big Al chuckled. "It worked, didn't it? Thinking that there was the possibility of an end run through Poland, the Germans were obliged to deploy three of their divisions on the Polish border, in part to block a threat that isn't there and in part to threaten the Poles if they allowed us to do so. This threat has caused the Poles to increase their state of readiness and send several of their divisions to the border. Now, even if the Germans find out they've been duped, they cannot pull those divisions away from the border so long as the Polish divisions are deployed."

"So," Lewis summarized, "you've eliminated several German divisions before you've even crossed the border."

"I hope so, Congressman. With three divisions on the Polish border, three divisions facing my fake deployment areas in the northern Czech Republic, one tied up with the French-German multinational corps, and one in northern Germany watching for the Marine Corps to come storming ashore, that leaves only one heavy division in reserve around Berlin and their airborne division free for immediate redeployment. The mountain division facing us to the west is more concerned with keeping an eye on the logistical units in Grafenwöhr and Hohenfels than watching the Czech border. With any luck, by the time they realize that we're going west through Bavaria and not interested in slipping the units in Germany east, it will be too late for them to establish effective blocking positions in Bavaria."

There was a pause as each man began to consider the next step. Those thoughts washed away the enthusiasm that they felt over the success of their maneuvers and manipulations to date. Finally Big Al spoke. "Will the President stay the course?"

"She is, General, committed. Like you and me, she understands what is at stake here and is willing to sacrifice her career, come what may."

That statement caused Big Al to grunt. "That's awfully big of her, considering that I've asked the people under my command to risk their lives in an enterprise that none of them understand and that I can't fully explain to them. I just hope that we can keep them together when the going gets tough. I have already ordered commanders to leave behind anyone whom they suspect won't be able to make it, physically or mentally. Besides some three hundred plus pregnant soldiers, I have over a thousand single parents and a couple thousand non-essential personnel staying in the Czech Republic. They'll be flown out via Austria and Italy once we get started. Still, a lot of good soldiers who start the march aren't going to make it to Bremerhaven."

"Will they follow you, I mean once they find out that you've been labeled a renegade and are, at least as far as the general public is concerned, acting on your own and against the announced wishes of the President?"

"I can safely say," Big Al said with an air of confidence, "that I have more confidence in the reliability of my soldiers than Chancellor Ruff has in his. To hedge my bets, I will maintain for as long as possible the Armed Forces Radio Network in order to feed my soldiers the information I want them to hear as well as to give the Germans public service announcements. The German public will no doubt use AFN to check the line their own government is handing them. I am, in fact, counting on it." There was a pause. Then he added almost as an afterthought, "Besides, once the shooting starts, it won't matter what anyone believes. By that time, we'll be deep in the heart of Germany and every man and woman in this command who's still with us will realize that their own road to salvation will be to stay with their unit and follow orders."

Lewis thought about that for a moment. "That, General, is rather cynical and manipulative, isn't it?"

"War, Congressman, always has been and always will be cynical and manipulative in the extreme. Cynical old men, too old and frail to wield the sword or pull the trigger themselves, have for centuries labored to manipulate the strong, young, and brave to do it for them, using some damned excuse or another. In that regard, I'm no better than Herr Chancellor Ruff. He has something against the United States and he's using his Army and his people to get back at us. I just hope that when Herr Ruff and I meet our maker, he, and not I, gets to join Hitler for eternity."

Lewis suddenly became quite solemn. "Have you ever thought, General Malin, that perhaps Herr Ruff is hoping for the same thing?"

MALIN'S MARCH TO THE SEA

CHAPTER 10

15 JANUARY

For over three hours, ever since the last of the mess trucks packed up and left, the company commanders of 3rd of the 3rd Mechanized Infantry Battalion had remained gathered about their battalion commander's humvee waiting. Except for them, the small train station bathed in a sickly dull blue light was abandoned. On the track beside them a train that disappeared in the darkness to the southwest, loaded with their combat vehicles, also sat waiting. Inside each of those vehicles strapped down on the train's numerous flatcars were the crews, who, like their commanders, sat huddled together in silence as they tried to protect themselves from the cold and boredom of waiting.

All good topics of conversation had been exhausted well before their last hot meal for many days was over, leaving the assembled groups of combat leaders with nothing of value to discuss. All the orders for the forthcoming operation had been issued. Rehearsals at every level, from battalion down to platoon, had been completed. Concerns had been aired and addressed. Pre-combat checks and inspections had been completed. Pep talks and the few final cheering words that the leaders could manage had been said. Now there was only waiting. Each commander, lost in his or her own thoughts, stood ready like a great jack-in-the-box ready to spring into action as soon as one word, like the latch on the lid, was released.

Standing next to a wooden lamppost at the railroad crossing where her commander's humvee sat, its silent radio waiting to blare out their final order to move, Captain Nancy Kozak pulled out the copy of the message that their corps commander had ordered all commanders, down to company, to read before their assembled units. As befitted Lieutenant General Malin, the corps commander, the message was to the point. In the faint light, Kozak reread the message dated January 14th.

Circumstances have placed this command in a difficult position. As you know, a nation that we had until very recently counted as one of our best allies has created an international crisis in which we, the Tenth Corps, are being treated as expendable pawns. The leaders of that nation, men who are no better than their Nazi forefathers, have seen fit to hold us, the Tenth Corps, collectively guilty for the errors and policies of our elected officials, officials who have seen fit to capitulate to the demands of the Nazi leadership in Berlin.

Although I am pledged to obey the orders of the superiors appointed over me in accordance with the Constitution, the oath of my commission also requires me to defend that very same Constitution from all enemies, foreign and domestic. After very careful consideration, I cannot view the surrender of this corps to the Germans as anything but detrimental to the maintenance of long-term peace and stability for the United States and Europe.

I therefore have decided to disregard the President's order to lay down our arms and allow Nazi aggression once again to threaten the world peace. Instead, I propose to march this command from the Czech Republic, through Nazi territory and to the coast, where I will deliver this corps, with all its equipment and personnel, into the hands of my superiors as an effective and combat-ready force.

I must underscore that my choice, my view, may not be shared by many of you. I am, after all, disobeying the orders of the President of the United States. I cannot ask you to blindly follow suit. Each of you, from division commander down to rifleman, must choose on his or her own. I cannot promise you success. I cannot promise you that you will be hailed as a conquering hero when we return to the United States. We may, in fact, be treated as criminals. Possible death and deprivation waits for us along our route of march. What I can promise you is that we will stand up to Nazi aggression, as our fathers and grandfathers did in

*World War II. If you go forward, with me, we go forward as
soldiers, masters of our own fates, ready to uphold our honor as
American soldiers and free men.*

*Those of you who in the depth of your hearts cannot bring
yourselves to commit to this enterprise are free to remain in the
Czech Republic, where you will be disarmed and returned to the
United States. I, and every member of this command, will respect your decision. You, like me, must determine where your
true duty lies.*

*I remind those of you who stay with the colors of what Captain
Charles May told his troopers of the 2nd Dragoons before they
charged Mexican positions at the Battle of Resaca de la Palma in
1846: "Remember your regiment and follow your officers." Together, with the help of God and the skill and determination that
have made the American soldier the most effective soldier in the
world, we will not only see this through but will serve notice to
the world that the United States is, and shall remain, a force to
be reckoned with. God bless you all.*

> *A. M. Malin*
> *Lieutenant General, U.S.A.*
> *Commanding*

The address to the corps was, Kozak thought, well thought out and
had had the desired effect on her company. Not a single soldier had
stepped forward to ask to be left behind. She had, when she had read
the message and after, taken every opportunity to ensure that no one
was being coerced through peer pressure or pride to do something that
they did not want to do. Though she knew that those forces were in
effect generally, Kozak was able to convince herself that the members
of her tiny command were there that night of their own free accord.
For that she was thankful.

Stuffing the piece of paper back in her pocket, where eventually it
would be forgotten and slowly destroyed as other items were shoved
in on top of it, Kozak folded her arms tightly across her chest as if she
were struggling to keep whatever warmth she had left from escaping.
The light snow that had begun to fall during their meal was becoming
heavier. While this, she knew, would cover their move into Germany
and give them the best chance to roll through the German countryside

to their point of debarkation without detection, it had its drawbacks. The wheeled vehicles of the battalion's field trains, moving by road after the border posts had been cleared, would have to negotiate the treacherous mountain roads made worse by the same fresh snow that would cloak the entry of the combat vehicles. And the follow-on forces, as well as the rest of the Tenth Corps sitting lined up and ready to move in fields and along the sides of roads, would have to deal with the foul weather that would hinder them as much as it aided Kozak's company. The whole operation, Kozak imagined, was like one of those giant domino contests run to see how many dominoes you could line up and then knock down with a single push. This operation, she knew, like the domino contest, depended on detailed planning and at times incredible luck. One domino out of place or falling wrong would stop the whole process.

Looking about her, Nancy Kozak suddenly got the feeling that she was alone. Standing there in the bitter night, every sound muffled by the falling snow, the world seemed to be at rest and asleep, not waiting to leap forward into battle. That leap, she knew, would come. What it would mean to her and her command, however, was beyond her comprehension. The whole enterprise was from beginning to end crowded with unknowns. Would they be able to make it through the mountains to their designated blocking positions and unload their vehicles unhindered? Would the Germans resist, and if so, how? How would her soldiers react to that resistance? How would she react?

While Kozak waited and wondered, eighty miles to the southwest, in a break in the mountains known as the Cheb Gap, Major Ilvanich and the rangers of Company A, 1st Ranger Battalion, 77th Infantry, were about to push over the domino of Big Al's gamble.

The sudden appearance of the Czech border patrol lieutenant and his two soldiers at the door of the German customs office didn't surprise the German customs sergeant. The German sergeant glanced up at the clock on the wall. Noting that it was just before midnight, he shrugged his shoulders and prepared to greet the Czechs. It was not unheard of for the men who patrolled the borders of their nations to pay social calls on each other while making their rounds, especially on nights like this. Looking up from his desk when the door flew open, allowing a flurry of snow and a blast of cold air to sweep into the building, the customs sergeant smiled and nodded at the Czech officer before shouting for the senior German Army sergeant on duty. The senior German Army sergeant, who had been enjoying the warmth of the back room with his squad where they had been watching television, threw his legs over the side of his cot onto the floor, pulled his uniform shirt on, and sauntered on out into the outer office.

The Czech officer, after shaking loose snowflakes from his uniform and stomping his boots just inside the door on a thin mat, came forward toward the long counter where the German customs sergeant sat. The sergeant, with a sweep of his right hand, invited the Czech officer to take a seat near the heater behind the counter. There they were joined by the senior German Army sergeant. Neither German paid any attention to the Czech border patrolmen who remained just inside the door where they unslung their rifles and checked the actions of their rifles to ensure they were not frozen. The sound of sliding rifle bolts caused no concern, for men coming in from the cold and snow were expected to check their weapons for operation. The Czech officer, taking a seat before them, held his hat in his lap over his hands, as if to warm them up faster. This didn't cause the Germans any concern who were more interested in warming themselves than watching their guests. Since the American operations in the Czech Republic had become a matter of international concern, both nations had reinforced their mutual borders. To ensure that things did not get out of hand, officials of both nations encouraged their people patrolling the border to maintain close and cordial contact during the period of crisis.

After allowing several seconds for the Czech lieutenant to open the conversation, the German Army sergeant finally spoke. "We were just getting ready to go out ourselves and follow the border trace for a while when you came in, Herr Lieutenant." The Czech lieutenant glanced into the back room where the soldiers of the sergeant's squad sat, stripped down to their T-shirts and lying about on cots or lounging on chairs watching the television. If they had been preparing for a patrol, they had the strangest pre-combat drill he, Major Nikolai Ilvanich, had ever seen. Still he said nothing about that, only grunting and nodding as the German sergeant continued. "I suppose that you have been out and around walking the trace itself. Perhaps, Lieutenant, you could show me where you were and we could coordinate our patrolling efforts?"

Ilvanich smiled, for he knew what the German Army sergeant really was after. If by chance the German sergeant found that the area he was responsible for had already been patrolled by the Czechs, he and his men wouldn't need to go out into the cold. The German sergeant could, in all good conscience, report to his lieutenant that the area was secured. It wasn't that the sergeant was being lazy or lax about his duties. It was just that he was being efficient. Ilvanich knew, as a soldier does, that it would be foolish to duplicate efforts. Although his German was impeccable, Ilvanich allowed some of his Russian accent to muffle his words, trusting that it would disarm the Germans further and that they wouldn't be able to tell the difference between German spoken with a Slovakian accent and German spoken with a Russian accent. "Let me see, please, your operations map, and I will show you where it was that we have just come from."

Happy that the Czech officer was more than willing to go along with his suggestion, the German Army sergeant got up and went into the back room to retrieve his map from his cot while the customs sergeant went to get Ilvanich a cup of coffee. Looking over toward the door, where his two companions still waited, Ilvanich gave Sergeant Allen Rasper and Specialist Kevin Pape a slight nod and smile. Both men, sweating as much from nervous anticipation as from the heat of the Czech Army overcoats that covered their own uniforms, returned Ilvanich's nod and waited for him to make his move.

"We have been," the German Army sergeant said, beaming as he returned with his map, "most anxious about how thin we are along the border." Plopping the map down on Ilvanich's lap, the German began to point out the location of the outposts his company had established along the German-Czech border. "The panzer and panzer-grenadier units were gone before we even got here. They're all up north around Chemnitz or Dresden. Our division is stuck here in a paper-thin outpost line trying to cover almost two hundred kilometers of frontier with lightly armed mountain troops. So, Herr Lieutenant, it is important that we cooperate whenever possible, in order to make best use of our men."

Looking back at the soldiers lounging about in the back room, weapons lined up against the wall without any magazines in them, Ilvanich felt both satisfaction and disgust. While he was pleased that the Germans were so unprepared and were at that moment giving him the disposition of their forces in the local area, he was upset that this sergeant was, through his lack of vigilance, endangering his men. While he and his fellow Russian officers knew that German soldiers were in all probability no better and no worse, man for man, than their own, the German military system had always held a mystique, an aura of evil efficiency that caused them great concern. To see it now close up and personal for the first time, in this light, made Ilvanich begin to wonder if through all these years his superiors had not been guilty of overstating the prowess of the enemy. While it was probably true, Ilvanich pushed that strange thought from his mind and began to listen intently while the German Army sergeant pointed out the clearly marked military symbols that represented the fighting positions as well as the outposts and patrol routes of the German Army company responsible for the Cheb Gap roadblock. The German sergeant, with a note of concern in his voice, ended by stating that except for his company covering the entire Gap and beyond, there wasn't an organized combat unit between where they sat and Nuremberg.

Taking the map and sticking it under his left arm, Ilvanich began to stand up. As he did so, his wool cap fell to the floor, exposing the 9mm pistol in his right hand. Noticing that the hammer of the pistol pointed at them was cocked back, the two German sergeants rose. First one, then the other, glanced at the two Czech soldiers who had been left standing at the door. Both had, while the Army sergeant was briefing Ilvanich, moved up to the counter. They now stood there, rifles raised and ready, staring at the German sergeants. Switching to his best High German, Ilvanich calmly began to issue his orders. "Now, if neither one of you gets excited, you and all your men will live to see the dawn. First, Sergeant, you need to assemble your squad out here without their weapons, where my sergeant can watch them. Then we need to call your platoon leader and company commander and convince them to join us here. Please, when you do so, be discreet, for although I really do not want to see you or any of your men dead, my American ranger friends here are quite upset about what your Chancellor has been saying and doing lately. Neither of them cares about your personal well-being like I do. They would, as the Americans are so fond of saying, just as soon shoot you where you stand as look at you."

When he was satisfied that the German Army sergeant understood, Ilvanich turned to the customs sergeant. "And as soon as my trusted American deputy arrives, a young lieutenant eager to practice his soldierly skills and not particularly concerned whom he practices them on, you and I will go to the station control room and begin to make some changes in the routing of rail traffic. This is going to be, I'm afraid, a much longer night than either of you expected."

Though he could see that both sergeants were quite angry, as much about the playful manner in which he was treating them as about the situation, Ilvanich could also see that they were confused and unsure. So long as he kept them that way, he and the rest of his American ranger company would have the advantage and, with just a little luck, be able to pry open the door into Germany for the rest of the corps.

16 JANUARY

Used to the night shift in the small town of Pegnitz, located in southern Germany, police Sergeant Julius Reusch found no difficulty staying awake and occupied. His silent companion, Ernst Ohlendorf, recently shifted from day duty, however, had long ago given up trying to entertain himself and had drifted off to sleep. Slouched in a seat opposite Reusch, Ohlendorf was hardly disturbed by Reusch's walking back and forth from his desk to the metal files as he sorted reports and documents that the day and evening shifts had not had time to file. Even when his lieutenant came in, flipping on the bright overhead lights, and told Reusch that he and Ohlendorf needed to go down to the rail yard and check out a report from an old woman that tanks were moving about down there, Ohlendorf didn't budge.

After a great deal of effort, Reusch managed to get Ohlendorf moving, though barely. Every move, every exertion by Ohlendorf, still half asleep, seemed to be in slow motion. Reusch, accustomed to the difficulties that even young men had when shifting from day to night duty, was patient with Ohlendorf. They had time. The lieutenant hadn't seemed terribly concerned with the old woman's complaint. She had made the same complaint when the American Army had moved into the Czech Republic the previous December, and when the German armored units deployed along the Czech border had suddenly been shifted north several days ago. No doubt, Reusch's lieutenant had been right when he offhandedly commented that some brilliant military strategist in Berlin had made the startling discovery that the Czech border faced Bavaria as well as Berlin and that it might be a good idea to keep someone there as well. It would be, Reusch thought, just like the Army to hustle troops north in a great panic and then hustle them right back where they started from. While he checked Ohlendorf to ensure he had his uniform on right, pistol belt on, and hat straight before stepping out into the bitter cold, Reusch felt like an undertaker preparing a corpse. Half to himself, half to Ohlendorf, Reusch mumbled that a corpse at least was cooperative.

Driving carefully along the slick, snow-covered streets, Reusch glanced about. There was no point, he figured, in going out without making the most of it. So he took a route to the rail yard that led him past some of the buildings and shops that needed to be checked on a regular basis. Though he would have preferred to have Ohlendorf do the checking while he tried to keep the police car from slipping and sliding, Ohlendorf had lapsed back into a deep sleep. So Reusch drove and made the checks on his own, steering with one hand most of the time.

He was in the process of looking closely at the front of one of the banks when a vehicle with headlights mounted high above the ground came tearing around the corner from a side street. Without realizing what it was, and only catching a glimpse of the vehicle from the corner of his eye, Reusch had seen enough to know that if he didn't do something immediately, there would be a collision. Jerking the steering wheel hard in the direction in which he had been looking, Reusch began to pump the brake. Despite his best efforts, however, the right front of the police car slid on the snow-covered street, hitting the rear of a parked car. This impact threw Ohlendorf forward and into the dash in front of him as the police car bounced off the parked car. Rather than bringing the car to a stop, the impact caused Reusch's car to spin out into the middle of the street, right into the path of the oncoming vehicle.

Realizing that he had lost control and unable to do anything but pray, Reusch stopped fighting the steering wheel and, ignoring Ohlendorf's panicked cries, turned to face the vehicle that they were fated to hit. As terrible as his sudden loss of control and the collision with the parked car was to Reusch, it did not match his shock when he looked and saw the tracks of an armored vehicle, level and in line with his eyes, bearing down on him just a few meters outside his car door window. Though the commander of the oncoming M-2 Bradley had seen his car and was attempting to stop, the slick, snow-covered pavement carried it forward several more feet toward Reusch. There was only enough time for Reusch to close his eyes as he prepared to be crushed.

From atop the turret of C60, the bumper number of her M-2 Bradley, Captain Nancy Kozak held her breath as the white and green German police car disappeared under the front slope of her Bradley. Preparing herself for the inevitable, Kozak winced, dropping down her open hatch and bracing herself. But instead of a sudden and crushing impact, Kozak felt little more than a slight shudder. Relaxing her grip, she slowly began to rise back out of her hatch, ever so carefully leaning forward as she did so in order to see what had happened to the German police car.

Instead of a mutilated car and body parts all over the street, Kozak saw that the slick road had in fact saved the Germans, allowing the German police car to bounce back down the street when her slow-moving Bradley hit it. From her perch, Kozak watched the driver of the German police car slowly open his door and, moving slowly, get out.

Rather than become excited, Reusch could only stand in the middle of the street looking first at his police car and then at the American Bradley that had almost run him and his car over. How he survived was at that moment beyond him. Not that it was important, other than the fact that something had saved him. Turning to face his attacker, Reusch realized for the first time that the front of his pants and his right pants leg were wet. In the excitement of the moment, he hadn't noticed the warm urine running down his leg. Only the cold night air hitting his wet pants caused him to notice. After looking down at his pants, Reusch looked back up at the Bradley, its commander now leaning out of an open hatch. Quickly replacing his shock and embarrassment with anger, Reusch began to step forward, toward the Bradley. As he did so, he mechanically unsnapped the flap of the holster for his pistol.

Even in the pale light of the streetlamps and falling snow, Kozak couldn't help but notice that the German policeman's look of shock had changed to one of anger. His sudden turn toward her and the unsnapping of his holster caused Kozak to ease back down into the safety of the turret just as her gunner, Sergeant Danny Wolf, was sticking his head up to see what was going on. When he saw the angry policeman, his right hand resting on the butt of an unseen pistol, advancing on C60 like Gary Cooper in *High Noon*, Wolf stopped. "Looks like the natives are restless, Captain."

Kozak simply shrugged off Wolf's concern. "Well, we knew someone was bound to get upset." Looking over at him, she added, "After all, most Germans don't take too kindly to having their country invaded."

Wolf, still watching the policeman as he stopped just off to one side of C60, chuckled. "I don't see why they should get so emotional over something like that. Hasn't everyone invaded Germany at least once?"

Unable to restrain herself at Wolf's attempt at humor at a time like this, after a long, tense rail movement through the Czech mountains and into Germany, Kozak laughed. "True, that's quite true. I guess they just don't see the humor in the situation."

As if his brush with death and his involuntary urination weren't enough to upset and anger Reusch, the sight of the Americans who had almost killed him laughing caused him to lose control. Pulling his pistol out, Reusch held it pointed at the Bradley commander and began to shout at the top of his lungs for him to dismount and surrender himself. He didn't realize, of course, that not only was the Bradley commander a woman, but that even if she wasn't, she was under orders to meet force with like force.

Seeing that things were getting out of hand, and sure that her laughing wasn't helping the situation any, Kozak dropped what Wolf called her official Commander Nancy face into place. Keeping one eye on the screaming German, Kozak slowly began to lower herself into the safety of the turret. When she knew her driver, Terri Tish, could hear her without the aid of the intercom, Kozak ordered Tish to slowly begin to move forward. Though she hoped that the German policeman would get the idea and move his police car, Kozak didn't much care what happened. Already the column of tanks and Bradleys coming up from the rail yard was backing up behind her, waiting to get out of Pegnitz and move to their blocking positions to the west of Grafenwöhr.

With one eye on the angry German policeman and the other on the street ahead, Kozak guided her Bradley forward. When it made contact with the police car turned broadside in the street, she noticed a second policeman, his head bleeding, jump out of the passenger side. The second policeman paused once he was clear of his derelict vehicle and watched the Bradley begin to crush it. Looking at his doomed car, then at the parade of armored vehicles coming up from the rail yard, he decided that this was more than they could handle. Turning on his heel, he began to flee down the street and out of sight.

An excited cry from Wolf, just as the police car began to crinkle and rip under the treads of the Bradley, caused Kozak to see what he was up to. Glancing over her shoulder, away from the irate policeman who was still screaming and waving his pistol about, Kozak noticed that Wolf had a grin from ear to ear. When he saw his commander looking at him, his smile grew larger. "I always wanted to do this, Captain. I just wish we could've gotten some pictures to send home."

Though she felt like saying something, Kozak didn't. It was at this point useless to try to explain to Wolf the seriousness of what they were doing, that they would be lucky if after this they would be able to send themselves home. Shaking her head, she looked back at the policeman, now standing on the side of the street watching as Bradley C60 finished grinding his police car into compressed scrap.

Though he was tempted to shoot the commander of the American Bradley, Reusch decided not to. Instead, he stood there and watched his police car reduced to a mass of twisted metal. It wasn't that he had any particular affection for the car. It was no different than any other police car operated by the police in Pegnitz. What really bothered Reusch was the total disregard for his authority and the blatant disrespect the Americans had shown him. It was the image of the American perched high above him laughing as he tried to perform his most difficult duties that upset Reusch the most. When he had seen that and realized that they were laughing at him, Reusch wanted to shoot him. And he would have too had he been able to control his anger enough to steady his shaking arm.

That he would have been gunned down in a matter of seconds didn't matter to him at first. His state of mind, and the minds of many Germans for days to come, would be unable to make the mental transition from peace to war instantaneously. Such things, as Big Al knew and counted on, took time. Even Reusch, standing in the street of Pegnitz waving his fist defiantly at the column of Bradleys and tanks as they rolled by him, failed to comprehend the deadly seriousness that the warlike Americans carried into this enterprise. Reusch's confusion and inability to deal effectively with the situation because of a lack of understanding and precedent were to be repeated time after time as Germans going about their daily routines ran into the lead elements of the Tenth Corps as it spilled out of the Czech mountains and into the peaceful, snow-covered river valleys of Bavaria.

Almost as if it were a routine occurrence, the guard opened the gate for the Territorial Army regional headquarters. Merging in with the line of cars waiting to enter the military compound, the driver of Scott Dixon's M-1A1 tank turned off the street crowded with early-morning traffic and rolled through the gate into the compound as if he were just another commuter going to work. Dixon, riding high in the commander's hatch with the confidence that war machines like the M-1A1 Abrams transmit to their crews like a battery supplies energy, gave the German gate guard a smart salute as he went by. Ignoring the stares of the reserve soldiers and officers of the German Territorial Army scurrying about in the predawn darkness of the neat, well-laid-out compound, Dixon directed his driver around the circular drive to the headquarters building. Cerro, riding high in the hatch of the M-577 command post carrier, followed Dixon's tank. Together, they represented the advance command post of the 1st Brigade, 4th Armored Division. Even more importantly, as they moved through the German Territorial Army compound, they represented the first test of official military reaction to the Tenth Corps march to the sea.

Scott Dixon and everyone in his small advance command post group understood the significance of what they were doing. Who went and how they traveled were all considered and discussed. Dixon favored a small party, but one that had a little punch. One tank, though not constituting by European standards much of a combat force, was sufficient to convey the message that they came ready to fight. Any more tanks, Dixon pointed out, would have been an outright invasion. Coming in anything smaller than a tank could have been interpreted as a bluff. Even the timing was critical. If they had come storming into Bayreuth and the regional headquarters before the alarm was spread, none of the key players would have been at their posts. By allowing them time to assemble and assess the situation, Dixon would be able to save a great deal of time explaining things and would be greeted with leaders who were awake and at least felt they were in control.

Bringing his tank to a halt in front of the main entrance of the headquarters building, Dixon took his time in dismounting, making great show of the fact that he was in no rush and did not feel threatened. Standing erect on the turret roof, Dixon towered above everyone as he made a great show of his indifference to the comings and goings of the German reservists who had been recalled to halt the invasion of their country by Dixon's command. By the time he had removed his armored crewman's helmet, replaced it with his Kevlar helmet, and pulled on his web belt and load-bearing harness, Hal Cerro was on the ground waiting dutifully for Dixon next to a German Army captain.

When Dixon finished climbing down, Cerro introduced the captain as the military region's Regular Army adjutant. Exchanging salutes, then handshakes, the adjutant led both Dixon and Cerro to the commander of the military region. Behind them, they left the gunner and loader of Dixon's tank up and manning the machine guns at the commander's and loader's position of the tank. Both guns, leveled and manned by alert soldiers with stern no-nonsense expressions on their faces, served as a reminder to anyone who saw them of the potential for open and armed conflict.

Rather than being led to the operations center, which didn't surprise Dixon but disappointed Cerro, who wanted to see what his counterparts had posted on their maps, Dixon and Cerro were taken to the commander's office. They were greeted there by the military region commander, the mayor of Bayreuth, chiefs of the city and state police for the area, and several other officers and civilian officials standing along the rear wall of the commander's office who were not introduced. The differences between the two groups were stark. Dixon in full battle gear looked and smelled the part of the combat commander just in from the field. The faint smell of diesel fumes that permeated his mud-splattered green, brown, and black field uniform contrasted sharply with the neat, freshly pressed gray dress blouse and tie of the German officers and the somber dark business suits of the city officials. After the principals were offered seats and served coffee, the German commander, Colonel Dieter Stahl, began by asking what exactly the Americans intended to do.

Dixon, hoping that Stahl had done his homework, took a sip of coffee before setting his cup down and answering. "You have, Colonel, no doubt heard the broadcast transmitted from Pizen by our Armed Forces Radio Network this morning." When Stahl nodded, Dixon continued. "That, Colonel, is Lieutenant General A. M. Malin's Fehdebrief to the German people."

Stahl's smile and nodding head told Dixon that he understood perfectly. The mayor of Bayreuth, however, was unfamiliar with the medieval term and asked Stahl in German what Dixon meant by a Fehdebrief. Apologizing for the interruption, Stahl turned to the mayor and in German explained. "During the Thirty Years' War and before, when marauding expeditions moved freely about Germany, the leader of the expedition, normally a knight, was obligated under the accepted codes of chivalry to deliver a formal challenge, or Fehdebrief, to the local inhabitants that explained and justified the knight's actions. If the local inhabitants chose not accept the knight's explanations for his actions as articulated in the Fehdebrief and resisted the knight, that knight, under those rules of chivalry, was free to wage cruel and destructive war on those inhabitants. If, on the other hand, the inhabitants chose to cooperate, the knight was obliged by the same code of chivalry to protect both the persons and the property of the region through which the knight's army passed. In our cold, cruel world of impersonal and scientific warfare, we would call Lieutenant General Malin's Fehdebrief an ultimatum."

Turning to Dixon, the mayor, whose English didn't match Stahl's, tried to make sure that he fully understood what the American colonel's intentions were. "You are, then, as I understand this, threatening us. You are telling us that if we do not cooperate, that if we attempt to defend our country against your aggression, you will devastate our communities. Is that the purpose of this Fehdebrief?"

Having anticipated this line of discussion, Dixon had already framed his response. When he spoke, he did so in an even, measured manner. "Please understand that it is not General Malin's intent to rain death and destruction down on Germany. We are not here to punish. To do so would be a waste of time and resources. It would be counterproductive to our true goal, which is to move the Tenth Corps to the coast where our Navy can evacuate us as a complete and coherent fighting force. You only need to consult with Colonel Stahl, your own military expert. He will tell you that General Malin has neither the resources nor the time to lay waste to your nation AND make it to the coast. To stop and destroy things just because we can would cause the people of Germany to rise up in a blood feud against us. Even if General Malin's real intent was to devastate Germany just for the sake of destroying things, I can assure you that no officer or soldier in the Tenth Corps would follow such orders. We are not animals. Our argument is not with the German people. So long as they do nothing to hinder our march to the sea, my soldiers will do nothing to harm them or their property. The damage caused by accident will be, as always, paid for by the government of the United States. We have been ordered by General Malin to use the same procedures and criteria for determining and processing damage claims by Germans due to our operations that we have used during past training exercises."

After listening to Dixon's explanation, and while the mayor considered what Dixon had said, Stahl began to carefully probe Dixon while laying out the position he was in. "You realize, Colonel Dixon, that I am under orders to resist your incursions and contain you as best we can until the Bundeswehr can redeploy. How can I, a soldier like you, do anything other than follow my orders. To do otherwise, to allow you to violate our national sovereignty and do nothing, would be treason."

Again Dixon was ready. "Who, Colonel Stahl, would you be betraying?"

Stahl looked at Dixon with a quizzical look on his face before responding. "Why, I would be disobeying my orders. I would betray Germany."

Dixon switched tactics. Leaning forward for dramatic effect, he looked into Stahl's eyes as he spoke with a clear, sharp voice. "Whose Germany, Colonel Stahl? Chancellor Ruff's Germany, the Germany of his dreams and ambitions? The Parliament, who are at this very minute debating the constitutional right of Chancellor Ruff's authority and actions? The mayor's Germany, one of working people and their families who have had no say in the past weeks over Chancellor Ruff's provocative actions and unreasonable demands upon my government? Or your Germany, a theoretical Germany that knows only blind duty to orders and traditions? Who, Colonel, will you be betraying, and, more importantly, what will the cost be to Germany if you do not?"

The mayor looked at Dixon, then at Stahl, as everyone in the room waited for him to respond. When he did, it was obvious that he was unsure of himself, that his comments were as much his thoughts as they were statements. "How can you possibly expect me to do other than follow my orders? You, Colonel Dixon, are a soldier. You know that we are expected to obey orders and do what we can on behalf of our nations. We are not like other people, free to pick those orders that please us and disregard those that do not suit us. If we were free to do so, anarchy would prevail."

"We are not, Colonel Stahl, machines. We are not puppets unable to think and act on our own. On the contrary, we are humans, with the ability to think and a conscience to guide that thinking. It is these qualities that we, senior officers in our respective armies, are selected for. While we do have our duty as prescribed by oaths of office, regulations, and orders written in black and white by men in distant capitals, we each are expected to interpret the solemn duties of our office and execute our orders using the high moral and ethical standards that our society has instilled in us." Dixon paused, leaning back in his seat. "I myself am guilty of disobeying the orders of my President. She ordered General Malin to lay down our weapons and leave Europe without them. She was wrong in her assessment of the situation and wrong to give such an order."

Shifting slightly in his seat, Dixon leaned forward, resting his elbows on his knees and holding his hands palms up out toward Stahl. "While I could easily hide behind those orders and blame her, I know she was wrong and that to follow her orders would have terrible consequences for the United States today and in the future. Just as Xenophon knew in 400 B.C. that it would have been a mistake to disarm his ten thousand and trust the Persian King, every officer in the Tenth Corps knows in their hearts that it would be wrong for us to allow the United States to capitulate in the face of nuclear blackmail. If we follow our President's orders and allow Germany to strip the United States of its military machine, other nations will follow suit. Every petty nation will seek to obtain nuclear weapons, legally and illegally, in order to threaten both its friends and enemies. Yes, I had my orders. But," Dixon added as he sat upright, bringing his hands to rest on the arms of his chair, "I also had my duty to those under my command and those we were pledged to defend. In all good conscience, I could not follow orders that were morally wrong. I do not ask you to betray your nation. I ask you to allow your conscience to guide your decision."

For several minutes there was silence. While the lesser German officials standing in the rear of the room who understood English finished translating Dixon's speech to those who didn't, the mayor looked at Stahl, then Dixon, then back to Stahl. Finally he asked Stahl if he could, in fact, refuse to do as Berlin had dictated.

Stahl studied Dixon's face for several moments before he answered. He knew that the American colonel's response had been well thought out and weighted for maximum effect. Stahl had come to realize that Dixon, though not saying so, had intentionally been hammering away at the question that had been debated in the Bundeswehr since its inception in 1955. The concept that a soldier was honor-bound to obey orders without question had allowed the German Army to be drawn into helping the Nazis create the nightmare that led ultimately to the death of over seven and a half million Germans and the near total destruction of Germany. Revival of the old Prussian concept that an officer was responsible for his actions and was expected to use his conscience in determining right from wrong had been the cornerstone of the Bundeswehr from its birth, its hedge against the recurrence of another nightmare. The American colonel, Stahl saw, was reminding him in a very circumspect way of the terrible results of a war caused by an army that had turned a blind eye to its moral obligations to the people it was pledged to defend. Without publicly rubbing his nose in the crimes of his fathers, Dixon was reminding Stahl of their terrible consequences.

Slowly Stahl, still looking at Dixon, began to nod his head. Then he turned to face the mayor. "It is the right of every German commander to decline an order that, based on his assessment, is not appropriate for the situation that the commander is faced with. This freedom to act according to his judgment, and not blind obedience, is the true Prussian military tradition." Looking over to Dixon, but still speaking to the mayor, Stahl continued. "I have been ordered to deter aggression. I intend to order my subordinate commanders to be vigilant and ready to protect the German people and property against any hostile acts, though at this time reports indicate that no hostile acts have been committed in this military region." Standing up, Stahl looked down at the mayor and smiled. "The Americans are guilty of conducting road and rail movements throughout this area without proper authority. That, however, is a civil and not a military matter. While the appropriate agencies of our governments address this issue, I urge the civilian and police authorities to cooperate with the Americans to ensure that damage to property and danger to the public is minimized."

Dixon, who had also risen, maintained his composure as he finished the meeting by offering the attachment of a liaison party to Colonel

Stahl's headquarters in order to facilitate communications and resolve any "difficulties" that might arise while the Tenth Corps was in his area. Stahl, taking Dixon by the arm, agreed as he turned and walked out of the room, leaving the mayor and the other civilian and police officials little choice but to follow the Army's lead.

Carefully unwrapping the last replacement computer circuit board from its protective covering, Sergeant Martin Hofer laid the fragile bundle of microchips on the stand, ready for the maintenance officer's inspection. Finished, he allowed the plastic wrapping to fall to the floor. "There, Captain Haupt," Hofer proclaimed with a flourish, "that is the last of them. There isn't another replacement board in all of Bavaria."

Looking up from the test equipment he had been fooling with, Captain Karl Haupt looked over at the bench where all the circuit boards that coordinated the fire-control system of the squadron's Tornado fighter-bombers sat, each board perched on its own stand and awaiting his check. "Thank you, Martin. Now go along and get something to eat."

Looking at the long line of circuit boards and then at Haupt, Hofer began to protest. "But if you try to check all of these out yourself, we will never be able to reinstall them in time. I heard that the squadron commander wants to be in the air at first light. Without a functional fire-control system, the squadron's aircraft will be useless."

Haupt didn't bother looking up as he continued to fiddle with the dials of the test equipment. "It will not take me long to do what I must do. There is nothing at this moment that you can do to help. Now go along and don't worry about the squadron commander. I will explain my actions to him when I am finished."

Not understanding why his captain was refusing his help, Hofer nevertheless shrugged and left the room. As he left the maintenance hangar, Hofer noted that the sun had not even begun to appear and already they had put in a full day's work. Pulling the circuit boards at the insistence of Haupt had taken time. Gathering the replacement circuit boards from other Tornado squadrons and the wing maintenance supply depot had taken longer. Putting them back, Hofer knew, would take just as long. Still, he was only a sergeant. Though he didn't understand the need for pulling perfectly good boards out of a system that checked out in the aircraft just to make a visual and detailed electronic bench check, his captain no doubt had a good reason. And if he didn't, then it was the captain's ass and not his that would be splattered on the runway by their commander.

Once Hofer was gone, Haupt walked over to the door and locked it. Turning around, he looked at the neat row of circuit boards suspended on little stands and ready to be hooked up to the electronic test unit. Taking a deep breath, Haupt reminded himself that he had his duty to perform and that there was little time. Walking over to a workbench, Haupt opened a tool drawer and reached in, pulling out a ball-peen hammer. Taking the hammer firmly in his right hand, Haupt walked up to the table where the circuit boards sat and began smashing them one at a time with his hammer. Convinced that Chancellor Ruff was wrong and that his actions against the Americans would only lead to misery for the German people, Haupt had decided that morning to do whatever he could to stop Germany from sliding back into the dark abyss. While he knew his actions wouldn't stop those who were determined to destroy his homeland, Haupt hoped that his actions would cause some of his fellow Luftwaffe officers to stop and rethink what they were doing. If nothing else, Haupt knew in his heart that he was right. Whatever became of him, he would have a clear conscience and the knowledge that he had taken a stand.

CHAPTER 11

17 JANUARY

The more Jan Fields-Dixon scrolled through the endless crop of news stories on her desktop computer monitor, the more confused she became. Like most major news agencies, World News Network subscribed to practically every domestic and foreign news and wire service in the world. The stories from these other news agencies were made available to the correspondents, producers, editors, researchers, and supervisors of World News through its interoffice computer network. Since it represented the most current and accurate information available, the staff of World News Network used that information from other agencies to alert them to developments in the world that they were not aware of, as background or auxiliary information to their own stories, and as a measure of the relative importance a particular news story or view was receiving, allowing them to adjust their own reporting efforts. Other news agencies, as well as the national intelligence agencies and the Department of Defense, tapped into the vast pool of information made available by modern communications for the same reasons.

While all the information available that morning substantiated the claim by the President of the United States, including General Big Al Malin's own statements, Jan knew in her heart that something was wrong with the picture that was being flashed around the world from Germany. While his actions made sense, and the statements released by the Tenth Corps information officer supported those actions, Jan knew that Big Al was incapable of leading an armed insurrection that would be so blindly followed by the officers of the Tenth Corps. She didn't question his ability to lead. She had seen that quality herself in Fort Hood, Texas, when her husband, Scott, was Big Al's operations officer. Scott himself, a person who was not easily impressed, had always spoken of Big Al's dedication to duty and leadership in terms of admiration bordering on awe. So when President Wilson began to paint Big Al as an outlaw and the news media labeled him America's twenty-first-century Benedict Arnold, Jan began to wonder how she and Scott could have been so wrong about Big Al.

That self-doubt, however, slowly began to disappear. At first Jan had started looking for some clue that would explain why a man like Big Al Malin would turn his back on his sworn duty and so endanger his command without the full support of his nation. But instead of finding answers and understanding, Jan just found more questions. Though everything taken in isolation seemed to make sense, when Jan put it together, it didn't come together into a nice neat bundle. With her intimate knowledge of what she often referred to in a half-joking manner as the military mentality as well as personally knowing several of the prime players in Washington and Germany, the story line handed out by the White House and the Department of Defense fell way short. Convinced that she was onto something, but that the raw news stories being dumped out onto her computer screen didn't contain the answer, Jan decided it was time to work her sources. While she left a story about German reaction from the Reuters news agency on the screen, Jan reached over, grabbed her phone, and dialed Ed Lewis's office number from memory.

When Jan was told by a staffer that Lewis was at an important meeting and wouldn't be available until noon, she asked to speak to Lewis's secretary, Terri Allen, rather than Lewis's assistant. Terri, who often knew more about what was going on in Lewis's office than Lewis himself, was the friendly type that got along well with just about everyone. If Jan was going to find out where Lewis was so that she could contact him before she finished preparing her program notes for the day, Terri, and not Lewis's male assistant, would be the person to talk to. After her call was routed to Terri's desk, Jan started the conversation in her usual casual manner. "Hi, Terri, this is Jan. I hate to bother you at a time like this, but I really need to talk to Ed as soon as possible. Is it possible for you to tell me how I can get ahold of him or transfer my call to where he is?"

Terri, with a hint of a Tennessee back-country accent, sighed. "Oh, gee, Jan, I'm sorry, dear. I'd love to, but Ed has been at the White House since six this morning, in the War Room, I think. He can call us but we can't seem to call him. The best I can do is to leave a message with the White House switchboard and hope that the Cro-Magnon security people there will get it to the right person sometime this century."

Ordinarily Terri's humorous comments about the White House staff would bring a smile to Jan's face. Today, however, it caused her to pause and think. If Lewis had been in the War Room that early and was still there, that meant that he would have been present for the early-morning update briefing, which, Jan knew, was a ritual for the military while operations were under way. This small shred of information served only to heighten Jan's feeling that there was more to what was going on than was being told. In an effort to get as much information as she could from Terri, Jan decided to subtly probe further. "I can't imagine Ed, who's probably madder than hell with the President, sitting that long with her. I mean, he's been blaming her for this whole mess."

There was an "oh, don't worry" manner in Terri's voice when she responded. "Well, to tell you the truth, Jan, we're all a little taken aback here by the way he's taking all of this. As a matter of fact, last night he went home early, and with a smile on his face."

"Well, I guess he has the right to gloat. Ed did, after all, predict that the President's plan was dumb and would lead to no good."

Terri hastened to correct Jan. "Oh, he's not gloating, Jan. I've seen Ed gloat. No, this is different. It's . . ." Terri paused. When she did continue, Jan noted that her voice betrayed a little concern. "You know, Jan, it's almost as if he was satisfied with the way things are going. You don't suppose he's up to something, do you?"

Though Jan suspected just that, she put Terri off and covered her tracks. She had gotten about all she could from Terri. "Ed working with the administration and smiling? No, too much to expect. Well, I've got another call coming in, Terri. Got to go."

"Do you want Ed to call you when he comes up for air?"

Jan, not wanting Ed to get wind that she was snooping about, for Lewis would know what Jan was up to, told Terri, no, that it wasn't necessary and then hung up. Glancing over to two battery-operated clocks on the corner of her desk, one set to Eastern Standard Time and the other Central European Time, she saw that it was midafternoon in

Germany and time for the American broadcast of the World News Network early-morning news show. Turning in her chair, she took the remote control unit that controlled the TV monitor that always seemed to be on in her office and cleared the mute button, allowing her to hear the top news stories of the hour. While she still mulled the question of what Ed Lewis was up to, Jan watched her morning-show counterpart run through the news of the morning. Nothing that he said made Jan feel any better or clarified the murky and disjointed drama that Jan saw unfolding in Central Europe.

Even the Germans themselves, sitting right in the middle of the crisis, seemed to be confused about what was going on and what to do. While the Chancellor's office in Berlin was pronouncing that a virtual state of war existed between Germany and the United States because of the "invasion," a majority in the Bundestag, or German Parliament, were demanding that the Chancellor curb his reaction to what they referred to as the "current American operations " in Germany. This divergence in views, the World News commentator pointed out, was not confined to Berlin. Based on stories from the German media as well as other crews in Germany covering the story, he reported that the population was divided on how best to react. Though reservists had been recalled to active duty, the commentator noted that early indications based on CIA reports showed that the response to these recalls had been very light. A Berlin newspaper pointed out that the confusion and conflict between the Chancellor's office and the Bundestag was to blame for this. That, the commentator pointed out, was substantiated by incidents throughout what one Munich newspaper editor was referring to as the "liberated" zone of Germany.

One incident, filmed in Nuremberg that morning by a WNN news crew following American forces, was telling. As Jan watched, the news correspondent explained how life in the city continued to go on despite the presence of American forces flowing out of the Czech Republic and staging for General Malin's announced march to the sea. At one train station, where he was filming the manner in which the citizens of Nuremberg were carrying on, a group of four German reservists in uniform and responding to the recall came onto the train platform to wait for their train. Almost immediately, and without any apparent prompting, several German civilians began taunting the German reservists. Unsure as to what to do, the reservists began to back away from the angry civilians. Their line of retreat, however, was blocked by other civilians who joined in condemning the confused reservists. Surrounded and in danger of being mobbed, the reservists had no choice but to stand their ground.

Just when it seemed that the verbal abuse would turn physical, two American military police, one male and one female, fully armed and in complete battle gear, came running down the train platform and began to work their way through the crowd. Parting reluctantly, the angry crowd allowed the Americans through. Once they reached the German reservists, the American MPs escorted the embarrassed reservists off the platform and to safety. As the television camera watched, the little parade of two American MPs protecting their erstwhile enemy marched out of the station followed by determined civilians who shouted angry words and shook their fists at the German reservists who represented to them the Berlin government's unjustified harsh and provocative actions. One civilian, speaking to the correspondent after the crowd had dispersed on their morning commute to work, summarized the view of his fellow protesters. "We have no argument with the Americans. They were wrong to bring the bombs to Germany. That was not proper. But that does not justify what that fool in Berlin, Herr Chancellor Ruff, is doing. It's crazy, just crazy, to turn our country into a battlefield just to teach the Americans a lesson. Let the politicians in Berlin come down here and fight if they want to. We just want to be left alone in peace."

Turning down the volume, Jan sat and looked at the television with a vacant stare while she thought about that story and allowed it to flow together with the bits of information she had gleaned from Terri and her own feeling that things were not what they seemed or were being reported as. The more she thought about it, the more convinced she became that her feeling, what old-time newsmen would call a gut feeling, was right. The military and the administration were up to something and they had no intention of telling anyone. In fact, Jan began to realize, there was the real possibility that the media, including her, were being manipulated in an effort to cover up some kind of operation aimed at saving American face and prestige or even, she thought, retrieving the weapons that the Germans had taken from the Air Force. That something was going on was to Jan a sure thing. What exactly it was, she could only guess.

For her, a savvy correspondent who had more than earned and re-earned her reputation for intelligence and journalistic skill and for meeting all challenges head-on, what to do with this revelation was the question. There was no hint in any of the stories jamming the news agencies that morning that anyone suspected that the situation wasn't as it seemed. Even the military "experts" and experienced correspondents crowding the WNN studios that morning didn't betray any sign that they saw anything beyond the immediate surface of the unfolding drama in southern Germany. Only she, Jan Fields-Dixon, seemed to see past the heavy official curtain that hid the true meaning of the actions shown on her nineteen-inch television monitor. But just as that knowledge pleased her, it also troubled her. Had this been another story in another part of the world involving different actors, she would have had no problem running her hunches and suspicions to ground until she had a story that would tear away the curtain of secrecy that she suspected hid the truth.

But this story involved the Tenth Corps, an organization led by a man she knew personally and to which her lover and husband belonged. What would happen, she thought, to Scott and his command if she was right about the conspiracy and a news story that she put together compromised it? Would her action save Scott from another foolish plan doomed to fail or would it condemn that venture to ultimate failure? Was it her duty to push a story that if true would further enhance her reputation, under the guise of defending the public's right to know the truth? Or did her first duty lie in allowing the suspected deception to continue without comment so that Scott and the tens of thousands of soldiers with him in Germany could carry on with their tasks? It came down, Jan realized, not to a question of what was truth and lie, or what was right and wrong, but to a question of responsibility.

She was still pondering all of this when an assistant to Charley Mordal, the senior producer, called Jan and asked if she had her notes ready for that afternoon's show. Looking down at the blank legal pad that sat in front of her, Jan told him, of course, they were just about ready. Hanging up, she looked at the television monitor one more time, then at the computer screen, before scribbling the first thing that came to her mind based on the information that she had pulled from the news stories from other news agencies. Until she had resolved her own concerns, she would stay with the pack and keep her own counsel. Too much, she knew, was at stake. Far too much.

* * *

From across the table, Pete Soares watched Abigail Wilson as she spoke to the German Chancellor. The conversation was conducted using speakerphones, which allowed the translators on both ends to hear not only the head of state whose words they were to translate but also to listen to the translation of their counterpart to ensure that the meaning was not altered by the translator's choice of words. This method also allowed both Wilson and Ruff to have selected cabinet members and advisors listen in, though they said nothing during the conversation between the two national leaders. Besides Soares, Wilson had her Secretary of Defense, Terry Rothenberg, the Chairman of the Joint Chiefs of Staff, and Ed Lewis. With Ruff were his Foreign Minister Bruno Rooks, Defense Minister Rudolf Lammers, Interior Minister Thomas Fellner, General Otto Lange, Chief of the German General Staff, and Colonel Hans Kasper, Ruff's military aide.

From the very beginning of the conversation, initiated by an excited and fast-talking Ruff, he took every opportunity to remind Wilson that this current crisis was her fault. In between those condemnations, Ruff pointed out that the American habit of conducting unilateral and aggressive international adventures could not go unchecked or unanswered. All of this, plus his habit of cutting Wilson off in midsentence, left little doubt in Washington that Ruff had no intention of opening serious negotiations. Each time Wilson attempted to suggest a means of peacefully resolving the crisis, Ruff fell back to his initial position that no discussions between their two countries could even be considered until all American forces were either withdrawn from Germany or disarmed. Wilson, maintaining her composure, reminded Ruff that unfortunately she did not have at that moment the ability to stop the movement of the Tenth Corps. "As I have told you before," Wilson reminded Ruff, "General Malin is a maverick, an unguided missile. We have attempted and will continue to attempt to bring him and his corps under control, but at this time neither he, his staff, nor his subordinate commanders are responding to our attempts to communicate with them."

"And, *Madam* President," Ruff responded, with great emphasis on madam, "as I have told you before, if you cannot control your own Army, the German Army can." In Berlin this statement caused both General Lange and Thomas Fellner to flinch. Both men, though for different reasons, were working to avoid a confrontation between the two forces in their own ways, though neither man knew of the other's efforts.

Unruffled by Ruff's threat, Wilson waited until Ruff was finished and then, in a voice that reminded Soares of a grade school teacher lecturing an errant student, attempted to put the seriousness of the situation in its proper perspective. "If I am to believe my own intelligence agencies, not to mention the international and German correspondents covering this situation, to date there have been no armed confrontations between your forces and mine. Except for a few unfortunate traffic accidents, no one on either side has been hurt. This fact alone, Herr Chancellor, leads me to believe that General Malin is doing exactly what he pledged he would—marching his command to the sea with as little disruption to the German public as possible."

"No! No. *You* don't understand," Ruff shouted. "You don't seem to appreciate my position. German sovereignty and national honor are at stake here. If I allow your mad general to go marauding through the heart of my country unchecked, I—no, Germany—will lose the respect of the rest of the world. That is, to me—to the German people—intolerable."

"And you must appreciate *my* position, Herr Ruff. The actions of General Malin and perhaps a few of his officers are his and his alone. There are thousands of good innocent American soldiers who are doing what they believe is expected of them, doing their duty and what they believe is right. Malin, and not the individual soldiers, must be brought to justice and punished. I have every intention of doing so at the earliest possible opportunity. If, however, you do not allow me that opportunity, and instead opt to use the German Army to stop the Tenth Corps by force of arms, you will be in a sense punishing the individual soldiers for the crimes of a handful of their leaders. That, Herr Chancellor, would be intolerable to the American public. Regardless of who was to blame in the beginning, regardless of who started this terrible sequence of events, I could not sit here and allow your military to butcher my innocent soldiers. I must tell you, Herr Chancellor, that if it comes to such a confrontation, and I pray that it doesn't, then I will have no choice but to bring down on Germany the *entire* weight of the American military in an effort to save as many of those poor misguided soldiers who are following General Malin that I can."

As if they were two boxers who had just finished flailing blindly at each other and then backed off by mutual agreement in an effort to recover from the blows they had received and to assess the impact of their efforts on their opponent, both Wilson and Ruff lapsed into silence. From across the room Ed Lewis couldn't hide a self-satisfied smirk. Abby, he thought, was doing well. Ruff had played his hand as they, including Malin, had thought he would. And Wilson, prepared for him, had come back without hesitation, without flinching, a fact, Lewis was sure, that wouldn't be lost on those listening to the conversation in Berlin. There would be, Lewis knew, little doubt in Berlin that Abby was ready to meet each German action, whether it be for peace or for war, with an appropriate response.

Pete Soares missed Lewis's expression. His attention, like everyone else's in the room, was riveted on Wilson. They all marveled at the manner in which she was handling Ruff. It seemed to them as if she and she alone had anticipated every word Ruff hurled at her and was ready with a sound, effective response. This, of course, should not have surprised Soares. He had seen Wilson use the same calm, easy manner in dealing with crisis after crisis in her long uphill fight to become the first female President. That she was now working from a base of strength and had a plan hidden away just out of view from even her closest advisors, just as she had done as the governor of Colorado and during the race for the White House, didn't dawn on Soares. This situation was beyond his comprehension. Everything about it was so foreign, so staggering to the imagination. For Wilson it was simply another challenge in a life full of the challenges that all women face when trying to deal with men in the world of politics as equals.

When Ruff finally broke the long pause, he seemed a little winded and slightly subdued. Taken aback by the fact that Wilson had so quickly responded to his threat of force with her own, without the slightest hesitation, put him at a temporary loss. In the exchange of verbal blows, Ruff had been bested and he knew it. "Well, *Madam President*," he stated slowly, still searching for an appropriate response that would soothe his bruised ego but preparing to break off the conversation, "you understand my position and the position of the German people. You have forty-eight hours to bring your mad general to justice or I will."

Knowing that this act was coming to a close, Wilson made sure her voice was smooth and calm yet showed firmness and resolve. "I will, as I have stated from the beginning, continue to work toward that goal. I do hope that, regardless of where this situation stands at the end of those forty-eight hours, we can continue to talk and work to resolve this without causing unnecessary deaths, civilian or military, or devastating your beautiful nation. To that end I will always be available to meet you or representatives of your government anywhere, anytime."

The mention of civilian deaths, which could only be German, and the devastation of Germany itself had its desired effect on the audience in Berlin. Even Lammers and Rooks, who were integral parts of Ruff's plans and dreams, flinched, for every man in that room had lost relatives in the last war. Every man there had vivid memories of growing up among the mountains of rubble that the allies had reduced Germany's cities to during World War II. Though the people gathered about her in Washington listening had a basic comprehension of what Wilson was really saying, everyone in the Chancellery's operations room knew only too well what she was telling them.

Stymied by Wilson's sharp response, it took Ruff several seconds to frame his thoughts. When he did speak, Ruff could produce nothing more than a subdued and halting reiteration of his previously stated position. "Germany cannot sit by idly while foreign armies move through it with impunity, endangering its people and sovereignty."

While Ruff groped for the appropriate words to follow this statement, General Lange wondered who in reality was endangering the German people. There was much that was being left unsaid by Ruff and Bruno Rooks, the Foreign Minister. Each time Lange or a member of the General Staff had been called in for consultation or to brief either man, their responses seemed to be preordained, already decided upon. Lange suspected that Colonel Kasper, Ruff's military aide, was overstepping his bounds and rendering advice that was beyond his assigned duties, but didn't know this for a fact. What Lange did know was that the Bundeswehr was being torn apart by raging debates. At every level of command, no one, including him, was sure what to do in this situation.

The first commanders to feel this uncertainty and indecision were the reserve unit commanders. Few reserve battalions, which accounted for two of the four battalions assigned to every combat brigade, were able to muster anywhere near their authorized strength. The men, one commander pointed out, refused to answer the call to

the colors until the Chancellor and the Parliament were able to resolve their differences and come up with a solid, intelligent policy. A
few put the matter in very human terms, stating that, as they saw it,
it was the leaders in Berlin, and not Washington, that were the real
danger. In an angry conversation between Lange and the territorial
region commander in Stuttgart, the region commander told Lange
that he could fill the ranks of the units in his area in a matter of hours
if he announced that their objective was to march against Berlin and
not the Americans. And to complicate Lange's position, this opinion
was shared by more than a few of the division and brigade commanders now scrambling to shift units from Germany's eastern borders
around Dresden back south to Bavaria.

Given the political uncertainty, not to mention the possible unre-
liability of the Army itself, Lange pondered what he would recommend when the Chancellor finished and asked him for his input.
There would be, he knew, no clear right or wrong answer. He could
easily and safely retreat behind the wall of duty, honor, and country
that would ostensibly relieve him of dealing with the morality and
consequences of his actions and those of the Bundeswehr. Lange and
his subordinate commanders after all were simple soldiers pledged to
defend their country against all invaders and to obey their national
leaders. Everyone understood that. That was the duty of all soldiers.
But for Lange and every German who had put on a uniform after 1955,
that comfortable defense had died in 1946 at the Nuremberg trials
when the leaders of the Wehrmacht were held accountable for their
actions in defense of a government that the victors deemed was evil.
Was this, Lange thought, a test? Was this some kind of strange Faust-
ian test to find out if the German Army had learned the real lessons
of the last war?

"General Lange, please, we do not have much time." Though Ruff's
comment was sharp, his voice betrayed the fact that he was at that
moment off balance, perhaps shaken by the conversation with Wilson
that, Lange suddenly realized, was now over. Shoving his troubled
thoughts into the back of his mind, Lange sat up and gave Ruff his full
attention. "When," Ruff continued when he saw that Lange was ready,
"will the Army be able to bring its full weight to bear on the Americans?"

Lange did not quite understand what Ruff meant by bringing the
Army's full weight to bear. He suspected that he knew but opted not

to ask for a clarification, because he might not like the answer. By leaving the question open and ambiguous, Lange could always say later that he had misunderstood Ruff's intent. Slowly he answered, carefully picking his words so as to leave himself the greatest amount of leeway in dealing with his own moral questions as well as the Americans. "I am afraid, Herr Chancellor, that we were caught in the midst of redeploying to the east. Everything, from intelligence assets to logistical support commands, was in the process of preparing to counter the threat from the Czech Repuublic and Poland."

"I know that, General, I know that."

Not to be rushed, Lange shifted in his chair before he continued. "Yes, Herr Chancellor, I know that you know that. But I tell you this because I need you to understand that what we must now do will be no easy thing. The combat elements of the units in the east are only a small portion of the mass of men and materiel which we must turn around. I cannot simply tell everyone to turn and go south. First we must decide where we should send those units. That will be determined not by where the Americans are today but where we think they will be in seventy-two to ninety-six hours from now. This determination is based on solid intelligence and analysis of what we think their intentions are."

"I can tell you, General Lange, what the Americans' intentions are!" Ruff screamed. "They intend to embarrass this nation and its people."

Lange ignored Ruff's outburst. "Once we have a grasp of what their objectives and routes of march will be, we then have to look at where best to stop them. Given that, deployment plans, along with the march tables to shift units in accordance with those plans in an intelligent and orderly fashion, must be developed and disseminated in the form of orders at every level. Equally important to the movement of the combat elements is that of the combat service support commands. The necessary support facilities, all of which are now moving or established in the east, must be shifted back west, one hundred and eighty degrees, to support our operations."

Rooks, seeing that Ruff was losing his patience, leaned forward toward Lange. "This is no time, Herr General, for a lecture on operational tactics. To the point, man, to the point. What do you recommend?"

Taking in a deep breath, Lange realized that both Ruff and Rooks were interested in pinning him to a definite course of action when he hadn't even decided in his own mind what an appropriate response for the Bundeswehr should be. He needed time. Time to resolve matters of conscience, and time to determine how well the German Army would do in a fight with the Americans, if it came to that. Time was needed to bring under control those Army and Luftwaffe commanders who had already decided and were taking unilateral action that ranged from the simple refusal to answer messages from higher headquarters to the actual sabotage of aircraft. "We must, Herr Chancellor, given the advantage that they have and the problems we face in redeploying our own forces, allow the Americans free passage through Bavaria. We are in no position to resist them there, and any effort to offer even token resistance would jeopardize our ability to stop the Americans further north."

Lange's statement, given in such a calm, almost casual manner, hit every man in the room like a slap in the face. Lammers, the Minister of Defense, almost jumped out of his seat. "We *can't* do that! We simply can't! Do you realize what you are saying?"

Looking at Lammers, Lange's voice was quite defiant, almost arrogant. "I know *exactly* what I'm saying. Do *you?*"

The point that Lange was making, using Lammers, was not lost on the others, especially Ruff and Rooks. For the first time they realized they were no longer in command of the situation that they had so carefully created. None of them had the background or knowledge to challenge Lange, who after all was "ein *General.*" For, despite years of demilitarization in Germany, the opinion of a senior member of the General Staff was something that demanded respect, especially among this particular group of men. Therefore, even though they found Lange's pronouncement distasteful, everyone in the room realized that none of them could alter the basic laws of time, space, and terrain that governed military operations. Lange, who had spent a lifetime dealing with such problems, would set the pace and tone of German reactions for the next few days. Rooks, looking first at Ruff and Lammers, turned to Lange. "Please, Herr General, proceed."

"From southern Germany, the Americans have the ability to move west through Stuttgart and into France, which may allow them to enter northwest through Mainz and into Belgium, or due north from Würzburg through Kassel to Bremen, where their Navy will be able to intervene. Though I personally believe that the Americans will strike

north for the sea, we cannot disallow the other possibilities. Therefore, I recommend that we commence redeploying our forces in such
a manner as will create in central Germany a huge cauldron, with the
5th and 10th Panzer divisions remaining in the west, the 2nd Panzer
and 4th Panzergrenadier deploying to form the eastern side of the
cauldron, and the 1st and 7th Panzer throwing themselves across the
Americans' line of advance to the sea in the north. The 1st Mountain
Division, with the 26th Parachute Brigade attached, will follow the
Americans, threatening their rear."

"Where," Ruff asked impatiently, "do you intend to stop the Americans?"

"*If*, Herr Chancellor," Lange responded with great emphasis on "if,"
"it comes to a fight, I expect it to be in the area south of Kassel. That,
however, will not be certain for several days. In the meantime, both
our forces and the Americans will be racing to see who completes
their redeployments first and can get moving first. If we can unsnarl
the massive tangle that our own divisions are in due to the need to
turn around, we will be in place and ready. If the Americans, however,
succeed in moving their forces out of the Czech Republic, gathering
up loose units left in Germany, and get moving first, we will find
ourselves fighting a series of meeting engagements with our forces
which may still be in the process of deploying throughout central
Germany. Either way, we still have several days in which the military
will be unable to do anything, leaving Herr Lammers free to seek a
peaceful solution to this crisis."

The unexpected reference to an effort to resolve the crisis through
other than force of arms caught Lammers off guard. He could not,
however, easily pass this off. If for no other reason than to keep Interior Minister Thomas Fellner, the voice of reason and the only figure
respected by all political factions in Ruff's cabinet, satisfied and in
line, Lammers had to respond in a positive manner. "Why, yes, that is
a very, very sound course of action. I will, of course, continue to
appeal to the Americans while the Bundeswehr prepares. But I must
warn you, I hold little hope for that."

"And I, Herr Lammers, must warn you and everyone else that the
Bundeswehr may not be able to deliver on the threats that you have
been hurling at the Americans. In the first place, every brigade deployed has for the most part only two combat battalions with it. There
has been insufficient response by the reservists needed in the two

reserve battalions of each brigade to bring those units up to strength. In effect, each of our six panzer and panzergrenadier divisions has only six, maybe seven, tank or infantry battalions with it. Instead of a three-to-one advantage, as the number of divisions deployed by the Bundeswehr and the Americans would suggest, we have less than a two-to-one advantage when counting the critical ground combat battalions.

"But even here," Lange continued after a slight pause, "our advantage in numbers is illusory. We have not fought since 1945. We have never in our existence moved the entire Bundeswehr at the same time. And the operation which we are engaged in is to say the least quite unusual and sensitive, politically as well as militarily. Regardless of what we say and do here, regardless of how much we talk and debate, the final military outcome, gentlemen, will be determined by the commanders and soldiers out there in units spread all over Germany. And right now those units are, without exaggerating, choking on their own supply lines, lines that run throughout Germany like a plate of spilled noodles. Added to all of this military movement is the mass migration of civilians, some seeking to get out of harm's way and some simply trying to carry on with their lives as if nothing has changed. It will be days before we know for sure if we can pull off the great plans which we so easily toss about here in the warmth of this building."

Unable to effectively counter Lange's argument, Ruff, Rooks, and Lammers let the meeting limp to an unsettling close. Lange for the moment had succeeded in buying the time he wanted. He had no idea what could happen to change what he was convinced Ruff saw as an inevitable confrontation. Until the first blood was drawn, there was always the chance of a negotiated settlement. The longer the conflict was postponed the better. Still, Lange could not delay forever. He knew that he could only buy so much time with which to allow the political situation to clarify itself by walking the fine line between performing his duty as a soldier and doing what his conscience dictated. At some point, and he had no idea where or when that would happen, time would run out.

The effect of shifting of forces from one place to another was a very real concern to Captain Friedrich Seydlitz as his column of Leopard II tanks rumbled back to the west down Autobahn E40 just outside of Dresden. The orders to move the two panzer, or tank, battalions of the brigade 230 kilometers by road to Erfurt, after having completed a 270-kilometer road march from the south, were greeted with little joy. Every officer took great pains to point out that the wear and tear on the machines as well as the men would leave the combat effectiveness of their units questionable at best. "One does not simply hop into a tank and go driving about Germany in the dead of winter," Seydlitz's battalion commander warned the brigade commander, "without paying a price."

As they moved along the westbound lane of the autobahn, Seydlitz could see that the price which his commander had warned about was already being paid. At regular intervals on both sides of the autobahn Army trucks of every description, Leopard tanks, Marder infantry fighting vehicles, and self-propelled artillery pieces sat idle, either broken down or out of fuel. In some instances armored vehicles had seized up in midstride, coming to a sudden stop in the center of the road. Left by the losing commander for the overwhelmed maintenance teams to recover, the rest of the unit, fighting civilian traffic as well as a tight timetable, would attempt to flow around the derelict vehicle. When road conditions did not permit vehicles following to pass on a paved surface, the other vehicles in the column and dozens of columns following would maneuver off the road, onto the shoulder, and then back onto the autobahn, dragging great trails of mud onto the road surface already made slick by freezing rain or wet snow. During the day, when the temperature rose above freezing, this mud made driving dangerous to any wheeled vehicles. The number of accidents involving German civilians speeding down the autobahn in their cars who unexpectedly hit this mud multiplied as rapidly as the number of broken-down military vehicles increased. At night or when the temperature dipped below freezing, the mud clods on the road froze hard as stone. The effect of hitting a patch of road smeared with these frozen fields of mud in a Mercedes was just as dangerous as it was when the mud was wet and slick. The image of smashed cars and civilian tractor-trailers along the side of the road, with their angry owners shaking their fists and shouting at Seydlitz and his company as they rolled by, did nothing to cheer up his confused and tired command.

As bothersome as this was to Seydlitz, his mind was on other, more pressing military matters. The military police and local authorities would deal with the angry and injured civilians. No one, however, seemed to be too concerned about the welfare of his command. Though he considered himself lucky that he had yet to lose a single tank to a breakdown, Seydlitz knew at this point that it was simply a matter of time before his luck ran out. And if a mechanical failure didn't stop them, lack of fuel would. For, although he had seen many fuel trucks moving about, all of them either belonged to another unit or were on the other side of the road headed in the opposite direction. The battalion's own fuel trucks, drained days ago, had been unable to find a fuel depot where they could top off. Suggestions by several of the company commanders in the battalion that they draw on civilian gas stations or fuel depots were rejected. They had, their battalion commander told them, no authority at that time to do so. That, and the desire to minimize the impact of military operations on the civilians, kept Seydlitz from topping off his tanks from a gas station that was less than one hundred meters from the assembly he had just left.

As if to mock the need to minimize their impact on civilians, Seydlitz's tank rolled by the remains of a bright yellow Porsche. Left on the side of the road, the front left fender was chewed up as though some great metal-eating cat had grabbed the fender and gnawed on it. In an instant Seydlitz knew what had happened. The impatient driver of the Porsche had apparently been following an armored vehicle too closely. Without having seen it, Seydlitz knew that at some point the driver of the armored vehicle had slowed for some reason, causing the Porsche to run into the rotating treads of the armored vehicle. Caught in the treads, the Porsche would be pulled up and into the drive sprocket of the armored vehicle to be ground up. If, like this Porsche, the civilian driver was lucky, the car would be thrown clear of the armored vehicle like a child's toy.

Such accidents, in a country where heavy military equipment shared the roads with everyone else almost on a daily basis, were to be expected. What was new to Seydlitz was the casualness and lack of serious concern with which his superiors and even his own men now treated this rash of incidents. It seemed as if, in the 2nd Panzer Division's rush to get at the Americans, all thought of maintaining the normally close and friendly civilian-military relationships that had highlighted every peacetime maneuver was forgotten. To Seydlitz, this didn't make sense. For rather than doing everything to defend civilians and their property, the civilians were being viewed as a nuisance to military operations. He had actually watched units along the division's route of march going out of their way to infuriate the very people they were supposed to be defending. When Seydlitz mentioned this to his friend Captain Buhle, the battalion supply officer, Buhle shrugged. "What, Friedrich, do you expect? We're being told to go out and defend those bastards, putting our asses on the line for them. Yet despite the fact that we need every kind of support imaginable, from fuel to rations, we can't requisition anything, not even toilet paper, from the civilians. 'Military operations,' the fools in Berlin tell us, 'cannot be allowed to interfere with the normal daily intercourse of civilian affairs.' Shit, Friedrich, just look at the mess that this division alone is creating and then tell me how in the hell we are going to keep from interfering with normal daily intercourse of civilian affairs. Fools, I tell you! We're being led by fools in the service of ungrateful swine."

Even the attitude that his superiors seemed to hold concerning the welfare of their own men and equipment during the marching and countermarching of the past few days bothered Seydlitz. For two days he and his company had sat in their assembly area south of Dresden waiting for their resupply of food and fuel to find them. Orders to move, however, found them first. If it were not for the soldiers going off on their own and buying the food themselves, no one in Seydlitz's company would have gotten a hot meal while they waited. Even their combat rations, as Buhle had so painfully pointed out, were running low.

Then, in the midst of bemoaning their fate, Seydlitz recognized the tactical symbol of his brigade on several fuel and supply trucks in the eastbound lane of the autobahn. Despite the orders to remain in radio listening silence, Seydlitz felt the need to inform his commander. Could they not, he asked, flag down the column in which their brigade's trucks were moving in order to refuel and draw rations?

Without any hesitation, his battalion commander informed Seydlitz that they could not. Both the battalion and, no doubt, the brigade's supply vehicles had to adhere to the march tables that controlled the movement of all units in the area. "If every commander stopped when and where he wanted to," the battalion commander explained to Seydlitz, "then this intolerable situation would become totally unmanageable." Reminding Seydlitz that the march orders they were

moving under had a maintenance and refueling stop set up by corps
supply units and scheduled in another two hours, the battalion commander went on to reassure Seydlitz that if everyone did what they
were ordered to do, everyone would eventually get to where they were
going.

Acknowledging his commander, Seydlitz gave up as he watched the
trucks carrying the fuel and food his company so desperately needed
roll away to the east into the gathering darkness. There was, of course,
no fuel and no food waiting for Seydlitz and his company at the end of
two hours. The corps supply unit responsible for establishing the refuel and rest stop was still on the road somewhere to the west, tied up
behind a broken-down tank and the armored recovery vehicle, also
broken down, that had stopped to retrieve it. With fuel almost expended, Seydlitz and his company, as well as the rest of the brigade,
would wait, lined up on the side of the road and unable to continue
due to a simple lack of fuel. For nearly twelve hours they would wait
while staff officers at corps and division desperately shuffled and re-
shuffled march tables and units without ever realizing that their efforts were for the most part creating more problems than they were
solving. It would take the direct intervention of both the corps commander of the 2nd German Corps and his division commanders, riding
up and down the route of march and herding and directing units like
cowboy trail bosses, and another twenty-four hours, to sort out the
2nd Panzer Division and get it moving again.

News that they had arrived at Grafenwöhr was greeted with moans
and groans by Captain Hilary Cole and the other nurses of the 553rd
Field Hospital. Somehow in their minds they had come to believe that
once they were out of the Czech Republic and back in Germany things
would be different, that everything would be all over. The long, seemingly pointless road marches in the back of a cold five-ton cargo truck
were supposed to end. There would be, they thought, no more endless
waiting as they sat on the side of nameless roads waiting for another
column to pass and gnawed at cold combat rations. And the jerky stop
and go, stop and go, as they wound their way through the Czech
mountains, would be over once they were in Germany.

So it came as a rude shock when the trucks pulled into a loose circle
in the middle of a large well-used gravel and mud parking area, and

they were informed that they were at Grafenwöhr. The unit first sergeant could have told them any other German name and, although Cole and the other nurses would have been unhappy, they would not have suffered the severe depression that hit them when the word "Grafenwöhr" was mentioned. Built as a training area with numerous tank and artillery live-fire ranges and maneuver areas by the Wehrmacht before World War II, elements of Erwin Rommel's famed Afrika Korps, as well as units of the elite and notorious Waffen SS, had trained there during the war. Taken over by the Americans after the war with little done to improve creature comforts, few soldiers serving in Germany escaped the horror of doing time there. Grafenwöhr was to those soldiers who went there to train synonymous with misery, discomfort, cold, wet, sleeplessness, and every other word that is used to describe the pain and discomfort a soldier experiences when serving in the field under the worst possible conditions. It was described by more than a few American soldiers as the armpit of the world.

It didn't matter why they were there. It didn't matter what they were supposed to do there. All that mattered was the fact that they were there, and not in some nice clean hospitable piece of Germany untainted by the foul reputation associated with Grafenwöhr. Even when a group of soldiers came by and shoved another brown plastic MRE combat ration into Cole's hand, she didn't react, though she felt like it. At that moment, she felt like sinking onto the ground and crying. It wasn't fair that they were being treated like that. This was not what she was trained to do. Cole could deal with the pain and suffering of others. She could watch and assist in a very detached manner as doctors pieced torn bodies back together. She could even handle the frustration of doing everything within her power to save a life and then watching that life slip away. All of that was manageable, reasonable, and expected. This, however, was beyond comprehension. Even worse than the horror before her eyes was the sudden realization that there was no discernible end. There was no well-defined conclusion to which they were headed. This terrible endless chain of suffering and wandering had to be endured without any chance of really influencing it in any way, no way of stopping it. That to Cole was the horror of it all.

Just when she was about to break, to give in to her desire to break down and cry, Hilary noticed that someone had beaten her to it. In the darkness she heard her friend Wendi. Looking about, Hilary could see her standing off from the group alone in the darkness clutching her arms tightly across her chest as she rocked from side to side and cried. Though her own pain and frustration were still with her, Cole handed her ration to another nurse standing next to her and went to Wendi. Wrapping her arms about Wendi, Hilary Cole gently pushed Wendi's head down onto her shoulder. Reaching up under Wendi's helmet, Hilary slowly began to stroke her friend's hair. As Wendi cried, Hilary softly repeated through her own sobs, "It's going to be all right, Wendi. It's all going to be all right. I'm here."

Under normal circumstances, Big Al Malin didn't like to bother his subordinate commanders when they were getting ready to start a major operation. He made sure that he had good people working for him and that he issued clear concise orders and directives. "The rest," he liked to tell people, "was in their hands and God's." This operation, now referred to as Malin's March to the Sea, was not a normal operation. Though it was planned and briefed to everyone in the same manner as a purely military operation, it was not. The intricate civil-military relationships that were woven into the entire fabric of the operation and designed to prevent or defuse problems between the Tenth Corps and the German populace that they would be moving through touched every aspect of the operation, both planned and potential.

Some commanders voiced strong reservations about the rules of engagement imposed by Big Al. The commander of the 55th Mechanized Infantry Division had on several occasions pushed Big Al to soften his order restricting the use of artillery fire to only confirmed enemy locations that were a danger to the command. Every chance he got, Big Al would remind his commanders that "We, an army used to the indiscriminate use of firepower, must look twice and three times before we pull the trigger. Otherwise we're going to leave in our wake a hostile populace that will cut our combat service support units to ribbons and deny us the use of their fuel and resources that the success of this operation depends upon. It is totally unreasonable to expect us to ask a German mother or father to allow us free and unhindered progress after we've blown up their home and killed their children. If you can't picture that, then just ask yourself before you make a call for fire, Would you still do so if your wife and child were in the target area?"

It was the need to stress such things that drove him to visit every command he could before they jumped off, and to talk to every officer and soldier in a position of leadership. In his own mind he wanted to ensure that he had done his best to convey his intent and that it was understood. Standing there that night in front of the commanders of Scott Dixon's brigade, Big Al went over what he intended to do and how they would do it. The formal review of the brigade's plan, given by Dixon himself, was Dixon's own effort to ensure that every battalion and company commander in his brigade understood what he intended. When he was finished, he turned the floor over to Big Al.

Slowly Big Al rose from his chair and walked over to the map showing most of Germany and the anticipated route of the 4th Armored Division. He made a show of studying it before slowly turning to face the captains, majors, and colonels seated before him. With his feet spread shoulder width apart, his left hand on his hip, and using his right index finger to point at the map, Big Al began. "It is 709 kilometers from here to Bremerhaven. That, for those of you still used to thinking like civilians, translates to 432 miles. In the States, it would almost be the same as driving from New York City to Cleveland, Ohio. During that trip the biggest threats you face are the Pennsylvania State Police. On a good day you could make that drive in eight or nine hours. *But*," giving great emphasis to the word "but," "this isn't the States. This is Germany." Turning around to face the map, Big Al placed both hands on his hips. "Germany is one of the most densely populated areas in the world. It has a long and proud history. It is one of the only European countries the Romans never conquered. It has been racked by great disasters, both natural and man-made. During the days of the Black Death, plague wiped out anywhere from a third to half the population. Whole villages simply died off. During the Thirty Years' War, a full one third of the population of Germany was again wiped out. And in World War II, what the Germans still refer to as 'The Last War,' they lost seven and a half million people, half of them civilians. They have not forgotten that, none of it."

Turning around quickly, Big Al stared at the assembled leaders. "To the Germans, a people who have a deep and long sense of history, we are simply another marauding army ripping up their fields, threatening their homes, and endangering their lives. They don't give a damn whether or not we are right or why we are doing what we're doing. We're just another group of soldiers passing through." Toning his speech down slightly, Big Al folded his arms across his chest. "Now, we have some advantages. First, because the American Army has lived with the Germans for more than fifty years, they know us and understand us better than just about everyone else that has gone before. The area of operations we'll be rolling through is used to seeing American GIs and dealing with us. So for many of those people this will be nothing new. Many of the procedures we will be using, from the recording of maneuver damage to the purchase of fuel from the civilian sector, are the exact same ones we used during peacetime training maneuvers. We're doing that because we have a reputation for paying in full all of our debts and doing as little damage as possible. I am hoping that reputation will allay any fears the civilians have and keep them from interfering with our operations."

Using his index finger, Big Al raised his voice as he jabbed his finger at his officers to emphasize his point. "That reputation, however, can be pissed away in a heartbeat if you and your people go through Germany like a plague of locusts or riding high and wild like Attila the Hun. Right now the media and the German people are neutral. I expect each and every one of you to do your best to keep it that way. We'll have more than enough to deal with when the German Army and Air Force get their acts together without having angry civilians chasing us with shotguns and pitchforks."

Allowing that point to sink in, Big Al wandered about the front of the room, folding his arms across his chest, then, when he was ready, stopping. Placing his hands on his hips again, he turned only partway to face his audience. "It will come to a fight. Somewhere at some time during our drive, it will have to come to a fight. The German Bundeswehr, despite the internal problems that you are hearing about right now, will eventually get itself straight. When it does, it's going to come at us with a vengeance. The Germans are fighters, proud and fierce warriors who have a long history of fighting against great odds, under the most adverse conditions, and winning. Now I fully expect that some German commanders and soldiers will choose not to engage us. The more the better. But we cannot count on that. What we can expect is that the bulk of their commanders will heed their call to duty and obey their orders. And once battle is joined, once we're locked in mortal combat on German soil, those who were undecided will no doubt join in their fight. Just remember that the words to the German national anthem, "Deutschland Über Alles," written in the mid-1800s, are a call for Germans, all Germans, to forget their petty loyalties and doubts and rally to defend the idea of a free and united Germany. Like I said before, we're nothing special, just the foreign army that happens to be passing through their nation today."

Big Al again paused to let his officers think about what he had said. While he did so, he looked at the map. When he spoke, it was almost as if he were thinking to himself. But he wasn't. "This brigade has a tough job. It's going to be the rear guard, not only for your own division but for the entire corps." Still staring at the map, Big Al stretched his arms out and made a big circle. "We're going to move through Germany like a herd of elephants. In the center, all of our supply trains and service support units will travel just like the cows and young do in an elephant herd. Outside, protecting the herd from all comers, the combat brigades will move, just like the elephant bulls, ready and vigilant." Pivoting, Big Al jammed his index finger into the air again. "You people are the bulls. Your job is not to collect trophies or conquer territory. You are there to protect those cows in the center. Because you all know, just like an elephant bull knows instinctively, that if the cows of the herd die the whole herd will cease to exist."

In an effort to lighten the somber mood of the assembled officers, Big Al was about to mention that he got the elephant idea from watching a National Geographic show on television with his grandchildren. The sudden thought of those grandchildren, whom he might never see again, was brutally painful. While still looking at the audience, Big Al wondered how many of those upturned faces, all younger than his and dutifully attentive, concealed similar thoughts. He, of course, knew that most of them did. So he decided to shy away from the mention of families and children. This, he knew, was already becoming hard enough without bringing such thoughts to mind.

Pointing his finger back at the map, Big Al picked up where he had left off. "It is 432 miles to Bremerhaven. That means that each and every M-1A1 tank in this command that makes it there will consume over 3,000 gallons of fuel. Fuel, ladies and gentlemen, not tactical genius or firepower, is going to make or break us. Remember that first, last, and always. We're going to suck dry every gas station between here and Bremerhaven, and still we're not going to have enough fuel.

If you, the combat commanders of the Tenth Corps, fail to save the cows, we'll all die. Period."

When he was sure that everyone had had sufficient opportunity to think about what he had just said, Big Al again toned down his speech as he prepared to wind it up. "This will be a team effort, one in which everyone must work together if we're going to hold it together and succeed. Blown bridges will need to be replaced by the engineers, or the herd stops. Air defenders will need to cover the herd from above, a tough job under the best of conditions made worse by the fact that we're moving. Maintenance units will need to keep up with the herd while doing their damnedest to deal with the many problems that will crop up as we roll north. And the medical services will be hard pressed when the time comes to deal with casualties while staying up with everyone else."

Big Al stopped again after mentioning medical services and looked down at the floor. In the audience, seated amongst her peers, Captain Nancy Kozak knew what was coming. She had seen the face of battle and understood the pain and concerns that were running through Big Al's mind. Nothing, she knew, ever took away the pain. You could justify it. You could soften it. You could even occasionally forget it. But you could never rid yourself of the pain of watching people entrusted to your care die in battle. Every commander carried the memories of those soldiers he had lost like open wounds, forever.

When he finally looked up, there was a reflective, thoughtful look on Big Al's face. As he spoke, it was in a soft, concerned tone that slowly began to increase in volume and harshness. "We're not all going to make it. War means fighting, and fighting means dying. You've all seen, I'm sure, my directive concerning the care of our wounded. I know that many of you do not agree with it. Well, to those of you who don't, to those who think that we need to drag our wounded about with us because you were raised to believe in some perverted warrior code that requires you to bring all your men out together or not at all, I say fuck you." Big Al's sudden use of vulgarity shocked most of the assembled officers, just as he had hoped it would. When he had their undivided attention, he made his point. "Some have used the Marine retreat from the Chosen Reservoir in November 1950 and the fact that they brought all their wounded and dead out with them in an effort to get me to change my mind. Well, I'll tell you like I told them. This isn't Korea and it's not 1950. Then the enemy couldn't even tend to his own wounded. Here today it's different. I have great confidence that the Germans will give our wounded the same regard and respect that they will give to their own. Both the German military and the civilian medical care system will be able to deal better with our wounded than our own medical units that will be almost continuously in motion. We'll keep those wounded that can make it, evacuate by air from Germany those in bad shape if that option becomes available, but if it comes to a question of life or death, we will turn our wounded over to the Germans, period."

Looking at his watch, Big Al glanced over to Dixon, then across the sea of faces that were watching his every move. "I've used up enough of your valuable time. But I felt it was important that you hear this from me one more time. This will be the last time that I'll be seeing many of you before we reach Bremerhaven. Until then, good luck. My thoughts will be with you. God bless you all."

On cue, Scott Dixon jumped to his feet and yelled, "Attention!" and saluted. Every officer in the room followed suit, leaping up and bringing their right hand up into a crisp, snappy salute. Big Al merely nodded in acknowledgment, quickly turning and leaving the room without further ado, hoping that none of the assembled officers saw the tears welling up in his eyes as he bid his soldiers farewell.

CHAPTER 12

18 JANUARY

The mood of the citizens of Niederjossa matched the gray, sullen sky as they trudged through the slush and around piles of old dirty snow that covered central Germany. Few paid attention at first to the German Army Volkswagen staff car, its canvas top down, as it pulled into the town center of Niederjossa without any flourish, without any haste. Like the rest of the midafternoon traffic, the staff car simply negotiated the narrow and winding streets of the small ancient German town built on the banks of the Jossa River. The German Army captain and his driver paid scant attention to the comings and goings of the civilians as they went about their daily routine. He was more interested in making sure that the five medium trucks that were supposed to be following were keeping up. Motioning to his driver to slow down, the captain turned his head around to the right to look for the trucks. As he did, he could not help but notice the stares from the civilians who, shaken from their gloomy preoccupation by the appearance of the German Army, stopped to watch when they saw the small staff car roll by.

As in most towns, there was a look of real concern on the people's faces. While everyone knew what was happening from the nonstop news coverage provided by the television and newspapers, the appearance of real soldiers, armed and ready for battle, on their streets could not be ignored. It had to be dealt with.

Many Germans had no real interest in the arguments put forth by their government. The Americans, they argued, were a benign presence. They had been there for years, one old woman told a reporter, and if they weren't, then someone else would have been. Better the Americans, she said, than the Russians or the English. Like the old woman, many Germans could not really understand why the men in Berlin were being so stubborn, so uncompromising in their dealings with the Americans. Most hoped that it was all a big bluff that, when the final call came, both sides would back down from.

The presence of real soldiers in their streets was to the people of Niederjossa proof that the government was prepared to make good its threats. And if that happened, the people of Niederjossa knew that the clash of arms would be played out in their town, right there in front of their own homes, before their eyes and the eyes of their children. It did not take a great leap of imagination either to picture what would happen when that clash came. Almost as soon as the Americans began flowing into Bavaria, television stations across Germany ran special reports that showed file footage from recent conflicts depicting the carnage that modern war leaves in its wake. Spliced in with older footage from the last war in Germany, the special reports had the effect of reinforcing the positions of those of the political center and left who were calling for immediate negotiations and efforts by the government in Berlin to defuse the situation. When the pleas of German legislators, news correspondents, local officials whose communities lay in the projected line of march, and concerned citizens fell on deaf ears, many decided to take matters in their own hands. So it came as no surprise to the captain when he saw several Germans, both young students on their way home from school and old women, stop in midstride and reach down to grab a handful of snow. Knowing what was next, the captain turned back to his driver and told him to speed up.

While the captain was able to make it through the center of town without much trouble, the trucks following the captain's Volkswagen caught the full weight of the German civilians' anger. When the first truck rumbled into sight, the citizens of Niederjossa had snowballs in hand and were ready. The soldiers riding in the rear of the truck were exposed to the full fury of the volley of snowballs, since the canvas sides of the lead truck were rolled up to allow the soldiers sitting on the bench seats that ran down the centerline of the truck's cargo bed to look out. The soldiers ducked and covered their faces as best they could while the truck's driver attempted to speed up. His efforts, however, were frustrated by the driver of a car that had slipped in behind the captain's Volkswagen and the lead truck. The driver of the car slowed down in order to allow his fellow townsmen a chance to launch a second and third volley of snowballs at the exposed and defenseless soldiers. Only the driver of the truck, a senior sergeant seated next to him, and a gunner who had been manning the machine gun set on a ring mounted at the top of the truck's cab escaped the full fury of the snowballs, but not completely. Several still splattered on the windows of the cab, some with a pronounced snap, indicating that some of the more vicious peace-loving civilians had put stones in the center of their snowballs. One particularly well aimed snowball even came in through the opening where the machine gunner had been standing and hit the machine gunner square on the head.

While the machine gunner jumped up to shake his fist at the shouting civilians and the sergeant tried to pull him back down into the cab, the driver of the truck inched closer to the slow-moving car until he lightly tapped the car's rear with the massive steel bumper of the truck. The driver of the car quickly understood the message. Knowing that the truck driver meant the first tap as a warning, the driver turned onto a side street as soon as he could, leaving the truck driver free to pick up speed and roll clear of the town center.

Only after they had cleared the last of Niederjossa's houses did the sergeant slap the machine gunner on the head with the palm of his hand. Recoiling from the sudden slap, the machine gunner yelled out in perfect English, "Hey, what in the hell did you do that for, Sergeant Rasper?"

"Because, Specialist Pape, I know you and you've got a big mouth."

Still angry and upset, Pape looked down at the floor of the cab, and then back to Rasper. "I wouldn't have said anything in English. I just wanted to give them the finger."

"That, you idiot, would have been just as bad. Germans use different hand and arm signals to communicate their displeasure with their fellow countrymen. Now if you can't do what you're supposed to and behave like a good little Nazi, I'll throw you in the back with the rest of the company." When he saw that Pape was finished pouting, Rasper stuck his thumb up. "Now get up there and see if the other trucks made it out and have caught up." While Pape climbed back up to man his machine gun and check to their rear, Rasper looked down at his map and spoke to the driver. "Let's start picking up speed and see if we can catch up with Major Ilvanich. We're almost at the bridge."

"Goddamned German Nazi sons of bitches. One town hails you like a hero and the next spits in your eye. I think the major's right. We should just say the hell with it, put on Russian uniforms, and let everyone hate us. At least we'd know what to expect."

Rolling his eyes, Rasper shook his head and repeated his order. "Quit thinking, Pape, and get back up there."

Ignoring the blast of frigid air that hit him as soon as he stuck his head up out of the cab, Pape grabbed the machine gun ring mount and pulled himself up. Planting his feet shoulder width apart on the cab's seat and bracing himself against the steel ring mount, Pape managed to get a good stable stance while the wind whipped at his back. Looking down the road back toward Niederjossa, he saw the last of the trucks carrying Company A, 1st Ranger Battalion, leave the town. Second Lieutenant Fitzhugh, whom everyone had begun calling Lieutenant Fuzz after the Beetle Bailey cartoon character, was in that truck bringing up the company's rear. Like the truck that Rasper and Pape were traveling in, Fitzhugh's truck had its canvas sides rolled up, exposing the soldiers of Company A. Wearing German Army uniforms and rank insignia, and riding in German Army trucks "borrowed" by Major Ilvanich at a German Army reserve depot, all the Caucasian soldiers of the company were grouped into one platoon. Led by Fitzhugh and nicknamed the "Salt" Platoon by Sergeant First Class Raymond Jefferson, the senior black soldier in the company and leader of the "Pepper" Platoon, this platoon was the up-front platoon, the one that Ilvanich intended to use when pretending to be the commander of a German infantry company. Jefferson and all the black soldiers in the company were formed into what Ilvanich referred to as his sneaky devil platoon, which would slip around any enemy while Fitzhugh held the enemy's attention. Riding in two of the covered trucks in the center, Jefferson and his platoon, retaining their own weapons and uniforms, kept track of where they were and what was happening by watching through holes discreetly cut into the canvas sides covering their truck's cargo bed. The third truck, in the center of the column, carried extra rations, fuel, ammunition, and the American uniforms and weapons for Fitzhugh's platoon.

Seeing that everyone had made it and was caught up, Pape bent down and informed Rasper. Standing back up, but before turning around, Pape pulled the gray German Army scarf up over his mouth and his goggles down over his eyes. Ready, he faced front just in time

to see the open Volkswagen staff car with Ilvanich and Sergeant Couvelha pull back onto the road from a small rest stop where it had been
waiting for the trucks. Off in the distance Pape could barely make out
the autobahn bridge over the Fulda River that they were to secure in
advance of the Tenth Corps. Though it was now less than a kilometer
away, it was partially obscured by fog and mist. The Russian major
kept telling everyone in the company that the gloomy, gray overcast
sky was good for the corps, since it limited aerial surveillance by the
Luftwaffe and German Army helicopters. The worse the weather, he
told everyone, the faster we go. To Pape, however, that same depressing scene only meant that they would spend another cold, dark, and
miserable night with their asses hanging way out in front of the rest
of the corps, waiting for someone to come along and relieve them
before the Germans found them out and killed them all.

Not that he wouldn't have preferred a good stand-up fight. Anything, Pape thought, was better than tromping around in enemy territory waiting for someone to discover who they really were. That, to
Pape, was nerve-racking. To a cocky young man full of piss and vin-
egar, infiltrating enemy lines in advance of the corps' main body to
secure key terrain and bridges lacked glamour, though he was finally
beginning to realize what being a ranger was all about. Slowly the
whole operation to him was turning out to be just like ranger camp.
The only difference was that instead of having to make long, grueling,
back-breaking treks through the Florida swamps, they got to ride.
That and the fact that if they screwed up this patrol there wouldn't be
a next patrol. For that matter, as he watched Ilvanich's Volkswagen
slow as it approached a roadblock on the highway manned by real
German soldiers, there wouldn't be a next anything. Reaching forward
with his right hand, Pape grasped the bolt lever in the palm of his
upturned hand and gave it a jerk back, cocking the weapon just in case
Ilvanich couldn't convince the real Nazis that they were, as Rasper
would say, good little Nazis too.

Too cold to leave the warmth of the fire they had started on the side
of the road, the two German Army engineers waved Ilvanich through
with no more than a glance. Angered by this lack of soldierly vigilance, Ilvanich was about to stop to yell at the German Army engineers for failing to challenge him. After considering the matter
carefully, however, Ilvanich decided not to. Though he knew that a
good German Army captain would do so, there was always the pos-

sibility that he just might play his role too well, causing the German soldiers to react by asking him for documents and identification that he did not have. Besides, he did not know for sure how his American rangers would react to such a challenge. Although he had no doubt that they were all good men, he'd had little time to work with them. Neither he nor the Americans had been able to establish the working relationship that allowed commander and soldiers to react intuitively as one in the short time that they had been together. So Ilvanich allowed the transgressions of the German Army engineers to go unpunished. They would someday pay for that. Turning away, Ilvanich motioned to Couvelha to head for a group of military vehicles parked under the autobahn bridge.

Even before he stopped, a young lieutenant of pioneers, German combat engineers, strolled up to Ilvanich's staff car and gave Ilvanich a casual salute. Without waiting for Ilvanich to return the salute, the young German lieutenant smiled as he spoke. "Well, can't say that I'm not glad to see you and your company. We've been finished for hours, waiting to get out of here and find someplace where we can warm up." Glancing beyond the lieutenant, Ilvanich saw the rest of the engineer platoon warming themselves around a barrel with fire in it. Again deciding not to criticize, Ilvanich simply nodded as he returned the lieutenant's salute. Looking about at the underside of the bridge to study the handiwork of the German engineers as he slowly got out of the staff car, Ilvanich, almost absentmindedly, began to question the lieutenant. "Must have taken most of the day to prepare this target."

"Actually, we started yesterday and finished this morning, Herr Captain. It was a bit too much to work on it during the night. The cold and all, you know."

No, Ilvanich thought, I don't know. These Germans, he thought, were not as good as he had expected. Perhaps, he thought, this was just a lazy unit. And if this unit wasn't an isolated case, if the whole German Army was as bad, the Americans just might be able to pull off this insane plan after all. Shaking his head, Ilvanich turned and faced the lieutenant. "Do you have written orders?"

The lieutenant nodded. "Well yes, of course."

Ilvanich didn't need to pretend that he was losing his patience with the German officer. He really was. "Well, Lieutenant, let me see them now."

Startled by Ilvanich's sudden demand, the lieutenant jumped slightly. "Well, I have to go get them from my map case, Herr Captain."

Narrowing his eyes into a piercing glare that sent a shiver down the German engineer lieutenant's back, Ilvanich leaned forward and snarled, "Well why don't you do that, Lieutenant."

While he waited for the orders, Ilvanich looked back at his own trucks. With little talking, the rangers of Company A had dismounted and were gathering around the rear of Fitzhugh's truck. Only Pape, manning the machine gun in the lead truck and providing Ilvanich cover, remained behind. And of course Jefferson and his Pepper Platoon were ready to pounce at the first sign of trouble. A few chuckles and muted laughter told Ilvanich that Rasper was using his fractured German to form up Fitzhugh's platoon. He had heard Rasper practice it and had found it amusing. Commands such as "Fallin zee in," and "Mockin much snell, now," mixed with Rasper's lazy Texas drawl, brought smiles to everyone, even the normally solemn Ilvanich. This, however, was not the time, Ilvanich knew, for such antics. Barking out in German to Fitzhugh to knock it off, Ilvanich's booming voice caused everyone in the area, real Germans and rangers, to stop what they were doing and turn toward Ilvanich.

At the rear of the column, Fitzhugh, realizing that Ilvanich was yelling to him, moved to the side of the last covered truck, where Sergeant Jefferson was, and stopped. With no idea of what Ilvanich wanted because he couldn't speak German, Fitzhugh looked toward Ilvanich but whispered to Jefferson, who spoke the language fluently. "What's the major want, Sergeant Jefferson?"

Seeing that he had an excellent opportunity to mess with what he called his favorite lieutenant, Jefferson took liberties with his translation of Ilvanich's order. "The major said, 'Lieutenant Fuzz, if you don't pull your head out of that lily white ass of yours and get that platoon under control, I'm going to come down there and stick my size twelve Russian boot up your butt.' "

Fitzhugh shook his head and smiled to himself. "But the major doesn't wear a size twelve. Please ask him, Sergeant Jefferson, to repeat his last order, just to make sure you got it right."

Silence followed by muted chuckles told Fitzhugh that he had stumped Jefferson. "Okay, fun's over. I'll get my people under control. Please do the same to yours. Supply trucks, especially German Army supply trucks, Sergeant Jefferson, don't laugh."

Back at the head of the column, the engineer lieutenant returned with the orders. Ilvanich took them and read them carefully. As he was doing so, the German lieutenant commented that he had never thought that he would be given such orders. Ilvanich, pausing, looked about at the gathered German pioneers, then up at underside of the autobahn bridge at the explosives that he and his rangers would soon be removing. A smile slowly began to creep across his face as he looked down at the German officer. "Funny," Ilvanich said. "Somehow I always knew that I'd be doing exactly this."

Struck by the captain's strange reaction, the engineer lieutenant didn't comment as Ilvanich went back to reading the orders. The captain, the lieutenant thought, was the hard, cold, and very proper Prussian type. He could see it in the captain's face, in his voice, even in the way he wore his short hair and uniform, all very military and very proper. The captain, judging from his accent, had to be an easterner, the lieutenant decided. He was right. He just didn't realize how far east Ilvanich really came from.

Finished, Ilvanich folded the orders and turned to place them in his own map case sitting on the side of his staff car's seat. The orders, official German military orders, gave Ilvanich documentation that he didn't have before that might be useful in bluffing his way through a tight confrontation with other, more alert German officers. When the German lieutenant protested Ilvanich's taking of the orders, Ilvanich demurred. "Your work here is finished. They told you to prepare this target for demolition and then wait for either orders to execute it or to turn it over to another unit that would guard it or execute it for you. My orders, all verbal unfortunately, are to relieve you of responsibility for this target."

Still unsure about leaving Ilvanich with his orders, the lieutenant countered. "I was expecting to be relieved by elements of the 2nd Panzer Division. A staff officer from that division was by here a few hours ago warning me that they would be delayed another ten to twelve hours at least. They are supposed to establish blocking positions here while linking up with the 10th Panzer Division to the east."

"Did this staff officer say where that link-up was to be made?"

Not suspecting that Ilvanich's question was anything other than idle curiosity, the lieutenant nodded. "Yes, Herr Captain. He said that the link-up would be somewhere east of Alsfeld. Once they had made that link-up, the staff officer said that the Americans would be forced either to stop and give up their race for the sea or attack. Quite frankly, Herr Captain, I think the staff officer was hoping that the Americans would attack. There are some officers I know who are looking for a fight."

Looking back at Fitzhugh and his platoon, ready to move forward and assume control of the massive autobahn bridge as soon as the German engineers were gone, Ilvanich shook his head. "Well, Lieutenant, if those officers knew the Americans like I do, they would think twice before messing with them. Now, unless there's something else that you need to tell me, I accept responsibility for this site and relieve you and your platoon."

Glad to be finished, the lieutenant told Ilvanich that as far as he could see all was in order. Saluting, he turned to gather up his men and equipment. The German engineers left the bridge without a second thought, leaving Ilvanich and Company A to disarm the masses of explosives the Germans had worked so hard to emplace and to pass on to the Tenth Corps G-2 the information Ilvanich had been able to glean from them.

While Ilvanich and the rangers of Company A secured the autobahn bridge east of Niederjossa, the lead elements of the 4th Armored Division prepared to make their next leap forward. Like a great Slinky toy moving across the face of Germany, each night the Tenth Corps would spring up, stretch out, move forward, and then collapse on itself further north than the night before. While that simple analogy might make Malin's "March to the Sea" understandable, the actual complex process of moving a corps with over 75,000 soldiers and 30,000 vehicles defied the ability of any one person to really understand the process. For it entailed more than simply lining up vehicles and putting them on the road.

In the first place, the Tenth Corps had to be prepared to fight. Combat maneuver units, armored cavalry squadrons, tank battalions, and mechanized infantry battalions marching in the lead, on the flanks, and in the rear of the corps, had to be arranged so that they could bull through a blocking position or turn and defend the rest of the corps from a thrust from a German unit. This requirement dictated the order and manner in which combat support units followed.

The march tables of artillery units had to conform to the movements of the tank and infantry units so as to allow the artillery units to rapidly set up and fire in support of the combat maneuver units if they made contact with German units determined to fight. The result was that the Tenth Corps, instead of moving forward as one large Slinky toy, in reality consisted of thousands of tiny company- and platoon-sized Slinkys. Moving at different times along different routes and to different locations, these separate companies and platoons tried hard to be at the right place at the right time without ensnaring with each other, a feat that they achieved most of the time but not always.

Mixed in with the combat maneuver units were the ubiquitous engineer units, ready to jump forward in front of the combat maneuver units to bridge a river or to clear an obstacle. To protect the ground elements from attack by German aircraft, which already were flying over the long columns with great regularity, were air defense units armed with heat-seeking and radar-guided missiles such as the Stinger and the Patriot. These units, relying on a system of interlocking early-warning radar, had to conform both to the needs of combat maneuver units and the leapfrogging forward elements of the radar network to cover the entire corps.

Within the complex and intricate layering of combat and combat support units were the combat service support elements. Signal units like the air defense radar units had to leap forward in well-planned jumps so as to maintain the communications between units and their superior headquarters. Supply and transportation units, collectively known as trains at every level from battalion to corps, had to move forward to refuel and resupply all elements of the corps, to include themselves. This process was extremely elaborate, made more so by the fact that the entire corps was moving up through Germany like a great bubble. Supplies and fuel, therefore, had to flow in all directions, out from the center and not just from the rear forward as was normally practiced. This complication alone made the already challenging task of meeting the needs of combat and combat support units while the support units themselves were moving a task that defied description.

Mixed in with the supply and transportation units as part of the trains were the medical and maintenance units, one responsible for retrieving and tending to wounded soldiers and the other for recovering and repairing, if possible, the damaged or broken-down vehicles and equipment left in the wake of the advancing corps. Like the sup-

ply units, the task of these elements of the trains was complicated by
the fact that this was not a normal textbook operation. Neither the
hospitals nor the maintenance units would be able to stop and fully
set up their operations. They, like everyone else, would be in an almost constant state of movement or preparation for movement. This
alone made it impossible to provide all the necessary services that
they were capable of. As with every other support element, the need
to deal with the evacuation of wounded in all directions, not just from
front to rear, made their tasks more arduous and demanding.

That, however, was not the most difficult part of the operation for
these dedicated professionals, both in the medical and maintenance
fields. The standing orders issued before the beginning of the march
established demanding criteria to be used in deciding which wounded
soldiers and damaged vehicles would be worked on and kept with the
corps and which would be left behind. Those wounded whose lives or
limbs would be endangered if kept with the Tenth Corps would be left
in the hands of German medical services at the nearest hospital. Damaged or broken-down vehicles and equipment would be abandoned
and destroyed if deemed unrepairable in the time available or if parts
were not available. While it could be easily argued that there was no
comparing the two, wounded personnel and disabled vehicles, the
dedication of the officers and soldiers in the maintenance units to the
accomplishment of their duties is no less real and pressing than that
of their counterparts in the medical units.

While Ilvanich and his rangers worked to clear the corps' line of
march, the personnel of the 553rd Field Hospital prepared for another
night of aimless wandering. Hilary Cole was charged that night with
supervising the transfer of three Tenth Corps soldiers injured in traffic
accidents over to the Germans. Leading the stretcher bearers carrying
the wounded personnel from the ward tent of their field hospital set
up in the parking lot of a German civilian hospital into the emergency
room of the German hospital, Cole pondered the wisdom of leaving
Americans behind. Though all three Americans had sustained internal injuries in separate incidents that required a recovery period of
rest and care that a moving field hospital could not provide, the idea
of leaving fellow countrymen in the hands of "The Enemy" bothered
Cole.

Leading the small parade of litter bearers and wounded, Cole was greeted by a German nurse whose English was about as bad as Cole's German was. The German nurse, an older heavyset woman with a round face and dressed in an immaculate white uniform, was seated behind a counter when Cole and her charges entered. After shouting out something in German to Cole that she did not understand, the German nurse stared at Cole for several seconds, looking her up and down with obvious disdain. Cole, like everyone else in her unit, had been unable to take proper care of herself or her personal needs. Moving about in what had appeared to her and the other nurses of the 553rd to be a totally random fashion, without ever knowing where they were going or when they would get there, unable to fully set up their hospital and the living areas for the staff, left Cole looking and feeling miserable, dirty, and haggard.

Realizing that everyone in the hospital was staring at them, half unsure what to do and half disgusted, Cole decided that she needed to assert herself. As much as she hated the idea of leaving her wounded here in the hands of foreigners, she knew in her heart that it was the right thing to do. The fact that she couldn't even properly care for herself made her realize how foolish it would be to saddle the 553rd with severely injured soldiers. When it became obvious that the Germans were not going to make the first move, Cole motioned for the stretcher bearers to set the wounded down, took off her helmet, and walked over to the counter where the big German nurse sat. Though she suspected that the German nurse wouldn't understand the words, Cole hoped that she would understand the meaning. Supplemented with motions of her hand, Cole tried to explain who she was and what they were there for. "I am a nurse. Those soldiers are injured and we cannot take them with us. We have an arrangement with your hospital to leave them. Who do I see to make the transfer?"

There was at first no sign of comprehension on the German nurse's face. She just sat there staring at Cole while Cole went about pointing at the wounded and talking. After a pause of several seconds, during which Cole became convinced that she had totally failed to communicate, the German nurse stood up and called for another nurse. A thin young nurse, her long blond hair pulled back and secured in a neat tight bun, who had been standing off to one side watching and listening, came up next to Cole and introduced herself. "I am Marie. The head nurse doesn't speak English, so I will assist you."

The smile on Marie's face caused Cole to relax. "Where can I take my patients? They are, I'm afraid, in the way where they are, and it's not a good idea to leave them for long near the doors. Drafts and all, you know."

Marie nodded and smiled. "Yes, yes, we know. If you would have your stretcher bearers pick up the injured, I'll take you to an examination room. Our doctors would like to examine them themselves and have them cleaned up before we send them to the wards and begin treatment."

Cole blushed slightly in embarrassment. "I am so sorry that they are not in better shape. We're very hard pressed to tend to even the most basic needs. These are hard times for us."

Marie glanced over at the big German nurse as she leaned closer to Cole. "Yes, I know," she whispered. "These are hard times for all of us. Her son," Marie said while nodding toward the big German nurse, "is a soldier with the 2nd Panzer Division. But don't worry. She is a good nurse, and your soldiers will be well cared for, just like our own."

The look in Marie's eyes, her efforts to ease Cole's concern, and the smile on her face told Cole that it would be all right, that she was doing the right thing. After thanking Marie for her kind words, Cole signaled the stretcher bearers to pick up the wounded and follow Marie. For the first time in days, Cole felt that something she was doing made sense. Perhaps, she thought, things weren't as bad as they had seemed. Perhaps, she thought, this would all work out in the end.

Within easy walking distance of the hospital where Cole was transferring her charges over to the Germans, men and women of the Tenth Corps' G-2 counterintelligence section were doing their part to blind or at least confuse German intelligence. Their current task of keeping German intelligence from gathering all the information that it needed to form a complete and accurate picture of where the Tenth Corps was and what it was up to at first seemed impossible.

The Tenth Corps was, after all, moving through the heart of Germany. Even in those towns and villages that dotted the corps' route of march with great regularity, where the populace supported the American efforts through noninterference, there were always a few who were outraged by what they called "the rape of our homeland by the foreign invaders." Together with local police officials dedicated to their duties, this network of informers provided the German intelligence agencies, both military and civilian, with a wealth of information. The Tenth Corps policy of noninterference with civilian property and operations seemed to aid this, since no efforts were made to cut the civilian phone system or hinder the movement of German civilian police. Even mail deliveries were still being carried out with great regularity between what was now referred to by Chancellor Ruff as occupied Germany and the rest of the nation.

Knowing full well that they would be unable to hide even the smallest piece of the corps from German eyes, the corps operations officer and intelligence officer decided that their deception plan would capitalize on this free flow of information. A special corps counterintelligence section formed a detachment manned by American personnel fluent in German as well as some trusted Germans, collectively known as the Valkyrie. This detachment, using a master deception plan drawn up by corps, used the same system and format utilized by the regular German informers to insert volumes of misinformation into the German intelligence system in an effort to both mislead the Germans and to discredit genuine information. By providing information that ranged from very nearly accurate to wild exaggerations, the Valkyrie matched the manner and the nature of the reports coming in from real informers who were zealous but untrained, and thus were indistinguishable from the real German information sources.

To assist this active program, a passive deception plan was also carried out corpswide. All distinctive unit markings and vehicle identification numbers and patches were removed from vehicles, equipment, and uniforms. In selected cases, however, some numbers were left on, while in other cases some numbers were changed to reflect a different unit. To totally confuse the Germans, and encourage the discounting of reports from real informers, some of the false unit markings placed on vehicles were those of units still stationed in the United States. So even if a real informer reported that a tank company rolled through his village at such and such a time headed in such and such a direction, the intelligence officer in Berlin would have to discount that report when the informer added that two of the vehicles had bumper numbers showing the tanks belonged to 1st Battalion, 32nd Armor, a tank battalion stationed at Fort Hood, Texas.

Inundated with masses of reports whose reliability was becoming more and more suspect, the German Army began to turn to its own intelligence-gathering efforts. Like tiny tentacles, air and ground reconnaissance elements crept forward in advance of the German combat units. Some of the recon units were very circumspect, relying on stealth and caution to close with and gather information on American forces. The techniques and methods used by German armored reconnaissance or *Panzeraufklärung* units ranged from the conventional to the artistic. One German cavalry sergeant, finding an ideal spot from which to observe a major north-south highway near Fulda, buried his eight-wheeled Luchs armored reconnaissance vehicle in a farmer's dungheap up to the turret ring and smeared the turret with dung. Only the keen eye of an American soldier who noticed an antenna waving gently in the breeze above the dungheap gave the German away.

Other German reconnaissance units were quite open and bold in their efforts. Taking advantage of the ambiguousness of the confrontation and the fact that no one had yet fired a shot, it was not unusual to see German Luchs armored cars parked on hilltops or right in the middle of a road, their crews sitting up on the turret roof as they counted the American vehicles that went by. In these cases, American vehicles with smoke generators, when available, were dispatched to pull up close to the German vehicles and then turn on their smoke generators. Depending on the mood of the American sergeant commanding the smoke-generating vehicle, the smokescreen was used to block the Germans' view or actually blow right across the German reconnaissance vehicle. This, of course, made it necessary for the German vehicle to move, which in turn caused the American smoke-generating vehicle to follow. Hal Cerro, watching one such pursuit with Scott Dixon, commented that it was like watching a cat run around with a can of rocks tied to its tail. Dixon, ever the realist, pointed out that this cat had big claws and sharp teeth that eventually it would use when it tired of these antics.

In support of the ground and air reconnaissance effort, units of the German Army responsible for gathering signal intelligence, called "sigint" for short, scanned the airwaves in search of units of the Tenth Corps. When a Tenth Corps radio was activated and its signal detected by a German Army signal intelligence unit, the Germans could eavesdrop on the conversation if it was not encrypted in an effort to find out what type of unit was making the transmission, what their situation was, and who they were talking to. If the signal was encrypted, then the Germans could at least locate the transmitter through a technique known as "resection" and, with this information available, create a picture of unit locations to confirm or deny information provided by informers. If all else failed, the Germans always had the option of jamming the American radio frequencies in use or recording the transmitters' locations for targeting at a later date.

To further hinder the reconnaissance efforts of the German Army, the Tenth Corps operations plan called for the bulk of the corps' movement to take place during periods of limited visibility. Since the sun set in central Germany before five in the afternoon during January and didn't come up again until after seven in the morning, the corps had plenty of darkness to operate with. Use of multiple routes, including countless logging and farm trails that ran through Germany like tiny capillaries through the human body, aided in confusing the Germans.

Darkness and fog, however, could not hide radio signals. In an effort similar to that of the Valkyrie informers, dummy headquarters were set up to simulate radio traffic of real headquarters. Consisting of three or four vehicles equipped with the same type of radios used by the real headquarters, these dummy headquarters moved about the Tenth Corps area in accordance with the Tenth Corps deception plan, the same used by the Valkyrie. While the real headquarters continued to move in radio-listening silence, using messengers or the German telephone system for communications, their dummy counterparts operated radio nets that normally would be used by the real headquarters. As they passed information back and forth, German signal intelligence units would track the dummy units, feeding that information into the German intelligence system. Of course, eventually most dummy headquarters were discovered for what they were. When the Americans were able to detect that a dummy headquarters had been compromised, those dummy headquarters were shut down and sent elsewhere to assume the identity of another headquarters, but not always. As an added twist, when everyone at Tenth Corps was sure that a dummy headquarters was in fact identified as one, the dummy headquarters was co-located with the real one. In this way, information provided by the German Army signal intelligence units claiming that a unit was a dummy actually discredited good solid information from other sources that identified the real headquarters and its associated units.

This war for information and intelligence that was being waged on the ground and in the airwaves over central Germany was not without its risks and costs. While flying back from the 14th Armored Cavalry

Regiment's forward command post in Fulda to the air squadron's command post, Major Bob Messinger, the squadron operations officer, noticed movement that he thought was a helicopter off to his left. He ordered his pilot, Warrant Officer Three Larry Perkins, to come around so that he could get a better look. After searching the area for several seconds, Messinger saw what he was looking for. "See 'em? Do you see them over there to the left?"

Perkins, watching his altitude and speed with one eye, glanced over to where Messinger was pointing. Finally, in the failing late-afternoon light, Perkins caught a glimpse of two German scout helicopters flying low and slow toward the west, side by side. "Oh, yeah. I see." Then as an afterthought he added, "Tryin' to be sneaky little devils, aren't they?"

Without taking his eyes from the German helicopters, Messinger mused, "Well, they're not being very good at it, are they? Look at 'em. Damn. There isn't more than a hundred meters between them. And I don't think they've seen us."

While bringing their helicopter around in a circle behind the German helicopters, Perkins continued to watch his instruments, where he was going, and the Germans. "Bad case of tunnel vision. You don't suppose they have someone flying cover, do you?"

Understanding Perkins's comment for the warning it was, Messinger began to look about for any sign of other German helicopters or aircraft. When he was sure there weren't any, he turned back to the two German helicopters. By this time Perkins had brought their own helicopter behind the Germans, slowing almost to a hover. Deciding that this was a good time to report, Messinger submitted a sighting report, called a spot report, back to the squadron command post. After providing his assistant operations officer at the command post with the location, number of helicopters sighted, their type, and their activity, Messinger turned to Perkins. "You feel like having a little fun?"

Knowing what Messinger was hinting at, Perkins looked at his fuel gauge, his other instruments, and the amount of daylight left, and thought for a second. When he was sure that they could afford to deviate from their flight plan, Perkins turned to Messinger and smiled. "Sure. You're the boss. Do we sneak up or dig our spurs in and charge home?"

"Let's shake these guys' trees a little. Kick her in the ass and overfly 'em. And, Larry, I want to see what color eyes the pilot of the right helicopter has."

Lining up his ancient OH-58 with the Germans, Perkins set himself like a sprinter in the starting blocks. Messinger, taking one last glance around to make sure there weren't any other Germans trailing or covering the two German scouts that they were about to pounce on, called out that the coast was clear. When all was ready, Perkins simply said, "Here we go," and began their run in.

Easing the joy stick forward with his right hand, Perkins tilted the main rotor forward by twisting the collective on his side with his left hand while manipulating the pedals with his feet to keep the tail boom straight. All these actions, done with the ease and grace of an experienced aviator who flew almost exclusively by feel and touch, put the helicopter in a nose-down position as the main rotor bit into the air and pulled the helicopter forward at ever increasing speeds.

By the time they were within one hundred meters of the two German scouts, Perkins and Messinger's helicopter had just about maxed out their airspeed. With a final quick jerk up on the cyclic, Perkins pulled their helicopter up and over the two Germans. Once he was sure that they had cleared the German helicopters, Perkins eased the collective down, causing the helicopter to drop right in front of the Germans. After holding this for a couple of seconds to ensure that the Germans got a chance to see who he was, Perkins made a hard left bank in order to get out of the Germans' line of fire.

Shooting, however, was the last thing the two German pilots were thinking of at that moment. They had been, as Messinger observed, totally oblivious to everything except where they were going. The sudden appearance of another helicopter overflying them at a high rate of speed and then dropping right in front of them just meters away caused both pilots to panic and overreact. The German to the left pulled up and made a sharp bank to the left in order to avoid a collision with the unknown intruder. He sought safety in altitude and speed. The other German attempted to do the same, but didn't quite gain enough altitude before he began his bank to the right. The result was that as his helicopter began to tilt to the right its rotors bit into the branches of a pine tree off to his side. Though the branches didn't shatter or break the rotors, the sudden blade strike, coupled with the shock of Perkins's overflight, totally unnerved the German pilot. At a loss as to what to do and unable to comprehend everything that was happening, the German flared out and crash-landed his helicopter.

While they were still coming around and slowing some, Messinger saw the effects of their maneuver. When he saw the blade strike and the crash landing of the German helicopter that had been on the right, he held his breath as he waited to see if the German helicopter caught fire. Perkins, also watching, said nothing. Instead he brought his own helicopter around in a tighter bank and headed for the crashed helicopter. As they approached, both men experienced a sinking feeling while they watched to see if their fellow aviators were able to make it clear of the wreckage. When they saw one, then the other, free himself from the downed aircraft, both men felt great relief. Messinger broke the silence by instructing Perkins to set down near the two downed aviators.

While approaching the crash site, two thoughts kept running through Messinger's mind. The first was a fear that their actions would be viewed in the worst possible light by the German government and serve as the pretext that it was so desperately looking for in order to start a real shooting war. Everyone in the Tenth Corps had been warned on a daily basis to avoid doing anything within reason that would give the Germans the excuse to start firing. Messinger himself had mouthed those words to the troop commanders in his squadron. It was because of this that the second thought or, more correctly, feeling kept gnawing at him. He felt, as Perkins prepared to land, the same feeling that he had when as a child he had broken something by accident and was trying to see if he could fix it before his mom and dad found out.

Once on the ground, Messinger was out of his helicopter before Perkins shut it down. Running over to the first German aviator, Messinger yelled, "Are you all right? Are you hurt?" The German was sitting in the snow, resting his elbows on his knees and holding his head in his hands. When Messinger finally reached him without getting any response, he bent over and reached out with his right hand, resting it on the German's shoulder before asking again, "Are you all right?"

The German aviator, finally recovered enough from the shock of the crash landing, looked up. Still too dazed to think clearly or be angry, he just nodded. "*Ja*, yes. I think so." Then looking over to the helicopter, he asked, "Otto! *Wo ist—*, where is Otto?"

Messinger, still with his hand on the German's shoulder, looked about for the other German aviator. He saw Otto on the other side of the helicopter standing next to a tree. Supporting himself with one hand, Otto was bending over, either trying to catch his breath or throwing up. When Perkins, carrying a first aid kit, came up next to Messinger, Messinger pointed over to where Otto was and told Perkins to head over there and see how he was doing. Perkins had no sooner left when Messinger heard two voices behind him. "Erich, Otto! Erich, Otto! *Wo sind sie?"*

Turning around, Messinger saw two Germans in flight suits approaching at a run. The other helicopter had, he decided, also landed to check on their comrades. As he watched them approach, Messinger noticed that the lead aviator had a drawn pistol in his right hand while the other one carried a submachine gun at the ready. Suddenly for the first time it dawned upon Messinger that landing might have been a bigger mistake than just flying away. Realizing that it was too late to do anything, Messinger stood up and waved to the approaching Germans. Having decided that bluffing it out was the best solution, he called out, "Erich is here. He's shook up but okay. Otto is over there with my pilot."

The German aviator wearing the insignia of a captain slowed down as he approached. There was a scowl on his face as he looked at Messinger, then at Erich, and then back up to Messinger. When he was ten feet away, the German captain let his right hand, which still held the pistol, drop to his side as he spoke. "You fool. You could have killed us."

Messinger did not miss the irony of the German captain's statement. Given the political and the military situation, that was exactly what they should have been doing. And yet, Messinger thought, just when it seemed that he had succeeded in doing just that, his first reaction and that of his pilot had been one of concern. They had come running out of habit to assist fellow aviators in distress, not to view their handiwork. And because it was so obvious that this was so, the German captain began to holster his pistol as he directed his observer to go help Perkins with Otto.

Squatting, the German captain placed his hand on the side of Erich's head and said something in German that caused Erich to respond with a weak smile that vanished as soon as it had come. Feeling out of place and uneasy, Messinger stepped back. "Hey, I'm sorry. We were only trying to scare you."

The German captain stood up and faced Messinger. "Well, Herr Major, you succeeded. Now you'd better go. There is a recovery team coming in with my battalion commander. He might take a dim view of seeing you here and decide to keep you."

Nodding, Messinger called to Perkins and began to walk. He had only gone a few steps when the German captain called out. "Major!" Stopping in midstride, Messinger turned toward the German. The German captain was looking down at Erich as he spoke. "Thank you for landing and your concern." Then he looked up at Messinger. "I wish our leaders could have been here to see that we are not in reality enemies."

Messinger looked about. "Yes, I know what you mean. Auf Wiedersehen, and good luck."

PART
FOUR

CENTRAL GERMANY

CHAPTER 13

19 JANUARY

Like someone hitting a light switch, the violent tugging at the bottom of his sleeping bag brought Staff Sergeant Joe Dallas out of a sound sleep. For a moment he didn't move, didn't make a sound. Perched on top of the turret of his M-1A1 Abrams tank, wedged in between boxes of rations, duffel bags full of personal gear, and boxes of .50-caliber ammunition, Dallas, known to everyone since his first day in the Army as Dallas Joe, just listened. It was quiet. Except for the sound of his own breath bounding off the nylon cloth that covered his face and protected it from the wind and weather while he slept, Dallas heard nothing. For a moment, lying there warm and snuggled up tight and secure in his Arctic sleeping bag, he could imagine that he was anywhere. He had even managed to learn over his years in the Army to ignore the discomfort of sleeping on the hard armor plating of his tank. During that moment before the distress of the circumstances crept into his conscious mind, before the bitter cold bit at his cheeks, before the responsibility of being a tank commander came crashing down upon his twenty-six-year-old shoulders, Dallas could enjoy a few seconds to himself, free from the misery and harshness of the circumstances.

Another tug at the bottom of the sleeping bag, followed by his loader's voice, punctuated by a hacking cough, ended Dallas's splendid isolation. "Sergeant Dallas, the LT wants you over at his tank right away. Says there's an order to move out in ten minutes."

With great reluctance, Dallas let out a grunt to acknowledge his loader's efforts. When he was ready, Dallas moved his right hand from where it had been resting mummy style on his chest and pushed the face cloth off. Though he was prepared for the cold, Dallas was not at all ready to be sprinkled with a shower of freshly fallen snow that had accumulated on the cloth. In an instant the peace and tranquillity that Dallas had felt just after waking was wiped away. Sitting up, he looked about but saw nothing. Even when he looked up, he couldn't see any sign of sky. The only thing he could detect was the soft, cold, wet pinpricks of falling snow on his face. It was, he realized, going to be another miserable day in Krautland.

With the speed and efficiency of a professional, Dallas was up, dressed, and on his way to his platoon leader's tank in minutes, leaving his gunner, Sergeant Tim Doyle, to pack up sleeping bags, camouflage nets, and to prepare the tank. When Dallas arrived at his platoon leader's tank, the lieutenant was standing in front of his tank with the platoon sergeant studying a map spread out on the front slope of the tank. Walking up to one side of the platoon leader to where he could see the map, Dallas made his presence known without interfering with the discussion between platoon leader and platoon sergeant. Though both of them realized that Dallas was there, neither acknowledged him nor broke off the discussion that had been in progress.

"You're right, Sergeant Emerson. I don't like the idea of running down the middle of a two-lane highway in the middle of the night either. But the CO was clear. He wanted us to physically make sure that Highway 84 was clear as far as Rasdorf and check out the reports from the division's cavalry squadron of tracked vehicles moving into that village. To me that means he wants us to roll along every inch of that hardball road."

The platoon sergeant, Sergeant First Class Emerson, looked at his lieutenant, thought for a moment, then leaned forward over the map. With a small red-filtered maglight, Emerson studied the map for several moments. "Look here, Lieutenant, there's this logging trail running parallel to the highway. If this map is right, there's a number of smaller logging trails that run from the logging trail out to the main road at regular intervals. I could take my wing man and run the logging trail, sticking my nose out onto the highway every now and then to take a look, while you and your wing man run the main road, but further back. When I see that the road is clear, I'll call. Then you can come up to where I am and hold while I drop back to the main parallel logging trail and go down to the next crossover point. That way we can satisfy the old man's desire to pound the pavement without stumbling down the middle of the road like a bunch of drunks."

Looking at the logging trail that Emerson had pointed out, the lieutenant thought for a moment. "It sounds good, Sergeant Emerson, but that's going to take a long time."

"Did the old man give you a time limit, sir?"

"No, no, he didn't. He just said do it."

"I don't see what the big deal is then. So long as we're doing exactly what he said, it doesn't make any difference how long it takes."

Conceding Emerson's point, the lieutenant sighed. "You're right, Sergeant Emerson. As always, you're right. We'll do that until we get here, just west of Rasdorf. There we'll set up on both sides of the road, with you on the north side and my section on the south. The only difference is that I'll take my section down the logging trail and you run the road. Gotta remember, I'm the platoon leader."

Emerson, trained long ago that there were certain things that you didn't argue about with a West Pointer, merely shrugged. "Okay by me. Unless you have something else, sir, I'm going to go and give Allston and his crew a swift kick and get ready to move."

Emerson, not waiting for a response, disappeared into the darkness. For the first time since his arrival, the lieutenant turned and faced Dallas. "Did you get most of that, Sergeant Dallas?"

Dallas, not pleased that his platoon leader had opted to take the logging trail, something that could be hazardous under the best of conditions, said nothing. Though the risk would have been higher, Dallas would have preferred to go down the road, especially on a night like this. Dicking around on a rutted logging trail at night when you couldn't see your hand in front of your face was not his idea of excitement. Just as Emerson had discovered a long time before, Dallas was finding out that there were some things that you just didn't debate with a young second lieutenant. Instead, Dallas just grunted. "Got it, sir, loud and clear. I'll be ready to roll in less than five."

Satisfied, the lieutenant brushed off the snowflakes that had fallen on his map as he carefully folded it in a manner that would show their route to Rasdorf. "Fine, real fine, Sergeant. Bring your tank around as soon as you're ready and meet me here." Giving his platoon leader a halfhearted salute out of habit, Dallas turned and stumbled back to his tank to prepare for the start of a new day.

Progress, as the lieutenant had anticipated, was slow because the condition of the logging trail was everything that Dallas had expected. The map that both the platoon leader and Dallas used, though it was the most detailed, couldn't show every twist and turn in the logging trail. At times Dallas even wondered if they were on the right trail. But after making the left turn and popping out onto Highway 84 a couple of times, as Emerson had suggested, Dallas stopped worrying. If there was one thing that his platoon leader could do well, it was use the position locator on his tank and read a map. Satisfied that all was going well, Dallas began to relax some by the time they reached the halfway point to Rasdorf.

Tracking their progress on his own map, Dallas figured that they should have reached the next turnoff. Looking up from his map, he saw the cat-eyed taillights of his platoon leader's tank slow and then turn to the left. After making a tick mark on his map case to indicate where they were, Dallas called to his driver, Specialist Bobby Young, to slow down and prepare to turn. Young, already aware of what to do, said nothing in response. He knew that it was just Dallas's way of checking on him and keeping the rest of the crew aware of what was going on. With the greatest of ease, Young began to feel his way into the turn while Dallas leaned as far out of his open hatch as he could to watch that the huge 120mm main gun didn't smack any trees as the tank turned onto the connecting trail that led to Highway 84. When they were on the trail and Dallas saw the taillights of his platoon leader's tank again, he eased himself back down into his open hatch and watched as his platoon leader moved forward slowly toward the main road.

Just before the two tanks reached the road, Dallas ordered Young to stop. He wanted to give the platoon leader some room to back up just in case he needed it. From the hatch of his tank, Dallas watched his platoon leader's tank break free of the woods, climbing up a slight embankment and traversing its turret to the right in the direction of Rasdorf as it went. To Dallas, who didn't like using night vision goggles, everything was black and shades of gray. Even his platoon leader's tank was nothing more than a large black mass before him, with the gun tube slowly moving to the right being the only clear feature of the turret he could see. Turning away for a moment to look down along the side of his own tank to check how well it was doing in negotiating the logging trail, Dallas was startled when suddenly the whole forest seemed to light up around him.

Young, the driver, hit the brakes when he saw a mass of flames leap out of the platoon leader's tank in front of him. Thrown forward and then back, Dallas struggled to regain his balance before looking up at his platoon leader's tank. That tank, now dwarfed by sheets of flame leaping up from the turret, was rolling backwards toward his own tank. Though he had no idea what happened, he suspected the worst. Looking to his left, then to his right, Dallas saw that there was no way to get around his platoon leader's tank, now being racked by a series of secondary explosions. Nor was there any way that he could fight his tank where it stood if he had to. Stuck on the narrow trail, and lit up by the fires from his platoon leader's tank, he would be a sitting duck. The only thing that Dallas could think of was escape. "BACK UP! Young, back up! NOW!"

There was no need for Dallas to repeat his order. Young was already shifting gears before Dallas said anything. When he felt the tank lurch, and then begin to move back, Dallas twisted about in his open hatch, facing to the rear as he prepared to direct Young. Dallas's night vision, however, was shot by the conflagration that was consuming his platoon leader's tank. He saw nothing of what was before him. Dots and blurred images of flames burned into his eyes, blinded him to where he was going and what was happening around him. Keying the intercom switch on the side of his crewman's helmet, Dallas told Young to take it slow and hold the tank straight. Though Dallas didn't hear a response, he could feel the tank slow slightly, telling him that Young had heard and understood.

Both Dallas and Young were calming down and getting their act together when the loader, watching back toward the road, yelled over the intercom, "Dallas! There's something moving on the road. It's—SHIT! It's a tank and he's looking right at us!"

To the west, sitting on the side of Highway 84 just around a bend in the road from where his platoon leader was supposed to come out of the woods next, Sergeant Emerson saw the ball of flame leap up over the treetops. Immediately following that he heard the crack of a high-velocity cannon firing. Someone, he knew, had fired, and someone had died. Without a second thought, Emerson ordered his driver to move forward slowly up to the bend in the road so that he could see what was going on. Emerson's gunner, unable to see anything, yelled out asking what was happening. In a voice that never seemed to betray excitement or stress, Emerson responded by simply telling his gunner to keep his eye glued to the sight and be ready to engage. Emerson in the same calm voice told the loader who had been riding with his head popped up out of the turret to get down, load sabot, and arm the gun. Even before he heard the loader's yell, "SABOT LOADED," Emerson had eased himself down into the turret so that only his head and shoulders showed above the lip of his open hatch. With his hand on the tank commander's turret override, he, like the rest of the crew, was ready.

Though the flames had died down some, whatever had been hit, and Emerson feared the worst, was still burning. The fire created an eerie light that lit the road and the trees that lined it at the bend ahead. Moving toward that point, Emerson slowly began to traverse the turret so that as soon as his tank rounded the bend the main gun would be pointed down the center of the road toward the east. Like everyone else in the crew, Emerson held his breath as he felt his pulse rate quicken in anticipation of what they would find. Taking a quick glance to his rear, he could see his wing man Sergeant Allston's tank, following at the same pace, off to one side of the road. Satisfied that he was ready, Emerson faced back to the front just as the front slope of his tank began to inch out around the bend. With a simple "Okay, here we go," Emerson prepared his crew.

The scene to his front confirmed his worst nightmare. The road leading toward Rasdorf was lined on either side by tall pine trees. Less than three hundred meters ahead, through the light snow that continued to drift down, Emerson saw the gun tube and front of a burning tank. Half protruding out of the woods, hanging on the road embankment and blocking one lane of the road, it was burning furiously. For a second he tried to confirm that it was in fact an Abrams tank. The motion, however, of another vehicle emerging from the darkness beyond the burning tank caught Emerson's attention. Instinctively he slewed the gun tube in the direction of this threat, more perceived than confirmed. Ordering his driver to stop, Emerson watched.

From further down the road, the black form moved to one side of the road as it tried to bypass the burning tank. Emerson was about to drop down and check out this vehicle through the thermal sight when he clearly saw it turn its turret to the left in the direction of the burning tank and fire at something in the woods beyond it. Without any hesitation, without waiting for any further evidence, Emerson shouted out a quick fire command. "GUNNER, SABOT, TANK!"

Both the gunner and loader responded in unison, "IDENTIFIED!" "UP!"

To which Emerson replied, "FIRE!"

At a range of three hundred meters, the flight time of Emerson's armor-piercing fin-stabilized discarding sabot round, which is a small depleted uranium dart launched at speeds greater than one mile a second, was indistinguishable from the rock and recoil of the main gun on Emerson's tank. By the time the muzzle blast had cleared, their target had already been hit and was beginning to be rocked by secondary explosions. Satisfied that the target was finished, Emerson dropped down to look at it through the tank commander's extension to the gunner's primary sight. When he did, the image that greeted him made his heart sink. The tank that he had just engaged and killed was without a doubt a German Leopard II. That, of course, meant that the burning tank sticking out of the woods was his platoon leader's tank. Knowing that German tanks, like American tanks, never travel alone, Emerson jumped back up and ordered his driver to back up around the bend. From there he could call, in an effort to find out what had happened to Dallas and even more important to inform his company commander that they had made contact with the enemy and report the results of that contact. The thought that he had witnessed the opening shots of the shooting war had not yet dawned upon Sergeant First Class Emerson. Such things were of no real concern to him. He was, as the commander of the German Leopard tank had been, simply doing what he was trained to do.

Impatiently, Big Al Malin waited for the morning update to end. He already understood both the nature and the severity of the situation that the Tenth Corps faced. The straight line between Alsfeld in the west and Hünfeld in the east was approximately thirty-five kilometers, or twenty-one miles. Between those two points, Autobahn A7 and Highway 27 ran north to Kassel from Fulda in the south. It was at this critical point amongst the hills and forests of central Germany that the Bundeswehr, prodded by Ruff, chose to strike first.

Neither the location nor the units involved were a surprise to the Tenth Corps' senior commanders. Big Al's intelligence officer had been tracking the progress of the 2nd Panzer Division from Erfurt in the east and the 10th Panzer Division coming up from Frankfurt in the west for some time. Warnings had gone out to the commanders of the 4th Armored Division and the 55th Mech Infantry Division to be prepared to block those thrusts, something that both commanders set about to do. Yet even as the commanders and staffs of the Tenth Corps and its two divisions went through the motions of preparing for the confrontation, many hoped that the maneuvers of the two panzer divisions were nothing more than posturing. That was why almost to a man the staff officers of Tenth Corps felt an uncomfortable sinking feeling that morning when they briefed Big Al on initial contacts, like Sergeant Emerson's. The hope of being able to make it to the sea without a serious confrontation was in an instant washed away by the blood of these first battles. It had come, as Big Al had predicted, to a fight. Now in a matter of hours it would become a death struggle for the Tenth Corps.

The corps G-2 intelligence officer himself presented the briefing that morning. Like the other briefers, he referred to a large map covered with clear plastic sheets that took up the entire wall of the expandable tractor-trailer van which served as the corps briefing area. In his usual clear and unemotional monotone voice, the G-2 presented as clear a picture as possible of the enemy's current situation and what he thought their intent was as he used his retractable pointer to indicate the unit symbols on the map he was talking about. The German units coming from the east and west were depicted in red. All major German maneuver units, down to brigade, were displayed with arrows to show where they were headed. This, of course, was toward Autobahn A7, the Tenth Corps' main axis of advance north. Between those arrows American units, shown in blue, reminded Big Al of a big bubble, a fragile bubble, which he realized was being prodded by ice picks.

In the west the American 55th Mechanized Infantry Division coming up from Würzburg aimed for Alsfeld. A relatively minor town, Alsfeld had no real strategic or tactical importance other than that was where two mechanized forces brought together by the roads that converged there collided on the morning of the 19th. It was, however, more of a cautious bumping together like bumper cars at a carnival than a head-on collision between two steaming locomotives. The commander of the 10th Panzer Division, Major General Albert Kiebler, unsure of the political situation, had intentionally moved slowly. Troubled by a light turnout of reservists, the 10th Panzer could only muster seven full panzer and panzergrenadier battalions by the 18th of January. And even the determination and combat value of the soldiers in those battalions was open to question as debate amongst the officers raged as to who was the true enemy of the German people. This left Kiebler with the impression that his division was at best a fragile weapon that he feared would shatter under heavy pressure.

Kiebler's tactics reflected his caution. Instead of the armored juggernaut that Ruff had envisioned, the 10th Panzer Division moved up from Frankfurt toward Alsfeld like a giant caterpillar. The two lead battalions, moving abreast, would stretch out a little and then stop. Once the lead battalions were set, the battalions following would move up behind as if they were providing the necessary boost to propel the lead battalions forward again. The official justification was that this technique was necessary in order to keep the division from being strung out and dispersed, keep supply and support elements up, and the division ready to fight. While this was true, it all but assured that the Americans, and not the 10th Panzer, would reach Alsfeld first. This, of course, suited Kiebler just fine, since in his heart he was willing to do anything to postpone any confrontation with the Americans in the hope that somehow the differences between Berlin and Washington could be resolved without a colliding of arms. Even as his units were clashing in the fields around Alsfeld, Kiebler continued to question the wisdom of his government and walked the fine line between obedience to his duty and following his conscience. Left to their own, the commanders of the 10th Panzer Division's lead battalions followed the example of their commanding general, restricting themselves to light probing actions that were easily parried by the 55th Mechanized Infantry Division.

The commanding general of the 2nd Panzer Division to the east had no such reservations. The initial confrontations, like the one involving Emerson and Dallas with his lead units, reflected this. A motorized rifle regimental commander in the former East German Army, Major General Erich Dorsch was reinstated with the rank of general in the unified Army under Chancellor Ruff's reforms. Dorsch drove the 2nd Panzer Division into the flank of the Tenth Corps like a lance. In part this was possible because many of his officers and soldiers were, like him, easterners. Having spent their formative years and early adulthood under communism, they had no great love for the Americans. Nor were they troubled by the conflict of duty versus conscience that had been hammered home into the minds of every officer of the old Bundeswehr, a handicap that now hamstrung them at the moment of truth. Even the turnout of reservists reflected this difference, with the 2nd Panzer Division boasting nine ground maneuver battalions, making it the largest German division in the field.

With the 2nd Brigade of the 4th Armored Division entering Kassel, and Scott Dixon's 1st Brigade still south of Fulda bringing up the rear, that left the 3rd Brigade the task of covering the division's eastern flank. Unable to cover every possible approach in strength, Colonel Andrew Bowman, commander of the 3rd Brigade, concentrated two of his three battalions to deal with an attack coming down Autobahn E40 running west from Erfurt to Bad Hersfeld, a city situated midway between Fulda and Kassel. The danger of this obvious avenue of approach made sense, for Autobahn E40 was the same road that Kiebler and his 10th Panzer Division were using as the axis for their advance from the southwest. To Dorsch, that approach was too obvious. Even before his own reconnaissance elements confirmed the information provided by the Luftwaffe and national-level intelligence agencies, Dorsch had already decided to use a more difficult but less obvious axis of advance into the flank of Tenth Corps. While holding the attention of the American 3rd Brigade with a supporting attack down the axis that the Americans expected the 2nd Panzer to use, Dorsch launched his main attack down Highway 84, which ran southwest from Eisenach into Highway 27 at Hünfeld. Six kilometers, or four and a half miles, to the west of Hünfeld lay Autobahn A7. In a single stroke Dorsch intended to push aside the Tenth Corps flank guard, inserting his 2nd Panzer Division between the American rear guard and lead elements while cutting both routes running north that the Tenth Corps so heavily depended upon.

By midmorning the series of sharp engagements that had begun with Sergeant Emerson's fight on Highway 84 just outside of Rasdorf left the tank battalion that Emerson belonged to battered and reeling back away from the relentless advance of the 2nd Panzer Division. Their line of retreat was toward the northwest and the 4th Armored Division's 3rd Brigade's center of mass. While this maneuver made sense to both the commander of the 3rd Brigade and the commander of Emerson's battalion, it opened Highway 84 all the way to Hünfeld.

Looking at his watch, Big Al decided that he could not wait for the briefing to continue as usual. His division commanders were waiting for orders from him. Although they were already reacting to the situation within their division areas of responsibilities, there was the danger that their decisions and actions, made independently, would handicap the corps' ability to deal with the twin threats effectively. When the G-2 finished his briefing, Big Al leaned over to his chief of staff, Brigadier General Buddy Bolin. "Buddy, I know that this briefing is as much a benefit to the staff as it is to me, but they're just going to have to get it later. We have work to do. Now I want you, the G-2, the G-3, the fire support officer, air liaison officer, and the assistant G-4 to stay behind. We need a plan and we need one right now. Otherwise my two headstrong division commanders are going to go charging off in different directions and tear this corps apart."

As the other staff officers left the expandable van, the G-2 grabbed a chair, seating himself facing Big Al with his back to the briefing map. Bolin, on Big Al's right, was joined by the corps assistant G-4, who took a seat to Bolin's right. On Big Al's left was Brigadier General Jerry Prentice, the corps G-3, with the corps fire support officer to Prentice's left and Colonel Tim "Big Foot" MacHaffry, the Air Force liaison officer, to his left.

When everyone else had left and the van was quiet, Big Al looked at the map for a second. He glanced at the somber faces of his battle staff, then back at the map. He already knew what he was going to say about future operations. That was simple. What troubled him was how to say it. He, like his staff officers, was tired, depressed, and deeply concerned to the point of being pessimistic. Placing his hands on his hips, Big Al pretended to study the map while he searched for the right words and prepared himself to deliver them. For he as their senior commander would set the tone. Everyone would watch him, studying how he carried himself and listening for the conviction behind his words. If his presentation was gloom and doom, that attitude would be carried over into the corps order and would be parroted by his own staff as they talked to the staffs of the two divisions. Such a negative attitude would in turn be passed on down by the divisions, who, unable to physically see Big Al himself, would assume that they were engaged in a questionable operation. There was no time for Big Al to personally visit each command as he had done a week ago. During this operation he would depend on his staff to convey both his, the commander's, actual and the psychological messages. Big Al, recalling a scene in the movie *Patton*, when Patton's aide-de-camp commented that Patton's staff didn't know when he was acting, Patton had smiled and informed the concerned aide that they didn't need to know. Only he, Patton, did.

With that thought in mind, Big Al forced a scowl on his face and turned to his battle staff. "As I see it, the real danger is the 2nd Panzer." To a man, the assembled staff officers nodded their agreement. This observation was based just as much on Big Al's personal knowledge of the two German division commanders as it was on the current situation. During several joint NATO and American-German command post exercises run while Big Al commanded the Tenth Corps, General Kiebler's 10th Panzer Division had operated as part of the American Tenth Corps. Though these exercises had used computers instead of real soldiers to wargame various scenarios and contingencies to deal with them, Big Al had been able to observe and learn how Kiebler thought and reacted. As a result, Big Al concurred with the G-2's assessment that Kiebler, while being both steady and reliable, was cautious. The movement of the 10th Panzer from Frankfurt am Main through Giessen reinforced this perception. Though Big Al didn't know that Kiebler's normal caution was intensified by his troubled conscience, that didn't matter. What was important at that moment to the assembled men was that they were able to agree that the 10th Panzer Division was of secondary importance.

The real danger to the corps for the next forty-eight hours would be the 2nd Panzer Division. Big Al's knowledge of the German commanders gained during both social gatherings and training exercises before this crisis again played a major part in his thinking. During two of the command post exercises that the Tenth Corps had run, Dorsch, the commander of the 2nd Panzer, had played the opposing force. Once, he had been the overall commander, and the other time he had played the role of a Polish armored division commander. In both roles, Big Al had been impressed with the manner with which Dorsch had combined the machinelike tactics of the former Red Army with the Teutonic precision that appeared to come as naturally to him as breathing. During meetings and social events associated with these exercises, Big Al had been equally struck by Dorsch's cold, standoffish manner. Both Big Al and other NATO commanders couldn't help but notice the aloof and cold manner with which he spoke to them. All agreed that this was the result of years of communist indoctrination and his early training, which had instilled into him the idea that the

Americans were the real enemy of Germany. This factor, just like the decision to go through Bavaria, where the people viewed the Americans in more favorable terms, was not discounted by Big Al and his assembled staff officers when determining which of the German divisions presented the greatest danger.

With that issue decided, how best to use this insight and knowledge to deal with the current situation was now discussed. Actually, a discussion per se never took place. The same men who were now assembled had already played out a series of "what if" scenarios over the past forty-eight hours collectively and within their own staff sections as soon as the danger posed by the two panzer divisions had been identified. Instead, Big Al stood up, moved over to the map, and looked at it for a moment before speaking, while the G-2 moved his chair around next to the assistant G-4. Turning to his staff officers, Big Al, using his finger as a pointer, began to talk. "With the 4th Armored's 3rd Brigade pulling back to the northwest, we're leaving the door open for the 2nd Panzer. It's too late to stop that maneuver, and even if we did, pressure from the supporting attack coming down Autobahn E40 as well as the main German effort would be too much for that brigade to handle. So for the time being we'll let the 3rd Brigade, 4th Armored, stand fast and cover Bad Hersfeld."

Big Al paused, turning to the map. When he continued, he remained facing the map, but still used his finger to indicate the units he was talking about, and ran his finger along the map to indicate where he wanted them to go. "Now, that decision leaves a big gap between the 4th Armored's 1st Brigade here, in Fulda, and the 3rd Brigade here, south of Bad Hersfeld. We could encourage the 4th Armored Division to hurry the 1st Brigade north in an effort to close the gap, but I don't think they'd make it. We could order the 1st Brigade to move directly north and hit the 2nd Panzer in the flank, but Dorsch would be expecting that. In this terrain the 1st Brigade would be easily blocked by a couple of German panzergrenadier companies. We would in short order find ourselves engaged in a slugfest here in the south and a standoff in the north, while Dorsch's lead brigade ran riot through our logistic areas. And that, gentlemen, would spell the end to this corps and our great gamble."

Big Al paused, stepped back slightly, moved his head about as he looked at the entire map, then turned to his staff officers. With his hands on his hips and a firm, determined expression on his face, Big Al made it known in his indomitable style that he intended to throw caution to the winds. "We knew from the beginning that this was a great gamble, one crapshoot after another. Well, people, it's time to roll the dice again." Without waiting for a response, Big Al began rattling off his concept for the corps counterattack. "Effective immediately, the 55th Infantry's 3rd Brigade, with no less than four maneuver battalions, is attached to the 4th Armored Division. That brigade will move due east, cross country if possible, and take up blocking positions at or west of Hünfeld. We'll lose the use of Highway 27 if Hünfeld falls, but we can live with that so long as the autobahn stays open. To do this, the 55th Infantry's 3rd Brigade will link up with the 4th Armored's 3rd Brigade. When and where possible, I want both brigades to conduct local counterattacks to stop or disrupt the German advance. In addition to the 55th Infantry's 3rd Brigade, the commander of the 4th Armored will have priority on the 10th Aviation Brigade's attack helicopter battalions. With a little luck we should be able to check the 2nd Panzer." Pointing to the symbol that represented the 4th Armored Division's 1st brigade, still south of Fulda, Big Al continued. "Our main effort to eliminate the threat posed by the 2nd Panzer will be made by the 1st Brigade. From Fulda, I want that brigade to strike northeast paralleling Highway 27 and head toward Highway 19. Just short of Highway 19, this brigade will turn north and cut behind the 2nd Panzer. Their mission is to tear up the 2nd Panzer's support elements and cause Dorsch to hesitate, maybe even turn around and go after the 1st Brigade. While all this is going on, we continue to push north. It is not my intent to fight a battle of annihilation here. Our goal is to get to the coast, not kill Germans. Now, having said that, I do want to make sure that everyone in this corps understands that does not mean holding back."

From where they sat, Big Al's staff officers could see the fire in his eyes as he balled his hand up into a fist. Pounding his fist on the map board to emphasize each point of his next announcement, Big Al drove home how he wanted his corps to fight. "Throughout this operation, I want every commander at every level to move fast, strike true, and hit hard. Our target is the German Army, not the German people. They are to avoid collateral damage whenever possible and heap terror and destruction on the German Army every time it comes to a fight. I want to serve notice to those gentlemen in Berlin that, while we may be running, we're not helpless." Toning down his enthusiasm, Big Al pointed out that if they succeeded here other German commanders not yet engaged might pause and think twice before striking.

Before turning his attention to the 10th Panzer, Big Al looked at MacHaffry. "Big Foot, talk to me about the Luftwaffe."

An F-22 fighter pilot by training, MacHaffry was labeled Big Foot because his six-foot-four frame was supported by feet that required size 13½ double-E boots. Leaning forward in his seat, MacHaffry placed his hands on his knees and looked up at Big Al. "Although rumors concerning the Chief of Staff of the Luftwaffe have yet to be confirmed, the fact is that there is a great deal of confusion at every level. We do know that pilots have refused to fly, sabotage is widespread, and base commanders have denied fuel to squadron commanders on their own base. Although we can expect some air activity, it will be limited."

After nodding a few times, Big Al turned to the map again and spoke without looking at MacHaffry. "Is Boomer ready for Operation Whirlwind?"

Boomer, the call sign for Colonel Wilber Smith, commander of the 79th Air Wing that had supported the Tenth Corps in Slovakia, was prepared to use Czech bases for as long as possible to support the Tenth Corps breakout efforts. Whirlwind was the name for what everyone believed would be a one-shot air offensive against selected Luftwaffe bases. The targets of Valkyrie would be those bases and Luftwaffe facilities that posed the greatest threat to the Tenth Corps. Though there was lively debate about whether Whirlwind would cause those in the Luftwaffe who were undecided about the wisdom of opposing the Americans to throw their lot behind Chancellor Ruff's government, it was agreed by every staff officer and pilot of the 79th Wing that they would support the Tenth Corps regardless of consequences. The worst that could happen was that each plane would fly one mission and then be interned by the Czech government upon its return. The best, the removal of the stain on the Air Force's name as a result of the capitulation at Sembach.

"We're ready, sir. We know that we'll be able to penetrate German airspace. Whoever has been feeding us the IFF codes for the Luftwaffe is continuing to do so." IFF, short for identify friend or foe, is an electronic system on every combat aircraft that emits a signal when interrogated by another aircraft or a ground-based air defense system.

If the correct response comes back from the aircraft being interrogated, it is considered friendly. If not, it is deemed to be hostile and engaged or tracked. With the Luftwaffe's IFF codes, the aircraft of the 79th Air Wing would be able to make it to their designated targets without interference from the German long-range air defense system. Even when it was discovered that the IFF codes had been compromised, confusion would reign and engagements between opposing aircraft would rely on visual rules of engagement rather than radar alone.

Looking back at MacHaffry, Big Al smiled. "Okay, get back to Boomer and tell him to stand by. I don't want to push the Germans too far, not until it's really necessary."

Satisfied that everything that could be done about the Luftwaffe was in hand, the assembled group looked to the portion of the map where the symbols of the 10th Panzer Division sat clustered west of Alsfeld. Prentice, the G-3, pointed out that the 55th Infantry Division, with two brigades and six battalions, was an even match for the 10th Panzer's three brigades and six battalions. Though Big Al agreed, saying that he intended to leave that fight up to the 55th's commander, he also stated that he would suggest a holding action at Alsfeld with one brigade, and a maneuver to the north and west with the other. To assist in this fight, Big Al directed Prentice to issue orders attaching one squadron of the 14th Armored Cavalry Regiment to the 55th. The rest of the 14th Armored Cavalry would cover the corps rear and the maneuver by the 4th Armored Division's 1st Brigade.

Finished, Big Al asked if anyone had any questions or comments. Prentice, looking at the map, asked if he thought that the 4th Armored Division's 1st Brigade would be able to cover the distance from Fulda to Highway 19 and still be able to strike north in time to influence the battle. Big Al smiled as he prepared to answer. "That's Scotty Dixon's brigade you're talking about. If I asked him to secure a bridgehead on the moon, the only question he would ask is what side of the moon we wanted it on." Then, on a serious note, he looked at the map. "If anyone can do it, he can." Unsaid was a follow-on comment that Big Al kept to himself: And if I'm wrong, Scotty's brigade will be wiped out and we fail.

While the general pondered and staff officers scurried about issuing orders to this unit and that, the first casualties arrived at the 553rd

Field Hospital just as the sky in the east began to lighten, announcing that another cold gray day was dawning. The appearance of real wounded soldiers whose bodies were torn, twisted, or burned in combat had the same effect on the personnel of the 553rd that news of the first battles had had on the staff of the Tenth Corps. But they hid any outward manifestation of that shock or dread behind the mask of medical professionals. For the task of the men and women of the 553rd Field Hospital was to save those who were suffering from true shock, the shock of physical and psychological trauma caused by what was being called the Battle of the Two Felds.

Working in pre-op, Hilary Cole, like every other nurse in the unit, walked a fine line between maintaining a detached professional attitude when dealing with the broken and traumatized soldiers entrusted to her care and opening her heart to their sufferings. In some cases, where the soldier was unconscious or under heavy sedation, this was easy. Then all she had to do was cut away those parts of the uniform that would interfere with the surgeon's work, remove old dressings, often hastily applied in adverse conditions and contaminated with dirt and mud, and clean the wounds as best she could.

It was when the soldier was conscious and able to talk that Cole had to be on her guard. Often these soldiers had no idea of how seriously they had been injured. They knew they had been hit, and they felt pain. But the shock of the wound, coupled with adrenaline dumped into their system by their bodies, and sedatives administered at battalion aid stations, masked for the most part the severity of their condition. Inevitably those who could would ask the question that the nurses working in triage and pre-op dreaded, namely, "How bad is it?"

Having worked in shock-trauma before joining the Army, Cole had seen serious injuries before and had learned to deal with that question. While working as quickly as possible, Cole would try every ploy she knew to change the subject. She'd ask the patient's name, where he came from, what his unit was, anything to take his mind off of his injury and save her from having to lie about it. That was not always possible. One soldier, missing his left foot from the ankle down, would not be put off by Cole's diversions. The more she told him to calm down and relax, the more upset he became. Finally, angry and upset, he began to struggle to sit up as Cole was trying to cut away the blood-soaked field dressings. Stopping what she was doing, Cole turned away from his left leg and leaned over the soldier, taking his face firmly between her hands. Mustering all the calm she could, she looked him in the eye and quietly told him his foot was gone. For a second there was a pause as the horror of her statement struck home. Then he closed his eyes and let himself slump back down as he tried desperately to absorb the reality of losing his foot. Finally, just as Cole finished and was preparing to leave, the soldier reached out and grabbed her arm. His face betrayed no more fear, no anger. He only nodded and whispered, "Thanks."

Taken in isolation, Cole and the other nurses could have handled such incidents. But as the day wore on, Cole's ability to keep her emotions in check, her efforts to isolate herself from the pain and suffering of the young men and women she worked on, oozed away like the blood that soaked through field dressings. By midmorning Cole could feel herself begin to lose it as she realized that no matter how fast she worked there were always two or three more waiting for her attention. Still, like the other nurses, she kept working, dealing with the screamers and those barely alive. She had to, as she watched two more wounded brought in. For a second Cole felt like she was the only one there, left alone to deal with cuts and gashes that measured a foot or more, burns that made the human body look like badly burned beef, severed limbs that refused to stop bleeding, abdominal wounds that revealed the intestines, and shattered bones that stuck out of the body in ways she never thought were possible. And there was no end, no letup.

Turning her attention away from the door, Cole forced herself to focus on the soldier lying before her. He was a young man, maybe twenty, twenty-one at most. From his waist down, blood seeped through his burned uniform from numerous wounds. Unable to deal with him properly, his battalion aid station had sent him straight to the 553rd with only hasty patching and treatment. It was now up to Cole to prepare him for the surgeons.

At first she didn't even bother looking at his face. Instead she mechanically began to cut away the charred uniform, stopping only when she exposed a wound that was bleeding too badly. The cutting was not easy, for the burned skin often stuck to the shredded uniform. When she ran across this, Cole was careful to lift the uniform slightly, and then separate the skin from the material with scissors or a scalpel. While she was doing this to one particularly nasty wound on the inside of his thigh, Cole noticed that the soldier didn't move or jerk.

Looking up at his face for the first time, she checked to see if he was breathing. To her surprise, he was awake and staring up. Finishing what she was doing, Cole moved over to check the soldier's vital signs. As she did so, he still didn't move as he continued to stare vacantly into space. Satisfied that he was still hanging on, Cole was about to go back to work when he softly called out, "Is it all there? Am I, am I going to be all right?"

Knowing that he was concerned about his genitals, Cole hesitated for a second. She didn't know, since she hadn't gotten that far. Torn between ignoring the soldier's gentle plea and responding, Cole flashed the best smile that she could and turned to face the soldier. With her right hand, she brushed several dirty strands of hair away from his forehead and leaned over close to him. "Well, honey, I'm sure you're going to be all right. I just need to do some more cleaning up so the doctors can take care of you. Now if you promise to relax and try to stay still, I'll do my best to finish as quickly as possible without causing you any more discomfort than I have to. Is that a deal?"

A weak smile was the best response that the soldier could muster before he returned to staring into space. Taking a deep breath, Cole straightened up, looked at his face one more time, then got back to work. Though she did her best to keep the amount of distress she was causing him to a minimum while working as fast as she could, Cole knew that she was putting the soldier through agony. Still he did not move. Every time she looked up, all he did was lie there staring at the ceiling. Only when she finished and turned back to tell him that she was done, did she find that at some point during her efforts the soldier had quietly slipped into unconsciousness and died.

Suddenly the full weight of all the emotions that she had been holding back, all the horror and suffering that she had been defending herself against, came crashing down on Cole. With her face stiff with panic, Cole stepped away from the table, unable to turn away from the soldier's eyes frozen open in death. Without realizing it, Cole began to shake and tremble. She didn't hear the high-pitched squeal that came from a soul unable to continue with her gruesome labors. Slowly, uncontrollably, Cole was beginning to break down under the stress.

From across the way, First Lieutenant Renée Ritter heard Cole's screech and looked up. In an instant Ritter knew what was happening. Shouting to an orderly to come over to where she was and finish cleaning a burn, Ritter rushed over and grabbed Cole's arm from behind and spun her around. Cole's face was taut with terror. Her eyes, wide open and unblinking, were focused on some unseen object past Ritter's shoulder. Holding Cole's arms firmly in her hands, Ritter gently shook her.

Finally Cole looked up and searched Ritter's face for a second before speaking. Even then Cole was able to utter only a few weak and fluttering words. When she did, those words were disjointed and almost whispered. "He died! He did what I asked and he died. He just lay there like I asked him and he died. I told him if he just relaxed and kept quiet, he'd be all right. And he died!"

On the brink herself, Ritter fought back her own tears as she took Cole's chin in her hand and tilted it up to look into her eyes. "Hilary, you're doing your best. You can only do so much. God, I hate to see this too and I hate to admit it, but not everyone in here is going to live. We can't stop that. You can't, I can't, even the colonel can't. We can only do our best to save those we can." Pausing, Ritter let go of Cole's chin and wiped away the tears that were streaming down her own cheeks. She didn't realize that in the process she was smearing across her own face blood that was still on her hands from the last casualty she had been working on. "Hilary, you've got to stay with me. If you don't, we'll lose more. Do you understand that? Do you hear me? You've got to stay with me."

Cole, fighting her tears with the last of her strength, looked into Ritter's eyes as she inhaled. She couldn't answer. All she could do was nod just before she wrapped her arms about Ritter. Putting her head on Ritter's shoulder, Cole began to cry. Without hesitation, Ritter wrapped her arms about Cole and leaned her cheek against Cole's.

While other nurses and orderlies around them went about their work, ignoring the two nurses, Ritter slowly rocked Cole, saying nothing, for there was nothing that could be said. No words could drown out the moans and screams of the wounded that waited to be tended to. No promises that everything would be all right could reassure Cole. Only the warmth of another human being, suffering and needing a kind and gentle touch just as badly as Cole did, could ease the suffering that was tearing at Cole's heart.

Though the wounded kept coming in, they would have to wait for a moment while the Army's caretakers took care of their own invisible wounds and suffered for a moment in silence together.

*　　*　　*

Outside, in any direction you cared to turn, officers and soldiers of the U.S. Tenth Corps and the Bundeswehr moved about through the woods and around the hills of central Germany hunting each other like animals. For at company and platoon level, the grand strategy and sweeping maneuvers discussed by commanders and staff officers at corps and division had no meaning. War to the company commander, platoon leader, and the soldiers entrusted to them was nothing more than a series of chance meetings, sudden firefights, and swift mad charges and countercharges as attacker and defender rushed forward to tear blindly away at their enemy whenever they were found. For the next two days, opposing German and American companies and platoons collided in the cold, damp, snow-covered hills, fields, and woods. When that happened, they would hurl themselves at each other, exchange fire, and push for an advantage. In this way they generated more wounded, more broken bodies, broken bodies that would eventually find their way to Cole, Ritter, and other nurses, German and American, working hard to undo the damage caused by officers doing their duty and national policies run amuck.

C H A P T E R 1 4

19 JANUARY

While the problems faced by all the commanders throughout the 1st Brigade, 4th Armored Division, up to this point of Malin's March to the Sea had been varied, complex, and numerous, they were for the most part taken in stride and carried out swiftly and efficiently. Even the sudden change in orders, jerking them from the nerve-racking task of playing rear guard for the corps to an offensive mission that would require them to charge off into the flank of an advancing German panzer division, was taken in stride with hardly a break in the tempo of the brigade. Scott Dixon, after all, had gone to great extremes during training exercises to stress and test the flexibility, both physical and mental, of all of his commanders. "Every conceivable problem and difficulty in war," he told his officers and noncommissioned officers at every opportunity, "is possible. The only thing that any of you can be sure of," he warned his subordinates, "is that in war, the next mission or next problem you face will probably be the one which you were never trained to deal with or weren't prepared to deal with." While these words were coming back to haunt every officer and sergeant in Dixon's command the further north they went, they had special meaning to Captain Nancy Kozak that morning.

Though everyone by this point was tired and a little ragged from the constant movement and stress brought on by maintaining a high state of combat readiness around the clock, the effectiveness of Scott Dixon's training paid off as the 1st Brigade went through the throes of changing its mission and direction of movement. Having received the new orders just after occupying a new defensive position, Kozak accepted the battalion order that would hurl them into the flank of the 2nd Panzer Division and without any fuss quickly prepared her own company order. With the efficiency of a well-trained drill, Kozak gathered her platoon leaders, described the new situation that they were about to face, and issued the necessary orders that would initiate their movement to contact in the clear, concise, and crisp manner that Fort Benning taught its young officers. With salutes that were as crisp as Kozak's orders, her platoon leaders had acknowledged their new orders and turned away to go back and brief their platoons, when without warning the company first sergeant presented Nancy Kozak one of those unexpected challenges that Scott Dixon had taken great pains to warn them about. The challenge came in the form of a Mrs. Emma Louisa Richardson and her two children.

As all good soldiers quickly learn, it is important to establish a routine, a disciplined routine, for taking care of oneself in the field and maintain it even under the most pressing of circumstances. Kozak, having discharged all of her responsibilities for the moment by issuing out a quick and complete operations order for their new mission, found herself with a few minutes to herself. Informing the executive officer that she was going to clean up and grab something to eat, Kozak climbed inside of her Bradley. Sitting on one of the seats free of personal gear and equipment, Kozak removed her helmet and dropped it to the floor. With both hands she violently began to scratch her head. As she did so, all she could think of was how filthy and oily her hair got during operations like this. At that moment Nancy Kozak would give just about anything to spend five minutes under a hot shower beating down on muscles that ached and skin that was so dirty that it almost made her cry. Knowing that such a dream, however, was only a dream, she pulled her rucksack over to her and began to dig for her ditty bag and towel, shouting up to Sergeant Wolf, who was standing radio watch in the turret, to keep an eye open for visitors and wave them off if possible. Within a few minutes, Kozak was stripped down to her T-shirt and preparing to spend the few minutes she had to herself getting as clean as her spartan conditions would allow.

She was just beginning to enjoy the warmth of the Bradley and fact that she had no web gear, bulky jacket, or itchy sweater on when Wolf yelled down to her. "Yo, Captain. First sergeant's coming our way."

Taking the washcloth she had been wiping the back of her neck with in both hands, Kozak wrung it out over the small bowl of soapy water that sat between her feet, dropped it into the bowl, and muttered a curse that Wolf couldn't hear. When she heard the first sergeant pound on the armor plate of the rear troop compartment door, the tone of Kozak's voice betrayed her disgust at being disturbed. "Come on in, Top."

Twisting the heavy metal handle, First Sergeant Gary Stokes let the door swing out, then stuck his head in. "Sorry to bother you, ma'am. But I got this little problem I'd like your opinion on."

Despite her anger at losing her only chance to clean up, Kozak couldn't help but smile at Stokes's shy country-boy approach when he was trying to tell her that something had come up that needed her attention. "What seems to be the problem, Top?"

"Well, ma'am, it seems some colonel's wife decided that she didn't need to go home with the rest of the dependents when they were evacuated last week."

Though she knew what was coming, Kozak didn't rush Stokes. Instead she brushed a strand of hair out of her face. "And?"

"Well," Stokes continued, "she and her two kids just showed up in front of 2nd Platoon's position and asked to see an officer about food and evacuation."

With that, Kozak let her head drop down between her shoulders and began to shake it from side to side. "Great, fine. We're about to go charging off with the mission of ripping off the head of a German panzer division and suddenly we have camp followers." Looking up at Stokes, Kozak sighed. "Where is she?"

"Right outside, ma'am."

That there was the possibility that the woman had heard Kozak's comment didn't bother her. Instead she told Stokes to help her into the Bradley while Kozak moved some gear out of the way. As Stokes helped Mrs. Emma Louisa Richardson climb into the vehicle that was so foreign to her, Kozak studied her. In her mid-forties, Emma Richardson looked haggard but still very dignified. Reflecting on her own state, dirty hair and stripped down to combat boots, BDU pants, and T-shirt, Kozak could only reflect how officers' wives, regardless of what the circumstances, always took great pains to maintain that look and air of dignity. Once she was settled, Emma Richardson looked over to Kozak, cocked her head to one side, reached out with one hand to touch Kozak's arm, and smiled. "Oh, thank God. *You're* a woman."

In an instant Nancy Kozak understood what the woman meant. Mrs. Emma Richardson apparently was under the impression that because Kozak was a woman she would be treated differently and that all her troubles were over. Though the worst was in fact over for Emma Richardson and her children, Kozak couldn't help but reflect how far from the truth that woman was about her. The very idea that Kozak would do something different than a male Army officer under the same circumstances slapped Kozak across the face like a wet towel. Though both women had been raised by the same society and as children and teenagers been molded and judged in the same manner, the worlds that Emma Richardson and Nancy Kozak moved through now bore no resemblance. For while Emma Richardson went to college and chose to follow a career and lifestyle acceptable to a female that allowed her to continue to move through life using her natural and learned feminine skills, Nancy Kozak had turned her back on the conventional and gone into a pursuit that was anything but feminine.

The art of war as practiced by Western societies is a most barbaric and brutal pursuit. The skills and practices of a soldier, when applied, are physically and psychologically demanding in the extreme, even to the strongest man. With few exceptions, the Western military traditions are a celebration of masculine values, virtues, and prowess. Anyone and everyone desiring to be a soldier and to be accepted as one has to accept those traditions and measure up to them without question, without fault. Early on at West Point Nancy Kozak learned that this requirement was more than a simple initiation or a rite of passage. It was a hard, brutal necessity. For soldiers in combat must be able to depend on each other and on their leaders. They must have unflinching trust and confidence in themselves, in their fellow soldiers, and in their leaders. Anyone who for whatever reason does not measure up to those demanding standards is viewed by any competent soldier as a danger to himself and those around him. So Nancy Kozak found that she had to leave the safety of being a woman, something that her parents and her society had prepared her for, and enter a gray area where, despite her skills, despite her achievement, she would always be on trial, a woman having to conform without question to a very male world. These hard truths, never far from Kozak's mind, weighed heavily on her as she listened to Emma Richardson talk.

"I'm so glad to be back in the arms of the American Army. My husband, Lieutenant Colonel Frank T. Richardson, the commander of the 126th Maintenance Battalion, always said that the Army takes care of its own, and, you know, he's right."

Forcing a smile, Kozak pulled her dark thoughts back to the matter at hand and shook her head. "Yes, Mrs. Richardson, I suppose he was right."

"But of *course* he was right, dear. Frank is *always* right."

The patronizing tone of Emma Richardson and reference to her, Kozak, as dear, irked Kozak. Yeah, Kozak thought, this is a colonel's wife, half of a "command team," a concept in which the Army expected a commander's wife to take charge of the other wives in the unit. Deciding that she didn't want to waste any more time with this woman and in a less than subtle move to put Mrs. Colonel in her place, Kozak let her face go into a stone-cold stare. "This, Mrs. Richardson, is a combat unit. We will be moving in the next few minutes and have little time to spare for civil-military concerns. My first sergeant will evacuate you and your children back to the battalion aid station, where they should be able to take care of you. Other than that, there's nothing that I can do. Now if you would excuse me, I need to finish washing up and get dressed. My company is waiting for me."

The reaction that Kozak elicited from Emma Richardson couldn't have been any more devastating if Kozak had punched Emma Richardson in the face. Like a child being scolded by a parent, Emma Richardson sat up straight as the warm smile that she had plastered across her face was replaced with a look of genuine shock. She couldn't understand, Kozak concluded, how another woman, especially one junior to her in age and status, could treat her like that. Though for a brief second Kozak felt bad about what she had done to the older woman, that thought quickly passed. Instead Kozak rationalized to herself that the pompous ass deserved it. Perhaps, Kozak thought, Mrs. Colonel Emma Richardson will think twice before treating an officer in the Army like she was one of her little Army-wife friends.

Turning to Stokes, who had been standing in the open door of the Bradley throughout this whole scene and trying hard not to laugh, Kozak nodded. "If you would, First Sergeant, arrange for transportation back to the aid station for this lady and her children so we can get on with the business of the day." Finished, Kozak reached down, fished the washcloth out of the bowl of soapy water between her feet, and paid no more attention to Emma Richardson as she made her way out of the Bradley.

Finished with his second briefing of the day to Chancellor Ruff and glad to be afforded the opportunity to flee the press of politicians and reporters that crowded the corridors and offices of the Chancellery, General Lange began his headlong flight back to his operations center. Even his brisk pace and choice of less well used exits, however, was not enough to ensure his unhindered escape. Lange was about to leave the building when a shout from Colonel Kasper, Ruff's military aide, stopped him. "General Lange, a moment of your time, please."

Upset that he had not even made it out the door without being summoned back to answer another absurd question, Lange paused and turned to face Kasper as he approached. That Kasper had framed his request more as a command and less like a question did not escape Lange and increased his anger. As the young colonel approached, the general watched him like a cat watches a strange dog. He did not trust Kasper. No one, in fact, on the General Staff trusted Kasper. He was to them an opportunist, a General Staff officer who used his training and proximity to the Chancellor to benefit his own career. A few who had dealings with him openly wondered if Kasper was singlehandedly trying to resurrect the old Prussian king's adjutant. Under that system, a relatively junior officer assigned to the king to handle administrative matters often served as a personal advisor to the king. Depending on how the king felt about the officer and the General Staff, the junior officer, or king's adjutant, could have power that was greater than his rank or experience warranted. The more Lange saw of Kasper, the more convinced he became that the talk of his staff might not be far from wrong. Looking at his watch just as Kasper came up to him, Lange gruffly reminded him who was the leader and who was the led. "I have, Colonel, already spent far too much time here. Whatever it is will have to wait."

Kasper, used to such efforts to brush him aside, ignored the general's rebuff. "This will not take more than a moment, Herr General. First I would like to apologize for the Chancellor's ramblings and short temper. You see, Herr General, he has been under a great deal of pressure and is not well equipped to handle it."

Though he felt like shouting back that everyone was operating under the same pressure, Lange merely grunted.

Though he saw the look of disdain in Lange's face and felt in his heart Lange's curt response, Kasper continued. "There is much concern with the manner in which the Army has been responding to orders. The Chancellor is not pleased with the lack of drive General Kiebler has shown in close contact with the American Tenth Corps. The Chancellor noted several times over the past days the vast difference between the performance of the 2nd Panzer and the—"

Lange cut him off, for he knew where the conversation was going. "General Kiebler is the commander of that division and he is carrying out his orders in a manner that he judges suitable for the situation, the enemy, and the terrain which he faces. I will not, so long as I am the chief of staff, second-guess my commanders in the field." He was about to add that Kasper needed to tell the Chancellor that there was a vast difference between the view in Berlin and conditions as they actually existed in the field, but again he held himself in check.

Not that he had to. Kasper already understood what Lange was leaving unsaid. Seeing that there was little use in easing into the subject, Kasper opted for the direct approach. "What I would like to convey to you, Herr General, is that the Chancellor is losing his confidence in certain senior leaders. He feels that they are intentionally holding back, that they are in fact attempting to do everything within their power to allow the Americans to escape and embarrass this government. The collapse of the Luftwaffe's command structure due to absenteeism, failure to follow orders, and the active sabotage of aircraft is only serving to heighten his suspicions."

By "certain" senior leaders Lange knew that Kasper was referring to those of the old Bundeswehr who unlike the easterners had been lectured for years that being an officer in a constitutional army required more than simply following orders. Seeing that the shadow boxing was over, Lange also got to the heart of the matter. "Doesn't the Chancellor appreciate the position in which he has placed us?" Lange, now animated, thrust his index finger at Kasper's chest. "You, Colonel, you are an officer. Don't *you* feel the pressure? Haven't *you* stopped to consider what's going on here?"

Lange paused, turned his head to look out the door at the leaden gray sky, then back at Kasper. What the hell, Lange thought. If he was here to feel me out for Herr Chancellor Ruff, he might as well get it all. Placing his briefcase on the tile floor next to his foot, Lange folded his arms across his chest and leaned forward closer to Kasper as he lowered his voice to a whisper. "My God, the Parliament has called for an immediate armistice, a call that Herr Ruff is happily ignoring as he continues to hide behind the emergency powers clause of the constitution. He, better than anyone else, knows! Every officer in the Bundeswehr, except for the easterners, has been taught that his first responsibility is to his conscience, and the selection process for our officers has always emphasized the need for officers who believe that morality and responsibility to the German people are more important than blind obedience. Every senior officer from the old Bundeswehr that I have talked to feels like he's being pulled by four plow horses all going in different directions. Herr Chancellor continues to run blindly off into the darkness, dragging us and the German people into a crisis of his own design. The Parliament insists that it has constitutional control of the Army and that the emergency war clause does not apply. The German people and our responsibility to them are not being served by blowing up our own countryside, and they are making it known. And finally, most of the officers of the old Bundeswehr cannot in all good conscience support a government whose motivations they do not trust."

Kasper listened in silence. He wondered if he had missed something. The frustrations of the German Army officers corps that Lange was pointing out to him were a surprise. Could they, his fellow officers, be so out of touch with the reality of the political situation? Could they be so absorbed by the military situation or their own mystical code of ethics that they did not see how precariously Germany's sovereignty and future hung? Or was he the one out of touch? Were the rumors true? Had Ruff adopted a bunker mentality and refused to see the situation as it really was? Were his actions those of a man serving the German people or were they self-serving? Kasper's head was still trying to absorb these questions when Lange continued.

"I do not know any longer, Colonel, what is right and what is wrong. Neither do the majority of the officers and the soldiers out there. Since the shooting started this morning, the debating has stopped. Now it is time to decide. And I will tell you and anyone here in Berlin with the good sense to listen that I do not know what is going to happen." Lange reached down and picked up his briefcase. When he stood up, he looked down at the floor rather than at Kasper as he continued in a very reflective, almost mournful tone. "As each unit closes with the Americans, our ability to influence the situation is slipping from our hands. Starting today, what is right and what is wrong is no longer ours to decide." As he looked Kasper in the eye, Lange's face grew taut. "That, Herr Colonel, will now be decided by each and every captain and lieutenant, every sergeant and every land-seer on the forward edge as the battle is joined. Your Chancellor may threaten and scream, shout and stomp all he wants. He can even roll on the floor frothing at the mouth and chewing on the rug if he pleases. That, however, isn't going to change a damned thing. It is, and probably always has been, out of our hands."

Kasper began to say something, then stopped. He didn't know what to say. For the first time, Lange realized that Kasper's face betrayed the confusion that Lange had just created in the young colonel's mind. Maybe, Lange thought, I have been wrong about this officer. Maybe he was after all really one of us? That he hadn't had time to determine that before saddened Lange. It would have been useful to have a reliable officer close to Ruff. There was no time, however, to concern himself over what should have been done. The American President was preparing to announce her response to the opening of armed hostilities, and Lange wanted to hear it firsthand. That response no doubt would overshadow the events in central Germany that were still in the balance and cause Lange and his staff long hours of hard work. As he had said himself, the debating was over. Now was the time of decision.

In a tone that was somewhat friendly, Lange excused himself and walked out into the cold Berlin afternoon, leaving Kasper behind to deal with his new concerns and, of course, Chancellor Ruff.

While she quietly sipped her coffee and listened to the White House spokesperson on screen deliver the prepared text, Jan Fields-Dixon glanced over to the President. She, like Jan, was listening intently to the spokesperson as she calmly sipped her second cup of coffee. Jan, used to working with politicians, knew this was a setup. She knew from the moment the conditions of the interview had been set that Wilson had something specific in mind and that she, Jan, was part of that plan. Still Jan, asked for by name, agreed. So with camera crew and notebook Jan tromped into the Oval Office fifteen minutes before the White House spokesperson was scheduled to go on and joined the President for a light breakfast of sliced fruit, danish, and rolls. The fact that the President was having her breakfast then and there made Jan suspect that she had been unable to have it upstairs in her private quarters before coming down to the Oval Office. Odds were, Jan thought, President Wilson had come up from the White House War Room instead, where she would have received an update on the current fighting taking place in central Germany.

Looking back at the screen, Jan watched as her colleagues from the White House press corps jumped up, to a person, madly waving their hands and calling out as soon as the spokesperson finished reading the prepared text. The camera couldn't help but catch the crestfallen expression on the spokesperson's face as he surveyed the sea of waving hands and tried to pick the easiest mark in the crowd. Again glancing over to Wilson, Jan smiled to herself. The President was no fool. She knew that the White House press corps would react like that. She knew that it would be impossible to control them. Therefore she had sent her spokesperson out to deliver the message and take the full brunt of the initial volley of questions while she, safely tucked away in the Oval Office, could watch and listen to the questions that the media felt were most pressing. Then with a single trusted member of the media, Jan, she would be able to answer those questions at her leisure in a calm setting where she would be able to think without competing with shouts, flashes popping, and hands waving to gain her attention. No, Jan thought, Wilson was no fool.

Wilson's abilities and skill as a politician, of course, were well known. She was good. She had to be in order to survive in a world that was not only male dominated but one in which her abilities and conduct were measured against standards established by those who had gone before her, all of whom were male. Jan had in a way highlighted Wilson's problem when she had asked Wilson how she felt about questions like "Is she tough enough to handle Congress?" or "Will she be able to fill the shoes of her predecessor?" during her race for the office. Wilson pointed out to Jan that skill and cooperation, not strength, were just as effective in dealing with people and securing their cooperation. Then with a smile Wilson also pointed out that she had no desire to wear her predecessor's shoes, since their style was not to her liking.

Jan understood all of this, having had to deal with similar concerns and issues in her own profession. So it was with a sharp eye that Jan watched Wilson as she redefined the image and role of the President to fit her. Though often accused of being "unpresidential," Wilson seldom failed to carry the day and come out every inch a leader and a lady. Today, Jan thought, was a perfect case in point. Rather than throw herself into a situation that was already degenerating into a shouting match, one in which passions and tempers would run high and words could easily be misunderstood, Wilson had chosen to distance herself from that while still dealing with it. Jan watched Wilson's face and her manner. Her face betrayed no strain, no apprehension. Instead, Wilson sat there rather impassively sipping coffee while studying the television monitor as she listened to her press spokesperson field the press's questions. Jan would be able to record Wilson's own version of those responses in a few minutes and then be able to have them on the noon broadcast, showing the nation and the world that the President of the United States was both in control of herself and the situation.

Turning back to the television, Jan listened, writing short notes in a spiral notebook that sat on her lap while she too sipped her coffee. The spokesperson, after finally succeeding in getting only one correspondent to ask a complete question, responded with carefully chosen words. "As I have stated in the text of the prepared statement, while President Wilson does not endorse General Malin's actions to date, she cannot ignore the fact that German reaction today, the resort to force of arms to stop General Malin, is placing innocent Americans in danger. The deployment of forces from the Mediterranean and the United States and the heightening of the readiness condition of Air Force units in England are all in response to the German decision to open hostilities and are intended to save as many innocent soldiers of the Tenth Corps as possible."

Another correspondent took up where the first had left off. He didn't wait to be recognized or for the spokesperson to finish. He simply jumped up and shouted, "But Chancellor Ruff of Germany is claiming that the soldiers of the Tenth Corps by obeying Malin's orders have made themselves willing accomplices to what he is calling a crime against German sovereignty."

The spokesperson, with specific instructions on what to ignore and what to respond to, turned his attention to this comment. "Chancellor Ruff might be right. Even if he were, however, the President feels that using the German Army to destroy the entire Tenth Corps, something that Chancellor Ruff has threatened to do, is the same as executing a person accused of a crime without a trial." The spokesperson paused, then added, "I would like to take this opportunity to point out again that even the duly elected German Parliament does not agree with Chancellor Ruff's decision. The call for an immediate cease-fire and an armistice negotiated by the European Council or the UN is a reasonable solution that President Wilson is more than willing to consider."

This last comment led to the next question. "Could President Wilson convince General Malin, who hasn't been willing to listen to Washington thus far, to agree to a cease-fire?"

The spokesperson, with a wry smile, responded. "That, at this point, is mere supposition. So long as the German government insists on resolving the issue by force of arms, I expect General Malin feels he has no choice but to respond in kind. It is now the Germans who have the responsibility of making the first move."

With that response, the balance of the press conference fell into a round of follow-on questions that attempted to draw out more details on the deployment of American forces to Europe. The spokesperson, not having this information, fended off these and other questions as best he could until they reached a previously determined time limit. Finished, he closed his folder and looked up; and over the chorus of shouts, he thanked the White House press corps and walked out of a room still reverberating from shouts of further questions. As she watched the manner in which her colleagues acted, Jan couldn't blame Wilson for opting to sit this press conference out.

Finished with her coffee and with watching, Wilson leaned over to the coffee table, put her empty cup down, and pressed the power button on the television's remote control. With a smile she sat up, looked at Jan, and told her that for the moment the show was over and she was ready to start their interview. Jan's cameraman and sound technician, who had been waiting in the outer office, were allowed in. While they prepared their equipment, Wilson prepared herself. She made no extraordinary efforts. Only a tug at her dark blue jacket, a smoothing of her skirt, and a quick check of her hair was all she needed. With a nod Wilson indicated that she was ready to start.

Well drilled, Jan's crew started to roll, giving her the thumbs-up when they were running. Skipping most of the preliminaries, Jan went straight to her first question. "President Wilson, I would like to pick up where Tim Allen of the UP left off during the press conference that was just held. While your prepared statement made it clear that the deployment of forces—including alerting the 17th Airborne, redeployment of elements of the Navy and Marine Corps into the Baltic Sea, and increased readiness of Air Force units in Great Britain—was in response to the German actions this morning and would be used to support the Tenth Corps, your statement said nothing about the conditions under which those forces would be used and did not set a timetable for their use. Have conditions, including a timetable, already been determined, and has the German government been advised of these?"

Without batting an eye, Wilson looked at Jan and began to respond. "To answer the first part of your question, as far as I am concerned, the conditions that would dictate the use of additional U.S. forces from outside the theater have already been met." Wilson paused to allow the implications of that statement to sink in before continuing. "If you recall, Jan, I stated several days ago that I would respond to any hostile actions against the innocent men and women of the Tenth Corps by the Germans by doing everything in my power to rescue as many of them as possible. The deployment of additional forces to that theater of operations is the initial phase of that effort. As to when they will be employed, I am still taking that under consideration. It is still contingent on German reaction over the next day or two."

"Then," Jan asked, "you are committed but it is not, in your opinion, too late?"

Wilson smiled. "It is never too late for sanity to prevail. I will be more than willing to entertain reasonable proposals and enter negotiations with Chancellor Ruff's government, provided the fighting stops and I have some assurance that he and his government are dealing with us in good faith and not simply stalling while seeking a military advantage while we talk."

"Then, Madam President, we have not crossed the proverbial Rubicon. Our forces have not taken any actions that threaten to escalate this crisis any further, for the moment?"

"That, as you know, is very subjective. For example, although our aircraft based in Great Britain have not violated German airspace, the Air Force has established round-the-clock patrols. They're already using aircraft based in Great Britain over both the North Sea and the

Baltic Sea, including E-3 airborne early warning and command and control aircraft flying in support of the Tenth Corps. Down links, using satellites and other secure communications nets, are already providing the Tenth Corps staff with information from the E-3s on German air operations."

The matter-of-fact manner in which Wilson was discussing the issue caused Jan to pause. Wilson was both calm and well prepared. This, coupled with no visible sign of stress or apprehension, made Jan wonder if the latest turn of affairs was not only expected but in fact had been planned for. Not wanting to lose momentum or give Wilson cause for concern, Jan popped the first question that came to her mind while she tried to figure a way of prying more information from Wilson. "Then it is your intention, Madam President, to use forces as they become available to assist the escape of the Tenth Corps?"

"As I said, Jan, employment of additional forces is contingent on German reaction." Shifting slightly in her chair, Wilson looked down at her nails, then back up at Jan. "I would like to take this opportunity to point out that I do understand the position of the German people and Chancellor Ruff's government. Yes, American forces, the Tenth Corps, have violated a number of international agreements. Yes, they have violated German territory and endangered the peace. But the Tenth Corps did not fire the first shot. Chancellor Ruff's government has over the past week continued to respond to my calls and those of my representatives for a peaceful and a negotiated settlement with demands that we cannot accept. I ask the American public as well as the German public to bear in mind throughout this crisis that it was the seizure of the nuclear weapons by force of arms at Sembach that started this chain of regrettable events. In the passions of the moment, we must not lose sight of the events that have brought us to this point, or of the real issues at hand."

Jan caught what Wilson was hinting at and jumped in. "You are, of course, referring to the nuclear weapons?"

A smile lit Wilson's face. "Exactly. The United States, operating as an agent of the Western nuclear powers, including Britain, France, Russia, and Israel, took direct action to secure nuclear weapons from an unstable government, one which had previously denounced nuclear proliferation. The seizure of those weapons by Germany, another nation that had previously denounced nuclear proliferation, the manner in which they were seized, and the resulting crisis are entirely separate issues from the intervention in the Ukraine."

"But we did contribute, Madam President, to this problem by bringing those weapons seized in the Ukraine to Germany. That was a clear violation of a previous agreement. Chancellor Ruff's government contends that that action on our part provided sufficient justification for their actions."

Knowing that Jan's husband was part of the Tenth Corps, Wilson decided to hit on a very personal note without making it seem like she was doing so. Leaning forward, her face set in a determined, almost angry mask, she said, "Does that violation of a treaty justify the murder of innocent American and German soldiers, not to mention the destruction of German civilian property? Does it justify the relinquishing of control of nuclear weapons to the Germans? No. Chancellor Ruff's justification for his actions over the past few days is far too thin. Rather than responding to this crisis in a responsible manner, as the commander at Sembach did, Chancellor Ruff has been obsessed with a desire to extract a pound of flesh when we in truth never threatened the safety or sovereignty of the German people in the first place. It is our soldiers, our sons and daughters, who are being endangered and unjustly punished without due process of law at the hands of the German military. And I will not tolerate it. Not as long as I am the President of the United States."

Wilson's angry and defiant response caught Jan off guard and, as Wilson had anticipated, hit her hard. The mention of American servicemen being endangered unnecessarily caused Jan to lose concentration as the image of Scott Dixon popped into her mind. The fact that the President of the United States was making a major policy statement as well as issuing a warning to a foreign government right there was forgotten for a moment. Scott and thoughts of his safety and well-being were what crowded Jan's thoughts. Because of this, an awkward silence of several seconds followed before Jan finally was able to pick up where Wilson had left off.

But the steam was gone from Jan's interview. When she finally realized that everyone was looking at her, waiting for her next question, Jan didn't have one ready. Instead she looked over to Wilson, thanking her for taking the time for the interview. With few formalities, Jan and her camera crew left moments before Ed Lewis, waiting in an adjoining office, came in. Wilson, who had already moved from where she had been during the interview with Jan Fields-Dixon, was seated at her desk but facing away, out into the Rose Garden. Seeing that she was deep in thought, Lewis quietly walked over to where the breakfast buffet was still laid out and helped himself to a cup of real coffee. As he went about this, he made just enough noise to ensure that Wilson was aware of his presence yet not enough to disturb her train of thought. When he was finished at the table, he walked over to the sofa that sat catty-corner to Wilson's desk, took a seat, and waited for her to finish whatever she was working over in her mind.

Without a word, Wilson slowly spun her chair around and faced Lewis. For a moment she simply looked at him. The expression on her face was one of pain. That, of course, did not surprise Lewis. It was in fact more of a surprise that she was holding up as well as she was when others about her, like Soares and Rothenberg, were losing their nerve and thrashing about the halls of the State Department and Pentagon like beached whales. For Wilson not only had the burden of the crisis to deal with, a crisis she was keenly aware her poor foreign policy decisions had precipitated, she was part of the three-way conspiracy that Big Al Malin was now playing out in central Germany. No, Lewis thought, she deserves to be concerned.

When Wilson finally spoke, it didn't have anything really to do with the matter at hand. Instead of discussing the battles raging in central Germany and her responses, she announced quite blandly, "Ed, I'm becoming a real bastard. A cynical, manipulative, grade A, government-inspected and FDA-approved bastard."

Caught off guard, Lewis's first reaction was to make light of her comment. "I think, Madam President, you're suffering from a little gender dysphoria this morning. I believe the female species uses a different term."

Looking at Lewis, Wilson showed her appreciation for his efforts by smiling slightly. But just as quickly as the smile came, it left. In its place was a serious stare. "No, Ed, I meant what I said. I've become one of them, one of those macho-asshole male professional politicians who don't give a damn who they step on or what they do in order to have and hold the power that this city has come to represent."

Seeing that she was stuck on this issue and his easygoing manner and humor wouldn't be enough to shake her off of it, Lewis put down his cup of coffee and prepared to deal with Wilson's crisis in confidence. "Abby, what did you expect? I mean, if the Lord on high was going to stage the second coming tomorrow and tempt the new messiah, he'd send him to Washington, not the desert. No one, Madam President, for all their good intentions, can do what you and others that have gone before you have to do and expect to maintain their eligibility for sainthood."

"Ed," Wilson said as she shook her head, "I know that. Damn it, I know that. People told me that before I started my race for the White House and told me that when I got here. But it still doesn't make it any easier for me. I mean, I really wanted to be different. And as the first woman President I thought that I could be different, that I could set my own standards and do things in a more human, open, and, well, loving and caring way. I mean, after all, I raised two children, maintained a marriage, and held down a career without losing my sanity. Why, I thought, couldn't I do the same thing here? Why couldn't I balance it all and still maintain my pride and dignity. Is that, Ed, too much to ask?"

"First off, Abby, I want you to know that you're the most human and caring individual that has occupied that desk that I've known. Despite all our differences, I admire the manner in which you have redefined the term 'presidential.' Perhaps this office was long overdue for a woman's touch and was just waiting for the right person who could retain her sense of femininity while dealing with the office and its demands." Lewis paused, picked up his cup of coffee, but set it down again without taking a sip. "Having said that, I must remind you, Abby, that you can't expect to play in a pigsty and not get dirty. Washington is the highest priced pigsty in the world, and this office happens to be in the center of it. That you've done as well as you have up to this point is nothing short of a miracle. Now tell me what's really on your mind. What brought on this sudden need for self-flagellation right in the middle of this crisis? Are you having second thoughts about letting Big Al make a run for the sea?"

Shaking her head, Wilson looked up at the ceiling. "No, no. I, like you, am still convinced that, given the situation, General Malin's option was the best of all the rotten choices we had. That's not what's gotten to me. No, it seems like the big decisions are easy to make and live with. It's when they become personal, human, that it gets to me." Looking down at Lewis, she waited a few seconds, then began to unload. "Jan Fields-Dixon was just here doing an interview after watching my spokesperson read the statement we prepared this morning. The interview was going fine until we got to a point where I saw an opportunity to make an impression on her, to play on her emotions. Knowing full well that her husband is in the middle of this mess, I used that connection to drive home the righteousness of my decision.''

Wilson paused as she took in a deep breath in an effort to hold back a tear. "I hurt her, Ed. I wanted to play on her female emotions, and when I did, and I saw that I had thrown her into a momentary panic, I felt a sudden twinge of pride.''

"I'm sure, Abby, you did what you thought was right. As I said, you are the President. You have a great deal of responsibility and many things that—''

Leaning forward, Wilson made a fist and pounded it on the desk. "That doesn't make me feel any better, Ed. I hear your words, but in my heart I feel like dirt. After despising and condemning male politicians all these years for doing the same thing to me and other female politicians, I suddenly realized that, given the opportunity, I would do the same thing.'' Easing back into her chair, Wilson thought for a moment before speaking again, this time with a softer, almost mournful tone. "It's, it's like I've lost the last of my innocence. I suppose that I've become nothing more than a political whore like everyone else around here, and it will be easier from now on.''

Standing up, Lewis walked over to the front edge of Wilson's desk. Leaning over with his arms resting on his knuckles, Lewis stared at Wilson. "Abby, no one will ever be able to call you a whore. And the fact that you feel like this should be enough to convince you that you'll never be like the rest of us. You are something special. Despite what your detractors say, you've made, and will continue to make, a difference. Don't buckle now. You've got too much going for you, and we've got a lot to do.''

"Do you think, Ed, that Ms. Fields knows that her husband is leading the main effort?''

Lewis, standing up, folded his arms and shook his head. "I really doubt it. But that doesn't make a difference. Scotty Dixon has a reputation for hanging his tail end over the edge. Jan knows without having to be told that Scotty is doing his duty and doing it from the front.''

"You know, Ed, I wish he weren't leading that effort. For Jan's sake, I wish he weren't.''

Leaning down, Lewis placed his knuckles back on the desk. His voice became rather stern. "No you don't, Madam President. Scotty Dixon is the best that you, the commander-in-chief, have. No. You, as the President and not the woman, want Dixon exactly where he is. Besides," Lewis concluded as he stood up, "he's a soldier. That means he's an expendable commodity. He knows that, Jan knows that, and you, the commander-in-chief, know that. It's when commanders become so concerned about the welfare of their soldiers that they are no longer willing to risk them in battle that men die needlessly and all is lost."

Wilson shook her head. "That might be true, Ed. But it doesn't make this any easier."

"And, Madam President, so long as you and those who follow you feel that way, this country will in my opinion be a cut above the rest." Finished, Lewis stood there for a moment. He suddenly felt very foolish for having lectured the President. It was, he realized, not the way things were done. But then again no one would ever accuse Lewis of doing things in a conventional way. Wanting to end this particular discussion, Lewis smiled. "Besides, Scotty Dixon's a brigade commander, a full colonel. There's so many people between him and the shooting that only an incredible stroke of bad luck could put him in harm's way."

Sensing that the mood had suddenly changed, Wilson sat up and looked Lewis in the eye. There was a hint of a smile on her face. "Ed."

"Yes, Madam President?"

"Thanks."

Though he didn't know exactly what Wilson was thanking him for, Lewis took it that the personal crisis she had been suffering when he had walked in had passed and that she was ready to get down to the business at hand.

Knowing that there was no time to lose, Captain Albrecht Benen ran up and down the line of flatbed rail cars sitting in the Dermbach rail yard in an effort to hurry his men. With the sound of the rest of the 4th Panzergrenadier Division's 1st Brigade already moving north through the town, Benen knew he didn't have much time to get his men and equipment offloaded and moving to their assigned forming-up point. Looking at his watch and seeing that it was not even twenty hundred hours, Benen wondered how the rest of the brigade, using roads, had gotten there before him, formed up, and moved to join the 2nd Panzer Division. But the noise of tracked vehicles and heavily laden supply trucks rolling through the town told him that at least some elements of the brigade had.

With no time to lose, Benen did his best to ignore the rumbling ground caused by tanks and tracked vehicles and to hasten the efforts of his soldiers. They had twelve Jaguar 1 anti-tank guided-missile tank destroyers, two trucks, and a small jeep to untie and get off the rail car. Doing it in the darkness of the deserted rail yard without the help of any railway workers only served to make things worse. The workers were no doubt screwing off with the police somewhere. No matter. The whole operation, from the first day that they had rolled out of their kasern to the receipt of the orders that had placed them on this train while the rest of the brigade had road-marched, had been a muddle. Why, he asked his first sergeant, should this be any different?

The first sergeant grunted his agreement. Then, looking in the direction of the town center, the first sergeant asked if maybe it would be a good idea for someone from the company to go into town and let someone from brigade know that they had arrived. Benen, embarrassed that he had arrived late, told the first sergeant that he would do so as soon as the company was ready to move. Besides, he needed every man he had to get the company's vehicles off the rail cars and moving. That decision, however, was countered by the captain himself with his next breath. Seeing that the lieutenant who commanded the one platoon that was already off the train had his men and vehicles assembled and ready to move, the captain shouted to the lieutenant to take his platoon of three anti-tank guided-missile tank destroyers up to the center of the town and wait there until the rest of the company was ready.

The first sergeant was about to point out that the personnel from that platoon could help offload the other Jaguar anti-tank guided-missile tank destroyers but didn't. Seeing that his commander was quite agitated and as confused in his own mind as the situation within the division appeared to be, the first sergeant shrugged and walked away. Officers, he thought, were sometimes difficult to understand. Tired from the long series of marches and countermarches that had taken them from one end of Germany to another, the first sergeant decided that this was neither the time nor place to argue with another confused and tired man. Better just to shut up and do as he was told while the officers sorted out this mess. Besides, the sound of tank engines growing fainter and fainter told him that whoever had been passing through the town's center had left. With the village cleared, at least for the moment, of military traffic, there would be little danger of their three tank destroyers getting mixed in with another convoy or adding to some other commander's confusion in the village. While the revving of engines of the lead tank destroyer platoon began to fill the rail yard, the first sergeant walked the line and shouted to his soldiers to hurry up and get a move on.

As the last tank of the 2nd Battalion, 4th Armored Division, left the north side of Dermbach, Scott Dixon and his tactical command post entered the town from the south. Leading the small convoy from his tank, Dixon was anxious to catch up to the rear of the 2nd Battalion, if for no other reason than to tuck up within it for security. The single M-1A1 tank, three M-113 armored personnel carriers, and one M-577 command post carrier didn't offer much in the way of defensive fire-power. In a pinch, against anything bigger than a platoon, the best Dixon could hope for was a valiant last stand.

Looking down to his left, Dixon watched Colonel Vorishnov for a moment. Standing upright in the loader's hatch of Dixon's tank, Vorishnov was leaning over on his folded arms that rested on the flat race ring of the loader's 7.62mm machine gun while he looked to the front, keeping track of where they were going while watching for any sign of trouble. Like Dixon, Vorishnov was bundled up in a heavy parka with its fur-lined hood pulled up over his armored crewman's helmet. A wool scarf wrapped around his neck several times was pulled up over Vorishnov's nose to protect his mouth and nose while a set of heavy plastic and rubber goggles were pulled down to keep his eyeballs from freezing in their sockets. Like every armored crewman who had to hang out of his vehicle and face the freezing temperature and the cutting winds, both Dixon and Vorishnov had every square inch of skin covered by as many layers of clothing as they could wear while maintaining their ability to function.

Vorishnov's desire to be up front where he could see what was going on was second only to Dixon's desire to have him nearby. Dixon had come to rely on Vorishnov's opinions and insights. It was like having a second pair of eyes that were just as keen as his own and trained to operate at the same level and speed. Vorishnov, understanding his role, never argued with Dixon and never tried to impose his own opinion on him. Instead he would stand back watching and listening. When he did have something to say or add, he would always start by saying, "Excuse me, Colonel, but could I make a comment?" By the time the order from division had come down to commence the flanking maneuver against the 2nd Panzer Division, no one on Dixon's staff would even consider commencing a briefing without the tall, stocky Russian colonel present. Vorishnov even shared Dixon's love of being a tanker, throwing himself into the task of learning how to function as a loader on an American tank. Though he couldn't help but comment every chance he had about how much better it was to have an automatic loader, like on Russian tanks, Vorishnov enjoyed being there with Dixon.

From the second-story window of his family's small corner apartment that overlooked the town's square, seven-year-old Hans Gielber watched in fascination as the line of three Jaguar tank destroyers moved from the rail yard toward him. Finally, he thought, the German Army had arrived. After watching American tanks and infantry fighting vehicles pass right under his own window for the last hour, someone was finally coming to stop them. Though he could only count three tank destroyers, that didn't matter. They were German tank destroyers, armed with either long-range TOW anti-tank guided missiles or the intermediate-range HOT anti-tank guided missiles. Either way, Hans knew that the big heavy American tanks would be no match for the fast, hard-hitting Jaguars that he and the other boys in his class had been learning about over the past weeks.

Like most of his classmates, he had great confidence in the abilities of the German Army and the effectiveness of its weapons. He didn't realize that the long-range anti-tank guided missiles on the Jaguars would be ineffective at very close range in street fighting due to the warhead's arming process that required the missile to fly a considerable distance before becoming fully capable. What young Hans Gielber knew in his heart was that both the soldiers and the weapons were the products of a nation with a long, proud military heritage that combined the knowledge of great engineers with the skills of master craftsmen. Nothing made in America, he told his friends in school, could ever hope to match a precision-made German machine in the hands of a brave German soldier. That he would be able to see the vindication of his arguments from his own window excited Hans no end.

While he intently watched the Jaguars move closer, Hans felt the floor of his apartment begin to vibrate as it had before when the last of the American tanks had come through. Pressing his face against the glass, Hans put his hands up on the window and looked in the opposite direction, down a side street that led to the south, to see if there were more American tanks coming. In the glow of the dim streetlights that circled the town square, Hans could just make out the image of a long heavy gun tube coming out of the shadows and into the town center. It was another American tank. Looking back to where the Jaguars were, Hans waited impatiently to see who would fire first. Not that it made a difference, he thought. The Jaguars would in short order reduce the American tank to a burning hulk. And he, out of all the boys in his class, would be there to see it.

Noting that they were about to enter the town's center crowded with shops and buildings, Dixon twisted about in his open hatch to look behind him to make sure that Cerro and the armored personnel carriers were keeping up. In his desire to make up for lost time, it was easy to forget about the slower, heavily burdened carriers. In the dim lights that lit the dingy little streets of the eastern German village, Dixon could make out the image of Cerro's personnel carrier as it wound its way through the narrow streets of Dermbach. He was about to key his intercom switch to order the driver to slow down so that the rest of the command post could catch up when Vorishnov, in a voice that was excited, yet clear and concise, cut Dixon off. "German anti-tank guided-missile carrier to the front, fifty meters!"

Snapping his neck about, Dixon instantly focused on the squat box-like tracked vehicle emerging from a side street directly across the town square from where his own tank was coming. While his body prepared him for battle, dumping adrenaline into his blood while his groin muscles tightened to keep from venting urine or bowel, Dixon's mind automatically flipped through a mental file of armored vehicle images and profiles. Without much conscious thought needed, a voice inside Dixon's brain shouted, Jaguar.

With that completed, Dixon's training as a tanker took over, treating the armored vehicle to his front as an enemy until such time as he could determine otherwise. With a single seamless order, Dixon shouted directions to his crew in the form of a fire command that did not come out as clear and concise as he would have liked. But that didn't seem to make a difference as the crewmen, including Vorishnov, responded to each element of the command. "DRIVER STOP! GUNNER—BATTLE SIGHT—ANTI-TANK!"

The driver, already alerted to the presence of an enemy by Vorishnov's acquisition report, had eased up on the throttle and was prepared to continue or stop when Dixon issued his fire command. With measured practice, the driver eased down on the brake, bringing the massive tank to a smooth stop.

The gunner, lulled into a near state of sleep, had also been jerked to life by Vorishnov's warning. By the time Dixon uttered his first word, the gunner had his eye on the primary sight, and the thermal sight switched from standby to on. Like Dixon, the gunner's training overrode any panic. Instead, his hand moved across the face of the primary sight's controls and knobs, ensuring by feel that all was ready to engage the target. Though Dixon had announced battle sight, the gunner intended to range to the target using the laser range finder integrated in the primary sight. In fact, the gunner didn't even have to think twice about that as his right thumb automatically twitched and depressed the laser range finder button on the top of the gunner controls. This action caused the 120mm main gun to jump as the computer received automatically the correct range to the target, computed a proper ballistic solution for the forthcoming engagement, and applied that ballistic solution to the tank's fire-control system, all done before Dixon had finished spitting out the last word of his fire command.

Vorishnov, steeled for action before anyone else, had dropped to the turret floor and plopped himself down on the seat he had been standing on. Reaching across, Vorishnov grabbed the long, crooked arm that served to arm the tank's main gun as well as deflect the wide base plate of expended main gun rounds into a container hanging from the gun's breech. Finished with that, Vorishnov pulled his whole body over to one side to escape the recoil of the main gun and hung on to the handles as he had been shown.

As he sat there watching Dixon in the dim blue-green light of the turret, he pondered whether he should ask what round Dixon wanted to load next but decided not to. Dixon's mind, he knew, was busy going over the shoot—don't shoot decision process. Vorishnov, knowing that they were facing an anti-tank unit, would load a high explosive anti-tank, or HEAT round next, once the armor-piercing, fin-stabilized anti-tank round already in the gun's chamber was fired. He would have to announce that to the gunner so that he could change the ammunition selection lever on the primary sight and allow the fire-control computer to provide a new ballistic solution. But that was easy and worth the effort. Though Vorishnov hadn't been told, he assumed that the Americans, like his own Army, preferred the HEAT round, a chemical round that caused a shaped-charge explosion on contact with target when engaging lightly armored vehicles and material targets. Armor-piercing rounds used against enemy tanks were nothing more than a depleted uranium slug that used kinetic energy to punch its way through the armor plate of the target. Against the Jaguar there was the chance that the armor-piercing round would sail through both sides of the Jaguar without destroying it. Though Vorishnov doubted that would happen, a HEAT round next time would be better.

If there was any doubt in Dixon's mind about whether or not he should engage the Jaguar across the square from him, he didn't dwell long on it. They were committed to war. First blood had been drawn, and this was neither the time nor place to determine if the crew of the Jaguar across from them was made up of good Germans or bad Germans. Only the fact that Vorishnov had forgotten to announce that he was UP, or ready for action, caused a delay. Out of habit, Dixon shouted, "LOADER! ARE YOU UP?"

Vorishnov, realizing his error, shouted, "UP," then silently cursed himself for being so stupid.

Dixon instantly shouted, "FIRE!" causing the gunner to respond with "ON THE WAY" just before he pulled the trigger.

The first engagement of the evening was over before the last of the reverberations from Dixon's tank died away in the close confines of the town's square. Like a giant dart, the depleted uranium penetrator sliced through the armor plate of the lead Jaguar 1 of Captain Albrecht Benen's company. Vorishnov's fear that such a round would have minimal effect against the Jaguar was ill founded, as the depleted uranium penetrator, pushing a chunk of the Jaguar's own armor plate in front of it, cut through stored ammunition into the Jaguar's fuel cell and out the rear through the engine compartment. The tremendous heat created by the transformation of the penetrator's kinetic energy into heat upon contact with the Jaguar set off first the propellant of the stored ammunition, then the diesel fuel.

Hans Gielber never had the opportunity to see any of this. By the time the lead Jaguar began shuddering from internal explosions, Hans was fleeing from the window, his face, chest, and upper arms shredded by glass that had been shattered by the concussion of the muzzle blast from Dixon's main gun. Though he would survive, he, like other children around the world, would pay for the decisions made by men who claimed to be their leaders and the men who were opposed to them. Like many of his countrymen caught in the middle of a conflict which few understood, Hans Gielber would carry the mental and physical scars of war with him for the rest of his life.

With the initial threat dealt with, Dixon now had to make a series of quick decisions. They were, relative to his rank and position, rather simple decisions. But that didn't make them any less critical. Knowing full well that anti-tank guns don't travel alone, Dixon knew there were more somewhere nearby, if not immediately behind the one he had just destroyed. The destruction of the lead Jaguar would serve as an effective, if somewhat bloody, warning to any German unit in the area that the Americans were there. So sneaking away into the darkness was out of the question. That didn't rule out the option of retreat. Dixon's tank was the only combat vehicle in the entire tactical command post. Though there might only be one more guided-missile anti-tank vehicle in the town, the chances of there being more were just as good, and Dixon had no way of knowing which answer was the correct one. So retreat was a prudent choice.

No one who knew Scott Dixon, however, would ever be able to accuse him of being conservative or prudent when it came to tactics. It was that reputation that had led his superiors to select his brigade for the foray into the Ukraine. It was those traits that gave them confidence that Dixon's brigade would be able to pull off the ride around the 2nd Panzer Division's flank. And in a moment of sheer panic Dixon's hard-hitting and aggressive nature overrode common sense and dictated his next series of orders. Keying the radio net, he ordered Cerro to find somewhere that the soft-skinned vehicles of the tactical command post could be protected by the officers and enlisted of the staff with the few anti-tank rockets that they had while they waited for the lead element of the next battalion to reach them.

Even before Cerro acknowledged Dixon's order, Dixon shouted for his driver to move out and told his gunner to keep his eyes open, that they were going to go around the Jaguar they had just destroyed and see if there were any more following. As the driver engaged the transmission, Dixon squatted on his seat and looked over to see how Vorishnov was doing with reloading. Dixon, just in time to see the Russian ram the next round into the gun chamber, noticed that he was sweating. Vorishnov, seeing Dixon watching, grunted and yelled over the sounds of the tank's turbine engines, "Automatic loaders are much better." Then he added after keying the intercom, "HEAT loaded."

With a quick smile and a thumbs-up, Dixon acknowledged the comment and popped back up just as his tank was about to pass the burning Jaguar. His gunner, who was not blinded by the flames of the burning German vehicle, shouted a new acquisition report. "Antitank, twelve o'clock!"

Dixon noticed that his gunner's voice was calmer now, even though he saw at the same instant that the new target was even closer than the one they had just engaged. Without waiting to give a full fire command, Dixon yelled, "INDEX HEAT—FIRE!" in a single breath. Before the gunner fired, Dixon looked and saw another Jaguar desperately trying to back down the narrow street behind the one his gunner was engaging.

The muzzle blast of his tank's 120mm main gun momentarily blinded Dixon, who had not heeded the gunner's warning of "On the way" and closed his eyes. Not that there was much to see. The second engagement ended as the first had, with a target hit on the second Jaguar at a range of less than forty meters. But there was no time to stop to catch their breath. For while the gunner was preparing to dispatch the second Jaguar, Dixon caught a glimpse of the other Jaguar halfway through the process of turning around further down the street. Suddenly Dixon began to doubt the wisdom of charging across the square in pursuit of Germans. For the briefest moments he understood how Custer could have allowed himself to get suckered into his own massacre.

But this was no time for half measures, no time for backing up. Dixon felt he was committed and that it was better to keep going than to back off now. Taking a deep breath, Dixon looked about as his night vision began to clear and ordered the driver to keep heading down the street toward what he thought was the rail yard. Though he was pushing his luck or, more correctly, the luck of his entire crew, Dixon had no intention of stopping while he thought he had an advantage.

In the rail yard, bewilderment was replaced by a panicked frenzy of activity as Captain Albrecht Benen and his first sergeant, once they realized what was going on, ran up and down the line of flatbed rail cars shouting at their men in an effort to get them to hurry. Not everyone was as panicked as their commander. One Jaguar commander, seeing that his crew was doing the best it could and noticing that the second tank cannon report was closer, climbed on his vehicle and began to mount an anti-tank guided missile. Even if they were still on the rail car when the enemy tank came, the Jaguar commander figured he would be able to get at least one shot off.

Benen, pausing after he heard a third tank round fired, realized that in moments the enemy would be right there in the middle of the rail yard itself. Knowing that it was useless to try to take on the enemy tank in the town, Benen decided to prepare to meet the Americans in the rail yard. There, the anti-tank guided missiles would have enough stand-off distance between the launcher and the target, for it took several meters for an anti-tank guided missile to arm itself after being fired, something that he couldn't count on in the narrow streets of the town. Leaving the first sergeant to take care of the vehicles at the front of the train, closest to where he expected the enemy tanks to come from, Benen ran to the end of the rail cars where he intended to deploy several of his Jaguars. Though it would be close, he was confident that they could do it.

Confidence, at that moment, was something that Second Lieutenant Tim Ellerbee could have used. Ordered to pick up his speed and get into the town of Dermbach as quickly as possible to protect the brigade command post from an enemy counterattack, Ellerbee and the rest of his platoon had left Captain Nancy Kozak and her slower Bradleys behind in the night in their efforts to reach the brigade command post before the Germans did.

The sudden burst of speed that allowed Ellerbee and his tanks to break free of the numbing convoy speed, heightened by the prospect of battle, shook any traces of sleep from Ellerbee's mind. They were going into battle again. This time he and his platoon would do everything right. The problems that he had experienced in the Ukraine would be washed away in a single smashing success. And he would be able to prove to the female captain who spoke to him like he was an idiot that he was as good a soldier, if not better, as she was. Of all the thoughts that ran through Ellerbee's mind as his platoon reached the southern outskirts of Dermbach, that was the most important one.

Which perhaps explains why Second Lieutenant Ellerbee missed the sign that indicated the main road, the one that would have taken his platoon to the center of town where the brigade command post was and where Scott Dixon and his crew were fighting for their lives. Instead Ellerbee found that he was rapidly leading his entire platoon down a blind alley instead of charging to the rescue. Not understanding what had happened, Ellerbee brought his tank to a screaming stop when he suddenly ran out of street and entered a factory complex. Pausing, he looked to his left, then to his right, then at his map while the sounds of Scott Dixon's lonely battle against Captain Albrecht Benen's Jaguar company reverberated through the empty streets.

While Ellerbee was trying to figure out what had gone wrong and what to do about it, Sergeant First Class Rourk, Ellerbee's platoon sergeant, came over the platoon's radio net. "Alpha Three One, this is Alpha Three Four. We missed a turn back there somewhere. Do you want me to get everyone turned around? Over."

Looking back down the line of tanks, Ellerbee realized that would take time, which the brigade command post might not have. Besides, if they missed the turn once, there was no guarantee that they wouldn't miss it again. Looking at his map again, Ellerbee noticed that there was a rail line that ran north to south. To his front, he could make out what he thought was a set of tracks in the factory's yard. Glancing back to his left, he followed the tracks toward the direction of the town center and the sounds of battle. It only made sense that the tracks in the factory yard had to be connected to the main rail line shown on his map.

Stuffing his map back down the open hatch he stood in, Ellerbee keyed the radio mike. "Negative Three Four. We're going to follow these tracks here to my front and into the center of the town. When we get close enough to the action, we'll cut up a side street and find the brigade CP. Over."

Though Rourk wasn't too keen on Ellerbee's idea, Ellerbee was the platoon leader and they had to do something fast. So with a less than enthusiastic "Roger, we're right behind you," Rourk and the rest of 3rd Platoon made a sharp left and began to rumble along the railroad tracks toward the sound of the guns.

In headlong pursuit down the twisting streets after another, and what he hoped to be the last, Jaguar, Dixon didn't notice that he had run out of street and was entering the wide-open rail yard. Not that this helped the Jaguar that they were chasing. When the gunner thought he had enough time, he yelled, "ON THE WAY." Without waiting for Dixon to give the order to fire, he fired the main gun. As before, this HEAT round found its mark.

The sudden report of a tank cannon and the series of explosions caused by the destruction of one of his Jaguars right there in the middle of the rail yard caught Captain Albrecht Benen and the rest of his company by surprise. In an instant the dark rail yard was bathed in bright yellow and red light as flames from the burning propellant of ammunition stored in the latest Jaguar destroyed leaped into the black night sky. Every one of Benen's officers and soldiers turned and watched before the image of Dixon's tank, with its huge 120mm tank cannon turning toward them, caused them to redouble their efforts. This was it. Fight or flight.

The sudden image of a dozen enemy armored vehicles, some still on rail cars but all of them pointing toward them, startled Dixon, Vorishnov, and his gunner. They were in deep shit with no good choices. Dixon knew that he had pushed his luck too far and it was now time to beat a hasty retreat if they could. Even the driver, without being told, understood their plight, had realized what was coming and had already applied the brakes before Dixon gave the frantic order to back up, repeating it several times, even after his tank had begun its rearward motion.

Like Dixon, the explosion of the Jaguar in the rail yard and the sight of multiple targets less than one hundred meters to his front caught Ellerbee by surprise. He and the rest of his platoon, however, had an advantage. All the Germans were looking the other way. Somehow he realized they had come up behind the Germans and were in a perfect position to hit them from the rear before they had time to react. Without looking to see if there was room to properly deploy, Ellerbee keyed the platoon radio net and ordered his platoon to deploy on line to either side of his tank and begin to engage the enemy vehicles at will.

Not waiting for acknowledgment from any of his tank commanders, Ellerbee let the radio mike go and issued a quick if somewhat confused initial fire command to his own gunner. The content of the fire command, including the target Ellerbee wanted to engage, didn't matter. Ellerbee's gunner had already laid his sights onto the rear of a Jaguar that was sitting on top of a rail car with its missile launcher up and ready to fire. When Ellerbee screeched his command to fire, the gunner gave a quick "On the way" and pulled the trigger on his right gunner's control.

While the destruction of the Jaguar to their front had been a surprise, the firing of a tank and the explosion of another Jaguar behind the men of Benen's company was a shock. Captain Albrecht Benen turned around just in time to see a second American tank pull up next to the one that had just fired and turn its gun on the Jaguar that he was standing next to. Realizing what was coming Benen threw himself under the rail car to his left just as the second American tank fired, destroying another Jaguar.

Rolling over onto his stomach and propping himself up on his elbows, Benen looked at his latest loss. He realized that all hope of salvaging this one-sided battle was gone. Though Benen had no idea that his company outnumbered the Americans engaged, that didn't matter. He had been unable to bring the weapons of his company to bear and had never been able to recover from the initial shock. As he lay there, Benen saw his men abandon their efforts to bring their Jaguars into the fight and, like him, seek safety behind cover or in flight. All thoughts of duty, honor, and country were forgotten as Benen crawled over the concrete rail sleepers and through puddles of waste oil, mud, and slush that dotted the rail yard and his path to safety.

Though the tide had swung back in their favor, it was several minutes before Scotty Dixon and his crew realized that. And even when they did, neither he nor anyone else on his tank showed any great desire to rejoin the fighting. They had done what they had hoped to do; they had saved their own lives. That they had killed other men in the process didn't matter. What mattered was that they were alive, that they were in one piece, and that the hope of making it home that way was still a realistic and achievable goal. There was no joy, no pride. Only four sweating men relieved that they had survived somehow and for the moment had nothing to do.

It was Vorishnov, in his indomitable style, who finally broke the silence and pulled Dixon and the rest of his crew out of their own personal reflections and thoughts.

Climbing up and out of the open loader's hatch, Vorishnov looked toward the rail yard, hidden by the twisting street but marked by many fires and secondary explosions. After taking off his helmet and wiping the sweat from his brow, Vorishnov looked at Dixon and pointed a finger at him. There was a stern look on Vorishnov's face. "You know, Colonel, it would have been much better with an automatic loader. This juggling act to load this cannon is too much for one man, especially an old one like me. You must tell your generals you need automatic loaders."

Dixon laughed. "Well, Colonel, remind me of that when we get to Bremerhaven."

Vorishnov nodded. "I will do that, Colonel. I promise you."

CHAPTER 15

20 JANUARY

In relative terms, the forces engaged were small given the area involved and the nations participating. The area defined by Giessen in the west and Eisenach in the east, Kassel in the north, and Fulda in the south belonged to the German state of Hesse and encompassed over 4,000 square miles, or slightly less than the state of Connecticut. The only river of any consequence was the Fulda, running north to south from the town of Fulda to Kassel. Most of the towns and villages scattered throughout this area were, comparatively speaking, small. Except for the major road networks that ran through some of them, few were of any significance.

It was the hills, forests, and small valleys that gave the Battle of Central Germany its character. Because of this, maneuver space was quite limited and the opportunity to use the sophisticated long-range weapons that both armies were equipped with to their maximum effective range was rare. The broken and hilly terrain, cluttered with forests, meant that the series of battles that took place seldom involved more than a single company on either side. There were no long-drawn-out battles of maneuver and massed firepower where generals and colonels maneuvered massed formations here and there. Instead, the Battle of Central Germany was a series of seemingly random and disjointed actions that were short but vicious. These confrontations, often fought at very close range, never involved more than a handful of tanks or infantry fighting vehicles, controlled by captains and lieutenants, and fought by soldiers who seldom saw more than one or two other vehicles of their own unit. Although violent

surprise attacks against strong points and ambushes were the preferred technique of both sides, chance meetings were just as likely as
the Tenth Corps shifted to deal with the aggressive 2nd Panzer Division and the leisurely probes of the 10th Panzer.

The weather added its own cruel touch to the battles fought
throughout the state of Hesse. Short days and long nights, nights that
lasted from 4:30 in the afternoon until almost 7:30 in the morning,
added to the difficulties of combatants and those supporting them.
Even when day did make its brief appearance, leaden gray skies filled
with angry dark clouds often shielded the soldiers of both sides from
the warming rays of the sun. It was perhaps the prevailing gloom of
winter weather and the discomfort it brought to members of the Tenth
Corps and the Bundeswehr that made the foul business of war even
fouler and more unpleasant.

In war the weather can be as deadly and vicious an opponent as any
human being. Freezing temperatures can kill the unprepared or care-
less soldier just as dead as a bullet. And even when the freezing temperatures rise long enough to melt snow, the weather gives no
warmth, no relief. Instead, warmer weather generates mud, mud that
coats both soldiers and their equipment. Mud that fouls weapons and
machines. Mud that grabs an infantryman's ankles and makes each
step an effort that further saps the soldier's diminishing strength and
stamina. With the approach of night, when the temperature dips again
below freezing, uniforms and jackets, now wet and covered with mud,
give their owners little protection from the bitter winter winds. Nor
do the cold and tasteless combat rations do anything to relieve the
sufferings of the soldiers. Together with the lack of dry clothing and
the inability to stop long enough to tend to personal needs, including
sleep, hope, as well as a soldier's ability to function, slowly erodes. As
physical discomfort and the frustrations of not being able to relieve
them continue, nerves fray and tempers wear thin, adding mental
gloom and despair to an already gloomy and desperate situation. With
each kilometer that the Tenth Corps moved north toward the sea and
the Bundeswehr fought to stop it, the hopes and spirits of the soldiers
sagged lower and lower. Only the efforts of the commanders on both
sides, who themselves suffered under the same conditions that were
slowly breaking their men, kept both armies going.

*   *   *

Seventeen kilometers south of Bad Hersfeld, Captain Friedrich Seydlitz stood shivering in the open hatch of his Leopard II tank, watching and waiting impatiently for the American mechanized infantry forming up in the wood line across from his company to make its attack. That they were there and that they were preparing for an attack was obvious to everyone in Seydlitz's company. Since moving west out of Hünfeld, the Americans had been putting continuous pressure on Seydlitz's brigade while it continued to make its way to Autobahn A7. Seydlitz, standing on the forward edge of battle and unaware of the activities of other units, couldn't understand why, after such a magnificent start, he and his company were now standing on the defensive. No one, not even his battalion commander, bothered to explain to him that the lack of fuel and the unexpected counterattack of an American brigade in the rear of the 2nd Panzer Division kept Seydlitz and his men from reaching their objective. Instead, Seydlitz was simply ordered to move to such and such a place, assume a hasty defensive position, and be prepared to beat back any and all counterattacks.

Turning up the collar of his field jacket, Seydlitz wondered what the Americans across from him were up to. They had been fooling around just inside the tree line five hundred meters across a narrow valley from his company for better than three hours. Every now and then one of his tank commanders or gunners would catch a glimpse of an American combat vehicle and ask permission to fire. Seydlitz, without exception, declined permission. They, not the Americans, were at a disadvantage in this situation and had to be careful. Better, he thought, to wait until the enemy came at him in force and in the open than to pick ineffectually at them and expose his own tanks to systematic destruction. Though Seydlitz, like his tank commanders, was chafing at the insufferable delay and anxious to do something, there was nothing to do but curse the cold and dampness that inflamed every joint in his body.

In the distance, a series of low rumbles broke the silence. The firing of American artillery announced the beginning of the attack. Never having been the target of an artillery barrage, Seydlitz didn't quite know what to expect. In training, he had seen and even directed artillery fire at old vehicle hulks and piles of scrap metal. That, however, had been under totally controlled conditions in which every effort had been made to ensure that no mistakes would be made and that no one would be hurt. This, Seydlitz realized as he dropped to the turret floor, pulling his hatch cover over his head, was different. He, and not some pile of scrap metal, was their intended target.

Any further thoughts were cut short as the first rounds of American artillery broke apart on their downward arc, disgorging baseball-sized anti-tank submunitions over most of the woods where Seydlitz's company was deployed. With his hatch closed and locked, there was nothing more for him to do but wait for the final impact and pray. The armor plate of his tank, while it served to insulate them from much of the noise, reducing the sound of the submunitions detonating to the point where they sounded more like firecrackers than lethal tank killers, could do nothing to diminish the fear and apprehension that Seydlitz felt as they waited.

Seydlitz looked around the turret at his crew. Across the turret, slouched down in his seat, was the loader, watching Seydlitz. As he tried to force a smile, Seydlitz noticed that he was sweating despite the fact that just moments before he had been freezing. Though the heat generated by the tank's heater made his overcoat unnecessary, most of the sweat running down his body felt cold and clammy. He was not suffering from overheating, just overexcitement and fear.

From his position, Seydlitz's gunner called out, "Smoke. They are laying down smoke to our front, Herr Captain."

Turning away from his loader, whose deadpan stare stayed fixed on him, Seydlitz glanced out of the clear vision blocks that surrounded his position. To his front he could see clouds of smoke that appeared to come billowing out of the ground. Artillery-fired smoke rounds no doubt were the cause. Putting his head up to his sight extension, Seydlitz saw that his gunner had already switched the view of the tank's primary sight from clear daylight to thermal. Even this did little to clear his view of the battlefield. Without moving his eye or directing his gunner, who was slowly scanning the area to their front by traversing the turret, Seydlitz mumbled, "Plastic white phosphorus." Then added, "I can't see a damned thing."

The gunner, keeping his eye to his sight while continuing to slowly traverse the turret, grunted. "Neither can I. Not a damned thing."

Unlike conventional smoke, plastic white phosphorus rounds contained a mix of white phosphorus and butyl rubber. On impact, the projectile ruptured, exposing the white phosphorus to air, which caused it to burn. The butyl rubber, mixed with the phosphorus, began to burn and flake off. Floating up and away from the ruptured projectile, these flakes of burning rubber created a curtain of heat that could defeat thermal sights. Seydlitz was still watching the clouds of heated smoke drift about in the opening between his position and where the Americans had been last seen when a new series of firecracker-like pops outside reminded him that they were under attack and that he needed to report his observations and status to his commander.

Without thinking, Seydlitz keyed the radio and called his battalion command post in preparation for reporting. He paused when he realized that he wasn't sure what to report. Not having received any reports from his platoon leaders since the artillery attack had commenced, Seydlitz naturally assumed that they had nothing to report. But that was just an assumption. If he was going to make a report to his battalion commander that his commander was going to use to make decisions, Seydlitz had to base that report on facts, not assumptions. Ignoring the calls by the battalion operations officer, Seydlitz switched his radio to his company net and contacted in turn each of his platoon leaders. Their situation, he found to his great relief, was very similar to his own. Artillery was impacting somewhere to their rear and smoke was obscuring their ability to see more than a hundred meters to the front. Warning them to stay alert and ready to move on a moment's notice, Seydlitz prepared to switch back to the battalion radio net to complete his aborted report.

He was, however, unable to do so, for as soon as Seydlitz flipped the battalion radio frequency on, the earphones of his headset came to life with reports streaming in from the tank company to the right of Seydlitz's and with orders from the battalion commander. Quickly it dawned upon Seydlitz that the brunt of the American attack had fallen on that company and not his. Surprisingly, the first thought that came to Seydlitz's mind was one of relief, relief that it was not his company that would bear the full fury of the enemy attack and in turn not his company that would determine, at least in the beginning, whether the battalion succeeded or failed. Though such a feeling was selfish and unprofessional, it was an honest reflection of Seydlitz's state of mind and priorities.

Seydlitz's salvation, however, was purchased at the expense of one of his fellow company commanders. From the radio traffic and reports, it was obvious that the American attack had come right under the cover of the artillery and smoke, catching the defending company momentarily off guard. Quick reactions and well-sited positions, however, cost the attacker dearly. In a matter of minutes, the lead echelon of the American assault force, consisting of M-1A1 tanks and Bradley fighting vehicles, was shredded and scattered.

When the two forces came together, it came down to a simple question of who saw who first. Though the artillery barrage managed to degrade the ability of the German company under attack to observe its sector of responsibility and caused them to button up, the artillery had little permanent effect on the Germans. And the artillery-delivered smoke, while covering the first three hundred meters of their advance, did nothing for the attackers during the last few critical meters. It in fact served to disrupt the attack in a few instances and separated the assaulting elements from those that had remained behind to cover the assault by fire.

Emerging from their own smokescreen, the Americans were greeted with a volley of fire from those Leopard tanks that were undamaged and waiting. There were only a few instances where an attacking American tank managed to fire first. Even here, however, that success was fleeting as German tanks that were not under attack or had dealt with the threat immediately to their front repositioned themselves to cover gaps created by the loss of a Leopard tank to their immediate left or right. Thus, before the German battalion commander was able to issue Seydlitz his first clear order, the critical point had been reached and the crisis was over. All that remained was the elimination of a handful of American vehicles that had made it into the German-held woodlot and the restoration of the defensive perimeter.

From his position on the periphery of this fight, Seydlitz waited impatiently for orders. While still relieved that he and his company were not involved in the fight, his ability to influence a battle that, if lost, could result in his own company being attacked from the flank and rear made him nervous and apprehensive. As he listened to the reports from the commanding officers in contact, Seydlitz followed the action on his map. As he did so, he began to notice that, while few American tanks and Bradleys were reported to have made it across the opening, those that had were beginning to work their way around the flank of the company next to Seydlitz's. If unchecked, they could find their way into his sector or, even worse, into the battalion's rear. Like many armor officers, raised to believe in the superiority of aggressive, offensive operations and trained to seek, strike, and destroy, the idea of simply sitting there while his peers were fighting for their collective lives just a few hundred meters away was becoming too much for him.

Opening his hatch slightly and popping his head up, Seydlitz noticed that the artillery barrage on his position had lifted. Satisfied that it was clear, he threw the hatch into the full open position, popped up, and looked about. The first thing that struck Seydlitz was that there were so few signs of the artillery barrage that his unit had just been subjected to. Since most of his images of war were based on films and photos of the devastation created by the massive and prolonged barrages of the two world wars, this should not have surprised him, but it did. Seydlitz looked in the direction from which the noise of battle drifted through the thick pines. He should, he knew, hold his position and await orders. There was still the possibility that the fight could spill over into his sector of responsibility or, having failed to achieve success in one part of the field, the Americans could expand their attack and hit his unit. On the other hand, the old military dictum that no commander could do wrong by marching to the sound of the guns kept buzzing through Seydlitz's mind.

He was in the process of weighing the pros and cons of moving parts of his company to the right into the fight when the sound of an M-113 armored personnel carrier coming up behind him caught his attention. Leaning over and looking to his rear, he noticed that it was the battalion's operations officer. With the same casual disregard for speed that most Germans display when driving their personal cars on the autobahns, the driver of the personnel carrier pulled around the rear of Seydlitz's tank without slowing down. When the battalion operations officer, riding in the open commander's hatch of the personnel carrier was even with Seydlitz, the driver of the personnel carrier brought his vehicle to a sudden stop. The operations officer, used to the driver's habits, hung on to the machine gun at his position with one hand and the rim of the hatch with the other as he absorbed the recoil of the sudden stop by merely swaying back and forth like a jack-in-the-box that had just been sprung.

Like many officers in the panzer corps, the operations officer freely demonstrated his individuality and devil-may-care attitude by wearing his cloth garrison cap instead of a steel helmet. Pulling the radio earphone from one of his ears, the operations officer yelled to Seydlitz as soon as he stopped swaying. "Seydlitz, your company will remain here and assume responsibility for the entire battalion's battle position. The rest of the battalion will move, as soon as the last of the enemy vehicles are found and destroyed, to an attack position south of here in preparation for a new effort to break through to the west. You will report directly to the 1st Panzer Brigade and remain in place until ordered to join us either tomorrow or the next day. Is that clear?"

Not sure that he had heard everything over the noise of his tank's engine and that of the personnel carrier, not to mention the ongoing fight somewhere off to their right, Seydlitz restated his orders as he understood them. "So, I'm attached to brigade with the mission of holding fast here until ordered to join you sometime tomorrow west of here."

The operations officer nodded. "That's right." Replacing the earphone over his ear, the operations officer yelled into the intercom for his driver to move out. With a jerk, the driver slammed down the personnel carrier's accelerator and went charging off back toward the sound of the battle. The operations officer, without so much as a look back, swayed this way and that, ducking low-hanging branches with a well-measured casualness as his driver picked up speed and disappeared in the direction from which they had come.

Though he was happy to have received definite orders and therefore relieved of the need to exercise his own initiative, Seydlitz didn't like the idea of being left behind. Success in holding empty woodlots in central Germany against attacks wasn't going to end this fight. Seydlitz knew this, as he was sure that his superiors did. Only by attacking would they be able to bring the renegade Americans under control and demonstrate for anyone who needed the lesson that Germany was a sovereign and independent nation. That he wouldn't be part of that effort suddenly overcame Seydlitz's common sense that should have told him that attacks in this terrain, just like the one that his battalion was still in the process of beating down, were costly and often led to failure. He was, however, a *Panzertruppen*, a tank soldier with a proud family heritage and the member of a branch of service that had once been the scourge of all of Europe. If he was to serve, he wanted to be in the forefront like his ancestors.

But Seydlitz was a soldier, a German soldier. And like all good soldiers who had orders that were clear and concise, he knew he had to obey them. Though his personal preference would have been to leave the defense to someone else, it was his duty to follow his orders regardless of how unpleasant they were.

With a sigh, Seydlitz noticed a slackening of noise. The fight to his right was ending. Settling down into his hatch, he reached for his map and began to study it as he considered how best to deploy his company once the rest of the battalion pulled out.

Just south of Autobahn E40 in what used to be East Germany, Company C, 3rd of the 3rd Infantry, lead element of Scott Dixon's brigade, ran into the flank guard of the 2nd Panzer Division. It was, like most of the engagements that Dixon's brigade was stumbling into on the 20th, a chance encounter. But the fact that these meetings between the 2nd Panzer Division's 2nd Brigade and Dixon's brigade were accidents didn't make them any less deadly.

Racing north along a muddy, deeply rutted road that cut through the forest south of the autobahn, Captain Nancy Kozak kept checking her map while watching for the vehicles of 2nd Platoon. Behind her the tanks of Ellerbee's platoon followed.

For the third time in less than twenty-four hours, Kozak found herself rushing into the middle of a crisis at full speed with little or no information. In Dermbach the night before Ellerbee and his platoon had charged into the middle of a street fight with anti-tank guided-missile carriers before she could get there. That morning her 1st Platoon leader, Second Lieutenant Sly Ahern, had made a wrong turn just after dawn and run head-on into a German artillery column that was in the process of setting up. And now her 2nd Platoon, which was acting as the battalion's advance guard, was in the middle of a hasty attack against an enemy force of unknown size. As she ducked to avoid low-hanging branches, the only thought that kept coming to mind, despite the desperateness of the situation and the mental exhaustion that was beginning to wear on her, was which would kill her first: enemy action or the antics of her platoon leaders.

Though Ellerbee's tanks were technically faster, the 63-ton M-1A1 tanks of Ellerbee's platoon with their wider chassis and oversized main gun protruding well to the front could not keep up with Kozak's Bradley C60 as it ran through the narrow, twisting forest trail that none of their maps showed. Through the use of such trails, the bulk of Dixon's brigade had been able to avoid hasty roadblocks and defensive positions set up to cover the obvious routes of advance that the Germans had thrown up between Dixon and Autobahn E40. With the goal of cutting across the rear of the 2nd Panzer Division and raising hell with its rear area supply and service units, Dixon had ordered his battalion commanders to keep their own supply vehicles tucked up close, ignore their flanks and rear, and run hell-bent for leather north until they hit the autobahn, destroying anything that belonged to the German Army along the way. The battalion commanders in making their plans had included Dixon's instructions word for word in their own orders. Company commanders, well drilled in Dixon's style of leadership and tactics, passed their commander's intent on to their platoon leaders and saw to it that those orders were carried out with a vengeance. It should have come as no surprise then that Gross had simply seized the initiative and gone right into the attack. He was, after all, following his brigade commander's intent to the letter.

That, however, did not excuse him in Kozak's mind from reporting to her what he was facing and what he was doing. As C60 bucked and swerved along the rutted trail, Kozak hoped that her young and energetic platoon leader hadn't bitten off more than he could deal with. Well aware of the pitfalls that most second lieutenants of infantry allow themselves to fall into, since she herself had been one, Kozak was hurrying forward with all the firepower she could muster as fast as she could. Though Ellerbee was still far from her favorite platoon leader, the performance of his platoon in Dermbach had shown that he was capable of reacting under fire and getting the job done. Of course, neither Dixon nor Kozak knew that Ellerbee's clever maneuver around the German anti-tank unit had actually been a mistake. The results had been good, and therefore the maneuver that had led to that success was termed brilliant.

In an effort to show that the infantry could be just as resourceful, and in response to Dixon's stated intent, Second Lieutenant Marc Gross had led his infantry platoon in what he considered to be a classic mechanized infantry action as they fell on two German Marders as they sat in a clearing refueling. The fight that developed turned out to be rather one-sided and over before it could even degenerate into a proper fight. In retrospect, Gross had made the right choice and Kozak's concerns were unfounded. But there were a few moments, after he had begun to maneuver his platoon and before they actually attacked, when Gross himself doubted that.

Coming up to a clearing that didn't show on his map, Gross stopped just inside of the wood line and dismounted to check out the area before sticking his nose out in the open. As he moved along the trail and left the noise of his own Bradley behind, he heard the noise of several diesel engines idling in the distance. Stopping, Gross used hand and arm signals back to his gunner, who was covering him from the Bradley, to have the dismounts come up and join him. When the fifteen dismounts of his platoon, stripped down for a fight, joined him, Gross deployed them in a line on either side of the trail they had been moving down. When all was ready, Gross, in the center of the line, began to advance, followed by his men. Gross kept looking in the direction of the sounds they were tracking. The three squad leaders with their dismounts watched Gross for his signals while ensuring that their men kept the proper distance and covered their assigned sectors.

At the edge of the tree line Gross paused and squatted. The dismounts followed suit, scanning the area to their immediate front. From where he was, Gross could see a stand of short pine trees. The clearing was, he decided after looking at his map, a tree nursery that had been planted to replace older trees harvested years before. Standing slightly less than three feet tall and covering an area that Gross estimated to be one hundred by one hundred meters on either side of the trail, the tree nursery provided the only open area of any note in this forest. Not that this was important. What did matter was that the short pine trees and the noise created by the German panzergrenadiers that he could now clearly see across the clearing gave Gross the opportunity to close with and surprise them.

The Germans, oblivious to the danger that was lurking less than one hundred meters away, were idly picking away at their first warm meal of the day at the rear of a mess truck while the drivers of their two Marder infantry fighting vehicles were refueling them using five-gallon cans taken off of two fuel trucks parked next to each of the Marders. Like Gross's own dismounts, the German infantrymen sought every chance they could to escape the cramped and confined spaces of their fighting vehicles. The presence of a mess truck and the need to refuel combined to negate any security measures that the platoon commander had set up. With such an advantage, Gross decided to take on the Germans without waiting for any reinforcements from the rest of the company.

Splitting his dismounts in half, Gross sent the two groups in opposite directions around the nursery to deal with each of the Marders while dispatching one of the squad leaders back to the Bradleys with his orders for them. Gross, leading one of the two teams of dismounts, would initiate the attack. Using hand-held light anti-tank rocket launchers and well-controlled small-arms fire, Gross intended to disable the German fighting vehicles and pin the German dismounts and crews without damaging the fuel trucks. With luck, the appearance of his four Bradleys charging across the tree nursery under the control of his platoon sergeant would discourage any desire of the Germans surviving the initial onslaught to continue to resist.

As with any operation, there are always the unknowns to contend with that do not become apparent until after the operation commences. That was why the battalion had an advance guard. That way, if something unexpected came up, like the two Marders, the advance guard could check it out, report, and allow the lead company commander or the battalion commander time to consider what to do without having the entire battalion stumble over the unexpected resistance. Gross knew this and kept pondering as he led his team along the edge of the nursery toward the Germans what he had missed in his hasty reconnaissance. What if there was a third Marder still tucked into the tree line out of sight? There could even be, he realized, a fourth, since German mechanized infantry platoons had four Marders per platoon. That, he began to grasp as they drew nearer, was a very real possibility that he had not properly planned for. It was, however, too late to stop and go back to reset the whole operation. He and his entire platoon were committed to the plan he had come up with and was about to spring. That he had neglected to report any of this to his company commander or seek her permission never entered Gross's mind.

When they reached the corner of the tree nursery just short of where the Germans sat, Gross paused for a few minutes in order to ensure that the other team of dismounts was set. Only when he was satisfied that he had allowed more than enough slack time for them to make it did Gross allow the squad leader with him to finish deploying his men and prepare to attack. As he watched his people slowly ease themselves into firing positions, Gross looked around and saw no sign of any other German vehicles. This relief was short-lived when he realized that the dismounts he was with were setting up in a way that would leave them open to friendly fire from the team deployed across from him. For a moment he considered pulling the men with him back, but then stopped when he saw a German sergeant walk out into the middle of the small cluster of soldiers and vehicles and begin to issue orders. Now was the time to strike. He would simply have to trust his luck to the hands of God, just like his company commander kept saying when she was in situations like this.

Just then the thought of Captain Kozak made Gross realize that he hadn't reported in. God, he thought, how stupid. How goddamned stupid. Looking back in the direction where the Bradleys were hidden, Gross hoped that his platoon sergeant had remembered to do so. He wondered if there was any way that he could before he attacked make sure that a report had been made. Looking over at the Germans, who were now beginning to move about as if they were preparing to leave, Gross dropped that idea. He was committed. Though he had screwed up by not reporting, this was not the time to worry about that. He had to play out his hand.

With that momentary crisis resolved, Gross refocused his attention on the matter at hand. To initiate the attack, he decided to take out the German sergeant giving orders himself. Raising his M-16 to his shoulder, he flipped the fire select switch off of safe and into the three-round burst mode. After taking careful aim, Gross squeezed the trigger just like the instructors at Fort Benning had taught him and began their one-sided battle.

Greeted by the presence of one of Gross's Bradleys covering the trail, Kozak ordered her driver to maneuver around it and over to where Gross and his dismounts were rallying. Though the other Bradleys were not visible, Kozak could see where they had come out of the wood line, deployed in the nursery, and charged across it toward the Germans. At the far side of the nursery she could see the two Marders, of which only one appeared to be damaged. The other simply looked abandoned, which it was. Sergeant Danny Wolf, not knowing this for sure, laid his sight onto the undamaged Marder and watched it while Kozak ordered her driver to bring their Bradley to a halt in between the two Marders.

Rolling out of the woods and into the small clearing that the Germans had been using for a resupply point, Kozak was greeted by Gross. Resting the butt of his rifle on his left hip, Gross waited until Kozak had brought her Bradley to a halt and dismounted before he saluted.

With a grin that ran from ear to ear and still pumped up from the rush that a soldier got who had just risked his neck and come out alive and successful, Gross reported. "Ma'am, Second Lieutenant Gross is pleased to report that 2nd Platoon, Company C has overrun a German outpost, destroying one Marder and capturing another as well as two fuel trucks, one mess truck complete with mess, and fifteen prisoners of war without loss."

While Kozak listened, she looked around. Unlike Gross, she felt only the full weight of her exhaustion and concerns, magnified by lack of sleep and the need to rush about from one crisis to the next. It was only with the greatest of efforts that she cleared her mind and focused it on the matter immediately at hand. From where she stood, Kozak could only see two of Gross's Bradleys, the one she had come across on the trail and Gross's own track that was being used to guard the prisoners. The others, she assumed, were deployed further into the woods. As she watched, a squad leader and his men were searching the prisoners while the platoon medic tended to half a dozen wounded Germans next to them. The dead, left where they had fallen, served as a grim reminder to Kozak that the success that Gross was so thrilled over had been purchased with human lives. Deciding that Gross needed to be brought back to reality, Kozak turned to face him, drawing across her face the mask of an angry commander. "Why in the hell, Lieutenant, didn't you report before you acted? What in the name of hell do you mean by charging off like that into the attack without permission?"

Kozak's response hit Gross like a slap in the face. Slowly dropping his salute, he thought for a moment before responding. When he did, his voice was subdued and unsure. "But, Captain Kozak, there were only two Marders. And they didn't look like they were expecting us."

"How did you know they were alone? How did you know that they weren't just the last two or the first two Marders in a whole column?"

Gross, remembering that he hadn't thought of that until he was well committed to his attack, didn't respond. His blank, almost sheepish expression told Kozak that her suspicions about him running off half-cocked had been correct. Deciding that she had made her point, far too tired to play mind games with Gross, and anxious to get on with the advance now that they had made contact with the Germans, Kozak considered what to do next before she issued her orders. Turning away from Gross, she watched the driver of Gross's Bradley as he ran back and forth to one of the fuel trucks, hauling five-gallon cans of fuel. Turning her head back toward Gross, Kozak pointed to Gross's driver. "Save that fuel for Ellerbee's tanks. Send a runner over to his tank and tell him to laager his tanks here and refuel. He has twenty minutes."

Gross looked over to his driver, then back at Kozak. "But we need the fuel too. All of my tracks are less than half full."

Kozak shook off Gross's response. "Ellerbee's herd of hogs need the fuel more than you do. Now what else do you have for me? I need to check in with the battalion commander."

"The prisoners. What do we do with them?"

Shaking her head, Kozak took in a deep breath as she struggled to hold her temper in check. "If you paid more attention to my orders instead of running off on your own little Rambo-fest, you'd know exactly what to do with them, Lieutenant."

Glancing over to the Germans, then back to Kozak, Gross leaned forward and lowered his voice. "You can't be serious. I mean, these guys are probably pissed off. After all, we just killed three of their buddies and damned near killed them. I know Colonel Dixon is a smart man, but I really don't think he's considered all the angles as far as prisoners are concerned. How do we know that they won't join the first unit they come across, get themselves rearmed, and come back looking for blood?"

"We don't, Gross. Odds are that's exactly what's going to happen. I know that's what I would do."

With a look of excitement on his face, Gross threw his free hand out to his side. "Then why in the hell are we letting them go? So they can come back and have a second chance to kill us?"

Angry at Gross's manner and persistence, Kozak reached down, unsnapped her holster, and pulled her pistol out. Pulling the pistol's slide back in a sharp exaggerated motion to chamber a round, Kozak flipped the safety off and offered the pistol, butt first, to Gross. "Well, Second Lieutenant Marc Gross, if you feel so strongly about leaving live prisoners behind, then here, go shoot them. Because that's the only other way we have of dealing with them. The entire corps has no transportation to haul them, no food to feed them, and no one to guard them. So if you're so hell-fired concerned about dealing with them, this is it. You said there's fifteen of them? Good! There's fifteen rounds in my pistol. Just enough to do the job."

The response by his company commander shocked Gross. She was normally a reasonable person who took great pains to explain everything to her subordinates, and Gross was not prepared to deal with her preposterous proposal or caustic response. Stepping back, Gross let his head hang down for a moment before looking back up at Kozak. Seeing the anger etched into her face, added to the signs of strain and lack of sleep, Gross knew that she was right. There was no good alternative. He also realized for the first time that this whole affair, the race for the sea and the fighting, had entered a new and very deadly phase, one in which there were no guarantees that they would make it. This was, Gross suddenly realized, a real life-and-death struggle, one which every one of his men, as well as Kozak and he, could very easily lose.

Looking up at Kozak, he began to apologize, but Kozak cut him short. "Listen, Marc. Odds are, unless we do everything right, you and I will be sitting over there with our hands on our heads in a matter of days. We, you, me, the battalion commander, Colonel Dixon, and anyone who calls himself an officer in this corps can't afford to forget that. We can't afford to make mistakes either. You understand that. I know you do, damn it. I taught you better than this. Now pull your head out of your ass and stop acting like a first-year ROTC cadet running around on a weekend maneuver."

Softening her tone, Kozak asked if he had anything more to report. After seeing him shaking his head slowly, Kozak turned and walked back to her Bradley, C60. As she did so, she looked over every now and then at the prisoners. For she knew, unlike Gross, that unless their luck changed soon they would indeed all be prisoners, or worse. All the plans, all the speeches, and all the pep talks, together with all the fancy maneuvers they had just done, had finally come down to luck and hard fighting, period.

That was what wars were all about.

Major Bob Messinger would have disagreed violently with Nancy Kozak's observation that luck was an important ingredient in military operations. A tried and true military technician by training, Messinger was proud to the point of arrogance of his skills as an Army aviator. Only his abilities as an operations officer, which had landed him the job as the battalion operations officer for the 14th Cavalry's air cavalry battalion, ran a close second. From that platform Messinger preached his doctrine that good combat pilots make their own luck. Praying that the enemy will make a mistake or depending on luck, he told his company commanders, was for weenies.

To this end he was meticulous with his planning. Nothing was left unaccounted for—fuel required for each mission; weapons mix carried by his squadron's attack helicopters; attack routes in and egress routes out; location of primary, alternate, and subsequent battle positions; command and control procedures; engagement sequence; suppression of enemy air defense; friendly fire support; forward rearm and refuel point locations and defense—nothing. And Messinger, unlike many of his contemporaries, had a natural skill for pulling all of these diverse elements together into a deceptively simple and coherent plan. Though he would have shunned being called an artist, for there is in fact a high degree of creativity involved when crafting a plan, few officers in the Tenth Corps could equal his skills. If there was one serious fault that Messinger did have, it was that he knew he was good and felt no shame in making sure that everyone around him knew that too.

Today, as he and Warrant Officer Larry Perkins stalked a column of armored vehicles and trucks belonging to the 4th Panzer Division's 1st Brigade as they moved north along Highway 19, Messinger was again afforded the opportunity to demonstrate his skills as a military artist. Ordered to screen the Tenth Corps' eastern and southern flank, the 14th Armored Cavalry Regiment ordered its air cavalry squadron, reinforced with two attack helicopter companies, to find and attack elements of the 4th Panzer Division, delaying and disrupting their deployment. Coming up from the southeast, that panzer division not only threatened to turn the maneuver of Scott Dixon's brigade into a trap, it threatened to add the weight needed to break the 2nd Panzer Division's deadlock as it continued to pound its way into the center of the Tenth Corps. In preparing his order, Messinger used the same words that regimental operations used when defining their mission: delay and disrupt. To these he added his own, reminding the company commanders that the best way to delay and disrupt the enemy was to kill them. To this end, Messinger laid out in detail how they would do it.

Working from an ancient OH-58D, an aircraft frame that was almost as old as he was, Messinger deployed his units. Scouts from one of his troops secured the ambush site, north, south, and east, keeping their eyes open for German attack helicopters as well as any anti-aircraft guns or surface-to-air missile launchers. If encountered before Messinger sprung the ambush, he would decide whether to press the attack or break it off. If the scouts ran across these threats after the ambush had been initiated, the scouts would deal with them as best they could and keep Messinger advised.

Messinger himself would be with the Apache company making the attack. From there he could judge the effectiveness of their fire and determine when they reached that point where a continuation of attack became counterproductive or too costly to them. Due to the increased work load placed on his squadron, insufficient time to properly maintain their aircraft, the exhaustion of critical spare parts, and the need to conserve fuel, none of the units of the Tenth Corps, particularly the aviation units, could afford to waste precious resources in pursuit of marginal gains. In most ambushes, the majority of the killing is done in the first few seconds or minutes when the enemy is surprised and off balance. When, because of the actions of the enemy commanders or an inability of the attacker to maintain the pressure, the unit under attack is given time to recover from that initial shock and rally, the tables are often turned and the attacker becomes the victim. Bob Messinger's primary job that morning was to insure that every one of his aircraft was long gone before that happened.

With well-measured ease, Larry Perkins slowly brought his aircraft up above the treetops until the golf-ball-like instrument dome mounted on top of the rotor blades had a clear view of the road. With one eye he watched the trees to his front and with the other the instrument screen. Messinger, his eyes glued to his observer's display, didn't speak. He didn't need to give Perkins directions or corrections, since the instrument dome had free rotation. Messinger himself could traverse his sight to cover the area that he was interested in, leaving Perkins free to fly the aircraft. When Perkins reached the proper height that allowed the instrument dome to clear the last of the tree branches, Messinger merely muttered, "Okay, that's good."

While Perkins held the helicopter steady, Messinger scanned the road. To his front a column of armored vehicles, Leopard tanks and Marder infantry fighting vehicles, interspersed with trucks and other vehicles, was moving north in a steady stream. Though he was interested in all of them, it was the tanklike Gepard armed with twin 37mm anti-aircraft cannons, and Rolands, tracked vehicles mounting surface-to-air missiles, that Messinger was looking for. They would be given priority when the killing started, since they were the most effective defense against just the kind of attack that Messinger was about to initiate.

When he found what he was looking for, he depressed the radio transmit button and called the other scout that was doing the same thing. "Kilo Nine Five, this is Kilo Five Three. I have a Gepard near the head of the column, three vehicles behind the lead. Over."

There was a pause while the observer in the other scout looked and confirmed. "Roger, Five Three. I see 'em. I've got nothing in the middle or rear. How 'bout you? Over."

Traversing the joy stick that controlled the instrument dome, Messinger scanned the entire length of the column a second time. When he was finished, he looked up from his sight, rubbed his eyes, and then put his head back down against the brow pads of the sight again before responding. "Negative. The Gepard in the front is the only gun I see." He was about to say that he would take out the self-propelled Gepard anti-aircraft gun but thought better of it. He was senior officer on the scene. He needed to keep himself out of the fight, exercising command and control for as long as possible. The other scout could deal with the Gepard, leaving him free to watch for other air defense systems they might have missed while keeping an eye on the attack of the Apache helicopters and the German reactions. With that decided, Messinger directed the scout to stand by to fire on the Gepard while ordering the commander of the Apache company, waiting in firing positions some five thousand meters away on the other side of the road, to stand by to commence firing.

When all was ready, he initiated the ambush with a simple, almost casual call to the scout. "Okay, Nine Five, let her fly."

When he was set, the observer in the scout helicopter with the call sign Nine Five hit the laser designator button, watched for it to illuminate the target, then fired a Hellfire missile. Once the Hellfire was clear of the trees and screaming in toward the Gepard, German air guards up and down the column began to yell their warnings to their vehicle commanders, who in turn relayed the warning throughout the column via radio. Though that warning came too late for the Gepard, which received Kilo Nine Five's Hellfire square on the side of the turret that housed the twin 37mm anti-aircraft guns, other vehicles began to turn away from the attack right into the sights of the waiting

Apaches. Without any need for orders, the commander of the five Apaches gave his order to engage and joined the fight himself by launching a Hellfire at a Leopard tank that he had been tracking.

With the attack coming from the direction that the fleeing vehicles had thought was away from danger, the surprise and chaos created had the desired effect. The commanders of the vehicles that survived the first volley ordered their drivers to turn their individual vehicles this way or that, to back up, or to stop and assess what was happening. The result was momentary confusion and loss of command and control. Some vehicles, their commanders and drivers trying to look in all directions at once, plowed into each other. Adding to the general confusion were clouds of smoke created when tanks fired smoke grenades in all directions. Here and there trucks ran off the road rather than be crushed by tanks wildly seeking safety as Marders dropped their ramps so that the precious infantry could scramble out and seek safety on the ground rather than remain boxed up in what might soon become a death trap. During this initial confusion, when none of the surviving German commanders could make sense out of what was going on or exert their authority, the Apaches launched a second volley, adding to the confusion and cutting down more leaders in midstride as they tried to sort out their commands.

From afar, Messinger watched. By now both he and scout Kilo Nine Five were long forgotten by the Germans on the road. The massed Apache attack was far too overwhelming to ignore. Though satisfied with the results of the initial strike and the confusion that reigned, Messinger knew it would soon end. Already he could see commanders of individual Leopard tanks turning to fight. Though a tank main-gun round was not the most effective anti-aircraft weapon, the sophisticated computer-driven fire-control system of the Leopard, like the American M-1A1 tank, gave them teeth that could not be ignored. Realizing that the longer he allowed the Apaches to continue the engagement the more the Germans would be able to respond, Messinger ordered the Apache company commander to fire one more volley and then break off the attack.

Though he could have stayed and taken out more vehicles, to do so would have increased his chances of losing aircraft and crews that could not be replaced. Since there were more columns further down the highway, all racing north in an effort to save the 2nd Panzer Division, Messinger knew he could repeat this performance again later somewhere else against another unwary column. For now, a dozen or more kills, a major highway temporarily blocked, a column scattered and in disorder, and the flow of combat forces north momentarily halted was good enough to accomplish what the 14th Armored Cavalry Regiment was tasked to do. When Messinger saw the last of the Hellfire missiles detonate on the rear deck of a Leopard tank and heard the Apache company commander announce over the radio that he and his company were out of there and en route to their next battle position, Messinger lifted his head from his sight and turned to Perkins. "Okay, Larry. We've done enough damage here. Let's head south and see if we can do it again."

With that, Larry Perkins allowed the OH-58D to drop down a few feet before he twisted its tail boom a quarter turn with a flick of his hand holding the collective, pointed the nose of the helicopter south and right into the gunsight of a German attack helicopter's gunner. The German gunner, seeing that his quarry was about to flee, let fly a stream of 20mm rounds at Messinger's aircraft. Though it had been a hasty shot, the German gunner's initial aim had been good enough. In a matter of a couple of seconds the crew compartment of Messinger's helicopter was shredded by a hail of 20mm high-explosive rounds, serving to remind anyone who cared to think about what had just happened that in war even the craftiest hunter can in the twinkling of an eye become the hunted.

CHAPTER 16

20 JANUARY

Though the evening briefing was a short affair that night, the information in it weighed heavy on Big Al Malin. Even if Big Al had been able to sit through it, none of the staff officers could have sat in one place for more than ten minutes without nodding off to sleep. For despite every effort to rotate the staff officers and enlisted staff members at the Tenth Corps command post in and out for rest, there were few who managed to snatch any meaningful sleep. It was not because things were going bad. On the contrary, the situation was for the most part conforming to the plan that this very staff had formulated and put into motion some thirty-six hours before. The fighting and maneuvering of both German and American forces then in progress was pretty much yielding the results that Big Al had hoped for.

The real problem wearing at Big Al and his staff was a problem that all senior officers in the modern age faced. Though he gave the orders, though he had the authority to initiate battles and determine when and where those battles would be fought, he did not, could not, do the fighting. At that moment Big Al or his staff didn't have much say over what happened. Neither he nor his staff, with all of its sophisticated communications equipment and collective knowledge, wisdom, and experience, could do anything to tilt the scale of the company and platoon battles being waged in the valleys, hills, forests, and towns of central Germany. The corps staff could order more fire support to assist a unit in contact in the form of attack helicopters or artillery. They could augment those units with reinforcements. But the one thing that Big Al and his staff could not do was to gain release through combat from their fears, apprehensions, and stresses.

Big Al's orders had set the divisions in motion. The divisions had issued their own orders that had sent their brigades attacking in just about every direction possible. Brigades had tasked their subordinate battalions to attack in a set direction with a definitive objective or to defend a key piece of terrain. From there the orders were transmitted to company commanders. At that level, in the confined spaces of darkened personnel carriers, the company commander issued his own instructions to a group of platoon leaders who were just as cold, tired, dirty, and confused as the soldiers that they were about to lead into battle. When that was finished, those young lieutenants or senior sergeants charged with closing with and destroying the enemy by use of fire, maneuver, and shock effect were left to wander on their own back to where their soldiers waited to hear the orders that for many would be a death sentence.

Often during the long, terrible wait for information and news from the units in contact and the results of those contacts, Big Al would stare at the map in his operations van. Every blue symbol on that map meant something to him. They were not simply marks on a plastic overlay; they were flesh and blood. They were his soldiers. That his orders determined how many of the soldiers represented by those symbols lived and how many died bothered Big Al greatly. So he like any competent commander did his best to ensure that he had all the information he needed to make sound, intelligent decisions. Though reams of information flooded into the corps headquarters every hour, only a shockingly small amount meant anything to the primary decision makers. It took time to collect a skilled staff to sift through and sort that critical information that Big Al would use when modifying his plans or issuing new orders. Until that was done, Big Al was left to struggle with his conscience, his fears, his personal battle, and watch the symbols on the map as they were moved from one place to another.

The operations map in front of him presented a picture that almost staggered the imagination. Throughout central Germany, units of the Tenth Corps were playing out a drama that defied definition or description. There were no longer front lines, rear boundaries, or flanks. There was at that moment no main effort, no center of gravity. All the corps staff could report to Big Al that night was a series of widely separated attacks under the control of brigade and battalion commanders that were attempting to achieve the objectives that Big Al had outlined the day before. To the west, the 1st Brigade of the 55th Mech Infantry Division was attacking south against the 10th Panzer Division's 3rd Brigade. The 55th's 2nd Brigade was attacking to the west while its 3rd Brigade was attacking, under the control of the 4th Armored Division, to the north and northeast in an effort to keep the 2nd Panzer Division's 1st and 3rd Brigades from linking up. Dixon's 1st Brigade was also attacking the 2nd Panzer Division's 3rd Brigade in one direction while putting pressure on the 2nd Panzer's 2nd Brigade and attacking the division's service support units in the opposite direction. Dixon's sister brigade, the 2nd Brigade, was doing likewise some fifteen kilometers away, sending one battalion northeast to hit the 2nd Panzer's 2nd Brigade, holding one battalion in place to fix the 2nd Panzer's 3rd Brigade, and attacking south with a third battalion against the 2nd Panzer's 1st Brigade. It was, one assistant operations officer dryly stated in a vain effort at humor while briefing, a high-tech barroom brawl.

The idea that he was unable to go somewhere to influence at least one of the chains of seemingly disjointed battles that the brigades of his corps were engaged in wore on Big Al's nerves as staff officer after staff officer stood up to brief him and the primary staff officers. The staff, in turn, was beginning to feel the pressure of having their commander standing about with nothing to do, watching them or staring at the operations map. They were used to receiving Big Al's guidance and then being left to deal with it while he visited units or division command posts. It was, one staff officer commented, like having a bear watching campers cooking their dinner.

Though Big Al tried hard to stay out of his staff's hair, the corps chief of staff felt the need to keep his commander entertained. This resulted in a steady stream of staff officers pulled from their normal duties and sent to update the corps commander on one thing or another. Though the staff officers did keep their commander informed and did receive some additional guidance, the wear and tear on each other's nerves was telling. Some of the staff officers were even betting how long it would take before Big Al finally blew a gasket and dumped on someone.

The victim of that eruption, quite innocently, turned out to be an artillery major. Midway through the evening briefing, while the major, an assistant fire coordination officer, was briefing, Big Al caught the attention of the chief of staff. Using the index finger of his right hand, Big Al made a small circular motion, indicating that he wanted the chief of staff to speed up the briefing. The chief shifted in his seat and cleared his throat in an effort to catch the fire support officer's attention.

The young major, caught up in his briefing, failed to notice Big Al's signal to the chief of staff and missed the meaning of the chief's cues. So rather than speed up or skip to the summary, the young major continued to dump hordes of numbers and heaps of data and information onto his reluctant audience like a tenured professor delivering a stale lecture. Though Big Al had no doubt that all the information being delivered had some importance to someone somewhere, the parade of digits and the major's monotone voice grated on Big Al's worn nerves like a child dragging his fingernails across a blackboard.

When it became obvious that the message had not gotten through, Big Al, unable to hold himself back and unwilling to give his chief a second chance, stood up, gave the chief a perfunctionary "Thank you," and began to walk out of the van. Though he knew his actions were rude and that the young major who had been briefing would catch hell for pissing off the old man, Big Al had bigger concerns on his mind. With his face distorted in anger, anger at his inability to do something more positive, more active, Big Al made his way through masses of staff officers who practically beat each other to death as they tried to get out of his way. Followed by his aide, who had been caught off guard and was trying to keep up with his boss while fumbling with helmets, jackets, and a notebook, Big Al fled the corps command post and out into the night.

When he caught up to Big Al, the aide found him outside the protective wire that surrounded the command post. Standing on the side of the road, Big Al stood alone watching a convoy of trucks and field ambulances go by. Moving around to the side, the aide made his presence known simply by placing himself so that his movement would be caught by Big Al's peripheral vision. Aides were trained to do that, to make their presence known without interrupting or interfering with conversations or reflective moments. Stopping a few paces short, the aide waited for Big Al to reach out and motion for the parka and helmet that the aide carried. But there was no movement, no beckoning call. There was only the silence of the bitterly cold night punctured by the steady grinding of trucks passing by and generators humming about the corps command post. In the faint light of dimmed headlights, the aide could see that Big Al's face was still screwed up like a twisted mass of raw nerves. He stood there alone, intently watching the trucks go by, one after the other, as they slowly inched their way north. Though the aide had no idea what was going on his commander's mind, he knew that Big Al had come here to escape.

After being in the warm vans that made up the corps command post all day, crunched in with other people and unable to go outside much, the cold night air sent a chill through the aide. Concerned that his boss was also cold, the aide moved closer to Big Al and prepared to hand him his parka. But at the last minute he stopped short. When he saw that Big Al's expression didn't change, the aide stepped back and waited. Though Big Al was cold, the aide also knew that there was something that was bothering his commander and that he was deep in thought. Good aides learned quickly when to say something and when not to. They learned when their commander wanted them and when they were expected to melt away into the background and wait quietly for their commander to summon them. It was time, the aide realized, to become a shadow.

The string of ambulances moving north did nothing to calm Big Al's concerns or feelings of inadequacy. In fact they only served to heighten his depression, for here, right in front of his face, were the by-products of his actions. The ambulances and trucks of a hospital unit were a terrible reminder that what he was doing in the command post behind him was no training exercise, no drill. The decisions that he made and the orders that his staff issued in his name were paid for in blood by the soldiers that his government and country had entrusted into his care. How terrible, Big Al thought, if after all was said and done his best intentions didn't measure up to their sacrifice. How terrible.

From the cab of the truck where Hilary Cole sat she could see the figures of two men standing on the side of the road. One man, a very short one with no helmet or jacket on, just stood there and watched as her truck went by. Though she couldn't see his face, his stance, with his arms folded across his chest, made him look important. The second man, holding a parka in one hand and a helmet in the other, stood a few feet away from the short man, as if he were waiting for the short man to notice him. Though she didn't know who the two men were, it was obvious that the short one was important.

But, Cole thought, he wasn't important to her, especially not at that moment. What was important was that she had an opportunity to escape the horrors of the day for a little while. There in the heated cab of the truck the steady hum of the engine served to drown out the screams that still rang in her ears. Though not the most comfortable seat she had ever had, Cole found it good enough. She rolled a blanket that she had brought along with her and placed it against the window beside her. When she had it set the way she wanted it, Cole leaned against it and folded her arms. With luck she would be asleep in a few minutes. It was important, she knew, that she take advantage of this opportunity to sleep, for she knew that once they stopped there would be much to do. Not only would the wounded they had taken along from their last site still need care, but there would no doubt be new wounded waiting. The battles, she had been told, had yet to reach their climax. That, for her and the other nurses, translated to more wounded, more suffering, more nightmares.

As she slowly drifted off to sleep, Cole wondered if the short man on the side of the road had anything to do with the battles. And if he did, she wondered if he really understood what his orders really meant to the soldiers who suffered as a result of those orders. Probably not, she thought. After all, if he did and he could see the suffering that his orders caused, he couldn't possibly issue them. No one could send men to their death or certain mutilation if he had seen it himself. No sane human that had seen what she had seen all day could continue to send men into battle. No, Cole thought as she drifted off to sleep, General So-and-So back there, warm and pampered in his little command post, had no idea of what his great plans cost. None.

The sudden appearance of the battalion's supply officer startled Captain Friedrich Seydlitz. Though he was still standing upright in the commander's hatch of his Leopard II tank, he had fallen sound asleep. Only after a great deal of shaking did the supply officer manage to awaken Seydlitz. When he did come around, Seydlitz jumped, causing the supply officer to laugh. "Well, Friedrich, I am glad to see the defenders of the Fatherland are alert and ever watchful."

Though he couldn't see the face, Seydlitz recognized the voice. Re-

alizing that he had fallen sound asleep but that there was no immediate danger, Seydlitz cleared his throat before he responded. "Fuck
you, Rudi."

Slapping Seydlitz on the back, Captain Rudi Buhle laughed even
louder. "Well, I am certainly glad to see that war has done nothing to
diminish your charm and eloquence, my dear Friedrich." Known for
his easy and friendly manner, Rudi Buhle was never at a loss for a
quick comment. His ready smile often served to cheer up the darkest
face. And if anyone needed a little cheer, it was Friedrich Seydlitz.

Left with only his company to hold an area that the entire battalion
had been stretched to defend a few hours before, Seydlitz had been a
nervous wreck. Throughout the early evening his tank platoons, now
spread out to the point where they could no longer support each other,
had sent him a steady stream of sighting reports. That the enemy was
still across from them and active was driven home twice when artillery barrages came crashing down on, around, and behind Seydlitz's
location. Of course, Seydlitz's tired mind never was able to make the
connection that the artillery attacks, normally lasting less than a few
seconds, came after he contacted the brigade command post he had
been ordered to report to. It simply did not occur to him that the
Americans were using his radio transmissions to locate him and his
company.

Stretching, Seydlitz yawned while Buhle sat on the turret of Seydlitz's tank and waited. Ready and more alert, Seydlitz turned to Buhle.
"I see that you have finally decided to venture out into the night to
find us."

Buhle grunted. "Finally? Finally? I've been on the road since before
dawn this morning looking for the battalion. Where the hell have you
all been?"

"We have been here all day. Don't you ever read the battalion orders?"

Folding his arms, Buhle leaned back. "My dear Friedrich, I have not
seen a copy of the battalion's orders in almost a week. I am reduced to
leading my little supply column around the countryside like a band of
gypsies asking everyone I come across, 'Ah, excuse me, good sir, but
have you seen the 26th Panzer Battalion? Yes, panzer battalion, you
know, a collection of tanks and soldiers.' " Seydlitz watched Buhle
gesturing while he spoke. Then he stopped and leaned forward. "And
do you know something, Friedrich? I have had to stop asking civilians.

I can no longer depend on the people we are supposed to be defending. One old man I asked this morning said he had seen you and gave me detailed directions on how to find you. It wasn't until we found ourselves running down a dead-end road that I realized that the old bastard had lied to me. A fellow German. Our countryman. And he lied to me."

Buhle's carefree manner had disappeared. In its place was a mixture of confusion and scorn. Though Seydlitz himself knew that not all Germans agreed with what the Chancellor was doing, intentional obstructions of the war effort, like the one that Buhle was describing, were an entirely different matter. It was, Seydlitz thought, treason.

After a long and heavy pause, during which Buhle calmed himself and caught his breath, Seydlitz reached out and placed his hand on Buhle's shoulder. "It will be all right, my friend. Surely you know that?"

Though Seydlitz's voice and reassurance were anything but convincing, Buhle nodded his head. "Yes, yes, I know." When he was ready, Buhle continued his story. "Now I just ask military personnel for directions. And even they are not very helpful. Christ, Friedrich, the whole division is screwed up. Brigades and battalions are intermixed. Supply trains and artillery units are stumbling over each other. Command posts are passing out information that is out of date. Even the *Feldjägers* don't know what they're doing. Earlier this evening they sent me south of here in search of the battalion. They told me that American units and raiding parties were roaming around throughout this area and that the battalion had pulled out of here earlier today. Everyone in the rear is running around like chickens without their heads. You are lucky, Friedrich, being up here where you at least know what you're doing."

When Buhle had finished, Seydlitz considered Buhle's last comments. Buhle obviously had his problems. But to imagine that it was better to be up front hanging your ass out and waiting for someone to swat it was not what Seydlitz would consider lucky. And the idea that he, Seydlitz, knew what was happening was a little much. Still Seydlitz said nothing. He was too tired and there was far too much to do. His company needed to be rearmed and refueled. But he could not let Buhle get away without comment. Though he found it strange that he would be defending the *Feldjägers,* or military police, a branch of service that Seydlitz never did like, he couldn't resist the urge to bust the supply officer's bubble. Leaning over, Seydlitz tapped Buhle on the shoulder. "Rudi, the *Feldjägers* were right, a little. The rest of the battalion left here late this afternoon. They are south of here, in an assembly area, waiting to continue the attack to the west. My company is the only one here."

The sudden realization that he had not seen an end to his seemingly aimless wanderings hit Buhle hard. Even in the dark, Seydlitz could see Buhle's shoulders slump forward. In the two years in which he had known Buhle, Seydlitz had never heard him talk so or be at a loss for a joke. Now finding that he had an opportunity to be the cheerful one, Seydlitz slapped Buhle on the arm. "Cheer up, my old friend. Things could be worse. You could be sitting on the side of some road waiting for the *Feldjägers* to figure out what they were doing instead of earning an honest living pumping fuel and passing out ammunition, both of which, by the way, my company needs."

Taking two deep breaths, Buhle prepared to climb down off of Seydlitz's tank, but paused. "You know, I'd rather face enemy fire than to tell my drivers that we're not staying here for the night. To a man, they're dead on their feet."

Seydlitz laughed. "Don't give me that shit, Rudi. Your drivers haven't used their feet all day except for pushing the accelerator down."

With a chuckle, Buhle corrected himself. "Okay, they're dead on their asses. Now let's get on with this. I have a feeling this will be another long night."

Though they were only five kilometers northwest of Bad Hersfeld when she woke up, Hilary Cole had no way of knowing that. As if awakening from a drunken stupor, it took her several minutes to realize that the truck was stopped, the engine was running at an idle, and the driver, leaning against the door and window on his side, was sound asleep. Looking outside the cab, she noticed that they were parked off on the side of the road right behind a truck only a few feet to their front. Though she wondered why they were stopped, she felt no great desire to go out into the cold and find out. The driver had left the heater on, the cab was warm, the steady hum of the engine had a tranquilizing effect, and she couldn't do anything anyway to improve their situation even if she knew. They were stopped, no doubt, by some MPs waiting for the road ahead to clear or for another convoy to pass. The military police were always doing things like that.

That they were sitting behind an engineer bridge unit that was waiting for their orders to move didn't matter to Cole. What did matter was that she was being left alone and that she could go back to sleep. Someone no doubt with more horsepower than she had was out there in the cold night stumbling around trying to sort the column out. Best to stay where she was and get some more sleep while she could. That, she knew, would end soon enough.

The rearming and refueling of Seydlitz's company had taken longer than Buhle would have liked. That it did shouldn't have been a surprise to anyone. Both his men and Seydlitz's were dead tired. Most wandered around during the resupply operations like zombies, barely knowing what they were doing or even where they were. While he watched, it amazed Buhle that anyone could expect men in that condition to think and act, let alone fight. Perhaps, he thought, this was what everyone meant when they said that war was insane.

Though he would have liked to coil up behind Seydlitz's tanks for a few hours and allow his drivers to sleep before pushing on back into the night, the news that the battalion was preparing to continue the attack to the west demanded that he continue. For if the fuel levels of Seydlitz's tanks were any indication, the rest of the battalion would not be able to go very far with what they had. So with great reluctance Buhle ordered his drivers to mount up, re-formed his column, and led it back out onto the hard-surfaced road that had taken them there.

When Buhle's column reached the juncture where the forest trail that they had been following met the hard-surfaced road that would take them back to Hünfeld, Buhle tapped his driver on the shoulder and pointed to his right. The driver, barely awake, simply turned the wheel and pulled out onto the hard-surfaced road. At first he slowed, since the trucks following needed time to make the turn and catch up to Buhle's little Volkswagen staff car. To make sure that all of his trucks were still with him and made the turn, Buhle opened his door slightly, leaned out, and turned his head to the rear to watch. His senior sergeant, riding in the cab of the last truck, would flash a green-filtered flashlight toward the head of the column when he was on the road. Until then, Buhle simply hung on to the door with his right hand, the dashboard with his left, and stared off into the darkness watching for the signal.

Actually, Buhle thought, this wasn't half bad. The cold air flowing around his neck felt good. It helped to wake him up and clear his mind. He needed to stay alert. He needed to keep himself, his driver, and every man in his column awake and alert. Before this night was over, Buhle mused, he was going to have to use every leadership and motivational skill and trick that his tired brain could conjure up.

Like a beacon at the end of a long dark tunnel, Buhle saw the green light from the last truck flashing. But he didn't react at first. It took several seconds for Buhle's tired mind to make the connection between the image of the green light and what he was supposed to do next. Finally a thought snapped and Buhle sat up, turned to his driver, and ordered him to begin to pick up the speed. While doing this, Buhle missed the red light to their immediate front, now only a few meters away, flashing wildly. Buhle's driver, however, didn't. Between Buhle's shaking him out of his stupor and the sudden appearance of a red light shining in his eyes, the driver shot upright in his seat, clutched the steering wheel in both hands, and slammed down the brake without hitting the clutch, stalling the Volkswagen and throwing Buhle forward into the windshield. A sudden jerk that shook the whole vehicle told Buhle that the truck behind them, still following closely since there had been no time to assume the proper convoy intervals between vehicles, had also been caught off guard by his driver's sudden stop. The thought that his little Volkswagen staff car could have been crushed by the huge Mann supply truck never crossed Buhle's exhausted mind. At that point it could only deal with one thought or one action at a time.

Pushing himself up and away from the dash, Buhle looked at his driver in wide-eyed surprise. He still had no idea why his driver, staring to the front with mouth agape, had stopped. It wasn't until he heard a rapping on his side window that Buhle turned away from his driver. When he did, he realized that his vehicle was surrounded by several figures. Where in the hell, he wondered, had they come from? Now it was Buhle's turn to gaze outside in wide-eyed amazement at the apparitions that had sprung up from nowhere.

After what seemed like ages, the soldier standing at Buhle's door opened it. Shining a red-filtered flashlight from Buhle's face over to the driver and then back to Buhle, the soldier said nothing. Only slowly did it dawn upon Buhle, now blinded by the flashlight despite its filter, that he not only didn't have any idea who these people were, he didn't even know whose side they were on. Seydlitz's warning that there were enemy units infiltrated into their rear drifted into Buhle's slow-moving mind and caused him to start.

Seeing this, the soldier with the flashlight paused but kept the flashlight aimed in Buhle's face. "Oh, excuse me, Herr Hauptmann. I was simply checking to make sure that you and your driver were all right. We seem to have given you quite a surprise."

As with everything that night, the fact that the soldier at his door responded in German with a heavy, very formal northeastern German accent took several seconds to register. When it did, Buhle could feel himself go limp with relief. The soldier also noticed Buhle's response and introduced himself. "Sorry to cause you such concern, Herr Hauptmann. I am Oberstleutnant Kramer, Feldjäger Company 75."

While this sank into Buhle's mind, dulled by lack of sleep and the stress of wandering about the countryside in search of his battalion, Oberstleutnant Kramer continued to talk. "I am afraid I must divert your column. This road is no longer open to German military traffic."

More alert, Buhle shook his head. "You mean that there are American units operating this far to the rear?"

"Yes, Herr Hauptmann. In fact, they are very, very close."

With the *Feldjäger*'s flashlight still in his eyes and his inability to deal with anything beyond the most immediate and obvious problems, Buhle never took note of the soldiers moving around or behind the lieutenant. Nor did his drivers, given a chance to lay their heads on the steering wheels in front of them and rest a minute, hear the movement of other soldiers as they moved out from the cover of the woods on either side of the road and crept up to the cabs of their trucks.

Standing upright and stepping back away from Buhle's door, the *Feldjäger* lieutenant named Kramer dropped the red-filtered flashlight from Buhle's face and turned to face toward the rear of the column. Buhle, wanting to talk to the *Feldjäger* lieutenant, began to climb out of his Volkswagen. This prevented him from seeing Kramer raise his red-filtered flashlight and wave it toward the rear of the column. Buhle, however, did catch the glow of green-filtered light at the rear of the column being waved at them.

For a moment he looked at the green light and thought. His sergeant, he was sure, had already signaled him that all of the trucks had made the turn onto the road. Why was his sergeant signaling him again? Perhaps the sergeant was tired, just like Buhle, and wanted to make sure that he had seen it. Or maybe, Buhle thought, the sergeant was under the impression that Buhle had stopped the column to allow the last trucks to catch up before continuing and it was he, Buhle, waving the red light. Well, no matter. Everything would be clarified in a few minutes. Turning back to the *Feldjäger* lieutenant, Buhle realized that he was looking down the barrel of a pistol held inches from his face.

Shaking his head to make sure he wasn't imagining things, Buhle began to step back, but Kramer, the *Feldjäger* lieutenant, whispered so that only Buhle could hear. "If you are very smart and very careful, you and your men will survive the next few minutes. If not, you all die. It makes no difference to me or my men."

Still not understanding what was happening, and working on the original premise that the *Feldjäger* lieutenant was who he said he was, Buhle began to protest. "What in the hell is this all about? Are you crazy?"

The sound of the hammer of the pistol held in front of his eyes being cocked back was the only answer Major Nikolai Ilvanich gave Buhle. But it was enough to convince Buhle that this *Feldjäger* lieutenant was perhaps not who he said he was and that he, Buhle, was in serious trouble.

Without taking his eyes off of Buhle, Ilvanich called out in English, "Sergeant Rasper. Lieutenant Fitzhugh and his men are ready."

Without any need for further instructions, Sergeant First Class Rasper of Company A, 1st Ranger Battalion, hit the horn of Ilvanich's commandeered German staff car three times. Rasper's three blasts served to startle the dozing German drivers and signal the rest of Company A to spring into action. As one, the rangers who had crept out of the bushes on either side of the road and eased up to the cabs of Buhle's trucks jerked both doors of the trucks open. Some drivers who had been leaning against the doors of their cabs asleep fell out onto the road. Their screams and yells were answered by rangers who shoved the muzzles of their M-16 rifles into their faces. In seconds, without a single shot being fired, the entire column—its precious fuel and 120mm tank-gun and 7.62mm machine-gun ammunition, all of which could be used by American tank units—was firmly in Ilvanich's hands.

Turning away from Ilvanich, Buhle tried to watch what was happening. Though he could see little, he heard everything. Surprised shouts and curses muttered by his drivers were answered by the rangers as they yelled to the German drivers to get up and put their hands behind their heads. Every now and then the clatter of a pistol or a rifle being torn away from a German driver and thrown onto the pavement of the road could be heard. Standing there watching his unit being taken over by the enemy caused Buhle to become angry. Then, realizing that there was nothing he could do, Buhle lost the last ounce of control he had and began to cry. He had been surprised, overpowered, and taken prisoner. Turning to face Ilvanich, who had in the meantime reached over and relieved Buhle of his own pistol, Buhle, with tears running down his cheeks, sputtered out in German, "Who in the hell are you?"

Ilvanich smiled to himself. Now was a good time to use some of the weird humor that had so fascinated him since joining this American unit. In his heavily accented English, Ilvanich responded to Buhle so that the rangers around him could hear. "We, Herr Captain, are the good guys. You, my prisoner." Then with a great flourish Ilvanich added, "On behalf of the United States Army and the Russian Republic, I thank you for these magnificent trucks and the supplies. They will, I assure you, be put to good use." On the other side of Buhle's vehicle, Specialist Pape, who was training his heavy German-made machine gun on Buhle's driver, began to laugh.

Angered at being the subject of a joke and at his momentary loss of self-control, Buhle turned on Ilvanich. Stomping his foot, Buhle shouted, "What do you intend to do with me and my men?"

Shrugging as he tossed Buhle's pistol into the bushes behind him, Ilvanich grunted. "I don't care what you and your men do. For all I care, they can go to hell. Now please step aside or we will be forced to run you over." Lifting his arm above his head, Ilvanich waved it in a circular motion and shouted, "All right, mount up and prepare to move. Spread the word down the line." Like an echo, Ilvanich's orders were relayed from ranger to ranger until from the very end of the column came three long blasts from Lieutenant Fitzhugh's truck.

With a casual motion of his pistol, Ilvanich signaled Buhle to move out of the way. Pape, on the other side, did likewise to Buhle's driver, who surrendered his seat to Pape. After seating himself in Buhle's place, Ilvanich turned to the still angry German captain. "I wouldn't be so hard on myself. I imagine that somewhere out there tonight one of your units is doing the same thing to one of ours. It's like that in war, you know."

Buhle couldn't tell if Ilvanich was trying to make him feel better or simply rubbing his nose in his own mess. Not that it made a difference. The fact was that he was still angry at himself and at the strange American commander for making fun of him in what was the most embarrassing moment of his life.

As he watched his supply trucks roll away into the darkness with their precious cargoes, now driven by the American rangers, Buhle wondered how he could explain losing them all without a single shot being fired in their defense. It would be several more minutes, after the sound of the last truck disappeared into the bitterly cold night, that Buhle realized that he had neither a map nor a flashlight. He and his men, stripped of their warm trucks, weapons, cargo, and purpose in life, were now reduced to a hopelessly lost and downcast mob of stragglers left to be brutalized by the weather and tossed about in the swirling storm of a very confused and vicious battle.

While Buhle stood in the middle of a deserted road wondering what to do next, his friend Seydlitz was busy running his company. Refreshed and under the impression that all was at least in some measure getting back to normal, Seydlitz made his rounds of his company positions as soon as Buhle and his supply column had departed. Upon returning to his own tank, Seydlitz's gunner informed him that the brigade operations officer had been trying to contact him. Pulling himself up back onto his own tank took most of Seydlitz's remaining energy. Though his mind was more alert, his body was far from refreshed. Pulling his crewman's helmet down over his dirty hair now snarled in knots, he didn't bother to tuck it all in and under the earphones. Standing on the back deck of his tank and leaning over the turret roof, Seydlitz looked down his open hatch to make sure that the radio transmitter was set to the brigade frequency before he began his broadcast. Satisfied, he keyed the radio, held it down for a moment, and then called the brigade operations officer. "Danzig Five Zero, this is Leo Four Seven. Danzig Five Zero, this is Leo Four Seven. Over."

There was no pause from the brigade operations officer. It was as if he had been sitting at the radio far off in the rear somewhere waiting for Seydlitz's call. "Leo Four Seven, this is Danzig Five Zero. You have a change of mission. Over."

Expecting nothing more than a request for a simple situation update, the quick response by the operations officer himself and the announcement that he was going to issue him an order caught Seydlitz off guard. Knowing that he would need his map and something to write on, Seydlitz yelled to his gunner to toss him up his map, his notebook, and a flashlight. Spreading the map out as far as he could, Seydlitz opened his notebook to the first page free of scribbling and notes and prepared to write. That his flashlight wasn't shielded from the enemy across the way didn't escape the notice of Seydlitz's gunner. Quickly, as his commander prepared to receive his order, the gunner pulled a poncho out from a storage rack. Standing on top of the turret roof, the gunner held it up so he and the poncho stood between the American positions and Seydlitz. Seeing what his gunner was doing, Seydlitz looked up and muttered a quick "Thank you" before rekeying the transmit lever on his crewman's helmet. "Danzig Five Zero, this is Leo Four Seven. Ready. Over."

"Leo, this is Danzig. The enemy forces that had been attacking your position have shifted their main efforts to the east. They are now hitting Düsseldorf and have forced Düsseldorf north of Autobahn E40. We must do something to relieve this pressure. Your mission will be to leave your present location, infiltrate to the north toward Bad Hersfeld, and conduct mounted raids throughout the enemy rear. Over."

Düsseldorf, the code name given the 2nd Panzer Division's 2nd Brigade, was supposed to be a supporting attack. Why he and his company were being sacrificed in such an obvious suicide mission to support a supporting attack didn't make sense to Seydlitz. To be sure that he was understanding his orders properly, Seydlitz rephrased them and asked for correction if necessary. "This is Leo. I am to move my unit north through enemy lines toward Bad Hersfeld and Autobahn E40, attacking enemy rear units as I go. Is that correct? Over."

"Leo, this is Danzig. That is correct. Over."

Seydlitz paused again to think. There was no mistake. He was being sacrificed to save someone's ass. Deciding that he'd be damned if he was going to go riding about in circles waiting to be pinned and wiped out, Seydlitz shot back to the brigade operations officer, "Danzig, this is Leo. How long do you want me to keep up my raids and where am I to go after I have done all that I can? Over."

The pause on the other end of the radio confirmed Seydlitz's suspicions. The bastards, he thought, hadn't thought about that. He and his company were truly being sent on a death ride. The gunner, listening to the exchange, looked down at Seydlitz. In the soft glow of Seydlitz's flashlight, the gunner's face betrayed the dark thoughts that were running through his mind. Finally the brigade operations officer responded. "Leo, this is Danzig. You are to use your own discretion as to how long you stay in the enemy's rear. Targets are your choice. When you feel you have done as much as you can, attempt to break out to the east, moving north of Autobahn E40 and link up with Düsseldorf. Over."

That, Seydlitz thought, was shit. Of course, he didn't take into account that the entire 2nd Panzer Division's situation was rapidly deteriorating. He couldn't. Left manning a thin outpost line on his own all day, Seydlitz had no idea what was happening even five kilometers from where he sat. That his superiors were rapidly losing all hope of cutting off the American march to the north and defeating them never occurred to Seydlitz. At no time did it enter Seydlitz's mind that instead of victory the fight now revolved around individual brigades, short on supplies and attacked from several directions at once, fighting for their very existence. Even the fact that the brigade staff of the 1st Brigade, which Seydlitz now was attached to, were issuing him orders that seemed pointless and suicidal didn't alert Seydlitz to the seriousness of their situation. Nor did it occur to him that the staff officers at brigade were just as tired and just as confused as he himself was. In the German Army, one expected the higher headquarters to be in control, to be able to think clearly and issue orders that were sound and well thought out. The idea that staff officers were only human and, like him, susceptible to exhaustion and error was the furthest thing from Seydlitz's mind. They were in charge and had to know what was going on. They had to.

Still Seydlitz instinctively continued to prod the brigade operations officer. "Danzig, this is Leo. When do you want this operation to commence? Over."

Tiring of Seydlitz's questions and anxious to join a briefing that the brigade commander was about to hold with the commanders and staff of the brigade a few meters from where he sat, the operations officer became terse with Seydlitz. "When you are ready, over." Then as an afterthought the operations officer added, "What is your fuel status? Over."

That he had been ordered to execute a mission such as this without first being asked if his unit was physically capable of executing it did not escape Seydlitz's attention. "This is Leo. We completed rearming and refueling an hour ago. Over."

The brigade operations officer's voice betrayed surprise. "Leo, who provided you with this fuel and where did they go?"

Why, Seydlitz wondered, was this so important? Were there problems that he wasn't aware of? Perhaps. But this was not the time to ask such questions. Instead he simply responded, "The supply column from my own battalion, of course. They left here some time ago headed to the assembly area my commander told me he was moving into. Over."

While Seydlitz waited for a response, the brigade operations officer turned to one of his sergeants and told him to check with the 26th Panzer Battalion to see if their supply column had arrived. As the sergeant was doing that, the operations officer returned to Seydlitz. "Leo, do you have any further questions? Over."

Taking a minute to look at his map and his skimpy notes, Seydlitz came to the conclusion that he had all he was going to get. The fact was the orders were sufficiently open to allow him almost unlimited freedom of action. To ask for more guidance might result in additional restrictions or orders that would eliminate that freedom. If he played this right, there was the chance that he and his company would survive the night. Satisfied, Seydlitz responded that he needed nothing more and then signed off.

Stretching as he looked down on his map, Seydlitz allowed himself to mutter a few curses and heard his gunner chuckle. "That good, Herr Hauptmann?"

Seydlitz, aware that he had erred by showing his displeasure with brigade in front of his gunner, looked up. There was, he realized, no hiding the truth. Seydlitz looked down at his map. "Oh, far better that you can imagine, Sergeant. I have no idea where the enemy is, no idea where our 2nd Brigade is, no idea what fire support is available, and no idea if anyone outside the 1st Brigade staff, in particular the Luftwaffe, knows that we will be going into the enemy rear. In short, we will be crawling out of the shitter into the asshole of the American Tenth Corps." Then with a tired smile Seydlitz looked up at his gunner. "Provided, of course, we can find where that asshole begins."

As Seydlitz prepared to translate his brigade operations officer's sketchy order into action, the sergeant on duty in the 4th Armored Division's division artillery intelligence section came bounding out of his armored command post carrier over to where a captain from the operations section sat. "We've got the bastards. We finally got a good fix on that German brigade command post south of Bad Hersfeld. Here are the coordinates, sir." Without waiting for a response, the intelligence sergeant went over to the wall map behind the captain and made a mark where the division's radio intercept unit, known as a collection and jamming unit or CJ platoon for short, determined the enemy brigade command post was.

Slowly the captain, tired from a long day made longer by two relocations of the command post done when he should have been sleeping, got up and walked over to the map. After looking at the newly plotted location, he thought for a minute. "We sure it's the brigade command post?"

The intelligence sergeant, anxious to have something to do that was meaningful, nodded. "Positive, sir. The enemy unit that's located seventeen kilometers south of Bad Hersfeld hasn't moved all day. The latest intercept was a long conversation between it and the brigade headquarters. The officer in charge of the CJ platoon thinks it was an operations order of some kind."

The captain raised an eyebrow. "Thinks?"

"Well, sir, the message was encrypted. We couldn't break it, but they talked long enough to get a good fix on the transmitter that we believe is the brigade headquarters."

The captain folded his arms. He knew about the enemy unit seventeen kilometers south of Bad Hersfeld. During the day several batteries of artillery had fired missions on its location twice with no noticeable effect. Its location and durability made everyone believe it was a front-line battalion or cavalry unit. Because the responses from the other unit or headquarters had been short, the collection and jamming platoon had never had enough time to get a good fix on what everyone assumed was the higher headquarters, probably the 2nd Panzer Division's 1st Brigade. Looking at the map, the captain decided that it was pointless to go after the front-line unit again. If it survived twice, odds were it would survive again. Having made his decision, the captain turned to his own operations section. "Sergeant Mears, get a copy of these new grids and pass them on to the MLRS battery. Have them dump a spill on those grids."

The intelligence sergeant thought about that. One spill, twelve rockets or one pod of a multiple rocket launcher, would be devastating, but maybe not devastating enough. Knowing that his boss had been waiting to catch the command post of the German 1st Panzer Brigade all day, the sergeant was determined to make sure that it got nailed good and proper now that they had it. "Sir, this is an enemy brigade command post, the command post of the lead enemy brigade that's controlling the enemy units threatening to cut off Autobahn A7. Don't you think we should dump more on them, just to be sure?"

The artillery captain thought about that while looking at the red brigade symbol on the map and its location. With a smile he nodded his head. "You're right. They do deserve everything we've got. Sergeant Mears, let's fuck 'em over real good. Three spills, followed up immediately with a battalion time on target from the eight-inch battalion."

The intelligence sergeant glanced over at the sergeant sitting in front of the TACFIRE computer. Both sergeants were grinning as the TACFIRE sergeant gave the intelligence sergeant a wink before he turned to input the necessary data for the fire mission. "On the way, sir."

Through the magic of computers and digital communications, Sergeant Mears communicated with rocket and gun batteries spread out all over the 4th Armored Division's area. The computer, accepting the grid and target description provided by Mears, determined all firing data needed by both the rockets and the eight-inch howitzers, relaying that data in seconds. When the computers of all firing units reported back to Mears's computer that they were ready, the same computer system gave the order to fire and initiated an artillery strike that would effectively wipe out the commander and staff officers that had given Seydlitz his last orders for the day.

21 JANUARY

When she woke again, Hilary Cole was completely disoriented. Looking around, it took several seconds for it to sink in that they hadn't moved from where they had stopped hours ago. When she went to sit upright, a sharp burning pain, caused by a muscle cramp and leaning against the door of the truck with only a thin Army blanket for padding, shot through her right arm. Pausing, Cole let the pain subside before she moved again. While she waited, she looked down at her watch. Three A.M. Four hours' sleep. She had been able to get four hours of uninterrupted sleep. That was the most sleep she had been able to get in one sitting since they had left Slovakia.

That adventure seemed years ago instead of just two weeks. Two weeks of traveling through hell, a hell that tonight looked an awful lot like a deserted forest road.

Ready, Cole finished sitting upright. When she did, she realized that she had a headache as well as a body racked with pain. Still she was thankful that no one had bothered her during the last four hours. That thought was soon replaced with one of concern for the wounded. How were they doing? Realizing that it would be a while before she would be able to go back to sleep, Cole decided to get out, stretch her legs, find some aspirin, and check on the wounded that were in the six ambulances immediately behind the truck she was traveling in. Looking over at the driver, who was sound asleep, Cole slowly opened her door.

Even before she had it fully opened, the blast of cold air hit her. It didn't bother her. Rather, it felt good, refreshing. Pushing on the door, Cole carefully swung her legs out and searched for the running board of the truck. When the toe of her boot found it, she slipped down, turned to face the driver, now stirring, and then closed the door as quietly as she could. When she was sure it was secure, Cole lowered herself to the ground, pulled her parka around her, zipped it up, and flipped the hood up over her head. Though she was sure she looked like something out of a Russian fashion magazine, Cole was warm and well protected from the cold night air.

As she moved over to the shoulder of the road, the pale moonlight allowed her to see the line of trucks that stretched off into the distance almost to a bend in the road. The trucks in front of her hospital's lead vehicle carried strange boatlike contraptions. An engineer unit, she thought. Had to be. They carried all kinds of unusual stuff like that. In front of the dozen or so engineer trucks at that bend there was an MP humvee parked in the center of the road. A lone MP sat upright manning the M-60 machine gun mounted on top of the humvee's roof while another MP, bundled up against the cold, slowly walked back and forth across the road in front of the humvee. With his rifle slung over his shoulder, Cole couldn't tell if he was on guard or waiting for someone and simply walking to and fro to stay warm.

No matter, Cole thought. They knew what they were doing. And she knew what she had to do. Turning her back on the MPs and the engineers, Cole began to walk toward the first ambulance. In doing so, she missed seeing the lone roving guard freeze in place, listening to a noise in the distance while he unslung his rifle.

Crashing through a series of logging trails and unpaved farm roads some six kilometers northwest of Bad Hersfeld, Seydlitz was beginning to realize that his orders, which seemed so absurdly simple, were becoming harder and harder to carry out. After backing his tanks out of position in pairs, he reassembled his company and began to infiltrate them en masse as he had been ordered. Though his attempts to contact brigade and notify them of his departure went unanswered, Seydlitz didn't care. He had his orders and he had verified them. Now all he had to do was to carry them out as he saw fit.

Doing so turned out to be almost as nerve-racking as sitting in one place for hours on end waiting to be attacked by enemy ground units or artillery. Fumbling forward into the darkness, Seydlitz's company managed to avoid contact with any American units. That soon became a problem. The routes into what he thought were the enemy rear areas were totally devoid of any sign of the enemy. It was almost as if the Americans had never existed. Slowly, as he pushed his exhausted company further and further north, he became bolder and bolder, picking up speed and heading for parts of the forests and countryside that looked like good places to set up rear area supply bases and facilities.

Under normal circumstances, Seydlitz's thinking would have been correct. But these were not normal circumstances for the Tenth Corps. Rather than concerning themselves with setting up and operating, the Tenth Corps' combat service support units were only concerned with getting out of the trap that the 2nd and 10th Panzer divisions were still trying to close. So instead of hiding in the woods where Seydlitz was hunting, the prey he sought sat in the open, lined up and exposed on the roads as they waited their turn to continue the long march to the sea.

Seydlitz's decision to leave the woods and begin to move along the roads was not based on any great revelation or protracted decision-making process. Rather, he was tired of screwing with the countless tree branches that slapped at him as his Leopard tank lurched back and forth over the heavily rutted trails now frozen stone hard. To hell with this, he finally said to himself shortly before 3 A.M. With a curt order over the company radio net that was almost a scream, Seydlitz ordered the lead tanks to halt while he took the time to study his map and decide where to go next. Satisfied that he had a good fix on his unit's location, Seydlitz noted with much joy that there was a hard-surfaced secondary road just a few hundred meters in front of his lead platoon. "There. That is what I want."

Seydlitz's gunner, waiting for his commander's order, thought that Seydlitz was yelling for him. "What is it, Herr Hauptmann? Trouble?"

"No, Ernst. No more trouble. We are going to get out of these damned woods and head east." Folding his map, he looked about. "If there are Americans here, then they are the best camouflage artists in the world. We tried as hard as we could. We went north, as ordered, and tried to find the Americans. Our duty is done. Now it is time to end this insanity." Keying the radio mike, Seydlitz contacted Sergeant Wihelm Zangler, the platoon leader of Seydlitz's lead platoon, and ordered him to make a left turn onto the next hard-surfaced road and follow it until they hit the first village. From there they would make their way to the autobahn and then, as per his orders, head east. Humans, even humans who were German soldiers, could only go so far. Seydlitz was reaching his end and suspected that his platoon leaders and tank commanders were collectively nearing theirs too. To continue would be a foolish waste of good men and machines.

Glad to finally be free of the worry of tree branches, the tanks of Zangler's platoon made the turn onto the hard-surfaced road as ordered and immediately began to pick up speed. Though they should have known better, since this left the tanks further back in the column still in the woods and struggling to reach the road, tired minds never think of everything. So when Zangler's tank came swinging around the bend and smack into an American military police vehicle sitting in the center of the road, his platoon was alone and instantly in contact. There was no time to think, no time to pull back. Without any hesitation, Zangler ordered his gunner to open fire and passed the word down to the tank commanders in his platoon to close up, follow him, and attack.

Hilary Cole had just reached the rear of the first ambulance when the chatter of machine-gun fire shattered the stillness of the night. Turning toward the sound, Cole watched as a great black lumbering form spewing orange tongues of flame came around the bend in the road and rammed the MP humvee without slowing down. In horror, she watched as the tank's left track rose ever so slightly onto the MP vehicle, then slowly crushed it under its full weight before any of the occupants, including the MP manning the machine gun, could escape.

Transfixed by the sight, Cole watched as another tank came up next to the first, which was still in the process of crushing the MP humvee. It slowed when it caught sight of the line of engineer trucks. Hilary watched as the second tank lowered its long menacing main gun, took a second to aim, and then fired on the first target that looked worthy of a tank main-gun round. Its choice of target had been a good one, for the fuel truck sitting near the head of the engineer unit's column ripped itself apart, sending a huge yellow fireball into the air and lighting the entire length of the column.

Cole, standing little more than a hundred meters from where the fuel truck blew up, could feel the heat of the fireball. As she watched the burning fuel run out from the sides of the ruptured fuel truck onto the road and into the ditch on the side of the road, Cole realized that she was standing on the edge of hell, and there was nothing that she could do about it. Without any further conscious thoughts, without any control of what she was doing, Cole turned and fled into the forest as a third Leopard tank came careening around the bend and began to charge down the road, machine-gunning anything and everyone who stood in its way.

After having done it, Zangler realized that ramming the American humvee hadn't been a good idea. It had proven to be a little tougher than he had originally thought. Because of his preoccupation with the wreck that had once been a humvee, the two tanks that had come up behind him had passed his. Now looking down the road, he saw them come together, almost hub to hub, and begin to run march down the road, firing as they went. The Leopard tank on the left, with its turret traversed forty-five degrees in that direction, was busy machine-gunning American trucks and personnel at point-blank range with all the machine guns that the tank's crew could bring to bear. The Leopard on the right was concentrating on trucks and personnel further down the road. Since it had greater range, that tank began to alternate between firing its main gun and its coaxially mounted machine gun. Because the loader was busy feeding the main gun, he couldn't bring the turret-mounted machine gun into play. Not that it mattered. By the time it had fired its second 120mm high-explosive anti-tank round, the chaos and confusion, not to mention the destruction, were complete.

Unable to lead, and seeing that it was not possible to get around the side of the line of American trucks and run down along the shoulder of the road, Zangler ordered his driver to slow down. Looking to his rear, he saw the fourth tank in his platoon finally come up. With a series of wild motions, Zangler directed the commander of the fourth tank to pull around and come up on the right side of his own tank. This formed a second pair of vehicles that stretched from one side of the road to the other. Ready, Zangler waved and ordered his own tank and his consort to begin moving down the road, following the first two at a distance of fifty meters and engaging any personnel or vehicles with their machine guns that the first two tanks of his platoon had missed.

The fireball that had marked the destruction of the engineers' fuel truck was the first indication Seydlitz had that the lead platoon was in contact. He immediately attempted to contact Zangler. His calls went unanswered. Still not on the hard-surfaced road yet, Seydlitz listened to the steady rattle of machine guns, punctuated on occasion by a main gun firing. Frustrated, he ordered his driver to pick up speed and his loader to change the radio frequency of his radio to Zangler's platoon frequency.

Pulling his head down to avoid the tree branches now wildly whipping over the open hatch above him, Seydlitz listened to Zangler's radio net for a second. To his surprise, Seydlitz didn't hear any of the excited chatter or confused orders that one usually hears on a radio during initial contact. Instead the radio was silent. Looking over to his own receiver-transmitter, Seydlitz made sure that it was on and set to the proper frequency. Satisfied that all was in order, Seydlitz keyed the radio and called to Zangler. "Leo One Five, this is Leo Four Five. What is your situation? Over."

Zangler responded without a pause. "We've run into a column of trucks. An engineer unit, I think. We're engaging them now." Though his voice was calm, his failure to use full call signs or radio procedures told Seydlitz that he was either busy in an engagement or directing his platoon. Since he was already engaging, there was little that Seydlitz could add.

Still he felt that he needed to say something. So Seydlitz rekeyed the radio. "Leo One Five, continue your attack and destroy everything on the road. Repeat, destroy everything on the road. I am coming up with the rest of the unit now. Over."

With nothing more than a quick "Affirmative," Zangler accepted his commander's orders and passed them on down to his tank commanders.

When they came across the red crosses on white backgrounds on vehicles further down the column, Zangler's tank commanders didn't hesitate. Why they didn't was lost in the confusion and panic of the night. For the moment, Zangler's tank crews had become mindless killing machines. Perhaps they simply looked at the trucks and personnel fleeing from them as nothing more than the enemy, someone to be acquired, engaged, and killed. Perhaps they saw this as an opportunity to repay the bastards who had attacked them the day before with artillery while they had sat buttoned up in their own tanks shitting their pants every time a round detonated nearby and praying that they would live for another minute. Perhaps some even had higher, loftier thoughts such as defending Germany against invaders. Perhaps.

C H A P T E R   1 7

21 JANUARY

By now Jan was used to listening to Colonel Edward J. Littleton, Jr., U.S. Army, retired. Littleton, located in a separate studio, was explaining the military situation in Germany. Jan, with a well-practiced smile on her face, sat and watched Littleton's face on a monitor while he explained the situation in central Germany as he saw it from Washington, D.C. Over the tiny earphone hidden in her right ear, the director whispered that they were ready to cut to the live feed from Germany. Excited at being given the chance to cut the pompous ass off, Jan jumped in while Littleton was in mid-sentence. "Excuse me, Colonel, but I've just been told that we have a live feed from Bob Manning, our correspondent in Germany."

With the camera focused on Jan's face, she leaned forward and with a look of concern spoke to the camera. "Bob? Bob, can you still hear me?" The man she was trying to talk to was Robert J. Manning, a British correspondent who was working for WNN. Right now Bob and a camera crew, using a satellite shot, were attempting to give a live feed for Jan's morning report.

In a flash, as soon as the technicians in the control room had a good clear picture of Bob, the video image was switched from Jan to Bob. "Jan, yes, I've got you now, thank you." Attired in a British Army camouflage smock with a black wool watch cap pulled down over the tops of his ears, it was obvious that Bob was more concerned about life and limb, not to mention protection against the cold, than he was about what his image looked like on the television screen four thousand miles away. The idea of wearing camouflage caught on very quickly when the losses amongst front-line correspondents began to mount. The bright yellow or international orange jackets and parkas, it seemed, drew far too much fire. The thought that a correspondent would be given special consideration vanished, along with many other illusions about war, as the viciousness and intensity of battle escalated.

"Bob, it's midafternoon there, isn't it?"

Before he could answer, the report from a small-caliber automatic cannon not far from where he stood caused him to flinch and look over to his right. When he saw that he was in no immediate danger, Bob looked back to the camera and responded to Jan's question trying to look as if nothing had happened. "Yes, Jan. It is afternoon. Of course, the time of day really doesn't seem to make any difference in this battle. The German mechanized infantry unit I'm with has been continuously engaged with elements of the American rear guard since early yesterday, day and night. The American cavalry unit that it has been playing a deadly game of tag with since then is now located just across the river behind me in a town named Burghaun."

Looking down at her computer-generated map of central Germany, the one used to show the home audience where the battles were taking place, Jan noted that there were no towns of that name shown. "Excuse me, Bob. But where exactly is that?"

"Jan, we're about four or five kilometers northwest of Hünfeld. If you recall, the Germans seized Hünfeld on the 19th but weren't able to go any further west due to the Tenth Corps' rapid redeployment of blocking forces. Now it seems that the elements of this German unit will be able to finally make it across the Fulda River here and link up with the 10th Panzer to the west."

"Is that due," Jan queried without betraying a hint of the deep concern she felt, "to a collapse of American forces?"

Jan could see Bob shake his head. "No, Jan. On the contrary. The American units that the Germans had hoped to bag have made it north and out of the trap. This is due in great measure to the skillful and valiant efforts of cavalrymen, like those across the river. It's almost become a regular drill these past two days. The American cavalrymen will set up in a town or blocking position and wait for the Germans in pursuit to catch up. Sometimes the Germans detect the Americans first and approach with caution. Most of the time, however, it is the Americans who initiate the action, usually with an ambush. This morning was a case in point."

Pointing over to a partially demolished bridge, Bob cued his cameraman to focus on the smoldering hulk of a German Marder infantry fighting vehicle sitting on the bridge.

"When the German unit I'm with lost contact with the American rear guard before dawn this morning, they took off and followed, as usual. For some reason, when we got here, they thought that the bridge was clear. Two Marders, the German equivalent of your Bradley fighting vehicle, rolled onto the bridge and began to cross. That's when the Americans in Burghaun blew up the bridge and fired on the Marders. You can clearly see, Jan, the results of that surprise."

While Bob talked and the camera continued to focus on the wrecked Marder, Jan felt a cold shiver. It was becoming harder and harder to watch those shots and talk as if they meant nothing to her. For while others viewed the film footage coming in with an eye to whether it supported their story or made a bold statement, Jan looked for anything that might give her a clue as to where her husband was and how he was doing. This was not easy, for some of the film showed wounded Americans and on occasion a corpse left sprawled on the ground in its own blood. Though she didn't know how well she could deal with seeing Scotty like that, Jan couldn't not look. She had to. It was there, and there was no denying it. So she looked and prayed in silence that she wouldn't find what she sought.

Just as Bob was finishing up his explanation, a series of loud screeches passed overhead. Automatically the cameraman, recognizing them for what they were, swung the camera away from the Marder on the bridge and over to a view of the town across the river. His reaction and timing were perfect, catching the impact of half a dozen German artillery rounds that had caused the shattering noise overhead. Looking over to where the camera was aimed, Bob then began to ad-lib. "What you're seeing, Jan, is an artillery barrage going in on what the Germans suspect to be American positions."

Watching her monitor, Jan shook her head. "Yes, Bob. We've got that here. Can you see any of the American vehicles or personnel from where you are?"

"No, Jan. And I doubt that the Germans can either. In fact, there's the very real chance that the Americans who blew up the bridge and destroyed the lead Marders are long gone. These cavalrymen are quite good at giving the Germans the slip."

With a look of mild surprise on her face, Jan asked, "If the Germans can't see the Americans, then why are they firing on the town, a German town that no doubt still has people in it?"

Bob pointed back to the Marder on the bridge. "It didn't take too many incidents like that to convince the young soldiers of this unit to shoot first before they stick their necks out."

Before she realized what she was saying, Jan asked, "Well, Bob, are you in danger of being fired on by the Americans?"

Jan cursed herself. That, she thought, was a dumb question, a really dumb question. Of course he was in danger.

"Well, Jan, of course there's always the danger that the odd shot will wander in our direction, but for the most part, no, we're in no real danger. The Americans have been very selective about how they use their artillery and where they shoot, so far. Though no one will admit it, the only times I've seen populated areas shelled by artillery have been when the Germans did it themselves."

Before Jan could ask her next question, the image of Bob disappeared from the screen. Jan pulled back, looked at the screen, then glanced over to the control booth. Over the earphone a technician announced that the feed had been cut from Bob's location. The German Army public affairs officer controlling the video feed hadn't liked his last comment. Jan looked up at the camera and did what most news anchors do when faced with a sudden interruption of their lead story. "It seems that we're having some technical difficulties with our live feed from Bob Manning in Germany. We'll continue to update you on the latest from Germany after this commercial."

While they waited, Jan sat back watching the commotion in the control booth while wondering what to do next. The logical thing was to go back to Littleton. The question was, however, how to tie Bob's interrupted report into a conversation with Littleton. As she pondered this, Jan heard the director suggest that she go back to Littleton and tie her questions into the last video somehow. Looking up at the director, Jan was about to say, "No shit, Sherlock," but decided not to. She could tell from where she sat that he already had more than enough on his mind and his hands full. He didn't need her smart-ass comment. Instead Jan simply smiled, nodded, and prepared to go back live.

When the red light flashed on the camera before her, Jan started in. "Good morning if you're just joining us. With us today in our Washington studios is Colonel Edward J. Littleton, Jr., U.S. Army, retired."

Glancing over to the monitor that showed Littleton's face, Jan's smile transformed itself into a serious mask. "Colonel Littleton, over the past few days we've seen an American force, outnumbered and deep in Germany, consistently outmaneuver and outfight the German Army, an army that has for centuries held the reputation as one of the best in the world. The German military machine, not to mention its skills in planning and its general staff, has been the model for many other armies in the world, including the American Army. How then, Colonel, do you explain what one could call the poor performance of the German Army over the past two weeks? It seems a simple thing to bring their forces to bear on the numerically inferior Tenth Corps and stop it."

When the video shot shifted to Littleton, he was smiling. "The myth of German military superiority has taken a long time to die. While the Germans have maintained a superb military force since the mid-1800s, it is not without fault and it is far from perfect." Shifting slightly in his seat, Littleton turned slightly away from the camera. "The fact is, Jan, the German Army has not fought in any wars since 1945. The United States Army, on the other hand, has had ample opportunity to blood its officers, so to say, in several conflicts. And," Littleton continued, pointing his finger at the camera, "there's more than simple combat experience. Since the breaking up of the Soviet Union, the German Army has not held a major maneuver training exercise. Most training exercises above battalion level have been command post exercises involving only the officers and assisted by computers. To my knowledge, there isn't a single German division commander who has had every unit in his command maneuvering in the field at the same time in years. An added problem was the creation of multinational corps. When the Germans pulled their units out of those multinational corps, in which officers from other nations held many key positions, the German effort to revert to all-German corps staffs in the midst of an active campaign created major problems at all levels of the German command structure that they still have not yet resolved."

"Then what you're saying, Colonel, is that the American Army is a better army."

Again Littleton smiled. "No, Jan, I'm not saying that. What I am saying is that the American Army was better trained and prepared going into this crisis than the Germans were. They, the Americans, have a solid corps of knowledgeable and experienced officers and non-commissioned officers who have made the difference when it mattered. Unfortunately for the Tenth Corps, the Germans are learning. In that particular instance at the bridge, the lesson cost them two infantry fighting vehicles and their crews. Our soldiers, who learned their lessons before the first shots were fired, are facing combat veterans now who have learned their trade the hard way."

Littleton's statement sent a chill through Jan. For a moment her face went blank as she tensed up. The director, seeing the sudden change, ordered the camera to hold on Littleton for a moment instead of cutting back to Jan for her next question. Only after Jan realized what had happened and had regained her composure did he allow the camera to cut over to her. As hard as it was for her to do, Jan asked the next logical question. "Will this newfound experience be able to make a difference in sufficient time to allow the Germans to stop the Tenth Corps?"

Taking a deep breath before answering, Littleton pondered the question, then looked up at Jan. "Perhaps. It is hard to say right now. Washington and Berlin must assess the results of the battle that's now winding down. It's really hard to say what either will do. The Tenth Corps has won, but it has paid for that success. The Germans have had their noses badly bloodied and will now step back to catch their breath and figure out what to do next. The only thing that we can be sure of, Jan, is that when and where the two armies come together again, it will be more violent and more vicious. The Americans now realize that they are fighting for their lives."

"And the Germans, Colonel? How will the German soldier react?"

Again Littleton carefully considered his next comment. He, like the rest of the world, was really unsure. Public opinion in Germany was solidly against the war. Anti-war riots in every major city outside the combat zone had resulted in martial law being imposed and the diversion of those reserve units that had responded to their call-up to controlling civil disturbances instead of reinforcing combat units facing the Tenth Corps. And yet the German Army continued to maneuver and prepare for the next fight. Taking another deep breath, Littleton finally answered. "I don't think anyone, even the German Army commanders themselves, can answer that question."

*　　*　　*

While Jan Fields-Dixon and Colonel Edward J. Littleton, Jr., U.S. Army, retired, pondered what would happen next, Captain Nancy Kozak had no illusions as to how the German soldiers would behave. From the side of the road, Kozak watched with cold and impassionate eyes as two soldiers from her first platoon carefully laid the charred and shredded body of her battalion commander on a poncho. Though they were careful, there was also a decided lack of true emotion on their part. They were, like everyone else in Company C, 3rd of the 3rd Infantry, beyond feeling. The stress and strain of battle, sleepless nights, long periods of tedium shattered by sudden spasms of sheer terror known as combat had beaten practically every human emotion out of them. They were, like Kozak, responding but no longer feeling. It was too late for that.

From down the road, the roar of the battalion executive officer's humvee failed to disturb Kozak as she watched her soldiers continue the grim task of removing the bodies of the battalion commander's crew from their smashed Bradley. Even when the executive officer's humvee stopped next to Kozak and he dismounted, Kozak made no effort to acknowledge his presence. She simply continued to watch her soldiers drape another corpse in a mottled green camouflage poncho. Coming up next to Kozak, the executive officer looked briefly at what Kozak's soldiers were doing, then, ignoring the stench of burned flesh that made his nostrils twitch, he turned to Kozak. "What happened?"

Kozak answered without taking her eyes away from the soldiers or enshrouded body. In a voice that was little more than a whisper Kozak responded. "The battalion commander's dead."

The executive officer stared at Kozak for a moment and blinked. He knew that. She was the one who had reported that to him. Not understanding her response, the executive officer continued. "Yes, I know that. What I meant to say is how did it happen?"

Still without looking at the executive officer, Kozak responded in the same soft monotone that she had before. "The Germans killed him."

Only slowly did it begin to dawn on the executive officer that Kozak's responses, her attitude, and her refusal to acknowledge him were not meant as disrespect or evasion. They were the best that she could do. Kozak, like most of the rest of the soldiers in her company, was at the end of her physical and emotional tether. After two weeks of giving all she had to give and enduring more than any reasonable person could expect, Kozak had nothing more to give except her life. And at that moment if someone had come up to her, pointed a gun at her head, and threatened to shoot, odds were she would have done nothing. Sometimes the soul dies long before the body does.

But the battalion executive officer, now the commander of the 3rd Battalion, 3rd Infantry, wasn't finished with Kozak and her company. The battalion, now the rear guard for the 1st Brigade and in turn the 4th Armored Division, had another important mission to fulfill. Though the death of the battalion commander was regrettable, it was part of being a soldier. The battalion commander knew this. The executive officer knew this. Kozak knew this. Yes, soldiers had died, the executive officer thought, all of them, like the battalion commander, good men. But the Tenth Corps had escaped being crushed by the 2nd and 10th Panzer divisions and the march continued.

After looking at the soldiers going about their grim task one more time, the executive officer moved so that he now stood between Kozak and the grisly scene. Finally unable to watch her soldiers as they tended to the dead, Kozak looked up at the executive officer for the first time. When he had her attention, the young major began to issue his orders. "Nancy, I want to take your company up this road about two kilometers to a place called Weiterode just outside of Bebra. Set up a blocking position oriented to the southwest. We have been ordered to keep Highway 27, which runs through Bebra, open until midnight. A Company will pass through you and deploy to the north of Bebra blocking 27 as it comes in from the north. D Company will be following and deploy to the south. B Company, which got beat up pretty bad this morning, will be reconstituting in Bebra and serve as a reserve."

Though Kozak was looking him in the eye without blinking and nodded in acknowledgment, the executive officer wasn't sure she understood. Patiently he tried to explain to her the importance of what they were doing. "Listen, Nancy, it's important that we hold here. The whole corps is shifting its axis of advance. Instead of pushing through Kassel directly north to Hannover, we're shifting to the northwest in the direction of Paderborn. The corps commander feels that we can do better there than staying in the hill country. Is that clear?"

Again Kozak simply stared vacantly into his eyes and nodded, causing the executive officer to wonder how much longer Colonel Dixon thought that he could push the brigade. The executive officer knew that when officers like Kozak began to teeter on the edge of total collapse, the end was in sight. He couldn't allow that to happen. He was a commander now, charged with a mission. "Okay, Nancy, I want you to get your company mounted up and moving. I want you in place before it gets dark. Is that clear?"

As before, Kozak stared at him and nodded. Realizing that there was nothing more that he could do there, the executive officer shook his head, turned, and began to walk away. He was about to get into his humvee when Kozak called out, "Major."

Stopping, the executive officer turned around and faced Kozak. "Major, I'm all right really. It's just that it's been a bad few days. I . . . I don't think . . ."

After Kozak lapsed into silence, the two officers looked at each other. For the first time in several days the executive officer felt compassion for another human being. Nodding, he said nothing at first. Then he said, "I understand. We'll talk about it in Weiterode. Is that all right?"

"Yes, sir. That will be fine. Thank you."

The executive officer looked at Nancy Kozak for a moment and realized that what she needed was more than another mission. She needed a calm and reassuring voice to talk to her, to reach in and wrap itself about her troubled and fatigued mind and ease her burden. But he couldn't do that right now. Several kilometers down the road another company commander, like Kozak, waited to receive his orders. The executive officer doubted if he would be in any better shape than Kozak. Though the image of Kozak shaken like this was very disconcerting to the executive officer, there was nothing that he could do about that. The war went on and they had a mission, a very important one, to execute. He would have plenty of time later, after Kozak's company had settled into their new position, to talk to her. Plenty of time.

With that, he turned, climbed into his humvee, and went speeding down the road in search of B Company, where he would play out the same scene with a different company commander. The executive officer didn't know that his tenure as battalion commander had less than thirty minutes left. Like his battalion commander before him, the executive officer was scheduled by fate to become a statistic.

*　　*　　*

Each day General Lange found the afternoon briefings at Ruff's office more and more intolerable. Everything about the briefings and the people who attended them bothered him. It bothered him as a professional soldier, as a German, and as a human being.

To Lange's right sat Rudolf Lammers. As the chief of operations briefed, Lange carefully looked over to the man who as the Minister of Defense was supposed to be his immediate superior. In the past three days, however, Lammers had been nothing more than a messenger for Chancellor Ruff, and not a very good one at that. Though he gave the outside world the appearance of still being in control, he was out of his depth. Whenever Ruff demanded action or a decision had to be made, Lammers hurriedly sought out Lange and with wide eyes simply asked, "Well, what do you think?"

On the other side of Lammers was Bruno Rooks, the Foreign Minister. While Lammers at least gave the appearance of being in control of himself, Rooks couldn't even manage this. Everything about the man, including body odor from lack of bathing, told of a broken man. Among the world community it was he, Rooks, who the press held up as the man who had been dealing with the other nations of the world before the crisis. So now it was he who the press watched as nation after nation slammed their doors in his face. While Ruff could hide in his office surrounded by his loyal staff and military men, Rooks suffered in person the abuse of diplomats who had once called themselves his friends. This, coupled with Ruff's own attitude of ignoring a man who had become unnecessary to his purposes, was too much for Rooks to bear. Just when he needed a friend, a person to confide in, he had no one; and no one except Lange seemed to notice.

Of the inner circle, only Fellner, the Minister of the Interior, seemed to be holding up. That, Lange surmised, was probably due to the fact that, although considered a part of the inner circle, he was not one of Ruff's men. Of the lot, only Fellner continued to maintain his dignity and speak for the good of the German people. Though he supported Ruff, who was after all the duly elected Chancellor, Fellner left no doubt that he stood for Germany and all of its people.

Finally in the circle of men who were driving Germany into the dark abyss there was Chancellor Ruff himself. If Fellner stood for Germany and the German people, what did Ruff now stand for?

Everything, Lange had been able to convince himself, up to the first bloodletting had been justifiable. Everything could be explained.

Ruff's indignation against the United States for not informing them of the Ukrainian operation, his seizure of the nuclear weapons brought into Germany against all treaties, even his use of the Army to blockade the American Tenth Corps in the Czech Republic were political maneuvers that could be defended. Those efforts, Lange had thought, had hoped, had all been bluffs. Now, however, after the battles in central Germany, Lange finally began to understand that Ruff had never been bluffing. Ruff had always been working for an armed confrontation with the Americans. But why? Why in the hell had this man who had earned an impeccable reputation as a man of reason, a strong unifying element in a troubled Germany, driven his people and his nation into a war that could only ruin decades of hard work, not to mention the lives of thousands of its people?

Leaning forward, Lange propped his chin on his hand. With a sly sideways glance he studied Ruff for several moments. There was something going on inside of that man's head that no one, even his most trusted supporters, knew about. But what? What could drive a man to sacrifice his fellow countrymen in such a manner? Perhaps this same thought had troubled the General Staff officers of Nazi Germany. Perhaps they too stared at their national leader and wondered what drove the man who drove their nation.

Lange's reflection on his commander-in-chief was interrupted by a civilian aide from the Ministry of the Interior who, after gaining access to the briefing room, walked straight over to Fellner and handed him an envelope. Without regard for the briefing officer, Fellner ripped open the envelope, ruffled the thin sheets of paper as loudly as he could manage, and made a great show of reading them. Finished, he folded the papers and turned to face Ruff. Again acting as if the chief of operations didn't exist, Fellner began to speak. "It would seem, gentlemen, that the stories about the destruction of a field hospital are quite true."

There was a moment of silence before Fellner continued. "Early this morning the Americans escorted French and British news teams to the spot and allowed them to film the recovery of wounded and dead personnel, both male and female, from vehicles clearly marked with the International Red Cross symbol. Those films are now playing on every news program around the free world. The British news team was the most charitable, referring to the incident as a massacre. The French preferred the word murder."

Unable to stand Fellner's gloating, Ruff slapped his hand on the table as he jumped to his feet. "BASTARDS! Who do they think *they* are?" The sudden outburst surprised everyone in the room except for Lange and Fellner.

As he looked about the room, red-faced and unable to conceal his anger, Ruff glared at everyone, who stared back until they averted their eyes. Only Fellner and Lange returned Ruff's stare with a defiant, almost contemptuous look. When he was ready, Ruff turned to Fellner. "I want you to make sure that we have complete control of all foreign correspondents. All of them. We cannot afford to allow them to run about freely, spreading lies and aiding the American propaganda campaign against us."

"But Herr Ruff," Fellner hastened to remind him in a warm voice, "the correspondents who shot those videos were then behind American lines. We cannot, as the past few days have demonstrated, control what happens behind enemy lines."

Turning about, Lange looked at Fellner. Was that last comment meant as an insult to the German Army? He was about to pass it off when Fellner added, "We could, of course, solve this problem by insisting that our Army refrain from committing atrocities except behind our lines."

Now there was no doubt. Fellner had declared himself, though it took Ruff, still steaming with rage, several seconds to understand this. But Lange knew that from that moment on the German war cabinet would begin to crumble. It was the beginning of the end. But what would that end bring for them and for Germany? How long, he wondered, would Ruff continue to play out this insanity?

Like a tiger whose paw was stuck in a steel trap, Ruff began to lash out at Fellner. "HOW DARE YOU? HOW DARE YOU SPEAK TO ME, TO US, LIKE THAT!"

Fellner, standing erect and calm, looked Ruff in the eye. "And how dare you, Herr Chancellor, betray the German people."

"BETRAY? You, Herr Fellner, are mad. If there be treason, you, and not I, are the traitor. There is no doubt, no doubt at all, that you have never fully supported this government during this crisis. You continue to work against our purposes."

"And what," Fellner shouted, "*are* those purposes? To destroy Germany *again*, for the third time in less than one hundred years? What in the hell are you doing?" Then looking about the room, Fellner asked everyone present, "What are we all doing? Have we gone mad, *again*? What are we doing dragging all of Germany and its people back to the gates of Armageddon? What?"

In the silence that followed, a captain of the operations section entered the room and began to head for Lange until he realized what was happening. Freezing in place, the captain looked at Lange, then back at the door. He was about to turn and flee when Lange caught his eye and signaled him to come over. Though he did so with the same reluctance that a man jumps into a sea full of sharks, the captain inched toward Lange and handed him a dispatch. For a moment, while the silent standoff between Ruff and Fellner continued, Lange read the dispatch.

When he finished, he thanked the captain and dismissed him. While the captain was fleeing the room, Lange stood up, cleared his throat, and began to speak. The sarcasm he felt showed in every word he spoke. "Gentlemen, excuse me for disturbing your, ah, discussions. But I am afraid the situation in central Germany has changed somewhat. It seems the Americans have entered Paderborn and are moving west and northwest toward Münster and Osnabrück. The enemy has managed to break out of our encirclement."

Dumbfounded, Ruff turned his attention away from Fellner and toward Lange. "How can that be? Just five minutes ago your chief of operations briefed us that the 7th Panzer Division had established blocking positions in front of Paderborn. What happened?"

Looking down at the message, Lange considered his response. When he spoke, he did so without looking at Ruff. "It seems the positions of the 7th Panzer Division were compromised."

"Compromised? What in the hell do you mean, compromised?"

"It means, Herr Chancellor, that enemy actions and maneuvering compelled the commander of that division to withdraw."

"And how many casualties," Ruff demanded, "did the 7th Panzer inflict on the Americans before they retreated?"

"I do not know, Herr Chancellor. This dispatch doesn't say."

"All right, Herr General, how many casualties did the 7th Panzer Division suffer before yielding Paderborn?"

With a quick glance down, Lange found the appropriate passage and read it. "The 7th Panzer Division reports suffering three casualties, all wounded, when their truck was sideswiped by a Leopard tank while leaving Paderborn."

"Three?"

"Yes, Herr Chancellor, three. It seems we were very, very lucky today."

Like a well-rehearsed stage play, the column of American tanks and infantry fighting vehicles of the 55th Mech Infantry Division approached the bridge held by elements of the 7th Panzer Division. When the lead Bradley was clearly visible, the senior German officer present, a panzergrenadier captain, walked out into the middle of the road. Upon seeing the German, the commander of the Bradley halted and reported. Within minutes the most senior American officer in the column, an armored major, came forth mounted in his tank. Stopping thirty meters away from the German officer, the American major dismounted with no undue haste, then walked up to the German captain.

After the exchange of military pleasantries, the German captain spoke first. "I have been ordered, Herr Major, to establish a blocking position here and prevent the passage of American forces."

The American major, responding in German, likewise stated his mission. "I have been ordered, Herr Captain, to seize this bridge and establish a bridgehead on the far side."

The German captain replied, "I must resist your efforts until my position is no longer tenable."

The American major nodded. "I understand." Then, turning toward the commander of the Bradley infantry fighting vehicle behind him, the major waved his hand over his head and then pointed to the bridge. Without hesitation, the commander of the Bradley gunned his engine and raced for the bridge, past German obstacles removed to clear the way and German Marder infantry fighting vehicles only partially hidden in positions meant to cover them.

When the American Bradley reached the bridge, the German captain, who had been watching its progress, turned to the American major. "Ah, if you would excuse me, Major. My position is no longer tenable. I must withdraw my unit to its next blocking position, which is seven point two kilometers further down the road."

"That is all right, Captain. I understand. Auf Wiedersehen."

Saluting, the captain also bid the American major farewell and returned to his unit.

*   *   *

Just short of the road junction west of Ronshausen, Major Harold Cerro saw a lone humvee half concealed in a stand of trees with two figures standing next to it waiting. Knowing one of the figures had to be his boss, Colonel Scott Dixon, Cerro ordered his driver to pull over next to it and stop.

Normally, when responding to a summons by his commander to meet at some isolated spot in the middle of the night, Cerro would literally jump out of whatever vehicle he was traveling in before it stopped and bound over to Dixon to receive the latest order or change of mission Dixon invariably had for him. Dixon and Cerro, having worked so long together, understood each other's work habits to the point where they could hold short, almost encrypted, conversations without any loss of clarity or meaning. Tonight, for example, when Dixon called the brigade command post and directed that Cerro meet him at a crossroads near the command post of the 3rd Battalion, 3rd Infantry, Cerro knew that Dixon had an important order that needed to be issued and there wasn't time for him to return to the command post himself.

Cerro, however, didn't leap out of his humvee when it stopped. Instead, he sat there for a moment almost as if he had to think about what to do next. Slowly Cerro had to gather the strength necessary to climb out of his vehicle. For Cerro, like everyone else in the brigade, from the youngest rifleman to Dixon himself, was pushing the limits of endurance. The Battle of Central Germany, now officially declared over by the American news media, had cost more than lives and materiel lost. Everyone, American and German, who had participated in the grueling slugfest was exhausted. And the exhaustion was not only physical. It was mental as well. Fear, stress, wild swings that took a person from near comatose exhaustion to the heights of sheer terror where they couldn't even control their bodily functions, tore away at the mental fiber of the mind and soul just as heavy labor tore at the cells of one's muscles. War, as von Clausewitz so correctly pointed out, was as much a contest of wills and minds as it was physical.

As he mustered the strength to move himself over to where the two colonels waited, Cerro looked at them. They were quite a contrast. Colonel Vorishnov was the storybook image of a Russian officer. He was big for an armor officer. The Russian Army still recruited only short officers and men so that their tank designers could create combat vehicles that had a lower silhouette. Unlike many of his peers, however, Vorishnov was not thick in the waist, though the heavy parka he wore made him appear to be quite pregnant. Dixon, a man of average height, seemed dwarfed by the tall Russian. The two had used their physical difference before the Battle of Central Germany for comic relief. Every now and then when he judged the mood to be right, Vorishnov would come up to Dixon as he was slouched over a map or document. Standing between Dixon and the light, so that the American colonel stood in the shadow of the tall Russian, Vorishnov would stretch his large frame out and up as far as it would go. When Dixon noticed the shadow of the tall Russian over him, he would stop what he was doing, look up, and with a look of terror on his face exclaim, "My God, they are ten feet tall." In response, Vorishnov would reach out with his hand, fingers upturned and spread out as if they were holding a ball. Bellowing so that his voice sounded like it came from the depths of a monstrous cavern, Vorishnov would say, "If we had known you were so puny, we would have crushed you a long time ago." In the past, such antics had never failed to bring a round of laughter from the staff of the 1st Brigade.

Sitting there, Cerro realized that those days were gone. The war had taken its toll. There was no humor anymore. There was no lighter side to look at. Even worse, after assessing the results of their recent battles, Cerro even wondered if there was hope. For as they sat there that night, there was no indication that the will of the German soldier to fight had in any way been diminished during the last battle. Fuel reserves within the Tenth Corps were almost nonexistent, casualties in some companies reached as high as 50 percent, equipment that had been damaged and could not be hastily repaired had been destroyed in place by their crews, the heavy freeze that had made the ground hard and easy to maneuver on was coming to an end. And they were only halfway to the coast with few surprises left up their sleeves. With such solemn thoughts as a backdrop, Cerro slowly unfolded his weary body from the front seat of his humvee and trudged over to where Dixon and Vorishnov waited.

There were no greetings, no pleasantries. Not even a grunt to acknowledge Cerro's appearance. There was only Dixon's announcement, made matter-of-factly. "Hal, you're to assume command of the

3rd of the 3rd. Jim Jensen, who's been filling in since their XO was wounded, will report immediately to brigade for reassignment." There was a pause before Dixon added, "You know the situation and the battalion's mission. I have no need to tell you how important it is that you keep the Germans at bay. We can't afford another incident like the one last night with the engineer company and the field hospital. We were lucky, you know. There was a supply convoy less than two kilometers down the road with a dozen tankers filled with diesel sitting on the side of the road. Had we lost them instead of the hospital, we'd have been in real trouble."

Neither Cerro nor Vorishnov, who was listening and watching, found any fault with what Dixon had said. They agreed that it would have been far worse if the fuel convoy had been lost. It was not that they had in a matter of a few days become unfeeling and inhuman monsters. All three knew what the 553rd Field Hospital incident had meant in human terms to the soldiers and patients of that unit. But there was no energy left at that moment in their exhausted minds, overtasked with the needs of dealing with the imperatives of the moment, to lament the dead and wounded of the 553rd. That action was over, completed. What was critical now was to get their brigade moving to the sea. The war had not stopped. The killing was not over. The next twenty-four hours would be critical. The commander of the Tenth Corps, Big Al, hoped to pull away from the last of the corps' battle against the 2nd and 10th Panzer divisions and posture the corps for the forthcoming battle with the 1st and 7th Panzers, now forming what was being called the Hannover line. It was believed that once this line had been broken, there would be no stopping them from reaching the sea.

To that end, Dixon assessed the effectiveness of his brigade, determined which units were still capable of offensive action and which were good only for defense, and positioned them in his line of march accordingly. The 3rd Battalion, 3rd Infantry, which had performed well and was still, on paper, a powerful battalion, had lost two commanders in less than six hours. That, coupled with a series of quick but brutal encounters with the 2nd Panzer, had left the leadership and troops of the battalion unsettled. After a quick conference with Major Jensen, Dixon had determined that Jensen was not capable of rallying the troops of the battalion and executing the rear-guard actions that Dixon had assigned it. Rear-guard operations, high risk under the best of circumstances, required a commander to have sound judgment, a will of steel, and, as Cerro himself had once said during a training exercise, "a commander with a set of brass nuts."

The first thought that came to Cerro's mind was one of confusion. "Why," he blurted out, "not Colonel Yost?"

"Because, Hal, I need Yost as the brigade XO. You're right, he should be the one. But I can better afford to lose a maneuver battalion than the field trains. Yost is the only person who is keeping this brigade's support units going and functioning."

The implication that Dixon was willing to write off Cerro and the battalion he was about to command in order to save the brigade's supply trains didn't bother Cerro. It was, after all, a simple statement of fact. Dixon had four maneuver battalions, two tank and two mechanized infantry. He had only one set of field trains to keep those maneuver battalions fed, fueled, and supplied. Without the field trains, the brigade died. Period. What bothered Cerro was that he was about to replace one of his peers under less than honorable circumstances. Jensen, by virtue of being the operations officer of the 3rd of the 3rd, was the next man in the chain of command and the proper choice for the position. That Dixon was relieving him and removing him from the battalion, to be replaced by an outsider, was a clear indication that something was wrong with Jensen, the unit, or both. Though Cerro wanted to find out what the problem with Jensen was, he knew that neither he nor Dixon had the time. Nodding, Cerro simply said, "Okay, sir. I'll head on down to their CP, transfer my personal gear over to Jensen's vehicle, and send him up to brigade. Any change in the mission or new orders?"

Having experienced a change of command under similar circumstances during the war in the Middle East, Dixon felt like giving Cerro some advice or a short speech to reassure him. But then he stopped. What could he say? What words could make this deplorable situation any better? None. Cerro was a professional and he had a job to do. It was that simple. Dixon decided to leave it at that. Instead he merely shook his head. "No, no new orders. You know what to do."

With that, the three men parted, Cerro to relieve a man who had once been a friend, and Dixon and Vorishnov to talk to the next battalion commander further down the road.

When Cerro arrived at the command post of the 3rd Battalion, he was surprised to find Major Jim Jensen waiting for him outside. Cerro's vehicle had barely stopped before Jensen was there greeting Cerro. "I spoke to Colonel Dixon. He said that I was to throw my stuff into your humvee as soon as you got here and report to Colonel Yost at the trains. I've got my gear ready to go." Turning, he began to rush over to his humvee parked several meters away, but then stopped as something occurred to him. "Oh, I had the commands and staff of the battalion already gather here. They're waiting for you inside. I thought that you'd like to talk to them." Then, without giving Cerro a chance to respond, Jensen continued to go for his gear.

Cerro, caught off guard by Jensen's behavior, yelled out, "Jim, hold it." Walking over, Cerro came up to Jensen, placed his right hand on Jensen's left shoulder and started to say something, then stopped. What in the hell do you tell a friend when you're about to relieve him of command? Cerro knew that this action, done under these conditions, would effectively destroy Jensen's career. As soon as Jensen got into Cerro's humvee and drove away, he would be viewed as a failure, a soldier who failed the test of combat. For a combat arms officer that was worse than the kiss of death. It would leave a psychological scar that Jensen would carry for the rest of his life. Cerro knew this. Jensen knew this. So what, Cerro thought, could he possibly say to make this better, easier, for Jensen?

While he pondered, searching his tired and confused mind for some words that were appropriate, Jensen saved Cerro from his embarrassment. "Hal, I asked to be replaced."

Taken aback by Jensen's comment, Cerro looked up in his friend's eyes and, unable to control his reaction, let his jaw drop open. "Yeah, that's right. When Colonel Dixon and the Russian were here, I asked them to be relieved." Jensen stepped back, throwing his arms out to his sides while letting Cerro's limp hand fall away. "I'm not the commander type. I just don't have it. You know the system. You know the peacetime Army. Majors who want to be lieutenant colonels have to be successful battalion XOs or ops officers. It's the system and I, just like you, played this system. I didn't know that there was going to be a war and I damned sure didn't know everyone was going to get themselves killed or wounded, leaving me to hold the bag. I don't want this. All I wanted to do was retire after twenty years as a lieutenant colonel. I can't deal with this. You can. I can't. I'm sorry, but that's the way it is. So don't worry."

Pivoting on his heels, Jensen again began to walk away but stopped a second time. Twisting his head slightly, he looked at Cerro, still standing dumbfounded, and called back, "Oh, yeah. Congratulations, Hal, and good luck."

Though he had been told to expect someone from Berlin, Major General Horst Mondorf, commander of the 7th Panzer Division, did not expect General Lange, Chief of the General Staff. After his aide had gone to escort Lange to Mondorf's office, Mondorf stood up, walked around to the front of his desk, straightened out his uniform jacket, and waited. As he stood there staring at the door, he kept repeating that he had been right. His decision to give way had compromised the entire Hannover line. Without the 7th Panzer Division, there was no way that the 1st Panzer could hold that line. He had through his orders opened the road to the sea for the American Tenth Corps and, he hoped, spared the German people further suffering. For the future of Germany as a nation, Mondorf had broken ranks with his fellow division commanders and, like the senior officers of the Luftwaffe had done a week ago, allowed his conscience to be his guide, consequences be damned.

Mondorf felt a strange peace as he prepared to greet Lange. He was about to be relieved of his command and no doubt be brutally criticized for failing to do his duty in the defense of Germany and to uphold the traditions of the German Army. Yet he had done what he knew was right. He had followed his heart and decided that for the good of Germany and the German people the current insanity had to be brought to an end. Though he knew his actions alone could not bring this sad chapter to a close, he had done all he could. He was prepared for whatever Lange did or said.

Preceded by a light rap, Mondorf's aide announced his presence and opened the door. With the precision expected of an officer of his rank and position, the aide announced Lange: "Herr General, the Chief of the General Staff, General Lange." Stepping aside, he made way for Lange. Lange paused at the door and looked at Mondorf. It seemed almost as if Lange was hesitant to enter. As the two general officers stared at each other, Mondorf couldn't help but notice that Lange's face, normally frozen in a hard expressionless stare, was haggard and worried. In his eyes Mondorf saw traces of doubt, worry, and uncertainty. There was something going on inside Lange's head that his years of training and self-discipline could not hide.

Pulling himself up to a more military stance, Lange entered the room and dismissed the aide, who without another word closed the door and disappeared. While he moved over to an armchair and removed his overcoat, Lange looked down at the floor. He said nothing to Mondorf and heard nothing from him. Finally, when he was ready, Lange dropped into the armchair and studied Mondorf, who remained in place at attention staring at the door. Lange knew what this officer, one of the senior commanders of the German Army, had done and he knew why. Now, Lange thought, did he himself have the courage to do the same? Was he prepared to follow the example of this officer, who was his junior, and turn his back on his sworn duty to his country and its appointed leaders and do what he as an individual deemed was right? Mondorf could be wrong. The senior commanders of the Luftwaffe who had resigned and the pilots who had flown their aircraft into Holland could be wrong. The individual commanders of the warships of the Kriegsmarine who had sailed out of port north to Norwegian fjords, where they dropped anchor and turned off their radios, could be wrong. And the reservists who had refused to answer their call to the colors could be wrong. They all could be wrong.

But what if they were not? What if their actions, and not those who still accepted Ruff's orders, were appropriate? And what at this point was right and what was wrong? It was all very confusing. All untidy and beyond explanation. The only thing that was clear to Lange, and he was sure to Mondorf, was that the point of decision had been reached. Each officer, as both he and Mondorf had been taught, had to decide between right and wrong for himself. Staff studies, regulations, orders, and philosophical discussions had no place here. This was, Lange knew, a critical moment in the life of Germany, and he alone should decide how that moment ended.

When his superior said or did nothing, Mondorf slowly turned his head and looked over to where Lange sat, lost in his own thoughts. He could see by Lange's furrowed brows and glazed, unflinching stare that the concerns and perplexed thoughts that were racing through his mind were weighing heavily upon him. Relaxing his stance slightly, Mondorf turned toward Lange and in a low voice spoke. "When it comes time, the difference between one's duty and one's conscience is hard to separate. I fear that perhaps we have been soldiers for too long, Herr General."

Lange looked up at Mondorf. He was right, of course. He was absolutely right. As a senior commander, Lange realized that he had allowed his duty and his conscience to merge into one. This, he suddenly realized, was why senior officers, far removed from the heat of battle, were having problems deciding what to do, while many junior officers saw clearly what needed to be done and did it. To them the choice was simple, fight or step aside and let the Americans pass. Finally he knew what he must do.

"Yes, Horst, you are right. I have forgotten." Then, like a man galvanized into sudden action, Lange jumped to his feet. "But I have not forgotten that before I was a soldier I was a German. You and other men of courage like you, thank God, have not forgotten that." Reaching down for his coat, Lange all but shouted like a man possessed, "Come, Horst, we have much to do and not much time."

"Where, Herr General, are we going?"

"We are going to Bremerhaven, now, tonight. We will use my helicopter. Turn your operations here over to your chief of staff."

Still bewildered, Mondorf hesitated as Lange raced for the door. He was halfway through the door when he noticed that Mondorf was not following. Stopping, he turned to Mondorf. "Come. We must reach our paratroopers before the Americans do."

PART FIVE

TO THE SEA

CHAPTER 18

22 JANUARY

"TEN MINUTES! TEN MINUTES TO THE DROP ZONE."

The sudden shouting of the jump master broke the long silence that had settled over both the crew and the paratroops in the ancient C-141 transport. From where he sat, the sight of nervous young men, younger than the airplane that had transported them across the Atlantic to their drop zones west of Bremerhaven, Germany, was not new to Major General Benjamin Matthew. With over thirty years invested in the Army, which had started during the dying days of Viet-Nam, nothing that he saw, heard, or smelled that morning was new.

Fighting the weight and bulk of the parachute and personal equipment strapped to his body, Matthew pulled himself forward and looked down the length of the aircraft at the young soldiers he was about to lead into battle. They were no different than thousands of other young paratroopers who had on many occasions in the past stepped out into thin air and jumped into hell. The big difference this time was that this would be the last time that Americans would do it. His division was scheduled for deactivation. There was, planners in Washington had determined, no place in the twenty-first century for airborne forces in the new model Army that was being built. "The airborne division," one brilliant young staff officer in the Pentagon had stated, "was like the dinosaur, big, clumsy, and unable to adapt to the changing environment of the modern battlefield of a new century."

Easing back into the nylon jump seat, Matthew shook his head.

Well, he thought, at least I'll be able to go out like my division, in a blaze of glory and doing what I was trained to do. Matthew had already decided that he would retire after this command. In fact, he had requested that his last day of active duty coincide with the day the 17th Airborne was scheduled to deactivate. If the Army was so ready to bury this old dinosaur, Matthew told his wife, they'd have to get someone else to kick the dirt into the grave.

But that was still in the future. Right now Matthew was preparing to throw the war in Germany into a new phase that would serve notice to Germany that the United States was not prepared to sit idly by and allow the soldiers of the Tenth Corps to be swallowed up, regardless of who was right or wrong. "Without us," he had told his command before leaving Fort Bragg, "the Tenth Corps doesn't even have hope. Only we can make a difference. Though some of us will die, we will die fighting in the only cause that really makes sense, to save our fellow soldiers."

On command from the pilot, the jump masters prepared for the jump. Opening the door and deploying the large spoilers that would protect the paratroopers from the blast of the jet engines as they exited the aircraft, the jump masters brought the 122 paratroops to life. Everywhere, in Matthew's plane and dozens like it following in formation, the men and women of the 17th Airborne checked their personal equipment, parachutes, and personal effects as they waited for the jump master's next command. Even Matthew was occupied checking his gear out for the fourth time when the jump master tapped him on the shoulder. Looking up, he saw the jump master holding his earphones, connected to the aircraft's intercom system, out to him. Over the roar of the engines and the air rushing in, the jump master yelled, "General, the pilot wants to talk to you." The pilot on this particular aircraft was no ordinary throttle jockey. Taking his cue from Matthew, and seeking to salvage the reputation of the Military Airlift Command after the Sembach debacle, the commander of the air division from which most of the transports in this armada came from, Major General Eddie Bower, flew the lead aircraft, Matthew's aircraft. Before leaving, he had told Matthew that if he didn't put him right on the money, he'd turn in his stars too. It was a show of faith that everyone in the 17th Airborne appreciated.

As he pulled his helmet off and slipped the earphones on, Matthew hoped that this operation was not being called off for some foolish reason by some weenie in Washington who had suddenly gotten cold feet. Ready, he pulled the microphone up to his lips and clicked the intercom button. "Eddie, this is Ben. What's up?"

"Ben, I just got the strangest damned message over the radio. A German who claims to be the commander of the German 27th Parachute Brigade is calling for you by name. Says he wants to talk to you. It's coming in over the clear on the commercial airlines channel. You want to talk to him?"

Matthew shook his head and thought. He had met the colonel who commanded the 27th Brigade twice before but couldn't remember the name. If he had the face right, he wasn't a bad sort of fellow. Friendly, tough, professional, and, according to Matthew's intelligence officer, straight as an arrow when it came to following orders. The 27th Parachute Brigade, charged with preparing the defenses of Bremerhaven, was a crack unit that would be the principal obstacle in the 17th Airborne Division's path into the city. Fact was, the 27th, with three battalions organized and ready on the ground, could be more than a match for the eight battalions the 17th was dropping that morning if the German commander reacted quickly and aggressively. That he knew Matthew and the division were on the way and near enough to communicate told Matthew that the German commander was ready. Seeing that there was nothing to lose, Matthew asked Bower to switch over his headset to the radio and monitor. When Bower passed on that his mike was hot, Matthew keyed the radio. "This is Major General Matthew. Over."

Ready and waiting, the German commander responded. "This is Colonel Fritz Junger, commander, 27th Parachute Brigade. The pathfinder detachment of my brigade has prepared drop zones for your division. We are ready to assist the drop of your division and will not resist. I repeat. We are ready to assist the drop of your division and will not resist. Acknowledge, please."

Looking up at the jump master with a dumbfounded look, Matthew was about to ask him if he had heard right but remembered that the jump master couldn't hear. Instead he keyed the radio again. "Eddie, did you hear the same thing I heard?"

"That's a roger. It seems the German commander has gone over and wants to help us."

Since Matthew's conversation was still going out over the radio, as he knew, the German commander heard his conversation with Bower. "I have, after conversations with the Chief of the German General Staff, General Otto Lange, ordered my soldiers to stand down and avoid contact with the soldiers of your command. I have declared, in cooperation with the civil authorities, Bremerhaven as an open city. You may jump if you desire or land at the military airfield. If you decide to drop, my operations officer is ready to turn on beacons to guide your aircraft in. All drop zones are marked using standard NATO markings and have smoke pots ready to be lit for wind direction and identification. Over."

Still unsure what to make of this, Matthew looked about at his men and pondered the most difficult question of his life. To trust this German, a man whom he was until seconds ago prepared to fight, could result in the failure of his mission and the loss of not only his division but the Tenth Corps. On the other hand, Matthew realized that if the German commander really had gone over, so to speak, to the American side, then a peaceful drop, assisted by the German Army, would mean a great deal when it came time to end this conflict. Matthew, as had all commanders, had been alerted that German commanders were starting to break with Berlin and that they were to take advantage of these defections whenever and wherever possible. "Ben, this is Eddie. Drop zone in six minutes. Right now we're committed to a jump. To make radical changes in direction would be difficult, not to mention potentially hazardous. What are we doing?"

With one more look at the upturned face of a young paratrooper seated across from him, Matthew decided. "Colonel Junger, have your operations turn on the beacons. We will drop using your drop zones. Please meet me on the ground as soon as possible. I will be the first man coming out of the lead aircraft. Over."

"I acknowledge that you will be dropping at our designated drop zones. Please have your lead pilot switch to frequency 27.05 for meteorological update and frequencies of guidance beacons. General Lange and I will meet you on the ground. Over."

"This is Matthew. I'll be on the ground in less than six minutes. Out."

Finished, Matthew took off the jump master's headset, handed it back to the jump master, and began to put his helmet back on. Ready, he looked up to the master sergeant who had as many years and jumps as he and shouted, "Okay, Sergeant, it's all yours now. Let's hit the silk."

On the ground, Colonel Fritz Junger, Major General Horst Mondorf, and General Otto Lange turned their faces up to the pale blue early-morning sky as the first olive drab parachutes of the 17th Airborne Division began to blossom over the flat, muddy German countryside. For a moment Junger looked around at his men standing idly about the drop zone, rifles harmlessly slung over their shoulders with their muzzles pointed down. He then looked at the two generals. "I am sure, General Lange, that you understand that we might be branded traitors."

Lange, without turning his face away from the spectacle of a mass airborne drop, sighed. "When von Clausewitz refused to submit to French rule and went over to fight with the Russians against Napoleon, the Prussian King called him a traitor. When the Saxon Corps, with drums beating and flags flying, marched across the fields of Leipzig in 1813, leaving the French and joining the Allies, the French, who had occupied Germany for years, called them traitors. When Count Von Stauffenberg planted the bomb on July 20th, 1944, in an attempt to assassinate Adolf Hitler, the Nazis called him a traitor. If I am allowed to join the ranks of men such as they, who put the best interests of Germany over their own, then I will lift my head with pride every time I am called a traitor."

Junger, still unsure, was about to say something more when he noticed that there was no sign of stress or strain on either Lange's face or Mondorf's. They simply stood there watching the American invaders slowly drift down to earth under their huge parachutes as if this were a peacetime NATO maneuver. These generals, Junger realized, were committed. They had made up their minds and were convinced that what they were doing was right. If that was so and they were right, Junger thought, how can I do otherwise. They were the voice and conscience of the German Army. It was, after all, his sworn duty to follow them. Satisfied, Junger turned to his operations officer standing next to the radio van and ordered him to start looking for the American airborne general after the first wave was on the ground and before the second wave began to exit their aircraft.

The major, untroubled by concerns of right and wrong, since there were so many senior commanders present to do that for him, carried out his orders as directed.

Like dozens of others separated from units that had ceased to exist or had moved north long ago, Hilary Cole was alone, frightened, hungry, cold, and lost. Fear and a sense of alienation dominated Cole's reactions. And the manner in which she dealt with her separation could only be termed reaction, for she had no clear idea of where she was, what was happening, or what to do. In fact, it could be said that Cole, like other ragtag survivors of the Battle of Central Germany, no longer was responsible for her actions. Nothing in all her training or even in her wildest dreams had prepared her for being so lost, so isolated, so miserable. She was in every sense hanging on to the lower rung of Maslow's ladder by her fingertips.

In a dreamlike state Cole wandered about without purpose, without direction. After days of being bombarded with horror after horror, that was the only state in which her mind could function. Even as she walked from tree to tree in the pale light of a new day, images of the dead and dying drifted before her eyes. And it didn't matter whether she was awake or asleep. The images came as they saw fit, confusing her efforts to deal with reality and causing her to swing from the depths of depression to an animated state of terror when she would start running in whichever direction she happened to be facing at the moment. Though she, like other members of her unit, had received rudimentary training in fieldcrafts and survival on the battlefield, no one and nothing had ever prepared her for the carnival of death that she had so recently been a player in.

In those brief moments when Cole was able to compose herself and think clearly, she was able to piece together some of what was happening. That she was alone, lost, and hungry was clear. All she had was the parka she had taken with her from the truck. She had no water, no food, no emergency medical kit, nothing. Even worse, she had no idea where she was and what was happening. There were only a few things that Cole did know. After watching the annihilation of her field hospital by German tanks, she was convinced that the Germans would kill her. So she never went back, even after the sounds of battle had faded. Nor did she dare approach any place where there might be Germans. They were the enemy in every sense of the word.

So Hilary Cole had spent the entire day after the destruction of her unit wandering about the woods aimlessly in the vain hope that she would somehow find another American unit. She didn't. Most units, once the word was out that there was a rogue unit roaming throughout that area, avoided it. That left Cole to spend another night alone in woods that were beginning to take on the appearance of a prison. With nothing but her parka to keep her warm, Cole threw herself on the ground and, between the shivers and sobs, cried herself to sleep.

On that morning, when stray beams of the morning sun came dancing through the trees and lit upon Cole's face, it took her several minutes to understand where she was. When she finally realized that her situation that morning was no better than it had been the night before when exhaustion had compelled her to drop to the ground and sleep, Cole began to cry. There was no sense to this. Crying would do nothing to improve her situation. Crying offered no solution. But then nothing made sense anymore.

In the midst of her own despair she heard a voice. It wasn't a very strong voice, and it had a rather mournful quality to it. But it was a human voice. Though she couldn't be sure if it was real or her imagination, that voice was the only thing she had. Pulling herself up with the aid of the tree she had slept huddled up against, Cole looked about, trying to determine where the voice came from. At first, with her mind still clouded by sleep and despair, Cole was unable to determine from which direction the voice came. It was as if the trees and her mind were playing a cruel trick on her, mocking her.

Then, as if it had suddenly been conjured up out of thin air before her very eyes, Hilary Cole saw it. At a distance of only twenty, maybe thirty meters, was the wreckage of some kind of overturned vehicle, half hidden by the wild chorus of trees that had been both a prison and a safe haven to Cole. She realized that she had spent the entire night not more than a few simple steps away from another human being who was probably as lost as she was. That she could have, in the state of mind that she was in the previous night, walked right past the man and his vehicle didn't dawn on Cole. The only thing important to her at that moment was that there, within easy reach, was another human being, a human who needed help, something that Cole was trained to deal with.

With a few easy bounds, Cole began to make her way to the overturned vehicle. As she drew near, the wreckage began to take on the appearance of a humvee. It was then that Cole realized that she hadn't paused to determine if the voice had been German or American. No matter, she thought as she weaved between the tree trunks. It was another person, a real person who was alive, and that was all that mattered. Only when she came to within a few feet of the vehicle did she slow down and then stop. Trapped under the vehicle, a hardtop humvee with a machine-gun mount on top, the gunner who had been manning the machine gun when it overturned lay silent, crushed to death. The sight of the body, still pinned beneath the humvee, drew Cole near. The soldier, a young man who couldn't have been more than twenty, still wore his helmet and web gear. His hands clutching the rim of the hatch and the grimace on his face told Cole that he had not been killed outright. Rather, he had survived the crash and had in his death throes struggled to free himself.

Cole turned away from that image but found no relief when her eyes fell upon the corpse of another soldier. This one, several meters away from the humvee, was that of a woman, a mere girl from the looks of her. Slowly Cole approached her, following the bloodstained snow that led from the humvee to her. When Cole reached the female, she slowly knelt down, reaching out to touch the face that was stone cold to feel. The female soldier, whoever she had been, was dead. Slowly Cole turned the body over. As the corpse came to rest on its back, strands of long red hair were caught by a slight breeze that stirred through the woods. A few wisps of hair fell across the dead soldier's face, now frozen in a sleeplike serenity. Were it not for the ashen color, it would have appeared to a casual observer that the young female soldier had fallen asleep instead of bleeding to death in the snow. For a moment Cole allowed herself to reflect on this tragedy and wonder why a girl who looked like she should have been at a prom instead of a battlefield had been shot and had died like this.

"She lasted most of the afternoon before she died."

The words, spoken by an unseen observer, startled Cole, causing her to jump back away from the female body and begin to scramble in panic back into the woods. Only when the voice spoke again, a hasty plea, did Cole manage to slow down and look for its source. "No! Don't go. Please don't go."

When she finally managed to stop and look around, she saw where the voice came from. Another soldier, a black man in his early thirties, sat against a tree across a small paved forest trail that she hadn't noticed before. He wore no helmet. His web gear and field jacket were pulled open in front, exposing his uniform shirt and a massive dark stain that covered his entire abdomen. As she looked, Cole could see that the field dressing that rested on the abdomen had turned colors and now was the same color as everything else that the soldier's dried blood had touched.

While Cole was still staring, the black soldier spoke again. "She lasted most of the day yesterday. Was able to get out of the humvee and crawl some." He paused, gasping for air while holding back a sob that threatened to cut off his story. "But she couldn't make it over here. And I . . ." There was another pause, now more to hold back the tears and sobs that so much wanted to come out. "I just couldn't, just couldn't get to her. So she just laid there, talking to me for nearly an hour before she finally stopped talking and . . ." Now there was no more stopping the tears. They just came. ". . . And she died. Right there. Right in front of me. She died. And I didn't do a damned thing. Not a damned thing." The last comments were angry ones, angry words spoken through tears that flowed down the black soldier's face.

With one quick rush Cole ran up to the black soldier, knelt down, and began to wipe the tears away with her bare hand. "It's okay," she said automatically in the same tone, in the same manner, that she used to talk to patients as they were carried into triage. "It's going to be okay. Now please relax, just lean back and let me look." Without waiting for a response, Cole, with one hand on the soldier's face, reached down and carefully began to pull the blood-soaked field dressing away from his abdomen. There was some resistance as she started, because some of the dried blood held the field dressing to the blood-stained shirt and the wound itself. Slowly, gently, Cole managed to free it slightly, pulling it away so that she could see what was behind it.

Just as she succeeded in freeing the field dressing, the black soldier stiffened as sudden spasms of pain racked his body. Cole felt this but continued until she could see behind the field dressing. When she could, she knew why he had jumped. Even before she had moved the dressing a fraction of an inch, dark red blood slowly began to ooze around the dressing and run down across Cole's hand. Though she wanted to stop, Cole eased the dressing a little further away in an effort to see how bad the wound was. This, however, stopped as soon as she saw a section of intestine fall away from his abdomen and against the dressing.

Having seen all that she needed to, Cole carefully eased the dressing back into place. Though she tried to do so without causing the soldier any further pain, that was impossible. With the same effort that Cole put into being as gentle as possible, the soldier fought off wave after wave of pain and the urge to scream. When she had finished and the soldier had managed to compose himself, Cole looked at him, face-to-face. "I'm a nurse. And you're hurt real bad. I don't know what I can do, but I'll do what I can. Okay?"

Still not recovered fully from the pain and his efforts to keep from yelling out at the top of his lungs, he merely nodded. He couldn't even open his eyes, still tightly shut. "Okay, soldier. I'm going to go over to the humvee and see if I can find an aid kit. Okay?"

Placing the soldier's left hand over the dressing in an effort to keep pressure on it, Cole looked at him one more time. "I'll be right back. I'm going to go over to your vehicle and look for a first aid kit. Is that okay?" Again there was no comment. Just another nod. Without waiting, Cole stood up and looked at the soldier one more time. Taking off her parka, she carefully laid it over him, turned, and hurried back to the humvee. There she got down on her hands and knees and crawled through the open door that both the dead female and the black soldier must have escaped through. As she searched the humvee for an aid kit, Cole worked her way around the lifeless legs of the machine gunner and a varied knot of personal gear, equipment, ammo boxes, maps, and sundry other items that made her search difficult. But Cole prevailed, finding not one but two aid kits. Pleased, she backed out of the vehicle, ignoring the dead machine gunner, got onto the road, and stood up.

Just as she did, a new voice from down the road shouted, "HALT!" Spinning about, she saw less than fifty meters away a pair of German soldiers, one of whom held his rifle up to his shoulder and pointed at Cole. It was the enemy. They had returned. Taking a step back, Cole glanced over at the black soldier.

Seeing Cole's action, the soldier had managed to turn his head enough to see that she was in trouble. With every ounce of strength he had left, he pushed away Cole's parka, grabbed the dressing with his left hand again and pushed it as tight against his abdomen as he could. With his right hand he reached down to his side, grabbed the M-16 rifle that had been lying there, and laid it across his lap.

The German who had been in the lead had also seen Cole's reaction and, looking over to where she had turned her head, saw the wounded black soldier, now preparing to bring his rifle to bear. The German, seeing that he himself was in danger, swung the muzzle of his rifle away from Cole, took a quick aim at the black soldier, and fired a short three-round burst.

At that range, the German's volley found its mark. Cole watched in horror as the first round struck the black soldier's left shoulder. The second round, due to the climb of the German's rifle muzzle, hit the soldier in the head. With the muzzle still climbing as the third round left the barrel, the bullet hit the tree just above the soldier's head. But Cole didn't see that. After watching his head jerk after being hit by the second round, his lifeless eyes rolling back into his head, Cole dropped the two aid kits she held, turned, and fled back into the woods followed by random shots from both Germans that missed her but kept her going.

When she finally stopped running, Cole found herself alone again, lost in the woods and more frightened than ever. What shreds of rationality she had managed to hold to until that morning were now gone. Dripping with sweat from her exertions but with no parka to protect her from the chilling winds that began to sweep through the woods, Cole slowly began to wander about without any thought, without any purpose. Only total physical exhaustion stopped her. At the end of her strength, Cole simply dropped onto the ground, curled up into the fetal position, and went to sleep.

It wouldn't be until the spring, when the forests shone in a wild blaze of lush greens and vibrant colors and the last of the melting snows had long disappeared, that Hilary Cole's body would be found.

"The chances of pulling this off, Madam President, are almost non-existent. There's just no way in hell I can support you in this."

Peter Soares's reaction didn't surprise Abigail Wilson. For days, despite the fact that he was still her Secretary of State, Soares had been looking for a way to distance himself from Wilson's administration. That he was using her recent decisions as a pretext for leaving it was both logical and, after his recent lack of support for her, a relief. "Do you, Mr. Secretary, see any reasonable alternatives?"

Like a slap in the face, Wilson's response caused Soares to recoil. The expression on his face changed in an instant from one of anger to a blank, almost embarrassed look.

Without asking for an explanation or making even the slightest effort to pursue the subject with him, Wilson looked down at some papers before her. There was, as she began to speak, the slightest hint of satisfaction on her face. "I find it strange, Mr. Secretary, that the same man who less than a month ago came into this very room and campaigned vigorously for this administration to invade a sovereign nation in pursuit of a more ambitious objective should, in the throes of an international crisis, back away from an operation which is aimed at doing nothing more than saving the lives of our fellow countrymen. This just doesn't make sense to me."

Soares resented having Wilson turn on him like this. He had watched her treat other men of power as if they were children, embarrassing them and making them so angry that they reacted in a manner that made them look like fools. In the past he had enjoyed watching his political enemies squirm under Wilson's subtle and manipulative attacks. He had on many occasions engineered such scenes during Wilson's climb to power. Now that he had become the target of just such a setup, Soares couldn't deal with it. "Madam President, I will let the American voters be *my* judge."

That Soares at a time like this should put this issue into political terms was to her distasteful. How could someone, she wondered, even think about elections and politics when the lives of Americans and the role of the United States as the leader of the free world hung in the balance? There were times, Wilson believed, when leadership, true leadership, demanded that hard decisions be made, political consequences be damned. Leaning forward with her arms resting on the table and her hands joined before her, Wilson responded with a voice that was clear and confident. "I, Peter, will trust to God to be my judge."

From the end of the table, Ed Lewis, who had been watching this outbreak building up for several minutes, finally added his own fuel to the flames that Soares was fanning. "You do understand, Mr. Secretary, that both the British and the French, not to mention the rest of NATO, agreed to support our expanded operations in Germany only if we would go in and secure the nuclear weapons that we lost control of after your failed adventure. Though we would have preferred to wait until the Tenth Corps had made it to the coast, it was decided that—"

With fire in his eyes, Soares leaned across the table and turned to face Lewis. "Who in the hell do you think you are, you little bastard, to come in here with these half-assed schemes and act as if you were the Secretary of State?"

Unable to resist the opportunity to take a slap at Soares, Lewis leaned back in his chair and smiled. "Well, it seemed to me, Mr. Secretary, that someone needed to act like the Secretary of State."

With that, Soares's face flushed with rage. Before Wilson could say anything, he was on his feet and shaking his fist at Lewis. "You bastard! You little slimy bastard!"

Wilson, upset by Soares's reaction, slammed the flat of her hand down on the table. "MR. SECRETARY! I will not have this meeting turned into a locker-room brawl. Now sit down and let's get on with this. There is much to do."

Eyes still wild, Soares turned on Wilson. "If there's more to be done here, you'll do it without me. My resignation will be on your desk within the hour."

With the measured control that had seen her through tough elections and had made her an effective governor, Wilson pushed her anger aside. Without any hint of disappointment or regret, she looked up at Soares. "I am sincerely sorry that you find it necessary to leave this administration *at this time*." Her emphasis was lost on Soares. Instead, he stood, growing madder by the minute as this woman sat there barely concealing a smile, talking to him in this manner. Still he let her finish. "I cannot tell you how much your wise counsel and support in the past have meant to me. For that I thank you. I do, however, understand your position on this matter and accept your resignation." Then, as if the whole incident had never happened and Soares was no longer in the room, Wilson turned to the Chairman of the Joint Chiefs of Staff. "Now, General, you were saying that General Malin has accepted Operation En Passant as reasonable and is already taking steps to prepare his corps for their role?"

Without so much as a second glance at Soares, the Chairman responded to Wilson. "Yes, Madam President, he has. I was on the phone to him just before we adjourned and . . ."

While the general spoke and everyone at the table listened, Soares realized that somehow, somewhere, he had lost control. He had suddenly fallen from being the power behind the throne to becoming an object of scorn. As the conversation went from one member of the Security Council to another, Soares's heart sank. He had for the moment lost. Now all that remained was to play out this hand, sit back, and watch what happened, hoping that somewhere along the line Wilson would stumble and leave him free of stain to pick up the party's political leadership and in a few years nomination for President. Without another word and with no one except Ed Lewis paying any attention to him, Soares left the room.

There was a light knock on the door, followed by the appearance of his aide's head. "General Malin, General Prentice has returned, sir."

Malin, who had been mechanically reading a stack of messages and requests for information with no great enthusiasm, looked up. "Great. Tell him I would like to see him as soon as possible, if not sooner." Then he added, "And tell the chief I need to see him after I finish with General Prentice."

Knowing that the first thing the corps chief of staff would ask was if the aide knew why Malin wanted to see him, the aide asked. "Sir, any particular subject you want to discuss with the chief?"

With a sweep of his hand across the scattered messages and reports sitting on his desk, Malin grunted. "Yeah. I want him to do something about all this bullshit the Pentagon dumped on us after we reopened our channels with them. Half of this stuff is pure crap that has no relevance to what we're doing, and I have no intention of providing a response."

The aide, who had organized the general's incoming correspondence, knew exactly what Malin was talking about. Though "officially" the Tenth Corps had severed communications with the National Command Authority when Malin had declared himself a renegade and begun his march north through Germany, selected channels had been maintained. In this manner, intelligence from the Defense Intelligence Agency freely flowed into the Tenth Corps and had given Malin information he needed that his own corps couldn't gather. Since this intelligence was sent out over a network that the Tenth Corps, like all the other major American commands scattered across the world, had access to, there was no compromise of Wilson's administration. The only direct two-way communication was between Malin himself and the Chairman of the Joint Chiefs of Staff, and was limited to a single phone conversation made each evening after Malin had received his last formal update for the day. This timing allowed the Chairman of the Joint Chiefs to report to the President in the late afternoon every day. The number of people who were involved in this chain was held to the bare minimum. Though no one had any doubt that the Wilson-Lewis-Malin conspiracy would eventually come to light, the longer they maintained the renegade corps commander story, the better, especially when dealing with other nations.

The commencement of hostilities, the refusal of the German Chancellor to open reasonable negotiations with Wilson, and the internal German conflict, with the Parliament demanding that Ruff accept a UN-mediated armistice and his refusal to do so, had altered the international political landscape. Careful manipulation of the stories fed to the media and well-worded press releases, not to mention round-the-clock discussions with members of NATO, were slowly shifting popular and official thinking. Malin, rather than being an insane and uncontrolled maverick was now being viewed by many as a hero, a man with the foresight and courage to stand up against an aggressive and resurgent German leader bent on altering the political, military, and nuclear balance in Europe. This, coupled with Wilson's pledge to the American public that she would not sit idle while the Germans destroyed the Tenth Corps, allowed her to broaden the conflict with the consent of the American public and all major NATO allies.

Hence, the commitment of the 17th Airborne to secure Bremerhaven, round-the-clock air cover from bases in Great Britain, and the dispatching of a Marine expeditionary force to the Baltic to threaten the German coast became possible. Along with these operations came the opening of all communications nets and channels, followed by a virtual avalanche of messages, requests for information, directives, and helpful advice from Pentagon staff officers who were far removed from the trauma of the battlefield. Tasked with updating their own charts and briefings, well-meaning Pentagon staff officers immediately inundated the Tenth Corps staff with message after message requesting information that the Tenth Corps staff had no need to accumulate or track. The Tenth Corps staff, which had been quite happy to operate as an independent entity, free from the curse of modern communications that allowed higher headquarters to talk to practically anyone, soon found itself in danger of being paralyzed by these requests.

All these requests came on top of the need to deal with the current battle, the drafting of new plans that would incorporate other American units coming into the theater, and the necessity of moving every twelve to twenty-four hours. When faced with the imperatives of dealing with the current battle and preparing for the next, the staff of the Tenth Corps, almost to a man, ignored the requests for information and the advice from Washington. When this happened, the well-meaning Washington staff officer informed his commander, who had tasked him to get the information, that the Tenth Corps was not cooperating. The higher-ranking officer in Washington in turn sent a message to a higher-ranking staff officer on the Tenth Corps staff repeating the request. The higher-ranking officer in Germany, with no more time to deal with outside requests than his subordinate, did as his subordinate had done; he ignored the request. Back in Washington this started a whole new chain of calls, message generation, etc., until finally almost all requests for information were being addressed to General Malin himself. It was a system gone berserk, and Malin intended to stop it.

He had to, for important orders and information were being crowded off the communications channels by mindless correspondence. Operation En Passant, a directive signed by the Chairman of the Joint Chiefs of Staff himself, had been lost in the flood of lesser messages. It wasn't until the Chairman called Malin and asked for Malin's opinion on the operation that Malin, who had still not seen the directive and was therefore caught off guard, began to appreciate the seriousness of the communications glut. Even Malin's chief of operations, Brigadier General Jerry Prentice, was unaware of Operation En Passant. A quick search found that the message was still waiting patiently in an electronic computer queue in Washington for its turn to be bounced off a satellite and down to the Tenth Corps.

Unable to apply the normal planning procedures, Malin, Prentice, and selected staff officers came together, quickly worked out their end of Operation En Passant, and then scattered throughout the corps area to personally issue the necessary orders to units that would play. Prentice, the senior officer involved, had himself gone to the most important Tenth Corps participant, Company A, 1st Ranger Battalion, 77th Infantry.

Without knocking, Jerry Prentice strolled into Malin's office and took a chair next to Malin's desk. "I almost didn't find them."

Big Al, looking for any reason to stop reading the drivel that overwhelmed his desk, smiled and eased back in his seat. "Map reading a little rusty, Jerry?"

Prentice shook his head. "No, the grids were right on. Couldn't have been any better. The problem was that they were too well hidden." Knowing that his commander appreciated a good story every now and then to help break the stress and strain of command, Prentice leaned back in his seat, accepted a cup of coffee from Malin's aide who had suddenly appeared as if by magic, and related to him his problems and observations. "The grid for Ilvanich's assembly area turned out to be in the center of a large abandoned warehouse complex just outside of town here. My driver and I came to the most obvious entrance but found it was blocked by a large disabled truck. So we went around the corner and found another entrance. It too was blocked. Doubling back, we went around the third side of the complex and, guess what?"

"It was blocked."

Prentice, seeing Big Al was enjoying hearing about Prentice's trials and tribulations, slapped his knee with one hand. "That's right. How'd you know? Anyway, we stopped and looked at the map and the warehouse complex. Now the fourth side of the warehouse butted right up against a wooded area that showed no access to any main road or the rail lines. That's why I didn't try that side. But seeing no way in from any of the roads, I decided, what the hell. We parked the humvee and I walked along the fence of the—"

"You walked? One of my staff officers got out? I don't believe this!"

He was definitely enjoying this, Prentice thought. This was the first time in almost a week that Big Al had actually laughed. So Prentice went on with his story. "Yes, sir. I walked. Read about that once. Seems the Army used to do that all the time. Anyhow, I started walking along the fence, and I found a section that looked like it had been cut, then wired back. Turning to the woods, I couldn't see any tire marks, but I could see a forest trail several meters inside the tree line. Going back to the fence, I shook the chainlink and tried to force my way in. I was about to succeed when I heard the bolt of a machine gun slide back, followed by a low, solemn 'Halt, who goes there?' "

"So what did ya do?"

"I did, sir, what any self-respecting general officer would do. I froze in place. Don't forget, these were rangers I was dealing with. After a minute or so, when the ranger had finished having his fun watching a general officer stand perfectly still while trying to keep from shitting his pants, a sergeant wearing an American Army parka, German Army field pants, and boots from God knows where came up to the fence and asked me for the password."

"Don't tell me, don't tell me, you forgot the password."

Prentice shook his head. "Sir, I never knew the password. That's my driver's job. Anyway, I'm standing there, hands on the fence, feet spread apart, waiting for the sergeant to do something while his sentinel, hidden God knows where, trains a loaded gun on me, when Ilvanich comes up. Now he's wearing a Russian Army field cap, a German Army parka, American camouflage trousers, fur-lined boots, and is carrying a shotgun that he got from God knows where in the crook of his arm. He comes up to me, stands face-to-face, and asks, in perfect German, *'Was wollen Sie?'* "

By now, Big Al had a grin that ran from ear to ear. "I would have loved to be there. It does my heart good to see a general reminded every now and then that they too are human."

"Well, if you'd been there, I have no doubt that you'd have been hanging on to the fence next to me. I finally convinced Ilvanich that I was the real thing, after taking out my wallet, laying it on the ground, stepping back ten meters, which by the way put me into the woods, and waiting there till they checked my wallet for ID."

"Well, Jerry, I would just like to say I'm glad there's still someone else besides me in this corps that knows how to handle general officers."

"Well," Prentice continued, "they finally let me in, escorted me to this warehouse where they're set up, and then offered me a breakfast of fresh bread, hot wurst, and cold beer, compliments of the German Army. You know, those guys eat better than we do. Anyhow, while I was there I didn't see a single soldier dressed the same way or any

American Army vehicles. And there was a detail painting new bumper markings on their trucks, getting ready to deal with the 1st Panzer Division."

"The morale of the soldiers, no doubt, was excellent."

Prentice nodded. "They were alert, appeared to be well rested, clean, and animated. Every weapon I saw was clean, properly lubricated, and handled with respect. Except for the ungodly uniform combinations, they were the best-looking troops I've seen in this corps in the past two weeks."

Malin got serious now. "Doesn't surprise me in the least. They're a good unit and they've got a great record. They have been given some of the dirtiest jobs and pulled every one off brilliantly. And when we've left them on their own, they've gone out and pulled off some really incredible stunts, every one of which has been of immense material benefit to us and served to shake up the Germans. And best of all, they've done it without the loss of a single man."

The smile on Prentice's face disappeared after Malin's last comment. Seeing the change in mood, Big Al also dropped his smile, looking down at the edge of his desk instead. Both men knew that the mission they had just assigned to Ilvanich and the rangers of Company A would be even under ideal circumstances a bloodbath. Prentice finally broke the silence. "After Ilvanich had assembled his senior leaders, I laid out the maps of the weapons storage site, the surrounding area, and the operations graphics. As I briefed them on the mission, no one said a word. When I finished, everyone, to a man, looked at Ilvanich and he looked at them. Finally he looked over to me and said, 'It shall be done.' There were no questions, no complaints, no sign of fears or doubts, no false heroics. Just Ilvanich's simple statement."

Leaning back in his seat as far as it would go, Malin folded his hands over his stomach and mused. "I wonder if those brilliant minds back in Washington, the ones who dream this stuff up, would issue the orders they do if they had to deliver them to the men expected to carry them out, face-to-face, like you did."

"Of course they would, sir. As long as there are young men in this world willing to accept orders from old men like you and me, people like those in Washington will continue to generate them and issue them."

Malin nodded his head but said nothing. Instead he took another minute to reflect on what they had just asked Company A, 1st Ranger Battalion, to do before pushing all thoughts of that operation to one side of his mind to make room for the next issue he needed to talk to Prentice about.

After sequestering himself in a corner office for the better part of an hour, Ilvanich called in Fitzhugh, both platoon leaders, their platoon sergeants, and all squad leaders. Taped up on the walls of the office were the maps, photographs, diagrams, and operational graphics of the nuclear weapons storage site west of Potsdam that this group of men were to attack and seize. Since most of the assembled leaders had heard Prentice's order to Ilvanich firsthand, Ilvanich skipped the preliminaries. Using a map spread out on the table set in the middle of the room he had used in developing his own plan, Ilvanich briefed his command. "This operation is rather similar to the one we executed in the Ukraine. We break in, secure the weapons, and prepare a landing zone for follow-on forces. Those forces are heliborne Marines coming in from the naval squadron sitting in the Baltic. When they arrive, we assist them in securing the area while the weapons are removed, and then we are evacuated." Ilvanich paused, looking around the room at the company's leadership as he waited for them to accept this. They, like he, knew this was not the same.

After an appropriate pause, Ilvanich folded his arms across his chest and continued. "Unlike the Ukraine, we will be outnumbered. The unit guarding the site is the 2nd Battalion, 26th Parachute Brigade, one of the best units the Bundeswehr has. That battalion has light armored vehicles, heavy mortars, and will outnumber us in riflemen by a factor of six to one. Add to that the following. Surprise will be minimal, since the Germans expect us to try for the weapons. Support from the Navy, Marines, or Air Force will be nonexistent for the first twenty to thirty minutes because the planners in Washington do not want to betray the purpose of the mission by having helicopters headed for or near the target until we have secured the weapons. And best of all, the storage site itself, built by the Red Army in the 1950s, is surrounded in all directions by flat fields, with no place to hide, for a distance of two kilometers."

From across the table, Sergeant First Class Rasper murmured, "They'll see us coming forever."

Ilvanich looked up at him. "Exactly. So stealth will be impossible."

"Hence," Rasper added, "the brass-balls approach."

Throwing a pencil that he had been using as a pointer down onto the table, Ilvanich sighed. "Yes, that's right. We go in there using the German convoy technique. Though the Germans guarding the site will suspect that we are not reinforcements, they will not know our intentions for sure. We go as far as we can go playing Germans, and then, when they move to stop us, we shoot our way forward."

Again there was silence. Finally Second Lieutenant Fitzhugh asked the question that everyone else had been pondering. "Major, do they really expect us to make it all the way to the weapons and secure them, and a landing zone?"

Having spent the last weeks with the American rangers as their leader and in word and deed becoming one of them, Ilvanich looked around the room at each man's face. Letting his arms fall to his sides, Ilvanich shook his head. "No, I truly don't think so. Though the general didn't say so in so many words, the Marines don't expect to find many of us still standing when they arrive."

The anger in Rasper's voice was unmistakable. "Then why in the hell are they throwing us away? Isn't that what they're doing, sir? Throwing us away?"

Leaning forward and resting the knuckles of his hands on the table, Ilvanich admonished Rasper. "We are not being thrown away. This is a desperate plan made necessary by a desperate situation. It is a political necessity. To secure the support of the other nations in Europe for the intervention of the 17th Airborne and the deployment of the Air Force from Britain, the American President pledged to stage a raid to secure the weapons immediately. For an operation against a target like this to succeed with minimal losses and a good chance of success, you need a great deal of time to gather intelligence, formulate your plan, rehearse that plan, and coordinate the efforts of all forces involved. When time does not permit, like now, you cut corners, go for what your planners call a quick and dirty solution by using whatever you have at hand, and hope for the best."

Easing off a bit, Ilvanich stood upright again and explained while the leaders of Company A listened in stone-cold silence. "The Germans are ready for an airborne assault. They are counting on that. Their heavy automatic weapons are placed to achieve maximum elevation and grazing fires across all likely landing zones within the storage site. Were the Marines to go in there with all these weapons in place, fully manned, even with a preliminary air strike, most would die before the first helicopter set down. Our sole purpose is to go in there and raise hell with the neat well-planned German defense. We are the first punch that will attempt to smash a hole into the defensive perimeter that the Marines will be able to exploit. Failing that, our goal will be to keep the German battalion in an uproar and off balance until the Marines arrive." Slowly Ilvanich began to walk about the room, placing his hand on the shoulder of each of the rangers assembled there as he went by. "That is why everyone who is a combat leader is here receiving the plan from me. When I go down, Lieutenant Fitzhugh will know what is expected and carry on. After he is gone, Sergeant Rasper will lead the company. Then Sergeant Johnson. Then the platoon sergeants. Then the squad leaders. And when they're gone, even when the last man in this room is down, I expect each and every ranger to carry on."

When Ilvanich stopped, his back was to the assembled group. Turning his head slightly, he looked over his shoulder. His voice was solemn now, almost hesitant. "We, the American general and I, do not endorse suicide missions. It is not part of the traditions of either of our countries. But, like he told me and I told you, desperate times call for desperate solutions. I therefore asked the general that I be allowed to leave behind any man who does not want to go. This will be a purely voluntary mission." Pivoting slowly on his heels, Ilvanich put his hands behind his back as he looked again at each of the rangers in the room. "Go back to your men and tell them what I have told you. Tell them what we will be doing and why. Then let the men decide, each one for himself. I place no time limits on their decision, no special conditions. If when we load the trucks tonight, they choose not to get in, then so be it. Is that understood?"

After all of them had nodded or mumbled a muted response, Ilvanich walked back up to the table and continued. "Now I expect each squad leader to bring his men up here and, using all of this information and photos, go over the plan with every man. I expect each and every ranger in the company to know where all of the heavy weapons are located and where the key points of the German defense are. Unless there are further questions, you are dismissed."

With that, the assembled rangers saluted and filed out of the room without another word, leaving Ilvanich alone to continue his study of the maps, photos, and graphics.

CHAPTER 19

23 JANUARY

Unable to sleep or sit, Abigail Wilson wandered about the room that served as her private study. Though she could have gone down and joined the others in the War Room buried beneath the house that had been home to some of the most important men in American history, Wilson knew that her presence there would only serve to heighten the nervous apprehension that always seemed to hang in that room like a cloud. Through years of practice Wilson had learned the fine art of hiding one's emotions and acting as those about you expected. Yet there were times when she simply could not stuff her emotions away like so much dirty laundry. She never made excuses for this, a trait that some of her male opponents in private referred to as a flaw. Instead she trusted her own instincts, for she knew there were times when it was wise to remove herself from public view and in private give free rein to whatever emotions swept over her.

Tonight her fears and doubts came forth like a spring storm. At first there was only a slight darkening on the distant horizon, so subtle that one hardly noticed it. Then came a gentle stirring of the wind, first that way, then this, as if Mother Nature herself was vacillating, unsure if she wanted to unleash her fury. But this lasted only a few minutes. With the measured pace of a great musical composition, the various elements began to make their presence felt. The clouds rolled in, casting their shadows across everything beneath them. The wind gave up its hesitancy and began to move across the face of the earth with purpose and force. Finally in the distance, like great kettledrums announcing a storm of war-horses, thunder warned all who heard that a great storm was coming. Finally, when all the elements were ready, wind, rain, darkness, and thunder, the storm unleashed its full fury and came crashing down.

In the beginning, during her first few years of public life, Wilson had discounted her feelings, telling close friends that they were nothing more than silly emotions that she needed to master. But as her political career blossomed and she grew in both importance and ability, Wilson also matured and found that she didn't need to deny herself or her emotions. For she found that, like the spring storm, an occasional venting of her fears or anger in private served to release her tensions and cleanse her soul in the same way that a spring storm unleashes the pent-up fury of the heavens and makes way for the cool, fresh calmness that inevitably follows.

So Wilson chose not to sit in the War Room with key members of her staff like mourners attending a wake. Instead she stayed in her private apartments and allowed her emotions and thoughts free rein for a while. In a few hours she would need to be in complete control of herself, for it would be in the aftermath of the operation to take back the nuclear weapons from the Germans, an operation that was about to commence several thousand miles away, while the wounded were still being tended to and the dead counted, that her struggle would begin.

In her wanderings, Wilson came to the window and stopped. Looking out, she could see the lights of the city that lit the streets and the many imposing statues and monuments that made the city of Washington an open-air museum. Even at this hour there was a fair amount of traffic, something that never ceased to amaze her. She still didn't understand cities, even after living in Denver for years and now Washington. They were alien places with their own rules, their own codes of ethics, their own ways of life.

In many ways, Wilson thought, her inability to understand the city was like her ignorance of the innermost psychology that drove the military machine that she now commanded. While the organizational charts and mission statements of each of the services and units were simple to understand and their use easily explained, she lacked a real appreciation of what it meant to be a soldier or an airman or a sailor. Nothing in all her years of college, life as a mother, member of Colorado's leading law firm, and governor of that state gave her any idea of what motivated young men and women to place themselves with

such casualness into harm's way in defense of a vague idea, a principle. How shallow such words as duty, honor, country, must seem
when facing death. Or were they shallow? Was there real meaning in
those words that only a person faced with his or her own mortality
could really understand and appreciate?

Leaning her head against the window, Wilson felt the coldness of
the glass against her warm forehead. When she had been a young girl
in Colorado and her head seemed so full of troubled thoughts that it
appeared that it must burst, she would go over to the window and
place her head against the pane of glass. Somehow, in the mysterious
ways that elude explanation or logic, the image of the soft, quiet
landscape and the feeling of the cold glass against her brow served to
calm her.

There was nothing more to do. She had done what she had felt was
right. Now it was up to others to do what was necessary, leaving her
to deal with her emotions alone and prepare for the consequences of
her decisions.

With every turn of his staff car's tires, he rolled closer to the front gate
of the storage site. Seated in the front passenger seat clutching the
assault rifle that lay across his lap, Ilvanich could feel his heart beat
louder, more violently. Though he tried not to, his eyes remained
fixed on the muzzle of a machine gun that protruded from the aperture of a concrete bunker that sat next to the front gate. Ilvanich knew
that behind that gun there was a young German soldier, a paratrooper,
with his finger wrapped around the trigger and his gaze fixed along the
sights of the machine gun that was locked on his vehicle. In silence,
while Sergeant George Couvelha seated to his left drove them forward
at a steady, unrelenting pace, Ilvanich waited for the machine gun to
fire. At this range there was little doubt that both he and Couvelha
would perish in the first volley. Yet there was nothing he could do. It
had to be this way. It was expected of him. He had known all of his life
that nothing less would be acceptable.

Still, sheer terror that tried to wrestle away Ilvanich's sanity
couldn't be denied. It was like the feeling of helplessness he got when
he sat in the front seat of a roller coaster. Slowly, with mechanical
precision, the roller coaster was cranked up the first incline. Ilvanich
hated roller coasters, hated them with a passion. To please a girl he

was with or a little nephew he was entertaining, however, he would always go, as was expected of him. There would be when the lead car reached the top nothing but sheer terror, panic that Ilvanich was expected to master because he was, in the eyes of those with him, the strong one. Today, as on those occasions, there was no other place he could be. He was where he was expected to be and nothing and no one could change that. It was his fate, and he accepted it in silence.

At the command post that served as the headquarters for the 2nd Battalion, 26th Parachute Brigade, Lieutenant Colonel Jakob Radek greeted the news that there was a convoy of trucks carrying troops approaching the front gate with a great sigh of relief. His pleas to Colonel Haas, his brigade commander, had been heard. It had been a stupid decision to strip away one of his companies and send it to Berlin for riot control just when the Americans were growing closer and the danger of a strike against the storage sites was at its greatest. Radek knew it. And Haas knew it.

In stormy conversations, both when he had received the order early the night before and again not more than three hours ago, Radek had told Haas exactly what he thought of the decision, not to mention the fools in Berlin who had placed such a demand on him. Though he knew he had been wrong to do so, it was, he felt, necessary to make his protest in the strongest possible terms. That Haas, or one of the idiots in Berlin, had finally come to his senses and realized what he had done didn't surprise Radek. Without further thought, he ordered the sergeant of the guard at the gate to have the company commander of the returning company report immediately to his office. Radek was anxious to get his third company back into the defensive positions inside the inner secure area where the nuclear weapons were stored. Hanging up the phone, he finally felt that he could breathe easy. Given the choice of having a strong force in the inner secure area at the expense of weakening his outer perimeter, Radek had opted for the strong outer perimeter. Since it was his mission, after all, to keep the Americans away from the nuclear weapons, it made perfect sense to Radek that the further away from the inner secure area he could keep the Americans the better. Besides, he reasoned, if the outer perimeter broke at some point, he could always withdraw units on the outer perimeter that were not under pressure into the inner secure area. That this gamble in deployment of his forces would never be put to the test was for Radek a great relief.

At the gate the sergeant of the guard looked at the receiver of the telephone, then at the corporal who stood across from him. Radek's last instructions, in light of the standing orders that no one under any circumstances was to be allowed in, did not make any sense at all. Of course, pulling one of the companies away from the battalion and sending it to Berlin for riot duty didn't make sense either. Carefully replacing the receiver, the sergeant looked at the convoy, now less than fifty meters away, and then back to the corporal. He shook his head before he gave an upward motion of his arm, the signal to his men to remove the barriers at the gate and let the convoy through.

At this range, Ilvanich knew that the machine gunner couldn't miss. There would be no chance to duck, no opportunity to strike back. He would fall with the first burst. It came as a shock when Couvelha shouted, "They're opening the gate for us, Major. The fools are going to let us in!"

Tearing his eyes away from the sinister black muzzle of the machine gun, Ilvanich looked over to the gate and saw a German corporal waving them through a now opened gate. For the briefest of moments Ilvanich was flabbergasted. What, he wondered, was going on? But quickly he recovered from his surprise and ordered Couvelha to continue forward. "They must be expecting someone and they think we are them. Go, go. Keep going but do not speed up."

Just as Ilvanich's vehicle pulled even with the front gate, Colonel Johann Haas's staff car came out of the wood line and into the open stretch of road that led to the storage site. He saw the convoy of trucks entering the storage site and wondered what was going on. Already angered by the tone of his last conversation with Radek, Haas began to slip into an absolute rage.

Under ordinary circumstances, Haas was a reasonable man. But these, as people kept reminding him, were not ordinary circumstances. Besides, he was not used to having his subordinates argue with him over such important issues. While Haas was always willing to listen to the thoughts and ideas of his subordinates, when he gave a final order he expected discussion to stop and for the order to be carried out. Radek's continued badgering and the tone of his conversations had infuriated Haas, who was already angered over his dealings with his own superiors. After Radek's second phone call of the morning, Haas wanted to run from his office, jump into his vehicle, and drive immediately to the weapons storage site and relieve Radek on the spot. But there were other, more pressing matters that needed to be tended to. The battalion he had sent to Berlin for riot duty had turned out to be woefully inadequate for the task. Though he didn't like the idea, he had ordered each of his other two battalions guarding the two nuclear weapons sites near Potsdam to send one of their companies to Berlin to augment the battalion already there.

This problem was only one that the parachute colonel had to deal with. Besides his own units, he discovered two battalions from the 3rd Panzer Division in Berlin. They had come into the city in the middle of the night after the President of the Parliament had made a personal appeal to the commander of the 3rd Panzer. By dawn Haas had learned that the President of the Parliament, fearing that Ruff had brought Haas's battalion into Berlin to intimidate them, felt the need to counter Haas's battalion with units loyal to the Parliament. So, although he had wanted to deal with Radek, Haas had felt that it was more important to meet with the commander of the 3rd Panzer's units in Berlin and ensure that they established a clear understanding of where each stood on the matter of loyalty to the government. The last thing Haas wanted to do was to have various units of the Bundeswehr start tearing away at each other because of misunderstandings.

Yet now, seeing the lead vehicle of the convoy start to roll through the front gate of the storage site, Haas regretted his earlier decision. Something was happening here, and he didn't like the looks of it. Haas began shouting to his driver and making gestures. "Go around. Go around this convoy and head for the front gate, now!"

Caught off guard by his commander's sudden shouts, the driver did exactly as he was told. Jerking the wheel to the left, he stepped on the accelerator and began to race down the road in the left lane so that he could pass the trucks as the lead vehicles of the convoy began to roll into the storage site.

At the gate the guard corporal turned his attention away from the trucks passing him as he heard the gunning of an engine. Looking down the flat, straight road, he saw a staff car headed right toward him and gaining speed. Throwing up his right arm and waving violently, he yelled halt three times in quick succession. The driver of the staff car only drove faster. Realizing that he was in danger, the corporal began to run for the cover of the bunker, yelling to the paratroopers inside to open fire as he ran by.

The sudden order to halt, followed by the rattle of the machine gun behind them, caused Ilvanich to snap, "NOW! STEP ON IT."

Like Haas's driver, Couvelha complied without hesitation. The inner secure area was straight ahead, less than three hundred meters away. With luck they could cover that distance in a matter of seconds and have a real chance to grab the weapons. Couvelha ignored Ilvanich as Ilvanich kicked his door open, leveled his automatic rifle, and began to spray the bewildered Germans along the side of the road as they emerged from buildings.

Radek had just opened the door of the commandant's building when the shooting started. Stepping out onto the front step, he gasped in horror as he watched a staff car career madly past him. It was going as fast as it could while the passenger on the side opposite from where Radek stood fired wildly out of his open door. Radek was still standing there, bewildered and disbelieving, when the first truck of the convoy went by. In the rear of the truck, the canvas sides were rolled up, revealing the German soldiers inside crouching behind the thin sides of the truck's cargo bed as it came roaring past. Like the soldier in the staff car, they too were firing their rifles as they went. Though their aim was wild, the volume of fire they put out more than made up for it. Hit in the shoulder, and then the chest, Radek was thrown backwards through the open door of his office. There, bleeding and unable to get up or even call for help, he lay listening to the sound of trucks rushing by, punctuated by screams of pain, panic, shooting, and every now and then a random explosion.

Outside the site, Colonel Haas pulled himself out of his overturned staff car. His driver, crumpled up like a ball of rags behind the steering wheel, was dead. And from what he could tell, he had two broken legs. Once he was out on the paved road leading into the site, Haas looked toward the gate, still gaping open. Like Radek, he listened helplessly to the sounds of battle as they moved away from him and closer to the inner secure area.

Specialist Kevin Pape ignored the wind whipping in his face, made harsher by the speed of the truck he was riding in. Instead, he prepared to fire the machine gun that he had cared for and manned for many days but had never had the opprtunity to fire in anger. Leaning into the weapon, Pape tucked his chin up against the shoulder stock, took careful aim at a group of three Germans running for cover behind a bunker near the gate of the inner secure area, and opened fire. Seeing his first burst of seven to ten rounds fly over his targets, he stretched himself up slightly and fired again. This time he was on target, sending the middle soldier tumbling down and causing the man behind him to make a quick leap lest he trip over his fallen comrade. With a slight correction, Pape caught the German in midair.

Absorbed by his engagement, Pape did not notice that a machine gun in the bunker where his targets had been running was now firing on Ilvanich's staff car. It wasn't until that car, its driver hit, made a sudden turn to the right and went crashing into the barbed-wire fence that Pape realized what was happening . The driver of his truck, Private Ken Hillman, cut the wheel to the left to avoid crashing into the rear of Ilvanich's staff car. In doing so, he lost control of the truck and, like Ilvanich's staff car, the truck went crashing into the barbed-wire fence. Unlike Ilvanich's car, the heavier truck continued through the fence and into the anti-vehicle ditch beyond. The front wheels bit into the soft mud of the ditch and buried the front fenders.

Even before the truck stopped, Sergeant Rasper slapped Pape on the side of his leg. "OUT! OUT! EVERYONE OUT!"

Reaching forward, Pape pulled the pin that held his machine gun in the truck's ring mount, dropped inside, and yelled to the driver as he started to duck out the door on the left. "Don't forget the ammo. Grab the ammo boxes."

As Pape began to go out the door, Hillman yelled, "Got it," and leaped from his.

Rasper, in the middle, was right behind Pape as a stream of bullets smashed the truck's windshield. "Go, damn it. Get your ass out of here." Excited, Rasper gave Pape a shove.

Caught off balance, Pape and his machine gun went flying down, face-first, into the mud of the anti-vehicle ditch.

Pulling himself out of his vehicle, Ilvanich paused only long enough to satisfy himself that Sergeant Couvelha was beyond help. Then, with his automatic rifle in his right hand, he jumped up onto the hood of his staff car, placed his left hand on top of the pole that the barbed wire was strung on, and boosted himself up and over the wire fence. Like any well-trained paratrooper, he brought his feet and knees together while he was still in the air and prepared to roll as soon as he felt the shock of hitting the ground. The mud in the ditch, however, was softer than he had anticipated. He sank several inches into it and never rolled until he remembered to do so.

His timing was impeccable. Ilvanich's gymnastics caught the attention of the Germans manning the machine gun in the bunker at the entrance of the inner secure area. Finished with the truck for a moment, the machine gunner brought the muzzle of his weapon around to the left and fired a burst at Ilvanich. He had, however, disappeared into the anti-vehicle ditch. Cursing, the gunner slapped the side of his weapon. "Why in the hell did they dig a ditch like that right in front of the bunker's field of fire? The Russians must have had a death wish."

The sergeant behind him smacked him on the side of his helmet. "Shut up and go back to the truck. The enemy are deploying."

But by the time the machine gunner had managed to bring the gun back to the right, the last of the rangers that had been in the rear of Rasper's truck were in the ditch and rushing forward to the wall of the anti-vehicle ditch nearest to the inner secure area.

Throwing himself against that wall, Ilvanich paused for the first time since the shooting had started to assess the situation. Twenty meters to his left he watched for a second while Rasper deployed his men against the wall and, like him, stopped to catch his breath and sort things out. Behind him he could hear firing from the direction of the buildings they had gone through. Lieutenant Fitzhugh, no doubt, was deploying the rest of the ranger company and engaging the bulk of the German garrison. Though Ilvanich didn't know what had happened that had allowed them to get so far, he knew that if they didn't do something in the next minute or so, the Germans to their rear would be able to assemble their overwhelming numbers. They would then be free to wipe out Ilvanich and the rangers, now trapped between the inner secure area and the main compound.

Desperate measures for desperate times. Over and over Ilvanich repeated that to himself. Desperate measures for desperate times. When he was mentally ready, he yelled over to Rasper, "Sergeant! We must get out of this ditch and into the secure area before the Germans recover. I am going for the machine gun. Cover me."

Rasper didn't stop to think about what Ilvanich was saying or what it meant. He simply turned to his men and yelled, "Everyone, up and fire. Up and fire." While his men did so, Rasper yanked a smoke grenade from his web gear, pulled the pin, and threw it over to where Ilvanich would be coming from.

Swinging the heavy German machine gun up, over, and down onto the dirt parapet of the anti-vehicle ditch, Pape took the best possible aim he could and began to fire at the bunker. As his bullets began to splatter against the concrete around the aperture of the bunker, the German machine gunner brought his weapon to bear on Pape and returned fire, throwing clods of mud kicked up by near misses back into Pape's face.

When Ilvanich saw this, he took a deep breath, pulled himself up out of the ditch, brought his rifle up to his hip, and began to race for the bunker at a dead run. Inside the bunker, the German sergeant's attention was drawn back to Ilvanich. From behind his machine gunner he pointed his finger toward Ilvanich. "To the left. Get that bastard." Without letting up on the trigger, the German machine gunner brought the muzzle of his weapon around, cutting Ilvanich down just as he reached the halfway point.

For the briefest of moments there was a stunned silence as the rangers with Rasper watched Ilvanich go down and roll over twice before coming to rest on his back. After all that they had been through in the past few weeks with him, to see him cut down like that was a shock. But it only lasted a second. Rasper knew what Ilvanich had been after, and he knew what needed to be done. Taking a second smoke grenade, Rasper pulled the pin, threw it out to his front, and watched its clouds of yellow smoke build up. Ready, he yelled to his men again. "I'm going for the bunker. Cover me."

Again the rangers in the ditch popped up and began to fire at the bunker as fast as they could while Rasper this time scrambled up over the edge of the ditch and headed for the bunker. And as before, the German sergeant in the bunker, despite the building clouds of smoke, saw the danger and directed his machine gunner's attention to it. Without a sound, without a single moan, Rasper pitched forward and fell flat, sliding to a dead stop only meters from where Ilvanich lay.

The thud of Rasper's body and the strange noise of the air leaving his lungs while he died caught Ilvanich's attention. Though his mind was drifting in an almost dreamlike state and he didn't seem to have any control over a body that he hardly felt, Ilvanich managed to bring his head around until he was facing Rasper. It took several seconds for his eyes to focus. When they did, Ilvanich quickly understood what had happened. Rasper lay there with bulging eyes and his face half buried in mud that had been plowed up as his body had pitched forward and slid along the mud. He had, Ilvanich realized, followed his lead and had for his efforts been killed.

Suddenly understanding that they were going to fail, Ilvanich began to sob. He still didn't feel any real pain, but he knew he was hit bad. Nothing except his head responded to his efforts to move. This was no way for a well-trained Russian paratroop officer, a man proud of his skills and abilities, to die. Not at the head of a foolish attack that was doomed to failure. No, these men deserved better than this.

In what appeared to be a foolish attempt to mock him even further, Ilvanich watched as another man came up and out of the ditch in an effort to reach the German machine gun. They were, he thought, doing exactly as he had asked them to do. And they were dying, for the ranger that had sprung up grabbed his face and fell backwards before he even managed to get both feet out of the ditch. Unable to watch anymore, Ilvanich closed his eyes and prayed to any god that would listen to take him now, before he had to see one more man die.

The shock of seeing Private Ken Hillman's body being thrown back into the ditch right next to him broke Pape. There, not more than a meter away, his friend Ken Hillman lay on his back clutching his bloody face with both hands, screaming at the top of his lungs and kicking wildly with his feet. Everything, the sudden rush from the front gate to the inner secure area, the truck crashing into the ditch, watching Ilvanich, followed by Rasper, and now Hillman, cut down like this was too much for Pape. Without any conscious thought, Pape let go with the yell of a man who had lost control. Hoisting his machine gun up to his side, he bounded out of the ditch and began to rush forward toward the bunker.

Across the field from him, through the thinning clouds of yellow smoke, the German sergeant saw the new target pop up out of the ditch and start running at him. "God in heaven! Are these men mad? Who are they?" For a second he, the machine gunner, and the assistant machine gunner watched in utter amazement as another man in a German uniform, screaming at the top of his lungs, came lunging toward them, a machine gun at his hip and firing as he went. Recovering from this spectacle, the sergeant simply said, "Kill him. Now." Seeing no need to rush, the German machine gunner prepared to comply, taking careful aim. When he was ready, he braced himself and pulled the trigger.

It took only a fraction of a second to realize that although the bolt had gone forward, the machine gun had not fired. Behind him, the sergeant, who had not heard the bolt go forward, yelled, "Fire! Fire, damn it."

Pulling the trigger a second time, the gunner confirmed that the bolt had gone forward. "AMMO! MORE AMMO. HURRY!"

Caught off guard and totally absorbed by the nonstop rush of events, the assistant machine gunner looked over to the gunner with a dumb look on his face. He stood there for the briefest of seconds before he realized what the gunner was saying. "AMMO. I'M OUT OF AMMO! HURRY!"

The sergeant, seeing the confusion, didn't wait for the assistant gunner to respond. Instead, he bent down and grabbed for the first ammo box that he could reach. The machine gunner, pushing the assistant gunner out of the way, raised the cover of his weapon, pulled the bolt back, and reached for the fresh belt of ammunition just as Pape stuck the muzzle of his machine gun into the aperture of the bunker and let go with a long burst of fire.

From across the anti-vehicle ditch, Fitzhugh, leading the rest of the company, had watched in horror as Hillman had gone down and then Pape, like a man possessed, had risen and rushed for the bunker. When he saw Pape cover the distance from the ditch to the bunker and stick his machine gun into the opening, Fitzhugh yelled to the men following him, "Okay, rangers, let's go. All the way. We're going all the way."

Without breaking stride, the rangers with Fitzhugh poured into the ditch through the hole in the fence made by the truck, ran through the muddy bottom, and scrambled up over the other side. Those rangers who had been with Rasper and were still in the ditch joined Fitzhugh and his men in the mad dash for the inner secure area.

Once they were clear of the ditch, their momentum carried them forward, overcoming any resistance that remained and leaving the German battalion, back in the main compound of the storage area, thrashing about in an effort to assemble and reorganize. Fitzhugh, short of breath but still fired up, paused for only a moment as he passed Pape and slapped him on the shoulder. "That was great! You did great. Now let's go. Follow me."

Pape, however, was in a daze. Allowing the muzzle of the machine gun to drop to the ground, Pape fell back against the side of the bunker and looked across the open field to the ditch. The last of the smoke from the grenades was being carried away by the breeze. There, under a thin veil of yellow, he could see both Ilvanich and Rasper lying still. In the ditch, though he couldn't see him, was Hillman. That much he knew. What puzzled him, and it would puzzle him for the rest of his life, was how in the name of God he had gotten to where he was now standing. Neither the eyewitness accounts nor the citation that accompanied the Medal of Honor he was given would ever satisfy Pape. What he had done, and why, during the longest and most important fifteen seconds in his life would always be a mystery to him.

From where he lay, Ilvanich could hear the sounds of battle move on. That and the trampling of feet past him and Rasper, accompanied by Fitzhugh's shouts, told Ilvanich that somehow the tide of battle had swung back in their favor. With nothing left to do but wait, Ilvanich closed his eyes and tried to relax. As he drifted off to sleep, he thought that he could hear above the din of battle helicopter blades beating against the cold winter air. That would be nice. Yes, it would be very nice if the Marines came now. Perhaps then this would have been justified. Yes, that would be nice.

Outside the storage site, Colonel Haas sat on the side of the road propped up against the wreckage of his staff car. Looking up, he watched the first of the dark green helicopters with large black letters spelling U.S. Marines stenciled on their sides come swooping down overhead and into the storage site. When he saw no anti-aircraft fire directed at them from the storage site and the helicopters following taking no evasive maneuvers, Haas knew it was over. Chancellor Ruff's great adventure in making Germany a nuclear power was at an end. Haas wondered if that meant that Germany too would soon be coming to an end. Though he hoped in his heart that such a thing would not happen, the specter of such a grim future for the country he so loved and had served so long suddenly became real.

Then, as if struck on the head, Haas realized that Germany had again placed itself into the hands of an ambitious man. "Maybe," he said to himself out loud, "we should disappear. Perhaps the German people are too great to live in such a small world."

There was a soft knock on the door of the study. Abigail Wilson, pulling herself away from the window seat, called out, "Come in, please."

When the door opened, one of her military aides stepped inside the study. Though he had never seen the commander-in-chief in a bathrobe and slippers, he pretended not to notice. Instead he submitted his report. "Madam President, we have confirmation that both storage sites have been secured. Though the inspection teams that went in with the Marines are still in the process of inventorying the nuclear devices, we're sure we got them all."

Wilson nodded. Then she looked up. "Casualties? How bad were our losses?"

The colonel smiled. "Initial reports say they were minimal."

Wilson frowned, looking down at the floor. Minimal, she thought. Minimal to whom? To us, the people who had issued the orders? How would she, a mother, like it if someone told her that her son had been one of the minimal casualties? She wouldn't. She knew that. But this was not the time to make an issue of the colonel's poor choice of words.

Instead Wilson simply thanked him and turned her head back toward the window. There, in the privacy of her study, she would be the first to mourn for those minimal casualties, whoever they were.

CHAPTER 20

24 JANUARY

At first, no one seemed to notice. The excuses rendered by those who failed to show up for work were, given the time of year and the advent of a new strain of flu, quite reasonable. Only when the flood of absenteeism spread to the General Staff did Colonel Hans Kasper begin to realize that the absences were not acts of God but wholesale desertion of Ruff's government. Following the example of General Lange, more and more officers openly declared their support of the unilateral cease-fire declared by the Parliament or simply failed to report for duty.

Even more ominous was the action of entire units that were declaring "Active noninterference" with American forces. Not satisfied that acceptance of the unilateral cease-fire was enough, commanders of battalions, brigades, and even divisions were lending logistical and medical support to American units as they streamed north. Some even intentionally maneuvered themselves between American forces marching to the sea and German units still considered loyal to Ruff, raising the danger of civil war. When Kasper, in a private conversation with the commander of the 5th Panzer Division, mentioned this, the general became quite blunt. "Your Chancellor Ruff will be gone soon. And I hope the devil takes him. But we and the German people will still be here to atone for his sins. Someone, Herr Colonel, has to defend the soul of Germany. Because when this is over and our day of reckoning comes, we will have to be able to stand up and show that we Germans truly understand right from wrong and that we deserve to sit at the table with other civilized nations."

Those words, like Lange's words to him a week before, haunted Kasper as he moved about the half-empty offices of the Chancellery, trying hard to catch up with the work that used to be done by those who no longer could support a man that they themselves had elected into office. This was not easy. There was no way that Kasper, with the aid of a handful of loyal staffers, could replicate the effort that had required twice their number. But they tried and for the most part succeeded by judiciously dealing with only those matters that were absolutely essential. Since Kasper was a trained General Staff officer, this was a relatively simple task. With a firm hand and a trained eye that was quick to sort out trivia from important information, Kasper was able to keep Ruff informed. This additional work was for Kasper a godsend, since it kept his mind busy and left him little time to ponder the questions of right and wrong, good and bad, and, even more pressing for an officer, duty versus a vague notion of personal conscience.

Still, Kasper had nagging doubts that Ruff himself did nothing to quiet. Rather than embarrass the General Staff, which was losing its officers to the Parliament at a prodigious rate, Kasper himself gave Chancellor Ruff the early-morning update on military operations in progress and those planned for that day. Kasper kept these updates brief, for he quickly realized that Ruff didn't seem to have much of an interest in the detailed workings of the military machine which he had so recently tasked to perform a mission that was now tearing it apart from within. Ruff was satisfied with a quick overview of where major American units were and what they were up to, where units still loyal to him were and what they were doing, and, most important of all to the Chancellor, how many Americans had been killed and wounded in the last twenty-four hours. His insistence on knowing the precise number of American losses, neatly broken down into the number of killed, wounded, and missing, bothered Kasper, since he showed no similar concern for the cost of this war to Germany.

At first Kasper thought he was imagining things. For three consecutive days he had briefed Ruff and after enumerating American losses had been dismissed before mentioning German casualty figures. This caused Kasper to wonder what was going on inside of his Chancellor's mind. So he decided while walking through the quiet halls of the Chancellery that morning to test a theory he had. He was going to present German losses first and not mention anything about American figures.

Looking at his watch, Kasper saw that he had only a few minutes to finish putting his update together and he still lacked the information from the General Staff. Reaching over to the secure line that went directly into the joint operations center used by the General Staff, Kasper punched in the number for the duty officer. When Colonel Siegfried Arndt answered, Kasper was surprised. "Siggie, this is Hans. I thought you were on duty last night? What are you still doing there?"

Arndt's voice was tired. "I'm still here because my relief hasn't reported for duty yet."

Since duty watches ran twelve-hour shifts and the night duty officer should have been relieved at six in the morning, over an hour ago, this meant that chances were good that another officer had come down with what was being referred to in private as the parliamentary flu. When Arndt spoke again, there was a less than subtle hint of disgust in his voice. "I'll tell you, Hans, if it weren't for the easterners who had been senior officers in the former East German Army that Ruff had insisted on reinstating, work over here would have come to a grinding halt yesterday. Word's out this morning that the entire operations staff has gone over."

This piece of news caused Kasper to stiffen upright in his seat. "Then who's in charge of current operations and the plans section?"

Arndt sighed. "They're still discussing that. I suppose another easterner will take over those duties."

"Yes," Kasper responded, trying not to betray his dismay, "of course. Listen, I called to get an update on what's happening. I brief the Chancellor in a few minutes."

"All right, here it is. The lead elements of the American 55th Division are just outside Bremen. We expect them to bypass that city to the west and strike north to Wilhelmshaven. Unless something stops them, which is unlikely, they will link up with the American forces in Bremerhaven tonight or early tomorrow. The American 4th Armored Division continues to screen the eastern flank of the American line of advance from a point just north of Paderborn, across the Mittellandkanal. And the 14th Cavalry Regiment continues to screen the rear and to the west."

"Who," Kasper interjected, "are they screening against in the west?"

Arndt chuckled. "Good question. The 7th Panzer, of course, has assumed a posture of active noninterference. It is the fuel from their supply trains that's keeping the American march going. The 5th Panzer, as you know, has assumed defensive positions in the east to protect the Ruhr east of Düsseldorf."

"And who are they protecting the Ruhr from?"

Ignoring Kasper's last question, Arndt continued. "The 1st Panzer expects to commence its attacks against the American 4th Armored later this morning with two brigades. Its axis of advance will be due west from Hannover north of the Mittellandkanal. The 2nd Panzer Division, which will not be in place until late in the afternoon, will join that effort, attacking on the right or north flank of the 1st Panzer. The commander of the Second Corps, coordinating the effort, expects to be able to penetrate the 4th Armored Division's screen and, with luck, isolate most of that division."

Pausing to look over his notes, Kasper asked why the 1st Panzer was attacking with only two brigades. "The other brigade, the 1st Brigade, is not responding to orders. They have gone into an assembly area south of Hannover and refuse to acknowledge all communications with their division headquarters."

"And the other divisions?"

Referring to a summary that he had prepared an hour ago, Arndt went through them one by one. "Well, as you know, the 4th Panzergrenadier was badly mauled and is unable to get around the rear guard of the 14th Cavalry Regiment. Those bastards continue to make the 4th Panzer bleed for every kilometer. The 10th Panzer, after its lackluster performance several days ago in central Germany, hasn't moved. It still needs time, according to its commander, to complete its reconstitution. The 3rd Panzer is watching the Poles, covering Berlin, and dealing with the riots while the 6th Panzergrenadier is waiting to see if the American Marines in the Baltic are going to land."

"So," Kasper announced, "we have more than three divisions that are no longer reliable, one, the 4th Panzer, that is approaching combat ineffectiveness, and two tied down in the east. That, according to my figures, leaves us less than two panzer divisions for offensive operations."

"Yes, Hans, that's about right. Even when you take their losses into account, we have, in effect, been cut down to near parity with the Americans."

"Well, that should be more than sufficient to severely punish the 4th Armored Division."

Arndt hesitated and then lowered his voice. "Well, yes of course, we can do that. But to what purpose, my friend? I mean, what exactly are we doing?"

This caught Kasper off guard. "Doing? What do you mean, what are we doing? We are defending Germany against its enemies."

Slowly, carefully, as if to feel out his fellow officer, Arndt spoke. "Are you so sure, my friend, that we are dealing with the proper enemy?"

Kasper wanted to ask Arndt to clarify that question, but he decided not to out of fear that he wouldn't like the answer. Instead, with a brisk voice, Kasper told Arndt that he needed to finish preparing his briefing for the Chancellor, thanked him for the information, and hung up the phone without so much as a good-bye.

When Kasper hung up, Arndt knew that he had gotten the answer he had expected. Looking about at the operations center, he listened to the dozen or so conversations that were going on about the room, watched as numerous staff officers went this way and that, and thought about his conversation with Kasper. Then without any further thought he stood up and turned to the young major sitting next to him. "I am going out."

The major, one ear glued to a phone, covered the mouthpiece. "I don't blame you, Herr Colonel. If someone asks where you are, I'll tell him you're taking a break."

Arndt smiled. "Yes, you do that." Turning, he walked out of the room, down the hall where their coats hung, grabbing his as he went by, then headed for the elevators. Taking the elevator to the ground floor, Arndt stepped out, walked through another series of corridors to the main entrance which led out to the street. Pausing as he put his cap on, Arndt smiled when he saw the sun. Returning the salute of the two guards posted at the main entrance, Arndt walked down the flight of steps to the street, made a right, and began to walk home. For him the war was over.

From where his tank sat, Second Lieutenant Tim Ellerbee had a clear shot straight down the main highway as it came out of the small German village they had evacuated less than an hour ago. Two hundred meters to his front right, and out of sight, sat Sergeant First Class Ralph Rourk and his tank, covering a side street that came out of the town and into a cluster of fields that surrounded the village. The Germans, Ellerbee figured, would probably use one of those two exits from the village. If they didn't, they'd have to take a long detour to the west. And if they did that, they would run smack into another platoon of Captain Nancy Kozak's company.

There was another way out of the village, a mere alley, that Ellerbee should have covered with a third tank. And he would have if he'd had a third tank. But he didn't. Like all of the platoons in Kozak's company, Ellerbee's platoon had been substantially reduced in strength through a combination of combat losses and mechanical failures. The first tank he had lost had been his wing man, A32. The platoon had just broken contact west of Kassel with the advance guard of a German panzer battalion and were making a high-speed run to their next blocking position when a pair of German attack helicopters sitting in ambush fired on both Ellerbee's tank and A32. Ellerbee saw the incoming missiles and took evasive maneuvers. A32 didn't. Though there was only one man wounded on A32, and Ellerbee was able to retrieve him and the rest of the crew after the German helicopters moved on, there wasn't time to recover the damaged tank. So it was abandoned. The wounded man was evacuated and the remainder of A32's crew was reassigned to one of Kozak's infantry platoons to make up for some of their losses.

Rourk's wing tank, A33, sheared a drive sprocket while maneuvering across the side of a muddy hill. Though the damage was not catastrophic, since a replacement drive sprocket could have been cannibalized from another damaged tank that had been written off, the fact that Ellerbee's platoon was part of the division's rear guard made recovery impossible. So, like A32's crew, this crew was forced to abandon their tank and join one of Kozak's platoons as infantrymen.

As every other platoon leader in the Tenth Corps had to, Ellerbee adjusted his tactics to compensate for his losses. Actually, Ellerbee found dealing with only two tanks much to his liking, especially since the other tank was commanded by Rourk, an experienced NCO who needed no real guidance from Ellerbee. That, coupled with his brief but sorry combat experience in the Ukraine which he had taken to heart, allowed Ellerbee to more than survive their recent battles in central Germany. Grudgingly, ever so grudgingly, Rourk and the other noncommissioned officers in the platoon began to recognize Ellerbee as a competent tanker.

Unfortunately, in the eyes of Captain Nancy Kozak, he was unable to shed his image of a bungling idiot. Ellerbee's actions of five days before that had saved Colonel Scott Dixon and his tactical command post were seen by Kozak for what they were, a happy series of lucky accidents and errors. In all her dealings, she continued to treat him as if he were a first-year cadet at West Point. In fact she had never dropped her requirement that Rourk, Ellerbee's platoon sergeant, be present whenever she issued orders to him. Determined to show that he was a better man than she, Ellerbee said nothing, knowing that when all was said and done and the fighting was over, his record and performance would speak for themselves and he would be able to show that it was Kozak, not he, who had been unreasonable and unprofessional. So Ellerbee said nothing, for this was not the time or place to deal with such trivial matters. Instead he concentrated on doing his duty and building a reputation that would allow him when peace came to extract a measure of revenge against the female infantry captain who had embarrassed him and his platoon.

Over the radio Ellerbee heard Rourk's voice calling, "Alpha Three One, this is Three Four. There's a German crawling along the ditch on the side of the road about fifty meters past the last house. Can you see him? Over."

Ellerbee keyed the mike. "Three Four, wait One. Out." Then, letting go of the lever that keyed the radio transmitter, Ellerbee called out to Specialist Wilk, his gunner. "Yo, Wilk. Can you see the German Rourk is talking about?"

With his eye glued to the gunner's primary sight, Wilk traversed the turret slowly to where Rourk had seen the German. When he thought that he was looking at the right spot, Wilk reached up and flipped the lever on the primary sight that moved the sight from a three-power wide-angle field of view to a narrow ten-power field of view. After a moment Wilk grunted. "Ah, there's the little bastard, LT, moving up next to that shot-up Mercedes about fifty meters beyond the last building in the village."

Leaning forward and putting his head up to his extension of the primary sight, Ellerbee saw what Wilk did. "Yeah, I see him." For a moment both he and Wilk watched as the German, moving with great care, inched his way forward. Every now and then the German stopped, popped his head up out of the ditch, and looked around before proceeding a little further. "Well, what do you think?"

Wilk laughed. "I think this guy needs to go back to basic training and learn how to low-crawl. God, look at that. His ass is sticking up so high a helicopter would have to swerve to avoid running into it."

When he was ready, Ellerbee rekeyed his radio. "Three Four, this is Three One. I see the German. From the way he's sneaking about, I think he's a tanker taking a look-see before his unit breaks cover. Over."

Rourk's response betrayed a slight chuckle. "Yeah, Three One, he's a tanker all right. Even the Germans, it seems, can't teach a tanker how to low-crawl right."

Ignoring Rourk's comment, Ellerbee issued his order. "Three Four, this is Three One. I think they'll come bounding out of town right down the main road. If they do, odds are every eye will be glued on where I'm sitting. So you wait until you've got a good flank shot and then pop the lead German vehicle. When you do, back up and get going to our next position. They may come down the street after you, in which case I'll be able to get a flank shot and cover your withdrawal. If the opposite happens and the Germans try to sneak out of town using the side street instead of the main road, I'll fire first and then you cover me. Do you copy? Over."

"This is Three Four. Good copy. I'll see you at the next position. Over."

"Roger, Three Four. Three One. Out."

Ellerbee and Rourk didn't have long to wait. With the confidence of a man who was sure that no one was watching, the German in the ditch stood up, walked into the middle of the road, and waved at someone in the village. In less than a minute Ellerbee could see the form of a Leopard II tank emerge from around a street corner in the village and begin to roll down the road toward him. Knowing that Rourk couldn't see the German tank yet and, from the manner in which the lone German on the road and the Leopard were moving, that his own tank hadn't been seen by them, Ellerbee keyed the radio. "Three Four, there's a Leo coming down the main road fast and dumb. Get ready. Over."

When Rourk responded, he betrayed no emotion. "Roger, Three One. We're ready."

Slowly, like an animal sticking its nose out to sniff for danger,

Rourk saw the end of the German tank's long 120mm main gun appear from behind the cover of the last house in the village. Then the front fenders, followed by the massive body of the Leopard tank. Finally, when the entire tank was visible, Rourk called out to his gunner, who had been tracking the German. "Not yet, Chuckie, not yet." For a moment, Rourk's gunner wanted to protest, but then stopped when he saw the German tank slow down. "Hold your fire, Chuck. We'll wait until the guy in the ditch begins to climb on board."

The gunner didn't respond to Rourk, calling over to the loader instead. "Billy, you up?"

The loader, watching his commander and gunner, reached over, threw the spent cartridge guard that also served to arm the main gun over to the ready position. Flattening himself against the side of the turret wall, he yelled back. "Yeah, I'm up."

When the German tank came to a complete halt and the German who had been in the ditch began to climb onto the front slope of the tank, Rourk all but whispered his command. "Fire!"

With his sight laid dead on the black German cross that adorned the side of the Leopard's turret, Chuck hit the laser range finder button with his thumb, glanced down at the range readout that showed up at the bottom of his sight picture, and yelled out, "On the way," before he pulled the trigger.

With that, the main gun of Rourk's tank spit out an armor-piercing fin-stabilized discarding sabot round. When the depleted uranium penetrator left the muzzle, it was traveling at over a mile a second. Inside, Rourk and his crew felt their M-1A1 tank shrug and lurch as the main gun recoiled, automatically opening the massive breech block, kicking out the small base plate of the expended round. By the time this action was finished, the loader already had a new round in hand, Rourk was sticking his head up out of his open hatch, shouting to the driver to back up as he went, and Chuck, the gunner, was searching for a new target.

There was no need to fire a second round at the German tank. Smacked in the side of the turret with a dart measuring little more than one inch wide and a foot and a half long, made from the densest metal available to man, the German tank was consumed by a catastrophic explosion.

From his position, Ellerbee watched. Two and a half hours of patient waiting had resulted in the destruction of another German tank and the successful completion of his mission. When he was sure that Rourk was well on his way and he saw that there were no Germans in immediate pursuit, he ordered his own driver to slowly back away from their hidden position. They had done what he had been ordered to do, delay the Germans. It would be at least a half hour before the commander of the German unit in the town figured out that their attackers were long gone. By then, both he and Rourk would be in their next position, getting ready to play the deadly game of hide-and-seek with the same German advance guard unit.

In silence, both Colonel Scott Dixon and Colonel Anatol Vorishnov watched as a sergeant from the brigade's intelligence section plotted the latest location of the 1st Panzer Division. With maddening regularity, the sergeant moved the red stickers that represented German tank and infantry companies further and further to the west. With the same maddening regularity, a sergeant from the operations section, paper in hand listing the location of Scott Dixon's tank and infantry companies, would move the blue symbols that represented them on the map to the west and away from the advancing red symbols. Every now and then, a blue symbol would be removed, like a chess piece that had fallen to an opponent's attack.

But these were not chess pieces. Every blue symbol removed represented a unit of fifty to one hundred men and women that had ceased to exist as an effective organization. Without taking his eyes away from the map that the two sergeants were working on, though they now had less than one hundred miles of their long and painful odyssey to go, Vorishnov summed up what Dixon already knew. "We're in trouble."

At first Dixon said nothing. Instead he waited until the two sergeants had completed posting their respective updates and then moved forward to the map. Vorishnov followed. Coming up to Dixon's left, Vorishnov jabbed at the symbol that represented Company C, 1st Battalion, 37th Armor. "This company, because of the terrain, cannot move west. It will soon be forced to move to the south, away from the rest of its parent battalion, if the Germans continue to advance."

Putting his hands in his pockets, Dixon looked at the company symbol, at the German unit symbols closing on it, and then at the other unit symbols scattered about the map. Taking a deep breath, he paused a little longer before he spoke. When he did, his voice betrayed the despair he felt. "And if that happens, ping, the Germans have a free road to the northwest. If the company retreats, it must retreat to the northwest."

Moving his finger down, Vorishnov placed it on another symbol. "That means that this unit, Company C, 3rd Battalion, 3rd Infantry, must speed up, get north across the Mittellandkanal, and block the Germans here. Because once the Germans find their route to the northwest blocked, they will simply deflect off the 1st Battalion, 37th Armor, advance to the southwest, and . . ."

Dixon nodded his head and finished the sentence. "And cut this brigade in half, leaving two battalions north of the Kanal and two south of it."

"Do you think, Colonel, that Major Cerro will be able to get north, across the Kanal?"

Turning to Vorishnov, Dixon looked at him for a moment. "What do you think?"

Without a word Vorishnov looked back at the map, mentally measured the distance that the advancing German units had to cover, then the distance that Cerro's battalion had to cover, before answering Dixon. When he was ready, he looked Dixon in the eye and shook his head. "No. I do not think so."

Dixon looked down. "I agree. Even if they managed to shake that German unit that has been dogging them all the way from Kassel, they wouldn't be able to get everything across the Kanal. The question, then, is what do we do?"

Vorishnov placed one hand over the symbols that represented Dixon's two battalions that were north of the Mittellandkanal, and his other hand over the two that were south of the Kanal. Pulling them apart, he moved the hand over the northern units further north and those south of the Kanal first to the west, and then north to the Kanal. "As much as I hate to say this, you must split your brigade, leaving those who have crossed the Kanal to continue to the north and those south—"

"To attempt to cross the Kanal further to the west and follow as best they can."

Dropping his hands to his sides, Vorishnov looked down at his boots, then back up at Dixon. "I am sorry, my friend. I understand what such an order means. But you must face facts." Vorishnov pointed at the map, moving his finger to indicate the units he was talking about. "If you order your 37th Armor to hold its ground, it will be overwhelmed, and you will still lose that company as well as the two battalions in the south. Better to save two battalions for sure than lose one trying to save two that are beyond help. Your four battalions, all of them approaching half strength and exhausted from the long march north, are no match for the full-strength well-rested battalions of the 1st Panzer Division. To make a stand would be to risk everything, even the uncommitted battalion in the north." Stepping back, Vorishnov allowed his observations to sink in.

For a long time Dixon said nothing. Instead he looked at the map, pulling his right hand out of his pocket and moving it from one unit and terrain feature to the next. Finally he looked at Vorishnov. "Even if we do this, someone will have to delay the lead elements here, just north of the Kanal, so the two battalions south of the Kanal can outrun the Germans to the next good crossing point to the west."

Vorishnov nodded. "Yes, that will be necessary. And that force will be sacrificed."

"Yes, I know." Sliding his right hand back into his pocket, Dixon stared at the symbol that represented Cerro's battalion, 3rd of the 3rd Infantry. "They will need to hold as long as possible, then when they're about to be overrun, they make a break and hope they can get out of the way of the Germans and find their own way north."

Placing his right hand on Dixon's shoulder, Vorishnov attempted to reassure him. "I understand. They are all your soldiers, my friend, but these concerns are best left to the commander on the spot, Major Cerro."

Dixon turned his head and smiled at Vorishnov. "As always, Colonel, you are right. I should leave that fight to the battalion commander. But I will be there to advise and encourage him, just as you have done with me, my friend."

Vorishnov raised an eyebrow. "You appreciate that, given the distance, you may not be able to control your entire brigade if you place yourself south of the Kanal."

"I have," Dixon countered, "no intention of attempting to control the entire brigade. When we split, I will go south with the tactical command post and command this half of the brigade. You will remain here with the main command post and command the rest."

For the first time since joining Dixon, Vorishnov was flabbergasted. He started to protest. "But I am a Russian officer!"

"And a damned good one. Listen, Lieutenant Colonel Yost has his hands full keeping the brigade trains together, functioning, and moving north. The same argument I used when I sent Cerro to the 3rd of the 3rd Infantry still applies. If Yost leaves, we stand a good chance of losing the trains." Dixon pointed to one of the northern battalions, then the other, as he spoke. "The commander of this battalion is a major, like Cerro, and the lieutenant colonel in command of this one has his hands full with what he already has. He's not brigade command material." Turning to face Vorishnov, Dixon tapped his chest. "So tag, Colonel. You're it. I'll leave you the tank and I'll take one of the personnel carriers. I want to go fast and be as inconspicuous as possible."

"Your division commander will never agree to my taking command, Colonel Dixon."

Now Dixon smiled, truly smiled for the first time in days. "Sorry, won't work. I've already talked to him about your succeeding me. He agreed."

Outmaneuvered there, Vorishnov turned his head toward the brigade staff and surveyed them. Those who were in earshot returned Vorishnov's stare. "And them?"

Turning his head also, Dixon let the smile on his face fall away. When he spoke, it was so that the staff officers and sergeants listening would hear what he had to say. "They, Colonel Vorishnov, are professionals, each and every one. They will do as they are told, regardless of who is in command." Finished, Dixon looked back at Vorishnov. "Besides, I am only lending this command post and those battalions to you. I intend to take them back as soon as I reach Bremerhaven."

Closing his eyes, Vorishnov smiled and nodded. "Fine. That will be fine."

With that, the two colonels parted. Dixon went out to gather his gear and head south before his route was blocked by the Germans, while Vorishnov turned to his staff and began to issue the orders that would be necessary to break contact with the 1st Panzer Division and continue the long march to the sea.

* * *

While he waited for Captain Nancy Kozak to arrive, Major Hal Cerro paced along the side of the road Across the road, the crew of his M-2 Bradley infantry fighting vehicle watched him as he would walk several meters, stop, look at his watch, turn, look at them, and then retrace his steps. When he had reached the limit of his small circuit, Cerro would stop again, look at his watch, look over to the Bradley again, and repeat the process. His gunner, sitting on the turret roof with his feet dangling down the open hatch, and his driver, half hanging out of the driver's compartment, watched, munched on tasteless rations, and exchanged comments.

"The major's in a hurry."

Swallowing, the driver wondered out loud, "How long do ya think he'll wait before we go lookin' for her?"

Even though the driver couldn't see the gunner, the gunner shook his head as he answered. "Don't think the major's in a hurry to get back on board. You scared the piss out of him on that last series of turns."

"I didn't mean to. He did say move out, didn't he?"

"You're going to have to take it easy," the gunner advised, "until the major gets used to us and the Bradley."

"I thought," the driver protested, "that he knew what he was doing. How the hell was I to know he'd never commanded a Bradley before."

Taking time to lick the tomato sauce off his plastic spoon, the gunner slowly responded. "Come on. Use some common sense. You see all those badges he's got? Master parachutist, jump master, pathfinder, ranger, combat infantryman's badge. That's a leg infantry collection. I'll bet he never spent a day in a mech infantry unit till he got assigned to us."

The driver grunted. "Yeah, ain't we lucky. We get to do some on-the-job training."

"It could be worse," the gunner reminded the driver. "We could have been stuck with the ops officer."

The driver shook his head. "I don't know. I really don't think it makes much of a difference. All officers get kind of strange when they get promoted to major. The best we can hope is that this one lasts longer than the last two."

The gunner was about to ask why he had said that, but caught himself. Of course the driver hoped that nothing happened to Major Cerro. Because his fate was now tied to theirs. Odds were, if something bad happened to the major, they'd be right there getting the same thing. "Yup. Sure hope this one's luckier than the last two."

The driver saw Cerro stop and look down the road. From the direction Cerro was staring in, the driver heard the whine of another Bradley's engine cut through the cold, damp morning air. "Looks like the Nose has arrived."

Turning his head, the gunner also looked to see if the Nose, the nickname Nancy Kozak had earned after breaking her nose during the campaign in Mexico, had finally arrived. From around the corner, a Bradley came into sight. When the gunner saw the black image of a wolf's head painted on the gunner's side of the turret, he knew it was Kozak. Sergeant Wolf had done the painting himself as a little extra show of pride. When Kozak saw what Wolf had done, she insisted that he do something similar on her side. Of course, all the junior NCOs in the battalion dared Wolf to paint the silhouette of a large crooked nose on her side. But Wolf, knowing that he'd have to put up with her for a long time, opted to paint a palm tree, resembling the symbol used by the German Afrika Korps during World War II, with a K in the center of the tree's trunk instead of the swastika. Kozak loved it and Wolf was harassed in a friendly sort of way by his fellow NCOs for weeks after that.

But that all seemed like ancient history to the gunner now as he watched Kozak's Bradley come to a halt across from Cerro's. Both Kozak and Wolf were riding low in their open hatches. Even from where he sat, Cerro's gunner could see that they were both exhausted. Neither Kozak nor Wolf looked as if they had washed their faces in days. While Wolf's face, stubbled with beard, looked bad, Kozak's was worse due to the dark bags that hung under her eyes and seemed to drag her cheeks down from their sheer weight. The gunner had no doubt that her eyes were just as bloodshot as Cerro's. That was becoming the first indicator that an officer was approaching. Though everyone was dragging tail, the officers, to a man, seemed twice as bad off as any enlisted man. There was, Cerro's gunner thought to himself, no way that he'd put up with all the shit that officers had to. No way.

From below, Cerro's driver shouted to get the gunner's attention. "Hey, you have something up there to trade for my dehydrated peaches?"

In the two and a half days since Cerro had assumed command of 3rd of the 3rd Infantry, Kozak had seen him nine times. At most of those meetings the format was the same. She'd give him a quick update on the status of her company, the location of her platoons, significant contacts or sightings, and what they were doing or about to do. Cerro, if time permitted, would explain what was happening elsewhere in the battalion and brigade area of operations, potential enemy threats that they needed to consider, and then issue Kozak new orders. When he was sure that she had a firm grasp of what was expected of her company, Cerro would mount his Bradley and head down the road in search of the next company commander. Only twice, due to the fact that they were in almost constant contact, was he able to muster more than two company commanders together at the same time. There just wasn't time.

Ordering Paden, her radiotelephone operator, to lower the troop ramp of her Bradley, Kozak dropped into the turret and through the small access door that led to the Bradley's troop compartment. Cerro walked around her Bradley and met her at the ramp. Kneeling down, he threw his map down on the ramp, took a notebook out of his pocket, and prepared to issue his order. Before he started, however, he asked Kozak, map in hand, which of her two infantry platoons was in the best shape.

Kozak didn't need to think about that. "2nd Platoon. Marc Gross's. He has three fully operational Bradleys and three dismount teams with four men each."

Cerro looked up at Kozak. "Is Gross reliable?"

Kozak nodded. "He's the best I have left."

Cerro, in a hurry and not keen on the order he was about to issue, snapped back, "I didn't ask for a comparison. I asked if he was reliable."

Cerro's sharp tone and the look on his face took Kozak aback. She realized that he, like her, was not thinking and tempers were short. Kozak rephrased her answer. "He is an experienced and capable platoon leader. The former battalion commander used him as an advance guard detachment on several occasions."

When Cerro spoke, there was no apology, no regret for his reprimand. He simply began issuing orders. "You're to take your company across the Mittellandkanal, here." With pencil in hand, Cerro pointed to a circle drawn on his map case. "Once across, Gross and his platoon will occupy a blocking position here. His mission is to hold up the advance of the German units moving along the Kanal for as long as possible. You and the rest of your company will move west, along the main road here, as quickly as possible and secure the cross point here. There you'll remain in place to cover the crossing of the rest of this battalion and the 35th Armor. Hold there until a company from the 35th comes up and relieves you. Once the brigade's across, we go north as fast as we can."

Kozak looked at the two points on the map that Cerro had marked and shown her. "You realize, Major, we wouldn't be able to support Gross and his platoon at all."

Cerro nodded. "I know."

"How long," she continued, "does Gross need to hold here?"

"Until he can't hold on any longer." There was, Kozak noticed, no emotion in his voice.

"Will Gross be able to join me when the 35th Armor relieves me or is he expected to join the 35th?"

Locking his eyes on Kozak's, Cerro leaned forward. "Let me make myself perfectly clear. Gross will hold that position until he is no longer able to hold it. I do not expect him to join us or the 35th. He digs in as best he can and he holds, period. If and when his position is overrun, the survivors will be free to make their way north as best they can, on their own."

Slowly the look of surprise on Kozak's face was replaced with a mask of horror as she realized that she was expected to order one of her platoons to literally die in place. That was not, she thought, the way we did things. Last stands, she thought, had been dropped from American military doctrine at the end of the nineteenth century. Besides, she wondered, how could she be expected to order almost half her remaining company to stand fast, fight, and die while she fled north to safety?

Cerro saw the look on her face and knew what she was thinking, for he had considered the exact same thing when Colonel Dixon had issued him his orders little over an hour ago. Looking down at Kozak, Cerro was suddenly struck by how out of place Kozak looked at that moment. As hard as this was for him, Kozak's big brown eyes and smooth round face, looking more like a hurt child's than a combat commander's, made all of this harder. Even with her long auburn hair, except for a stray wisp that always seemed to fall across her face, wrapped and tucked-up into an olive drab wool watch cap, and layers and layers of bulky winter clothing that made Kozak look more like a stocking doll than a woman, Kozak was for an instant a female, someone he suddenly felt the need to protect, to comfort. Only with a great effort was Cerro able to pull his tired thoughts back onto track. She's an officer, damn it, a captain in the United States Army. A company commander. Nothing more, nothing less. Taking several deep breaths, Cerro continued.

"Look, Captain, the Germans are crashing down on the corps' flank with two panzer divisions. If we don't get out of the way, we'll be crushed. As it is, the units north of the Kanal are already giving way. Our only chance is to turn to the west and cross somewhere else, and then run north as fast as we can. And we can make it in less than twenty-four hours. Unfortunately, so can the Germans. The Air Force can chew 'em up and delay them some. Unfortunately they can't stop them. Only ground forces can do that."

"And Gross has been elected." As soon as she said it, Kozak was sorry she had.

Angry, Cerro clenched his fists. He didn't like what he was doing any more than she did. But he had been convinced that it was necessary, had accepted the order, and now he expected Kozak to do likewise. He could have blamed Dixon, who had originated the order. That, Cerro knew, would have been easy and would have made Dixon the bad guy. To do so, however, would be wrong, for the order did make sense, and it was after all an order.

Barely holding back his anger, Cerro glared down at Kozak. "Yes, goddamn it. Your Lieutenant Gross has been elected. He elected himself when he took his oath of office and put on the uniform. No officer who understands his or her responsibility to his profession and duty should ever imagine that there's always an easy or safe way out. It just doesn't work like that. Being a soldier means killing, and sometimes being killed. Well, I'm here telling you that I expect your Lieutenant Gross to take his men there, north of the Kanal, and kill Germans. And they will continue to kill Germans until they can't kill any more. This is no time to debate the wisdom or merit of orders regardless of who generated them. You have your orders, and I expect you to issue Gross his. Is that clear, Captain?"

Kozak sat there on the ramp of her Bradley and looked up at Cerro. There was a rage and anger in his eyes that she had never seen before in a human being. He was, she realized, a man beyond reasoning. What kindness or emotions this man had once possessed had been crushed by the weight of his responsibilities and the horrors of war, just as her own spirit and hope had been extinguished as she had watched the soldiers of her company drop or disappear one by one during the long march. That none of this made sense anymore seemed a moot point. All that seemed to matter anymore was to follow orders and keep going north, regardless of cost, regardless of consequence. To stop now was not possible. They had all gone too far and paid too much to stop or allow this enterprise, right or wrong, to fail.

Slowly, as if the weight of the entire world were on her shoulders, Kozak pushed herself up off the cold metal ramp and faced Cerro. Though in her heart she was dying, Kozak choked back her tears and saluted him. "Yes, sir, your orders are clear."

Unable to speak, and not knowing what to say anyway, Cerro reached down, grabbed his map, and fled across the road to his own Bradley, leaving Kozak to pass on the order.

24 JANUARY

Despite the fact that she had been finished several hours ago, Jan Fields-Dixon couldn't bring herself to leave the World News Network studios. In Germany, where it was still midafternoon, the flow of Tenth Corps units into the perimeter held by the 17th Airborne Division, south of Bremerhaven, was beginning to turn into a flood. At checkpoints all along the southern tier of that perimeter, news teams stood by recording what some correspondents called completion of the greatest military march since Xenophon led his ten thousand Greek mercenaries out of Persia in the year 400 B.C. Like everyone else, the experts, real and imagined, sat by television monitors shaking their heads in disbelief and watching as the soldiers of the Tenth Corps finished what many had said could not be done. "Every man and woman in the corps," one retired colonel had told Jan during an interview earlier that day, "should be proud of what they have accomplished."

Jan, ever watchful for any sign of her husband, could see no hint of pride in the vacant eyes of the survivors as column after column of soldiers rolled past the electronic eye of the news media. Few in Germany seemed to share the wild joy most Americans back home felt now that the great march to the sea was coming to an end. Instead, when a correspondent managed to make his way to a group of survivors, his questions were often left unanswered as the soldier stammered or simply lapsed into a stunned silence. At one assembly area, where the remains of a tank battalion had been marshaled, a reporter found every man, officer and enlisted, spread out over the fenders and tops of their tank turrets asleep. It was, the reporter commented as his cameraman panned the slumbering crewmen, as if the only thing that had kept the men and women of the Tenth Corps moving, in spite of the terrible hardships and odds, was stubborn pride and fear of failure, and now that they were safe, they could go no further.

Having been long associated with the military, Jan knew better. Men like her husband, Scott Dixon, his operations officer, Harold Cerro, and the corps commander, Al Malin, went on doing things that often could not be explained and defying common sense because they couldn't do otherwise. There was a vague and indefinable force known as duty that drove her husband and those that followed him to keep putting themselves in harm's way. Jan, like others, knew that stubborn and mindless male pride, coupled with a childlike fascination with danger and the primeval animal-like drive to kill, played a part in the process. But these drives alone could not justify or explain what Scott did for a living. Neither could high-sounding words, such as duty, honor, country, justify the brutality that Scott and others like him meted out to others and suffered in return. That was something that defied explanation. Something kept Dixon in the Army and allowed the soldiers of the Tenth Corps to do what everyone in Washington had termed impossible.

While such thoughts were never far from her mind, there were other, more pressing concerns that Jan had to deal with. For in spite of the fact that the end was clearly in sight, the dark and nebulous forces that had driven the Tenth Corps on were still at play. With the same blind and mindless determination that had kept the Tenth Corps moving north, units still responding to the orders of the German Chancellor continued to hack away at the rear-guard elements of Big Al's tattered corps. It was in the words of one of Jan's male co-workers as if some Germans couldn't admit defeat as long as they had a chance to strike out and hit an American unit. Forgetting for a moment that her husband was still very much a part of the story, Jan's friend predicted that there would be one more final killing frenzy, one last mindless battle, regardless of how pointless it was, before serious political negotiations could begin. Though she hoped that everyone in Germany would simply allow the battle to die away quietly, Jan knew in her heart and soul that as long as men like her Scotty still stood on both sides of the battle lines that wouldn't happen.

So she watched the videos as they were beamed in live from Europe and prayed that somewhere on one of them she would be able to catch a glimpse of his face.

Flanked by Secretary of Defense Terry Rothenberg and the Chairman of the Joint Chiefs of Staff, President Wilson moved with such a brisk pace down the corridor that those following began to think she was trying to run away from them. They didn't realize how right they were. Tired of briefing after briefing on the military situation, Wilson was looking for any excuse to shake her entourage of stern-faced military bureaucrats and generals. So when Wilson saw Ed Lewis come around the corner out of a side corridor quite by accident, she called out, "Ed, before you return to the State Department, there's something I need to go over with you."

Without even a polite smile, she turned to Rothenberg. "Terry, if you'd excuse me, there's a few things I need to discuss with the Secretary of State designee before he leaves." Not waiting for a response, Wilson stepped away from Rothenberg and his gang of military men. Grabbing Lewis's arm, Wilson snatched him away from his assistant and started to head for the Oval Office as quickly as she could. Only after they were in the office and a member of the Secret Service closed the door behind them did she let her newly named Secretary of State go.

Walking over to the front edge of her desk, Wilson stopped, placed her hands palms down on it, and leaned forward. "How much longer do *you* think it will be, Ed?"

Walking over to one of the overstuffed chairs, he allowed his tired frame to drop into it and settle before he answered her. "From what I've been told, maybe another six, seven hours before the last of the rear guard makes it to the 17th Airborne's forward outpost, providing the Germans don't cut the road again."

Shaking her head, Wilson corrected Lewis. "No, not that. I know about the counterattack that the Germans are preparing." Spinning around, she folded her arms across her chest. "No, what I'm talking about is how long before everyone figures out that we, with the help of General Malin, duped them?"

There was no need for Lewis to consider that question. "Never." For a moment Wilson stared at Lewis before he continued. "There is no need for anyone to know. There are only four people who know exactly what happened and how this whole thing got started." Lewis held four fingers up. As he named each of the conspirators, Lewis dropped a finger. "To start with, there's you. But I don't think that you're going to go on national television and announce, 'Guess what, folks, I fooled you.' No, even if you had a burning desire to repent for your sins, this country has had far too rough a time. The last thing you need to do is follow the Ukrainian adventure and the German crisis with a Washington scandal like this."

Holding herself close, Wilson considered what Lewis had said. There had been times, especially when she was alone, when she'd considered doing exactly that. But she didn't tell him, or anyone else, for she still wasn't sure which way she would go on that issue. Even as Lewis continued, Wilson decided that she was still undecided.

"Then, of course, there's me. I can assure you, Madam President, this has not been the highlight of my career as a public servant. Yet I have no intention of slitting my own wrists in public. You see, as much as I hate what we did, I consider what we did the best choice from a whole stableful of bad ones. I am confident that in time our actions will be able to stand on their own merit."

"What about Malin? Remember, I'm obligated to relieve him as soon as he reaches Bremerhaven and bring him to Washington to stand court-martial."

Lewis dropped his hand and let a slight chuckle slip. "Yes, I know. And I've noticed that he has not been seen by anyone, especially the media, since his corps started re-entering friendly lines."

Not having made any special effort to track him, Wilson pondered this for a moment. "Do you suppose he's trying to skip out, escape or hide?"

"No, no need to worry about that. He's just waiting until all of his units are safe. When the last of the rear-guard units make it back safely, he'll turn himself over to the most senior commander on the scene and come back here to face his court-martial, just as we agreed to."

"But then the nice little story about a renegade commander will be exposed as a lie."

Lewis shook his head. "No, not at all. He'll ask for a trial by a military judge only, which will eliminate the jury. Since much of the evidence that will be brought against him deals with national security issues, the session will be closed-door. And his defense attorney will be able to present only that information that Malin himself provides. So the trial will be quick. General Malin will be found guilty, sentenced, and after a few weeks forgotten. After all of his appeals have run out and the trauma of this crisis has been replaced on prime time news by another hot issue, you will pardon him."

"Do we have to go through this charade?"

Shrugging his shoulders and clapping his hands together, Lewis sighed. "'Fraid so, Abigail. The German Parliament, which is on the verge of gaining control in Germany, is watching your every move. They are looking for anything that will allow them to bring this affair to an end. You see, the German Parliament, through their own little staged trial, will bring Ruff to justice, as they see it, just as you will bring your renegade corps commander to justice. Ruff, who took the nuclear weapons from us and placed unreasonable demands on you, will be gone. Malin, who violated German territorial integrity and started the German crisis, will be gone. Since neither the German Parliament nor you had any direct control over those events, the ones that precipitated the actual shooting war, there'll be no barriers to open and free negotiations. Resolution of outstanding issues will be quick, and everyone will trip over themselves as they rush to re-establish the prewar normalcy, whatever that was."

Though she knew Lewis was a tough character, she had never viewed him as being a cynic. Unfortunately that happened to anyone who worked too long within the Beltway. She looked at Lewis. "Who's number four? I thought there were only three of us?"

"Number four, Madam President, is Colonel Scott Dixon."

"The same Dixon that's married to Jan Fields, the correspondent on WNN?"

"The very same. Malin insisted that Dixon, whom he considers one of the brightest minds in the Army, be in on the initial discussions when we were considering the feasibility of this whole escapade. Dixon made a quick study, came up with some initial planning guidance, and turned it over to Malin so that it appeared that Malin had done it on his own. The plan I brought back from Prague and that Malin executed was Dixon's."

"And how will he react when Malin takes the fall for this whole affair?"

"Scott Dixon, Madam President, is a professional soldier. He will do what he is told. Before I left Prague over two weeks ago, General

Malin, in my presence, asked Dixon to promise that he would never divulge any of the conversations that Malin and I had."

"Dixon will adhere to that promise?"

"Abigail, Dixon's a soldier, not a politician. Of course he'll keep his word. Besides—" Lewis stopped.

"Go on, Ed. You were about to say something?"

Lewis looked down at the floor a little sheepishly before he answered. When he did, there was a hint of remorse in his voice. "You know, of course, that the rear-guard detachments from the 4th Armored Division are part of Dixon's brigade?"

Cocking her head, Wilson tried to remember if she had been told about that, but in the blizzard of military briefings she had been given, she was sure that she had never made the connection. Finally shaking her head, she responded, "No, to tell you the truth, I really didn't. But what has that to do with this?"

Slowly Lewis explained himself. "The 2nd Panzer has not been stopped by naval or Air Force aviation from Britain. They're the ones that took a hammering back in central Germany, and if reports are to be believed, they're out for blood, anyone's blood. Since that unit is mostly easterners who have remained steadfastly loyal to Ruff, we expect that they'll make one more effort."

"But why? I mean, it's over. They have no more nuclear weapons. Most of the Tenth Corps has made it to the sea. What possibly is there to gain from one more battle?"

Lewis stood up and looked over to Wilson. His face was a mask betraying no emotions. "The 2nd Panzer Division will attack for exactly the same reason that Scott Dixon will keep his mouth shut. A sense of duty that even soldiers can't explain."

It suddenly dawned upon Wilson what Lewis had left unsaid a moment ago. Dixon, who was still out there exposed to danger, might not make it, leaving only three people to share their secret. Standing upright, Wilson was about to call Lewis a bastard, but then held herself in check. Not that she had to, for the look on her face told Lewis what she was thinking.

Lewis said nothing. There wasn't anything more to say. Whatever happened in Germany in the next twelve to twenty-four hours was out of their hands. The fate of Dixon and the soldiers who rode with him was back where it probably always had been, in the hands of tired and exhausted men and women, armed with the best weapons their nations had to offer, lurking about under leaden gray skies in search of each other.

With the roads leading west finally cleared of wreckage caused by ceaseless air strikes and hordes of refugees that always seemed to be in the way, Major General Erich Dorsch was free to unleash his 2nd Panzer Division. Though there was little chance of his division's doing serious damage to the American 4th Armored Division, Dorsch felt a certain amount of satisfaction that the little chunks of that unit he was about to scoop up and crush were the same ones that had frustrated his operations a week before in central Germany. The attack of the 4th Armored Division's 1st Brigade into his exposed flank had slowed and then stopped his advance, denying him a great victory. For that he intended to make every soldier in that unit pay.

So with the same ruthlessness that he had driven his motorized rifle regiment in the old East German Army, he drove the soldiers of the 2nd Panzer Division on. The final fight, he promised himself, would be his alone.

Far removed from the command post of the 2nd Panzer Division, the weary soldiers of the 2nd Panzer prepared for one more effort. In the gathering darkness, under cloudy and forbidding skies that told of a new winter storm coming, Captain Friedrich Seydlitz grimly led the pitiful remains of his company forward one more time. That this would be the last battle, there was no doubt. Already the word had filtered down throughout the division that the bulk of the Americans they had been pursuing across Germany were already safe and out of reach. Only a few stray rear-guard units remained to be eliminated. Though Seydlitz had no idea why these units needed to be dealt with, he'd said nothing when he had been given his orders.

The attack, scheduled to commence just before dawn, would be a difficult one. The rash of warm weather had softened the ground and restricted cross-country maneuver to a few patches of solid ground, trails, and hard-surfaced roads. Were it not for the low cloud ceiling that was preceding the new weather front, this restriction on maneuver would have meant an end to the attack. For the Americans controlled the air. Even German Army aviation no longer was available, as it had been in central Germany. There would just be a handful of panzer and panzergrenadier battalions, backed up by field artillery, for the morning's fight.

But that, Seydlitz decided, would be more than enough to satisfy his division commander's honor, pride, or whatever foolish emotion was driving him to continue this insanity. That there was no good reason to do what they were doing was obvious. It had been obvious to his loader over two weeks ago. Only Seydlitz, of all the men in his company, had been unable to see what they had seen. Perceiving the obvious, however, was not the same as knowing what to do. That was where they, the men in his command, had failed and where Seydlitz himself now failed. By all rights, Seydlitz realized as his company prepared to move out, he should refuse to follow his latest set of orders. Others, particularly the pilots in the Luftwaffe, had done just that. They simply refused to do what they had been told. But then their failure had cost the German Army a sure victory. Even worse, the absence of the Luftwaffe had cost German soldiers their lives. Most of those who had fallen had been good Germans, men who had been guilty of nothing more than doing their duty and following their orders. Was the refusal then justifiable? In the course of the past two days, whenever an American ground attack aircraft had rained down destruction on his company, Seydlitz had felt anger at the German pilots who had refused to do their duties. How could fellow country-men allow this to happen?

Those feelings, those thoughts, were like a great trap. When he questioned the loyalty of the Luftwaffe pilots, Seydlitz realized he was questioning his own. How would he be able to condemn them if he himself failed to carry out his own orders and as a result allowed an attack by a sister unit to fail in a bloody repulse? He couldn't. Right or wrong would not be determined by him or the men in his unit. All they could do was trust that their commanders were looking out for their best interests and those of Germany. In the meantime, all Seyd-litz could do was what he had always done, his duty.

So when the time came, he keyed his radio and gave the order for his company to start engines and move out to the west for one more battle.

It was several moments before Chancellor Ruff noticed that he was no longer alone in his office. Seated at his desk, with one leg held straight out to one side to ease his discomfort, Ruff had been staring at the open box that glistened under the harsh light of the desk lamp. With all other lights in the room extinguished, the highly polished box with its bright red lining and black-sheathed knife sat in the center of Ruff's desk as if it were on a stage under a spotlight. With his hands resting on the arms of his padded chair, Ruff sat for the longest time looking down at the box and the knife.

To Colonel Kasper, who had quietly slipped into the Chancellor's office, Ruff looked as if he were watching a little television set or a child's video game. He half expected something to come popping up out of the box that Ruff was staring at so intently. But nothing happened. Ruff simply sat there looking at the box. Kasper, leaning against the wall in the shadows, watched, waited, and began to have second thoughts.

Finally, without any indication as to what alerted him, Ruff looked up from the little wooden box and straight at Kasper. For a moment Ruff's eyes betrayed the look a child gets when a parent catches the child doing something wrong. Leaning forward in his chair quickly, Ruff reached out with his right hand, slapped the lid of the wooden box shut, and sat up straight in his seat. With a gruffness in his voice that barely concealed his anger, Ruff called out, "What is it you want, Colonel?"

For the longest time Kasper said nothing. He merely stayed there in the shadows looking at Ruff and wondering what this man, considered by all who knew him to be a great politician and a wise statesman, was thinking. Loved, until he had initiated this crisis, by Germans in both the East and the West, Ruff had brought the nation together like no other man could have done. Not since Konrad Adenauer had a single German commanded such respect. Why, Ruff thought, had he thrown all of that away? Why?

Becoming angry at the failure of Kasper to answer his question, Ruff slammed his hand on his desk and shouted, "What do you want, Colonel? Either tell me or leave."

In a whisper that made the question more of a plea, Kasper simply said, "Why?"

Already agitated, Ruff twisted his face in anger. "Why what, Colonel? What are you talking about?"

"Why, Herr Chancellor, this foolish war? We have lost so much and gained nothing. Nothing!"

Ruff fell back in his chair. "You think, Colonel Kasper, that we have gained nothing? You think all of this was a waste? How could you not see what we were truly fighting for? How could you be so blind?"

Kasper didn't move. Remaining at the wall near the door, he spoke out. "We have gained nothing. The precious nuclear weapons that started this whole thing are gone. Not only was the German Army unable to stop an enemy force a fifth its size and was crippled while doing so, that pitiful performance created a split in the officer corps and left the Army racked by internal dissent. The Luftwaffe has turned its back on the Army and dishonored itself and Germany. The streets of our cities are being torn by riots against this government while police stand aside and watch. In the world councils, nations who had once been our allies condemn us. And years of patient rebuilding of our nation and its image have been endangered. What possible reason can you or anyone give that could justify all of this?"

Slowly Ruff stood, pushing his chair away from his desk. With the look that had won him election after election, Ruff puffed out his chest. Pulling back the coattails of his suit jacket, Ruff placed his hands on his hips. "We have, Colonel, regained our pride and our honor."

With a deep sense of dread, Kasper looked down at the floor at his own feet as Ruff continued. "For the first time in over sixty years, Colonel, Germany is almost free of occupation forces. Once all this internal foolishness has been given a chance to settle, we will sit with those whom you call our former allies. With the same determination and skill that led to the removal of Russian forces from Germany, we will negotiate away the remains of America's broken forces as well as the others. Freed from the heavy hand of occupation and the stigma of our defeat in the last war, Germany will be able to resume the role of leadership in Central Europe that is Germany's by right. Don't you see, Kasper? What I did was no different than what Arminius did to the Romans in 9 A.D. Arminius and the German tribes, united in their hatred of the Romans, hounded the Roman legions until they were wiped out. We are within a hairbreadth of doing the same to the Americans. Don't you understand? Can't you see that?"

"Then, Herr Chancellor, you intend to continue this war?"

Ruff drew in a deep breath. "I see no other options that make sense. It is the heart and soul of Germany that I fight for. What Germany once was can be again. But we must have the courage of our convictions. We must do what is right regardless of the consequences, regardless of the cost." Ruff paused. When he spoke again, his tone was like that of a father talking to a son. "You know, Colonel, being a German has never been easy. We, our people, have always been at the crossroads of European history. Sometimes we have served as the bridge between East and West, sometimes as the West's shield to protect them from the terrors of the East. But always we have been here, a proud, free, and strong people. This business of collective shame and perpetual atonement for the Holocaust and occupation by foreign armies must end. It is time to put all that foolishness behind us and go forward, as our ancestors always did. Surely you see that?"

Pulling himself upright to the position of attention, Kasper finally stepped out away from the wall and advanced to the edge of Ruff's desk. "You are right, Herr Chancellor, this foolishness must end. But not by looking back into our dark past for answers. To compare yourself to a hero like Arminius is to denigrate his name and memory. The gift your actions are bestowing upon this land is not honor or freedom. No, it is a plague, the same plague that Adolf Hitler brought to our people. Any illusions you have that what you have done is good for Germany is a sin against logic and humanity. So I am here to bring this to an end."

Ruff looked at Kasper. He was totally unprepared for seeing his loyal military advisor standing before him speaking to him in such a manner. Dropping into his chair, Ruff looked up and was about to admonish Kasper when he saw the pistol Kasper held tightly at his side. Slowly Ruff dropped his head, took a long hard look at the pistol, then looked back up into Kasper's eyes. "So, you are to be my Graf von Stauffenberg."

Lifting his pistol up to waist level, Kasper shook his head. "No, Herr Chancellor. I am no Von Stauffenberg. You are right in many respects. Germany has lived in the shadow of its past for too long. But we must shake ourselves free of our own brutal history, not relive it."

"And by killing me you believe that you will solve Germany's problems? That we will be able to make right what you believe is wrong?"

Again Kasper shook his head. "No. We cannot make the past right. But we can make the future right. You must atone for your crimes against our people. You must be held responsible and brought to justice."

Ruff smiled. Pointing a finger at Kasper, he warned the colonel.

"Yes, you do that. You bring me to trial. Stand me before the German people and let them judge. And when you do, when I stand before them, I swear to you you will be sorry. For they and history will judge me to be right, and you, all of you who would castrate this great nation and leave us pitiful eunuchs serving foreign masters, will see your errors."

Unwilling to allow Ruff to continue, Kasper took two deep breaths, as if steeling himself for carrying through what he had started. Ready, he spoke deliberately, as if he were reciting a well-rehearsed speech. "There will be, Herr Chancellor, no public trial, no chance to make a mockery of Germany again. Even if you were found guilty of something, you would live, for we have no death penalty, even for murderers like you. No, you cannot be allowed to spread your distorted vision of our future, not from the courtroom docket, not even from the cell of a prison. No, Herr Chancellor. Your dreams of Germany, your rape of my country will end here tonight, now."

Allowing his arms to fall to the padded armrests of his chair, Ruff half smiled. "Am I to understand that you, a simple colonel in the Army, have decided to take justice into your own hands?"

"No, Herr Chancellor. As I have said, I am no Count von Stauffenberg. I cannot do what I believe needs to be done." With that, Kasper threw the pistol onto the desk. "Instead, I am going to allow you by your own hand to bring an end to this insanity of yours."

For a moment Ruff looked at the pistol, and then up at Kasper. "What makes you think that I would do such a thing, Colonel?"

"Because, Herr Chancellor, the devils that have driven you to extract a blood revenge against the Americans have by now been satisfied. Even you realize that once the last of the Tenth Corps is within the perimeter of the American airborne division, the fighting will stop. And if there is no more fighting, no more Americans can be killed."

In utter amazement, Ruff looked at Kasper and tried to figure out how he had discovered his deepest and darkest secret. Had his justification for this war been so transparent? Had this colonel seen through Ruff's mask of German nationalism and into his very soul? How had he betrayed himself?

Satisfied by the silence and the look on Ruff's face that he had hit his mark, Kasper continued. "A public trial will do your reputation and your lust for revenge no good. Your story and all your great high-sounding claims that what you did for Germany was in the name of the German people will be revealed for what they were, false words spoken by a false prophet. What you have done in the past will be forgotten as your name is dragged through the newspapers of the world day after day, as the real purpose behind this war slowly comes out. And as the trial reduces your stature from that of a head of state to that of a mad, demented murderer, you will very soon live to regret allowing yourself to be held up to such scorn and ridicule."

After considering Kasper's statements, Ruff looked around the room, then back at Kasper. There was the hint of a smile on Ruff's face when he spoke. "And so, Herr Colonel, you think that I will take your suggestion and end my life with my own hand?"

"I am only giving you that option."

"And if I don't?"

Kasper brought himself to a rigid position of attention and said nothing. Ruff waited for Kasper to say more, but then realized that the colonel had said all he intended to say. Ruff was about to make a comment but stopped. He knew that there was nothing more to say. Over the past few weeks he had said everything that he had wanted to say. And even more important, he had done everything that he had set out to do. His life's work, he realized, was finished. There was nothing more that he could do. His task to punish those who had destroyed his nation, who had killed his father and made his family suffer, had been completed. Looking at the pistol, then up at Kasper, Ruff thanked his military aide, asked that he be given five minutes alone, and then reminded him to close the door as he left.

When the heavy wooden door of his office was closed, Ruff reached out with his left hand and opened the wooden box sitting on his desk. With his right, he took the pistol and lifted it to his head. As he sat there looking at his Hitler Youth dagger, he regretted that he had never had the opportunity to use this cherished symbol of his childhood for its intended purpose. Yes, he thought, that was unfortunate. With that, he pulled the trigger.

CHAPTER 22

25 JANUARY

From his M-1A1 tank south of the 17th Airborne's perimeter Colonel Anatol Vorishnov had a clear view of the hard-surfaced road that ran south like a straight black ribbon through the muddy brown fields to either side of it. Along that road on the right side sat a farmhouse and barn approximately one thousand meters to the south. That farmhouse, clearly marked on all their maps, was the designated link-up point where he was to make contact with Scott Dixon and the remaining battalions of the 4th Armored Division's 1st Brigade. Dixon's forces, coming up from the south along the road, would come out of a tree line that sat just a little over two thousand meters past the farmhouse.

Looking about to his left and right, Vorishnov watched the young company commander of the unit he was traveling with deploy his tanks to cover the link-up. Not that he had very many tanks to deploy, Vorishnov thought cynically. The company, commanded by a second lieutenant who had finished the armor officers' basic course just three months before, had a grand total of six tanks. The other four officers and eight tanks that had begun the march a mere ten days ago hadn't made it this far. Like every unit in the Tenth Corps, this small company had taken its losses, reorganized itself, and kept going. Whether that effort had been worth the cost had yet to be determined. Soldiers only pay the price. It's the diplomats and the deals they strike afterwards that fix a value to those sacrifices.

Edging his own tank forward as far as he dared go, Vorishnov looked beyond the obvious and studied the terrain more closely. From his new vantage point, he noticed a cluster of trees sitting about twelve hundred meters due east of the farm. There was an elevated trail that cut across the muddy fields and connected that group of trees with the hard-surfaced road running south past the farm. From his map, he couldn't tell for sure how far that trail continued to the east into the woods. Looking back up from the map and over to the woods, he was about to order the company commander he was traveling with to send a platoon over to occupy those woods when an armored personnel carrier came screaming up behind him. Turning around, Vorishnov saw the man standing in the carrier's commander's hatch shout something into the intercom. Getting off onto the left shoulder of the road, the driver of the carrier waited until the last possible moment before he slammed on the brakes. The sudden stop caused the M-113 armored personnel carrier to lurch nose down and then rock backwards. The commander, anticipating the sudden stop, hung on to the barrel of the .50-caliber machine gun mounted at his position and rocked back and forth with the motion of the carrier. Even the two people riding in the rear, heads popping up out of the open cargo hatch of the carrier, took the sudden stop in stride. Only when the carrier finally came to rest did Vorishnov notice that one of the two people in the cargo hatch was the commander of the Tenth Corps, the man everyone called Big Al.

Deciding that he had best dismount and go over to brief the corps commander, Vorishnov ordered the driver of his tank to cut the engine at the same time that the man riding the commander's hatch of Malin's carrier had his driver cut their engine. The sudden silence enveloped the patch of woods, Vorishnov, Malin, and the tiny tank company like a blanket. Now all the subtle noises, like people talking or sponson box doors being slammed shut, that had been masked by the sound of diesel engines drifted throughout the cold, damp morning air. With one eye on Malin and an occasional glance down the long straight road to the south, Vorishnov started to dismount when Malin from his carrier waved over to him and yelled, "No, stay where you are, Colonel. I'll join you over there on your tank." Without waiting for a response, Big Al ducked down and out of his carrier through the troop door in the rear.

Vorishnov saw that Malin, like everyone else in the corps, was tired. His walk and the way he carried his head reminded Vorishnov of a man carrying a heavy load. Of course, Vorishnov knew that the general did have a heavy load, several in fact. He just didn't know which one, the responsibility of commander or his anticipated arrest and trial for disobeying the American President, was weighing heaviest on him at that moment. Climbing up, Malin smiled at the driver, who could only manage a simple nod in return. Even the loader, a large jolly fellow, was slow in coming to attention as he stood on his seat and saluted the general. Pulling himself up and onto the turret, Malin came up next to Vorishnov and squatted down on his haunches. "Any contact with Dixon yet?"

Pulling his combat crewman's helmet off and setting it down on the roof of the turret, Vorishnov nodded as he ran his gloved fingers through his matted hair. "Yes, General, about ten minutes ago, just before we broke out of the tree line here. Colonel Dixon, who is traveling with the lead element, announced that he expected to reach the link-up point within fifteen minutes." Looking down at his watch, Vorishnov studied it for a moment, then pointed down the hard-surfaced road to the tree line three thousand meters to the south. "I expect them to be coming out of there any time now."

Malin followed Vorishnov's outstretched arm, looked at the far tree line, and simply nodded. "Good. Good. I'll be glad when Scotty and his wandering strays are finally back with us."

Vorishnov was about to ask Malin if it was a good idea for him to be so far forward when he heard a call for him come in over the headphones of the crewman's helmet that he had laid on the turret in front of him. Picking it up, he recognized Dixon's voice. "Excuse me, General, that's Colonel Dixon calling now."

Smiling, Malin reached out. "Here, Colonel, could I have that?"

Knowing of the close relationship Malin and Dixon had, the request did not surprise Vorishnov. "Of course, General."

Without bothering to put the crewman's helmet on, Malin put the earphone as close to his ear as he could and pulled the boom mike over to his mouth. Then, before he spoke into the mike, he glanced over to Vorishnov. "This thing in the secure mode?"

Vorishnov nodded.

"Good." Then depressing the transmit lever, Malin called Dixon. "Colonel Dixon, this is Big Al. What took you so damned long?"

For several moments there was silence. Finally Dixon, realizing that it really was Malin, came back with the best response that he could think of. "Sorry, sir. But I forgot something in Prague and had to go back for it."

This caused Malin's face to light up. Watching, Vorishnov knew for the first time that all was going to come out all right. The Americans were beginning to regain their terribly unmilitary and inappropriate sense of humor.

"Scotty, this is Big Al. You almost at the link-up point? Over."

"Affirmative. I have the farmhouse in sight. Over."

"Great. I'm in the wood line to the north of the farm with your Russian counterpart. How about I meet you at the link-up point? Over."

There was a pause. "Roger. As soon as we fire the recognition signals. Over."

Turning to Vorishnov, Malin asked about the recognition signal. Having heard Dixon's request, Vorishnov was already reaching down for the two star clusters. "Here, General, a green star cluster followed by a red. They respond with a green and white."

"Okay, then fire away."

"Before I do, I need to bring a tank up to go with you to the link-up point."

Malin smiled. "I don't think that'll be necessary, Colonel."

Vorishnov insisted. "We are still, as you would say, in Indian country. I am afraid as the senior tactical commander here I must insist that you have an escort."

Knowing that Vorishnov was right, Malin nodded. "Okay, Colonel. Bring up your tank and fire the star clusters. I'm going over to my carrier to get ready."

Without a salute, Malin stood, moved over to the edge of the turret, and climbed down. As he went, Vorishnov felt a sudden pang of sorrow. This would be Malin's last official act. For once Dixon and the two battalions traveling with him had passed through this point, his career would be over. How terrible, Vorishnov thought, to end such a great effort on such a melancholy note. Then, with a slight shake of his head, as if it were necessary to shake his mind free of his last thought before he could move to the next, Vorishnov yelled to the young company commander to have one tank prepare to move out to the link-up point as soon as he fired the star clusters.

From his position behind the lead tank of his column, Seydlitz looked up through the barren tree branches to the west at the brooding gray clouds. He had greeted this cruel winter day with mixed feelings. The low gray clouds would limit the interference they could expect from American ground-attack aircraft. Though capable of flying, finding their target, and hitting it in just about any kind of weather, the American pilots showed a distinct distaste for coming in low and exposing their expensive aircraft to the murderous anti-aircraft fire that Seydlitz's company and the attached Gepard anti-aircraft guns threw up at them. Still that didn't mean they were impotent. Even at an altitude of ten thousand feet the guided weapons and deadly 30mm cannons of the ground-attack aircraft took their toll. And the further north the 2nd Panzer went, the worse it became. Of the seven tanks that Seydlitz had lost, four had been to air strikes.

So there was much to be thankful for today. If only the ground would freeze again. Then, rather than being restricted to roads and a few patches of high ground, Seydlitz would be able to freely maneuver his company. Again, the further north they went and the closer to the sea, the worse things became, especially in this area. Marshes in this part of Germany were numerous and, to a tank, as deadly as a mine-field. Already that morning they had passed three Leopards and two Marders that had strayed onto what they thought were fields of solid ground that had turned out to be bottomless pits of mud. Mired in the soft black mud all the way to their fenders, the tanks were as useless to the battalion as if they had been hit by an enemy anti-tank missile. The only good thing about this miserable weather was that the Americans too would be confined to the roads.

Taking one more glance at the skies, out of habit, since he was sure there would be little flying today, Seydlitz was about to turn around and check on the progress of the tanks behind him when the blazing trail of a star cluster to his front right caught his attention. Standing up as far as he could in the open hatch, Seydlitz watched as the star cluster reached the highest point of its flight, then burst into a sudden flash of green. This star was no sooner beginning to fade when a second star cluster, this one red, followed the first and burst. Judging the distance to be not more than fifteen hundred meters due west, Seydlitz keyed his radio and issued a warning to all the tanks in his column to stand by for action. Switching the radio to the battalion net, Seydlitz began to report his sighting but stopped in midsentence when from the south he saw a green and white star cluster fired as if in response to the first. Correcting his initial report, Seydlitz updated his battalion commander with his latest observation and then dropped back to the company radio net as he prepared to close with the enemy.

From across the open expanse to his front, Dixon could see a tank move out of the tree line three thousand meters north of his position and head straight down the hard-surfaced road for the farm even before the green and white star clusters Major Harold Cerro fired in return went off. Though he couldn't see it, he had no doubt that Big Al's personnel carrier was following close behind the tank. For a moment, Dixon wondered if the tank was his own tank carrying Vorishnov out to greet him. That would be a bit foolish. He already felt a little uncomfortable at allowing Big Al to come out like that before the area was secure. Senior commanders, after all, just didn't do things like that. Not even brigade commanders. But in this case he could understand why Malin was doing this. For even if, after all was said and done, Big Al was allowed to retire gracefully, this would be the last time he would ever ride into battle in the service of his country.

Ready, Dixon took one more look around to make sure that everything and everyone at his end were set. Captain Kozak and her small company were just about in place. She had her one remaining tank deployed to the left of the road, while the two infantry squads of her one infantry platoon were deployed in the woods to the right. Kozak's Bradley sat on the right side of the road keeping a watch to the northeast while Cerro sat on the left side of the road watching the farm and road itself from his Bradley. Satisfied that all was ready, Dixon ordered his driver to move out and head for the farmhouse.

Just as the Leopard tank to Seydlitz's front was about to break out of the tree line, the tank commander of that tank stiffened upright in the open hatch. He stood there for only a second before he disappeared into the turret of the tank with such speed that it looked as if someone inside had pulled him down. Immediately after that the turret of the lead tank made a quick, short jerk to the right, or northwest. For a moment it stopped and then slowly began to move back to the left, as if it were tracking something moving south. Seydlitz, guessing what was going on, was about to call to that tank commander when he heard the tank commander report in. There was great excitement in his voice as the tank commander of the lead tank reported that he was about to engage an American tank moving south along the road.

Not sure that he wanted to initiate such an engagement before he had deployed at least some of the company out of the column formation, Seydlitz was about to order the lead tank commander to hold his fire when that tank fired its main gun, shattering the cold winter air with a sharp crack.

Ordering the commander of his personnel carrier to pull over to one side of the road, Malin stood up as high as he dared and leaned over the side in an effort to see around the damned tank that Vorishnov had insisted come along. Suddenly, without any warning, the tank to his front was engulfed in a huge shower of sparks, flame, and black smoke. The terrible screeching noise of metal tearing metal cut through Malin like a knife. Even before he had time to twist his head the fraction of an inch necessary to look from Dixon's personnel carrier to the tank less than fifty meters to their front, the first of the tank's large metal blow-off panels that covered the ammo storage area had already been torn free. Like a dead leaf, the blow-off panel was flipped off the turret and sent flying straight up, followed by a solid sheet of flame. Allowing himself to fall back into the personnel carrier, Malin continued to rotate his head to the left in the direction from which he thought the attack had come.

When he finally was facing the east tree line, Malin saw the sinister form of a Leopard II tank, its main gun still smoking as it emerged from a clump of trees. They were, he realized, in trouble.

His personnel carrier, moving as fast as it could roll, was about to reach the tank leading Malin's personnel carrier when out of the corner of his eye Dixon saw a flash. Instinctively his head cut over in that direction, but then, when the tank on the road to their front began to tear itself apart, he twisted his head back in that direction. Not needing long to assess what was happening, Dixon jumped up, hit the sergeant that was serving as the commander of his personnel carrier on the left shoulder, and yelled, "Get behind the burning tank. Go left and get behind the burning tank on the left. Ambush from the woods."

The sergeant, having seen the same thing, was already preparing to do that, since he knew that it would have taken longer to turn around and run back to the woods they had just left. The driver, on the other hand, who had been shocked by what had just happened, immediately let his foot off the accelerator. The sergeant commanding the vehicle heard the engine change pitch and yelled, while Dixon was yelling to him, "NO! DON'T STOP! DON'T STOP. GO! GO!"

When he heard both the sergeant and Dixon, the driver quickly overcame his initial panic and stomped his foot down till it couldn't go down anymore. With a sudden jerk, Dixon's personnel carrier lurched forward and went screaming toward the burning tank, still being racked by secondary explosions, and the farmhouse.

Unable to get the commander of the tank in front of him to acknowledge his calls, Seydlitz watched helplessly as that tank commander allowed his tank to continue to roll west, out of the tree line and into the open. Though Seydlitz still couldn't see around the lead tank, it was obvious that he was preparing to engage another target. Seydlitz watched the turret of the lead tank jerk to the right a little and then as before begin to drift back slowly to the left. Not waiting any longer, Seydlitz ordered his own driver to move off the trail to the left and then instructed his company to commence deploying.

From where she sat, Kozak had only seen a faint muzzle blast from the tank to the northeast that had fired. At that moment it was still too far in the woods and masked by trees. Still, as she had on many occasions before, she dropped into her seat, issuing her initial fire command to Sergeant Wolf, her gunner, as she did so. "GUNNER! MISSILE! TANK!"

Wolf, who had not seen the telltale muzzle blast, yelled back, "Cannot identify!"

Once she was settled in her seat and had her eye pressed against her sight, Kozak grabbed the control handles and slewed the turret to the right until the sight was sitting at the edge of the tree line to the northeast some two thousand meters away. Believing his commander had made a mistake, Wolf yelled again, "Cannot identify!"

Kozak was animated. "The tree line, Wolf. The enemy tank is still in the tree line. Keep your eyes open and be ready to pop him when he sticks his nose out."

Leaning as far into his sight as he could, Wolf watched and waited. Then he saw it. At a range of two thousand meters, the 120mm gun tube of the Leopard tank, even in the Bradley's high-powered sight, looked like a thin pencil line. Still Wolf was able to see it, yelling when he did. "Okay! I got 'im! Here he comes." Depressing the palm switches on the turret controls, Wolf tried to traverse the turret but saw that it didn't move. Immediately, without taking his eye from the sight, he yelled out, "I see the enemy tank, Captain. Let go of your controls!"

In her excitement, Kozak had forgotten that she was still hanging on to her matching set of turret controls. As with a tank, the commander's controls override the gunner's, denying the gunner the ability to traverse the turret or elevate the gun until the commander releases the palm switch on his control. When Wolf yelled, Kozak let go of the turret control as if she had been shocked by an electric current. That, she thought, had been dumb. Really dumb.

With the turret under his control, Wolf watched the gun tube. As soon as the German tank began to appear, Wolf started to track it. He was about to announce the launching of his first TOW missile when, to his surprise and Kozak's, the German tank jerked suddenly, was bathed in a shower of sparks, and then began to spew black smoke.

Leaping up on her seat and sticking her head back up out of the turret, Kozak realized that an American tank in the tree line due north of their position had also been tracking the German tank and been able to get its shot off first. As she peered across the field, a sudden feeling of disappointment swept over her because they had missed a shot, though she didn't stop to think that in truth they had never had a clear shot. That feeling was quickly pushed aside when she heard Cerro calling her on the auxiliary radio receiver. Reaching down, Kozak flipped the remote radio frequency selection lever, taking her off her company command net and over to the battalion command net.

Waiting a second for the radio to reset, Kozak was about to respond to Cerro when the distinctive boom and screech of a TOW missile launch to her right caught her attention. Glancing over in that direction, she didn't see any indication that the 1st Platoon Bradley next to her had fired. It had to have been the other 1st Platoon Bradley. Looking out across the field, back to the northeast at the woods where the German tank had come from, she saw no sign of another enemy tank or a TOW missile headed that way. Something, she realized, was coming up on their flank through the woods. Anxious to reset her radio to the company net and find out what was going on, Kozak blurted a quick report on the battalion net. "Hotel 60, this is Charlie 60. I think we're in contact over on our right flank, in the woods. I'll report back in a minute. Out."

Without waiting for any sort of acknowledgment, Kozak flipped her frequency selection lever back to the company net and began calling her 1st Platoon.

Sitting next to the road, Cerro, perched atop his Bradley, felt overwhelmed. In quick succession he had watched the M-1 tank coming south toward him blow up, leaving his brigade and corps commanders on the road and exposed. Then he had watched a German tank come trundling out of the woods to the northeast while he was talking on the radio and had done nothing. Finally, just as things seemed to be getting under control, the commander of the company he was with called in, told him she thought they were in contact with enemy forces due east of their position, and then disappeared off the battalion radio net. Though he could clearly see Kozak's Bradley to his right, less than thirty meters away, it could have been a million miles away for all the attention she was paying him. Determined to solve one of his problems, he ordered his driver to back up and then move over to where Kozak's Bradley was sitting. If they couldn't talk on the radio, they could at least shout at each other.

Inching his way out to the edge of the tree line, Seydlitz, hunched low in his open hatch, scanned the open field to the south and west for any sign of danger. His gunner, able to see the hard-surfaced road to the west for the first time, saw an American personnel carrier racing north on that road toward the burning American tank and yelled out his acquisition report. *"Achtung!* Personnel carrier!"

Seydlitz, who was looking for more dangerous targets, ignored the gunner's sighting. His vigilance was rewarded when off to their left he caught sight of a Bradley in the wood line to the southwest backing up. Now he was ready to issue his fire command. *"Achtung!* Bradley, traverse left!"* The gunner, aware of what was happening, complied until in the center of his primary sight he caught a glimpse of the retreating Bradley. Seydlitz, who had allowed the driver to advance a little further out to the edge of the tree line, finally ordered him to halt and prepare to engage the Bradley.

Unable to see anything from where his tank was, Second Lieutenant Ellerbee ordered his driver to move forward slowly. As they did so, Ellerbee ordered his gunner to keep his eyes open for the clump of trees across the field that would appear to their right once they had cleared the trees they had been hiding behind. With his head up out of his open hatch, Ellerbee looked first to his right at the trees to the southeast and then south down the hard-surfaced road where he watched Colonel Dixon's personnel carrier pull up next to another one behind the burning tank. They were using the destroyed tank as cover. He was thinking about how clever this was when his gunner screamed, "ENEMY TANK! TWELVE O'CLOCK IN THE WOOD LINE!"

Without even looking, Ellerbee dropped back into the turret, ordering the driver to stop and issuing a fire command as he went. As the gunner and loader yelled their responses, Ellerbee gave the command to fire before he even got his eye to his primary sight extension. Used to the rock and recoil of the powerful 120mm main gun by now, Ellerbee eased his eye up to the commander's extension just as the tank was settling back down from firing its first round. Though he could see from the fading whiffs of smoke that they had hit the Leopard tank, he knew they hadn't killed it, for its 120mm main gun, exactly the same type that was mounted on Ellerbee's tank, was now being trained on them.

At first neither Seydlitz nor his gunner realized that they had been hit. A sudden shudder and a soft scream from the driver's compartment, more of an excited exclamation, were the first clues that something was wrong. Only when Seydlitz noticed his tank jerk to the right did he call out, "Willie, what are you doing?"

"Captain, we've been hit. Right track I—"

The gunner's scream cut him off. "ACHTUNG! PANZER!"

Looking back up to his sight, Seydlitz saw the American tank that had just fired on them as it appeared in the far right corner of their sight for the first time. "Forget the Bradley, engage the tank, now!"

Laying his sight on the center mass of the target, the gunner announced he was ready. Knowing that the American would continue to shoot till he saw his tank burn, Seydlitz didn't hesitate. "FIRE!"

They had hit it. Ellerbee knew they had hit the damned thing. But it wasn't dead. Without another thought, he yelled his new command as he watched the German's gun come to bear. "TARGET! RE-ENGAGE!"

Without waiting for the loader to finish announcing "UP!" Ellerbee's gunner screamed, "ON THE WAY!"

In quick succession, as if one finger had pulled the two triggers, both the Leopard and the M-1 fired. And with the skill and precision of veteran gunners aided by high technology, both gunners hit their marks. It was Ellerbee's tank, however, that got the worst of the exchange. Punching its way through the frontal armored plate on the left side of the turret, the armor-piercing round fired by Seydlitz's gunner scattered hot scraps of metal and debris as it continued through the crew compartment and into the ammo storage racks to the rear of the turret. There it ignited the propellant and the warheads of several rounds, beginning the process of destroying Ellerbee's tank.

The scream of the loader, the sudden discharge of the on-board fire extinguishers, and a searing pain that shot though Ellerbee's body told him he needed to get out now. There was no real conscious thought. He didn't feel the pain or comprehend everything that happened in the few seconds it took him to pull himself up out of the turret and onto the turret roof. Nothing registered. No pain, no thoughts. Not even when he rolled off the turret, hit the right front fender, and bounced off it like a rag doll and onto the ground did he understand what he was doing. Only vaguely was he aware of his gunner and driver, who both came down next to him, grabbing him by either arm and dragging him back into the woods as his tank, the last of four tanks in his platoon, tore itself apart.

Shaken, but alive, Seydlitz looked about the turret of his tank, first at the loader, then the gunner. "What happened? What in the hell happened? Did we get him?"

The gunner, anxious to see, put his eye to his sight, then cursed. "SHIT! He got our sight."

Putting his own eye up to his sight, Seydlitz saw that the primary sight was gone. "The telescope. Is it still good?"

From above, Seydlitz watched the gunner pull his head away from the eyepiece of his shattered primary sight and move over to the telescope mounted on the side of the main gun's cradle. "Yes. Yes, it's still good. And the American tank, it's burning!"

Popping his head up, Seydlitz looked across the field and saw that their shot had been true. Though he couldn't see Ellerbee and his crew as they fled back into the woods, that didn't matter. Looking back to the left, where he had last seen the American Bradley, Seydlitz confirmed that it was now gone. With no primary sight, one track shot out, and no targets in view, he decided that he needed to check in and find out what was happening to his left and right and then report to battalion.

From his vantage point, Vorishnov had no idea who was coming out on top. He could see that both Dixon and Malin were for the moment safe to the right of the burning hulk of the tank that had been Malin's escort. To the southeast, in the woods that the Germans had come out of, there was at least one German tank destroyed and a second one that had been hit. Due south, where Dixon's force had been, he could see dense clouds of dirty black smoke rising on what should have been the right flank for those forces and another column of dense black smoke to the left of that. While Vorishnov didn't quite understand exactly what was going on, he realized that the enemy attack had two prongs, only one of which, the one coming from the woods to the southeast, that he could do anything about. Contacting the commander of the battalion he was with, Vorishnov ordered him to deploy more forces to their left and prepare to send infantry over into the woods where the first German tank had come from. In the meantime, he ordered his fire support officer back at the brigade main command post to call for every piece of artillery he could find and begin to pound the woods to the southeast.

When Dixon and Malin finally realized they were safe, Dixon pulled himself out of the rear of his personnel carrier and stood on its roof. Carefully he looked up and over the burning tank that was giving them cover. From below, Malin, who was just now catching his breath, called up, "Can you see what's going on, Scotty?"

Just as Malin asked that question, Dixon saw a muzzle flash from the German woods to the east. A flash of tracer streaking from those woods came to an abrupt halt in the tree line not far from where Malin had come from. A sudden bright flash, followed by a sheet of flames, told Dixon that another American tank had been hit. His reaction told Malin that something bad had happened. Finally ready, Big Al pulled himself up and jumped over onto Dixon's personnel carrier. Together they stood there side by side powerless to do anything effective to influence the battle as they watched the next series of exchanges.

Just as they came around a bend in the forest trail and caught sight of the 1st Platoon Bradley guarding the right flank, Kozak watched in horror as it was struck by a high-explosive anti-tank round fired by an unseen assailant. Because the back ramp was down, left open after the dismounted infantry had exited, much of the force of the explosion was vented out and in her direction. Still that didn't seem to make much difference to the Bradley's crew. Of the three men she suspected had been left to man the Bradley, only the driver popped up and out, leaping onto the ground and rolling across the trail as soon as he hit the ground. With no time to lose, Kozak pulled herself up, reaching for her rifle and gear as she went. "I'm going forward to find that squad of dismounts," she yelled to Wolf as she prepared to jump down. "Have

Paden grab some LAWs and follow me. You get the Bradley into a good position here and cover the trail." Kozak didn't wait for Wolf to acknowledge. With a small hop she jumped down off her Bradley onto the soft floor of the forest. Even as she struggled to slip the straps of her web gear over her shoulders, Kozak was trotting forward to where she thought the dismounted infantry squad of the stricken Bradley would be.

Seeing a soldier hugging the ground for all he was worth, Kozak came up next to him and dropped to one knee. "Where's Sergeant Manning?"

Without a word the soldier pointed to his right. She glanced to her right, saw Manning, and then pushed herself up off the ground and headed for Manning. Behind Kozak, Specialist Pee Paden came running, carrying the AT-4 light anti-tank rockets Wolf had ordered him to grab. Called LAWs, the AT-4s were designed to be man-portable and disposable, each AT-4 LAW being a single round of ammunition. Paden, carrying three of them, first headed to where Kozak had stopped by the soldier for directions and then, seeing her shift to the right, changed directions to join her and Manning.

Even before she reached him, Kozak called out. "Manning, what have you got?"

At first he said nothing. He didn't even look over at his company commander. He simply pointed east as he whispered, "Leopard, twenty, maybe thirty meters straight ahead."

Looking in the direction that Manning was pointing, Kozak listened for a second, then heard the deep throaty rumble of the Leopard's diesel engine. From the sound of it, it was sitting still, idling. No doubt the commander of that Leopard was either waiting for orders or uncertain how to proceed. Looking to her left and right, she saw that each of Manning's dismounts had an AT-4 LAW. "Okay, Sergeant Manning, go get it."

Again Manning didn't look at his company commander, staring intently instead in the direction from which the sound of the Leopard's engine came. Like Kozak, he had been listening for any change in pitch, any sign that it was moving or being joined by another tank. Only when he was ready did he bring himself up to a half crouch, reaching down for the AT-4 LAW that had been lying next to him. Calling out to his squad, he gave his orders. "Larson, Evestus, grab your rockets and follow me. The rest of you, cover us." From a short distance behind, Kozak, followed by Paden, went forward with Manning and his tank hunters.

Pulling up to where Kozak's Bradley should have been, Cerro discovered it was gone. Confused for a second, he looked down on the ground next to his own Bradley. Seeing where the tracks of Kozak's Bradley had torn up the ground when it had pulled back out of position, Cerro knew that he was in the right place. Kozak, however, had moved. Looking up to his right, he saw a second Bradley some thirty meters away. Cerro was about to dismount and go running over to it, hoping to find out if the commander of the other Bradley had seen where Kozak had gone, when he saw that Bradley launch a TOW anti-tank guided missile. Turning his attention across the open field to the woods to the northeast, Cerro watched the TOW as it streaked across the muddy field toward a target that he couldn't see.

The gunner of the Bradley that had fired, however, could. The TOW blew up as soon as it reached the far tree line and disappeared behind the trees that had been masking Cerro's view of the target. A ball of black smoke was already rising above the trees when the sound of the warhead's detonation reached Cerro's ears. Shaking his head, he turned back to look at the Bradley that had just fired and watched as it pulled back to hide in the woods. Fearing that he was going to lose contact with this Bradley, Cerro had just begun to wave at the commander of the Bradley when the sound of several small explosions further to his right came echoing through the trees. Since there was no distinctive high-pitched crack that characterized a tank cannon firing, or enough of a report to indicate the launching of a TOW, Cerro guessed that someone was firing anti-tank rockets on the battalion's right flank. Though he had heard Kozak's report of enemy activity over there, he hadn't imagined that it was so close or a major threat, since the obvious danger to the front across the field had so dominated his attention.

Grabbing his map and spreading it out before him, Cerro forced himself for the first time that morning to consider everything that was happening and come up with a clear, effective, and coherent plan of action.

When the first round of artillery came screaming in and impacted somewhere in the woods behind him, Seydlitz thought that the artillery battalion firing in support of his company had made a horrible error and was shelling his position instead of the enemy's. Pulling his hatch to the opened covered position, Seydlitz was about to call the fire support officer at battalion and tell him to cease fire when he saw across the field a series of explosions shake the farm buildings. That, he suddenly realized, was his artillery. The rounds behind him were American. While he was watching to see what effect his artillery had on the enemy and listening to the drumbeat of their artillery on his position, he wondered why he had discounted, almost without thought, the possibility that the enemy would respond with artillery too. He shouldn't have. And he knew he shouldn't have, since they had, until recently, been allies. Still Seydlitz reminded himself that all too often one allows himself to fall into the common pitfall of feeling that his side is superior or he is clever and his foe is dumb. The worst foe in war, Seydlitz had been told by one of his instructors, was often one's own arrogance.

Seeing that the first volley of his artillery had fallen too far to the west, Seydlitz calculated in his head how much of a correction he needed to give to his fire support officer before they fired the next volley. When he was ready, he attempted to contact the fire support officer. As he waited for him to respond, Seydlitz glanced over his shoulder, then to the northwest where the American vehicles had first come from, wondering if some American company commander wasn't doing exactly the same thing at that moment.

The first volley of German artillery had caught both Malin and Dixon standing on top of Dixon's personnel carrier watching as a momentary lull set in over the morning's fight. Without having to look about to decide what had happened, both men dropped onto the top of the personnel carrier as if someone had pulled their feet out from under them. When he was sure that the last round had landed, Malin looked up and over to the farmhouse, now ablaze. "Scotty, they know we're still here and want our asses."

Lifting up his head, Dixon looked over to where the shower of tiny cluster munitions had come down. "Jesus, that was close."

Looking to his rear, in the direction that he had come from not more than five minutes ago, Malin could see the tree line through the smoke of the burning tank that was offering them cover. "Yeah, we're lucky this time. Think they'll make a correction and try again?"

Dixon looked at Malin, in the direction that he was still looking, then back at Malin. He knew what Malin was thinking without asking. "Do you think we could make it?"

Slowly Malin turned his head toward Dixon. "Well, Scotty, we bet our lives if we stay here that the Germans won't shoot at us again. And we bet our lives that the smoke from the burning tank and the speed of these tinker toys will get us back in one piece if we make a run for it. What do you think?"

Dixon didn't need to think. It wasn't in him to sit and do nothing. "Do we go by road or trust the fields?"

Looking back again, Malin considered that. The fields to the west of the hard-surfaced road were a good three feet lower than the level of the elevated roadway. "Fields, I think. There's a chance we'll get stuck. If we do, we unass and go it by foot."

Dixon nodded. "Okay, General. I'm right behind you."

The loss of the two lead tanks in his column attacking into the flank of Kozak's position convinced the German commander of the tank company moving through the woods that staying in the woods was more dangerous than pulling out into the open. With a crisp, curt command he ordered his driver to make a hard right, taking a trail that led out of the woods. Once they broke the tree line, he ordered his driver to hug the tree line and his gunner to keep a sharp eye out. If they ran into someone, he told his gunner, it would be very close. He knew they would have to get the first round off or die.

The call by Dixon that both he and Malin were making a run for it in his direction didn't surprise Vorishnov. From his position, he had watched the first German volley go in at the farmhouse, and like Malin he had wondered if the Germans would try again. With a quick call to the brigade fire support officer, Vorishnov ordered him to switch to high-explosive mix with smoke rounds and continue to repeat the mission against the German woods to the southeast until he, Vorishnov, gave permission to cut it off. Though not as effective as a dual-purpose conventional round that spewed out dozens of submunitions, Vorishnov felt the high explosive and smoke slamming into the edge of the tree line would serve to disrupt any gunner's aim long enough for Malin and Dixon to have a chance.

"There they go! The Americans are running."

Seydlitz looked first to the northwest, the direction he thought that his gunner was talking about, then, seeing nothing, to the west, toward the burning farmhouse. Without his primary sight, he couldn't see what his gunner was talking about. "Who? Who's running and where?"

The gunner, excited and already tracking his new targets, shouted back to Seydlitz, "The American personnel carriers, two of them. On the other side of the roadway. They're running from the farm north."

Leaning forward, Seydlitz looked hard. Only after a second of intense search did he manage to see the very tops of two vehicles, mostly hidden by the elevated hard-surfaced road, crawling north. "Yes, I see them. Prepare to engage."

The gunner hesitated. He had not used his telescope in a long time for a main-gun engagement. Like many of his peers in the German Army, he had come to rely on the computer-driven electronic/hydraulic fire-control system that gave the Leopard such a high probability of first-round hits. With the primary sight out and only the telescope available, he, the gunner, would have to make many corrections, such as target tracking and range estimation, that the automated system had done for him. Still, as he looked, he figured that he had more than enough time to get off three, maybe four shots before the Americans reached safety among the trees in the north. A miss with the first round, therefore, would not be catastrophic.

Unable to see or do anything where he was, Cerro ordered his driver to slowly move forward. With his gunner looking to the left and he watching the German woods to the northeast, Cerro allowed his Bradley to inch out of the protective tree line slowly. If all went well, he would have the driver cut to the right and follow the tree line looking for somewhere to duck back in a little further to the east. Though this didn't make good sound tactical sense, Cerro was tired of being left out of this fight and was looking for the quickest way to find Kozak so he could get an accurate assessment from her and start exerting some command and control.

Unfortunately, when you defy good tactical sense, you often get caught. No sooner had the Bradley come halfway out into the open than the image of a huge gray Leopard tank, its gun pointing right at him, struck Cerro square in the face. "BACK UP! DRIVER, BACK UP! NOW! NOW!"

Cerro's sudden screaming and the decibel level told the driver they were in trouble. Without hesitation, he slammed the transmission into reverse and began to back up. The gunner, seeing what had caused Cerro to yell, slew-laid his sight onto center mass of the German tank and squeezed the trigger, firing whatever ammunition and weapons were ready, without waiting for Cerro to issue a fire command. In this case, unfortunately, it was only the 25mm cannon and not the TOW anti-tank missile.

Across the way the German gunner had been as surprised to see the American Bradley pop into his sight. He was about to alert his command to this when suddenly the American Bradley began to shower his vehicle with a volley of 25mm high-explosive rounds. Though not particularly lethal to a tank's frontal armor, the hail of 25mm rounds served to startle the German crew and delay their first round. When the commander yelled fire without giving a proper fire command, the gunner took a snap shot that passed within inches of Cerro's Bradley as it gained speed and disappeared into the woods, firing as it went.

The wild firing of Cerro's gunner also served to alert one of Kozak's Bradleys to the danger. With a quick glance to the right, the commander of that Bradley saw the German tanks being well marked by the tracers from Cerro's wild volley and issued his fire command. Since he had been looking for tank targets at long ranges, the Bradley commander had his TOW missile pod up and in the ready-to-fire position. It was a simple matter for him and his crew to dispatch the German tank company commander that had frightened Cerro so badly and sent him scurrying back into the woods.

While Cerro was recovering from his near calamity, Seydlitz gave the order to fire. With great deliberateness, his gunner watched and tracked the two personnel carriers. Estimating their range, based on the range that he had used during his last engagement, the gunner took what he believed to be a good proper lead and prepared to fire. Ready, he announced he was shooting and squeezed the trigger.

Well on their way, Dixon dodged the great mud clods that the tracks of Malin's personnel carrier were throwing up as he endeavored to keep his personnel carrier as close to Malin's as prudent. They hadn't gone fifty meters before Dixon began regretting their decision to go by field instead of the road. Both his personnel carrier and Malin's were sliding about this way and that in the mud as their spinning tracks grabbed for traction and found little. He was about to call over the radio to recommend that they get onto the hard-surfaced road and make their run up there when a large geyser of dirt and rock sprang up from that road. Looking to his right, Dixon quickly saw that someone from the German woods to the east had seen them and was engaging them. Knowing that it was too late to switch to the road now, Dixon dropped the idea. Fixing his stare on Malin's head as it bobbed this way and that in the open cargo hatch of his personnel carrier, Dixon tightened his grip on the lip of his hatch and began to pray.

Without having to think about it, Vorishnov knew what needed to be done. With cold, emotionless determination, he ordered his driver to move out and head south down the center of the road. When he heard the transmission slip into gear and felt the tank lurch forward, Vorishnov reached down, grabbed the tank commander's override, and brought the main gun to bear on the woods to the southeast where he thought the Germans firing on Dixon and Malin would be. "Gunner, look for a German tank in the tree line to the left."

As they came out of the tree line and began to gain speed, the gunner looked and tried to track but realized that he didn't have control of the turret yet. With no sign of distress or fear, the gunner called out to Vorishnov, "I've got the tree line in sight. Let go of your controls, Colonel."

Releasing the tank commander's override, Vorishnov looked first at the woods, then at the two personnel carriers struggling through the muddy fields. He wondered as he watched if this crew with him realized that he was setting them all up as a decoy, a diversion. Vorishnov knew that as soon as the Germans saw his tank sitting high atop the hard-surfaced road, they would forget the personnel carriers and go for him, the more dangerous target. That was, of course, provided that there was only one German tank shooting. If more than one enemy was in a position to engage them and the two personnel carriers, then he, his crew, Malin, and Dixon all stood a good chance of getting killed, making his sacrifice an empty gesture.

Watching, Seydlitz felt like he needed to say something. He felt the urge to make some sort of correction, issue an observation. Something. But he knew his gunner had seen his first round strike short. The gunner had yelled out a short, crisp "Shit," while he continued to track his intended target and correct the lay of his gun.

So Seydlitz said nothing to the gunner. From his position, half in and half out of the turret, he watched the loader fumble about with the large tank cannon projectile. Now he wanted to speed up the loader. Shouting at him, of course, wouldn't do any good either. The loader was a good man and there wasn't anything that Seydlitz could say or do at this moment that would improve his performance. With nothing to do, he stuck his head out of the open hatch, looked across the field at the two personnel carriers, and waited.

Finally, after what seemed like an eternity, the gunner announced, "Shooting now," just as Seydlitz caught sight of the American tank, its gun aimed directly at them as it came charging south down the hard-surfaced road at full speed.

"Enemy tank twelve o'clock in the wood line." Jerking his head to the left, Vorishnov caught sight of the German tank's muzzle blast. Doing as he had seen Dixon do, Vorishnov dropped to his sight, yelling as loud as he could on the way down, "GUNNER—SABOT—TANK!"

In unison, the gunner and loader yelled out, "IDENTIFIED" "UP!"

Without a pause, Vorishnov responded, "FIRE! FIRE!"

The heat and the brilliant bright flash of the penetrator impacting on the front of the turret's armor plating blinded Seydlitz. Though his tank did not blow up and the onboard fire extinguishers kept the tank from burning, Seydlitz was now blinded, his gunner was dead, and the loader, panicked by the whole process of being hit again, abandoned the tank, fleeing into the woods just as the artillery mission Vorishnov had requested came crashing down about them. He would survive, making his way to the next tank just before it pulled out of position and, like the rest of Seydlitz's company, withdrew to the east away from the battle to regroup.

That the battle was over was not immediately evident to Cerro from where he sat. Looking out over the vast open field, he had watched with macabre fascination the duel between the personnel carriers, the German tank, and the American tank that had come charging down from the north in an effort to save the personnel carriers. That the tank had managed to save one of the personnel carriers was both fortunate and, considering the intensity of the battle, lucky. Before turning back to the matter of finding out what was happening within his own battalion, Cerro looked back at the road north of the farm. He watched for a second as the tank came up and stopped on the road, shielding the two personnel carriers from any future attacks from the woods to the east. On the left side of the road, Cerro studied the two personnel carriers through his binoculars. He could see that they were now sitting side by side, with the crew of the undamaged personnel carrier working frantically to pull out the crew and passengers of the damaged personnel carrier before it was totally engulfed by flames. On the hard-surfaced road the tank stood motionless, guarding the carriers and their crews.

Though he knew who those personnel carriers belonged to, Cerro didn't pause to wonder whose had been hit. There was a battalion he needed to get in hand. If his performance and luck up to this point of the fight were any indication, it would be a while before he would be able to achieve that. For some reason nothing was working right that day for him. Nothing.

C H A P T E R   2 3

26 JANUARY

There was a certain strangeness to everything. Somehow, when Second Lieutenant Tim Ellerbee was finally able to open his eyes and keep them open, he noticed that everything had changed. The early-morning light filled the room he was in and made everything seem so bright, so white. Looking straight ahead, he could see the ceiling, the light hanging from the ceiling, and the pole next to him. Still this didn't help him. With his head still clouded from drugs and painkillers, Ellerbee didn't have any idea where he was. He wasn't even sure, for that matter, if he was conscious or in the throes of a seriously weird dream. With an effort that required every bit of conscious thought he could muster, Ellerbee forced his head over to one side. Unfortunately, once it started moving, Ellerbee felt a momentary panic when he realized that he couldn't stop it. So his head rolled to the side until the side of his face flopped down on the thin pillow.

For a moment he rested from this exertion, gathering the strength and presence of mind he would need to continue his explorations. Ready, he pried his eyes open again, noting that everything was terribly blurry, making every object soft and ill defined. Eventually, after his cloudy brain was able to identify the objects he saw, Ellerbee realized that he was looking at a bed, a hospital bed, with someone in it. Taking this discovery into account, it wasn't long before Ellerbee was finally able to deduce that since he was looking at a hospital bed, this meant that this was a hospital. If this was true, his erratic logic ran, then he must also be in a hospital bed. If all of that proved true, he finally concluded, he was wounded and not quite dead yet. After working all of that out, Ellerbee allowed himself to relax and rest. There was, as he did so, a certain feeling of joy, but not for having survived, because it was way too soon to come to such sophisticated levels of self-awareness. Instead, his source of joy was having been able to figure out where he was.

When he was ready to continue, Ellerbee looked closer at the patient in the bed across from his. His fellow patient was sitting up busily writing away at something on the little hospital tray that sat suspended over his lap. Clearing his throat, Ellerbee attempted to speak but couldn't muster any coherent words on his first try. That effort, however, was not wasted, since the patient heard his croaking and turned his head toward Ellerbee. Having the other patient's attention encouraged Ellerbee to redouble his efforts. Ready, Ellerbee slowly forced the words out of his mouth, almost syllable by syllable. "You Am-er-can, or Ger-man?"

The other patient, without any change of expression, responded, "Russian. And you?"

Not sure if he heard right, Ellerbee had to think about what he had asked and what the response had been. Blinking, he decided to try something else. "Tim Ell-er-bee, second lieu-ten-ant, U.-S.-Ar-my. You?"

"Nikolai Ilvanich, major, Russian Army. Welcome to Bremer-haven."

At first Ellerbee couldn't understand what a Russian major was doing in Bremerhaven. Closing his eyes, Ellerbee tried to sort this out. If this major was a Russian, whose side had he been on? Only slowly was he able to recall that many Russian advisors had stayed with their American units after the Ukrainian operation. With that problem resolved, Ellerbee opened his eyes again.

When he did, the room was different. The overhead lights that had been on were now off. The major across from him was no longer writing. He wasn't even sitting up. Instead he was lying down. Ellerbee didn't realize that a couple of hours had passed. Anxious to find out more, Ellerbee called out as best he could. "Ma-jor, you a-wake?"

As before, the head turned. "Yes, Second Lieutenant Tim Ellerbee. And you?"

"Yes, I'm a-wake. What un-it?"

"Company A, 1st Ranger Battalion, 77th Infantry."

Ellerbee sighed. Without thinking, he replied, "Lucky."

"Why do you say I am lucky, Second Lieutenant Tim Ellerbee?"

"No wom-en. My com-pany com-mander. A fe-male in-fan-try cap-tain."

After pausing to think about what Ellerbee had said, Ilvanich re-sponded, "Oh, I see. She failed to get the company back."

Ellerbee surprised himself when he shook his head. He was getting better, he thought. He could now move his head and control it at will. "No. Com-pany made it. All the way."

"Oh. Then she lost every battle you were in. Wasted a lot of lives."

Again Ellerbee shook his head. When he answered, there was a hint of pride in his voice. "No. We did good. Didn't fail any missions. Took all objectives."

"Oh. Then she mistreated you and your men. Didn't get you food or supplies on time."

"No. We ate what-ever was on hand. Never went hungry. She only yelled at me when I did some-thing—" He was about to say wrong, but changed the word. "Something dumb."

"Oh. Then her tactics caused unnecessary losses?"

This one didn't require any thinking. All their losses, Ellerbee had noted throughout the march to the sea, had seemed reasonable and unavoidable. And when compared to the damage they had done to the Germans, they had always been light. "No. We lost, lost a lot. But really punished the Ger-mans. Kicked ass."

"Then," Ilvanich exclaimed, "what's the problem with your com-pany commander? I don't understand. You are here. Your company did the best it could. Succeeded in all of its missions. Won battles. Suffered losses but reasonable losses. And it finished the march. It sounds like this company commander, other than the fact that she's a woman and you don't like that for some reason, is good."

This was almost too much for Ellerbee's mind to absorb as it floated about in a state of drug-induced bliss. While the Russian major's com-ments were good ones, each and every one, there was something that Ellerbee and the Russian were missing. Perhaps if he rested a little while, the missing element that would justify his dislike of Captain Nancy Kozak would come to mind. Closing his eyes, Ellerbee quickly drifted back to sleep.

Roused from a fitful sleep at 3:05 A.M., Jan Fields-Dixon was not prepared to greet her unexpected visitor. Her mind was so clouded with sleep that she didn't even make any effort to consider who would be disturbing her at this hour. Not that this was an unusual occurrence. After working for an outfit like World News Network for as long as she had, Jan had learned that nothing, not even her home life, was ordinary. Just about everything that could have happened had happened to her, sometimes more than once, in her years as a correspondent. Still there were times when even a hardened news veteran like Jan could be caught by surprise. Reaching the doorknob, Jan stopped, swept back the stray hairs that had cascaded lazily across her eyes, and opened the door.

In her worst nightmare, Jan couldn't have imagined a sight more frightening, more terrible, than the image of the Army colonel standing before her in the open doorway. For a moment the two of them stood there staring at each other. Jan in an old white terry-cloth bathrobe faced the colonel, standing erect and alert in his overcoat topped with a green scarf that covered his neck and a hat pulled down so low that it hid his eyes in the shadow of its brim.

Slowly, ever so slowly, Jan could feel her knees begin to tremble. Grasping the doorknob with her left hand, Jan almost fell over as she reached out with her right to steady herself on the door frame. Though her mouth fell open and she wanted so to scream, she couldn't. Nothing, not even a wisp of air, came out. It was as if her entire being, everything that she was, had suddenly locked up and come to a sudden, terrible dead stop. Without having to be told, without having to hear it, she knew that Scott was dead. The one man who had touched her heart and soul as no one ever had was gone.

After an embarrassingly awkward moment, the Army colonel reached out ready to catch Jan but did not touch her. Finally with great trepidation the colonel leaned down and spoke. "Mrs. Dixon, are you going to be all right?"

Responding to the words, Jan looked up at the eyes under the highly polished hat brim, nodded, and even managed a weak, stoic "Yes."

Taking her word for it, the colonel took a deep breath and prepared to carry out his orders. But before he could, Jan spoke first. "How, how did it—" Then she stopped. How stupid. What difference did that make now? Why in the hell was it so important to know how? Wasn't it bad enough that it had?

Confused, the colonel looked at Jan, who was obviously having a problem with his being there, and started again. Though he thought it probably would have been better to go inside, and he wondered why this woman in front of him didn't invite him in, the colonel decided to go ahead and just blurt it out. "Mrs. Dixon, I'm here on behalf of President Wilson. She sent me to personally inform you that your husband reached Bremerhaven."

There was silence as Jan's expression quickly changed from pain to confusion, and finally to wonder, all of them reflecting the jumble of thoughts that raced through her mind. When Jan looked up at the colonel, he wasn't ready for her next question. "Then," she said with great trepidation, still struggling to keep her knees from buckling, "his body has just been recovered?"

Now it was the colonel's turn to be confused. Cocking his head to the side, the colonel asked quite innocently, "Excuse me, ma'am, what body?"

Looking up with wide eyes at being asked such an extraordinarily dumb question, Jan shouted, "Scott's! My husband's body."

Finally it became clear to the colonel. With a quick shake of the head, as if to clear it, he almost laughed. "Oh! Oh, my God, no, Mrs. Dixon, you don't understand. Your husband isn't dead. He's alive. He made it back with the last of his brigade. When I said that he had returned to friendly lines, I meant that—"

Jan didn't let him finish. In a flash her near paralysis caused by the grief she felt over Scott's death turned to anger. "YOU BASTARD! You *rotten* bastard! How dare you wake me in the middle of the night, scare the living shit out of me, and then stand there and laugh at me?" Without waiting for a response, Jan slammed the door in the colonel's face and fled to her bedroom. There she threw herself on her bed and let go with a flood of tears brought on by an avalanche of emotions that she had up until that moment held in check.

Back at Jan's front door, the Army colonel stood motionless for several seconds in front of the closed door, not quite sure what he had done or what to do now. Finally, satisfied that he had accomplished his assigned mission and not wishing to disturb the crazy woman inside the house again, the colonel slowly pivoted about and headed back to the sedan that was waiting to take him back to the White House. As the driver pulled out of the driveway, the colonel looked back at the house one more time and wondered what he was going to say when he got back. Finally he decided that in this case the truth was the safest bet. With that decided, he pulled the brim of his hat down over his eyes, folded his arms across his chest, slumped down in the passenger seat, and went to sleep.

Though the Thirteenth Corps had assumed control over all tactical operations in northern Germany and relieved the battered and exhausted Tenth Corps staff of that responsibility, the press corps continued to hover about the final command post site of the Tenth Corps like a pack of wolves waiting for food. Located only a few kilometers from the flat sandy beaches that bordered the North Sea, the staff throughout the Tenth Corps command post waited for the same thing that the media did—the appearance of Lieutenant General Alvin Malin, the renegade general. The correspondents, like the rest of the world, waited to see if Big Al, the most controversial American military figure since MacArthur, would stay true to his word and surrender himself to American authorities.

Though rumor abounded that Malin had in fact returned to American lines the day before, no one outside the staff of the Tenth Corps knew where he was. This failure to report immediately as he had promised was causing problems for the President in Washington and delaying the scheduling of her talks with representatives of the German Parliament. Though both were anxious to put a quick end to what both sides were now referring to as a regrettable affair, the issue of General Malin had to be cleared up before anything on the diplomatic level could go forward. The silence surrounding the whereabouts of the man who had led the Tenth Corps in the dead of winter from the mountains of the Czech Republic to the North Sea seemed to weigh heavily on everyone's mind.

It was in the late afternoon, just as the pale winter sun was preparing to fade off in the distant southwest, that the reporters and camera crews of the media pool, camped out across the road from where the Tenth Corps main command post sat, noticed a stirring throughout that headquarters. Alone and in pairs, the officers and the noncommissioned officers of the Tenth Corps staff emerged from their expandable vans and tents and began to line the road in front of the headquarters main entrance across from where the newsmen sat waiting. As the newsmen watched, the officers and NCOs gathered around the corps chief of staff, who was standing at parade rest, legs slightly spread apart and hands held together loosely in the small of his back.

The look on his face, one of great sorrow, was no different than that of other staff officers and NCOs as they lined the road to either side and assumed a similar stance. Not knowing what was going to happen next but sensing that something was amiss, newsmen and camera crews began to record their observations with words and images.

Critics would later claim that the grim procession was staged for the eye of the camera that caught every moment, every participant. Nothing could have been further from the truth. Even if someone had thought of doing so, neither the corps staff nor the soldiers who made up General Malin's escort would have agreed to such a cynical plan.

As the sound of an armored vehicle moving north along the road became audible, the chief of staff of the Tenth Corps, in his best parade-ground voice, shouted out his commands. "CORPS STAFF, ATTEN-TION!" With that, every man across from the newspeople came to a rigid position of attention with a snap. When the armored vehicle that had caused the chief of staff to call his staff to attention came into sight just down the road, he shouted out his next order. "PRE-SENT ARMS." As before, the response was immediate and snappy. Only the soft hum of generators in the background, the muted comments of correspondents talking into tape recorders, and the wail of the mournful winter wind blowing in off the North Sea disturbed the silence of the headquarters that had been the eye of an international storm for so long.

In the lead was a young female captain riding low in the open hatch of her M-2 Bradley fighting vehicle. The haggard expression on her face made Nancy Kozak look ten years older than she was. Next to her, Sergeant Wolf, her gunner, grimly looked ahead with eyes that didn't seem to blink at all. As Kozak's Bradley came abreast of the corps chief of staff, Kozak turned her head slightly, saluted the chief for a moment, then, after dropping her salute, she turned her attention back to the front without changing expression. Immediately behind Kozak's Bradley came a second Bradley, the only other combat vehicle of her company that had survived the long trek north. The other eleven Bradleys and four tanks, as well as far too many of their crews, littered their route of march that started in Bavaria and ended here. Though the abandoned hulks of her vehicles were only metal, rubber, and plastic, each stood as a temporary headstone that marked where an American had fallen and where a little more of Captain Nancy Kozak's heart had died.

Next came the battalion commander's Bradley. No one on the

ground realized that the young major riding high in the hatch had not started out in that position. Not that Major Harold Cerro's story was any different than that of hundreds of other officers and sergeants in the Tenth Corps. Military necessity, a term often applied to something that was often unpleasant, had resulted in the sudden shifting of officers and NCOs into positions vacated by those who had fallen in battle, collapsed due to stress and strain, or proved incapable of dealing with the responsibilities of the position. In peacetime, Cerro, like many of his fellow officers, had joked about the wonderful opportunities that war offered a professional soldier. The reality of how such opportunities came about, coupled with the grim realization that a friend or peer had to fall in order to advance in such a manner, made such a promotion a thing to dread. For Cerro, because he lived, there was no escaping the price that others had paid so that he could be where he was. When his Bradley slowly trundled by the corps chief of staff, he like Kozak saluted him. After passing, Cerro looked to the north, toward the sea, and returned to his own grim thoughts and memories.

Next came an ancient M-113 armored personnel carrier with a Russian colonel standing upright in the open cargo hatch. With his field cap pulled down low over his eyes, Colonel Vorishnov looked neither left nor right until his vehicle came abreast of the corps chief of staff. He too saluted and then looked back to the front, his gaze, unblinking like Sergeant Wolf's, fixed straight ahead at nothing in particular.

Finally came the tank. As it came up even with the corps chief of staff, the chief seemed to stiffen his already rigid position of attention just as every officer and NCO gathered about him did. There was no loader in the hatch of this tank. Only Colonel Scott Dixon, commander of the 1st Brigade, 4th Armored Division. Dixon stood in the commander's hatch of the tank, exposed from his hips up. Holding on to the open hatch with his left hand and the machine gun with his right, Dixon never altered his expressionless stare from a fixed point on the distant horizon to the north. He did not salute the corps chief, for the salute that the corps chief and his staff were waiting for from this vehicle could not be returned. For Lieutenant General Alvin Malin, whose body lay wrapped in a poncho and strapped over the loader's hatch next to Scott Dixon, had been killed in action on the morning of the 25th, just as his greatest military feat was coming to an end.

Only after the procession had passed did anyone take the time to tell the press what had happened. When they found out, there was an immediate rush north to follow the procession. This rush, much to their anger, was stopped short of the coastline. Only the five vehicles of General Malin's funeral procession were allowed onto the flat wind-swept expanses of the desolate cold beach. There, the deputy corps commander and the corps sergeant major waited to receive the body of their former commander. Behind them stood a small honor guard with the corps flag and the national colors. Behind them in an extended line that stretched out to either side, stood representatives from all the units of the Tenth Corps, each with its own unit flags, flags that represented all of the units that had made the long march north. As before with the corps staff, when the procession had passed the main command post, the party assembled on the beach saluted the arrival of their commanding officer.

Slowly and in turn, the lead vehicles of the procession moved to one side to make way for Dixon's tank. When they were all clear, Dixon ordered his driver forward until, finally, the treads of his tank were only meters away from the edge of the North Sea. By the time Dixon had stopped his tank and climbed out of his hatch, Cerro and Kozak had come up to his tank and climbed aboard. Together they undid the straps that held Malin's body securely to the top of the turret. Dixon, dismounting, was joined by Vorishnov, the deputy corps commander, and the corps sergeant major on the left side of Dixon's tank. When these four men were ready, Cerro and Kozak slowly, carefully passed Malin's body down to them.

Hoisting the general's body aloft on their shoulders, with the dep-uty corps commander on the front right, Dixon to his left, and Vor-ishnov and the sergeant major in the rear, this party carried Big Al's body the few feet that separated them from the sea. When they reached the surf, the party in unison lowered Big Al's body down until it rested on the beach so that the waves rushed about his lifeless body. Having completed their last duty to General Malin, the four men took several steps back, lined up, and, without any order being necessary, saluted their former commander.

For several moments as the sun began to dip below the horizon behind them, the assembled mourners stood there in silence looking at their fallen commander; and then, to a man, each lifted his gaze beyond him to the sea.

EPILOGUE

14 MARCH

Neither Nancy Kozak nor her family were ready to deal with each other when she came back to her childhood home west of Lawrence, Kansas, on leave. Though everyone was anxious to see her, they were put off by the cold aloofness with which she held herself. Even when her mother hugged Nancy, whom she still called her baby, she felt no emotion, no warmth in her daughter. Everything about her homecoming was uncomfortable for all involved.

It was only when they went to visit Nancy's grandfather that she finally found someone with whom she could talk, someone that understood. After a quiet dinner, which everyone but Nancy and her Grandfather George enjoyed, the bulk of the family returned to the living room, leaving Nancy and George Kozak to go to his den. For Nancy, this was home, a room filled with books representing knowledge, adventure, and wisdom.

She had always had a special affinity for her Grandfather George, a man who had dedicated his life to study and teaching after he returned home from Europe in 1945. Earning his master's, then his doctorate in history, Grandfather George had spent the rest of his life in an effort to understand what had driven a handful of ambitious men to wage a war that had denied him his youth and his friends their lives. That there wasn't an answer, a really good one, took years to accept. Yet whenever he had been ready to accept this as true, deep in his soul a voice told him he could not dismiss the savagery of war as mindless, random, and meaningless. So he studied and read more, keeping more and more to himself. Only Nancy, of all the many grandchildren that he could claim, had found a way into the heart of a man who had allowed his spirit to die a little each time a friend had fallen from the line of march that led from Normandy in France to the streets of Regensburg, Germany.

In the quietness of the den, neither spoke for the longest time. Grandfather George busied himself in the little open-hearth fireplace until the fire was going. Satisfied with his efforts, Grandfather George settled in a chair next to the one that Nancy sat in. With the stacked logs engulfed in flame, they both sat and watched in silence, each recalling names and faces that were burned into their minds forever. Finally Nancy looked over to Grandfather George. "They never go away, do they?"

He answered without looking at her. Instead he stared into the fire as he spoke. "The memories? No. They will always be there."

In the silence that followed, Nancy wanted to ask Grandfather George how he had dealt with the burden. Turning away from the warm fire, she looked about the room, as if that would provide the answer. As she slowly looked at the rows and rows of books standing silently waiting for the grandfather, Nancy Kozak began to realize that his many hours in quiet reading and meditation in this room had been his refuge, his place to go where he could find the strength and wisdom necessary to put his memories in their proper perspective and carry on a useful life. That he had allowed Nancy when she was a child to enter this private world was something she had never understood the full significance of. That he had seen in her the future, a future that could be free of the horrors of war that still tortured his mind, was never appreciated by anyone but him.

Now as Nancy began the long and arduous task of healing herself, her Grandfather George sat with her in silence, saddened by the fact that his hopes for her had come to naught. *At least if I can't protect her from this terrible burden, I can be here to help her with it.*

And so they sat there in silence. *Perhaps her children would escape. Perhaps when she is my age, she will have children free from the sins of their parents. Perhaps.*

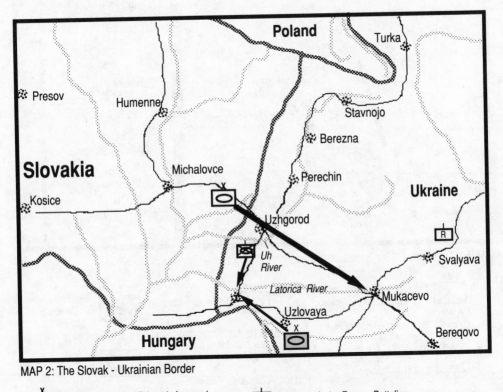

MAP 2: The Slovak - Ukrainian Border

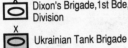 Dixon's Brigade,1st Bde, 4th Armored Division

 Ukrainian Tank Brigade

R Company A, 1st Ranger Battalion

Kozak's Company
Company C, 3rd Battalion, 3rd Infantry

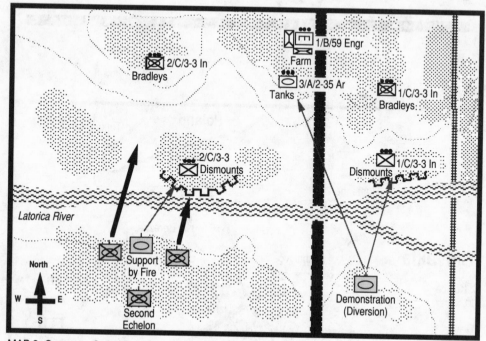

MAP 3: Company C, 3rd Battalion, 3rd Infantry (Mech), at the Latorica

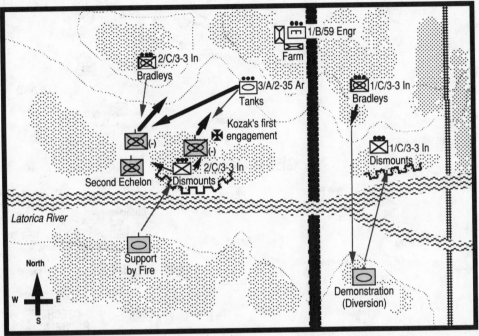

MAP 4: Company C's counterattack at the Latorica

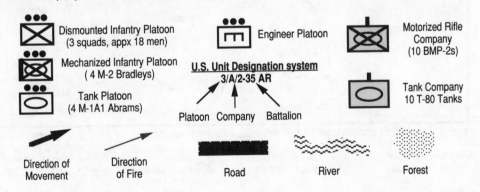

MAP 5: Tenth Corps deception plan & German redeployments in response

German Panzer (Armored) Division	German Gebirge (Mountain) Division
4th U.S. Armored Division	14th U.S. Armored Cavalry Regiment
55th U.S. Mechanized Infantry Division	False (Deceptive) Unit location

German Panzergenadier (Mech Infantry) Division

Tenth Corps supply trains

German Fallschirm (Airborne) Brigade

Corps logistics (supply) base

MAP 6: Tenth Corps enters Germany & initial German reaction

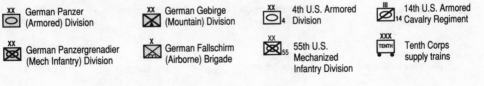

	German Panzer (Armored) Division		German Gebirge (Mountain) Division		4th U.S. Armored Division		14th U.S. Armored Cavalry Regiment
	German Panzergrenadier (Mech Infantry) Division		German Fallschirm (Airborne) Brigade		55th U.S. Mechanized Infantry Division		Tenth Corps supply trains

MAP 7: First battles

German Panzer (Armored) Division	German Gebirgsjager (Mountain) Division	4th U.S. Armored Division	14th U.S. Armored Cavalry Regiment
German Panzergrenadier (Mech Infantry) Division	German Fallschirmjager (Airborne) Brigade	55th U.S. Mechanized Infantry Division	Tenth Corps supply trains

✕ Armed Confrontations

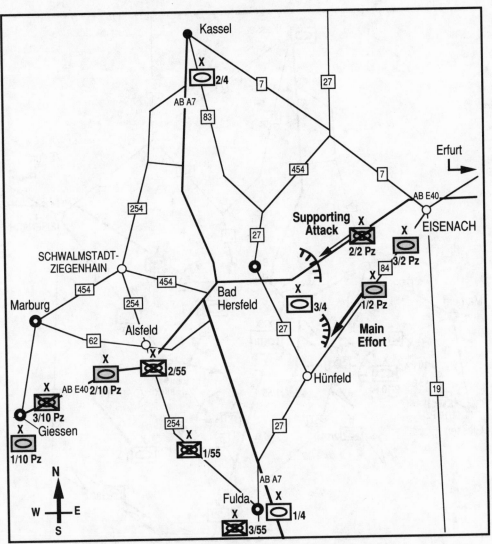

Kassel

X 2/4

AB A7

7

27

83

Erfurt

454

7

254

AB E40

Supporting Attack

X 2/2 Pz

X 3/2 Pz

EISENACH

SCHWALMSTADT-ZIEGENHAIN

454

254

454

Bad Hersfeld

27

84

X 1/2 Pz

X 3/4

Marburg

254

62

Alsfeld

Main Effort

27

X 2/10 Pz

X 2/55

Hünfeld

X 3/10 Pz

254

19

X 1/10 Pz

Giessen

X 1/55

27

N
W — E
S

AB A7

Fulda

X 1/4

X 3/55

MAP 8 "The battle of Central Germany"; Initial unit locations and maneuvers

Map not to scale and not all roads are shown

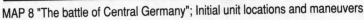

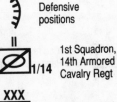
Defensive positions

1/2 Pz
1st Brigade, 2nd Panzer Divison

X 1/4
1st Brigade, 4th U.S. Armored Division

II 1/14
1st Squadron, 14th Armored Cavalry Regt

3/10 Pz
3rd Brigade, 10th Panzer Division

X 2/55
2nd Brigade, 55th U.S. Mechanized Infantry Division

XXX TENID
Tenth Corps supply trains

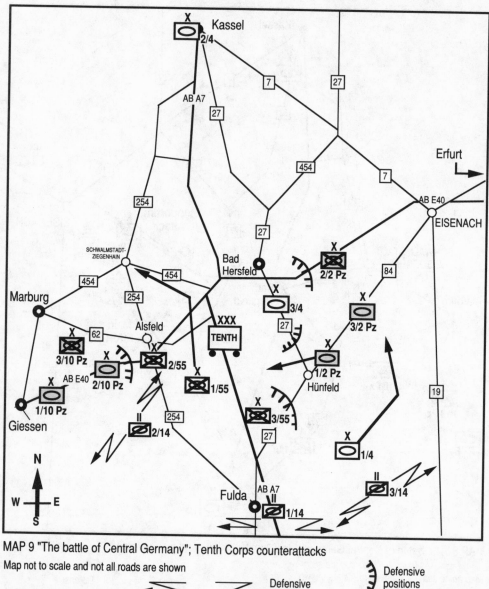

MAP 9 "The battle of Central Germany"; Tenth Corps counterattacks

Map not to scale and not all roads are shown

 Defensive screen

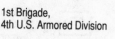) Defensive positions

 1st Brigade, 2nd Panzer Divison
1/2 Pz

 X 1st Brigade, 4th U.S. Armored Division
1/4

1st Squadron, 14th Armored Cavalry Regt.
1/14

3/10 Pz 3rd Brigade, 10th Panzer Divison

2/55 2nd Brigade, 55th U.S. Mechanized Infantry Division

TENTH XXX Tenth Corps supply trains

536

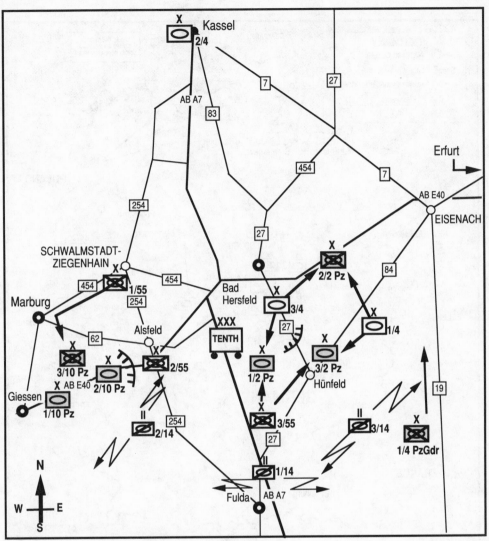

MAP 10 "The battle of Central Germany"; General melee

Map not to scale and not all roads are shown

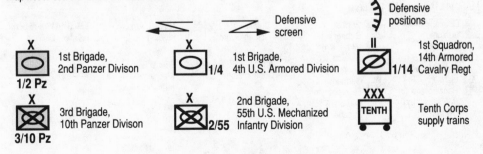

537

GERMANY

★ National Capital

Bonn ■ City

— International Boundary

0	Kilometers	161
0	Miles	100

NAVAL TASK FORCE
& MARINE AMPHIB GP
FROM MEDITERRANEAN

DENMARK

Kiel

Rostock

Schwerin

Hamburg

Emden

Bremerhaven

27

Bremen

POLAND

6

Berlin

26

Potsdam

Magdeburg

3

Hannover

1

PATTERBORN

Halle

Leipzig

Görlitz

7

55

Düsseldorf

Kassel

TENTH

Dresden

Chemnitz

Cologne

5

4

Erfurt

2

Decin

Liberec

Bonn

14

Teplice

Fulda

4

Chomutov

10

25

Wiesbaden

Frankfurt

Würzburg

Bayreuth

Cheb

Praha
(Prague)

Mainz

1

Plzen

CZECH
REPUBLIC

GERMANY

Saarbrücken

Grafenwöhr

NETHERLANDS

BELGIUM

LUXEMBOURG

FRANCE

Nuremberg

Hohenfels

Stuttgart

Augsburg

Munich

Freiburg

AUSTRIA

SWITZERLAND

MAP 11: The race for the sea

German Panzer (Armored) Division	German Gebirgsjager (Mountain) Division	Defensive Screen/Guard
		Armed Confrontatons
German Panzergrenadier (Mech Infantry) Division	German Fallschirmjager (Airborne) Brigade	

4th U.S. Armored Division

55th U.S. Mechanized Infantry Division

17th Airborne Division

14th U.S. Armored Cavalry Regiment

TENTH — Tenth Corps supply trains

538

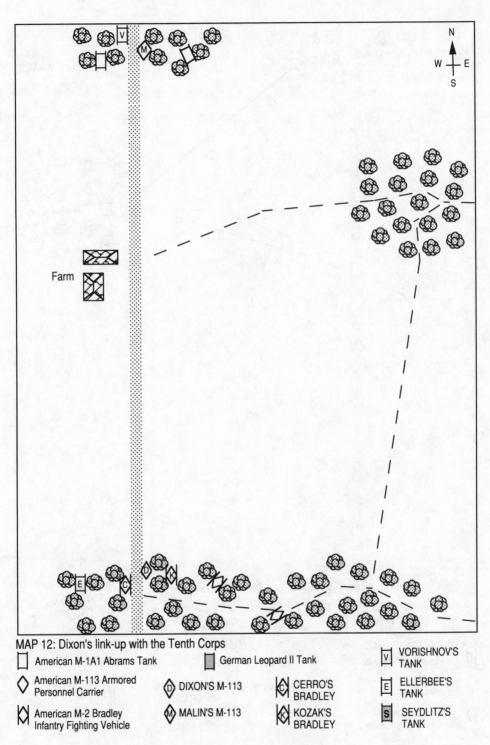

MAP 12: Dixon's link-up with the Tenth Corps

☐ American M-1A1 Abrams Tank	▨ German Leopard II Tank	Ⅴ VORISHNOV'S TANK
◇ American M-113 Armored Personnel Carrier	◈ DIXON'S M-113	⬖ CERRO'S BRADLEY	Ｅ ELLERBEE'S TANK
⬖ American M-2 Bradley Infantry Fighting Vehicle	⬖ MALIN'S M-113	⬖ KOZAK'S BRADLEY	▨ SEYDLITZ'S TANK

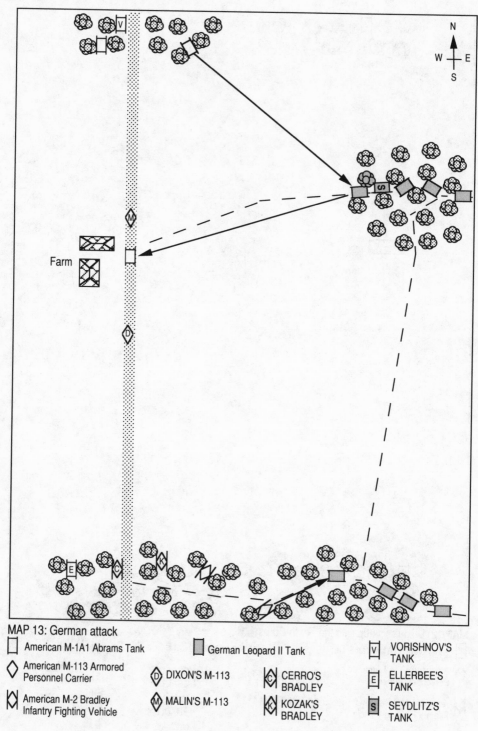

MAP 13: German attack

☐ American M-1A1 Abrams Tank	▨ German Leopard II Tank	Ⅴ VORISHNOV'S TANK
◇ American M-113 Armored Personnel Carrier	Ⓓ DIXON'S M-113	Ⓒ CERRO'S BRADLEY
		Ⓔ ELLERBEE'S TANK
Ⓚ American M-2 Bradley Infantry Fighting Vehicle	Ⓜ MALIN'S M-113	Ⓚ KOZAK'S BRADLEY
		Ⓢ SEYDLITZ'S TANK

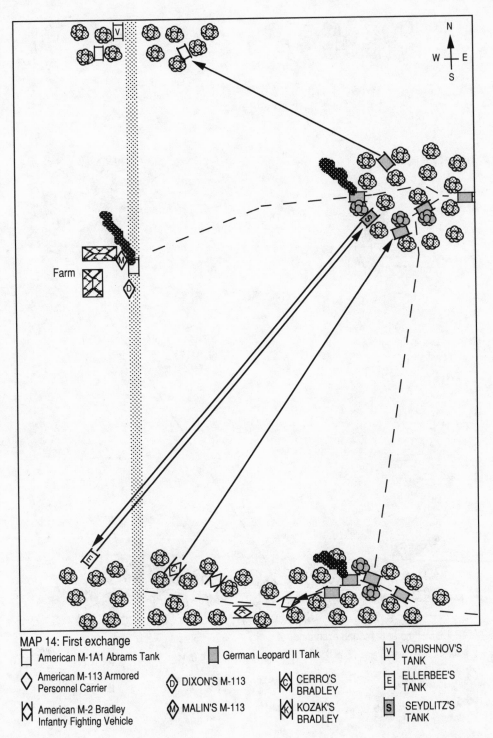

MAP 14: First exchange

American M-1A1 Abrams Tank	German Leopard II Tank	VORISHNOV'S TANK
American M-113 Armored Personnel Carrier	DIXON'S M-113	CERRO'S BRADLEY	ELLERBEE'S TANK
American M-2 Bradley Infantry Fighting Vehicle	MALIN'S M-113	KOZAK'S BRADLEY	SEYDLITZ'S TANK

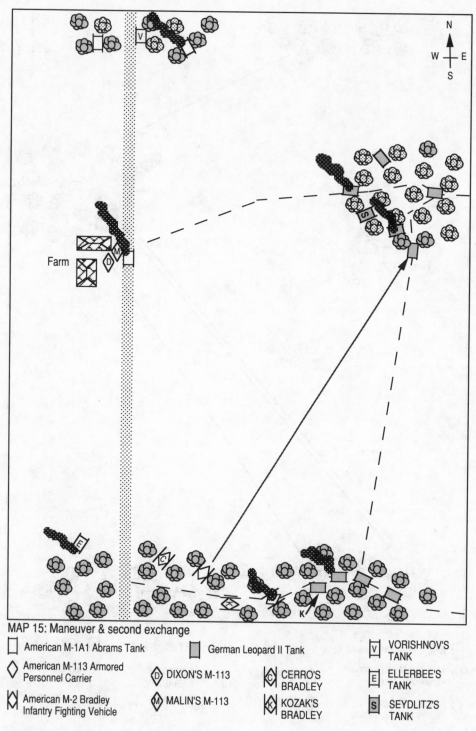

MAP 15: Maneuver & second exchange

□	American M-1A1 Abrams Tank		▨	German Leopard II Tank			☑ V	VORISHNOV'S TANK

◇ American M-113 Armored Personnel Carrier

⬙ D DIXON'S M-113

⬙ C CERRO'S BRADLEY

☒ E ELLERBEE'S TANK

⬙ American M-2 Bradley Infantry Fighting Vehicle

⬙ M MALIN'S M-113

⬙ K KOZAK'S BRADLEY

▨ S SEYDLITZ'S TANK

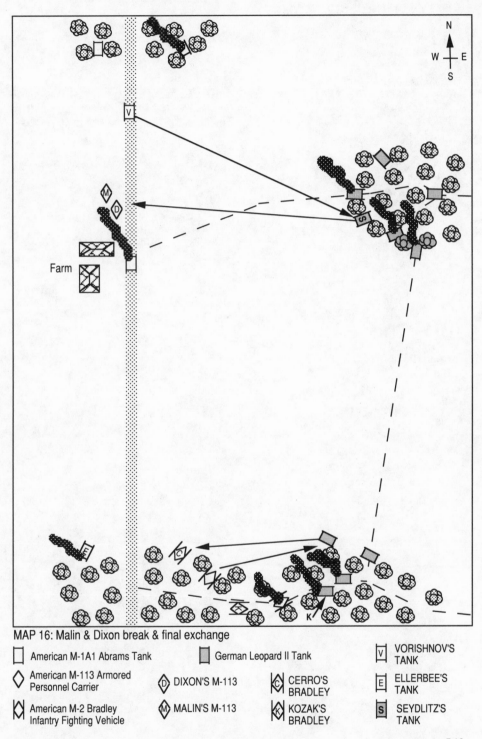

MAP 16: Malin & Dixon break & final exchange

☐ American M-1A1 Abrams Tank	▨ German Leopard II Tank	⊻ VORISHNOV'S TANK
◇ American M-113 Armored Personnel Carrier	◈ DIXON'S M-113	⧖ CERRO'S BRADLEY	⧖ ELLERBEE'S TANK
⧖ American M-2 Bradley Infantry Fighting Vehicle	⧖ MALIN'S M-113	⧖ KOZAK'S BRADLEY	⧖ SEYDLITZ'S TANK